THE *Ariana* TRILOGY

THE MAKING OF A QUEEN
A GIFT MOST PRECIOUS
A NEW BEGINNING

THE *Ariana* TRILOGY

THE MAKING OF A QUEEN
A GIFT MOST PRECIOUS
A NEW BEGINNING

RACHEL ANN NUNES

DESERET
BOOK

SALT LAKE CITY, UTAH

Page 376: Janice Kapp Perry, "A Child's Prayer," *Children's Songbook* (Salt Lake City: The Church of Jesus Christ of Latter-day Saints, 1989), 12. Used by permission.

Visit us at DeseretBook.com

Ariana: The Making of a Queen first published November 1996
Ariana: A Gift Most Precious first published August 1997
Ariana: A New Beginning first published January 1998

Library of Congress Cataloging-in-Publication Data

Nunes, Rachel Ann, 1966-
  Ariana : the trilogy / Rachel Ann Nunes.
    p. cm.
  ISBN 978-1-59038-907-2 (pbk.)
  1. Mormon women—Fiction. 2. Mormons—Fiction. 3. Religious fiction, American. I. Title.
  PS3564.U468A6 2008
  813'.54—dc22   2008006615

Printed in the United States of America
Worzalla Publishing Co., Stevens Point, WI

10   9   8   7   6   5   4   3   2   1

*To my mother, who taught me to read when
I was four, instilling in my heart a
lifetime passion for words.*

*To my father, who tried to teach me proper
grammar and who gave me a love of
foreign places and people.*

*To my husband, TJ, my best friend and biggest fan.
Thank you for giving me Jewels (my computer) and for
never giving up faith in my abilities.*

*To Jordan, Cassi, Cátia, Kaiden, Jared, and Liana,
my wonderful children. Thanks for your patience and support.*

*And special thanks to Jean Hanvey, for sharing touching
experiences with her premature son, Wyatt.*

ARIANA

THE
MAKING OF
A QUEEN

CHAPTER ONE

Warm rain fell softly in the dark Parisian night, yet strongly enough to mingle with the tears that fell down my face, masking them completely as I stood against the balcony railing in the cheap hotel. Not that there was anyone around to see that I was crying, or to care about my pain. It should have been one of the happiest days in any woman's life—full of wonder, discovery, and love. But on this night, my first since becoming a wife earlier that day, I was alone and crying.

My new husband, Jacques, was out drinking with his friends, celebrating our marriage in the way he knew best, and shattering my dreams—dreams that had already been thin enough to begin with. Still, I guessed I was lucky he had gone through with the wedding in the first place. One thing I did know was that I loved him with a first love's passion, even though he had left me alone on this of all nights.

Noise blared from the next-door window—another American song idolized for its irreverence and suggestiveness, a typical theme of the nineties. Ordinarily, I would appreciate the music; but tonight it only intensified my loneliness.

The rain came down faster now, and I could see figures scurrying to the subway where it was dry. The hole seemed to swallow the people as they ran down its stairs, their heads bowed and bodies huddled against the rain. It was summer; the tourist season was upon Paris, and the weekend crowds seemed undiminished even by the late hour and the rain. Along the road I could see the bars, lighted and beckoning. I wondered idly which of them held my new husband, and a fresh batch of not-so-quiet sobs erupted at the thought.

If only Antoine were alive! The thought came suddenly but not so unexpectedly. The rain would always remind me of Antoine and how he had been ripped from my life, my world changed forever. I would never forget how, up until nine months ago, Antoine had been my world. He had always taken care of me.

"Come on, let's go do something!" Antoine would shout at me whenever I was depressed. "There's no use in hanging around feeling sorry for ourselves!" Then he'd grin at me, and I couldn't help but smile back. I'd put my hand trustingly in his, willing to go anywhere with the brother I adored, knowing that with him my problems would disappear.

My brother had been loved by everybody who knew him. He had the sort of face even strangers felt attracted to and trusted. He always kept their trust and mine—except when he died and left me all alone. But I really couldn't fault him for that; he would never have left me on purpose.

"Where are you children off to today?" Father beamed down on us that last day we spent together. He laid a proud hand on Antoine's shoulder. "You will take care of Ariana, won't you?"

Antoine, seeing my frustration at his words, replied, "She's hardly a baby, Father. But I will look after her, and she after me, as we always have." That made me feel better, since we were the same age—the only difference being that he had been born a boy and I a girl. Of course, with my father's double standard, that alone was enough. Though we would soon be entering the twenty-first century, my old-fashioned father believed boys were somehow more competent in all areas of life than their helpless female counterparts.

"What time will you be home?" my mother asked.

"I don't know," Antoine said offhandedly. "Sometime before dark, I assume." He flashed her his smile before she could object, melting her instantly as usual.

Oh, I didn't mind that my parents loved Antoine so. I did, too. In my eyes, as in theirs, he could do no wrong. He always included me in everything he chose to do, giving me the freedom I would never have known otherwise. He never made me feel I was just something extra that had happened when my parents had tried to have the baby boy they had longed for, though that was the truth.

Together we spent many days roaming Paris where we lived, using the subway to take our explorations further, until I felt I knew Paris and the surrounding area better than I knew my own bedroom. Yes, I had many good memories of Antoine. I had especially loved walking along the Seine River, where numerous artists and others set up to sell their talents and various pieces of junk they called "souvenirs" to the many tourists. It was fun being near people who were so different from me, yet somehow the same. I adored watching and studying them, particularly when they weren't aware of me.

"It's getting late," Antoine had said to me that last day in September, now nine months past. He glanced at his watch. We had been walking near the river at the end of our adventure-filled day of roaming the catacombs in several of the nearby cathedrals. "We just have time to get home before dinner. Mother will be expecting us." I wanted to protest, but he was right. She would be expecting us, and Antoine was a good son to remember that. He was always good to everyone. Seeing my understanding, he smiled, making me glad I had not objected.

We took the subway home that night, and for some reason the train stopped between stations. The lights went off, and we were alone in the dark. Worry crept up inside of me; I had never felt comfortable in dark, closed-in spaces. "Don't worry," Antoine said, ever aware of my feelings in the way that close twins were. "They'll come back on soon."

As if to obey him, the lights flickered on. But still the train did not move. I tried to peer out into the dark tunnel but could see only my worried expression reflected in the glass.

"Look at this!" Antoine shouted. He had hold of two of the bars that were meant to steady standing passengers at rush hour, and he was hanging upside down on them like a monkey.

"Are you crazy, Antoine?" I exclaimed. We were alone in the car, but people from the next car could see him if they glanced though windows in the connecting doors.

"Come on!" he cried, doing a flip and swinging further down the bars.

"We're not ten anymore, Antoine!" I protested, remembering the time when we had perfected our antics on similar bars at the playground. But that had been more than seven years ago—we were nearly adults now. In six months we would be eighteen.

"Oh, Ari!" Antoine tossed his dark head around to gaze at me, his deep brown eyes dancing. Then he uttered the prophetic words that would echo in my mind forever: "We're only seventeen; we're not dead and buried yet!" At that I had to join him, my fear of the stopped train vanishing completely. Of course, looking back, I know that to comfort me was the only reason he had hung on the bars that night. He had always taken care of me.

Pain ripped through my soul as it always did at this point in the memories, for the train incident had happened the night before he died.

Now I clutched tightly at the balcony railing until my hands turned white and began to ache. The light from the hotel room came through the tiny glass door, its feeble rays barely reaching me in the dark. Dressed in my thin, dark blue nightgown, I felt suddenly cold. But still I lingered at the railing where the rain could reach me, almost wishing it could wash me away—or at least wash away the feelings that tortured my heart.

"Oh, Antoine," I whispered into the night. "If only you hadn't left, then things would not be so mixed up." But he was gone forever, and anything I said to him wouldn't make any difference. Antoine existed no more, except in my memories.

I continued to stare out into the night, but I didn't see the streets or the cobblestone sidewalks—only the frozen expression on my father's face the day Antoine died. It had been raining all morning long, turning from a soft pitter-patter to an earnest downpour. Antoine had already left for his early class at the private school we attended. Unlike me, he never passed up a chance for the early classes. He rode the bus and trains, as we all did; it was the fastest way to get anywhere in crowded Paris, where parking spaces were few and far between.

My parents and I were finishing up our croissants and coffee at the table when the phone rang shrilly into the silence; there was always a lot of silence when Antoine was absent. My father stood and reached for the phone. "Hello?" he said in his decisive voice. "This is Géralde Merson."

As the person on the other end of the phone continued, my father's face grew stark white, contrasting sharply with his dark hair and moustache. "No! No! It can't be true!" he exclaimed suddenly and painfully, but his voice sounded defeated. He listened further before asking shakily, "When did it happen?" And then, "What time should I come down? Okay. Thanks for calling."

When he turned to us, he was no longer the man I thought I knew. "Antoine is dead," he said. "A car hit him on his way to school."

"Oh, no!" my mother gasped and began to cry. "What happened?"

"He's dead, Josephine!" My father's voice was harsh. The pain in his eyes was too terrible for me to bear. "What does it matter how?"

The reality that Antoine was never coming back hit me like the weight of an anchor, and my anguished words exploded into the air. "Oh, please, not Antoine! Why did it have to be Antoine?"

My parents turned slowly to face me, seeming almost surprised at my presence. I thought for a minute they would reach out to me, that we could turn to each other in our shared grief. But they didn't. My father turned on his heel and went into his office, shutting the door firmly behind him. My mother stared after him for a long moment, the hurt evident on her face, and then she also turned and ran down the hall to her room, her loud sobs filling the sudden silence.

"Oh, Antoine," I whispered. "We're lost without you!"

I stood in the dining room alone, not knowing what to do. I lifted my eyes to the large mirror on the wall opposite me. There I could see my face, still tan from summer, with my short, dark hair and large brown eyes—each feature a feminine version of Antoine's. No wonder my parents couldn't bear to look at me!

For a very brief instant, I saw my brother's face instead of mine in the mirror. I could almost hear him speak the words he'd said on the train the night before: "Oh, Ari! We're only seventeen; we're not dead and buried yet!" I gasped and ran to the mirror, but he was gone, and I was truly alone. My face was now white beneath my tan, but I didn't cry. I bit my lip until the blood came, but I still didn't cry. Not then.

I didn't know it at the time, but my parents' reactions that day were to develop into a more permanent reality. My father spent more time at work, and I often went days without catching so much as a glimpse of him. When I did see him, he was cold and withdrawn, the light gone from his eyes. Mother was worse, sinking into a shell of her own making. She talked to me but seemed to see right through me, her face a bitter mask of pain and loss. I spent less and less time at home, but my absence went unnoticed. I knew they would never love me as they had Antoine, that I could never replace him in their hearts. And I began to hate them for it.

The day of Antoine's funeral, the rain finally stopped. The sun shone brightly down on the mourners, but its warmth did not reach our hearts. I stood dutifully by my parents during the short graveside service and while they lowered the coffin into the hole that seemed to ravage the earth. But I fled from the cemetery as they began to throw the dirt on the coffin. I couldn't bear to see them do that to Antoine; it was too final. At that moment I knew my life was over; how could I possibly live without my other half?

I ended up at my favorite section of the Seine where we had spent so much time, Antoine and I. Breathless and sweating when I arrived, I lifted my face to gaze out over the water, hoping for a breeze and maybe some kind of comfort. There was neither—only boats, faceless people, and squawking seagulls.

I walked blindly and aimlessly for a while. Suddenly I stopped and stared, surprised to see a group of young men with short hair and suits, singing in the street. Several young women were among them, holding up a big sign proclaiming "Families Are Forever!"

What a bunch of idiots! I thought. *Nothing is forever.* I had learned that lesson only too well.

Other young men and women with the singers were stopping people passing nearby and talking with them. One of the men—a tall boy, really—with a shock of bright red hair approached me with a pamphlet. His accent betrayed that he was a foreigner, probably from America by the sound. "Here," he said, thrusting the little booklet into my hand. "Did you know that families can be together forever?" His voice was sincere, his blue eyes clear; I knew he believed what he was saying, but in my grief-induced haze, I didn't care.

I stopped in my tracks and whirled on him. "You don't know what you're talking about!" I sneered. "Has anyone you loved more than life itself ever died? Someone who was so much a part of you that you'd rather die than live without him?" The red-headed boy shook his head and opened his mouth to speak, but I continued quickly, "Well, I know how it feels, and anything you can make up won't change the fact that my brother is dead and gone from me forever!"

I crumpled the thin pamphlet in front of his face and threw it to the ground. Then I added cruelly, "Now get out of my way and leave me alone!" The young man stepped back, and I glanced up at him. I expected to find hurt and anger in those clear blue eyes, but all I saw was pity and, strangely, love. It made me even more furious that the only one who seemed to show me what I so desperately needed was a red-haired stranger from another country.

"I am sorry," the young man said softly and hesitantly in his uncertain French. "I hope you find what you need. I will pray for you."

How dare he! I thought, and I was about to say something even more unkind, but he was already gone, leaving me alone as I had requested. I went home and cried as I hadn't been able to since Antoine's death earlier in the week—red-hot tears that seared my cheeks as they fell. There seemed to be no end to the bitter flood. My throat felt raw, and my eyes were swollen, but the ache in my heart was worse. I thought I was going to die, even hoped that I would.

At last the torrent subsided, and through my abating tears I spied my parents' liquor cabinet. I had never been drunk before, but I had often had alcohol with dinner. I knew it would give me a euphoria that would make me temporarily forget. I began to drink, and an unnatural warmth flooded through me.

Yet I didn't forget, not even for a moment, and all my drunkenness did was to put another wedge between me and my parents when they came home to find me nearly passed out. They utterly forbade me to drink. I didn't give it up, though; I continued drinking at home or with friends in the months that followed. My parents' anger was better than their indifference.

A loud knocking at the hotel door brought me abruptly back to the present. I came in from the balcony, hardly noticing my wet hair and the thin nightgown clinging to my body. I glanced at the TV, which I had left on. The sound was muted, but I could see the latest Disney movie filling the screen. Special TV channels were the only modern concession the run-down hotel had made for its questionable clientele. I had always enjoyed Disney cartoons—one more thing I had shared with Antoine—but this time I didn't stop to watch.

The knocking sounded again. Could it be Jacques? And it was only one o'clock in the morning! With a hopeful heart, I hurried to the door and threw it open to reveal not Jacques but Paulette, the girl who had become my best friend after Antoine's death.

My heart sank. "Oh, hi, Paulette." I stood back and let her enter the room. As she swept past me I could smell the cigarette smoke in her hair and the alcohol on her breath. Involuntarily I flinched. In the months after Antoine's death, those things had been my constant companions—but no more. I had someone else to think of now.

When I had shut the door, she turned her plain face to me. "Ariana, you're soaking wet! Haven't you got any sense? I—" She broke off when she saw my pain. "Oh, I'm sorry, Ariana, I know you wanted Jacques, but he's not coming. I was just down at the bar and saw him with the gang. That's why I came. I knew you were alone and thought you could use some company. Come on." She put her arm around my shoulders. "Let's get you out of these wet things." Numbly, I let her lead me to the bathroom.

A short time later we sat together on the large bed. I was now wearing a long T-shirt and my robe instead of the negligee. I drew my feet onto the bed and lay back on a mound I had made of the pillows, my fingers plucking carelessly at the green coverlet, faded and worn but clean. Paulette drew out a thin, homemade cigarette and lit up, breathing deeply. She offered it to me, but I refused as I hadn't in the weeks and months following Antoine's funeral.

Antoine had never liked Paulette, who lived nearby, though she would have given anything to be noticed by him. "I don't think you should hang around with her," he had told me. So I hadn't; I was too busy with school and spending time with him, anyway. Then he died, and suddenly I didn't care about anything. I stopped going to school and began to hang out with Paulette, who hadn't been to school for years.

"It's too bad about your brother, Ari," she had said the first day she found me drinking alone in the park. That had been the day after Antoine's funeral.

"Ariana," I said dully. "Don't call me Ari ever again." In my eyes, Ari had died with Antoine.

"He was one good-looking guy. He . . ." Paulette had talked on, but I hadn't really heard her; it was just nice to have someone to sit with. She pulled out some of her thin cigarettes. "Want one?"

For the first time, I looked into her clouded eyes. "What is it?"

"Marijuana. It will help you feel better."

I took the cigarette and breathed in, hesitantly at first and then more deeply, coughing some but at last finding some relief for the aching pain in my heart. I didn't realize at the time that drugs would bring much more misery to my life than I could ever imagine.

After that day at the park, Paulette and I became inseparable. We hung out with a group of teenagers like us, brave on the outside, yet each hurting in some way on the inside. We drank all the time, went dancing, and smoked. Sometimes I never even bothered to go home. At times my parents didn't notice, at others they yelled at me, but it made no difference. I was living my own life, and they had no influence over me.

Then I met Jacques. I had just turned eighteen, and we were at our favorite dance club celebrating when I saw a good-looking young man with dark blond hair come from across the room toward our group. Several of the guys got up to meet him.

"Hey, welcome back, Jacques! How did things go on the Riviera?"

"Good, good," Jacques replied, a sincere smile on his handsome face. "But I missed you all." His eyes suddenly spotted me. "Who's this? Someone new to our little group?"

"I'm Ariana," I said with a smile. "It's my birthday, and we're cele-brating."

Jacques came to sit beside me and put a casual arm around the back of my chair. "I'm glad to meet you, Ariana." His brown eyes burned into my own. "Very glad."

"Oh, yeah, I'm sure you are," I joked dryly. "I've heard all about you, Jacques, and your way with women."

He smiled impudently. "Good. Then you will let me help you have a great birthday, won't you? I'll make it one you'll never forget!"

And he did. We danced together all night, laughing and joking. He was so handsome and attentive, always saying just the right thing. He knew how to treat a woman, how to flatter her and make her feel loved and cared for.

I didn't go home at all that night, not wanting to be separated from the dashing Jacques. The magic between us was strong, yet I feared it would vanish if we were parted, even for a few hours. The group of us crashed at someone's apartment, and we stayed up all night watching videos, smoking pot, and drinking. At last I went to sleep in the crook of Jacques' arm, feeling more content than I had since Antoine's death.

Jacques and I became a couple. The group seemed amazed that the wild Jacques had finally settled down, and I secretly worried that he would leave me. I didn't understand what he saw in me, a girl who had been rejected by her own parents, but he seemed genuinely fascinated and wanted to be a part of every aspect of my life—including my parents. I took Jacques to meet them a few days later, but they refused to accept him and even forbade me to see him. So less than a week after we met, I moved to Paulette's, so Jacques and I could spend every minute together. How could I have known I was only getting into more trouble? I had still been so innocent, even then. That had been just three months ago.

And now we were married, a thing we had decided to do only two days earlier—or rather, something I had convinced Jacques to do. When he finally agreed, Paulette and I had thrown together what kind of a ceremony and party we could. It wasn't much, but our friends pitched in to see that it had a least a semblance of a real wedding. My parents hadn't bothered to show up. They simply sent a substantial check, like some kind of a payoff. I wanted to rip it up into a hundred little pieces and send it back to them, but I had learned the importance of money in the last three months and knew that I would probably need it. I took the check immediately to the bank my father owned, careful to choose a time when he wouldn't be there. I cashed the check, withdrew my own childhood savings, and took the money to another bank, where I opened an account that I kept secret even from Jacques. I wanted to save it for an emergency and couldn't trust him to do so; he seemed to live only for the moment.

"Ariana!" Paulette's voice was insistent. "Are you okay?"

I looked up at her, shaking away the memories. "Yes, I was just thinking."

"About Jacques?"

"Yes." I stared out the open balcony door into the wet night and added softly, "And about Antoine." It was the first time I had said my brother's name to anyone since the day he died, and Paulette seemed taken aback.

"I'm sorry, Ariana. I know things haven't been easy for you. But now that you and Jacques are married, things will get better; you'll see. He's got a job now, and you can get one." Paulette's homely face was serious for once. The curious light of the room made her brown hair seem dull and lifeless, matching the look in her drugged eyes.

I smiled gently at her. "Yes, it just has to be okay." We hugged each other impulsively. I brought my hand to rest on my slightly swollen stomach, where my true hope for the future lay. There the baby I had conceived nearly three months ago, a week after meeting Jacques, was already making its welcome presence felt. For this baby, I had given up drinking and drugs. I was determined to do right by this life inside me, no matter what.

CHAPTER TWO

When Jacques came home three hours later, I was long asleep. I felt him slip into the big bed next to me, and his movements woke me. Sighing contentedly, I rolled over to him; but he was snoring almost before he hit the bed. Once again the tears came, and I blinked them back angrily. After all, he had at least come back to me.

For long moments I stared into the darkness, hearing Jacques' even breathing, yet feeling utterly alone. The night was finally still, broken only by an occasional shout or a lone car. The rain had stopped sometime while I had been sleeping, and I was fiercely glad. Now things would be all right again.

Almost unconsciously, my hand went to where my baby was growing. Sleep finally came, giving me a welcome relief from my lonely thoughts.

"Wake up, my love!" Jacques sang to me the next morning, kissing my face all over. He threw back the covers, and his hand slid down to my stomach. "Hey there, baby, wake up. Daddy wants to talk to you!" He made a show of kissing my belly noisily.

I opened one eye and then the other and held out my arms for him. The dashing man I had fallen in love with was back!

He lay next to me, our arms entwined. "I've brought you breakfast," he whispered, kissing my ear. "Though we've slept so late it's more like lunch!" One brown eye closed in a wink.

I smiled and sat up slowly so I wouldn't feel nauseated; I still had morning sickness most days. While I ate, I examined Jacques carefully. His handsome face showed no signs of a hangover, though his eyes were still clouded with drugs.

"So what are we going to do today?" I asked, trying not to sound too hopeful.

He raised his eyebrows a couple of times suggestively, making me laugh. Then he said seriously, "Well, I thought we could find an apartment. I've got a few leads to follow up. I've had everyone I know out looking since we decided to get married. It has to be something we can afford."

I knew that meant a dump, but I didn't care because we would be together. I smiled. "At least we'll be able to pay for the first month's rent." I was referring to the paycheck Jacques had received just the day before our marriage.

His smile suddenly vanished. He pushed his longish hair back with a nervous hand. "I, uh, spent some of the money last night," he said.

I wanted to scream at him, but I didn't. More than anything, I wanted to keep the peace. Besides, getting upset would only make my morning sickness worse. "How much?"

He told me, and it wasn't as bad as I had expected. We would still be able to get the apartment; we just wouldn't be able to eat for more than a few days. But I knew we would manage somehow. At least he had a job, and I would look for work tomorrow.

After breakfast and a quick shower, we left the hotel. Outside, the June day was hot and sweltering, and many times I felt dizzy. Heat always seemed to do that to me since I became pregnant. But I was determined to spend as few days at the hotel as possible. We went from one old apartment building to the next, and just as I was giving up, we found an apartment. It was a real dump, but at least it was a place to put our few belongings. The real selling point was that it was available immediately.

We paid the landlord and took a second look at the apartment. The paint was peeling, and the room lacked air conditioning. The bathroom was so small that I couldn't go in without leaving the door open or I would feel claustrophobic. The vinyl tile in both the kitchen and bathroom was loose and coming up, the grayish carpet in the living room had dark stains everywhere, and the bedroom had no carpet at all, just heavily pocked and scratched hardwood flooring. I was suddenly glad my parents wouldn't be coming to see me in such a place, far removed from their elegant apartment on the better side of town.

We checked out of the hotel immediately. Paulette helped me move my few belongings from her mother's apartment, and one of the guys helped Jacques move his things from his cousin's where he'd been staying. There wasn't much to move, but the gang had found an old bed, a worn couch, and even a small table for us.

After helping us settle in, our friends laughed, making jokes about newlyweds, and left us to our honeymoon. But Jacques and I spent the day cleaning, or at least I did. Near dinner time, Jacques kissed me and went to get something for us to eat. He didn't come back until after eleven. By that time the apartment was liveable, though not completely clean.

I heard Jacques come in, and I glanced up at him tiredly from the kitchen floor where I was finishing up. "There must have been a long line," I said dryly, eyeing the plastic bag he held in his hands.

He grinned the beautiful smile that always made my heart skip a beat. "I got waylaid down by the bar, but I'm back now." He leaned down to kiss my cheek and handed me the sack. I grabbed it eagerly; I had eaten only bread since lunch and was feeling sick from the lack of good food. But all the bag held was wine, some pastries, and a few thin marijuana cigarettes.

I shook my head at him in anger. I knew that if I didn't eat soon, I would be very sick. "Jacques, I can't eat this junk! You heard what the doctor said when we went last week. I'm supposed to eat *healthy* stuff!"

But Jacques only smiled. He walked to the door and picked up another sack that he had left outside. "I know, gorgeous. That's why I brought you this." He handed me another sack full of yogurt, fruits, cheese, and various other healthy items I had asked him to buy. The food was still cold, so he must have just gotten it down at the new market on the corner that was open all night. "I must have mixed up the sacks," he continued as I tore off the lid on one of the drinkable yogurts.

I drank the yogurt before I replied, needing to stave off the nausea I was feeling. "Thanks, Jacques." I smiled and pulled my husband down to the floor to kiss him with all the passion of a young wife. He loved me so much. It would mean a lot of work and adjusting, but together we would make everything turn out right.

Morning dawned all too soon, bright, hot, and bustling. Jacques left early to go back to his job at a distribution warehouse, where he loaded boxes of clothing and other items into trucks all day. After kissing him good-bye I went back to bed, feeling sick from the late night before. But the sounds from the street and the heat that seeped in from the thin windows and poorly insulated walls made me even more ill. I made myself get out of bed and eat more of the food Jacques had brought me last night. I also spied the wine and marijuana on the counter, but, with a hand on my belly, I resisted the impulse. I was going to do right by my baby.

After breakfast, I showered and left the apartment to look for a job. Though still hot, the streets were better than the apartment because of a cool breeze that blew fresh air into my face. I set my jaw determinedly and started out. I tried nearly every supermarket and café in the area—it was the only work I was qualified for—with not even a hint of an offer. Half of the owners turned me away the minute they found out that I was expecting, so I soon stopped mentioning my condition. I didn't feel good about it, but I needed to eat, didn't I?

The June sun was hot on my head and back as I reluctantly started searching the bars for openings. Not even a breeze broke the afternoon heat. I didn't like the idea of working in a bar, not appreciating the environment for my unborn child because of the smoke and the rough handling of the customers, but I felt I had no choice. Several of the workers told me there were openings and asked me to come back the next day or later in the evening to talk to the managers. I saw a glimmer of hope but was depressed nonetheless; I didn't want to work in a bar.

On the next street, I saw two young men in white shirts and short haircuts walking toward me. With a flash, I remembered the young American with the bright red hair who had talked to me the day of Antoine's funeral nine months before. Pain washed over me, and I hurried across the street to avoid them.

"And he said he'd pray for me," I muttered. "Then why doesn't his God get me a decent job?" Of course, I wouldn't pray for myself; I didn't believe in a God that would let Antoine die. Besides, I had done well enough without Him, hadn't I? I had a husband and a baby—what more did I need? Certainly nothing that confused young man could have offered.

I shrugged the thoughts aside and hurried down the street to the next bar and the next. I had no luck at either. I was only two streets away from our apartment when I suddenly saw a little café squeezed in between a shoe store and a cheap clothing outlet. Above the shop, as above many shops in Paris, loomed a three-story apartment building that appeared old but well-maintained.

I sighed, almost unwilling to risk rejection again. But something urged me over to the café. "Now would be a good time for you to pray," I murmured to the absent red-haired American boy. Again thoughts of Antoine flooded my mind, but I shoved them away. He was dead and gone forever; he couldn't help me now.

The shop had obviously just finished with the last of the lunch crowd, for it was nearly empty. I arranged my blouse carefully over my slightly rounded stomach, though it was really not noticeable to those who didn't know how thin I had become since Antoine's death. Still, I felt as if a neon sign pointed to the baby inside me.

The stout woman at the counter glanced up as I entered. One hand went up to push back a piece of gray hair that had escaped from her bun. She smiled wearily. "What would you like?"

Looking down at the splendid array of sandwiches and pastries, I felt suddenly hungry. I had stopped several times during the day to nibble at the cheese and bread I carried in my purse, but it was long past time for me to eat again. Nausea rose up in my throat, and I fought it down.

"I'm—I'm looking for work," I said as clearly as possible. "Do you have any openings?"

The lady studied me a full minute in silence before saying severely, "I don't hire people on drugs."

"But I'm not," I protested as the room around me began to spin. I felt the blackness coming as it always did if I didn't eat at least every three hours, and suddenly I knew I was going to either be sick or pass out.

I turned from the woman as quickly as I could, hoping at least to make it out the door. The room whirled faster, and the blackness ate at the edges of my consciousness. Desperately, I clutched at the nearest table to try to steady myself. Then everything went black.

The next thing I knew, someone was dabbing my face with a cool cloth. "Wake up," said a woman's voice. It was the woman from the counter, but this time her voice was softer.

I sat up quickly, only to feel a return of the sickness. I lay back down on the cot and looked around the small room anxiously for my purse.

"My purse," I whispered urgently. "Where is it?"

The woman clenched her lips tightly but handed me the purse. She obviously thought that I was going to pull out some drugs. I ignored her as I fumbled through my bag, my fingers eagerly closing around my one remaining cheese sandwich. I took a big bite and began to chew while the lady watched me curiously, a puzzled expression replacing her former disgust. After swallowing the first bite, I forced myself to eat more slowly; it would make my embarrassment even worse to throw up now.

After the small sandwich was gone, I glanced up to see the woman still staring at me. I brought one hand instinctively to my stomach that jutted out, still small but tellingly from my thin body as I lay on the cot. The woman saw the gesture, and her gray eyebrows raised slightly.

A bell rang in the distance, and the woman spoke. "I've got customers. You rest right here a moment, and I'll be back." She smiled ever so briefly and disappeared through the door.

I sat up slowly and surveyed the small, windowless room. A desk, a chair, the cot, and a large bookcase took up most of the space, obviously the woman's—or someone else's—office. I stood up and walked to the office door, which led into a large kitchen. Through a door beyond that I could see the stout woman helping a man at the counter.

There seemed to be no way out of the shop without passing the woman—unless one of the closed doors in the kitchen was a hall leading to her living quarters and perhaps a back door. It was likely, but I didn't want to make the situation worse by being caught snooping. I went back and sat on the cot.

The woman returned in minutes. In her hands she carried a glass of milk. "Here, drink this," she said gruffly, handing it to me. "You should drink a lot of milk for the baby."

I took the milk and did as she asked. "I'm sorry," I said between sips. "I didn't realize I had gone so long without eating. I've been searching for a job all morning, and I was almost home when I saw your shop.

I thought it couldn't hurt to try." I looked down at the floor and blinked back tears. Whatever hope I had of getting a job at this particular café was long gone.

"What's your name?"

"Ariana. Ariana Merson, I mean Ariana de Cotte—I got married recently."

"I'm Marguerite Geoffrin," the woman said. "My husband and I own this café and the apartment building over it. That's where he is right now, fixing a shower in one of the apartments while we're not too busy." She paused, and her next words surprised me. "Business is very good, and in fact we do need someone to work the lunch and dinner shifts, Tuesday through Saturday. If you are willing to work, we'll give you a chance."

I looked up at her quickly, hardly daring to believe my luck. "But why?" The words came out before I had a chance to stop them. "What about when the baby comes?"

Marguerite smiled. "We'll cross that bridge when we come to it, Ariana. First let's see if you're a good worker."

I returned her smile eagerly. "Oh, I will be, I promise!"

Marguerite held up her hand. "But there is one condition." Her expression became serious. "You will not use drugs of any kind."

"I smoked pot for a few months," I confessed hesitantly. "But since I found out about the baby, I quit. I want to do what's right for it."

"Then it's agreed. You will earn the minimum salary plus two meals daily—or four half meals if you prefer, given your condition. Be here tomorrow at noon. I think that you already have been too long on your feet today."

"Oh, thank you, Madame Geoffrin! And I won't let you down, I promise!"

"I hope not, Ariana," she said softly. Her eyes grew very sad. There was something more she wasn't telling me, some reason why she was giving me a chance, but I didn't want to push her. There would be time enough later to find out her secrets.

Jacques and I celebrated that night, using our last money to pay for an inexpensive dinner at a restaurant, saving just enough to buy bread until payday. Since Jacques also ate a meal at work, we would survive.

After dinner, he drank a lot of wine, but I was used to his doing so. I was content to see my handsome husband enjoying himself.

The next weeks went by happily for me. The work at the café was constant but not strenuous, and the customers were nice. I had plenty of opportunities to rest my feet when business wasn't so brisk. Marguerite, as I soon began to call Madame Geoffrin, even brought a tall stool to put behind the counter where I could sit and take the customers' money while she filled their orders during the rushes. Together, we developed a system that efficiently took care of customers in the minimum amount of time, and this only increased our business. In the kitchen her husband, Jules, was busy preparing the foods we served to the many customers. I felt more needed than I had ever felt in my life, even when Antoine was alive. He had never needed me, only loved me.

Marguerite mothered me, and I responded to her care. She filled a void in my life that I hadn't realized even existed. She and Jules became my closest friends besides Jacques and Paulette.

Summer turned into mid-October, and I blossomed—in more ways than one. Of course my stomach grew, and in fact I gained needed weight all over. But I also became more sure of myself and more positive about my future. The only strain on my new happiness was Jacques. Two months before the baby was due, four months after our marriage, he came home in a rage.

"I quit!" he exclaimed as he walked through the door. It was nearly noon, and I was getting ready to leave for the café.

"You *what?*" I asked in amazement. He had been doing well at work, and together our wages were paying nicely for our expenses. We had bought a few new things for the apartment and for the baby, and I was already dreaming about moving to a better home—someplace where the plumbing didn't need to be repaired, where there were no cockroaches, and where the neighbors didn't party all night long. Not that I ever complained about the parties; we were as bad as our neighbors in that respect. Many nights our friends were over very late, watching our secondhand TV and smoking pot or drinking. I didn't mind it as long as they stayed out of my bedroom and didn't make us pay for the liquor. But still, things would have to change once the baby was born. I wanted my child to *be* something, not grow up to be a junkie.

"I quit my job," Jacques repeated. "They accused me of being on heroin, and I won't stand to be treated that way."

I didn't say anything for a time, my suspicion growing by the minute. He hadn't exactly denied taking the drug. "Well, are you?" I finally asked.

He glared at me. "It's none of their business what I do in my off time. It isn't affecting my work any."

My heart began to race. Marijuana was one thing, but heroin was something quite different. I had been in the gang long enough to see what kinds of lives were led by those who were addicted.

"It's no big deal," Jacques said, understanding immediately my expression of horror. "Everyone in the gang has been trying it lately, even Paulette."

"When?" I still couldn't believe it.

He shrugged. "While you're at work in the evenings. Sometimes here, sometimes at one of the others' apartments. What difference does it make? The fact is, the stuff is wonderful. It makes you forget all your problems and—"

"I didn't know being married to me was a big problem," I blurted. Tears came to my eyes. "I thought we were moving up in the world, that we could be like normal families and leave this life behind!"

Jacques stared at me. "I don't *want* to leave this life behind! I want to live, to feel, to experience life to the fullest!"

"Is that what you're doing when you're all drugged up?" I spat at him. "Experiencing life? That's some reality for you!"

"I didn't know you wanted to make us over to be like your parents!" he rejoined cruelly. "Or maybe your sainted brother!"

"How *dare* you!" I was crying hard now, smearing the mascara I had just applied. Jacques turned from me and stalked into our room. I followed him.

"What are you going to do now?" I asked. "What about our baby? I can't possibly pay for the bills alone! Please, Jacques!"

He flung himself on the bed. "Don't worry, Ari. I'll get a new job after I take a little vacation. We've already paid one month's advance rent, so I deserve a rest." He lay back and closed his eyes.

What about me? I wanted to scream at him. *What about* my *rest?* I felt the baby inside of me move restlessly, responding to my emotion, and I forced myself to be calm. "Don't call me Ari," I said through grit-ted teeth, keeping my voice calm. "My name is Ariana." Leaving him there on the bed, I turned and ran out the door, pausing only to snatch up my coat from the couch. The October weather was cold, but I was warm from the sparks of our fight. I almost wished I never had to see Jacques again.

I arrived at the café slightly late, but Marguerite didn't say anything. She took one look at me and hustled me to the bathroom, leaving Jules to man the café. Working quickly, she cleaned away the streaked mas-cara under my eyes and gave me some powder to cover the red blotches on my face.

"What happened?" she asked softly.

"Jacques and I had our first fight." I nearly started crying again at the words. "He lost his job, and he's taking heroin," I added, searching her face beseechingly. "I don't know what to do. I thought we could make a better life for our baby, but he doesn't seem to want to. At this moment, I wish I'd never met him!"

Marguerite listened intently. "You've good right to be upset. Not only is heroin addictive, but it can kill. You must not get involved with it, Ariana, no matter what!" A shadow passed quickly over her face. "You asked me once why I hired you, and I'll tell you now. I had a daughter who hung out with a group like yours. She left home and soon got into heroin and prostitution. She ended up dead." Marguerite paused, and tears rolled down her wrinkled cheeks. "When you came here, I saw my little girl again, asking for help before she was drawn into the depths. I couldn't help but think that if someone had been there to help her, she would still be alive today."

The bell hanging on the outside door tinkled suddenly. Then again and again. Marguerite wiped her tears away with the back of her hand.

"I'm so sorry," I whispered, suddenly understanding much more about this woman who had befriended me.

"Just don't let me down," was her reply. She hurried back to the counter to help Jules with the customers, leaving me to follow thoughtfully.

CHAPTER THREE

*O*ctober went by in a rush of work—for me, anyway. Jacques mostly moped around the apartment in the mornings and complained because I wasn't spending enough time with him. I kept urging him to find a job, but it was a month before he did. During the first few weeks he didn't even try to find a job but would spend hours with his friends, drinking and shooting up. I knew he was still using heroin, though I didn't know where he got the money. As soon as I got my check, I paid the bills and bought groceries. After that, there was nothing left. Jacques murmured several times that it wasn't right for us to live in such poverty while my parents lived in luxury. He wanted me to ask them for money. "You could say it was for the baby," he suggested several times.

"But I don't want their help!" I told him finally. "Besides, they never loved or wanted me; why would they want to give me money?" But even as I said it, happier times when Antoine was alive came to mind. I could see now that they probably had once loved me in their own way. And as for money, the large check they had sent me for my wedding—something I was now grateful I had never told Jacques about—showed they at least felt some responsibility toward me.

"They'd pay just to get you off their backs," he insisted, his sensitivity clouded by his habit.

I sighed. "Jacques, I will not ask my parents for money. You're perfectly healthy, and there's no reason you can't find a job." I wanted to add that even if my parents gave me money, I certainly wouldn't give it to him to spend on drugs. I tried to encourage him but carefully, so as not to offend his already bruised ego. "You're a good-looking, smart guy," I said, reaching to wrap my arms around his neck and get as close as my huge belly would let me. "There must be a hundred companies out there looking for someone like you." I kissed him tenderly and left for work, hours before I should have, bundled up against the increasing November cold.

I went down the sidewalk, not noticing where I was wandering, and thought about Jacques. Today he hadn't gotten mad at my suggestion that he find work, like he had all the other times. That was a very good sign. Maybe things would work out after all.

I made my way mindlessly to the subway and from there to the Seine River, where I sat on a stone bench and watched the boats pass by. From where I was, I could see the Cité—one of the islands that rose in the middle of the Seine. I walked along the parapets next to the river, pausing at several bookstalls without buying anything. Their prices were never low; they sold more to the tourists than to the natives. At the moment, business was very slow because of the off-season, and many of the vendors had simply packed up and left, waiting for spring to return again.

An old woman was selling hot chestnuts from a cart and I eagerly bought some, holding them close to my chest for their warmth. Then I turned back to the Cité, where I could see the tall spires of the Cathédrale de Notre-Dame de Paris standing out majestically against the more modern lines of the hotel next to it. A feeling of longing overwhelmed me, and I knew that it was for Antoine.

I shrugged off the feeling and began walking, peeling and eating the warm chestnuts as I went. Soon I could see the Palais de Justice. I paused as I always did when seeing it. Somewhere among the buildings lay La Conciergerie, where prisoners like Marie-Antoinette had been held and later beheaded during the French Revolution.

Antoine and I had always loved to hear about the Revolution—how Marie-Antoinette's children had been taken from her and adopted by others and how Mme. Roland, on the scaffold, had uttered the famous words, "Oh, Liberty—what crimes are committed in thy name!" We had acted out the parts with passion. But it had all been a game, for neither of us had yet felt the touch of death.

I turned my head quickly from the memories. Realizing the hour was growing late, I raced down the street at a rate quite unbecoming a woman eight months pregnant. Against the cold, I scrunched my neck and head down in the thick coat that didn't quite reach around my belly—a remnant left over from the easy days with my parents.

I literally ran into them before I even saw them . . . two young men in dark suits and overcoats. For a moment I was scared, until I looked up into their innocent faces filled with concern.

"Uh, excuse me," I said, disengaging myself. Futilely, I tried to pull my coat lapels together to hide my stomach and laughed self-consciously when I saw them watching me.

"Well, it's just as well we ran into you," the tallest said in accented French. "I'm Elder Walton, and this is my companion, Elder Fredric. We're missionaries from The Church of Jesus Christ of Latter-day Saints, and we have a message to share with you. Do you have a family?"

"Yes," I said, not bothering to hide my reluctance at answering. I knew without a doubt that they were going to start that foolishness about families being forever like the red-haired boy had done over a year ago, the day of Antoine's funeral. His words had never stopped haunting me, and I didn't want to hear anything else from his friends. I would put a stop to it right now. "But he's dead and gone, and you can't bring him back. It's over—now, leave me alone!" I skirted around them quickly and continued my wild flight to the subway, resenting them for talking about something that I still so desperately wished could be true.

I made it to the café barely on time, throwing myself into my work so as not to think about Jacques, Antoine, or anything serious. But I still felt restless and unhappy. Marguerite eyed me strangely but didn't say anything, letting me work out my own problems. I was grateful for her patience.

Just before the dinner rush, Jacques, with Paulette in tow, came to see me. For once, my husband's eyes were clear of drugs, unlike Paulette's, whose light brown stare was clouded and who moved as if in a dream.

"I got me a job!" Jacques exclaimed, his beautiful smile transforming his features into those of the man with whom I had fallen in love.

I ran around the counter to hug him. "That's great! What will you be doing?"

"Well, my uncle works for the train station, and he got me a job as a ticket taker. No more heavy lifting for me!" Jacques picked me up and whirled me around somewhat awkwardly.

I felt my happiness flood back. "I'm so happy, Jacques! I knew you could do it!" Jacques swaggered around a bit, basking in my praise like a small child. He kissed me quickly and turned to leave.

"I'm going to tell the gang," he called over his shoulder when he reached the door. His eyes darted to Paulette. "You coming?"

She shook her head. "Naw. I came to talk to Ariana. Tell them I'll come by later." Jacques shrugged and left, whistling happily to himself as he walked out into the cold.

I took my break in the kitchen, bringing Paulette with me. "I've only got a few minutes before the rush starts," I warned. "Speak fast."

Paulette focused her eyes briefly on me, as if trying to remember what she had come to say. "Oh yeah, it was your parents. I saw them outside your father's bank. They recognized me and asked about you."

The knowledge startled me. "Did you tell them about the baby?"

She shook her head. "No way. I know you don't want that."

"So what did you tell them? How did they look? Did they ask to see me?" My heart beat rapidly as the questions rushed out one after another, with barely a pause in between.

Paulette closed her eyes for a moment to let the questions sink into her drugged brain. "Let's see. I told them you had a job at a small but very nice café, that you and Jacques were still desperately in love, and that you weren't drinking anymore. They asked specifically about that, but I don't think they believed me. And . . . what else did you want to know?"

"How did they look?" I prompted.

"Not good. Older than before—when your brother was—"

"Did they ask to see me?" I interrupted, not wanting Antoine dragged into the conversation. "Or say that I was welcome there or something?"

Paulette shook her head. "No."

I sighed. I don't know what I had been expecting. Like me, they were still grieving for Antoine. At least I had new hope in my baby.

I glanced out to the counter, where people were beginning to line up. "I've got to go now, but thanks, Paulette." We left the kitchen, and I climbed up on my high stool, watching her leave.

Marguerite was staring at me, and I turned my attention to her, raising my eyebrows questioningly.

She pointed to the door with her chin. "That one is just about done for," she said sadly. "She looks like my Michelle the last time I saw her. A few years later, she was dead." Marguerite turned from me, putting on a mask of happiness for the next customer—but not before I saw the devastating loss in her eyes.

How horrible to lose your only child like that, I thought. My hand went to where my own little one grew, stretching the skin on my stomach so tightly that I feared it would break. *I'll never let you near drugs,* I vowed, setting my jaw firmly. *I'll keep you safe—even if it means keeping you from your own father.*

Wistfully, I turned to my work, masking my thoughts as had Marguerite. Life always went on its speeding course, not caring if one had time to think out the important things.

———

Jacques kept his job for only a short time. He was fired two weeks before Christmas for fighting on the job—not once but on three different occasions. The company had to pay damages on two of the cases and was taking no more risks with him. His pay for the two weeks had taken care of the rent for one more month, as well as the carpet cleaning I insisted on before the baby came, but I had expected much more.

Jacques plunged once more into his drunken, drug-filled world, this time with a vengeance. I withdrew from him, despairing of what I could do to save him and myself.

"What about when the baby comes?" I asked him a couple of days before I was due, a week before Christmas. "I'm not going to be able to work for a while. How will we eat and pay the rent?"

He turned on me. "This whole baby idea wasn't mine," he sneered. "But I did right by marrying you, didn't I? Leave me alone!" He stalked out, slamming the door behind him.

Once more I was late for work, making things worse by bursting into tears the minute I walked in the door. Again Marguerite took me into the back, leaving Jules with the customers. "What did he do *this* time?" she asked almost menacingly, helping me off with my coat and gloves.

"He got fired, the baby's coming, the doctor tells me that I won't be able to work for two or three weeks . . ." The words came out in a rush as I hiccupped and sobbed my way through my problems.

Marguerite listened sympathetically. When I had calmed somewhat, she said, "Well, your doctor is right. I remember with my Michelle, I was in bed for a week and couldn't walk without pain for another two. They told me that second babies are better, though, so remember that it shouldn't be so bad the next time."

"The *next* time?" The idea sounded so ridiculous that I laughed in spite of myself. I had learned a thing or two in the last nine months, and there was no way I was going to have another baby until Jacques straightened out completely.

Marguerite smiled. "And Ariana, you don't have to worry about how to pay your rent. You have become very valuable to us. Your friendliness and quickness at filling orders have helped increased business substantially, and we've decided to raise your wage. You can also take your vacation with pay earlier, instead of after a year's work, so you can receive money while on maternity leave. And when you get well, you can bring the baby with you to work. We'll put a crib in the office where the cot is, and you can come and nurse or take care of him or her anytime you want. Jules and I will help you."

I threw my arms around Marguerite. "Oh, thank you! How can I ever repay you?"

Marguerite sniffed. "You have already become the daughter I lost, and I am very proud of you. I should have told you before this, but . . ." She shrugged as her voice trailed off. We sat in comfortable silence, and then she spoke again.

"There's one more thing, Ariana. We have several small, one bedroom apartments above us that are or will soon be vacant. I know you want a better environment for your child, and while our building is old, it is well cared for and the renters very carefully screened. We would offer you a rent as low as your other place if you want to move here, but . . ." She hesitated as if choosing her words carefully, "we wouldn't accept anyone on drugs."

I nodded, knowing that she meant Jacques. "Thank you, Marguerite. I am very grateful to you, and I will think about it, but I do mean to stay with my husband, if I can. I still love him."

Marguerite stood up. "I understand that, Ariana," she said softly. "I simply wanted you to be aware of an alternative if you should come to need it."

We went to work, relieving Jules, who was swamped with orders. Together Marguerite and I handled the rush easily, talking naturally with our customers, most of whom we knew by name. Through the afternoon, I felt my stomach tighten and relax as it had been doing for the last week. False labor, they called it, and while it wasn't really painful, it did give me a sense of what was to come.

In the late afternoon, I noticed the contractions were coming at regular fifteen-minute intervals. They still seemed no harder or more painful than before, but it drove me to distraction. Could the baby be coming?

The dinner rush was hectic as usual, and I worked as quickly as possible to take the customers' orders. During any slowdown, no matter how brief, Marguerite or I would slip over to the dining area to clear the tables. At first, I didn't notice that the contractions were coming even closer and more severely, causing me to catch my breath. I thought I was just tired from the long day. Then, all at once, I doubled up in pain near a table I was wiping clean. I sat abruptly on the chair in surprise. I knew without a doubt that I was in real labor. There could be no mistaking it.

"Marguerite!" I shouted, oblivious to the many curious stares turned my way. My pain and excitement must have been written on my face, because she dropped what she was doing immediately.

"We're closing early tonight!" she pronounced, raising her voice. "Ariana's going to have her baby!" Everyone clapped, and a few regulars crowded around me. Marguerite brought my coat and helped me into it.

"You take her to the hospital," Jules said. "I'll close and see if I can find Jacques before I follow you." He put his hand on the shoulder of one of the regulars. "Will you take them in your car?" The man nodded, and he and Marguerite helped me out the door into the freezing night air.

As we left, I noticed someone had already put up the "Closed" sign on the door to the café, with a bigger one beneath that read: "Ariana's having her baby!" The words brought a lump to my throat and tears to my eyes.

I remember little of the mad dash through Paris to the hospital, only the pain that seemed to come and go like waves in the ocean. I do remember calling Antoine's name and my mother's, but neither was there to help me. Just Marguerite, whose rough hand clasped mine and helped me through the pain.

When we got to the hospital, I was already fully dilated. The doctor told me I had probably been in labor since the early afternoon yet hadn't recognized it. He offered me some drugs to dull the pain, though he was doubtful they would take effect before the baby came. Regardless, I refused. There was no way I would allow drugs into my body—Jacques already used more than enough drugs for his whole family.

I didn't once think of my husband as I pushed and pushed, feeling that my insides were about to explode. Through it all, Marguerite was a solid rock in my storm. Sometime near the end, Jacques came into the room. His eyes were glazed, and he reeked of alcohol. For an instant I was happy to see him, until I realized that he was mostly unaware of what was happening. When he suddenly leaned over and retched on the floor, I glared at him angrily.

"Not even for this could you be sober! Get out! I don't want you here to sully our baby!" Anger flared briefly in his eyes, but he turned and left without uttering a single word.

Someone cleaned up the mess while I tried to rest between contractions, which were coming more quickly by the moment. Soon I could no longer tell when one ended and the other began.

"I can see the head now, Ariana," the doctor said suddenly. "Just a couple more big pushes, and it'll be out."

My labor had already gone on much longer than the doctor had expected, and I was exhausted. Still, I gathered up my scattered energy and pushed for all I was worth. Five more pushes and the head was finally free, followed immediately by the body. Relief flooded through me—never had I known such a wonderful feeling!

"You have a little girl," the doctor said, bringing the baby to me. "Healthy and beautiful."

I knew as he spoke that I had wanted a girl all along. I hadn't been able to afford an ultrasound to determine the sex of my child, but in my dreams, the baby had always been a girl. "Oh, my precious Antoinette," I cooed. "You're so beautiful! I've waited so long for you!"

"She's so perfect!" Marguerite exclaimed in awe.

We sat there looking down in speechless admiration at my baby for long minutes, until the doctor whisked her away for a few tests. I felt a great loss when they took her from me, almost an ache. But before I knew it, she was back again in my arms, and Marguerite was showing me how to nurse her.

A sudden commotion came from down the hall as Jacques pushed past Jules, who on Marguerite's instructions was guarding the waiting room door. "It's my baby too!" he yelled. "And I want to see her!"

I was afraid of what I would see when he barged his way in, but someone had given him lots of coffee and made him shower and change. There was only a trace of the drugs in his eyes, and not even the smell remained of the alcohol.

Jacques stared at the baby in amazement. "She's so tiny, so beautiful," he whispered reverently. He reached out to glide a finger over Antoinette's cheek.

"Would you like to hold her?" I asked, keeping the reluctance from my voice.

Jacques stared at the baby for a minute before replying. "May I?" I nodded and carefully handed Antoinette to him. As I did, she opened her dark eyes to gaze into her father's. Wonder spread over his face. Happiness blossomed in my heart as I watched my husband tenderly cuddle our daughter, our little angel from heaven. Sighing, I lay back on the pillows. From the corner of my eye, I caught a glimpse of Jules hovering outside the room.

"Jules, come in here and see the baby," I called. He came eagerly with the same reverence on his face that Jacques had shown.

After a few minutes, Jacques awkwardly handed the baby back to me. "I think she's hungry, she's trying to suck on her fist." I gratefully took my daughter back into my arms.

"I didn't know what it would be like," Jacques continued, his voice clearly showing amazement. "I had no idea I would feel this way." He tore his gaze from Antoinette and looked at me earnestly. "I do want to be worthy of her—and you, Ariana. I'll make good, you'll see. I'm through with drugs."

I knew he was sincere, and I wanted to believe him. But something told me that such a change wouldn't come easily.

CHAPTER FOUR

I got a job!" Jacques exclaimed triumphantly the day before Christmas. Little Nette was six days old. I felt a sense of déjà vu; this was the third time Jacques had said this exact phrase to me since I first met him, once before our marriage and twice since. I wondered how long this job would last.

I stifled the thought quickly. "That's great, honey!" I said. "Doing what?"

"I'm a doorman at that hotel near Notre Dame!"

I was surprised. "Why, that's really something! I can't believe it! How did you do it?"

He told me in detail, but my thoughts wandered as he spoke. It didn't matter how he had charmed his way into the job, just that he had gotten it. The week since Nette's birth had passed in a sea of happiness for me, marred only by the fear that Jacques would not live up to his promise. But each day he had searched diligently for work and then had come home to attend to Nette and me faithfully. I hadn't seen him drugged up or drinking the whole week, though I had smelled alcohol on his breath a time or two, and I was happy that he seemed to be keeping his promise. I was proud of Jacques and felt all the love I had for my handsome husband brimming to the surface again.

While I was happy with Jacques and basked in his tender care, I still felt afraid to trust and love him completely. With my precious new baby, I had no such reserves. I delighted in Nette and lavished upon her all the love I felt I hadn't received from my own mother—all the love I had once cherished only for my twin brother. She was a miracle, and I couldn't believe the incredible love and awe that glowed in my heart each time I looked at her soft, perfect features. I gave her my whole love as only a mother can. In return, she was a good baby, fussing only when she was hungry or tired.

I was relieved to have my own body back after being pregnant for so long, though my breasts were sore and cracked from nursing. I shrugged the pain aside, knowing it would not last.

"How about a party to celebrate my new job?" Jacques suggested, coming to sit with me on our old couch. He had finished a very prolonged explanation of how he convinced the manager at the hotel to hire him, a feat that included showing pictures of me and little Antoinette.

While I hadn't been listening closely to his story, I stiffened immediately at the mention of a party. "I don't think that's a good idea, Jacques," I protested, choosing my words carefully. "The baby is too young to be exposed to all that smoke and excitement."

Jacques looked doubtful but still seemed determined to do what was best for his daughter. "Well, maybe you're right. We can have a party in a few weeks, when she's older."

So we spent a quiet and happy Christmas, cuddling together against the cold outside that seeped in through the thin windows and walls. We bought each other small gifts—a new pair of gloves for me and a wallet for Jacques—and we ate Christmas dinner with Marguerite and Jules. Because of the baby, we all agreed to have dinner on Christmas Day instead of the traditional one at midnight on Christmas Eve. For presents, Marguerite and Jules gave us clothes for Antoinette, and I happily dressed her up in each outfit to model for us while Jules snapped photographs. To my wonder, Jacques was charming and full of fun; even Marguerite was impressed with him.

The next week sped by quickly. Paulette and Marguerite came to see me often, cooing and cuddling the baby. I loved Marguerite's visits, but I was always nervous to let Paulette hold Nette. She was more often drugged than not, and I was afraid she would drop the baby. I didn't let the rest of our gang in the apartment at all, using the sleeping baby and my recovery as an excuse; but the better I became, the harder it was to keep them out. It helped that Jacques worked mostly nights; I simply didn't answer the door when they came, justifying my actions because of Antoinette.

When little Nette was two weeks old, I returned to work. I felt good, though I still tired easily. "That's because you're nursing," Marguerite said as she showed me the small crib with wheels that she and Jules had purchased. "See? It rolls. That way if she's awake, we can roll her into the kitchen to be with Jules while he's cooking, or even to the counter with us if we're not too busy. Of course, when she's a little older we'll have to block off part of the kitchen and put some blankets down to let her crawl—we can't have her growing up confined to a crib, you know."

Her expression was serious, and I laughed. "Yes, I know, Marguerite, and I'll be careful never to leave her in a crib too much at home." I didn't tell Marguerite that I didn't even have a crib for Nette at the apartment, that she slept peacefully next to me on our bed. This made it easier for night nursings, and Jacques and I both loved to cuddle with her.

At first it was difficult for me to leave Nette in the office or kitchen. It was as if a part of me was missing—and I guess in a way it was; Nette, after all, had been a part of me for nine months. She slept most of the time, and the few times she was fussy I carried her next to my chest in a baby carrier, or Jules sang to her in the kitchen. I was very happy.

We had more customers than ever that week, as many people were still on holiday from work or school. News about the baby spread quickly, and nearly everyone insisted on seeing her. Many of the regulars brought gifts. "Where is that baby?" people would say as they approached the counter, and I would proudly show her off. "She looks just like you with that dark hair and big brown eyes," they would always continue. I thought that she did too, though she had her father's slight cleft in her tiny chin.

My life seemed perfect. Oh, I still complained about my apartment and secretly missed my parents, but I was so full of wonder and love for my daughter that those things made little difference. To me, it seemed almost as if my beloved brother had been restored to me in the form of a baby, though I did not believe that exactly.

Jacques had been at his job for three weeks when he brought up the party again. We were spending a quiet night alone in front of the TV. For once it hadn't been busy at the café, and Marguerite had sent me home early. Little Nette was already asleep on our bed.

"Let's have a party to show off the baby," he said abruptly.

"But the smoke—"

"We won't let anyone smoke—pot or tobacco. Afterwards, they can move down to one of the bars. Or," he cast me a boyish glance, "they can smoke in the hall."

"Okay," I agreed reluctantly, seeing his excitement and determination in the matter. "But no drugs, no shooting up. Not around the baby."

"It's a deal! Tomorrow night, then. It's Sunday, and we're both off." He jumped up abruptly, glancing at his watch.

"Where are you going?"

"To get some drinks for the party. The liquor store's still open. And I'll call a few of the guys to spread the word." He threw on his coat and shot out the door.

I was left alone.

"This is one hoppin' party!" a man shouted at me above the dance music. I tried not to wince at the reek of alcohol on his breath.

I nodded and turned abruptly to search the crowd for Jacques. The front room and kitchen were full of people, half of whom I had never even met. They were dancing, necking, playing cards, and drinking. So far, they had all scrupulously obeyed Jacques when he said no smoking or drugs in the house, but it had made little difference. They went just outside in the hall to do both, leaving the door wide open so the smoke drifted into the apartment. Many of our guests were already passed out in the hall and on our floor.

"Have you seen Jacques?" I asked Paulette when I found her sitting in the hall, squeezed in among many others.

"In the kitchen, last I saw," Paulette said. "But relax, Ariana. He's just having a good time celebrating his new job and Nette. Loosen up a little and have some fun, like in the good old days before you got pregnant." She pointed down at a needle in her hand. "Want a little?"

"No!" I said tightly. I had already taken a few drinks but quit when I started to feel dizzy. I couldn't risk not being able to take care of Nette should she need me.

I found Jacques in a crowded corner of the kitchen as Paulette had said, having a drinking contest with five of his friends. I saw at once that he was already too far gone to move the party to a bar somewhere, but still I tried.

"Jacques, it's time to go to the bar!" I shouted above the din.

He stared at me dumbly for a few moments, as if trying to remember who I was. "Oh, it's you, Ariana," he said finally. "Have a drink?" He held up his glass with an unsteady hand.

I turned away, disgusted, making my way as quickly as possible to our small bedroom where I had left Nette after her brief, one-minute introduction to her father's friends. I had made sure the room was off limits, marking it with a large sign and verbal threats. So far no one had dared enter, but I was afraid to leave Nette for very long; these were people who thrived on breaking the rules. Fleetingly, I wondered what I had ever seen in such a life.

Yet as I pushed through the thick mass of bodies, a sinking despair flooded through me. *Maybe this is what life's all about,* I thought. Suddenly, I was tempted to throw myself into the party, to drink myself crazy in order to rid myself of this growing hopelessness. Only the thought of my precious little Nette saved me.

I finally reached the bedroom and opened the door. My anger flared as I saw a couple wrestling around on my bed, threatening at any second to roll over my one-month-old daughter. I raced up to the bed, fury and fear flooding my mind and body, blotting out the former despair; it was a savage blaze, ripping through my soul. Abruptly, I was the fear-strengthened mother protecting her young.

"Get out!" I screamed, pulling them off the bed and onto the floor with a strength I didn't know I possessed. They landed with a bump and a chorus of complaints. "Get out of my room!" I yelled again. I wanted to scream stronger words at them, words that until then I hadn't realized I even knew; but ever conscious of my little daughter, I refrained. Grabbing the couple by the necks of their T-shirts, I hauled them over to the door, practically strangling them. They were too weak with drugs and drinking to protest much. I reached to open the door to shove them out. As I did so, two more couples burst in.

"Not in here!" I shrieked. "I swear I'll call the police!" That finally got them all out the door, but I knew it wouldn't keep them for long.

I swept over to the bed to make sure Nette was all right. Still shaking with fury, I forced myself to focus on what to do next. We had to get out of the apartment. I dressed the baby as quickly as possible in her warm body coat, shoving extra items into the baby bag someone had given me. Nette's eyes opened, and her lips curled in a sweet, angelic smile.

"I'm getting you out of here, Nette," I whispered. She closed her eyes trustingly, already dozing off again to dream of things that babies dream.

I added an extra layer to my own clothing and wrapped Nette in two more blankets to protect her from the winter cold. We left quickly, stopping only at the closet to get my own coat. From the corner of my eye, I saw another couple head toward my room. Anger again flared in me, but getting Nette somewhere safe was more important now. I shrugged and turned my back resolutely on the crowded apartment. No one paid any attention to us as we left.

Though it rarely snowed in Paris, it did get very cold in the winter months. This January night was no exception. An icy wind was blowing furiously outside, and I put Nette inside my coat, making sure she could still breathe but protecting her face from the biting wind. "We'll go to Marguerite's," I said softly to the baby, though she was asleep. "Only two blocks away." I watched the shadows carefully as I hurried down the sidewalk. These streets were not the safest at this hour, and I had never walked them alone after dark. Either Jules or Jacques had always walked me home after my shift at the café. Cold fear arose in me, but I didn't know what else to do.

All at once, I remembered the red-haired American missionary and thought, *Now's the time I really need a prayer.* But I didn't pray for myself, at least not consciously. Nette's coming had made me rethink my former disbelief in God, but I hadn't yet figured out exactly what I did believe.

As I neared the café, I realized that someone was following us. "Please, let us make it," I mumbled, not realizing that such a fervent wish was actually a prayer. We arrived at the café, and I began to ring the buzzer insistently. I could now see three youths coming down the street, angling for where I stood. My heart beat wildly as I thought about what I should do. *Should I run? Face them? What?* I pushed again and again on the buzzer and then turned to face the three young men. I felt helpless to protect myself and my daughter.

"What's a pretty thing like you doing all alone on a night like this?" one asked as they neared. "We can help you out!"

"I don't need help, thank you," I said stiffly, trying to hide my fear. Inside my coat, Nette began to wriggle in her sleep, and I shifted her position awkwardly.

"Hey now, what you got inside that coat?" the youth asked, genuinely curious but menacing as well. I knew in a moment he would rip my coat open to see for himself.

At that moment, the door opened behind me, and Jules appeared. He sized up the situation immediately and turned a gruff face to the boys, holding up a large fist. "Go on now. I'll take care of my daughter. Or do you want my wife," he motioned to Marguerite, who had appeared at the counter behind him, "to call the police while we fight about it?"

The boys examined Jules, who was short but strong looking, and backed down. "We don't want any trouble, mister," said the one who had spoken before. "We just wanted to make sure she got in okay."

"Yeah, right," Jules said, his voice full of irony. He whisked me inside and closed the door in their faces.

"What's wrong?" Marguerite came to me quickly as Jules locked up.

I began to shake with delayed fright. "Here, take Nette," I said, holding out the baby, afraid I would drop her. As Marguerite swept the sleeping baby up to her warm breast, I began to tell my story. "Can I stay here tonight?" I said when I had finished.

"Of course." Marguerite led the way through the kitchen to their own apartment. I had been there only a few times before, but I knew they had a couch that folded down into a bed in their sitting room. It was to this that she took me.

"What's wrong with my life?" I asked her while she made up the bed. I was sitting back in a comfortable chair with Nette asleep on my chest. "I don't know what to do!"

Marguerite stopped what she was doing and looked down at me. "It seems you have a lot of decisions to make, Ariana. You still have your whole life before you."

"What would you do if you were me?" I asked softly.

She shook her head. "Only you can decide that. But you might start with deciding where you want to end up in life and work from there. To get there, you might have to go back to school, make up with your parents, maybe make some decisions about Jacques. But the point is, only you can do it."

I frowned and then nodded. "I guess you're right."

Suddenly out of nowhere came the thought, *Oh, Antoine, why did you leave me?*

CHAPTER FIVE

The next day the biting wind continued, but it didn't seem to stop the flow of people to the café. I was grateful to immerse myself in work, putting aside my feelings and the decisions I would soon have to make. Regardless, I felt their weight as heavy upon me as sin upon the soul.

Jacques didn't appear at the café all morning or afternoon, but shortly before the dinner rush, Paulette came in, her face flushed and excited.

"Boy, did you miss all of the excitement last night!" she declared, leaning against the counter. "Someone called the police, and the whole place got busted. They took most everyone to the tank, including Jacques. I didn't get busted because I slipped into one of your neighbors' apartments. You know, the ones that have that so-called band. Anyway, I went down to the jail to see what was what and Jacques was there, asking you to come and bail him out."

I stared at Paulette in horror and then looked to Marguerite for advice.

She shrugged. "Honey, if it was up to me, I'd let him rot in jail. But it's you that has to live with him, not me. However, if you're going to get him out, it would be best if you went now, before the dinner rush. That way, maybe he won't lose his job."

"Yes, you're right. Will you watch the baby for me?"

"Sure." Marguerite's eyes fixed on me sadly. "Do you have enough money?"

"I think so." I wasn't sure if I did, but I wasn't about to ask her for more than she was already giving me. If I had to, I would take some money out of my secret bank account.

Paulette and I hurried up the street to the subway. The sky was overcast and gloomy. A perfect day for what I had to do. I had barely enough cash to pay the police officer to get Jacques free—money I had been saving to pay the rent that was due in just over a week.

"What about the rent, Jacques?" I asked tightly as we left the station.

"When's it due?"

"End of next week." I couldn't believe he didn't remember.

"No problem," Jacques said confidently. "I get paid next week. We'll have enough to pay the rent. Don't worry about that, Ari."

"Ariana," I corrected him tersely.

"Oh, sorry." He turned to Paulette. "But wasn't that some party, eh, Paulette?"

"Sure was," she agreed, a stupid smile on her face.

I stopped dead in my tracks. "I don't believe you, Jacques! Smoke was filling the whole apartment, there were drunken and doped people everywhere, couples making out on our bed, practically rolling on top of Nette! Then Nette and I nearly get mugged or worse in the street trying to find someplace to sleep, and you end up in jail! And you call that a party?" I let out all of my pent-up anger in one rush, and Jacques cringed in the face of my rage. "Is that how you want your daughter to grow up? Doing drugs and sleeping with anyone she meets? Well, that's not the kind of life *I* want for her—or for me! I want to grow up and get on with living, and if that's not what you want, you can have your drugged life. But it's us or them. You can't have both!" With that I turned on my heel, leaving a stunned Jacques behind me.

I spent the rest of the day angry at Jacques, but gradually my rage cooled. At closing time, he appeared with a bouquet of flowers. Jules and Marguerite scowled at him suspiciously, but he seemed clearheaded.

"I thought a lot about what you said," he began as we were walking home. "You know, about what kind of a life we want for Antoinette." He motioned to the baby in my arms. "You're right. I don't want her to grow up like this, and I don't even want this life for you and me." His eyes grew thoughtful. "Like at Christmas, when we ate dinner with Marguerite and Jules, I thought how it would be having a place like that and doing well like they are. I really want that for us, but sometimes the yearning to drink comes so hard that I just can't fight it. And the heroin is worse." He held up his hands quickly. "I swear I've done it only once or twice since Nette was born. But the whole point is that I'm going to do better, Ariana. I promise." He put a hesitant arm around me, and I leaned into him slightly.

"Okay, Jacques, we'll try it again. But no more parties."

"I agree. And we'll look for someplace nicer to live, now that we both have jobs."

"Maybe we should go back to school," I suggested.

"Maybe."

I could tell that he was humoring me. He was sincere in wanting to do better, but that didn't include being locked up in a room with books. I sighed. I guess it was all I could expect, for now.

I seemed to hold my breath as the next two months passed by. Jacques was impossibly well behaved. We laughed a lot and spent more time as a family. During March, as the weather warmed, I would even take him to some of my favorite places along the Seine, recounting the stories of my youth.

"You were very lucky to have Antoine," Jacques said to me one day as we walked along the river. It was the morning before my nineteenth birthday. "I feel almost jealous when you talk about him. Your whole face lights up, and you look so beautiful. I hope I can make your eyes light up like that someday."

My hair, having grown long during my pregnancy, fell into my face, and I flipped it back to look up at him. "I do love you, Jacques," I said earnestly. "I really do. These last two months have been good for us, haven't they?"

His expression was serious. "The best in my whole life." But as he said it, a shadow passed over his face. "I wish that—" He broke off suddenly. "Oh, look at the time! We've got to get to work!" He kissed me tenderly and took Nette from my arms and kissed her, too. Together we headed toward the subway.

I hummed as I worked that afternoon, noticing how the sun shone through the window, casting a glow about the café. I was happy, but something whispered that it was too good to last. I pushed the thought away forcefully; problems came easily enough without my searching for them.

But the feeling had been right; things were too good to be true. Paulette came into the café after lunch and dropped the bomb. Her words exploded in my heart and broke the tentative trust I was developing in Jacques.

"I have something I think I should tell you," she said, staring at me unhappily from across the small table in the kitchen where we sat. I froze instantly. Nette, in my arms, felt the difference and looked up at my face curiously.

"What is it, Paulette? Is it Jacques?" I asked quickly, trying hard to breathe normally. I remembered only too vividly the problems Jacques and I had gone through before Nette's birth.

She nodded. "I'm really sorry, Ariana, and I shouldn't be the one to tell you, but you deserve to know." She avoided my gaze as she rushed on quickly. "Jacques quit his job about three weeks ago. He said he was tired of being treated like a servant."

I shut my eyes and breathed deeply. Still, if that was all, maybe we could . . .

"And that's not all," Paulette continued as if reading my thoughts. "He's been with the gang during the day, drugged up like the rest of us. He does it early in the day, and it wears off a bit so he can still walk you home without you noticing too much. Then he sleeps it off." Her voice grew quiet. "He sometimes brags about fooling you, and I just couldn't stand it any longer. Even though you aren't really one of us anymore, you'll always be my friend."

I thought carefully about what she was saying. Jacques had been quiet at night, and I had often felt he was hiding something from me—but drugs? *How could I be that blind?*

"I guess I wanted to believe him," I said despondently, more to myself than to Paulette.

"Today I asked him what he was going to do for money." Paulette obviously wasn't finished with her story, and I steeled myself for more. "He said that he'd just live off his old woman—don't take offense, it was the drugs talking. Then he said maybe he'd find an easier way to live." Paulette met my gaze straight on. "Ariana, I think he went to see your parents."

Anger erupted inside me. *How dare he beg for money when he wasn't willing to work for it!*

The rest of the day, I practiced in my mind the things I would say to him when he came to pick me up. But after closing he didn't come, and Jules ended up walking me home. It began to rain, and I was reminded again of Antoine.

Jacques was not in the apartment when I arrived. After putting Nette to bed, I paced the floor restlessly, waiting in the dim lamplight for my husband's return. I knew our marriage was ended, that we had to separate, at least until he got his head on straight, but I didn't know if I would have the courage to tell him. Somehow, for my daughter, I had to be strong.

Sometime after one o'clock in the morning, Jacques stumbled in. He didn't see me at first, but when he did, he held open his arms.

"Hi, honey."

I didn't move to greet him. "You lied to me."

Jacques stopped short. "I didn't want you to worry about the job. I'll find a better one."

"Will you? And what about the drugs, Jacques? You said that you were finished with the drugs!"

"I am," he said.

"Oh? Then you won't mind if I take a look for myself." I turned on the brighter overhead lights while Jacques covered his eyes at the sudden glare. I pushed his hands away from his face and saw what I had tried so hard not to see these past months. I checked his coat pockets and found the hard evidence.

"No wonder we don't have any money!" I shouted, holding the drugs in front of his face. "You spend it all on drugs, even when you're working! Well, I can't do it anymore! I can't support you and your habit! You see only what you want to see—you're blinded by the drugs! Don't you know that I need you, that I love you?" I shook my head. "But not like this."

"We've got plenty of money, Ariana," Jacques responded coldly. He pulled his wallet out of his pocket to reveal a fat sheaf of large bills.

My eyes opened wide. "Where did you get this?"

"Little Ariana, pretending to be so innocent," he said mockingly. "I got this money where you got yours, though I don't know where you've kept it all this time. I got it from your parents. I told them about our baby and how we desperately needed the money. Your father wanted to know what we did with all the other money he gave us for our wedding. Remember that, dear Ariana? I told him we had to pay extra hospital bills when the baby was born, because of complications. But now, you tell me. What did you do with the money?"

"I was saving it for the baby! Or for an emergency!" I exclaimed. "What would you have done with it? Tell me, Jacques! No, let me tell you. You would have had a party or spent it on drugs. You certainly wouldn't have wanted to work. Just like now. I wanted us to make something better of ourselves, not only for our baby but for us! I wanted you and me to spend that money to help us in school, but you just want to waste your life away!"

His face became livid. "No, Ariana," he hissed through clenched teeth, "that's what I *have* been doing—wasting my time away here with you, when I could be out really living and enjoying myself!"

That stung, because despite our problems, I believed Jacques stayed with me because he loved me. "Okay, maybe I was wrong not to tell you about the money," I admitted reluctantly, trying to see his point. "But I wasn't wrong in what I wanted to do with it."

"It doesn't matter anymore, Ariana," Jacques said, his voice weary. "I'm leaving."

My laugh was short and bitter. "That's funny. I was going to tell you the same thing." But it didn't feel funny. It hurt almost as bad as Antoine's death.

He looked at me. "Well, I guess there's nothing more to say."

"I guess not." Then I added more softly, "But tell me one thing. This morning you said these past few months were the best you'd ever spent. Was that also a lie?"

I could tell he wanted to say that it was, but he couldn't. "It's true, Ariana. I got a glimpse of the life we could have had together under other circumstances. But I'm not good enough for you, and I don't know if I want to be."

"And Nette?"

He shook his head. "She's better off without me." At that he scooped up his wallet and all the bills. Draping his coat over his arm, he headed for the door. "Tell your parents thanks for the money," he said over his shoulder. "They know our address and will probably show up here one day. They wanted to see the baby."

Then he was gone, and I was left alone again, listening to the rain falling in the empty streets.

CHAPTER SIX

*T*he morning of my nineteenth birthday dawned, though I had surely thought that after my separation from Jacques nothing in the world could possibly be the same. I awoke early, and without thinking felt the side of the bed where he slept. Of course it was empty. I looked down at Nette sleeping peacefully beside me, her little body curled into mine. A deep sadness filled my heart. As my father had distanced himself from me a year and a half ago at Antoine's death, so had my baby's father distanced himself from her—and just as permanently.

Listlessness settled upon me, and I didn't want to even get out of bed. I lay there for an hour, gazing alternately at the ceiling and my sleeping baby. She stretched and slowly opened her eyes, looking up at me with such love and trust that it forced me to think seriously about our future.

"We're all alone, Nette," I said to her softly. "But that's okay because we have each other, and women have been raising children without men since time began." I bit my lip, unwilling to let my child see how much the thought frightened me, though I knew she wouldn't understand. Nette smiled and giggled softly, reaching up to put her hand in my mouth.

Suddenly a loud shout came through the thin walls. Some of my neighbors were fighting, even this early in the morning. Abruptly, I made my decision.

"The first thing to do is get out of this hole," I said, bringing Nette to my breast to nurse. "After you eat, we'll get up and bathe and see if Marguerite still has an apartment for us." Strength and determination cascaded through my body. Tears were for late, rainy nights, but days were for action.

Less than an hour later, we were at the café. It was also open for breakfast, but they had another girl, Dauphine, helping out in the mornings, so Marguerite was free to talk with me when I arrived.

"What? Here so early?" she asked with a smile, reaching out to hug and kiss Nette. "How about some breakfast—on the house? It is your birthday, after all."

I returned her smile. "No thanks, I've already eaten. But what Nette and I do need is a small apartment, if you've got one open. Jacques and I have separated."

Marguerite watched me without speaking for a moment before saying quietly, "I'm sorry, Ariana. It's a rotten thing to have happen on your birthday, but maybe you can see it as a new beginning or something."

I bit my lip hard so my strength wouldn't suddenly fail me. "That's how I'm looking at it. I'm starting anew. I'm going to go back to school, too, if I can find a program that will allow me to do much of the studying at home with Nette, and then on to college. We're going to build our own life, Nette and I."

Marguerite hugged us both. "Good for you! I'll be here to help you out. And I'll have an apartment free next week. I've been interviewing people for it but haven't promised it to anyone yet. So it's yours, and half-price this month because of your birthday."

"Oh, thank you, Marguerite!"

I had a few hours before work, so I searched out a couple of schools in the area. Because of my age and the baby, it was relatively easy to find a program that would work around my schedule. The program I chose would begin in a month, and I could learn at home and take the tests when I was finished. I had to use a good chunk of my parents' wedding gift to pay for it, but I knew it would be worth it in the long run. I figured it would take me about four months to finish my last year of high school, even with only mornings to study. Of course, I would have to find someone to watch Nette during the tests, but I was sure Marguerite and Jules would help.

I had time afterwards to walk by some of my favorite places along the Seine. When we arrived near the Palais de Justice, I told little Nette the story of Queen Marie-Antoinette. "She must have been very beautiful, as you are going to be," I concluded. "But the point is that she was a queen, and that's what we are both going to be. That's one of the reasons I named you Antoinette, you know. I want you to be as wonderful as my brother, Antoine, and as noble as a queen. Not the kind who rules over others but the kind who rules herself and is not afraid to love and be kind, even though it sometimes hurts so much." Sorrow and pain clutched at my heart when I thought about how much I was hurting for those I had lost, but I blinked back the tears quickly and walked on.

I stopped at one of the vendors along the river and bought a stuffed bear for Nette. It was fluffy and as white as snow and so cuddly. She grabbed at it immediately, smiling, but shortly lost interest. I didn't mind; I knew that as she grew older she would learn to love it as much as I had once loved my own stuffed bear, now long gone.

I kept walking until I found a bench where I could sit down. Though Nette was only three months old, I had been lugging her around all morning and was beginning to feel even her slight weight. She had fallen abruptly asleep as she always seemed to do, but I was content to look down on her peaceful, angelic face. Emotion welled up in my heart, and I knew I loved her more than I had ever loved anyone in my entire life, including Antoine. She was a perfect miracle.

After a while I heard singing from a distance, and my curiosity made me go see who was causing the commotion. Several young men and women like those I had seen the day of Antoine's funeral were singing on the cobblestone sidewalk overlooking the river. They held up a sign as before about families being eternal and also another one that read: "Jesus Christ Loves You!"

I felt a warm, unfamiliar glow inside me. I once had decided that God didn't live because Antoine had died; but now I had little Nette, and the love I felt for her was so strong that I couldn't help wondering if God had sent her to me. Maybe He existed after all.

"Oh, Nette," I whispered to the sleeping baby. "I wish it were all true, that we could see Antoine again somehow and that you could be mine forever."

Glancing at my watch, I suddenly realized I was late for work and hurried in the direction of the subway. A young woman held a pamphlet out to me as I passed, and I hurriedly took it and shoved it into my coat pocket. It was well and good to dream, but I had to come back to the real world now. There was work to be done.

A week later, Jules and Marguerite helped me move my few

belongings to the new apartment. They absolutely refused to let me keep the couch, however, saying that it was flea-infested and dirty beyond saving. "We have one that you can have," Marguerite said. "I ordered a new one for our apartment only last week to go with the new wallpaper, and the old one has to go."

"You mean the beautiful one with the bed in it?" I asked. She nodded. "Well, in that case, let's leave the old bed behind, too," I said. "We'll sleep on the couch-bed until we can buy one of our own. I—I think it would be easier for me if I didn't have to sleep in the same bed."

"Well, I can certainly understand that," Marguerite agreed immediately. "And that's one less thing we'll have to move!"

We did take the small kitchen table with its two chairs, the TV, the TV stand, the lamp and corner table, and the crates I had been using to store our clothes. It wasn't much, but it was enough.

The new apartment was everything I could have wished for. It was as small as the one we'd come from, except for the bathroom, which was twice the size. It had new-looking carpet and vinyl flooring, and the walls had been freshly painted. Everything had a clean look and smell about it, which made me love it immediately. I wasn't afraid to lay Nette on the floor, even though she could roll off her blanket.

During the moving, Marguerite and Jules kept disappearing and reappearing with odds and ends to make the apartment more comfortable. "This dresser was left in one of the apartments last year," Jules said once. "It needs a little paint, but it'll be better than those crates for your clothes."

About the same time, Marguerite came in with some wall hangings. "I bought these just last month, but they don't go with the new wallpaper."

On and on they went until my apartment really did look like a home. Not even once did I let myself think about Jacques; that part of my life was over. Only at night was I unable to forget, and then I cried. But morning would soon dawn, and I would start anew.

A week later, my parents showed up at the café. It was during the evening rush, so I pretended I hadn't seen them and worked furiously, hoping they would go away. But they waited until things slowed down.

"Who are they?" Marguerite asked, smoothing her white apron over her large bosom.

I grimaced. "My parents."

"Well, they don't seem so bad."

I looked at them, trying to see them from her point of view, but all I could see were the cold faces that had shut me out of their lives when my beloved brother had died.

"I don't want to talk to them," I whispered suddenly.

But Marguerite wouldn't let me run away. "You're going to have to face them sometime. Remember that they lost not only Antoine but you as well. They've got to be hurting. Try to be nice to them." Her words reminded me of how I had told Nette on my birthday that we were going to be queens. It was time for me to act like one.

I wiped my hands and went over to the door where they waited. "Hello," I said, trying to make my voice as steady as possible.

"Hello, Ariana," my mother said quickly. "You look good. I like your hair long like that."

"We went to your old apartment, and they told us that you work here, so we came," my father added. "We wanted to see how you were doing."

"I'm fine."

"And the baby?" my mother asked. "Where is she?"

For a moment I wanted to lie and say there was no baby, but I told myself a queen would never lie. "She's in the kitchen." I motioned to the door with my chin. "Probably asleep."

"May we see her?"

"Sure." I reluctantly went to get Nette. She wasn't asleep and was all smiles when I walked in the door and picked her up from the blanket on the floor.

"Come on, little queen," I said. "You've got some grandparents to meet. Try to be polite now."

I held the baby close as I presented her to my parents, not offering her to them to hold.

"She's beautiful!" My mother reached out a finger for Nette to grab.

"I think so." Then I added, just to see how they would react, "She looks a lot like Antoine."

My father's face tightened, as if a mask had suddenly covered it. My mother's eyes watered, and she looked away. It seemed they still had not come to terms with Antoine's death.

"Don't, Ari," my mother begged.

"My name isn't Ari anymore. It's Ariana," I said bitterly. "You have both buried Ari as surely as you buried Antoine! But you still won't talk about it, will you? Why are you even here? Did you decide that since your beloved son is gone, I will finally have to do?"

Neither of them spoke for what seemed like long minutes. Finally, my father coughed and began. "We wanted to see if you needed help with the baby. Your husband said money was tight, and we thought that if you needed us to, we could take care of her for you, to make sure she had everything she needed."

That made me furious. "Everything material, you mean! Why, Father, I do believe that is the longest thing you've said to me since Antoine's death—except to bawl me out about drinking. What you don't seem to realize is that Nette already has everything she needs with me. I love her as you two never loved me! I'm in school, and I'm going to make something of our lives. And I'm never going to make my daughter feel as if she's a half-brained idiot just because she's a girl. No, I can raise my daughter alone, thank you very much! We don't need you, and we don't need your money. Do you know where the last money you gave to Jacques went? Well, I don't know exactly, because he left me the day you gave it to him. But you can be absolutely sure he's on a heroin trip or something worse. That's where your precious money went!" I glared at them, daring them to refute my words.

My father only shook his head. "We shouldn't have come. I can see you are just as unreasonable as before."

"Me, unreasonable!" I exclaimed, feeling my heart harden even further against them. "You're the ones who come in here thinking you can rescue my daughter from her horrible situation. Just what makes you think you can raise her better than I can? You don't exactly have a good track record with raising daughters. Even now, you can't admit you are partly at fault for what happened to me after your precious Antoine died!" I was practically screaming at them now, and nearly everyone in the café had stopped eating to listen. But I didn't care.

"You left me all alone! Both of you! When Antoine died, part of me died as well. Don't you see? He'd been with me since the moment we were conceived, so in a way he *was* me, because I had never learned to be myself!" I took a deep, shaky breath and said more calmly, "I think you should leave now."

My mother was crying openly, and my father put an arm around her to lead her out the door. "Come on, Josephine. Let's go."

At least they seem closer than they were when I left home, I thought. I put my face into Nette's hair and whispered, "I didn't do too well, did I? I guess acting like a queen takes more practice than I thought." I turned and went into the kitchen where Marguerite was waiting.

"Well?" she asked, as if she hadn't heard the whole conversation.

"They wanted Nette," I said sadly, cuddling the baby to me. "They still don't want me."

Marguerite put her arms around my shoulders. "Maybe it just seems so, Ariana. Maybe they simply don't know how to show you they care."

But I didn't believe her.

CHAPTER SEVEN

School came as a wonderful surprise for me. I had never had much interest in learning before, but now I lost myself in the various texts, especially anything to do with mathematics. Equations seemed to practically solve themselves on the page, and I delighted in my new-found talent—one I had never expected. I wondered I hadn't noticed it before. Maybe it was because for the first time in my life, I was serious about making a career for myself—and, most important, a good life for little Nette.

The days, weeks, and months slipped by as I immersed myself in work, school, and my daughter. On the few occasions when I had to take tests, either Marguerite or my next-door neighbor, Jeanne, a mother of two young children herself, would baby-sit Nette.

I was strangely happy and content with most of my life, though I was alone with only Nette for company most of my free time. I hadn't seen any of the gang except for Paulette, who came in regularly in the afternoons during the rush to play with Nette in the kitchen. During these times she was mostly sober and clearheaded, though I knew she was still using many different drugs. Because she never asked to take Nette anywhere and they seemed to delight in each other's company, I allowed their relationship to continue.

"Do you miss him?" Paulette asked me one afternoon after the lunch rush, when Nette had just turned eight months old. We were sitting on the floor on a large blanket, eating a late lunch. I had my back propped against the door to the small office, with Nette curled up in my lap, nursing. While she did eat some solid foods, she was late getting teeth and was still dependent upon me for most of her nourishment. Since breast milk was the cheapest food available and because nursing enhanced our closeness, I didn't mind.

"Do I miss him?" I repeated Paulette's question while I seriously thought about it. I didn't have to ask who "him" was. "Well, yes, I guess I do. I miss the way he used to look at me with his head tilted back, as if wanting to catch every word. I miss feeling him in the bed beside me at night and seeing his tousled hair in the morning. And I miss watching him play with Nette." As tears began to form in my eyes, I blinked and purposely made my voice hard. "But I don't miss the uncertainty of life with him, the drugs, or the alcohol."

"Would you take him back?" Paulette picked up her sandwich and took a halfhearted bite. Drugs had seriously dampened her appetite. "I mean, if he just showed up one day," she said a trifle unclearly as she chewed.

I took a bite of my own sandwich before I answered, holding it with the hand that wasn't supporting Nette. "I guess that would depend. I mean, I'm not willing to go back to what was before. I'm stable now and working toward a goal, and if I'm not completely happy, well, it's still much better than what life was with him."

"But what if he had changed?"

I snorted. "I don't know if I could believe him—he lied to me so many times before." I sighed. "I guess I would probably give him time to prove himself, though I wouldn't hold any great hopes in the matter."

For once, Paulette looked directly into my eyes. "You still love him, don't you?"

I wanted to deny it but found I couldn't. "Yes," I admitted reluctantly. "But I don't want to. And I don't hold any hopes of his coming back changed. He's chosen a different way of life, and that's that."

"I'm not sure I believe it. I think he really loved you."

I shrugged. "*Loved* is the key word here, Paulette. It's past tense. I think it's time I filed for divorce." As I said it, I became determined. It would probably take a good chunk of my savings, but it was a necessary step. I had to cut ties with my unhappy past. I should have done it long ago.

My conversation with Paulette spurred me to action. During the next few days I went to see several lawyers about my divorce. Thursday morning, two days after our talk, I chose one—not the cheapest but the one I felt would get the job done the fastest. I didn't anticipate any problems from Jacques.

I arrived at work that afternoon feeling a little more depressed than normal but firm in my decision. I found Marguerite busily showing another woman around the kitchen. She looked much like Marguerite herself, yet fatter and more disapproving and stern.

"Oh, Ariana, come meet my sister, Françoise!" Marguerite motioned to me. As I approached, she scooped the giggling Nette out of my arms to hug and kiss her. "How are you today, precious? Boy, am I going to miss you while I'm on vacation!"

I started at her words. I had completely forgotten that Marguerite and Jules were leaving the next Monday for a month of well-deserved vacation. Her sister and her niece had come to take their places while they were gone, as they had done in other years.

"It's nice to meet you, Françoise," I said, kissing the woman's cheeks several times in the French custom.

"And you, Ariana," Françoise rejoined with a tight smile. Her rolls of fat jiggled as she shifted into a more comfortable position. "I've heard quite a bit about you from Marguerite."

"Oh, Ariana here is a wonder!" Marguerite exclaimed. "Everything is pretty much the same as the other times you came, Françoise, but if you have any problems, just ask Ariana. She knows the job better than I do. And don't worry about little Nette here; she's an absolute angel. We block off part of the kitchen with crates to keep her away from the stove, and she just plays all day. Your daughter, Colette, will probably love her." Marguerite turned to me. "You'll meet Colette on Monday. She's getting married next spring, you know."

I hadn't known but nodded anyway. Then Marguerite was off again, reacquainting the corpulent Françoise with the café. I stared out the large window and sighed. I wasn't looking forward to life without Marguerite and Jules, even if only for a month, but they certainly had chosen a perfect time to go—the last week of August and the first three of September. I wished I could go with them, but I had tests the next week, and they needed me here at the café. Still, maybe when they got back, Nette and I would go somewhere really special for our own little vacation. Not somewhere costly but where we could be alone for a few days and relax from all the pressures of work and school.

The next morning, the day after I paid the lawyer, I got up early for a test at school. After this one, I would have to take only two more the following week to graduate. I had no doubt that I would pass; I had done nothing but study every morning for the past four months.

I readied Nette to take to my neighbor, Jeanne. Since Marguerite was busy packing for her vacation, she would not be able to sit with her. Nette actually preferred going to Jeanne's because she loved playing with her children. I had often gone there in the mornings during study breaks to let them play together, especially when I had realized that Marguerite wouldn't always be able to watch Nette during my exams. I hadn't wanted Nette to cry when I left her with Jeanne.

The doorbell rang suddenly, and I ran to answer it.

"Hi, Ariana."

I gasped, feeling my eyes widen as I saw Jacques standing there. I had been so certain I would never see him again, that he was out of my life forever. I couldn't believe he was actually standing in front of me.

"Why are you here?" I asked, holding a hand up to still my heavily beating heart.

He was leaning against the door frame gazing down at me, his head cocked slightly to one side. His eyes were clear and seemingly drug free, although I knew I could not trust myself on this. I had been fooled before.

"I came to see you, Ariana." His voice was soft. "I've missed you terribly."

I steeled myself against the ache in his voice. "I've filed for divorce."

Jacques frowned and then sighed. "Well, I guess I should have expected as much. Still, it's not final yet. Could you give me another chance?"

"But I don't want to be hurt again, Jacques!" I retorted. "I can't trust you!"

"I won't hurt you, I promise!"

"Your promises haven't been very good."

He grimaced. "That was five months ago, Ariana. I've changed." His voice was pleading. "Please, just think about it."

I didn't say anything but stared at the ground, trying for all I was worth to avoid looking at the face of the man I knew I still loved. Simply seeing him made my emotions race crazily, compelling me to throw myself into his arms. During the ensuing silence, Nette crawled over from near the couch where I had left her. She stood up, using my legs to steady herself.

"Why, she's so big!" Jacques exclaimed. "Is she walking already?"

"Not alone." I smiled down at the chubby baby. "But it won't be long now. She walks along anything she can hold on to. Most babies don't walk until they're around eleven months. Nette's just extra determined."

"Like her mother," Jacques commented. He knelt down and called Nette to him, but she clung to my legs. Undaunted, he continued to play with her until her cherub face crinkled in a smile. He glanced up at me in triumph. "She likes me!" He continued his play. "She looks so much like you with those huge round eyes and dark hair." He touched his own dark blond locks with a finger. "Doesn't look much like her dad, that's for sure. And a good thing, too."

"Nonsense, Jacques. You've got brown eyes, too, and look at the dimple in her chin—it looks like yours." I crouched down to point it out to him. Little Nette giggled. She had taken hold of Jacques' fingers and actually took a step in his direction.

"She needs a father," Jacques said suddenly, looking deep into my eyes. "Please, give us another chance."

I suspected he was using Nette to get to me, but I knew I wanted to try again anyway. "Okay," I agreed. "You can come and see us, and we'll see where things go. But you can't stay here."

Disappointment flared briefly in his eyes, but he seemed willing to live with my rules. "I'll show you, Ariana," he said sincerely. "I still love you, and I know that you love me, too."

I shrugged. "Love isn't everything, Jacques. It doesn't pay the rent, and it's useless without trust."

"Things are going to be different now. You'll see."

I sighed. "Yes, I guess I will. But for now, I've got a test to take." I gathered up my school supplies and slung Nette's diaper bag over my shoulder. "Come on, Nette." I picked up the baby in my free arm and motioned to Jacques to shut the door and to see that it was locked. We started off down the hall towards Jeanne's. At her door, I rang the bell.

She answered almost immediately, flanked by her two toddlers. "Why, good morning!" she sang cheerily. "Do you want to play, Nette?"

She held out her arms to take the baby, but Nette kicked to get down with the other children.

"It shouldn't take more than a couple of hours," I said.

Jeanne smiled. "Take whatever time you need." She peered behind me at Jacques and added teasingly, "Who's this handsome guy?"

I grimaced slightly and replied, "This is Nette's father, Jacques. He came to visit this morning, but he's just leaving."

"It's nice to meet you, Jeanne." Jacques held out his hand and smiled his most charming grin. Jeanne practically blushed, and I wanted to roll my eyes in disbelief. Instead, I changed the subject.

"Thanks so much for watching Nette, Jeanne. Will you still be able to watch her Thursday evening?" I had two tests left, and since one was offered only at night, I had decided to take them both Thursday night, one right after the other. That way I wouldn't have to find a baby-sitter again.

"It's no bother, really," Jeanne said. "And Thursday's fine. Did you get time off at the café?"

"Yes, I traded for Monday." I glanced at my watch. "Goodness, I've got to get down to the school or I'll miss my test!" I gave Nette a final kiss before running to the elevator. Jacques followed me down the hall.

"I could have watched her," he said as we waited.

I snorted incredulously. "She doesn't even know you! And there's still that little matter of trust. Don't push it, Jacques."

"Okay," he agreed hastily. "But can I walk you to wherever you're going?"

"If you can keep up."

———

The next few days, Jacques seemed to be everywhere I turned. That first day, he waited for me after my test, walked back with me to get Nette, and stayed until I went to work. Later, he came back to eat dinner at the café and waited for me outside after I closed up.

"You don't have to walk me home, Jacques," I said, pointing to the apartment building door that stood five paces down from the café. "I'm quite safe as long as I check the streets before I make a run for it."

"But I want to, Ariana." He pointed to the sleeping baby. "May I carry her for you?"

"Sure." It had been a long day, and I was happy to let him do some of the work for a change. I unlocked the outer apartment door and held it open for him. Then I went in myself, turning to make sure the heavy door clicked shut behind us.

Once in the apartment, Jacques carried Nette to my recently purchased bed. "You've got a nice place here," he said as he looked around the room.

"I've been working hard," I said softly.

His face darkened slightly. "I'm sorry for everything, Ariana. I really am. I want to be the man that you want and need—and love."

"Let's take one day at a time, Jacques. Right now I'm really tired, and I've still got to work all day tomorrow."

"What about in the morning? We could walk along the river like we used to."

I smiled. "Okay, Jacques."

After he left, hope and fear wrestled within me until I was too tired to think. At last I fell asleep, cuddled to the warmth of Nette's tiny body.

CHAPTER EIGHT

Saturday morning dawned bright and shining, giving more than a hint of the heat to come later in the day. Jacques came as promised, still clear-eyed and hopeful, and we spent a wonderful morning together. Little Nette warmed up even more toward him; it was as if she somehow remembered him from before.

We walked along the river, and once again I showed Nette the Palais de Justice and told her the story of Queen Marie-Antoinette. She laughed and babbled back to me as she always did, not understanding anything except the love in my voice.

"Your daughter is going to be a queen, did you know, Jacques?" I said, smiling and looking tenderly at Nette.

He returned my smile with a grin. "She already is. Just like you." I wanted to tell him no, that we weren't yet, but he reached over to kiss my cheek, sending chills throughout my body.

We made our way back to the café, and Jacques stayed for lunch. He returned later for dinner and to walk us home. He was trying his best to be charming and considerate, and I couldn't help the feelings of love that arose in my heart.

"What about tomorrow?" he asked. "Let's spend the whole day together. You still have Sundays off, don't you? We'll take a picnic and go somewhere or something." He stroked Nette's soft cheek and then reached out to touch mine. A shiver ran through me at his touch, as it had that morning when he kissed my cheek.

"Okay, Jacques. I'd like that."

He quickly tucked Nette into her bed and whirled me around. "You don't worry about food or anything," he said excitedly. "I'll take care of it all!" He kissed me once, hard, on the mouth. "I love you, Ariana de Cotte!" He was out the door and gone before I could say another word.

I suddenly, desperately, wanted things to work out. It was difficult and sometimes very lonely raising a child alone. How much easier it could be with a husband to share the responsibilities!

I was dressed and waiting Sunday morning when Jacques showed up at ten with a huge basket filled to brimming with different foods. He kissed me on the cheek and turned to hug little Nette. This time she didn't pull away. On the way to the elevator, we passed my neighbor, Jeanne, in the hall. "Good morning, pretty lady," Jacques said with a winning smile.

Jeanne laughed. "You've got yourself a charming one there!" she said to me.

"You can say that again!"

We were quiet on the ride down the elevator and out into the street. Jacques headed purposely toward a waiting taxi. "Where are we going?" I asked.

He grinned. "It's a secret, just wait and see. But I'm sure you'll enjoy it."

We sat in comfortable silence as the taxi careened through Paris to the city's outskirts, where the countryside became a beautiful green, so unlike the crowded city. I had almost forgotten such things existed. Too much time had passed since I had visited similar places—since Antoine died. "Oh, this is beautiful, Jacques!" I exclaimed, breathing deeply the fresh air.

Jacques looked so happy he could burst. "You go on ahead, honey, and I'll arrange with the taxi driver to come back for us later."

I did as he requested and found a calm, shady spot under a tree, out of sight of the narrow road. Nette laughed in delight and immediately tried to eat the soil. I laughed until I choked while Nette eyed me curiously, as if trying to figure out what had overcome her mother.

The day was inconceivably perfect. Jacques was so wonderful—so normal and caring. I thought that all my dreams had finally come true. The only damper on the whole day turned out to be from Nette. When time came for her nap, she refused to sleep and cried and cried. The only thing that made her feel better was to nurse, but she soon became full and cried because there was too much milk. "What's wrong with her?" Jacques asked, looking as frustrated as I felt. I knew he'd been hoping for romantic time alone that Nette's nap would have permitted us.

I shook my head. "I don't know; she rarely does this. It could be that she's finally teething. Marguerite says it's quite painful for some babies."

"Don't you have anything to give her?"

"At home I do. But she's never needed it. I certainly wasn't expecting her to do this today."

Jacques sighed. "We could give her some of this wine." He motioned to the half-empty bottle in the picnic basket. I shook my head vigorously. He sighed again and put the bottle back into the basket. "Well, the taxi driver won't be back for an hour yet."

"Let's go for a walk," I suggested. "Maybe she'll calm down."

"It's worth a try." Jacques jumped up.

I carried the whimpering Nette in my arms and followed him down a small path. The trees still hid us from the mid-afternoon sun, making the heat tolerable and even pleasant. It was beautiful there, but I found it hard to enjoy myself through Nette's cries. Occasionally Jacques cast a worried glance at us, holding stray branches back so that I wouldn't have to duck or push past them.

We had walked only a short way when we spied a small stream. Immediately, I made for the water. "This ought to do it." I took off Nette's shoes and socks, as well as my own, and put our feet into the water. Nette stopped whining abruptly and stared, fascinated, at the stream. It was all I could do to keep her from plunging in altogether.

Jacques and I relaxed and sat with our feet in the coolness, talking quietly. The area was peaceful and undisturbed, the silence broken only by our voices, the birds chirping, or the unhurried movement of the little stream. We seemed to be the only three people in the whole world. But eventually the taxi driver came, and we went home, listening to Nette's renewed screams nearly the whole way. At our apartment, I found the teething remedy and immediately gave it to her. She screamed for another half hour, nursed again, and finally fell asleep. With a sigh of relief, I put her into bed.

"Whew! I didn't know she could be like that," Jacques said.

I laughed. "Neither did I. She's full of surprises, that's for sure." I sat down on the couch and laid my head back, exhausted.

Jacques sat down beside me. "You still have Mondays off?" he asked hopefully.

"Normally I do. But Marguerite is leaving on vacation, and she wanted me to be there the first few days to make sure her sister and niece can manage. So this week I agreed to trade for Thursday. It works out so I can take my tests."

"What about in the morning?"

I shook my head. "No, I've got to study, Jacques, really I do. This is very important to me."

"But I'm back now, and I'm going to take care of you."

I sat up stiffly. "Oh, Jacques, that has nothing to do with my going to school! I like school, and I want to finish. Plus, I'm going to take a college accounting program in January so I can get a job at a bank or someplace when Nette is old enough for school. That way I can be here for her when she comes home. But it's something I want to do for myself, as well as for her."

"But you can stay home all you want now, because money's not an issue anymore," Jacques insisted.

"Did you suddenly get a job that pays millions?" I asked, a little angry. He didn't seem to understand that not only did I *want* to further my education but that I still didn't trust him.

"Not quite, but I make about ten times what I used to."

I regarded him suspiciously. *Could this be another one of his lies?* I wondered. Aloud I said, "What do you do, Jacques?"

"I'm self-employed."

"Doing what?"

He shrugged. "Nothing out of the ordinary. I sell things door-to-door. And I have people who work for me." He moved closer and put his arm around my shoulders. "But the point is that I can get you anything you want now, even a bigger apartment. With room enough for the three of us." He leaned over and nibbled on my ear.

For the first time, I noticed Jacques was wearing clothes of the finest make, similar to the clothes I had been accustomed to when I had lived with my parents—clothes I now saved for special occasions like school, appointments with the doctor, or college registration. I glanced down at my own worn jeans. Could he be telling the truth? I wanted to believe in him, but I was so afraid. I needed time to think.

I pulled away. "I need time, Jacques. I—I'm still not certain things will be different from the last time. Give me time, please?"

He studied me for a minute and then nodded once, sharply. "Okay, we'll leave it for now, Ariana. But I will win out, you'll see." He stood up, leaned down to kiss my forehead, and made his way slowly to the door. "I'll be by again. See ya."

After he left, I went about straightening the apartment and getting Nette's bag ready for the next day. As I set it by the door where I wouldn't forget, I noticed that my extra set of keys was not on the hook near the door. I wondered briefly if I had put them in my purse or perhaps given them to Nette to play with as I sometimes did. But tiredness overwhelmed me, and I shrugged the matter aside. They would turn up eventually.

On Monday I didn't see Jacques at all. It was a normal day for me, yet I longed for the light and love his presence had brought back into my life. Work at the café went smoothly and efficiently under the firm control of the massive Françoise. I didn't take to the woman, but I readily liked her daughter, Colette, who at twenty-one was two years my senior.

"She is so beautiful!" Colette had exclaimed the minute she caught sight of Nette. She eyed me up and down. "And looking at you, I can see why. I wish I had smaller bones. But, alas! I inherited my mother's large ones. Oh, well, I guess I'll make do." She sighed dramatically, and her mother rolled her eyes. I laughed. Colette wasn't lying when she said she had large bones, but she was very pretty, regardless.

That night after work, a strange depression settled upon me. I knew that I had been hoping to see Jacques. Nette's sleeping form felt heavier than usual, and I wished he were there to carry her to my apartment. Like the day before on our picnic, she had cried and cried all day at the café. I was sure she was teething because her gums were red and sore-looking. I had given her two more doses of the pain remedy, and it had helped a little. Not for the first time, though, I wished I didn't have to work at the café at all but could stay home and take care of my baby properly. I was so tired.

Nothing felt different when I put my key into the lock of my apartment. But when I opened the door, I gasped. At first I was so shocked that I wondered if somehow I had entered the wrong apartment by mistake.

The entire room was filled with my favorite flowers—pure white roses. Everywhere I looked there were vases and more vases of white roses in all shapes and sizes. A bit of red caught my gaze. On the short coffee table in front of the sofa stood a large vase with two dozen long-stemmed roses of the darkest red.

I went to put Nette down in the bedroom, where more white roses adorned my dresser and even the floor. A quick scan around the apartment showed that the kitchen and the bathroom held more of the flawless blossoms. I returned to the living room and sat down on the sofa to read the short note that accompanied the vase with the red roses: "To Ariana with love, Jacques."

Suddenly, I knew what had happened to my other set of keys.

I sat speechless, looking around the room in amazement. This was every young girl's dream. But I was a mother first and an impoverished one at that. Instead of enjoying the flowers and basking in the love with which they had been given, I swiftly calculated that the roses cost more than two months' rent, which I actually could have used a lot more. That made me laugh. Still, if Jacques could waste money like this, maybe he *had* changed.

The next day I gave some of the roses to Jeanne, telling her what Jacques had done. "You should hang on to that one," she said laughingly.

"We'll see." I wasn't quite so ready to trust him yet.

I also took some of the flowers to the café, where I worked half-heartedly, hoping Jacques would visit me. He came in shortly after noon, wearing dark sunglasses. Two wealthy-looking gentlemen were with him. "Hi, honey," he said. "I wanted to come and see you earlier, but I've been working." He motioned over his shoulder to the men. "These are some of my . . . clients. Could you get us the best meal you've got and bring it to the table? These guys are used to posher places, but I couldn't wait to see you." He counted out various bills and laid them on the counter. "And keep the change, love."

I tried not to show my surprise. The "change" would be more than half the money he had given me. "Keep it for Nette," Jacques urged when he saw I was going to refuse.

That made sense. He was, after all, her father. "For Nette," I said. "And thank you for the roses, though it was way too much, Jacques."

He grinned. "Nothing's too much for you, Ariana." I wished his eyes were uncovered so I could see his expression, but the glasses hid them well. I couldn't help the dark suspicion that he was hiding something from me—and perhaps from his clients as well.

I smiled anyway and motioned him to the corner table. "Sit down, and I'll bring it out to you." I rang up the special order and then slipped into the kitchen to give it to Colette. I stopped briefly to kiss and hug little Nette, who was deeply involved in playing with a set of spoons that Colette had given her. Beside her on the blanket, Paulette was trying unsuccessfully to build a tepee with some of the spoons.

I tucked Jacques' extra money into the diaper bag. "That's from your daddy, Nette. It sure is easy to act like a queen when that's how you're treated." The baby grinned, her mouth opening to show the sliver of a tooth that had nearly broken through. For the moment, she seemed to be free of pain and content. I hoped she stayed that way. But at least Paulette would be there to help for a while if she did start screaming.

When I returned to the counter, the lunch rush began in earnest. I worked feverishly to clear the customers so I would be free to take the food to Jacques' table. But people kept coming, and when Colette was finished with their plates, I couldn't get free. Françoise was also very busy and unable to take my place at the register. I shrugged and motioned for Colette to carry the food to Jacques' table, hiding my disappointment. I told myself there would be plenty of time for us later. The rush of people continued for hours, and I didn't even see Jacques when he left or have time to ask him for my keys.

———

I didn't see Jacques again until the next morning, when he arrived at my apartment door unannounced. Like the previous day, he wore his dark glasses.

"Come in," I invited. "Care for some orange juice?"

Jacques shook his head. "I've got to run. Business, you know. I just wanted to come by and give my girls a kiss." He kissed me quickly on the lips and reached down for Nette.

"Mamma," Nette gurgled.

"No, I'm your daddy, silly girl." Jacques kissed her, and Nette smiled. "Hey, she's getting a tooth!"

I nodded. "And more coming. I hope she doesn't keep being so ornery. At least yesterday I had a rest, though. She was an angel." As I spoke, Nette reached up for Jacques' glasses and pulled them off before he could stop her. My heart pounded furiously as I saw what Jacques had been hiding: he was still using drugs.

Jacques shoved the glasses on again quickly as if nothing had happened. He gave Nette another kiss and handed her to me. "Well, I'll see ya. Have a good day. I'll come by tonight." He left, and I stood in the doorway, watching him go. At the same time, Jeanne and her two children left their apartment. They entered the elevator with Jacques, laughing and talking.

I shut the door slowly. Nothing had changed, not really. As long as he was using drugs, things would be exactly as they had been before. Eventually he would lose or give up even this latest job that seemed so lucrative.

Tears came rapidly as I slid down to the floor with my back pressed against the closed door, arms tightly wrapped around my innocent baby.

"I wish he hadn't come back," I told Paulette later that afternoon. I wanted to strangle Jacques for giving me hope and then failing to live up to my expectations. To make things worse, Nette had been screaming constantly almost all day. The only time she even stopped for a breath was when I was holding her. I had given her the baby medicine to no avail and had finally strapped her to my chest until Paulette had shown up sometime after the lunch rush ended. My back and legs ached, and I felt miserable.

"Hey, at least he can give you some money to help out with Nette," Paulette said.

"But what about me?"

Paulette shrugged. "He isn't good enough for you. You're special, Ariana. Even I know that."

"I don't want to be special, Paulette. I just want to have someone to depend on."

But it seemed I couldn't depend on Jacques, even to come and see me when he said he would. That night I had planned to tell him it was over between us, but he didn't show up at the apartment. Nette screamed for hours before we both finally fell asleep on the couch, exhausted.

In the morning, I awoke to find Nette nursing. I didn't remember pulling up my nightshirt, but there she was, gulping down milk as if there wasn't going to be any later on. She appeared rested despite the horrible night we'd shared and smiled up at me as I looked at her. Returning her smile, I tried to stretch my stiff body. My neck ached from sleeping on the couch, and my back was still sore from the day before. I sighed. At least I didn't have to go to work. Today was Thursday, the day I would finish school.

I took the morning easy, not even opening a book until I got Nette to sleep after lunch. She was cranky but tired and fell asleep quickly. I was relieved because I had used the rest of the pain medicine the night before. After she dozed off, I began reviewing the test material, but I already knew it well and found my mind wandering. Soon, I too was fast asleep.

Hours later, we awoke together. I nursed Nette again and got her ready to take to Jeanne's house. "It's only for a little while," I chattered to Nette nervously. "And when you see me again, I'll be a graduate—or near enough, anyway." I hugged her and covered her face with kisses until she laughed with delight. "Oh, I love you so much, Nette," I whispered against her cheek. "And no matter what, I wouldn't take back a second of my life if that meant I wouldn't have you."

I glanced at the clock and saw it was time to go.

"I hope she doesn't scream for you, Jeanne," I said as I dropped the baby off. "I ran out of that teething medicine, but I fell asleep after lunch and didn't have time to buy more."

"That's okay, I have some if it's needed. And I'm used to babies crying. Just go on and do a good job on your test."

"Thanks, Jeanne. I don't know what I'd do without you."

"Well, you'd manage somehow, I'm sure. Besides, it doesn't seem as though you'll be needing me for long, with that handsome husband of yours back in the picture."

I didn't have time to tell her the truth about Jacques, but I would tell her all about it later when I picked up Nette. As I left the apartment building, warm rain started falling lightly and then more heavily. By the time I reached the school, I was soaked.

The tests were long but not especially grueling. The first was mathematics, and I flew through it, finishing early. That meant I had to wait an hour to even start the last one. But soon I was on my way back home, anxious to see Nette. It was still raining hard, odd for August but greatly needed by the dry earth. I hurried quickly through the wet streets, trying to avoid the deep puddles on the cobblestone and cement sidewalks, hating the rain for the memories it brought of Antoine's death. The cloudy sky was darker than usual, and there was lightning nearby, thunder sounding loud and threatening like a dire warning. My heart began pounding loudly in my chest and in my ears. I started running.

The hall seemed eerily quiet when I arrived at Jeanne's door. For no reason I could define, I felt my heart constrict in fear. I rang the bell quickly. "Hi, Ariana," Jeanne said brightly when she opened the door. "What do you need?"

I blinked. "What do you mean? I came to pick up Nette."

"You did?" Her face showed surprise. "That's strange. Your husband came to get her hours ago. He said you told him to and that he was going to take Nette to wait in your apartment. He had your keys and everything. I thought it would be okay, so I let him take her. I even stood here and watched him go into your apartment. Did I do wrong?" she asked anxiously.

"I hope not, Jeanne." But I couldn't stop the horrible worry that clutched my breast or the pressure that had begun in my head. "Did you hear her crying or anything?"

Jeanne nodded. "My husband did. You see, I left to visit my mother for a little while, and when he came home he heard the baby crying. He went to pick me up at my mother's, and when he told me Nette was crying, we came right home. But we couldn't hear her crying anymore. I guess she'd fallen asleep." She paused a moment. "I'm sorry if I shouldn't have given Nette to Jacques, but I thought everything was worked out between you two."

"I should have told you," I mumbled and started quickly down the hall. It seemed to take forever to reach my apartment. The door was locked; I shoved the key in and opened it quickly, hoping that everything would be all right.

But I already knew, deep inside, that my world had changed forever.

CHAPTER NINE

*P*aulette sat stiffly on my couch. Her dark eyes were large and frightened as she looked at me, tears rolling down her cheeks.

"What is it, Paulette?" I asked, my voice sharp with worry. I glanced around the apartment. It appeared as if someone had thrown a wild party. Used cups and plates littered the floor and coffee table, and food was ground into the nice carpet. "Tell me!" My voice was beginning to sound hysterical. I ran to the bedroom, frantically searching for my baby. "Nette? Where are you, Nette? Come to Mommy!" But she was nowhere to be found.

I ran over to Paulette and shook her. "Where is my baby? Did Jacques take her?"

Paulette shook her head almost violently. "No, not like that. He wanted to surprise you, to show you he could take care of Nette. But she kept crying, so he went to the café and called me down at the bar. He was pretty upset and mumbling about how he was going to get a phone installed here, and how there was no one home next door, and how he couldn't find the baby medicine. I could hear Nette crying over the phone, and some of the guys and I came to see if we could help. I played with her like I do at the café, but she just kept crying and crying and chewing on her fist." Paulette bit her lip as the tears came faster. "Jacques couldn't stand seeing her in pain, and he wasn't thinking right. None of us were. We'd all been shooting up and stuff. Jacques had given us a lot of free stuff. He's been dealing, you know, though I only found out last night, or I would have told you before."

I shook her again. "Paulette, my baby! Tell me about my baby!"

Paulette gazed at me sorrowfully. "Jacques shot a little bit of stuff into her. You know, just a little, to try and get her to calm down—"

"No! He didn't!" I shook my head. *Could anyone be so stupid as to give drugs to a baby?*

71

Paulette gulped. "She calmed down after that and seemed happy. She went to sleep, and everyone began to celebrate. But I was worried about Nette, so I kept checking on her. And once she wasn't breathing, so I told Jacques. He gave her mouth-to-mouth, and she started breathing again, but she didn't wake up. Jacques got real scared and took her to the hospital."

"Is she all right?" I demanded, holding my breath for the answer.

"I don't know!" Paulette wailed tearfully. "It's all my fault, Ariana! I shouldn't have let it happen!" She bit her lip again until a trickle of blood appeared. The pain seemed to help her concentrate. "After Jacques left, I went and called the police, and they sent someone to the hospital. I told them I'd come back and wait for you here, and we'd meet them down there. I'm so sorry, Ariana!"

I was out the door before she finished talking. I didn't wait for the elevator but shot down the stairs and into the stormy night, running for all I was worth. Paulette followed behind me, trying to keep up.

Jacques was pacing the hospital halls when I arrived. If he had been drugged before—and I didn't doubt that he had—all traces were blotted out by the stark realization of what he had done. Nearby, two policemen waited to take Jacques to the police station after Nette's condition was known.

I ran to the desk, tears blocking my vision. "My baby! How is she?"

The nurse didn't ask who I was. She just shook her head gently. "I don't know. The doctor should be out as soon as he knows."

I waited there with my heart aching, hardly believing that such a thing could actually be happening. Surely this was a nightmare, and I would soon wake up. I shook myself repeatedly, but it seemed this nightmare was real.

Jacques came close to me, his face lit eerily by the fluorescent lights of the hospital. "I'm sorry." His were eyes pleading, begging for absolution. "It seemed the right thing to do at the time. She was in pain."

I turned on him in contempt. "And what about now, Jacques? What kind of pain is she in now? Oh, I wish you had never come back! We were happy without you. Why couldn't you just leave us alone?" I retreated from him, backing down the orange carpet that contrasted so harshly with the stark white walls. Jacques started to follow me, but I held up a hand to motion him back. "Stay away from me!" Defeated, Jacques stayed where he was.

The doctor came out minutes later, and the nurse at the desk guided him over to me. "This is the baby's mother," she said softly.

The doctor looked at me, his face somber. "I'm sorry. Her body couldn't handle the drugs in her system."

"No!" I whispered. "*No!*" The doctor and his words seemed unreal. I stared at him, noticing the short hairs growing stiffly out from his face as if he hadn't had time to shave that day.

"If it helps to know," he said kindly, "she didn't feel any pain at all. She just went to sleep."

My heart ached so badly I thought I would die. "Can I see her?" I asked hoarsely, not bothering to wipe away the tears streaming down my face.

He nodded. "Of course. Come with me." We turned to go through the door, but Jacques put his arm out to stop me.

"Please, Ariana!" he sobbed. "I didn't mean it!"

Anger swept over me like a fire raging out of control. "I don't care what you say!" I hissed at him. "Nothing can change the fact that you murdered our baby—the only person alive that means anything to me! You are a murderer, and I hope you rot in hell forever!" I wanted the words to burn into his soul, destroying him as surely as he had destroyed me.

His face was stricken. "Ariana, I—" But I turned and followed the doctor. Out of the corner of my eye I saw the policemen leading Jacques down the orange carpet, a broken parody of the man I'd once loved.

The doctor led me to a room crowded with equipment. In the center was a large table with a still figure on it, seeming small and lost in the midst of a huge expanse of white. Nette looked as though she were asleep, so perfect and angelic. At any moment, I expected her to open her eyes and smile at me. Strangely, I felt her presence in the room, though I knew she was dead. I touched her white cheek softly and then picked up her limp body and cuddled her to my chest. Already, my milk was letting down in anticipation of the baby who would never nurse again.

"Oh, Antoinette," I whispered. "I should never have left you. I'm so sorry. Now you will never grow up—but you will always be my little queen." As I said her name, I remembered Antoine and how he had also died during a rainstorm nearly two years before. I also thought of Queen Marie-Antoinette and how she had been beheaded. "I shouldn't have named you Antoinette," I sobbed suddenly, sinking into a nearby chair. "People with that name never live very long."

I don't know how much time passed as I sat there, holding my precious baby close to me. Eventually the doctor took her, and I let her go because the essence that had been Nette was no longer in the little body. The presence I had felt in the room had also gone. Nette was lost to me forever.

I stood to go home but found my strength waning. I made it as far as the waiting room before I sank onto one of the brown couches in a haze of inner pain.

"Ariana." I looked up to see a young woman in a nurse's uniform. Somehow she seemed very familiar to me. "It's Monique. We had the same dance class in school when we were children."

I stared at her dumbly, wondering what difference that fact could possibly make to me. Yet uninvited, the memories came flooding back. She belonged to the happy times when Antoine had been alive—times that were gone and better forgotten.

"I was with your baby from the time she came in tonight," she added softly. "I left when you came in to see her. You didn't notice me, and I wanted you to have time with her alone, so I didn't say anything." She had tears in her eyes. "I want you to know how sorry I am. It's horrible to see these things happen, even though I know the children go straight to heaven."

"There is no heaven," I replied dully. "She's dead, and that's all there is." I got up quickly and went out into the rainy night, leaving Monique to stare after me. I didn't want the stranger she was now to see my pain. Besides, I knew deep inside the accident was my fault, that somehow I deserved what had happened. I kept seeing little Nette's face before me, crying in Jacques' arms, wondering where her mother was. I had failed her miserably.

The rain had let up while I was in the hospital. The drops still came down but only halfheartedly. I made my way slowly, almost blindly, to the subway. It was very dark, and I saw no one in the street. The hospital district seemed quiet and peaceful in the early morning, as if denying the innocent death that had occurred. The narrow roads and sidewalks were full of large puddles, but I apathetically sloshed through them; it was too much effort to go around.

A revving car sounded in the distance and soon came careening into sight around a corner. The windows were open, and I could hear the laughter of young teenagers, as yet unburdened by the sorrows of life and death. They came down the street at an incredible pace, swerving purposely into the deep puddle at the edge of the street. They laughed with renewed glee as the dirty water flew up to completely soak me. Abruptly they were gone, and I went on, barely noticing or caring about the indignity. What difference could a little dirty water make when my baby was dead?

I made it home somehow, though I remembered little of the journey. I didn't turn on the lights in my apartment but sat on the couch in the darkness, clutching my daughter's white stuffed bear, the one I had bought her the day after Jacques had left us, and feeling my breasts fill with milk until I wondered if they would burst.

I must have dozed off, because the apartment was suddenly bathed in morning light. Still I sat clutching the bear. I went to use the bathroom sometime later and noticed the white roses there. One by one, I pulled the petals from the flowers and let them fall to the tiled floor. I did the same to all the other flowers in the apartment. Vase after vase of white blossoms hit the floor, followed by the single vase of red. Their remains mixed red and white, like blood against pale skin, with the clutter and mess that Jacques' friends had left behind. I felt a tempest of anger inside of me, but worse still was the horrible emptiness in my arms.

And I kept seeing Nette's crying face, calling to me hopelessly.

Several times my doorbell rang, but I didn't answer. I was slumped to the floor in my bedroom, once again clasping Nette's bear to my swollen breasts. Night fell, and still I did not move. My breasts became sore and rocklike. The ache of a breast infection came swiftly after, with alternating chills and fever. But I didn't care; the fever at least gave me some mental relief from the pain in my soul.

The next morning, I heard someone ring the doorbell. This time they didn't go away. A key turned in the lock. "What a mess!" someone said; and then, "Ariana? Are you here? Colette, why don't you check that way, and I'll look back there."

"Oh, I hope she's all right," Colette said. "I knew something was wrong when she didn't show up to work yesterday."

"We've got to find her," replied the other voice that seemed familiar to me, but I couldn't quite place it. "I've even been to her parents' apartment searching, after I came here yesterday and got no answer. But she hasn't been there, and no one has seen her since the hospital."

The voice had moved from the living room to the bathroom and now into my room. At first she didn't see me in a heap on the floor, but then she gasped and ran to my side. I looked up at her almost unseeing. It was Monique from the hospital.

"Colette, she's in here!" Monique cradled me for a moment until Colette came into the room. "Go get my bag, please, and bring a cup of water from the kitchen." Colette quickly obliged.

"How do you feel, Ariana?" Monique asked, but I just shivered.

"What's wrong with her?" Colette's voice was worried.

"Breast infection, I'd guess." She reached out tentatively to touch my left breast. "Yes, it's hard and swollen. She ran out of the hospital before I could get the doctor to give her something to suppress the milk. Now she needs an antibiotic, but I can't get her any if she doesn't go back to the hospital."

That brought a reaction from me. "No, I won't go! Let me be!" I was nearly hysterical as I struggled to get away. If they thought I was going back to that place of nightmares, the place that had taken my baby away, they were crazy.

"So what are we going to do, Monique—carry her?"

Monique shook her head. "She won't die from this. The body has a way of curing itself, and I brought some things to help. An antibiotic would do the job faster, but she's a bit incoherent right now." Monique's words weren't cruel; they were simply stating a fact.

"Who could blame her?" Colette's voice was rough with sympathy.

Monique began removing items from her bag. "Vitamin C. She should take a thousand milligrams every hour until she's better. We'll also give her E, at least four of the garlic capsules, and four of these cayenne capsules. We should repeat these doses every four hours or so."

"How do you know all this?" Colette asked Monique. "I thought most medical people were against all this natural stuff."

Monique smiled. "I think that mostly we medical people are an impatient bunch and just don't like to wait around for nature or the herbs God gave us to take their course. But my grandmother, who raised me, knew all about herbs and vitamins. Many people would come to her for help, and I sort of learned by watching. It's part of why I became a nurse."

As she was talking, Monique had taken the capsules from the bottles and was making me swallow them. I did as she asked, too spent from my previous outburst to protest. Besides, a fiery pain had begun inside my chest, and I couldn't breathe without feeling a sharp agony.

"Now what?" Colette asked.

Monique wrinkled her nose. "A bath, I think. How did you get so dirty, Ariana?" I shrugged indifferently, but as she started to lift me, I fleetingly remembered the youngsters and the dirty water splashing up to soak me. "We've got to get this dirt off," Monique continued. "Then I can put a poultice on to help you get better."

They helped me into the bath. The hot water felt good and seemed to ease the pain somewhat. Monique found my hand pump and made me express my milk to relieve the pressure. It hurt incredibly but didn't compare with the suffering in my soul. Afterwards, I lay on the bed while Monique made up the poultice.

"Some slippery elm powder mixed with warm water, add a little comfrey, lobelia, and goldenseal, and there you have it." She spread the mixture on two rectangular cloths. Carefully she applied them and wrapped them with plastic. "This is to keep the herbs moist. We'll leave it on overnight and see how it does."

"Well, I've got to get down to the café," Colette said. "But I'll be back for a minute every hour or so to check on you, Ariana. And don't worry about the café. Mother and I can handle it, and if we can't, we'll find someone to fill in. I'm also calling Marguerite." She reached down to kiss my cheek and tears flooded her eyes. "I'm so sorry about Nette," she whispered, looking so miserable that I felt I had to say something.

"Thank you for coming, Colette."

She smiled slightly. "I'll be back later." She turned and left the room.

That left Monique and me alone. "Thank you," I murmured and drifted off into oblivion. But even there, I was not freed from the aguish in my heart or the throbbing emptiness of my arms.

During the next few days I slowly recovered. At least my body did. Inside I still ached for Nette and for Antoine as well. On the fourth day the fever was completely gone, though I was still weak. Monique was with me, as she had been constantly except for when she had to work at the hospital. She had cleaned the apartment, washed my clothes, and put most of Nette's toys in a box out of sight. Now she was making dinner, singing snatches of different songs as she worked. I mostly just sat and stared into space.

Monique finished adding the final ingredients to her soup and came to where I sat on the couch. She looked at me earnestly. "Oh, Ariana, you're going to make it! I know it doesn't seem as though you will right now, but you will. I know that when my parents . . ." She gulped audibly. " . . . that when my parents died, I thought my life was over. But there was Grandma, and I found a new life and the gospel of Jesus Christ. It explained the reasons for why everything happened and gave me the strength to go on. And you'll make it, too. You were always so strong, even when we were kids. I admired that in you."

I shook my head. "It wasn't me; it was Antoine."

"No, it was you, Ariana. Antoine had strength, too, but you were his source. He loves you so much."

I began to cry. "*Loved,* you mean. Don't you know that he's dead?"

She nodded. "I read about it in the paper. I felt bad, because I had run into him a couple of weeks before, and we had met a few times for lunch after that. We had planned to meet again the day after he died, but he never showed up or called. I thought he had dumped me."

"No. Antoine would never have done that to anyone." Her story called up memories I had long forgotten, as I suddenly remembered Antoine telling me about running into the friend from my childhood dance class. He had wanted me to go to with him that last time. But then he died.

"Just as you would never have done that to anyone," Monique agreed. "I understood that afterwards, but at the time I didn't know him well enough, though I was crazy about him. I thought I had finally found my Mr. Right—even if he was a year younger than me. He was such a good person." She paused a moment before adding, "You and Antoine are a lot alike, you know."

"Well, we're twins. Or were."

That seemed to spark something inside of Monique. "Are! You still *are* twins! Don't you see that this life isn't the end? The body dies, yes, but our spirits are eternal. Don't you believe in God and that He created us? Well, I do. I know we're His children, and we are as eternal as He is, only we haven't progressed as far. Oh, Ariana, He loves us so much! Don't you think He has a plan to reunite us with our loved ones? He does! I feel it! Please believe that!"

I looked at her, really seeing her for the first time. Something she said seemed to speak directly to my soul, to all my treasured hopes hidden deep within. And yet the part of me that hurt so badly was afraid to hope and didn't want any part of it. Closing my eyes, I saw Nette's beautiful, perfect face as it had been in the hospital. I had felt her there, just for a moment, hadn't I? But the thought that she might still exist somewhere brought even more agony to my soul. "Where is my baby now, Monique?" I asked, feeling my heart breaking all over again. "Who's holding her? Who's singing to her and telling her how much she's loved?"

She gazed at me with understanding. "People often ask me that same question in the hospital," she said quietly. "I personally think your little Nette is with Antoine. And I think he is holding her and loving her and telling her all the things you want her to know. He'll watch over her until you are able to be with her again. And knowing she is well taken care of, you can do something meaningful with the time you're apart from her."

Dumbfounded, I stared at her. For the first time since Nette died, I felt myself focusing on something other than my loss and my feelings of guilt and pain. I didn't know exactly where heaven was, but I suddenly wanted to believe in it. I could almost see Antoine holding and kissing Nette. And in that moment I knew what I had to do. Antoine had died for no reason, but I would not allow Nette's death to be in vain.

Monique watched my reaction closely. "I have some friends from my church who spend two years out of their lives to teach these things. Wouldn't you like to listen to them?"

I shook my head. "No, Monique. I know what I'm going to do." She regarded me curiously as I continued. "I'm going to make Nette's death mean something. I'm going to call that coalition against drugs they're always advertising on TV, and I'm going to volunteer. What happened to Nette should never happen to anyone, and I want to make sure no one ever has to go through this hell that I'm living!"

Monique nodded. "That's a definite step in the right direction. I knew you would find a way to come out of this."

I nodded, but I think we both knew that I was just hiding the pain away so I didn't have to look at it right then, masking the hurt with anger and action. Still, I had survived terrible loss before, and I knew that time would dull the pain.

After lunch, we went down to the café, where I called the drug hotline and told them my story, still so fresh and painful. The woman on the phone seemed very interested and said she'd get back with me after talking to her supervisor. I went back to my apartment, grateful to leave the pitying stares of the café customers behind. Again I sat on the couch clutching Nette's bear, staring into nothingness. I didn't notice when Monique left for work.

The next day, two women and a man from the Anti-Drug Coalition appeared outside my apartment. They talked with me for hours and finally asked me to be the focus of a new television campaign. I would have to tell parts of my story on camera, and they would use the footage to warn others of the terrible potential of drugs. Posters and personal appearances would also be required. I was overwhelmed with their plans, though grateful for something to focus on. We made a date for the following week to begin working on the campaign. *Somehow,* I told myself, *I will do this.* But the pain in my chest made it almost impossible to breathe.

They also planned to attend Nette's burial the next day. "We'll stay in the background," one of the women promised. "You won't even know we're there."

Indeed, I didn't see them among the few people who came to the short graveside service. Marguerite and Jules had come back from vacation and attended, along with Colette and Jeanne. We were all dressed in black—except for Monique, who stood out from among the others in her rich mauve dress. Instead of being offended, I found she was the one bright spot in the whole day.

My parents also came to the cemetery, though I hadn't told them when the funeral was to be held. We stared at each other from across the gaping grave, not knowing what to say. I was close enough to see the tears on their cheeks and that their eyes were swollen and red. I didn't cry, though, until they lowered the tiny coffin into the dark hole. Then I began to sob, helplessly and horribly. I had lost one more part of myself, and I knew that nothing could ever fill the resulting void in my soul.

A few days later, several lawyers came to see me about testifying at Jacques' trial. I also received near-perfect scores on my school exams, though that victory seemed hollow now.

A week after Nette's funeral, I returned to work. Marguerite and Jules had canceled the rest of their vacation and were home to stay. Françoise and Colette had gone home, so I was needed again at the café. I found relief in work, until closing time, when I went into the kitchen to get Nette ready to take home. A terrible grief washed over me as I realized that she wasn't there, that she wasn't ever going to be there again. Blinking back the tears, I hurried out the door before Marguerite understood the mistake that had caused me fresh pain. I cried all night, hugging Nette's stuffed bear, and slept in late the next morning. I was getting ready to go down to the café when the doorbell rang. Opening the door, I found Monique, but she was not alone. Two young men in white shirts and dark pants were in the hall with her.

"I know you said you didn't want to listen to my friends," she said. "But when I told them about you, they wanted to come and see you. Please, even if you don't want to listen to them, at least let them come in and leave a blessing in your house."

I sighed. "Oh, Monique, I accepted what you said about there maybe being a heaven, and I'm grateful for the hope it gave me. But I'm not ready to talk about all this. I'm getting back on my feet; isn't that what you wanted?"

"Yes, but I didn't want you to bury your feelings. You're so angry inside. I just want you to understand our Father's plan and learn to be happy again."

Sorrow and pain filled my heart. "I don't know if I will ever be happy again," I said. "Or even if I want to be."

"There's one more thing I have to tell you, Ariana," Monique said, looking at me beseechingly. "I told you Antoine and I had been meeting. What I didn't tell you is that he had also been taking the discussions, the lessons the missionaries have, and that he wanted to be baptized into my church. But he wanted you to hear the lessons first. You were supposed to come with him the day he didn't show up. Think back . . . didn't he mention meeting with me that day?"

I nodded and closed my eyes to stop my tears. "He did, Monique. But that makes no difference now. Please go. I have to leave for work."

One of the young men in the poorly lit hallway stepped closer, his features suddenly revealed by the light from my doorway. "Please," he said. "Give us a chance."

I gaped at him. This was the same tall, red-haired missionary who had stopped me by the Seine River two years ago, after Antoine's funeral.

"You!" I exclaimed.

He nodded. "You didn't forget, then. I wasn't sure if it was you when Monique told us about you—until now. Still, I didn't want to take the chance of missing you. You see, I've always been sure we would meet again. I was supposed to go home two months ago, but I asked for an extension and a transfer back into this area. I kept seeing how your eyes looked that day, and I've wanted the chance to see you again—to teach you."

His voice took me back to the day when I had crumpled up the pamphlet in his face and thrown it to the ground. And how he had not been angry but kind and loving.

"Did you pray for me?" I asked, a trifle unsteadily.

He nodded, and when he spoke, his voice also shook. "Every single day. I never forgot your face or the look in your eyes. It was as though it had been burned into my memory. I wanted to help you that day we first met, but I couldn't. Please, let me have a chance now." His clear blue eyes bored into mine, imploring.

I started to shake my head, wishing he would go away so I wouldn't have to think about my dead brother or little Nette, just two weeks dead. I pulled my coat tighter around me; the weather had turned exceptionally cold for September, and I would need the coat later on that evening. Besides, it seemed I was always so very cold now that Nette wasn't there to warm me with her sunny smiles and affectionate hugs. I thrust my hands deep into the large pockets.

I felt the paper there and brought it out before remembering what it was. There in my hands was the homemade pamphlet the young woman missionary had given me the day after Jacques had left me all those months ago—the day I had told little Nette how she and I were going to be noble queens who ruled themselves and weren't afraid to love and be kind, even though it sometimes hurt so much.

I had to blink twice before my eyes cleared enough to see the picture on the pamphlet. It was of a mother and a baby cuddling, and over it were the words: "You can have your baby with you forever. It's true! Our Heavenly Father has a plan for families."

The pamphlet and the memory of that day decided me. How could I refuse, when I had told Nette that we must be kind despite the pain in our hearts? This missionary wanted, even needed, to teach me, and just maybe I needed to hear what he had to say. "Okay," I said finally, looking into the red-haired missionary's pleading eyes. "But not right now. I have to go to work."

"How about tomorrow morning?"

I shook my head. "I've got an appointment with the Anti-Drug Coalition."

"What about the day after—on Saturday? Would ten o'clock be all right?"

I nodded. "But I've got to be to work at noon, so be on time."

I left them without a backward glance, using the stairs instead of waiting for the elevator, hugging my aching memories of Nette to me as tightly as possible so the tears wouldn't come. They had already seen enough of my pain.

All that day, I couldn't keep my mind off the red-haired missionary. I had to admit I was curious. What was it about this church that had made Antoine want to join?

CHAPTER TEN

The next morning Marie, one of the women from the Coalition who had come to my apartment the week before, appeared with three men in tow. She introduced me to the men, and they went to work quickly, setting up their lights and cameras. They moved my TV into the kitchen to make room but brought a large picture of Nette from there to place beside me on the couch.

"Now, here's what's going to happen," Marie said. "You tell your story, and occasionally we might stop you to ask a question or ask you to retell a part of the story. Later, they'll splice everything together to make the commercial. Enrique, here," she pointed to a short man with long black hair, "will also take photos of you while we videotape—for the posters and billboards. Just tell me your story the way you did the other day."

I sat on the couch and tried to do as she asked but couldn't. I kept looking at the cameras and feeling awkward with the strange men watching me. After more than an hour of failure, Marie called it quits.

"Let's take a break, boys." They all stretched and stopped staring into their cameras for a moment. Marie came to sit with me on the couch. "Look," she said to me, "I know this is all kind of awkward, but it really will help others."

"I'm sorry." I motioned to the cameras and lights. "I can't seem to do it with all this stuff here." As I spoke, I spied Nette's bear where it had fallen beside the couch during the setting up. I picked it up and held its fluffy white body close to me.

"Was that Nette's?" Marie asked.

I nodded. "I bought it for her when my husband left me, when I was still so full of hope for her. She didn't pay much attention to it until a couple of months ago, when it became her favorite toy." At that I had to bite my lip to stop it from quivering. "But now she'll never hug or play with it again."

"How did you meet Nette's father?" Marie asked suddenly.

In response to her questions, I slowly told my whole story again in more detail than I had the other night. I told her of our separation, my schooling, and everything leading up to Nette's death. I don't know when I started crying, but suddenly there were tears making their way slowly down my cheeks.

"It's just not fair!" I said when I'd finished. "My baby never had a chance to even take her first step alone! Jacques killed her, that's true; but it never would have happened if it hadn't been for the drugs. People must realize the ruin drugs make of lives—and not just our own but the innocent ones like Nette's!" I hugged the bear tightly and looked down at Nette's picture. "Now my heart aches, my arms are empty, and Nette's gone. It has to stop somewhere—it has to stop *now!*" I looked up at her, my eyes pleading. "Please tell the people."

Marie smiled at me. "I think you just have, Ariana."

"What?"

She motioned to the men, who, unbeknownst to me, were back at their cameras. I saw tears on two of their faces. "It's an old trick, Ariana," Marie said gently. "Pretending to stop filming but not turning off the cameras. I think we'll have enough now to make our commercial. Could we borrow some of Nette's photographs?"

At first I was upset at what Marie had done, but relief came quickly after. Enrique took a few more photographs as the others packed away their equipment and put my apartment back the way it had been. Soon they were ready to leave.

"Thank you so much." Marie hugged me as she left. In her hands she held several photographs of Nette. "You're a strong woman. I'll be in touch."

After they left, I cried until I thought my head would explode from the pressure. "Oh, Nette," I moaned over and over in despair, rocking myself to and fro on the floor. "How can I go on without you?"

But I knew that I would.

Abruptly the tide was over, and I went around the apartment and gathered up all pictures, clothes, or any remnants of my baby. I left only the bear and a large picture of Nette in my bedroom, storing the rest in the closet where Monique had already put most of her toys. Someday, I would be able to look at her things without anguish; but I knew that for now, I had to put them away where I would not be assaulted by the memories and the grief at every turn.

I noticed the calendar on the wall. It was September 10, the day my brother, Antoine, had died two years earlier. I was nineteen years and six months old, and I felt that my life was over.

Saturday morning, the missionaries rang the bell ten minutes before I expected them. I opened the door to see their smiling faces. Monique was with them. "We're on time," she said cheerfully.

"No, you're early. But come on in and have a seat anyway." I motioned to the couch with a sweep of my hand.

The missionaries sat on the couch, and Monique and I used the kitchen chairs which I had moved into the living room. The red-haired missionary waited until we were all settled before beginning.

"Well, now, let's properly introduce ourselves. I'm Elder Kenneth Tarr, and this is my companion, Elder Robert Cocteau. We're mission-aries from the . . ." He now spoke fluent French but still had a slight American accent. I listened intently, enjoying the sound. Soon he was explaining about prayer and asking Monique to offer one.

I found her prayer curious, yet intriguing—far different from the memorized ones my mother had taught me as a child. Monique talked to God as if He were a real person, someone who actually cared about us individually. And somehow I felt He really was listening to her.

Afterwards, Elder Tarr began talking about God and Jesus and the method God always used to communicate to His people—through prophets. "Ariana, this is what He has done in our day," Elder Tarr said in a soft voice. "In 1820, there was a young boy named Joseph Smith . . ."

The missionaries took turns explaining about Joseph Smith and the Book of Mormon. They often bore their testimonies, looking sincerely into my eyes as they spoke. Monique also told how she had been con-verted to the gospel shortly after her parents' deaths. I knew they all believed what they were saying, and I felt strange and wonderful at their words.

"Do you think it is important to know if this book is true?" Elder Cocteau asked me, showing me the book he claimed Joseph Smith had translated. I nodded, and he continued, "It really is important, because if you know it's true, you will know Joseph Smith is a prophet of God and that everything else the Church teaches is true." He turned to a page near the back of the book and showed me verses that promised I could know the truth of this and all things if I but asked. "This is yours now, Ariana," he added, handing me the book.

I took it and promised to read several marked sections. We also set up another appointment for the following Monday. I waited for them to leave, but Elder Tarr looked at me. "Would you offer a closing prayer for us?"

"I don't know how," I said, remembering the easy, eloquent prayer Monique had offered.

"Well, you simply say, 'Heavenly Father,' and then thank Him and ask Him for what you need. Then close in the name of Jesus Christ."

"Okay," I said softly, surprising myself. I wasn't completely sure I even believed in God. We knelt on the carpet around the coffee table, and I glanced about nervously until the others bowed their heads and closed their eyes. Finally, I closed my own.

"Heavenly Father," I began hesitantly. "Thanks for my friends. Please help me to know if You exist and if You love me." His certain love was something they had stressed during the discussion, but I couldn't understand how He could love me and still let Nette and Antoine die. "And please," my voice broke, "if there is a heaven, please take care of my baby. In the name of Jesus Christ, amen."

We were all crying when we stood up, but I didn't know exactly why. For the first time since Nette's death, I felt strangely comforted. We stood around looking awkwardly at each other until the elders left. Monique stayed. I still had an hour before work, so I asked her if she wanted some coffee.

She shook her head. "No, I don't drink coffee, Ariana. It's got caffeine in it, you know, and that stuff's a drug. It's even addicting."

"I guess you're right. I never thought about it that way, probably because it doesn't do damage like other drugs."

"Yes, it does."

I didn't argue because she was a nurse and would know better. I poured my cup of coffee down the drain and had juice instead.

"Tea is bad, too," Monique said suddenly. "Not certain herbal kinds, though."

I raised my eyebrows. "Anything else?"

"Just drugs and alcohol and stuff like that. Anything that harms the body."

Light suddenly dawned. "Does this have something to do with your church?"

"Well, yes, but not just. You see, the Prophet Joseph Smith received a revelation counseling the early members not to use such things, years before our doctors began finding out they were bad for our bodies. That was one of the reasons I looked into the Church in the first place. It was incredible to me that an uneducated man could be so right."

"Anyone who counsels against drugs can't be too bad," I agreed. I found I liked the idea of such a standard for a church. "I wish I'd had an influence like that in my life. Maybe then—" I couldn't continue.

"Ariana, would you like to go to church with me tomorrow?" Monique asked, covering my sudden silence. "We have a meeting in the morning."

I thought of the church services my parents had taken me to at Christmas or for christenings. I had never felt comfortable there. Still, I had nothing else to do, and Monique was good company. I had to admit I was very curious. "Okay," I agreed. "But I don't have anything appropriate to wear. My few good dresses that fit are pretty worn. Some of my dresses from before my marriage are still in great condition, but I'm bigger in places. Not that you can tell. I was such a twig before." *Before I had Nette,* I added silently, feeling the emptiness in my arms again.

"Let me see them," Monique said. "You're still thin; they can't be all that difficult to fix." I took her to my room and pulled two dresses from the closet that my mother had bought at her favorite shop. They were expensive and well-cut, much better than anything I could afford now. Monique turned them inside out immediately. "Why, this can be let out a little, and I think I could add some material to the other. Try it on for me, and let's see what's what." I tried each on in turn. The waist was fine on both, but the hip and bust were definitely too tight.

I found some thread, and Monique went deftly to work, pulling out the stitches and placing tiny, even ones of her own. "This one I can do by hand, but the other I'll take with me. I have a machine at home." Her fingers flew in and out quickly, becoming almost a blur.

"So where did you learn this?" I asked enviously. "Is it one more thing your grandmother taught you?" My own grandmother had died before I was born, during the long years my parents had tried to have a child.

"Oh, no," Monique said quickly. "My grandmother hated sewing. But after she and I joined the Church, the sisters there taught me. We get together once a month, or more often if necessary, to teach each other different homemaking skills. You would hardly believe the many different talents they have to share." She laughed. "Why, even I have to give a lesson on home remedies next week."

I laughed with her but wistfully. "I wouldn't have anything to offer."

"Oh, Ariana!" Monique stopped her sewing abruptly. "That's not true! In fact, what you have to offer I think would be a lot more important than what I could ever teach!"

I stared at her in disbelief. *What could I possibly know that Monique didn't?*

My thoughts must have been obvious, for Monique continued softly, "Well, if you don't know, maybe it's best to let you find out for yourself." She put her sturdy hand on my shoulder. "But trust me on this, okay? You have so much to share inside of you. Maybe you're just not ready." She turned back to her sewing while I readied for work, still puzzling over her words.

That night after closing the café, I began to read the book the elders had given me. They had assigned me 3 Nephi 11, but I didn't stop there. I read until chapter 17, where Jesus blessed and wept over the little children. Suddenly, I felt His love around me as tangible as anything I had ever touched. Though I had always believed I was alone, I never really had been. The concept was amazing.

I thought of Nette and cried, but this time hope mingled with my tears—hope that she might actually be with Jesus and Antoine. I didn't quite understand it all, yet I wanted to. Slipping into my schooling mode, I read far into the night, searching for scriptures that had anything to do with children or resurrection. Hours later when I finished reading, I knew for certain that I would see Nette and Antoine again. This knowledge, after the dismal feelings of finality before, made my heart sing. I still hurt terribly inside, but at least I could see a tunnel and a light at the end. The light was my Savior, Jesus Christ, and I knew that He loved me and understood what I was feeling.

The next morning Monique arrived early, but I was awake and ready in the dress she had let out the day before. I hadn't slept much that night, but I didn't feel the lack; I was alive with questions. "I need more to read about the Church," I told her when she couldn't answer my questions fast enough.

"Okay, okay," she said laughingly. "After church we'll stop off at my apartment and get all the books I have. I have quite a few of them, some I haven't even read. I never was much of a reader."

The church building was quite unlike anything I expected—large and spacious without being pretentious. We were greeted at the door by a friendly man Monique introduced as the bishop. A score of young people gathered around us excitedly, talking and laughing. Entire families filed past us into the chapel to sit on padded benches, their faces smiling and relaxed. As we talked with the young people, several sets of missionaries arrived, among them Elders Tarr and Cocteau.

"Hey, Elder, I hear you're finally going home!" someone said to Elder Tarr. "Or are you going to try and extend again?"

He laughed and shook his head. "No, I think I've done the work I was supposed to do." He looked directly at me as he talked. "Haven't I, Ariana?"

I think I had always known Elder Tarr's church was my destiny, ever since I had seen his kind face on the day of Antoine's funeral. I didn't know how he knew I had accepted the teachings, but I did know that he was the only missionary who could have broken through my shell of hurt and anger to make me listen. And it had only taken that once.

"Yes, I want to be baptized," I said softly. "Why didn't you ask me yesterday?"

"Because you weren't ready yet," he answered with a smile. "But how about next Sunday. Is that soon enough for you? I go home the Wednesday after."

"I have to wait that long?" I asked. The group of young people around me burst into laughter at my words. I hadn't realized until I spoke that they had all been holding their breath, waiting for my reply.

"Well, we need to give you the rest of the discussions," Elder Tarr replied. "Just to make sure you understand the covenants you'll be making."

We confirmed the appointment we had already made for Monday and made two more for later in the week. They would teach me two discussions the first two days and the final one on Friday.

"And you might want to start thinking about people you want to invite to your baptism," Elder Tarr added. "It's a very good way to share the gospel with people you care about."

I immediately thought of my parents, but the gulf between us was so great that I didn't know how to go about breaching it. In my heart, I partly blamed them for my life since Antoine died and especially for Nette's death. *Why hadn't they wanted me?* I shut out the feelings quickly because I wasn't ready to deal with them. Someday, perhaps, when my wounds weren't so fresh.

The week went by quickly in a flurry of reading and learning. On Wednesday, the missionaries taught me the fourth and fifth discussions. They showed me the film *Families Can Be Together Forever.* I found myself crying when the boy's mother died; I knew so well what he was feeling. "Are you all right, Ariana?" Elder Tarr asked me, concern apparent in his eyes.

I nodded. "It's just that I wish I had listened to you two years ago. I can't help but think what a lot of pain I could have spared myself . . . and my baby."

The elder's sadness glistened in his eyes, but we both knew nothing could change the past. "Sometimes we don't always understand why things happen," he said, "but we must trust in the Lord. He knows what He's doing. And whether we appreciate the trials or not, we always learn and grow from them."

"Well, I'd like to stay this size for a while, if you don't mind," I said, trying to make my voice light.

My tone didn't fool Elder Tarr. He gazed at me sincerely as he spoke. "I think you will, Ariana. The Lord knows you better than anyone, and He knows when the growing needs to ease up. But never forget that the Father loves those He tests. If He didn't care, He wouldn't want us to progress and become more like Him. That's what the trials do for us, you know. They make us more like Him. And I believe with my whole heart that He suffers right along with us."

I nodded. We had always wanted to be queens, Nette and I. We just hadn't realized exactly what kind. And I knew that to be like our Heavenly King would be even more difficult than I had thought—but also much more rewarding in the end.

That Sunday, three and a half weeks after Nette's death, I was baptized. It was a beautiful, cloudless day in late September. Marguerite, Jules, and my next-door neighbor, Jeanne, attended. Marguerite was mostly disapproving, feeling as though I was being taken advantage of because of Nette's death, yet even she felt the Spirit at the baptismal meeting and shed a few tears. Jeanne came gratefully, happy to know I didn't blame her for what Jacques had done. We hadn't talked much since that terrible day, but slowly our relationship was returning to normal.

I emerged from the warm baptismal water feeling new and reborn. As I received the Holy Ghost, I knew there would still be many trials ahead in my life, but now I would never feel alone again. My Savior would be near, and I would also have the constant companionship of the Holy Ghost.

Life changed drastically after my baptism. When I wasn't at work, I was involved in Church service. Almost immediately, I was put into the Young Women organization, where I learned by teaching. I avidly read every Church book I could get my hands on and spent hours researching my lessons.

Church was much like an extended family, and I loved being there. People were friendly and caring. There were many young adults my age; but while I enjoyed being with them, and maybe even resembled them on the outside, I realized that my experiences distanced me from them. Not in a negative way but in a manner that actually made my observations and comments help them understand life and the gospel. Monique was right; I did have something important to offer. In turn, the older sisters helped me come to terms with my loss, as well as the anger and guilt that still burned in my soul. Slowly, as the weeks and months went by, the pain I felt at Nette's passing dimmed in the light and love of the gospel.

Of course, I still found time in my busy schedule to volunteer once a week at the Anti-Drug Coalition and make a few personal appearances. The new media campaign was a huge success, and the Coalition received not only many new calls for help but also much additional funding. Unfortunately, this also meant that my face was plastered from one end of France to the other, and often I felt embarrassed when people would recognize me in the street. I cut my hair very short again to reduce such recognition, and to some extent the disguise worked.

My divorce from Jacques was final in the middle of November, and shortly afterward he went to prison. I learned about it when the lawyer prosecuting the case came to see me at work. "He's pleaded guilty so you won't need to testify against him," he said. "It's just as well, because our main witness, Paulette, has disappeared somewhere. She wasn't too reliable anyway because of her drug habit."

I drank in the information slowly. "I haven't seen her since that night," I said. "I haven't wanted to." I felt guilty as I said it, but I was telling the truth. "How long will Jacques go to prison for?"

"Well, the judge will decide next week, but since he was under the influence of drugs at the time, he probably won't get more than seven years. That means with time off for good behavior, he'll probably serve around five."

Five years didn't seem like much of a punishment compared to all the years he had stolen from Nette, but I didn't become upset. I told myself that ultimate punishment would come from the Lord. Meanwhile, I couldn't help but hope that Jacques would be miserable in prison. The feeling wasn't very Christlike, but I was helpless to shake it.

"So where do you go from here?" the man asked, really seeming to care about the answer. Maybe it was because he had three little ones of his own and needed to know how I could cope with my loss.

"Well, I'm starting school in accounting in January," I told him. "From there, I'll take one day at a time. I know I'll see my daughter again someday." Feeling compelled, I began to explain some of my beliefs and even gave him a pamphlet with the missionaries' phone number on it.

"Thanks," he said as he left. "Maybe I'll check it out."

The year passed quickly for me. I kept busy learning, teaching, and just plain surviving. For the most part I did well, except when it rained at night. Then I was alone, so very alone. Often I would relive Nette's death—and Antoine's, as well. During those nights, only my growing testimony of the Lord kept me sane. Crazily, I found that at those times I even missed Jacques.

"You'll find someone else," Monique assured me. Indeed, she kept trying to introduce me to every eligible bachelor in the Church. Those I did date either weren't my type or they couldn't get beyond my past. I told myself it didn't matter. But deep inside, where I didn't let anyone see, I hoped I would find someone special. At times I despaired it would ever happen. I felt lonely and unfulfilled.

Until I met Jean-Marc, and my life once more changed forever.

CHAPTER ELEVEN

*I*n January, three months before I turned twenty-one and more than a year since my baptism, Elder Jean-Marc Perrault, from Bordeaux in the southwest of France, was transferred into my area. From the moment I set eyes on him, I knew that somehow he was different from any of the other missionaries I'd known before.

He wasn't much taller than I was, and I had never been very tall, but he was large in presence. He was my age and incredibly handsome, with black hair and wonderful green-brown eyes. He had an engaging grin, yet a serious way about him that appealed to me.

"I know you," he said to me the first day he saw me. It was Sunday, and Monique and I had just arrived at the chapel for an early morning meeting called by the missionaries in our ward. We had been introduced to the new missionary, and since that moment he had been staring at me curiously. "You've cut your hair, though, and you're much prettier in—" He stopped talking, as if suddenly remembering he was a missionary, one who still had five months left to serve.

We all laughed at his expression. "Yes, that's me on the TV commercials," I admitted.

"Don't worry about it, Elder Perrault," said his companion, Elder Jones from America. "We all forget ourselves the first time we meet Ariana." We laughed more, but I could see that Elder Perrault wanted to ask me if what the commercials said was true; everyone always asked me that, even though the commercial came right out and said it was a true story before I even began talking. Usually I didn't like to dwell on my loss, but somehow I felt it important that this particular missionary understand the truth about me right from the first.

"It's all true," I said quietly to him as the others found their seats.

His eyes locked onto mine. "Somehow I knew you wouldn't lie about such a thing. I'm so sorry."

I smiled wistfully. "I've gone on now, and I know I'll see her and raise her someday. I'm stronger for it."

"Yes, I guess you are." The look he gave me was admiring, without pity. "Anyway, I'm pleased to meet you after all this time. To tell the whole truth, I'd hoped to meet you one day."

"It's nice to meet you, too, Elder," I returned, though I was thinking it was a little strange that he should want to meet me because of my commercials. Usually men seemed turned off when they heard about my past. But Elder Perrault was a missionary, and he certainly didn't mean he had wanted to meet me in the romantic sense . . . or did he?

I was saved from having to think about it further when Elder Jones motioned for us to sit so he could begin the meeting. After a song and a prayer, he came right to the point. "We need volunteers to help with the missionary work," Elder Jones said. "Those who want to help will be divided into member-missionary teams to work with the different missionaries in your area. They will visit you each week and help you understand how to do missionary work with your friends and relatives and set specific goals to reach. Our mission president feels that by work-ing through our members, we will not only find and baptize more people but have them stay active because of your love and support for them. We need every one of you. Now who wants to volunteer?"

I raised my hand immediately. Ever since a year ago, when I had talked to the lawyer who was prosecuting Jacques' case, I had wanted to learn how to share the gospel. I always felt so strange and unsure of myself when talking about it with others. Even when spiritually prompted to speak up, I didn't know what to say.

We divided into teams. Monique and I were put with another girl, Aimee, and a young man named Claude. We were assigned to Elders Jones and Perrault, the missionaries in our area.

"Well," began Elder Perrault, looking at the other teams who each had at least twice as many members, "we're outnumbered. But we all know that quality is better than quantity." We laughed.

"What we want you to do is to make a list of ten friends or family members by the time we visit you this week," Elder Jones said. "People you love or those you feel might be open to hearing the gospel."

"And you don't have to worry that we're going to beat down their doors," joked Elder Perrault, as if reading my thoughts. "We just want you to have the names on paper so we can discuss them and what steps you can take to make their introduction to the Church a positive one."

"Will you do that?" Elder Jones asked each of us in turn. We all committed ourselves.

I struggled with my list that week, taking their challenge seriously and prayerfully. Though I had many friends in the Church, I hadn't reached out to any nonmembers since Nette's death. Marguerite and Jules were already at the top of my list, but I was plagued with doubts about who to put next. To make things worse, it rained all week because of a sudden warming in the weather. I was reminded forcefully of Nette and Antoine and spent much of the week crying alone in the night.

Luckily, I had school and work to keep me busy. I was in my second year of accounting and enjoying it thoroughly. Soon I would be looking for a job in my field and leaving the café behind forever. That was one of the reasons why Marguerite and Jules were on my list. I owed them so much and yet couldn't find a way to share with them the most precious gift I could—the gospel.

The rest of my list grew slowly: Jeanne and her husband; Dauphine, the girl who worked the café in the mornings; a certain regular at the café; and one girl at school. This brought me up to seven people. And there it stayed. I knew deep down who at least two of the remaining three people should be, but I couldn't write their names. Not yet.

"Well, let's see that list," Elder Perrault said to me on Friday afternoon, when he and his companion appeared at the appointed time at the café where I was taking a break.

I gave it to him reluctantly. "I've only got seven so far," I confessed. "But I want to have more."

He smiled at me and ran a hand through his thick, black hair as if to push it back, forgetting that it was already cut very short and no longer needed such attention. "We'll work on it, Ariana," he said. "That's what we're here for." The way he said my name seemed caressing, but he was unaware of it—or of how my heart beat so quickly when he was near. I was surprised to find myself reacting to him that way. It was the first time such a thing had happened since Jacques. Not one of the men Monique had introduced me to had made me feel anything similar.

Instead of pressuring me about the rest of the list, Elder Perrault talked with me about Marguerite and Jules and what I could do to help them. "You love them, don't you?" he asked me after we had gone over the steps of missionary work.

"More than anyone alive, besides Monique," I said.

"Then you have already finished many of the steps. Now you need to prayerfully decide how to approach them. Remember, the only thing they can say is no. It shouldn't change your relationship."

"So should I ask them to meet with you?"

Elder Jones shook his head. "Maybe try something else first. How about asking them to church? They believe in God, don't they? Church is a good way for them to feel the Spirit without being threatened."

"All right, I'll do it," I said determinedly. It did seem a lot easier to ask Marguerite and Jules to church than to ask them to listen to the discussions. After the elders left, I began fasting with a goal to ask them to go to church with me on Sunday. But the rain continued, and I felt despondent. No matter how I tried, I couldn't seem to find an opportunity to ask them. When Saturday evening rolled slowly to a close, I knew that it was now or never.

"Uh, Marguerite," I began hesitantly as we finished putting away the food. I could hear Jules in the office, putting the day's proceeds into the safe. "You know, you and Jules have been like family to me these past two and a half years . . ." My voice trailed off. I didn't know how to continue.

"As you have been to us, Ariana."

I plunged on. "Well, after Nette's death, I found my church, and I know you thought I was jumping into things. But I've been very happy there, haven't I?"

Marguerite nodded. "Yes, I think I was wrong. It's been very good for you."

"Well, I wanted to know if you and Jules would come to church with me tomorrow. I think you might enjoy it there. And it would be nice to spend some time together outside of work. What do you think?" I stopped talking and held my breath. I was so afraid she would say no.

"That sounds nice," Marguerite said, as if it were the most natural question in the world. "I think I'd enjoy going. Jules and I haven't been inside a church since we buried our Michelle. Maybe it's time we go back. I'll tell Jules about it, but I'm sure he'll come."

I wanted to tell them what to expect, to prepare them for the difference from their own church, but something stilled my tongue. Maybe it was something best experienced.

The next morning the January sun shone weakly but insistently over Paris, and my depression had completely lifted. Jules, Marguerite, and I all went to church in Jules's car. There they were greeted with the same love and enthusiasm I had experienced more than a year before. I saw the amazement on their faces at the simple beauty of the chapel and the services. Afterward, I proudly introduced them to the elders.

"I do believe you can do anything you set your mind to, Ariana," Elder Perrault said to me privately. I thought again that his deep voice was tender, and I blushed like a child. Seeing my discomfort, he grinned. But he didn't understand that I was reacting to him and not his compliments.

Things went quickly after that, with the missionaries giving Marguerite and Jules the first discussion the very next day. The elders also began to come daily to the café for lunch, where Marguerite clucked over them like a mother hen and Jules regaled them with stories of his youth. Two weeks later, the elders and I taught the Geoffrins the fourth discussion. As they heard and understood how families can be eternal, I knew for certain that they had finally accepted the gospel.

"You mean we can be sealed to Michelle?" Marguerite asked. "We will see her again and be a family?"

I nodded. "It's part of the plan our Father has for us. We're all going back to live with Him someday, if we are worthy, to become more and more like Him and to inherit His kingdom."

Her gaze was intent. "Then everything you used to tell little Nette about being a queen someday was real," she said with sudden insight. "She is going to be a queen someday, isn't she?"

Tears came to my eyes, and I couldn't speak. But Elder Perrault said softly, "Yes, just like her mother." My eyes flew to his in surprise. How could he know how I struggled to act as a queen would, to be worthy of raising my baby one day?

"Based on our worthiness, we will all be like our Heavenly King,"

Elder Jones added. "But first we have to live our lives in . . ." He continued on, leading the conversation away from the doctrine that was generally hard for investigators to understand. But I knew instinctively that he was wrong in this case; we all needed to know about Nette and how my dreams for her would come true, even though she was dead.

A week later, Marguerite and Jules were baptized, and attending the special meeting were the next five people on my list. The missionary spirit burned in my soul, and suddenly it was easy to share the gospel. I felt the Lord really did bless those who opened their mouths despite their fears and insecurities.

Over the next month, our member missionary team worked hard to bring the gospel to those on our lists. We began baptizing new members every few weeks, to the surprise of the other teams who had not yet gotten so involved. In the first week of March, after working almost daily with Elder Perrault and his companion, we baptized the rest of the seven people on my list, along with some of their friends and family members.

"You've done better than you expected, haven't you?" Elder Perrault asked me that Sunday.

I smiled. "Yes. I was scared at first, but now it seems to come easily."

"You'll make a good missionary," he said with a special light in his eyes. His companion beside him nodded in agreement.

I stared at him in wonder. "Me?" In the last few months I had often longed to go, but because of my past, I didn't think they would let me. Even so, my desire to serve a mission had increased as my twenty-first birthday grew closer. Now it was little more than a week away.

"Why not, Ari?" Elder Perrault asked.

His sudden use of my old nickname froze me in my place. For a long moment I couldn't breathe as I stood and stared at him. Finally, my throat loosened up, and I could speak. "Ariana," I whispered hoarsely. "Not Ari. Still not Ari." And despite my efforts to the contrary, I began to cry. I turned and fled out the door, with the elders staring anxiously after me.

Rain drizzled slowly but incessantly the next day when the elders came to see me at the café. It was my day off, but we had planned to meet because of the missionary team. As usual, Marguerite fussed over them and introduced them to everyone who came into the building. But at last I was left alone with them.

"How are you?" Elder Perrault asked with concern. He looked as if he had not slept well the night before, and since he refused any food, I knew he was fasting.

"I'm okay," I said. "I'm sorry about yesterday. There are just some things I haven't told anyone about . . . about my family."

The elders and I were seated at a table in the corner of the nearly deserted café. Elder Jones pulled out his notebook and retrieved my sheet of names. The last three spots were still blank.

"What about your family?" Elder Perrault asked me, indicating the list in his companion's hands. "Why aren't they on this sheet?"

I sighed and closed my eyes for a minute. The rain fell softly against the window in a continual assault, and I wanted to scream at it to stop. "I hate the rain," I said suddenly. "Why does it have to rain so much?"

Elder Perrault stared at me, his expression sincere. He was going to say something, but his companion beat him to it. "It doesn't rain all that much here," Elder Jones said. "You ought to see how much it rains in Washington, where I'm from."

I didn't care in the slightest how much it rained in Washington, so I sat there silently.

Elder Perrault looked hard at his companion before turning to me. "It has been wetter than in past years, so I've been told. I think—"

"I guess I just notice it more than others," I interrupted bitterly.

Elder Perrault didn't even blink at my retort but sat watching me. His handsome face was calm, his eyes caring. When he spoke, his voice was soft yet compelling. "Tell me, what happened to make you hate the rain?"

I took a deep breath. I found that I wanted to tell him. I wanted to bury myself in his arms and tell him everything. Of course, I couldn't throw myself at him, but I could at least explain. "I had a brother once—Antoine," I began before I could change my mind. "We're twins. My parents tried for many years to have a baby, and finally they did. Only they had two instead of just one. Antoine was everything I ever could want in a brother. Everyone adored him, my parents included. He had a way with people, yet he never abused his gift. I loved him so much." Tears rolled slowly down my cheeks, and I brushed them away impatiently. "He used to call me Ari. Everyone did. Three years ago, he died on a rainy day like this one. My parents shut down inside themselves, and I felt that Ari was gone forever, buried in the earth with Antoine. I went crazy for a while but finally settled down and had Nette. Then she died." I paused and gave them a watery smile, trying desperately to stifle the sobs that threatened to burst from my throat. "It was raining that night, too."

"And you never see your parents?"

"Once, a few months before Nette died, and again at her funeral." I looked at them seriously. "I know they are supposed to be two of the last three people on my list, but I don't know if I am able to contact them or if they even want me."

"How could they not want you, Ari?" asked Elder Perrault with tears in his eyes. The eyes suddenly widened when he realized he had called me Ari again. "I'm sorry. You just look like an Ari to me. Over the months I have thought of you as such, though no one ever used the name. I finally decided to see how you liked it. I'm very sorry. I won't do it again, if you don't want me to."

I smiled slightly. "It doesn't hurt so much today, now that you know about my brother," I said, surprised to be telling the truth. "And if there ever was anyone to call me that, it should be you." Now I had to choose my words carefully, because he was still a missionary and I wouldn't compromise his calling for anything. "You are very special, like my brother was. You are very similar."

"Then that makes two of us," he replied. "You are also very like you described Antoine." He paused and added softly, "So what do you think he would do in relation to your parents?"

I laughed shortly but without real mirth. "I knew you would ask that. I've asked myself the same question almost every day for the past year. Maybe it's time for me to talk with them. Maybe I can finally do it."

"You can, Ari. I know you can." Elder Perrault looked so confident that I felt I really could succeed.

"Did you mean what you said about me being a missionary?" I asked suddenly. "Would they accept someone who has been married and had a child?"

"It does happen," Elder Jones said. "You'll have to talk to your bishop, of course, to get things going."

"You'll be wonderful!" Elder Perrault smiled at me, and I felt myself tingle all over in a way that I, a woman who had been married and given birth, barely recognized. "And I'll write to you every week."

My eyes met his. "Really?"

"I guarantee it." His eyes were full of promise.

The next morning the sun was shining brightly again, making my spirit warm. Eagerly I went to see my bishop at his work without calling first. He was a supervisor at the local telephone company and was in his office most of the day.

"I want to go on a mission," I blurted out the second his secretary left the room. "Can I go? Even though I've been married before?" I didn't mention that I'd also had a baby; Bishop Rameau already knew my history.

He was silent for a moment, and I held my breath, fearing his answer. "Oh, Ariana," he said finally. "I think that's a wonderful idea. I don't know why I didn't think of it myself. You will be an exceptional missionary." His face was so sincere that for a moment I wanted to cry. "But I think because your divorce took place after your baptism, you will need an interview with a member of the Area Presidency."

"What! Why?" I asked, nervous again at the thought of actually talking alone with a General Authority. They were men to be revered.

Bishop Rameau seemed to read my mind. "They are people, as we are, but with a special calling. There's nothing to be afraid of. As to why you need to see him, it's Church policy for youth who have been divorced or who have had moral transgressions. But I think you will enjoy the encounter."

I didn't agree but nodded anyway. "So how soon can I do this? I want to go on my mission as soon as possible." I knew that even once the interviews were completed and the papers sent, I would have to wait weeks, maybe months, for my call.

He smiled. "I'll bring the papers to the café this evening. It won't take long to fill them out. I'll make an appointment with the stake president for Sunday, and he'll make one with the Area Presidency for whenever one of them is available. I'll tell him how anxious you are."

I wasn't sure that was a good idea, but I thanked him and left.

As promised, Bishop Rameau brought the mission papers by the café that evening. By Sunday, two days before my birthday, they were completed and ready to go, and I was interviewed by my bishop and the stake president. I was happy and content that they were both excited and positive about my decision.

But as I walked out of the room where the stake president had held my interview, I was startled to see an American man in a dark suit. By his very posture, I knew he was a General Authority, though I didn't recognize him personally. Bishop Rameau was at his side and introduced the man by name. I heard only "Elder"; the rest of the name escaped me.

"He came today because I told him how anxious you are to go on your mission," the stake president explained as I shook hands with the tall man. "He is flying to Utah tomorrow to counsel with the Brethren and won't be back for several weeks. He wasn't sure he was going to make it today, but he did."

I smiled faintly. I was happy I wouldn't have to wait weeks for my interview but felt mentally unprepared for it today. "Thank you," I said mechanically.

The man smiled and motioned to the room we had just left.

"You don't want a translator?" Bishop Rameau asked.

"I think not," the man replied in heavily accented French. "Thank you." He gestured again, and I went inside. He followed me and closed the door. I gulped audibly; I was alone with a General Authority.

He began our interview by asking me brief questions about my life and my desire to serve a mission. His French was bad and my English worse, but somehow we communicated. He was well-informed about my past, thanks to Bishop Rameau, who spoke fluent English, and it made things easier for me. Even so, I was in tears as I told him about my baby. To my surprise, he was also crying. I watched as large tears rolled slowly down his long face, and I wondered that he could feel so much for me, someone he didn't even know. It reminded me of how the Savior loved. Truly this was a man of God!

"Ariana," he said after we had talked for more than an hour, "I feel that your Father in Heaven loves you very much and is pleased with the way you are living your life. In His estimation and in mine, you are worthy in every way to serve a mission."

I didn't know what language he was speaking, but I understood him perfectly. With tears streaming down my face and blocking my vision, I said, "Oh, thank you. Thank you so much."

"No," he said, shaking his head, "thank you, Ariana. Thank you."

We were quiet for a comfortable moment. I felt as if I had known this man all my life, and I didn't even know his name.

"Can we pray?" he asked.

I nodded mutely. We knelt down on the rough carpet and he began to pray. He called down the blessings of heaven upon me and pleaded with the Lord in my behalf. I had never felt so much love before. The feeling permeated my whole being until I couldn't hold another drop.

When he was finished, I hugged him; I couldn't help myself. I wanted to thank him again, but my voice would not obey. Yet I knew he understood because we had been communicating with our spirits.

As I left the room, he held up my papers. "I'll take care of these, Ariana. You'll get your calling soon. You're going to be a wonderful missionary!"

I left him, my heart full of love and singing with joy. But as I walked down the street to the subway, it started to rain softly, making me recall my conversation of the previous week with Elder Perrault and how he had made me feel that it was time for me to see my parents. With this new love inside me, I suddenly knew I couldn't leave on a mission without clearing things up with them. I had to at least tell them I loved them, regardless of the distance and bad feelings between us.

Darkness was already beginning to fall when I arrived near the expensive apartment building where my parents lived. As I hesitated outside, several people emerged from the outer door and held it open for me so that I wouldn't have to use my nonexistent key to open it. I thanked them and smiled, but as soon as they were out of sight, I left the building and let the door shut behind me. Then I went to stand before the row of buttons that rang in the individual apartments above. It wasn't fair for me to simply appear outside my parents' door; I would at least give them the few minutes it would take for me to reach their fourth-floor apartment to prepare themselves for my visit, as I had tried to prepare myself on the way over. I pushed the black buzzer and waited for an answer.

Suddenly I was afraid.

CHAPTER TWELVE

W ho is it?" came my mother's voice through the speaker.
"It's Ariana. May I come up?"
I heard a swift intake of breath and a shocked pause. Then the
buzzer at the door sounded as the outside door unlocked. I made my
way up to their apartment slowly, using the stairs instead of the elevator
to give them more time. I imagined my mother rushing into the sitting
room to tell my father I was coming. Would they be planning what to
say? Or would they simply look at each other without speaking, their
hearts racing as wildly as mine? Or maybe they didn't care. I didn't quite
believe that last thought, though it made no difference; whether they
accepted me or not, I had to make my peace with them before I could
serve the Lord on a mission. It was something I had to do.

The fact that it was raining outside didn't escape me, and a sense of
impending doom was constant. But I pressed on. Suddenly I was at the
door, and it opened before I rang.

"Come in, Ariana," my mother said softly. Her expression was
hopeful, and for the first time I had an inkling that maybe I had judged
her wrongly in the last few years.

We went to the sitting room and sat down. Clean and elegant, the
room looked nearly the same as when Antoine and I had lived there.
Memories of happy times when I was a child chased each other through
my mind. I also saw my parents as they had once been—young, hopeful, and loving.

I sat on a comfortable chair opposite the sofa where my parents
were settling themselves. In the quiet of the room, I studied them. They
seemed older than before and somehow softer. I couldn't help hoping
that the year and a half since Nette's death had changed them as it had
changed me.

"I came because I wanted to say that I am sorry for the past few years," I began, looking at the floor, feeling like a small child again. I was certainly grateful that I had rehearsed my speech on the way over. Maybe I would finally be able to tell them everything. "For years I've hated you for blocking me out after Antoine died. Instead of his death bringing us together, it tore us apart. I blamed you both for everything that happened afterwards—my drinking, doing drugs, even getting pregnant. I was just so lonely, and you weren't there." I began to cry silently. The tears fell from my eyes, but I paid them no heed. "Then you came to me after Nette was born, and I hoped deep inside that you wanted to be a family again. But instead you asked for Nette—the one thing I had left in my life. You wanted her, not me." I looked up at them now. "Don't you see that I needed you, that I just wanted your love?"

"We do love you, Ariana!" they said together.

My mother came to kneel next to my chair. The bright light from the lamp nearby lit up her face, and I could see the love in her eyes quite clearly. "We *did* want you in our lives. We were just afraid that we were too late. We feared that how we acted when your brother died pushed you so far away that you'd never be able to forgive us!"

My father also came to kneel by my mother. The telling light showed that he was no longer stiff and withdrawn but reaching out to me with hope. "We asked to take care of Nette, but we meant for you both to come back here to live with us." He gazed at me earnestly with tears in his eyes. "We wanted to help you, but we didn't know what to do!"

I nodded, looking at each of them in turn. "I think I knew inside that you loved me—or wanted to believe it. But I guess even when Antoine was alive, I knew I was always second-best."

"What?" my parents said again in chorus, seeming genuinely surprised.

"But we've always loved you, Ariana," my mother said. "As much as we ever loved Antoine."

I shook my head. "No. No one was ever like Antoine. He was special. I didn't mind being second to him."

"But you're special, too!" my mother said. "The way you always knew how to bring a smile to our faces. The way you always stuck up for what you believed in. We loved you every bit as much as we loved Antoine. You have your own special talents, some similar to your brother's and some very different."

I felt the truth of her words spread through me, but I wasn't ready to let it go that easily. "But you always treated him differently. You let him do what he wanted, and yet I couldn't go to the corner flea market without company!"

"That's true," my father said. "We did want to protect you from people like . . . like Jacques and Paulette, and Antoine always was a good judge of character. But our wanting you to be with him was for him as well as for you. You were always a steadying influence on him. We hoped that your common sense would rub off on him, even just a little. He could be so impulsive at times, but when he thought he was taking care of you, he was always more responsible."

"I never saw that in him," I said, but as the words came, I remembered that my brother had been impulsive, doing daredevil things that he would never let me do. I remembered how once I had cried out in fear that he would fall off a steep wall to his death and how he had promised me never to do such a thing again. My brother had been wonderful, full of infectious laughter, caring, and trustworthy. But he had also been heedless of many hidden consequences, things that had been so clear to me. Maybe I had been as important to him as he had been to me.

If only I had been with him on the morning he died.

"Can you ever forgive us?" my father asked. "For what happened to you after Antoine died, as well as for Nette's death?"

I started at his words. "But that's really what I came to tell you. I don't blame you anymore for any of it. I've learned that we all make our own decisions and have to live with them, and some things, like death, aren't even in our control. What happened wasn't your fault or mine; it was just because we didn't know any better."

"Will you . . . come back home?" my mother asked hesitantly.

I didn't know until she asked that I even wanted to come home, that I longed for my parents to want me with them.

"Do you really want me to?" I asked.

"Yes, we do," my father replied. "We always have. We need you."

I smiled through my tears. "Then I want to come. But I'll only be able to stay a month or so, because I'm going on a mission."

"A mission?"

As I talked, I prayed they would understand. "Well, after Nette's death, I was in a bad way, but I had a good friend who helped me a lot. And through her I found that the Church of God has been restored to the earth! My whole life has changed now—that's part of the reason I came tonight—and I want to tell other people about it."

My mother looked steadily at my father in the lamplight and then at me. "Any religion that brought you back to us must be good."

My father was more practical. "How long will you be gone?"

"A year and a half." I saw their sadness at that, so I hurried to add, "But I'll write to you every week, and I probably won't even go for six weeks or more. I haven't gotten my call—my assignment—yet. But it's something I have to do."

"You're an adult," my father said, "and you make your own decisions. But we had simply hoped for more time. We have so much to make up for."

"But that's just it, Father," I said earnestly. "We'll have plenty of time. With each other and with Antoine and Nette. That's what is so wonderful about the gospel—knowing there's so much more than what we see. We can be a family forever, even after death!"

My parents appeared skeptical, but they didn't reply or verbally reject what I had said. That alone showed how much they had changed.

⁓

The next day, Monday, I moved back home after my morning classes, even though I would lose the last two weeks' rent from my old apartment. I didn't mind. The important thing was that I had my family back. And Marguerite and Jules weren't upset in the least, only very happy that I had patched things up with my parents.

"I always knew they loved you," Marguerite said. She hugged me and then sent Jules to help move my things.

"So now what?" my mother asked as we settled my few belongings in my old, familiar bedroom. It had been kept virtually the way I had left it years ago. Since it was fully furnished, my other possessions, such as Nette's toys and clothing and my couch and bed—the only furniture really worth keeping—went into my parents' storage room in the basement of their building.

"Well, I'm going to finish out my school course and work until I get my mission call."

"But you don't need to work anymore," my mother protested, trying to hide her grimace as she unpacked my worn clothing. "We want to take care of you while you're in school."

I stood up and took her hands in mine, looking earnestly into her eyes. "I know, Mother, and I'm so grateful. But I'm trying to earn as much as I can to pay for my mission, so my church doesn't have to do it."

"You have to pay money to go?"

"Only my expenses—food, clothing, a place to stay."

"Oh." My mother's voice was thoughtful.

I forgot about our conversation until later that night, when my father knocked softly on the door. I had just settled into bed and called for him to come in.

"Your mother tells me that you have to pay for this mission of yours," he said bluntly. "I'd like to help you out." He held up his hand before I could speak. "We've got more than enough money to do so, and it would make us feel better, knowing that we are helping our little girl."

His words reminded me of how much I'd wanted to give to Nette and how time had taken away that chance. "Thank you, Father," I said, understanding what it meant to him for me to accept. It meant a great deal to me, too. I could almost feel the weight of my monetary worries vanishing as if they had never existed. "I would appreciate it greatly."

"I also want you to come to work for me at the bank," he said, reaching out to hold my hand. I was almost overwhelmed at the love I felt in his grasp. "You'd earn a lot more money, and when you come back you'd have a good job waiting. You'd be good, too, from what you tell us of your grades, and you'd learn a lot."

A job at the bank! "Oh, Father, I would love to!" I blurted out without thinking. Then I remembered the café. "But I'd have to talk to Marguerite first."

"Of course." He kissed my cheeks and left.

I lay in bed thinking of the new life opening up before me. My parents back, a good job. If only . . . Thoughts of Nette overcame me, and I held her bear to my chest tightly. But I didn't cry. Suddenly I was thinking of Elder Perrault and how my heart fluttered every time I saw him. Quitting work at the café would mean that I wouldn't see him every day, only on Sundays. But maybe that would be for the best, in view of how I felt about him and the fact that he was a missionary.

I fell asleep thinking about Elder Perrault, dreaming of the day when he would just be plain old Jean-Marc.

"You don't have to give me notice," Marguerite said cheerfully when I told her of my father's job offer. "I've been waiting for a chance to introduce my niece, Colette, to the gospel, and now I can call her and say that I'm desperate for her. She's not expecting her baby until the end of next month, so we'll have plenty of time to find a replacement for you." She hugged me suddenly. "But that doesn't mean I'm not going to miss you terribly. You're like a daughter to me." She stopped to wipe a tear from her eye with the back of her rough hand.

"And don't worry about your apartment. The people the missionaries were living with had a new baby and want to use the missionaries' room for a nursery. They came by last night and told me, so I said they could rent your old apartment. Someone in the ward has already donated twin beds and a couch. With the furniture you left, they'll have things pretty good—for missionaries." She laughed. "So I'll give you back two weeks' rent for this month to go for your mission. They'll be moving in this afternoon, if it's all right with you."

Things were working out wonderfully. "That's great! But I still have a few things I forgot—pictures and stuff."

"Well, you can run up and get those things after the lunch rush."

The afternoon sped by as we helped and laughed with the customers. During a brief lull, Marguerite called Colette, who promised to be there the very next day. I had a bittersweet feeling, knowing everything I did that day at the café was for the last time. I had many good memories there.

Finally, things slowed down during the late afternoon. "Why don't you go now?" Marguerite asked.

I glanced around the nearly deserted café. "Okay. I'll be back in a few minutes. It shouldn't take me long."

Marguerite shrugged. "Take as long as you want."

The hall was strangely quiet as I made my way to my old apartment. Memories of Nette and days gone by fluttered through my mind like the ghosts they were. But I felt no regret at leaving. I had to go on with my life.

The door was slightly ajar when I arrived. It seemed the missionaries were already moving in. "Hello?" I called.

"Come on in," someone said. So I pushed the door open and walked in.

"Surprise!" yelled many voices as I stood there blinking in surprise. "Happy birthday!"

I laughed. I had completely forgotten it was my birthday. Everyone close to me in the ward was there, as were my parents. There were so many people in the room that I practically had to squeeze my way into the apartment. The small kitchen table had been dragged to the center of the room and, along with the coffee table, was loaded with treats.

Marguerite arrived shortly after me with additional food and drinks from the café. "Don't worry about going back to the café tonight," she said. "I got Dauphine to cover for you. I'm going to stay with you myself until the dinner rush begins."

It was a birthday party like those I had known when Antoine was alive, and I found myself laughing and talking as I hadn't for years. I received many presents, mostly books and Church-related items. Towards the end, when people started leaving, the elders finally showed up, carrying their suitcases.

"You're a little late," I teased.

"Yes, we know," Elder Perrault rejoined. "But it's your fault."

"What?"

"Some lawyer called us this morning and asked to see us this afternoon. He said he was the one who prosecuted Jacques' case a year and a half ago. We've just spent hours in a first discussion with him and his family." He shook his head in amazement. "You never cease to surprise me, Ari."

At his use of my nickname, my mother looked up quickly. But

during the week I had grown used to his calling me that. In fact, I loved hearing it said in his caressing voice.

"These are the elders, Mother, Father. They're the missionaries in this area. I'm going to be doing what they're doing," I said.

"What is it exactly that you do?" my father asked. Elder Jones immediately began explaining.

Seeing that his companion had things well under control, Elder Perrault picked up the luggage. "Which way to the bedroom?" I pointed it out and even walked over with him to open the door. He smiled his thanks and went inside as I returned to the living room to listen to Elder Jones, my parents, and the few remaining party guests discuss missionary life.

Through the open bedroom door I could see Elder Perrault unpacking his suitcase, putting most of his clothing on hangers in the closet. I saw him take something else out of his suitcase and slide it under one of the twin beds. But not before I had seen what it was—a poster of me from the Coalition's campaign. *Why does he have that?* I asked myself hopefully. A warm feeling spread through my chest.

"Ariana." My mother's voice called to me as if from far away. "Are you ready to go home?"

"Uh, yeah. I've just got to get my pictures." I went around the room quickly, taking down the few pictures I wanted to keep. I handed them to my mother.

"Is that all?"

I shook my head. "I've got a few more in the bedroom. One more of Nette and one of me." I turned to go into the bedroom but stopped at the door. Elder Perrault had taken down the photograph of me from the wall and was staring at it. One hand reached out to touch the glass, as if stroking my face. I coughed delicately, and he started. Our eyes met. We stood there not speaking, as a current of something wonderful and priceless seemed to pass through us.

He spoke, his voice suddenly husky. "You left this, Ari." He came across the room to give it to me. "And this one as well." He took a picture of Nette off the dresser near the door. "This is a very good picture of you," he said, indicating the first one. As he talked, his companion and my parents came over to look at it. The strange intensity of my emotions made me glad they had come. I knew Elder Perrault would never do anything to jeopardize his missionary status, but I didn't have the same confidence in myself. At least not when I felt the way I did at that moment.

"Here."

I accepted the picture from Elder Perrault's reluctant hands. Was I only imagining his reluctance? "Thanks," I said. "Monique took it, and she liked it so much that she had it enlarged and put in a frame to give me for Christmas." Looking at his familiar face, I added impulsively, "Would you like to keep it, Elder Perrault?"

His eyes told me how much he did before he spoke. "I would, Ari. It'll be a great remembrance of our most successful missionary team member. Right, Elder Jones?" He glanced over at his companion, who nodded.

We said our good-byes, and on the way home I was very quiet. I wasn't sad, only aware of my budding feelings for Elder Perrault. Somehow I knew he was very special.

Three weeks after my birthday, I received my mission call. I was called to the Bordeaux mission, due to leave the first of May, three weeks away.

"Only three weeks?" my mother asked when I told my parents.

I smiled. "That only means I'll be home sooner," I replied.

"I know." My mother sniffed and reached out to hug me. Her embrace was just what I needed. I felt loved and happy.

The weeks passed by quickly. I enjoyed both school and my new job immensely. Spring was beautiful, and I found myself taking walks again along the Seine, contemplating my life. Compared to where I had come from, it seemed nearly perfect. I was so excited to serve a mission! A week before I left, I received my endowments at the temple in Switzerland. To my joy, while in the temple I felt I could almost glimpse beyond the veil to see my baby.

With a rapidity that scared me, Saturday night arrived, two days before I was due to leave. My mother and I were packing my clothes into two suitcases. Most of the items were new and in very good taste, all picked out and paid for by my mother.

"Does this go?" she asked, pointing to a picture of Nette on my dresser.

"No. I already have tons of them in my suitcase. I'll leave that one for you."

"Thanks," she said quietly, holding the photograph to her slim body. She turned her gaze on me intently, as if searching. "Do you . . ." she began hesitantly. "Do you ever wish you could go back and change things so that those years after Antoine's death had never happened?"

I shook my head violently. "Never! Not ever! That would mean Nette would never have existed. And I could never wish for that."

"Yes," she nodded. "That's how I feel. Even though Antoine's death hurt us all, I could never wish that he hadn't existed."

We stared at each other, caught up in our thoughts. We had both been through the worst a mother could face and had survived, though not unmarked. Of the two of us, I was better off; I at least had hope for a future reunion, while my mother did not.

The next day at church, I said good-bye to all my friends. There was a flurry of address exchanging and hugs and kisses. Marguerite was especially emotional. "Thanks so much for everything," she said.

"No, I should thank you," I returned.

But she shook her head. "I mean for introducing us to the Church. Now it looks as though Colette and her husband will be baptized, and my sister is even taking the discussions." I could hardly picture the large, terse-faced Françoise agreeing to listen to the missionaries, but I was happy for her. I was even more excited to know that Colette was accepting the gospel. She had returned home about the time I had received my mission call and I had not had word of her since, except that she had given birth to a healthy baby boy.

"I'm so glad!" I hugged Marguerite and Jules both.

A cough sounded behind us. I turned around to see Elder Perrault and Elder Jones.

"I've got something for you, Ari." Elder Perrault held out a paper in his hand.

"What is it?" I asked as I reached for it, but I immediately saw that it was a list of ten names.

He grinned. "Well, your mission area covers where I live, and just in case you serve anywhere near my home, I've written down the names of ten people for you to go and see. You did it for me, so I want to do it for you. I've been writing to these people and preparing them since I've been on my mission."

"Well, thanks," I said. "But I never did give you ten names, you know."

He looked at me seriously. "You're only one short." He motioned to his companion, who took a paper out of his notebook. "We've decided to give it back to you until you finish it. If not for us, then for the other missionaries who follow." I took the proffered sheet and saw that someone had written in my parents' names. Now only one space was left blank.

"Thanks." I put both papers carefully away and turned to leave the building. Outside, clouds had gathered, blotting out the sun. I sighed in frustration. After weeks of beautiful sunshine and warmth, the rain had chosen this day to return.

I glanced back to see Elder Perrault watching me. "You'll write to me?" I asked. "After you finish your mission?" He had only a few weeks left now.

"I will write, Ari, as soon as I'm released," he said softly. "And please believe me when I say that someday the rain will remind you of Nette and Antoine, without the pain."

Once again I heard the promise in his voice.

Chapter Thirteen

I had been away from home several weeks when I received Jean-Marc's first letter. It was mid-May, warm and sunny, with only occasional rain showers to remind me of my past. I was serving in Tours at the time, feeling homesick and sort of lost, and I tore the envelope open greedily.

My dearest Ari,

How wonderful it is to write to you and to finally share my feelings without fear of breaking any rules. Though I'm not with you, I feel closer to you since I'm no longer a missionary and can consider our possible future.

I hope you are settling into your mission life. I am at home now with my family, but in a couple of months I'll be leaving to serve my time in the army. I promised them, and so I'll do it. I'm lucky I was able to go on my mission first. Beginning today, I will write to you weekly as I promised.

I think of you every day. It's time I risk my feelings (and your possible rejection) and confess that I have felt something special for you since I first saw your commercial over a year and a half ago. It touched me in a way I can't describe. I wanted so much to comfort you. I did some checking and found that you lived in Paris, though I never dreamed you were a member. When I was transferred to Paris, I took my poster of you, knowing somehow we would meet.

And we did! What a wonderful day for me! The fact that you were already a member only made me even more sure that you were as special as I had thought. As we started to work together on the missionary team, my feelings for you grew—first as a friend and then . . . Well, I didn't dare think beyond that, except to begin praying that you would go on a mission so I could at least have a chance with you when my army service is over. (Otherwise, I'm sure some lucky guy would have convinced you to marry him!)

It's raining here as I write this, and, Ari, I love the rain because it reminds me of you. I hope you will also think of me when it rains and not just of sad things. If you give me a chance, I promise someday I will help you love the rain.

Write to me soon.

Yours,
Elder Jean-Marc Perrault

P.S. Your lawyer friend, his wife, and their three children were baptized yesterday by Elder Jones and his new companion! He (the lawyer) called and asked me to tell you thanks for your great example. He will be a bishop one day, I think.

P.P.S. I'm glad you think I am similar to your brother, but don't ever make the mistake of thinking my feelings for you are brotherly!

I laughed with joy and even cried a bit. His feelings for me were all I could hope for at the moment. The next preparation day I wrote him a long letter, recounting everything I had been doing and how much his letter meant to me. I also admitted my budding feelings for him. Thus began a year and a half of weekly letters. With each long letter, my love for him grew. I learned about him—things I had only suspected before. I found he shared my love of numbers, of rivers, and of watching people. And most important, we had the same eternal goals.

But that was only the beginning of what I would learn about my Jean-Marc.

I had been out in the mission field a year when I found I was to be transferred in a week to Bordeaux and I would serve in Jean-Marc's home ward. He was thrilled. "Go see my family, lovely Ari," he wrote from his army barracks. "I've told them all about you. They will make great members of a missionary team. Show them my list of people, and tell them I said they'd help."

I was transferred on a Monday, and that night my junior companion, Sister Moura from Portugal, and I went to see the family, armed with Jean-Marc's list. My companion had been in the area two months and knew them well.

I felt nervous as we rang the outside bell to their apartment. "Who is it?" they asked through the speaker.

"The sisters," my companion answered. The buzzer sounded, and soon we were on our way up the elevator.

"This is my new companion," Sister Moura said as we were ushered into a modest apartment by a plump woman and a thin girl of about sixteen. "She knew your son in Paris. Her name is Sister Ariana Merson." I had taken back my maiden name after my divorce.

Jean-Marc's mother stared at me incredulously. "You mean you're Jean-Marc's Ari? How glad I am to meet you at last!" She hugged me effusively and then settled me on her flowered sofa. "You may call me Louise, and this is my daughter, Lu-Lu." She indicated the young girl. "Jean-Marc's brother is working at our store. You knew we had a grocery store, didn't you?" I nodded because Jean-Marc had mentioned it in his letters. "Now tell me, how did you and Jean-Marc meet?"

I was swept up instantly by Louise's warmth and charm, and soon I was telling her of my time with Jean-Marc in Paris. When I was finished, she sighed heavily. "Yes, that is what he told me. Ah, that boy has been a blessing to me, he really has, and I miss him every day." She straightened up on her chair, flashing me a smile much like Jean-Marc's. "Still, I know he is in the service of the Lord, no matter where he is, and that's what's important. But to think he met you as he dreamed of doing since your commercial came out on TV! And you a member; that is a miracle indeed."

She paused a moment, and I sat there with a silly smile on my face, suddenly speechless. What does one say to the mother of the man she loves? I turned my head to look around the comfortable room, especially noticing the photographs lining her piano in the corner of the room. Impulsively, I went to examine them.

"That's Pierre," Louise said, pointing to a picture of a man who resembled Jean-Marc. "He's a year older than Jean-Marc." She touched another photograph. "This is their father. He died when Lu-Lu was still a baby, shortly after we joined the Church."

"How did you manage?" I asked.

"We had the store. At first, other family members helped me with the store, but finally my boys were old enough to do the work. And by the time Pierre went on his mission, Lu-Lu also could help. Then Pierre was home, and Jean-Marc went on his mission—a little later than most boys because he was helping me, but he took it all in stride. He has great trust in the Lord. He has always been a good example to us."

"I miss him." Lu-Lu spoke for the first time, and her green-brown eyes, twins to Jean-Marc's, were wistful. "Only home for a bit and then gone again."

"I miss him, too. But he'll be back before we know it." Louise traced a finger along the frame of a recent picture of Jean-Marc. She glanced up at me. "He wrote us when your commercial came out. He said he was going to find you and baptize you someday, that there was something different about you. Of course, by the time he did get there, you were already a member." Her voice grew quiet. "My son says you're a special person, and from all he's told me, I think he is right. I'm glad you're here."

"He never told me," I said softly. I was happy to hear her words, but I suddenly felt very uncomfortable. I looked to my companion for help.

"Show them the list, Sister," she said helpfully.

"Oh, yes." I crossed to the couch to pick up my appointment book. Carefully tucked into the flap at the back were the two papers Jean-Marc had given me that last Sunday—the two lists of names, one mine and one his. I drew his out and showed it to Louise.

She smiled. "Yes, he told me about this list and who was on it," she said as she held it in her hands. "The first person is Elisabeth, our next-door neighbor. For two years I have been trying to send her the missionaries, and she has always refused."

I was puzzled. "Why does Jean-Marc think she will accept me?"

Her eyes met mine. "If she ever would accept a missionary, it would be you," she replied enigmatically. She crossed the room to the couch and sat down with the others.

"Why me?" I asked.

But it was Lu-Lu who answered. "It's because of your commercials and posters." That explained a little. Often during my mission, people had been curious about my past and it had led to discussions, especially the past few months when they had begun to play my commercials again after nine months of having focused on other similar commercials. Marie, the lady in charge of my campaign, had written to tell me that mine had been the most successful, so they were giving them another try.

Louise sighed. "You see, Elisabeth lost a baby two years ago in a car accident, shortly after she moved here. She hasn't been the same since."

Understanding dawned. I too had lost a baby, and maybe I could give this woman hope where no one else had been able to. "Well," I said, "I'm willing to give it a try." I gazed down again at the photographs of Jean-Marc. A fresh May breeze came through the window and touched my face like a whisper or a caress. *I will try my best, Jean-Marc,* I promised silently. Aloud I said, "Can we go now?"

The others looked at me, startled. "Right now?" asked Louise.

I shrugged. "She'll either accept or she won't. I feel we should go now." Hope flashed briefly over Louise's face, and I felt myself drawn to this woman who cared so deeply about her neighbor. *Jean-Marc is very lucky to have such a mother,* I thought.

I could see that my companion was nervous. I too felt my stomach churning. To hold the salvation of another person in one's hands was almost too much to bear, even if only temporarily. *Please, Father,* I prayed. *Let me be enough to get her to listen. Let Nette's death be worth this one thing more.* As I prayed, longing for my baby came over me, and I almost wept. I shut my eyes momentarily against the pain, knowing it would abate.

But it didn't. We were at Elisabeth's door now, and it was as if my emptiness and longing grew by the moment. The grief I felt seemed fresh. *Why, Father?* I pleaded. Then suddenly I knew I was being reminded so distinctly of Nette's death in order to understand how real it still was for this woman who didn't have the gospel to help her understand her devastating loss.

Louise rang the bell but didn't back away as I had expected. She stayed in front of me with a determined expression on her face. I was glad, because I wasn't sure if I would be able to speak past the bitter lump of sorrow forming in my throat.

"Oh, hi, Louise," said the woman who opened the door, as she looked up at the taller Louise. I knew instinctively that this was Elisabeth. She was young, maybe five years older than I. She was not slim but not fat either, and with her dark eyes and auburn hair, she was very pretty. Everything about her appeared normal, except for her eyes, which had the same hopelessness mine had held before I had joined the Church—empty, longing, alone, and so afraid of trying again.

"I have someone I want you to meet, Elisabeth," Louise said softly in the stillness of the hallway. "Jean-Marc sent her to you." Louise's hand reached out, lightning quick, and squeezed mine reassuringly. Then she moved her bulky figure to the side, and I faced Elisabeth alone.

Her eyes focused on my name tag first. "Louise, we have gone over this," she began, but suddenly she saw my face and stopped talking. She gasped. "The girl on the poster, the one whose baby died!" Her eyes began to water. "You're a member of their church? But how? Why? How can you serve God after what He did to you?"

I met her gaze steadily, seeing the anguish in her face, and I couldn't help the genuine tears that fell from my eyes and onto my cheeks. "Because," I said softly, remembering the thing that had bothered me most once I had begun to believe in a heaven, "I know where my baby is and who is holding and loving and singing to her. May I please come in so that I can tell you about it?" As I spoke, a vision passed through my mind of Elder Tarr standing in the poorly lit corridor outside the apartment Nette and I had shared. Now I knew how he felt that day two and a half years ago—anxious, hoping, fearful, accountable, and loving. Yet how could I love this woman I had never before met? Why had Elder Tarr loved me? I knew the answer, of course, being a missionary and having felt the pure love of Christ before, but each time the feeling came as a new wonder.

She stared at me, and for a long moment our souls communicated; we were bonded by our loss. Then, "Yes," she said in a whisper, full of hope and longing. "Please. Oh, please come in."

Chapter Fourteen

*T*he July day was hot and sweltering, but my companion and I didn't notice the heat. With smiles on our lips and a song in our hearts, we made our way from the church to Louise's apartment, where an informal gathering was celebrating our ward's latest converts, Elisabeth and her husband, René. They had been baptized only that day by Pierre, Louise's oldest son, Jean-Marc's brother.

We'd spent two long months working with them, weaving the discussions into my story so they would listen. Getting Elisabeth to pray had been the most difficult, but her husband's eager willingness to do anything at all that might bring his beloved wife back to herself helped things along. Many days Elisabeth and I had simply cried together. But finally, she gained a testimony for herself and had begun to live again, even thinking of having another child one day—something her husband had been urging but that she had utterly refused to consider. "To bring another child into the world so that God can take it away?" she said contemptuously the first time I had brought it up. But gradually her misplaced anger at the Lord grew into acceptance and even understanding. She began to smile and read the Book of Mormon and at last had asked to be baptized.

"Thank you, Sister Merson," she said afterwards. "I can never thank you enough for giving my baby boy back to me again, and my husband, and my faith." I hugged her and cried, not knowing how to tell her that I hadn't done anything someone hadn't already done for me.

My companion, a new one since Sister Moura had been transferred only last week, and I were a little late to the baptismal celebration at Louise's because of the next three people on Jean-Marc's list. They were all young, single people from Jean-Marc's school days, and we had taken them to see the baptisms. Afterward they had many questions for us, so we had stayed to teach them. We had been impressed to challenge them to be baptized, and two had immediately accepted. I felt the third would soon follow. As many missionaries would be content to baptize only one person during their entire mission in France, I felt considerably blessed.

On the way to Louise's apartment, I was thinking about the long letter I would write to Jean-Marc the next preparation day when I saw a scrawny figure slumped, unseeing, against an apartment building near Louise's. From the looks of the thin legs jutting out at odd angles from the rag-clothed torso, I knew it was a woman. She had her head thrown back against the wall, her dull brown hair swept up and over to cover her face entirely, dirty arms limply dangling, fingers with broken nails caught between loose cobblestones on the sidewalk.

We stopped and stared, as did several other people. It was a repulsive sight, and part of me wanted to flee. Yet somehow, the figure was strangely familiar. People shifted uncomfortably in the hot sun. A sight such as this was familiar to some but certainly not on this side of town.

"Call the police," said one man somewhat tersely.

"Yeah, we don't want any whores around here," said another next to him.

"She needs help," I heard myself saying. I drew closer to the sprawled figure, glancing only once at my American junior companion, Sister Osborne, who followed somewhat nervously.

"Be careful, girl," warned the first man. "These people are sometimes dangerous."

"And you might catch something," murmured the second man, almost under his breath.

I was standing beside the woman now and gingerly pushed back her hair. I gasped in shock.

"Paulette!"

I was kneeling beside her in an instant, shaking her and trying to wake her. When my efforts failed, I simply hugged her tightly.

"Is she dead?" the first man asked.

I shook my head. "Unconscious."

"You know her?"

I nodded. "She was my best friend—once. She needs a doctor." I peered up at the two men who had come closer, pleading. "Please, will you help me? There's a doctor nearby, a friend of mine." Even though Paulette looked thin, she was dead weight. There was no way I could get her back to the apartment alone, and my companion wouldn't be much help because of all our books and discussion guides.

"Not me," said the second man, backing away.

The other man regarded me intently for a moment. "Hey, you're the girl on that drug commercial, aren't you?"

"Yes, that's me. Will you help me?"

"Yes, I will," he said. "I'd do just about anything for you. Your commercial helped me get my own daughter off drugs." He bent to pick up Paulette, while I reached for the dirty duffel bag that was half under her.

"Thanks." I cast a hard glance at the second man who had refused to help, but he and the others were already moving away to find something else to do with their lives.

"Is that from your drug organization?" the man asked me, motioning to my name tag.

So I began to explain about the Church, about how I joined and what I had been doing since. When I was finished, the man smiled at me for the first time. "It sounds as though your church is something my daughter needs. Maybe you could come by and meet her."

I couldn't believe my ears. It seemed as though the promise our mission president had made to us was coming true: "People are out there waiting to be baptized. They are practically falling out of the sky and into the baptismal font. Keep the mission rules, pray hard, and most of all, open your mouths, and people will find you."

We took Paulette to Louise's, where the party was in full swing. At Louise's insistence, the man who carried her stayed for refreshments. I asked Lu-Lu to be a temporary companion to Sister Osborne and help her watch over the man who unknowingly had just become our newest investigator. Then I went into the back bedroom where Louise, Elisabeth, and René were standing over Paulette.

Now, I had exaggerated when I said I knew a doctor. René was only studying to become one and still had years left to complete his studies. But he had always planned to specialize in drug rehabilitation, so I figured he must know something.

"Will she be all right?" I asked.

He sighed. "I don't know, Sister." He pulled up her sleeve and showed me the needle tracks on her arm. "I mean, she'll come out of it this time, but the next she may not be so lucky. She'll have severe withdrawal symptoms, and there's nothing we can give her that will dim the cravings. She'll do almost anything to get drugs. It's my bet that she's already done things she never dreamed of doing."

I knew he was talking about prostitution, and I looked down at my once-best friend sadly. "Isn't there anything we can do for her?" Even my time on the drug hotline hadn't prepared me for this. Mostly I had talked to depressed teenagers who were thinking about doing drugs, not ones who were truly addicted.

"Yes, we can keep her away from drugs," René said. "But none of us has the money to put her into one of those fancy programs, and the free ones don't have the constant supervision she'll need until she's stronger. That is, assuming she even wants to be free of the drugs."

"We can do it," said Louise without hesitation. "We can get volunteers from the ward to stay with her while we're working, and she can sleep here." Her voice was firm. "Don't worry, Ari," she added softly, for the first time forgetting my missionary title. "We'll help your friend, won't we, Elisabeth?"

Elisabeth nodded. "Remember, you told me that's what a ward was for—to help each other. I'll take a shift with her each day after work. And René will be our medical advisor."

"We'll start with volunteers from the party." Louise was already out the door, followed by the other two.

I stayed behind to study Paulette's lifeless face, the lavish makeup smeared, a blackening bruise covering one side. She looked so old and ravaged. "This is partly my fault," I whispered to her, remembering the many times she had come to the café to play with Nette. "I never imagined how you must have suffered with Nette's death. I'm so sorry." I bent down to kiss her pale cheek.

Paulette didn't wake until late the next afternoon. Lu-Lu and another girl in the ward were with her. They helped her bathe and dress and fixed her something to eat, all the while talking and laughing like the youngsters they were. I had been calling after every teaching appointment to see how she was doing. Finally Lu-Lu announced that she was awake and wanted to see me.

We had just finished giving the first discussion to the man who had helped us with Paulette. He, his wife, and two daughters seemed very open and willing to learn. The daughters even offered to take turns sitting with Paulette when they heard what had happened. After our lesson, they let me use their phone to call and check up on Paulette.

"We'll be right there, Lu-Lu!" I practically yelled into the phone. I turned to the others. "She's awake. We'll let you know what happens." In seconds we were out the door and waiting to catch a bus to Louise's apartment.

Paulette was on the flowered couch in the sitting room when we arrived. She looked impossibly thin and somewhat rebellious. "The girls say I can't leave without them," she remarked. "Am I a prisoner here, or what?"

I smiled. "Don't be ridiculous. We just want to take care of you for a while. Will you stay?"

A tired expression came over Paulette's face. "Yes, I'll stay—for now. But I'm not promising anything, Ariana."

"I want you to promise me one thing." I crossed the room and sat next to her. "That before you leave, you'll say good-bye. You didn't the last time, you know."

"You didn't either," she muttered evasively.

"I know, and I'm sorry." For a moment she seemed close to tears. I reached over to hug her. "I love you, you know," I whispered. She didn't reply.

The shakes started the next day. By the time I saw her again in the evening, she was nervous, hyper, and unsteady as her body cried out for the drugs. She talked too fast, didn't listen to what was being said in return, and was rude to those who reached out to help. But the many volunteers had been warned, and they came prepared with iron-clad feelings and projects that might keep Paulette's thoughts off drugs. The young adults in the ward took her to activities, service projects, and even home to their own families. I was continually amazed at their dedication.

But despite their help and our first successful week of keeping Paulette off drugs, I could see she wasn't going to make it. Everyone was working for Paulette except for Paulette. She kept talking about leaving, about finding something to relieve her tension—drugs. Yet, she didn't go. I wasn't sure why until we stopped by on Saturday morning.

The door to Louise's apartment was opened by Pierre, Jean-Marc's brother. He looked a great deal like Jean-Marc, and every time I saw him my heart leapt, though when he spoke, it was clear he wasn't the man whose letters were making me love him more each week.

"Sisters! I'm so glad you're here!" Pierre's honest face shone with relief. "Elisabeth was supposed to be staying with Paulette, but she's gone. I don't know what happened. I was in the sitting room with Paulette, talking about her past—I thought it would help her to understand why she got so involved with drugs in the first place—and Elisabeth was in the kitchen listening to us, but she suddenly left. I went and knocked on her door and she wouldn't answer, but I know she's in there. Now I'm late for the store, and Saturday's our biggest day. I've called a few people, but no one's home or they can't come to sit with Paulette. But that's not the worst thing. Paulette says she's leaving now. She's packing that dingy old bag she has with the clothes we all gave her, and she's leaving! Can you stop her?"

The rush of words finally ended. I watched him with interest. For some reason he was very upset by Paulette's pending departure, much more than I would have thought. Of course he had been spending a lot of time with her, as had Elisabeth.

Thinking of Elisabeth brought me abruptly around. As a very new member whose testimony was still fragile, she had to be my first concern. "Okay, Sister Osborne and I will go talk to Elisabeth, quickly, just for a minute. After that we'll talk to Paulette while you go to work and see if we can get her to stay. Then we'll call someone to sit with her. If we can't find anyone, we'll take her proselyting."

Pierre blinked once or twice at that and then smiled the endearing grin he shared with his brother. "I like that idea." We all laughed.

"Now don't let her leave, Pierre," I said. "Tell her she promised to say good-bye to me." He nodded, and we turned and headed down the hall to Elisabeth's. She opened the door on the very first ring, as if she had been waiting for us.

"I saw you through the peephole," she admitted. "I was trying to decide whether or not to go back to Paulette when you came." She began to wring her hands as she talked, glancing around her small entryway, avoiding our eyes.

"What happened?" Sister Osborne asked.

Elisabeth sighed and looked at the ceiling, blinking rapidly to stop the tears from falling. "They were talking, Paulette and Pierre, about what happened before she came here, how she used to do drugs, but how after your baby died she went totally crazy. She said that for a long time, she didn't even know what town she was in or where she was sleeping. Just a blur, she said. But the part that got me was where she sat and watched your husband give drugs to that tiny little baby without stopping him. I suddenly couldn't stand to be around a person who could sit and watch a baby die! I can't believe I even spent so much time with her this week—I feel sick when I think about it!" She glared at me defiantly, but I nodded in understanding. I too had hated Paulette for what she had done—until I had seen her sprawled on the sidewalk nearly a week before. I didn't know exactly what had changed me or when it happened, but I didn't blame Paulette anymore.

Then Elisabeth asked the question I knew was coming. "How can you stand to help a person who did that to your baby? I don't think I could do it. If the person who killed my baby hadn't also died in the car accident, I think I would hate him still!"

I blinked and took a big breath before replying. "I hated Paulette for a long time—blamed her, even. But you don't know how manipulative my ex-husband could be. He killed Nette; Paulette didn't. She was even under the influence of drugs at the time it happened. She did try to stop him, and she called the police. But all that doesn't matter, not really. The fact is that she is repentant; and no one, not you, not me, can judge her or say that Jesus' atonement doesn't apply to her." Until I said the words, I hadn't realized I felt them that strongly. "Jesus loves Paulette just as much as he loves us. We *have* to forgive her. Remember that by the same spirit we judge and forgive, we will be judged and forgiven. Please, Elisabeth, see if you can't find it within yourself to forgive Paulette. She needs us now, and I know she has become especially attached to you. I'm afraid that without all of us, we will lose her."

I hugged her, but she didn't return the embrace. "We'll be over at Louise's if you change your mind," I added softly. "I hope you come." My companion and I were silent as we made our way quickly back to Louise's.

"Thanks," Pierre said as he left, pausing at the door to cast a pleading glance at Paulette. "Please be here when I come back." She shook her head violently, but he was already out the door.

"Don't try and stop me, Ariana." Paulette picked up her duffel bag. Her hands were shaking, and I could tell she was suffering more withdrawal pains, maybe not as severe as before, but still very real and compelling.

Our eyes met from across the entryway, hers looking so scared and young without her mask of makeup. "Were you going to leave without saying good-bye?"

She shrugged indifferently. "You're the only reason I've stayed as long as I have—you and Pierre. But I didn't think you would want me to say good-bye under the circumstances."

That made me angry. "What circumstances—because you're going to get a fix? Do you think I don't know what you're feeling? Maybe not exactly, but I do know that you're suffering! Your face is haggard, you've got the shakes, and you're downright rude! But everyone here has opened their hearts to you, given you a place to stay, helped you. Everyone except you, Paulette. It all comes down to you in the end. What do you want to do with the rest of your life? Do you even *want* a life?" I shook my head slowly. "No, that's it, isn't it? You don't even want to live. You don't care about any of us."

She didn't reply but dropped her gaze. I moved closer to her, fighting to contain my desire to shake her. "Paulette, look at me! Can you at least tell me why? I know it's hard, but with so much help, you could beat the drugs. Tell me, why quit now?" Tears flooded my eyes.

Paulette clenched her jaw, and for a moment I thought she would flee, but she didn't. "It's you, Ariana. I keep seeing your face the night Nette died and knowing I was responsible. Every day here you have come to see me, and I see your pain again, and I don't know how you can ever forgive me for what I've done!" She began to sob. I reached out, not to shake but to hug my friend.

"But it wasn't your fault, Paulette. And I did forgive you. It took a long time, but I don't blame you anymore. And now you've got to forgive yourself." I swallowed hard. "I know for me, forgiving myself took even longer." I held her back to stare into her eyes again. "But look at my face now. Do you see pain, unhappiness, anger? I hope you don't, because that's all gone now, since I've accepted the truth. Take a good look at me."

She did as I asked and abruptly stopped crying.

"Paulette, we are much more than we seem. We are eternal creatures, and we have to see things with an eternal perspective. Nette's not gone forever. Haven't you heard any of what we've talked about each time I've visited you this week? The plan of our Father in Heaven allows families to be together forever, despite death. One day we will both see little Nette, clothed in all the robes of a queen in heaven."

"You really believe that?" Paulette asked hesitantly, afraid to hope. "Nette's still alive somewhere, waiting for you?"

"I do. And you can know for yourself that it's true. God loves you every bit as much as He loves me!"

"But I've done so much wrong since Nette died," she said earnestly. The regret in her voice cut deep into my heart. "Things to earn money for drugs. I've about done it all."

Her words were exactly what I had been waiting for. We began to teach Paulette about repentance, my companion and I, slipping easily into our role as missionaries. Finally, Paulette was open to our teachings, and I knew that she was hearing them for the first time, though we'd already talked about them earlier in the week. It was as if her hearing my forgiveness and seeing my face without pain reached the place deep inside her that still wanted to try.

After a long time we got up to leave, already late for our morning street meeting with the other missionaries in our zone, planned for the flea market nearby. Paulette agreed to go with us. We met Elisabeth at the door, her eyes red and tearful.

"I'm sorry," she said. "You're right, Sister Merson. Paulette, can you ever forgive me?"

Paulette was genuinely puzzled. "For what?"

"Never mind," Elisabeth smiled, knowing instinctively that to tell her would only reopen her barely closing wounds. "But René and I were talking yesterday, and we want to know if you would like to stay with us until you're completely back on your feet and maybe longer. Louise doesn't have as much room as we do, and it's not proper for you to stay in their house with Pierre feeling the way he does about you." At her words Paulette reddened, and I laughed. I was not the only one, it seemed, who had noticed Pierre's unusual devotion to Paulette. "Anyway, Louise and Pierre always need a hand at the store, so they'll give you a job—they've asked already, haven't they? I thought so. Well, what do you think?"

We all knew Elisabeth was really asking if Paulette was going to stay and kick the drug habit that had imprisoned her for so long. If she was going to let us love her.

Paulette was quiet for a long time and then she nodded, meeting Elisabeth's eyes. "Yes. I want to stay with you, if you really mean it."

Elisabeth hugged her. "Oh, I do."

Even though Elisabeth had forgiven Paulette and everything was happy again, they both ended up going with us to the street meeting. Paulette had never seen one before and was curious. We even got them to sing with some of the missionaries and hold up signs while we contacted people in the streets. When I glanced at Paulette a short time later, I could see the happiness on her face and knew she was going to make it.

Two months later I was transferred, just a week after Paulette's baptism and engagement to Pierre. Sister Osborne and I had only baptized two-thirds of Jean-Marc's list, though we had contacted all of them. I left the list for her to finish. As I took it out to give her, I noticed my own list with the last number still blank. *Should I fill in Paulette's name?* I asked myself. But something stopped me. Somehow I didn't feel that last name would be so easy.

Once I was settled in my new area, Elisabeth wrote to tell me she was expecting another baby. "I'm almost scared to love it when I remember what happened to my first child," she wrote. "But knowing I will have my little boy again someday gives me the courage to love again. Indeed, I already love this baby with an intensity I didn't believe I'd ever feel again. Thank you so much for everything. And one more thing: if the baby is a girl, I'm going to name her after you."

Paulette also wrote to me, though her letters were rare and very short. But she was drug-free, in love, and happy again—and that's all that mattered.

I served the last two months of my mission in Nantes. As the end of my service approached, I felt excited and scared all at once. Jean-Marc was also nearing the end of his army service, but as he had recently been stationed not far from Paris, he had promised to come see me at our stake baptisms after I returned from my mission. Our meeting would be brief because he would need to get back to his base and then to his family in Bordeaux, but it would be enough.

In my mind I imagined the conversations we might have, the feelings our hearts would feel, the expressions our faces would show. But nothing, I knew, would equal the real thing.

Chapter Fifteen

*F*og, deep and dark like a heavy blanket in winter, covered Paris in the early mornings of late October. I didn't mind. It was a lot better than the rain and the fading memories it still brought to mind.

I had settled happily into my parents' apartment and was savoring their pampering. Father insisted I take a week off before returning to the bank, and Mother enjoyed herself thoroughly by giving away my worn missionary clothing and buying new things. I spent the foggy mornings sleeping in and dreaming of my promising future with Jean-Marc. The days I spent visiting friends, reading, or writing letters. I also organized my mission mementos, putting pictures in albums and throwing away papers that no longer had meaning. In the cleaning out I came across my list of ten people, already yellowing and torn in several spots. The last name was still blank. I felt the urge to throw the list away—hadn't I already done my share? But I knew that though my mission was over, my life's mission had just begun. And I would start that service by filling in that last name—when I could think of someone. Smiling, I slipped the sheet into the extra Book of Mormon I always carried in my purse or briefcase.

The first friends I visited were Marguerite and Jules. They were doing so well at the café that they had opened a second one which Colette and her husband, who had both been baptized long ago, were managing. The missionaries still lived in Marguerite's building, and the café had become a great contact place for them as well as a hangout for ward youth.

I looked up other friends—even Monique, who had since married and moved to another city and ward. She was now expecting her first baby. I was happy for her, happy for all my friends whose lives had gone on while I had served a mission. I missed the way things had been, but I was too excited about my own love for Jean-Marc to begrudge them their new lives and loves.

Sunday morning, I went to church and spoke in sacrament meeting. To my surprise, my parents attended. I was grateful for their support, because there were many new members in the ward I did not recognize. As people congratulated me on my successful mission, my parents beamed with pride. After the meeting, the missionaries asked to give them the discussions. "No, thank you," my father quickly declined in his firm way that brooked no argument.

"Maybe some other time." My mother smiled at the elders to soften my father's terse reply. The missionaries smiled back and shrugged. They turned to talk to others nearby while my parents and I started for the chapel doors.

"Well, welcome home, Ariana," said a sweet, drawling voice behind me.

"Aimee?" I said in surprise, turning to exchange the customary cheek-kisses with the blonde girl who had once been on Jean-Marc's missionary team with me.

She lifted her head slightly, the better to show me her long, curly locks. "Do you like it?"

"Yes, it's very pretty." And it was. She had grown out her hair and had lightened it slightly so that with her expertly applied makeup, she looked like an American movie star. I felt suddenly dowdy, with my dark brown hair cropped short and little makeup on my face.

"Are you coming to the baptisms?" she asked. I nodded, and she continued. "It will be the last time we can see Jean-Marc, since he's going home." She smiled at me prettily, revealing her perfect white teeth. "Of course, I'm going to go visit him soon. I don't want him to forget me."

It took a while for me to realize that she was talking about *my* Jean-Marc. But, of course, no one knew about how close we'd become. I hadn't told anyone but my parents and Monique, and Jean-Marc certainly wasn't discussing me with Aimee. I almost laughed.

"I'll see you there, Aimee," I said lightly. "I want to see Elder Perrault, too." She must have seen something she didn't like in my smile, because she frowned.

"Until later, then." She walked off, mincing as she went. My eyes followed her—as did those of every unattached man in the ward over the age of twelve.

Maybe it was because of Aimee that I took such great pains in getting myself ready that afternoon, but I didn't think that was my only reason. I wanted to look good for Jean-Marc, so I wore a flattering new dress. My thick hair was brushed to a shine and makeup applied carefully but not heavily. I surveyed myself in the bathroom mirror and felt pleased with what I saw—eyes dancing with excitement, smooth, white skin flushed in anticipation, love beckoning in my expression.

"You look beautiful, Ariana." My mother glanced up from the couch as I came to say good-bye.

"Thanks," I said breathlessly. "But I'm a little nervous."

"Would you like us to go with you?" my father asked.

I smiled. At any other time, I would have jumped for joy that my parents were volunteering to go see the baptisms, but today I wanted to be alone. "No, thanks. I think this is something I want to do myself."

My mother returned my smile. "We understand. Good luck."

By the time I arrived, the church was already teeming with missionaries, members, investigators, and those to be baptized. People stood laughing and talking quietly in the halls and foyer. Almost immediately I saw Jean-Marc. He was near a group of missionaries, and Aimee was with them, talking animatedly and fawning over Jean-Marc as much as she could without being too obvious. He looked up and our eyes met. The intensity of his expression and my echoing feelings surprised even me. I could actually feel the magnetism between us. Suddenly, it was as if we were alone in the foyer, the many people disappearing as if by magic. No one else existed for either of us. It was all I could do not to run across the room and throw myself into his arms.

As if from a long distance away, I heard a pouting voice saying, "Are you listening to me, Jean-Marc?" I knew it was Aimee, and I also knew that he wasn't hearing a word she said. His eyes were still locked with mine, as were his emotions and thoughts. I crossed the few feet between us in an instant.

"Ari!" he reached for my hand and grasped it tightly. "You're really here!"

"Of course I am! You think I'd give up a chance to see you before you left? Just wait until—"

"Excuse me," a loud male voice said, cutting me off. I turned to see one of the missionaries watching us. "Aren't you going to introduce me, Elder? Not that I can't tell who she is by all the photographs you have of her." He laughed, and to my delight, a slight blush crept over Jean-Marc's features.

"Sure. Elder, this is Ari—Ariana to you, however. I reserve Ari for myself. Ari, this is an elder, and that's all you have to know about him!"

The elder laughed. "He's afraid I'll charm you away from him. I'm Elder Madsen." The tall elder stuck out his hand, and Jean-Marc reluctantly let mine go so that I could shake hands with him. As I did so, I saw Aimee behind them, red with anger. She flipped her hair at me and stalked off. The others didn't notice her leaving.

The garrulous Elder Madsen was still talking. "Now, Jean-Marc here keeps telling me—and everyone else he meets—about you and showing a picture he keeps in a cardboard envelope in his notebook. He keeps telling us how many people you are baptizing, what a great example you are, and how much more beautiful you are than anyone else's girlfriend." He leaned toward me conspiratorially. "Now, of course, I didn't believe him until now. But he was right. And now I want to know one thing." He turned to Jean-Marc. "What makes you think you deserve this woman? I mean, besides being the top-baptizing elder during your mission, what else have you done to prove yourself to her?" We all laughed at that, and the conversation went on. But through it all I felt Jean-Marc's eyes on me, drinking in my presence as I was his. I felt happy and content.

Before long the baptisms were over, and it was time to go. "Good-bye," I told Jean-Marc softly. "For now."

I expected him to smile and tell me when he was going to call so we could begin carrying out the future we'd been planning for months in our letters. But instead, he frowned and looked at me seriously. "Ari, I need to do some thinking about things. I'll call or write you soon."

A chill swept through me, and I looked at him sharply. But he stared at me with such longing and love in his eyes that I dropped my suspicions immediately.

The next few weeks passed by, agonizingly slow and painful as I waited for Jean-Marc to call or write. Countless times I picked up the phone myself, only to put it down again before I dialed. I knew it was my pride that was stopping me, but I wouldn't force myself on a man who didn't love me.

My depression deepened, and through it all I kept questioning myself. Had I imagined that he loved me? Imagined the look in his eyes? Was it only me who had fallen in love? I brought out the letters he had written during my mission, and there was no mistaking the words. He had loved me, had been planning a future with me, but something had happened. What? Try as I might, I couldn't find the answers.

Another side of me reasoned that Jean-Marc was busy at home after being away for so long. Even now, he was probably thinking up a creative way to propose. I remembered his engaging grin and the laughing, green-brown eyes so full of love, the way his voice had caressed my name, the long letters that had promised so much more.

What had happened?

"He's probably having problems," Monique said to me one Sunday at the end of November, exactly a month since I had seen Jean-Marc. We had arrived a little early for sacrament meeting and were talking quietly in the chapel. I enjoyed having Monique with me again. She and her husband were visiting our ward to show off their new baby, a little girl with light brown hair and dark eyes. Envy of Monique and her life swept through me as I remembered what I had lost, but I forced the feelings down. Monique, too, had been through a great deal with the death of her parents before finding the Church and eventually a good, worthy man to take her to the temple. I didn't begrudge her that life; I just wanted it for myself.

"You know," she continued, "when my husband got out of the army, he acted really strange at first, like he was in shock or something. Then suddenly he came around, and everything fell into place."

"Yes, but why wouldn't he at least write?" I glanced around the chapel with its beautiful organ music sounding softly through the room, cushioned wooden benches, many chandeliers, and the smiling congregation gathering. But it seemed that no matter where I looked, I saw Jean-Marc. "Paulette has written once, but she didn't say a word about Jean-Marc, even though I asked her about him. Oh, why doesn't he call?"

"Well, did *you* write to *him?*" Monique asked quietly as she cuddled her baby close to her. Seeing her, I felt my arms ache with emptiness.

I shook my head. "He as much as told me not to that last day I saw him—to wait until he called me. I didn't understand how he could say that while looking at me like he did. I still don't."

Monique nodded in agreement. "He always did stare at you like that—his eyes filled with love and longing. After you left, he carried that picture I took of you everywhere." She frowned sympathetically. "I'm sorry, Ariana. What he's doing now doesn't make any sense. I don't know what to tell you. I can't figure out why he hasn't called or written."

At that moment, a sweetly malicious voice came from the bench behind us: Aimee. I stiffened immediately. How much of our conversation had she heard? Monique and I both turned our heads to see the blonde beauty sitting forward on the bench behind us, elbows coming to rest on the back of the bench we were sitting on.

"I thought I heard you mention Jean-Marc," she said with fake innocence. She flipped her long hair over her shoulder with a practiced hand and threw a teasing glance at a young man a few rows over who was staring at her. "Have you received a letter from him?"

I wanted to lie or tell her it wasn't any of her business, but I couldn't find words. I didn't need to. She already knew I hadn't heard from Jean-Marc, if not by my desolate expression, then by her eavesdropping. I simply shook my head.

"Well, I received a letter from him only this week, and I've talked to him many times on the phone." Her beautiful green eyes glittered, but beneath the beauty I saw the hardness of her white face. "I'll be going to see him soon."

I stared at her, not wanting to believe my ears, though I could hear the truth in her voice. She actually *had* received a letter from Jean-Marc.

I didn't cry or hit her smug face as I wanted to but carefully masked my feelings. There was no way I would let her see how deeply her words cut into my heart. I'd had much practice with pain, and I could hide it well.

Yet I couldn't help the thoughts of Jacques that came fleetingly to my mind and how terribly he had let me down. *Were all men that way?* I asked myself bitterly. *Even those who are members of the Church?*

Now Aimee turned to Monique and began to gush over the baby. "What a beautiful baby, Monique! She looks just like you. I can't wait until my future husband"—she shot a meaningful glance at me—"and I have one. May I please hold her?"

"I'm sorry," Monique said pleasantly enough. But I, who knew her well, could feel the chill in her voice. "I promised Ariana that she could hold her next." As she spoke, she was handing me the baby.

Aimee frowned. "Another time, maybe. The meeting will begin soon, and I've just got to talk to Henri over there before it starts." She motioned with a careless hand to the young man who had been staring at her. "Good-bye now." She stood and walked away, leaving us in a cloud of her expensive perfume.

"Don't mind her," Monique whispered. "There's no way Jean-Marc could love a girl like Aimee. She's not real. He'd see right through her."

I had thought so too—until now.

"She's not really that bad," Monique continued. "She just has a lot of growing up to do."

I nodded, relieved when Bishop Rameau stood at the podium to start the meeting. Now Monique wouldn't expect a reply. I felt my heart break, threatening to plunge me into the abyss of gloom and despair I had felt after Nette's death, when I had believed myself all alone.

The only thing that saved me was the precious gift from heaven cuddled in my arms. I buried my face in Monique's daughter's fuzzy hair, breathing in all the baby smells of her, holding her to my chest, feeling her trusting innocence. She opened her eyes to look at me. Those dark eyes, so wise, still filled with heaven's glory. Eyes that reminded me of Nette's.

I felt the pressure of Monique's hand against my leg. I looked over to see tears in her eyes. "You hold her for as long as you want," she whispered. I smiled and nodded. But after a time I gave the infant back to her mother. She was rooting around to nurse, and I had no milk to give her.

CHAPTER SIXTEEN

$\mathcal{A}$imee caught me at church a week later. This time Monique was not there to buffer her attack. It had been raining steadily all morning—wet, cold, and depressing. I had participated in the church meetings, had drunk them in like a man stranded in the desert drinks the clear waters of his rescuers, but now I had to go out into the dismal, cold day.

I stood staring out the double glass doors before I left the church building, trying to sort out my future. I was planning to go back to school in January and had already moved up a position at the bank. In fact, I was fast becoming my father's right hand. I loved the work and adored being with my father, but I missed Jean-Marc endlessly. I still hadn't given up hope of working out whatever it was that had come between us.

But what?

Aimee?

I thought not, but men were sometimes hard to decipher.

"Oh, it's raining," said Aimee's sweet soprano voice behind me, interrupting my thoughts. "Now I'll have to ask one of the men for a ride home." Her voice didn't sound disappointed. She studied me closely, beautiful as always in her modern dress, hair arranged just so, makeup accentuating her green eyes and thin face. "Have you heard from Jean-Marc?" she asked suddenly, her voice almost too casual.

I sighed. "Oh, Aimee. What does it matter to you?"

Her chin raised slightly, her eyes held mine. "Because I love him. Oh, I know you were close and that he wrote you while you were on your mission, but I got to see him a great deal. I often went to visit him on Sundays where he was stationed. He was always glad to see me.

We're good friends, and now that he has finished his army service, I intend to make him see me as much more than a friend."

"What makes you think he wants you as more than a friend?" I asked. I wasn't trying to be rude; I really wanted to know.

She pulled back as if I had slapped her. "He at least has written *me*," she hissed spitefully. "He still hasn't written you, has he, Ariana? I thought not. You see, it's one thing to be friends and to write letters, but when it comes down to choosing a wife, a man has to consider a woman's past. A man has to be sure that such temptations as drugs, immorality, and such won't get in the way of an eternal relationship." She glared at me pointedly. "And we both know your past is none too good, Ariana. Maybe you're not worthy of a man like Jean-Marc."

I would have slapped her for real then, but she whirled away before I could do anything. And I might have also sent words as evil and hateful as her own ripping into her back, but my missionary training prevented me. Instead, I shook my head in amazement. How could she talk about eternity and my past in the same sentence? My life before I knew the Church was gone, forgiven, and forgotten, or so I had thought. Evidently some people did not forget easily.

I left the church, whose steeple rose high and beckoning into the low, dark clouds. Not bothering to pull my hood over my head, I made my way to the subway, hoping the freezing, snow-like rain would hide my tears and wishing I had accepted my father's offer to use his car. Unpleasant and dangerous as driving in Paris sometimes could be, at least I wouldn't have had time to think about the words Aimee had said—words that were eating away at me as I walked.

Those words never left me that week as I struggled to work and to forge a new life without my dreams of Jean-Marc. I was failing miserably, because deep down inside I knew Aimee was right. Why would a man choose a woman with a past when he could choose one who had always been in the Church? No, not Aimee; I could never believe that Jean-Marc would choose a woman like her. But maybe there was someone else. Perhaps a woman like Monique, who had never broken the law of chastity or stooped to drinking and drugs. Was that why Jean-Marc hadn't written? Was he worried about my future faithfulness? Had he turned to someone else because of this fear?

The more I thought about it, the more likely I thought it to be true. *Should I call him and tell him not to worry?*

I was at work when I had the idea to call him, but even as I thought to do so, I began doubting myself. Was I really on the strait and narrow? Could I be truly free from that old life forever? What if I actually wasn't worthy of Jean-Marc? I loved him so much and wanted him to succeed in life and especially in the Church. What if I wasn't the woman who could help him reach his eternal goals? Suddenly the ache in my head matched the one in my heart. I put my head in my hands and closed my eyes.

"Why don't you knock off early today, Ari?" my father said. I looked up from my desk at the bank to see him standing anxiously over me. "You've put in enough time as it is this week, and you deserve a couple of hours off today."

I shook my head and stared down at the papers I was going through. But I couldn't focus on them. I sighed. "Maybe you're right, Father. Besides, I can always take these with me."

He smiled. "Sometimes I think you're too much like me."

I stood up to hug him. "I like that idea."

"It's going to be all right," he said, tightening his arms around me. "I know you're going through a tough time right now, but you'll find your way. And your mother and I are here for you—this time." The last two words were said with regret, and I knew he was thinking of Antoine.

I would have gone home, but as I was leaving, someone stopped me just inside the bank.

"Hey, Ariana!"

I looked over to see a man my age coming from one of the tellers. He had long brown hair that hung like strings around him. His thin, crowlike face boasted a hooked nose, evasive brown eyes, and a chin blackened with beard stubble. An unlit cigarette dangled from his lips. He was wearing old jeans that were ripped at the knees, dirty tennis shoes, a faded green sweater, and a worn jacket.

I didn't know who he was.

"It's me—Maurice," he said, seeing my blank expression. "One of the old gang. Jacques' friend . . ." His voice trailed off as he waited for me to remember, to look past the years and lifestyles that separated us.

"Oh, yeah, I remember. It's been a long time." We were walking out the door now.

"Hey, come have a drink with me for old times," he urged, holding up a white envelope. "My parents sent me some money for Christmas, so I'm good for it." He smiled, revealing yellowing teeth. I was revolted at the sight, but he looked at me so hopefully that I felt pity in my heart. "Please," he said as I hesitated. "There isn't anyone left from the old gang anymore. We all went our own ways. Can't you spare a few minutes to talk about old times? Remember, it's Christmas. You know, goodwill and peace on earth and all that."

Christmas was still more than two weeks away, but I nodded. "Okay. But only one drink and nothing alcoholic. And I choose the place."

His expression was puzzled, but he shrugged his agreement. We walked together down the street and to the next, finally finding a café with a bar that didn't look too sleazy. I went in, and Maurice followed. He immediately ordered two beers, but I asked for hot chocolate. "I forgot about the no alcohol," he said sheepishly.

I took off my coat and laid it on my lap over my thin briefcase. "That's okay. So what have you been doing these past years?" As I asked the question, the bartender brought the two beers and hot chocolate.

"Nothing much. Just hanging out, working from time to time. I get kind of lonely for the good old days. I sometimes go see Jacques at the prison, but he's different now. Ever gone there?"

I shook my head. "No reason to. You knew we're divorced, didn't you?"

"Yeah, but you never know."

"I have seen Paulette, though." I told him how she was living in Bordeaux and planning to be married in February. We also talked a lot about our shared past. The memories hurt more than I cared to admit.

The small bar was rapidly filling with people, mostly men coming from work. The wild crowd, the kind I had always run with, usually didn't come in until later. I remembered how out of place I had felt at first when I had joined them, but they had accepted me and loved me when I didn't have anyone else. I also remembered how the drinking had dimmed the pain of Antoine's loss; even now I could feel the taste of it on my lips, the warmth spreading through the cold in my heart.

Oh, how I could use that warmth now! Temptation struck hard and quick, and feeling as hopeless as I did about my own future and self-worth, it was almost too much to bear.

"I always liked you, Ariana," Maurice said suddenly. "I would have tried for you if Jacques hadn't come along." He watched me for a minute before continuing. "You look pretty depressed now. Tell me, what's wrong? Or wait, I have something better." He reached into his coat pocket and withdrew a thin, homemade cigarette that I knew was full of marijuana. He thrust it into my hand, and I sat clutching it in surprise.

I was embarrassed to be holding it, but worse was at that moment I would have given almost anything to smoke it, for it would temporarily make me forget that I wasn't worthy enough for Jean-Marc, or any other good man in the Church. And what was my future worth without Jean-Marc, whom I loved more than I could express? Better to drown myself in alcohol and drugs than to risk disappointment time and time again.

But something inside me rebelled at that, and at the last instant before giving in, I remembered to pray to the One who had never let me down. *Oh, Father, please help me out of this!* I begged silently. *I don't know what I'm doing, and I'm so afraid!* And at that precise moment my salvation came, though certainly not in the form I would have chosen.

Aimee.

I glanced up to see her watching me from the cashier where she was buying a bottle of soda, triumph etched on her face. The homemade cigarette slipped from my fingers and instantly I was saved, freed from the almost magical hold it had over me. What on earth was I thinking? Could I forget my daughter and how she had died? I knew better than this! Suddenly everything was clear, and I found myself again.

Maurice chose that second to lean over and kiss me, clumsily but passionately, his arms reaching around me in a tight embrace. As if in slow motion, I saw Aimee's green eyes grow even wider, her triumph more pronounced. I pushed Maurice forcefully away. "I'll be right back," I muttered, slipping off the bar stool to confront Aimee, who had turned to leave.

"Aimee! Wait!"

She was already outside in the cold December afternoon before she turned to face me, a mocking smile on her pretty lips.

"So, Ariana," she began before I could explain, "I see you have
fallen back into your old ways. Jean-Marc will be sad to hear that his
precious Ari has been drinking and smoking and even has a new
boyfriend."

"It isn't what it seems," I protested.

"Isn't it? There you are in a bar, with a beer in front of you and a
cigarette in your hand, kissing a man who's obviously a drug addict.
Those things add up to one thing, Ariana. Don't the scriptures say
something about a dog turning back to his vomit? Well, that's what
you're doing, and I'm glad Jean-Marc has thought to reconsider his
involvement with you. What kind of wife could you possible make
him?"

I could feel my face burning as my anger grew. All at once it
exploded. "You hypocrite! You talk about my past as if it's something
you personally have to forgive, as if you're the judge of my worthiness!
Oh, yes, you even had *me* wondering. But not anymore. I suddenly see
everything clearly. I know my Savior loves me and that He died for my
sins! They are gone, every one of them. And if you don't believe it, you
have a lot of searching to do, because that means you don't believe in
the Atonement of Jesus Christ, that He can really do what He promised: take away our sins so we can be free of them forever. Well, I see
the truth now. When I looked up to see you there, so ready to judge
me, I suddenly realized that you haven't the right! No one on earth has!
And as for Jean-Marc, if he does feel the way you claim, if he can't forget my past, then *he's* not worthy of *me!* No future husband of mine will
ever doubt the power of Jesus Christ!"

I left her and went back into the bar, letting her spiteful retort disappear into the air: "I'll tell Jean-Marc about you. I promise I will!"

It made no difference to me. I was free of her, and what she thought
no longer mattered. The change in me wasn't complete; but I had seen
the situation as it truly was, and now I needed time to sort it all out.
But first I had to face Maurice.

"Maurice, I don't feel romantically about you," I said firmly. "In
fact, I'm in love with someone else, though I don't know how things are
going to work out between us. Besides, my life is different now. You and
I don't live in the same world." Then my missionary spirit kicked in.
"But I would like to introduce you to my world, if you're willing. It's

not an easy way, but it's much better. Paulette found it, too." He just stared at me, and I knew he didn't know what to say. I hastily pulled my extra Book of Mormon out of my briefcase. I opened it to write my phone number below the missionaries' number I had already printed there, along with my testimony. As I did so, my sheet of ten names fell out. I looked at it for a moment before placing it back in my briefcase.

"Here, consider this your Christmas gift." I handed him the book. "If you're curious, call the first number. You'll reach the missionaries, and they can tell you all about it. The other number is mine. Call whenever you want to talk. Leave a message if I'm not home, and I'll call you back. Or come to the bank. Will you do that?"

"Yeah, sure, Ariana." His eyes went curiously to the book; but I had been a missionary long enough to know that if you left it up to the investigator, sometimes things never got off the ground. "What about your number? Do you have one?" Maurice nodded, and I wrote it in my address book. I slipped it back inside my briefcase and shut it with a decisive snap. "I have to go now. I've got a lot to do."

He nodded, and I touched his shoulder briefly. "It was nice seeing you." I turned and left, walking purposely though I didn't have any destination in mind. I knew only that I had to sort out what had happened, to understand it completely. My feet traced the familiar path to the Seine River, and I walked along it as I used to with Antoine and later with Nette. It had been a long time since I had come, maybe too long. The wind was blowing slightly, and the cold air hurt my lungs. I pushed up my scarf to cover my mouth so that my thoughts could race unhampered by the searing in my throat.

Jesus died for me! He paid for what I did in the past! How could I have lost sight of that? I thought of Paulette and how she had been so afraid that her sins were too deep and too many ever to be forgiven and how I had assured her that the Atonement was expansive and profound enough to cover anything, if we were willing. Jesus, a God, had done the suffering, and He would remember our sins no more. The familiar and beloved scripture played across my mind: "Though your sins be as scarlet, they shall be as white as snow; though they be red like crimson, they shall be as wool."

I thought about Aimee, too, and I suddenly saw that she was hurting. She might be right about Jean-Marc worrying that I might not be worthy, but she knew he didn't want her, either. In the words "his precious Ari," she had revealed to me that there was more to her story than she wanted me to know. But it made no real difference. If Jean-Marc loved me, he would have contacted me. What Aimee said or did shouldn't make any difference.

Sorrow nearly overcame me at the thought of Jean-Marc, his gaze so intense and caressing, the words of love in his many letters. I loved him so much—more than I had ever dreamed of loving even Jacques, the man I had once married.

I stopped walking now and set my briefcase on the short stone wall that looked down over the Seine. I stood leaning there with my hands pressed against the rock, feeling them slowly numbing from the cold and wishing the feeling could extend to my heart, at least to the part that ached for Jean-Marc. Boats passed in the river below, some cargo, a few with passengers, leaving paths of rough water in their wakes, unmindful of their solitary observer and the tumultuous feelings within my soul.

Oh, Jean-Marc! How can I go on without you?

At the same time, a thought came so firmly into my mind that it seemed as if I was hearing it with my earthly ears instead of my spirit: "Trust in Me." Hoped filled my heart. Yes, that is what I would do. I would have faith in the Lord and believe that He would do what was best for me. I would believe that even if things didn't work out the way I wanted, they would work out somehow, and I would be happy. I clung to this thought as a drowning man clings to a piece of flotsam wood. For eighteen months I had taught others about faith and repentance, but only now had I truly begun to understand how they applied to *my* life.

"I will make it!" I said aloud and triumphantly. The cold breeze lifted my words out across the river like a promise.

I still loved Jean-Marc, still yearned for him, but I knew that I could—and would—survive without him. The thought, though aching and raw, came as a welcome relief. Within myself I had discovered the power to be happy, with or without Jean-Marc. My thoughts once again turned to the Savior and the plan of redemption. I realized that once and for all, I had finally and completely forgiven myself for Nette's death, as I had Paulette. There was only one more thing I had to do.

With numb hands, I opened my briefcase and retrieved the list of names I had given Jean-Marc so long ago. The cold air began to blow more forcefully in my face, but I didn't stop, not even when my scarf fell back and let the searing wind into my nose and throat. Filled with purpose, I unfolded the paper and reached for a pen. Firmly, I wrote in the last name.

Jacques de Cotte.

I remembered what I had told Elisabeth the day she learned that Paulette had been with Jacques when he had given Nette the drugs—how we would be forgiven through the same spirit in which we forgave. The scripture I had been referring to was in Luke 6:37: "Judge not, and ye shall not be judged: condemn not, and ye shall not be condemned: forgive, and ye shall be forgiven."

Once, I had believed that God would punish Jacques for killing Nette. It never occurred to me that he wouldn't go to hell and burn forever; indeed, the thought had given me comfort in those first lonely months without my daughter. That he might repent and be forgiven didn't even cross the far reaches of my consciousness. But, after all, he hadn't murdered our baby in cold blood; it had been a horrible, drug-induced nightmare, and just maybe he was ready to go on with his life.

And I knew I had to forgive him.

I didn't have to love him or visit him daily, but I had to start him on the path back, to free him from my anger and accusations. After feeling Aimee's scorn and seeing how desperately Paulette had yearned for my forgiveness, I knew I had to at least give him that. The thought frightened me, and my heart beat rapidly and painfully. How could I face him again?

CHAPTER SEVENTEEN

Two weeks passed before I found the courage to go see Jacques at the prison. I wanted to make sure that I really had forgiven him deep down. Forgiving Jacques was much more difficult than it had been to forgive Paulette, because he had betrayed my love, all my hopes, and my trust. I finally decided there was only one way I would know for sure: to see him face to face.

I went on Christmas morning. My parents were sleeping in after the eating and present-opening we had done at midnight, and I didn't tell them I was going. This was something I had to do alone.

The morning was very clear and cold but windless. I was dressed in thick black stretch pants and a dark brown ribbed shirt. I had chosen the outfit carefully; it was sober but flattering to my coloring and features. I had always looked good in dark colors. I didn't know why I cared how I looked, but I spent extra time that morning getting ready for my visit. At least the confidence my appearance gave me helped calm the pounding of my heart.

There was almost no one out on the streets yet, and I walked toward the subway, moving briskly to keep myself warm. My heavy, thigh-length coat was more than adequate, but I felt a chill of terror spreading out from my heart in anticipation of what I was about to do. The public transport was operating even on Christmas, and as I settled into my seat in the train, I felt grateful I would not have to drive. My hands were shaking badly—and not only from the cold.

The rhythm of the underground train soon had me relaxing, and my mind recalled the previous Sunday when I had borne my testimony. It hadn't been fast Sunday, but a few days earlier I had been called in to talk with the bishop, who had asked me to be the new Young Women's president. I accepted with trepidation. During our conversation, I told him about Jean-Marc, about Aimee and the incident at the café, and also about my plans to go see Jacques. There were tears in our eyes when I finished.

"I wish everyone could understand the Atonement as you are learning to," Bishop Rameau said quietly. "I think too many times we are hard on ourselves and too quick to judge others in an attempt to ease our own feelings of inferiority." He paused. "Do you feel able to tell your story to our members? I feel it could greatly help them."

Hesitantly, I agreed.

The next few days I had prayed about what I would say and about choosing my counselors. Strangely, a particular name kept coming to mind. On Saturday, I gave Bishop Rameau my names written on a piece of paper, and he smiled when he saw them.

"I'll ask them tomorrow," he said almost laughingly. "These are just the people I would have chosen myself. But I want you to talk in church before I ask them. I know it's unusual to call a president without counselors, but I want them to hear your testimony first."

Sunday dawned bright and cold. I went to church, once more accompanied by my parents. When the bishop read my name to sustain me, I looked at Aimee. She stared at me, and I almost expected her hand to be raised in opposition. But she didn't raise her hand at all, not even to sustain.

"Now," the bishop continued, "I'd like our new Young Women's president to speak to us."

I smiled nervously at the bishop as I approached the podium. The congregation seemed much larger from in front, and I swallowed once or twice before beginning. I was used to talking and teaching others, but today was different; I no longer had the mantle of a missionary to sustain me. My parents smiled up at me encouragingly, and Aimee's green eyes fixed on my face. The others around them blurred, and I felt that my talk was only for these three.

The words came slowly and then more quickly as I told of my feelings of self-doubt, the experience in the bar, and my ensuing understanding of forgiveness. I told them about Paulette and Jacques, but I didn't mention Aimee or Jean-Marc. My testimony rang out strong and true, and I saw many people with tears in their eyes. Finally, I was

finished and sat down, my eyes once again searching for Aimee's. She
was crying and gazing at me sorrowfully.

Afterward, she came up and hugged me. "I'm so sorry. I didn't realize what I was doing. I was blind, I think. Please forgive me."

"Does that mean you'll serve as Ariana's first counselor?" Bishop
Rameau asked, suddenly appearing at my elbow.

Aimee's eyes widened in shock. She turned an incredulous face to
me. "Me? You want *me?* Why?"

"I don't know. I just do." I hugged her, and we both made fools of
ourselves, weeping like babies.

"I—there's so much I want to tell you about Jean-Marc," she whispered in my ear. "I was just so hurt that—"

"It doesn't matter, Aimee." I cut her short. "Neither of us needs
Jean-Marc to live. We'll become the best we can be. And we will be
happy."

She nodded, her golden locks bouncing. "But I still want to tell
you."

I sighed, suddenly feeling the weight of the extreme emotions I'd
been through that day. "Later. In a few weeks, when things calm down.
Not today."

Aimee agreed, but since then I had seen her only at a planning
meeting where we hadn't been alone to talk. My other counselor, secretary, and my mother had also been present, each coming up with ideas
for the Young Women. Not for the first time, I had found myself thinking that my mother would make an excellent member. Caught up in
my new responsibilities and thoughts of converting my mother, I had
forgotten Aimee's comments at church—until now.

My thoughts came slowly back to the present, and I found I had
almost reached my destination. I stood and walked carefully to the
doors, remembering how Antoine had hung on the bars our last night
together in the stopped train. I smiled. This time there was no pain
associated with the memory.

The train slowed, and as it stopped the doors slid open to let me
out. I still had a good walk in front of me to reach the prison, but I
didn't mind. I had called several days before to ask about the visiting
hours and procedures, and now my watch told me I had plenty of time.

When I reached the prison, I was immediately ushered to a desk where I had to show identification and sign some papers. Afterward, I went through a metal detector and into a hall, led by a strong-looking guard who whistled Christmas tunes. One side of the corridor was made of glass windows; I could see the inmates inside, sitting at long tables with various friends and family members. Some seemed happy, some sad and sullen. *I guess we choose our attitudes no matter where we are,* I thought.

I saw Jacques before he saw me, and I stopped a moment at the glass to study him. He was waiting at one end of a table. At the other end, a fellow inmate was deep in conversation with two friends who had come to spread Christmas cheer. Jacques watched them wistfully, his dark blond head tilted to one side. His hair was cropped shorter than I'd ever seen it; other than that, he hadn't changed much physically, except that maybe he was a little thinner. Like all of the other inmates, he was dressed in prison blue.

Memories of the past shook me, and I wanted to flee, to run back the way I had come and be rid of Jacques forever. But deep inside, I knew this was the only way we could both be free. I had loved him once, we'd had a child together, and despite the anguish raging through my heart, I would do this.

I watched him a minute more and then shook myself. I wasn't doing any good here, peering through the window like a child spying. I resumed walking, quickening my pace to reach the guard who was waiting at the entrance to the visiting room. He smiled gently, which surprised me, but all at once I felt the fear on my face as well as the pain. Glancing at the long glass window beside the door, I saw my white face, just for an instant, stark and stiff against large eyes and brown hair—alabaster framed in dark shadow. My lower lip was trembling, and I bit it to still the movement. I swallowed once, closing my eyes briefly to find courage, praying for strength, and then walked into the room.

He looked up as I entered, sad brown eyes fixed on me, never flickering for an instant, a tentative smile on his face.

I sat across the table from him. "Hi, Jacques."

"Hi, Ariana," he replied warily. "I never thought I'd see you again."

I returned his steady gaze. "Nor I you."

"You look really good," he ventured. "You've cut your hair short, like when we first met."

I didn't reply but sat there staring at him. The old attraction I had felt for Jacques was completely gone. Instead of the wild, desperate urge for him to love me, I felt only sadness and acceptance.

"Why are you here?" he asked. His hands clutched the edge of the table as he steeled himself for my response. I knew he was afraid of what I might say. In his eyes there was also a glimmer of hope, which he quickly squelched before it began to mean too much.

I glanced away for an instant, trying to find a way to begin. At the other end of the table the inmate was telling a story to his two visitors, arms raised in animation as he spoke. On one thick arm he had a tattoo of an anchor. I was feeling lost and scared, but the anchor seemed to strengthen me, to remind me that my anchor was my God and that with Him nothing was impossible.

"Ariana." Jacques' voice was agonized. "I never did drugs again after that night. It's been three years now. It wasn't because I was in here, either; those who want them know how to get drugs. But I didn't want to ever forget what I did that night. I will never forgive myself—ever—for what happened to our baby." His voice was dead, and I abruptly tore my gaze away from the tattoo anchor to see the terrible mask of suffering that was Jacques' face. His eyes were now completely devoid of hope.

My eyes flashed again to the anchor and then back to Jacques' face. "But I forgive you," I said softly.

The incredulous, wondrous expression on his face made me glad I had come. Under my very gaze, he became more alive. And as I watched that change take place in him, somehow I too was freed from the chains that had bound my spirit to the past.

"But why? How?" he asked. His hands still gripped the table so tightly that the fingers were dead white against the dark hairs, the blood vessels standing out grotesquely.

I gave him my best missionary smile. "That's a long story."

"Well, I've got time," he said seriously.

I began from the first time I had seen the missionaries to the present, leaving nothing out, not even my feelings for Jean-Marc. At times Jacques' eyes showed disbelief, yet at others I knew he understood and accepted. We talked the entire time allotted at the prison. When it was time to go, I handed him a blue book.

"The Book of Mormon," Jacques read the cover aloud. He opened it to see my testimony and the missionaries' number, pamphlets, a list of reading assignments, and one thing more: a picture of his daughter.

He started to cry, taking in loud, heaving breaths, and I thought my heart would break all over again for him. "Thank you," he whispered when he had recovered slightly. "Thank you so much."

"Will you see my friends the missionaries, Jacques?" I asked him fervently. "Will you at least let them explain? Maybe then you can make sense of all this and forgive yourself."

He nodded. "Yes, Ariana. For you I will."

I stood to leave, but he reached out a hand to stop me. "Jean-Marc would be a fool not to see what he has in you." He glanced down at the ground and added, "As I was." After a brief moment he looked up at me again earnestly. "You are a true lady, Ariana. A queen like you always talked about. And you'll get the best, because that's what you deserve. I only wish I hadn't hurt you so much."

I smiled and shrugged. "I also wish it had never happened. But, Jacques, the making of a queen or a king is never easy, you know, though terribly worth it in the end." We stood looking at each other without speaking, sharing a bond that could only be felt by those who had faced joint tragedy and survived.

I said softly, "Good-bye, Jacques. I hope you have a good life. I hope you can be happy."

"You too, Ariana. And thanks for coming."

"You're welcome, Jacques." I left without a backward glance, feeling lighter and happier than I had since Jean-Marc had deserted me. What was it Jacques had said? Oh, yes, that Jean-Marc would be a fool not to see what he had in me.

And Jean-Marc had never struck me as a fool.

CHAPTER EIGHTEEN

After leaving the prison, I went straight home. The afternoon was very cold, and an icy breeze had started blowing, yet my heart was warm. I was filled with a strange kind of contentment I had never felt before. I realized that these past few weeks I had learned to have faith in the Lord and accept His will, knowing it would be the best thing for me. I no longer needed others to make me happy but could rely on my inner self that was buoyed by the constant power of my Savior. At last, I understood what it meant to have a testimony.

A part of me still ached for Jean-Marc and the love I had so hoped for, but I knew that time and the gospel would heal my wounds as they had the last time—wounds far deeper than I had now.

I was so intent on my inner thoughts that I was upon the man before I realized who he was. Suddenly, there was Jean-Marc, sitting on the cement steps outside my parents' apartment building! I had no time to prepare my reactions or steel myself to pretend that I didn't care. I felt my face light up with the love I had for him, though I could feel the hurt there as well.

"Jean-Marc, I—I didn't expect you," I stuttered as he jumped up to greet me. His face was reddened by the cold and his hair tousled by the light breeze. His expression was anxious as his green-brown eyes searched mine. I suddenly wished desperately for night to fall, to quickly hide my face, but the afternoon sun shone clearly and did nothing to mask my feelings. "Why have you come?" Tears gathered in my eyes.

"It's Christmas, Ari," he said in a hoarse, emotion-filled voice, blinking his eyes rapidly as if trying to stop his own tears. "I *had* to come."

"Why?" I really wanted to know. Almost two months had passed since I had seen him at the baptisms, and I had been sure it was over between us.

Until now.

Jean-Marc stared miserably at me, his eyes filling with tears. "Why? Because I love you, Ari!" I could feel the warmth of his breath against my face, and it was too much to bear. I dropped my gaze to the ground as he continued. "I have always loved you, since the very first day I met you. It wasn't just the way you looked. It was the way your soul touched mine, the way you threw yourself into the gospel so wholeheartedly after going through the worst nightmare any woman could imagine! It was the way you made up with your parents and helped Paulette, even though she was partly responsible for Nette's death." He paused and gave a short, mirthless laugh. "I wouldn't be surprised if you had already forgiven Jacques and invited the missionaries to visit him." He stopped talking as a sob shook him. I was still staring at the ground, unable to believe what I was hearing. After all, there was still the matter of those two months between us. Why had he left me so long without even a letter? He had hurt me deeply—shattered my dreams. How could I trust him again?

I knew I had to at least hear him out. I needed to understand why he had acted as he did so I could begin to heal properly, putting it behind me. Besides, I had learned that to be kind was important, even when—no, *especially* when it hurt.

"Oh, Ari!" Jean-Marc's voice was anguished, and he fell to his knees on the cobblestone sidewalk before me so he could look up into my downcast eyes. "I'm so sorry I haven't called you! You see, when you got off your mission and came to the church that day, you were so beautiful and confident, a true queen, worthy of all the blessings of the eternities—and I felt unworthy of you!" Now it was his turn to look down at the ground while I gazed upon him in amazement. The torment of self-doubt that I had felt came back to me vividly, self-inflicted but powerful and wrenching. I understood exactly what Jean-Marc was saying.

He paused a moment, as if organizing his thoughts, and then stared up into my teary eyes with a love so unmistakable that I wondered how I had ever doubted him. "If you remember, it was a missionary who posed the question that day," he continued. "What made me think I deserved you? And I knew deep down that he was right. I kept staring at you, unable to get his words out of my mind. You had been through so much, refined way beyond me by fires I could not begin to imagine! You made it, despite where you came from, despite the horrible death of the daughter you loved more than life! You came up fighting, long after others would have given up, and I felt I had nothing to offer you. I've been a member almost all my life—I never even knew what it was to have a testimony until I went on my mission. I've never had to fight for anything or prove that I would stay true to the Lord no matter what.

"And there you were, a potential queen, and I suddenly knew that only a king could help you become a true queen one day. And, Ari . . ." His voice broke. "Ari, I didn't know if I could be a king, but I knew you deserved one. I loved you so much that there was no way I was going to hold you back."

Tears streamed down both our faces now, and I sank to the sidewalk with him, pulling him back to sit on the cement steps that led to my building, pressing my cheek hard against his so that our tears flowed together. A few passersby who had braved the cold Christmas weather watched us curiously, but we paid them little heed, being so caught up in our emotions.

I tried to speak, but Jean-Marc put a finger over my lips and continued. "So that's what I've been doing these past two months. I've been trying to see if I had the potential within me, no matter how deeply hidden, to become your eternal partner. I wanted to know without a doubt that you and our children could rely on me, as I knew I could rely on you." His face took on a pained expression as he remembered. "I was so afraid I would come up short. I studied, I prayed, talked to my bishop and my mother, prayed some more. And, Ari, I think that with your help, I can make myself the man you deserve—the man who will never let you down and who will love the Lord as much as you do!"

"Oh, Jean-Marc," I whispered, so afraid but knowing I was going to give him another chance, knowing I still loved him. "I could have told you that!"

He smiled a little sheepishly through his tears. "I realize that now. You see, only yesterday my little sister, Lu-Lu, brought it to my attention that I should give you more credit for picking a potential husband.

She said you probably knew me better than I knew myself and that I was a dummy not to have told you how I was feeling right after your mission!"

"She was right."

Jean-Marc laughed and gazed into my eyes, wiping away my tears with his fingertips. "I promise never to try to solve the important things myself ever again, Ari. We'll do it together—as long as you promise to be my queen!"

"I will, Jean-Marc! I will!" I said exultantly, lifting my lips to his. After he kissed me, I added, "But let's keep this queen thing to ourselves, okay? You know how we French feel about royalty . . . remember what they did to our last queen, Marie-Antoinette." I made a neck-chopping motion to emphasize my point. We laughed helplessly until the cold from the cement seeped into our bones, making us so stiff we could hardly move.

"Come, let's go inside and tell my parents," I urged, getting to my feet and pulling him with me.

He kissed me once more on the lips, passionate yet tender, full of promise. "Okay, Ari." He paused and added teasingly, "But remember, I'll not have you smoking in front of our children!"

"What?" I exclaimed, trying to figure out what he was talking about. Then I had it. "Aimee—she *did* write to you! I hope you didn't—"

"Of course I didn't believe her! I realized there was probably more to the situation than she knew or was telling. I knew that whatever had happened that day, you came out on top! I figured she was just mad because I had written her to say I didn't feel romantically about her. You see, she had called and written me repeatedly, asking to come down to visit, alluding to our future together. I had to tell her she and I had no future. She was the last thing I needed right then!"

"She's very beautiful," I said, just to see what he would say.

He shook his head. "No, she's very pretty but never beautiful. *You're* beautiful, Ari!" He still had one arm around me, and with his free hand he stroked my hair. "I love your hair, so soft and cut short so I can see the curve of your neck, and those dark eyes that see into my soul. But there's more—the inside beauty that's even more important, your heavenly aura. You're everything to me, Ari!"

"I was tempted that day Aimee saw me," I admitted suddenly. I wanted only truth between us.

Jean-Marc smiled. "But once more you proved yourself, and it's over and done with. Now come, are we going to announce our engagement to your parents or not? I rang a few hours ago but didn't go up since you weren't there. Now I'm so cold from waiting here that your parents will probably think I'm shaking in fear of them."

"You're not afraid of anything, Jean-Marc!" I turned to open the door with my key.

"That's not true," he said suddenly, his voice full of emotion. "I was so afraid you'd tell me no."

I left the key in the lock and threw my arms around him. "Make no mistake about it, Jean-Marc. I love you, and I'm going to marry you!"

CHAPTER NINETEEN

*T*hat Christmas was the best I'd had for some time. The weather was freezing, and we even saw a few flakes of snow in Paris; but Jean-Marc and I were warmed and comforted by the new light of our love. He didn't return to Bordeaux, except to get his things, and I went with him to do that. He stayed temporarily with Marguerite and Jules until we could find an apartment for him. We were determined to not be separated too far ever again.

In January, Jean-Marc began to work at my father's bank and to attend college, studying—of all things—accounting, for he shared my fascination with numbers. I too was taking classes, though we didn't share any since I was three semesters ahead of him. We rented a small apartment near my parents where he stayed, a place we would soon share. My bed and couch looked very good in the stylish apartment, and weekly we added new items to make it more comfortable. My mother especially went wild, buying things until, laughingly, we had to beg her to stop.

Paulette and Pierre were married civilly in February. They had chosen not to wait for Paulette to be a member one year before marrying. Considering their ages and their growing closeness, it was the best decision for them. We drove with my parents to Bordeaux to attend the wedding. My parents, who had gone principally to meet Jean-Marc's family, were amazed at the change in Paulette.

Paulette herself seemed more amazed than anyone. "I can't believe I'm actually marrying Pierre!" she whispered to me just before the ceremony. We were in one of the classrooms in the church, standing before a huge mirror that Elisabeth, now large with her pregnancy, had set up for the bride.

I stared at Paulette in wonder. She had changed so much since that day I had found her sprawled on the sidewalk. Her light brown eyes

161

were clear of drugs and shining with love. Her rich brown hair now gleamed lustrously and was arranged in artful waves. Her hands, once dirty with broken nails, were now clean and strong, the nails cut short and even. Her skin was clear, and the pain and sadness that had aged her were gone. But the biggest change was in her spirit—the confidence and vigor she had for life, the faith in her Savior, the love she had for Pierre and, at long last, for herself.

Shortly after Paulette's wedding, I received a letter from Jacques saying that he was to be paroled within the year. He had seen the missionaries a few times and was taking school courses in the prison as well. Maurice was also coming to church and listening to the missionaries—befriended by Aimee, of all people.

The first week in April, Jean-Marc and I were married at our church house in Paris. A few weeks after our civil marriage, we went to the temple in Switzerland to be sealed for time and all eternity. I was grateful that years earlier, Church policy in Europe had been changed to allow those without access to a temple but who held recommends at the time of marriage to be sealed as soon as they could go to the temple instead of waiting an entire year. I was saddened that my parents were unable to attend my temple wedding, but Jean-Marc's family was there in force, including aunts and uncles and many cousins. Even Pierre and Paulette were there, though Paulette could not yet go through the temple.

Before our sealing, Jean-Marc was baptized and endowed in behalf of Antoine. Only then did we go to be sealed for time and all eternity. Having previously obtained Jacques' consent, we also had Nette sealed to us. Feelings of absolute contentment radiated through my entire being. My baby at last had an eternal family!

After the short ceremony, we went hand in hand to the celestial room to sit together before leaving the temple. I glanced at the couch opposite us and noticed with surprise that the man sitting there had a baby in his arms. I looked over at Jean-Marc to see him staring at the same thing.

"He looks like you . . . it's . . . your brother!" he whispered, and I quickly looked again to see Antoine with little Antoinette in his arms. Both seemed happy and content.

Jean-Marc and I turned to each other in amazement, but when we glanced back at the couch, they were gone. "Did you—?" I began, feeling a warm happiness spread through me.

"Yes, I did, Ari! I did!"

Rain beat against the windows in a steady torrent, as it had done for the past few days. I sat by the window, looking out into the February night. Occasionally, lightning shot through the darkness, and thunder sounded like a giant screaming in agony, echoing the swelling pain in my body. *I'm happy,* I thought fiercely with joy, even through the terrible, crashing pain.

Indeed, the last ten months had been the happiest of my entire life. There had been no real period of marriage adjustment for Jean-Marc and me; our missions had prepared us well for constant companionship and sharing. Our love had already learned patience and faith; and that, I knew, was half the battle.

Thunder crashed again both outside and within, and with the glow from the lightning, I saw my parents' car. "They're here!" I yelled, gritting my teeth against the contraction that seemed to pulse throughout my entire body.

Jean-Marc helped gather my things and carried them down to the waiting car. We had our own car now, but I wanted my husband beside me, holding my hand through the contractions instead of fighting the traffic. So I had called my parents the minute I realized that the false labor I'd been having for weeks had finally become real. Besides, this time I wanted my whole family with me.

Four hours later, I gave birth to twins—a girl, whom we named Josette after my mother, and a boy, called Marc for his daddy. The love that swelled in my heart as I touched and kissed them seemed to equal the fervent emotion I had felt for my first baby, Nette. My happiness knew no bounds. Yet I knew that I felt the joy of my present life more intensely because of the pain I'd experienced in the past—and it was worth it.

"Uh, I guess I won't be working for you anymore, Father," I said, looking up into his happy face as I lay on the bed with a warm baby cuddled in each arm. Jean-Marc sat beside me, stroking my hair and gazing down at our children with reverence and love and not just a little awe.

"Well, under the circumstances, I won't require a month's notice," my father said, smiling.

My mother also looked happy. "It's a lot of work, Ariana, having twins, but they'll take care of each other later on." She wiped a tear from her face, and I knew she was thinking about Antoine, but this time the memories were happy. "And I'll be over every day to help, if you want me to."

"I do, Mother. Thank you." There was silence as we stared at the babies, so recently come to earth from heaven.

"Just so you don't go on Wednesday at seven, Josephine," my father said. "Remember, we have an appointment."

"What!" I said, pretending indignation. "What's more important than these two precious babies?" To emphasize my words, I kissed each little forehead and looked up at my father.

"Well, uh, we . . ." I had never known my father to fumble for words and wondered what could cause such a thing. I waited curiously while he got himself under control. "You see, the other day some young missionaries from your church knocked on our door, and we decided to hear what they have to say. Not," he held up his hands quickly, "because we want to join but because we feel it's time we understand our daughter and what she believes."

"That's wonderful!" I exclaimed with a silly smile on my face. I suddenly remembered seeing Antoine and Antoinette in the temple on my wedding day. *We'll see our whole family there yet,* I promised them silently. *We have time.*

My eyes moved to the window, where rain was still beating at the panes. But the sight of the falling drops no longer brought sadness and despair to my heart as they once had. They would always remind me of those I had lost, but the emptiness was completely gone. And now I had a new, happy memory to add to the good rainy-day recollections Jean-Marc and I had already made together.

"It's just as you promised, Jean-Marc," I said softly, looking up into his sparkling green-brown eyes. "I think I'm really starting to love the rain."

ARIANA

A GIFT
MOST PRECIOUS

FOUR YEARS LATER

CHAPTER ONE

*T*he fluorescent lights hurt my eyes, already burning from the tears I had shed the night before and again today. Around me, people moved with purpose; only I sat slumped motionless against the wall, waiting to hear if she would be all right. I hadn't been to the hospital except for the times I'd had a baby . . . and when Nette died. The memory made me suddenly afraid that Paulette, too, had come here to die. *Please tell me she's all right!* The thought was a silent prayer.

It was what Jean-Marc would term a perfect ending to a really rotten day. Of course he wasn't here to say it, and even if he were, I'd be too angry to listen. *It's all his fault,* I wanted to mutter, but I knew I had no one to blame except myself.

The carpet in the waiting room was brown instead of the unsightly orange that had lined the floor in the hospital where I had lost my daughter; the observation offered meager comfort. A nurse at the nearby desk glanced up at me from the paperwork in front of her. She smiled kindly, but I felt it was more from habit than from any feeling of compassion. Her smile didn't reach her tired eyes, and I knew she would much rather be home with her family than working the night shift.

Even at this hour, the lights on the hospital phone winked furiously. I wondered who could be calling so late and what emergencies had driven them from their beds. The wild blinking echoed the raging emotions in my heart and contrasted sharply with the quiet intensity around me. Crossing my arms over my chest, I rubbed the flesh under my long-sleeved shirt for warmth, ignoring the chestnut-colored jacket thrown carelessly across my lap. I wondered if Paulette was dying—or perhaps the baby she carried inside. Even as the thought came, I prayed more fervently for it not to be so. Paulette had been through too much already. Besides—it was impossible to stop the selfish thought—I needed her, especially since Jean-Marc had walked out on me last night, suitcase in hand. I still didn't understand how I had let that happen.

Though my current troubles had begun months ago, they had come to a climax the morning before. I had been in the kitchen frying eggs, wishing I had earplugs to block out the clamor the twins and André made as they banged their spoons against their dishes in raucous discord. André's rice cereal sloshed out of his bowl, making the high chair tray look like a war zone. I was sure he had put more cereal *on* his body than *in* it.

"Good morning, Ari," Jean-Marc had said from the kitchen doorway. My husband's trim figure was smartly dressed in a dark gray suit, a wool and polyester blend. On his face was the familiar grin I adored. He crossed the room and gave me a kiss.

Peering into the shiny metal surface of the toaster oven, I ran a quick hand through my dark brown hair that was cut short to fall in wisps about my neck. I noted with satisfaction that I hadn't really changed all that much since Jean-Marc and I had met while he was serving his mission here in Paris. My laugh lines were deeper and I was more experienced, but that was all.

I turned to see Jean-Marc trying to get the baby cereal out of André's ears. Our son cried and tried to push the cloth away.

I walked over. "There, there, André. Poor child." I took the baby out of the high chair and away from Jean-Marc. "There's no hope, honey. He needs a bath."

He threw the cloth at me, but I ducked, and it landed on the stove. We both laughed and hugged each other tightly. André objected loudly to the squeeze.

"See you tonight," Jean-Marc said, releasing me.

"But I've got breakfast nearly ready," I protested. I usually didn't bother with more than a few croissants and hot chocolate, but I had wanted to make this day different. Jean-Marc adored eggs in the morning—a habit acquired from one of his American missionary companions.

He sniffed the air appreciatively. "It smells good, but I really have to go. Your father and I are visiting the new branch today, and we want to get an early start. He's probably waiting outside. We'll grab something at the corner bakery on the way."

I sighed. Sometimes I hated the fact that my father, Géralde Merson, was president and partial owner of the bank and that Jean-Marc was rising ever higher in the bank hierarchy. "But you'll be home early, won't you? Remember our date?" There was an adult dance at the church building, and we were going. We hadn't been out alone together for months, and I had finally taken a stand and made plans to attend. My mother would baby-sit our four-year-old twins and one-year-old André.

"Yeah, I remember." He bent to kiss the children. "You guys are getting so big," he cooed. Briefcase in hand, he was nearly at the door before our son stopped him.

"Wait!" little Marc yelled accusingly. "Prayer. You forgot!"

Jean-Marc returned and stood against the wall, bowing his head as Marc prayed. He kissed us again and jogged down the hall. "Good-bye!" He tossed the word over his shoulder like a bag of laundry. I felt a little upset at his hasty departure, but I was determined to enjoy myself that night, and I wouldn't be able to do so if I held a grudge.

The time for our date came and went with no word from my husband. While I was hurt, I wasn't really surprised. I tried to call the bank, though I knew it was an almost hopeless endeavor. Jean-Marc spent most of his workdays out of the office with clients or on the phone, staying long after closing. At least the receptionist was still there.

"This is Ariana," I said when she answered. "I need to speak with Jean-Marc."

"He's not here. Shall I transfer you to the other branch?"

"Yes, thank you." But he wasn't at the second branch either, and they didn't know where he was. I left a message and hung up. Next, I called my mother to tell her I didn't need her to watch the children after all.

My anger simmered inside me hotter than the soup I had made the children for dinner. "Bedtime," I said when they were finished eating.

"I'll get the Book of Mormon!" Josette shouted.

"No, me!" Marc was out of his chair in a flash.

I read them the story of how the brother of Jared made sixteen small, transparent stones to put in the eight boats and how they shone when the Lord touched them with His finger.

"And then Jesus showed Himself to the brother of Jared," I explained, "because he had so much faith."

"I wish I could make stuff light up," Marc said.

"Where are those rocks now?" asked Josette. I didn't know and told her so.

"I bet Daddy knows," Marc said.

I rolled my eyes. "We'll ask him tomorrow. It's Saturday."

"Saturday! Maybe we can play tiger!" the twins shouted. Saturday morning was the one time Jean-Marc usually spent with the children—or had, up until a few months ago. The children would come into our room and wrestle on our bed until finally hunger took control and Daddy got up to make breakfast. Then I would enjoy a leisurely bath alone, without any peering eyes. I wondered that the twins still remembered.

"Aren't we going to the Saint-Martin tomorrow?" Marc asked.

"Daddy promised," Josette added quickly.

The Canal Saint-Martin in Paris was the world's only underground urban canal. We had promised to take the children there months ago after they had seen a special about it on television. We had already changed the date twice because of Jean-Marc's work.

"Then we'll go," I assured them.

It took another half hour to put the children to bed. It wasn't an easy task alone but one I had grown used to in the past year. And all the while my resentment built inside me until I wondered if I might explode.

Jean-Marc came home around ten. "Are you still in your pajamas?" he joked when he found me in bed reading a book. With his green-brown eyes twinkling, he looked vital and alive.

I glared at him.

"What is it?" he asked. Suddenly realization dawned, and he smacked his forehead with his open palm. "The Church activity! I forgot. I'm really sorry, Ari."

"It's okay," I murmured untruthfully, as I had so many other times.

"Well, I practically closed the deal I've been working on," he said, looking relieved. "Tomorrow I'll wrap it up."

"Tomorrow?" I felt my eyes narrow. "But it's Saturday, and we're taking the children to the Saint-Martin canal. We've been planning this for months. They're so excited about it—we can't let them down again."

Once more he smacked his forehead. "I forgot about that. I can't do it, Ari. We'll go next time. They'll understand."

I pictured the disappointment on the twins' faces when they learned their father had once again canceled on them—on us. The anger I'd held in check for months boiled to the surface as I got out of bed and began to pace around the room. "They'll understand that your work is much more important than they are," I said acidly. "Or me."

"I'm working for us," he retorted. "As soon as we're set, I'll slow down. I'm only doing it for—"

"We don't need your money! We need *you!* The children, especially." Now that I had begun, I couldn't stop the hot torrent of words. "I'm sick of waiting in line for time with you. Home is not just where you come to sleep! I see the man at the corner bread store more than I see you!"

"That's not fair," he said. "Stop charging around like an angry bull, and let's talk about this reasonably." He tried to draw me close, but I was sick of listening to "reason" tinged with his bias. Besides, his touch always affected my judgment. I pulled away.

He released me and ran a hand through his hair. His face had grown stiff, and I felt a wall forming between us. "We've been through this before, Ari. It's only for a short time."

"Is it? I'm not so sure. Not even my father, who *owns* the bank, works as much as you do. He at least came home at night before Antoine and I were in bed. Tell me, how often do you see your children? Saturday mornings and Sundays? Yes, that's about it. And half the time on Sunday you're at Church meetings. You're not around or available at the important intersections of life. You sleep here, but that's all." I put my hands on his shoulders and stared into his eyes. "Jean-Marc, we need you *now*, not ten years from now. In ten years, if the children haven't learned to trust you and go to you with their problems, they won't *ever* do it. It'll be too late!"

He took my hands from his shoulders and held them. "It was for this new branch, Ari. That's all."

"And what was your excuse last year?" I took my hands from his, threw open the closet, and pulled his suitcase down from the top shelf, driven by my anger. "Maybe if you don't want to be with us, you should leave," I said, thrusting it into his arms. "Maybe our children would see you more if you didn't live here."

I was trying to make a point, trying to show him how serious the situation had become. He wasn't just a man who worked overtime during deadlines but a man so obsessed with his job that he neglected his children, his family. Me. I was through simmering about it; the time had come for a change.

I met his eyes and saw hurt there, but it seemed deeply buried beneath his own anger. "Fine," he said through gritted teeth. "I'll leave."

His words pierced me. My insides seemed to tear apart as I watched him hastily throw a few things into his worn case. I loved him. What was I doing? What were *we* doing? Weren't we married for eternity? I wanted to throw myself into his arms and tell him I didn't mean what I had said and beg him to stay.

But I *did* mean what I'd said. We had been sealed in God's temple for eternity, but I didn't want to live my life alone, waiting for eternity to come.

He clicked the suitcase shut and left the room, pausing momentarily at the door but not looking back at me. His jaw worked and he seemed about to speak, and then he shook his head once and stalked down the hall, leaving whatever it was unsaid.

I couldn't believe he was actually leaving. He wouldn't do that. He couldn't! I waited in our room for him to come back. He didn't. Tears came, searing and painful. *What have I done?* But even as the question came, I resolved to see it through. I had to protect my children.

By losing their father? The accusing words seemed to come from the oppressive silence.

I was almost relieved when a cry came from the twins' bedroom. Unlike little André, they still had difficulty sleeping through the night. I wiped my tears on the long sleeve of my nightgown and went down the hall, wondering how I would tell them tomorrow that not only was their daddy not taking them to the canal but he wouldn't be coming home at all. Perhaps I would take them by myself. The sad thing was that they might not notice the difference.

CHAPTER TWO

*Y*ou can see her now."

I started at the voice and looked up to see a nurse standing over me. At once the sights, sounds, and smells of the hospital came rushing back, firmly pushing aside the raw memories of the night before. I stood and followed the nurse down the hall to a room where Paulette lay on a tall bed, seeming very small and weak despite the mound of her stomach. She had an oxygen tube in her nose and a machine monitored her vital signs. An IV dripped steadily into her arm. She seemed to be unconscious or perhaps sleeping.

I glanced up at the doctor, who stood near my friend. He was an older man with white hair, sagging cheeks, and sad brown eyes that made him look like a basset hound. He was tall for a Frenchman and very thin. He studied a chart with an engrossed expression and then said something quietly to a nurse who replied with an equally soft voice. It was all I could do not to yell at them to speak louder. I bit the soft inner side of my cheek and moved restlessly in the doorway, finally drawing the doctor's attention.

"Hello," he said, his eyes coming to rest on my face. "I'm Dr. Flaubert."

"I'm Ariana Perrault, Paulette's sister-in-law."

"You were with her when she collapsed?"

I nodded and swallowed hard, forcing my feet to take a few steps into the room.

"Tell me exactly how it happened." I had told the nurses before, but it seemed Paulette's doctor wanted to hear for himself. I was happy, at least, that they had found him. With her difficult pregnancy, Paulette was better off in the hands of her own doctor than those of a stranger.

As I spoke, guilt once more assailed me. It was my fault Paulette was here. This morning I had decided to take the children on our outing without Jean-Marc rather than to see their disappointment. Knowing that her husband was out of town on business, I called Paulette to ask if she and her daughter, Marie-Thérèse, would like to go with us.

Paulette was my sister-in-law and best friend and had been for years. She and Pierre used to live in Bordeaux but had moved to Paris after Pierre sold the family grocery store to a larger competitor who had a chain of stores throughout France. Now he worked for that same company, overseeing the stores in Paris and surrounding areas. His mother had retired and still lived in Bordeaux with her youngest, Lu-Lu, who was twenty-two.

"Want to come?" I asked, after explaining where we were going. "Please?"

Paulette was expecting her second child after three disheartening years of trying to conceive. She had been sick this time, almost to the point of being bedridden, but now that she was five months along, she had begun to feel better. "Canal Saint-Martin?" she said. "I'd love to. Marie-Thérèse has been wanting to go ever since she heard you were taking the twins."

"Are you sure you're feeling up to it?"

She laughed. "Not really. I've gotten a cold from somewhere and a cough as well, but I can't spend the next four months doing nothing. I'm coming, Ari."

I hung up the phone and looked down into the eager faces of the twins. "They're coming with us," I said.

"What about Daddy?" Josette asked, her large brown eyes luminous.

"Yeah, I thought he was taking us," Marc added.

I frowned. "He's working." Both little faces drooped. "But we'll have fun anyway." I ruffled their dark brown locks and tickled their stomachs until the sadness vanished. It didn't take long; they were accustomed to their father's absence.

"It's underground!" Marc said importantly when he had stopped laughing. "We get to ride on a boat! And underground for two kilometers!" He stumbled slightly over the last word.

Josette glared at him, unimpressed. "I know, I know." She turned to me. "Mom, don't you think we should go get André? He's awake. I heard him a little while ago."

I started guiltily. Oh, yes, André. My youngest was so well-behaved that I sometimes forgot he existed at all—quite a treat after the rambunctious twins. He had just turned one and had only recently weaned himself from nursing.

"Go get dressed," I said to the twins, backtracking down the hall to the baby's room. "Make sure it matches!" I added. "And bring a jacket." It was mid-May, and though the day would most likely be pleasant, the underground canal would probably be chilly—if I remembered anything from my days of exploring Paris with my twin brother, Antoine.

André was awake, standing up inside his crib, waiting patiently. When he saw me, he smiled and jumped up and down, holding out his arms in anticipation.

"Good morning," I sang, picking him up and kissing him.

"Ma-ma," he said, grinning. Then he continued babbling, as if explaining something unquestionably important. I didn't understand his baby talk but pretended I did. Otherwise, he would become so frustrated that I would never get him calmed down. It was his only true shortcoming, and I loved him for it. Besides, I couldn't really consider it a shortcoming; after all, each of us craves understanding.

After taking care of André, I showered and exchanged my nightgown for chestnut-colored pants and a matching jacket; the dark colors served the dual purpose of setting off my brown eyes and announcing my disheartened mood to the world. Part of me kept listening for Jean-Marc's step, but it didn't come.

When we arrived in front of Paulette's apartment, only five minutes away, she and Marie-Thérèse were waiting outside. Marie-Thérèse held her favorite doll in her arms—one Paulette had made for her at last year's Christmas Homemaking meeting. Marie-Thérèse was four and a half, four months older than the twins, with light brown hair, brown eyes, and a slightly upturned nose. Taller than the twins, she took after her mother's side of the family rather than her father's. The cousins greeted each other eagerly, but as Paulette and Marie-Thérèse slid into the car, my friend's face darkened. "What's wrong?" she asked. "You're wearing brown. That's your best color, but you only wear it when you're upset. What's going on?"

I shook my head slightly, moving my eyes toward the children.

"Okay," she agreed. "For now. But you won't get away with it for long."

I smiled. She was really a good friend, and I loved her. I was closer to her than anyone, even Jean-Marc, though that hadn't always been the case. Once Jean-Marc and I had been best friends—and once I had wished Paulette dead. I shook away the unwanted memories.

Paulette sneezed and drew out a tissue to blow her nose. I studied her anxiously. She looked thinner than I remembered her being even a few days earlier. Her brown hair hung limply on either side of her face; it also seemed thinner somehow, though surely a few days could make no real difference. Her stomach poked out hugely from her thin frame, dominating the scene. Though she was only five months pregnant, she looked almost like a caricature in an artist's chalk drawing. There were several artists who worked along the Seine, mostly taking money from the many tourists, and only last week Paulette and I had had our portrait done. When the artist finished, Paulette's stomach had taken up nearly the whole page, though in reality she was small compared to most pregnant women. It was just because she was so thin that her stomach jutted out so tellingly.

I drove to the yacht harbor near the Place de la Bastille where the canal tour began. The children were competing to speak louder than each other, and the din grew until I wanted to shout at them to be quiet.

"Children," Paulette said in a composed but firm voice, "you all need to calm down a bit, or we won't be able to find a parking place and we won't go on the tour. It takes concentration to find a place to park." The children grew silent, and I was amazed, as I always was with Paulette these days.

We finally parked and made our way down the sidewalk to the canal, where several boats floated in the water. We didn't have a long wait, as the tourist traffic hadn't reached its peak, and were soon comfortably settled in a medium-sized craft. A group of other people had joined us—mostly tourists—and Josette was already talking enthusiastically to a woman seated on the bench next to her. Marc peered over the edge of the boat, making me nervous, and Marie-Thérèse sat quietly between me and her mother, playing with André, who was cuddled on my lap.

Before entering the corridor leading to the nineteenth-century tunnel, we sailed under the roundabout and the lofty, 180-ton Colonne de Juillet—Column of July—where the names of the five hundred who had died during the 1830 revolution were inscribed. Once we entered, the light faded, and we had to blink several times before our eyes adjusted. Skylights positioned every fifty meters cast a misty blue light into the passageway. It was a romantic setting, and I found myself missing Jean-Marc.

Above us we could see the stone base of the Colonne de Juillet, which served as a crypt for the bodies of those whose names were etched in the towering column above ground. The canal was more than impressive, and I settled down eagerly for the three-hour ride. Nostalgic memories of my twin brother softened the longing I had for my husband.

"Did Jesus make this?" Josette asked, coming to stand beside me.

"Actually, this used to be an open canal," I explained. "But then, a long time ago, the people lowered the canal bed and covered it over."

"Why?" asked Marie-Thérèse.

I shrugged. "I think they wanted to use the space above for cars and buildings."

"But Jesus told them how, didn't He?" Marc said. He still stood near the side, but at least now his feet didn't leave the boat's floor in his eagerness.

Paulette and I glanced at each other, trying to hide our smiles. This was one of those great teaching moments, one of the times I was so grateful to be a member of The Church of Jesus Christ of Latter-day Saints. At least I knew what to tell my children.

"Yes," I said. "Jesus is the source of all knowledge. Every great idea man has comes from the light of Christ. Every invention ever made."

"Even boats?" Marc asked.

"Even boats," I affirmed.

When the canal ride came to an end at the Bassin de la Villette, we made our way to a bread shop to buy something for lunch. The small boulangerie was filled with different breads, and I ordered two bagettes.

As the lady handed me the long bread, the children clamored for *pain au chocolat*—bread with chocolate baked inside.

"Okay, okay," I said. The lady at the counter smiled and rang up my order. I paid and waited outside while Paulette ducked into the shop next door for cheese and fruit. Purchases in hand, we walked down the street until we found a bench overlooking the canal and settled on it. The children scampered on the cobblestones nearby, eating and trying to attract the pigeons flying overhead.

Paulette dabbed at her nose with the tissue she carried in her hand. "So what's up?" she asked. "You've been going around all day glowering and looking like you lost your best friend."

I scowled. "Maybe I have."

"Jean-Marc?"

I nodded.

"He loves you, Ariana."

I wasn't so sure. After all, he had left. And not knowing where he was and who he was with drove me crazy.

She put her arm around me. "I'm here for you, you know."

I leaned my head on her shoulder. "Thank you. I do need you."

"I'm glad."

Something in her voice made me look up. Her eyes had the faraway glaze that signaled a return to the past. "Don't," I said softly. "Leave the past alone. We're happy now."

She smiled, her hands moving to her stomach. "Do you remember how I longed for this baby?"

I remembered well. After having Marie-Thérèse, Paulette had been unable to conceive until five months ago.

"I worried I wouldn't ever have another child," she continued. "I think I must have felt like Queen Marie-Antoinette. Do you remember what she did?"

"What? You mean how when she couldn't conceive, she took the child of a peasant woman to raise as her own?"

"Something like that." Paulette's laugh was low and husky.

"You'd never steal a child," I said, smiling at the idea.

"No," she agreed. "But I wanted to. I understand Marie-Antoinette's need."

"I remember reading that she was criticized for doing it," I mused.

"And later, that child—a son—became one of her worst opponents during the Revolution."

"But that's because she neglected him after finally having her own children," Paulette said. "I would never neglect any child. Not now, anyway."

And I knew she wouldn't. Once she had been able to discard the heavy weight of the drugs, Paulette had uncovered the inner part of herself that was good almost to the extreme. At times I envied her.

"So what happened with Jean-Marc?" she asked, returning doggedly to the subject of my husband.

I shrugged and looked away. "I'm not sure. Let's walk, okay?" I knew I was hiding from the issue, but Paulette would let me, at least until I felt I could talk about it. That was one of the reasons she was such a good friend.

We walked for a short time, until Paulette began wheezing. "We'd better head back now," I said. She nodded and coughed into a handful of tissue. Her coughs and sneezes had become more frequent during our outing, causing her frail body to shudder with each exertion. It didn't take me long to realize that she had come today because of something she had heard in my voice rather than any desire to leave her warm bed. Suddenly I was anxious to get her home.

We took the subway back to near where we had parked the car. On the train, André sat on my lap, yawning. The girls were also tired and sat languidly across from me next to Paulette.

Marc stood on the seat and tried to climb the bars next to it. A man standing and holding onto the bar in the crowded train eyed him indifferently, but I grabbed my son and pulled him down, shaking my head. He frowned, huffing emphatically. I hid a smile in André's hair. Marc was impulsive and wild, just like my brother had been. Antoine had always hung on the bars, especially to amuse me. The memory made me warm.

After leaving the subway, we walked the short distance to our car. Near where we had parked was a short stone wall encircling several trees, the only greenery in sight. Marc immediately jumped up on the wall and stuck his hands in the soil. Then he stood up, extended his arms for balance, and began walking the length of the wall.

"Get down, Marc!" Josette cried.

"No!" Marc said, sticking out his tongue. He started to lose his balance.

I dropped André into the car and rushed to grab Marc. I was too late. He fell to the cobblestone sidewalk, his head making an ugly cracking noise as he hit, face first. There was a brief second of stunned silence before he started to wail. I turned him over to see a small river of bright red coming from his chin.

"Here." Paulette shoved a wad of tissue in my hand, and I held it tightly against the wound. Marc was still crying, and I pulled him onto my lap and cuddled him.

"Try to lie still," I said. "Let me see what's happened." He tried bravely to obey, letting me remove the tissue and take a peek. My insides churned at the sight of the deep gash.

"That's definitely going to need stitches," Paulette said.

Marc started to cry again, louder this time. I soothed him as best I could. "It's all right. I'll be there with you."

I held him on my lap as Paulette drove to the hospital. Once there, she sat with the children in the waiting room while I talked to the nurse. I wished I could call Jean-Marc, but even if my pride would let me, I had no idea where he was.

At last the doctor arrived, an older man with graying hair and a kind face. He looked like someone's grandpa, and Marc gazed at him trustingly.

"Let's put this over your face so the light won't hurt your eyes," the doctor said gently. In his hand he held something that looked like a sheet of white wrapping paper with a hole cut in it to expose the chin area. I knew its real purpose was to hide the sight of the shot needle they would have to use. Despite the doctor's gentleness, Marc screamed as he received the injection of painkiller in his chin. He clutched my hand, and tears squeezed from the corners of my eyes. I wished I could spare my little boy this suffering.

After the stitches were in place, I went into the waiting room. Paulette was sneezing again, and her face glistened. I felt her forehead. "You have a fever," I said.

She groaned and clutched her chest. "I thought I was feeling strange, but I figured it was being here at the hospital."

"Come on. I'll get you home."

Marc fell asleep in the car on the way, sporting a row of tiny stitches on his chin. Josette watched over him, occasionally smoothing his forehead. Maybe she would be able to protect her brother as I hadn't my own.

We were nearing our area of town when Paulette started coughing violently. In the tissue she clutched in her hand, I saw blood. She was in no condition to be alone. "You're coming home with me," I said.

"I don't want to get in the way," she murmured. "I'm sure Jean-Marc is waiting for you."

I gave a short, bitter laugh. "No, he won't be." She gazed at me, a question in her light brown eyes. "He left last night with his suitcase," I explained quietly.

Her eyes grew sorrowful, but she said nothing as another bout of coughing shook her.

The apartment was ominously quiet when I finally succeeded in opening the door with my key, burdened by Marc's sleeping form. I felt my hopes dwindle; Jean-Marc hadn't come home. I laid Marc in his bed, disturbing him only enough to remove his shoes. I was sure he would wake up before I finished dinner; a small accident like this wouldn't cause him to lose his appetite.

"Mommy, come quick!" Josette's worried voice called from the bathroom. I hurried from the twins' room and found her and Marie-Thérèse watching Paulette, who sat on the edge of the tub, hunched over the toilet. The water inside was red.

I pushed past the anxious girls and little André, who stood in the doorway. "Are you all right?" I said, reaching out to Paulette.

"I feel so tired," she said, "and my chest is hurting."

She looked exhausted. Her face was pale against the red of her lips, stained with bright blood. A streak of crimson marked her cheek.

I pulled some tissue from the roll and wiped her face tenderly. "Can you walk?"

"I think so."

"Let's get you to bed, and then I'll call your doctor."

Paulette gasped in pain as I put my arm around her and helped her to the door. She pasted a smile on her face as we passed the children, but Marie-Thérèse wasn't fooled. She watched her mother without speaking, her eyes plainly showing fear.

We were almost to the bedroom when Paulette collapsed in the hall, unconscious. I nearly dropped her as her weight sagged against me. The children started to cry.

"Wake up, Paulette!" I cried, gently slapping her face. There was no response. She lay on the floor, pale and still.

"It's going to be all right," I said to the children as I ran to the kitchen and called the ambulance.

I had been terrified—more terrified than I had ever been since the night my firstborn had died. Nette had been so young, only eight months old. And now, as I stood next to Paulette's bed, the vivid memories of my daughter's death vied with the more recent ones of Paulette's collapse.

"Then we waited until they came and got her," I found myself saying to the doctor, closing my eyes for a moment to gain composure. It made no difference; open or closed, I could still see Paulette's inert body on the white sheets—and Nette's as well.

"I took the children to my mother's and came here," I added, though the doctor couldn't possibly care about such details. "Is she going to be all right?"

Dr. Flaubert shook his head. "I don't know yet. She's stabilized for now, but there's something wrong. She seems to have pneumonia, but it shouldn't affect her the way it has. She's normally a healthy person. We're going to know more in a few hours when the test results come in."

Guilt ate at my insides. I shouldn't have hauled Paulette on my family outing. The cold in the tunnel couldn't have helped.

"Could she die?" I asked.

"She's in very serious condition," the doctor replied, his jowls shaking as he spoke.

I wished he would give me a straight answer. "But could she die?" I repeated.

He nodded slowly. "Yes, she could. The next twenty-four hours are crucial."

I didn't dare ask about the baby, but thoughts of that innocent spirit tortured me. I didn't know what Paulette would do if something happened to her baby.

CHAPTER THREE

I called my apartment just in case Jean-Marc had come home, telling myself it was for Paulette. I needed to find someone to give her a blessing. There was no answer, but I hadn't really expected one. Next, I telephoned the hotel where I knew Pierre would be arriving later and left a message at the desk. After calling the bishop for the second time that evening and again receiving no answer, I left a message on his machine. I didn't know Paulette's home teachers' numbers, or my own, nor could I find them in the book. The point was moot anyway, as I had run out of change and had left my checkbook at home. For all their smiles, the nurses weren't allowed to let me use the hospital phone.

Giving up, I settled into a chair, refusing to leave Paulette's bedside the rest of the night. Occasionally she awoke, and each time she clutched at her chest as pain racked her body.

"Why does it hurt so much?" I asked the nurse who went mechanically about filling the doctor's request for additional tests. Her gray-speckled hair was swept on top of her head in a tight bun, and her thin lips were pursed in disapproval. I wondered if, like the woman at the desk, there wasn't somewhere else she would rather be.

She withdrew a needle from Paulette's arm, full of dark red blood, before replying. "Pleurisy," she said. "A complication of pneumonia. It's very painful but should get better in a week or so."

"Stay with me until Pierre comes?" Paulette asked during one of her short lucid periods.

"Of course I will."

"You're such a good friend," she murmured. "Much better than I ever was to you."

I knew she was thinking of Nette and how she hadn't been able to prevent her death. Though she knew I didn't blame her and that God had forgiven her for being drugged up that night, she still remembered it with a certain degree of pain. As did I. But our Savior, who had endured so much more, helped us survive even the most severe bouts of memory. I opened my mouth to comfort her, but she was already asleep.

⁓

Pierre came in about seven o'clock Sunday morning, his short black hair tousled and a worried expression on his face. He closely resembled Jean-Marc except that he was taller and his large eyes were a simple brown instead of my husband's unusual green-brown color. He also had an ample waist, whereas Jean-Marc had always been slender.

"Is she all right?" he asked, as he came into the room. Paulette was sleeping.

"But you were supposed to be out of town!" I exclaimed.

"When I called to tell the hotel I'd be delayed a day at my first stop, they gave me your message. I drove all night to get here." His eyes never left Paulette's face as he spoke. "How is she?"

"It's pneumonia," I said. "The doctor says she's stable for now, but—"

"Oh, thank you, Father," Pierre whispered, falling to his knees at the foot of the bed. He stayed there for a full minute in silent prayer before adding aloud, "I don't know what I'd do if something ever happened to Paulette."

Tears gathered in my eyes as I remembered how they had first met: Paulette, a drug addict, and Pierre helping her to overcome the insufferable craving that ate at her body. His love for her and forgiveness of her past was what had saved her in the end, when her testimony of the gospel hadn't been strong enough to sustain her.

I remembered, as if it were yesterday, how he had proposed to Paulette. She had been off drugs for a month and was living with his next-door neighbor, Elisabeth. We thought we were over the worst of her drug problem when a large sum of money came up missing at the Perraults' grocery store, where Paulette worked. Pierre called me as soon as he discovered the missing money, and my missionary companion and I went to his house immediately. I remember wishing that Jean-Marc was not still serving in the army so he could be there to help us.

Together we went to Elisabeth's, where we found the outside door ajar. Paulette was alone in her room, staring at an empty suitcase on her bed.

"Going somewhere?" Pierre asked. His voice clearly showed his suffering.

She nodded, not speaking, and slumped to the bed in complete abjection.

"You took the money from the store," Pierre said. It was not an accusation, only a statement of fact.

Again she nodded. She reached for her brown handbag, lying on the bed next to the suitcase.

"No, I don't want it," Pierre said hoarsely. Both Paulette and I stared in surprise.

"Everything I have is yours, Paulette," he continued. "Everything. Including my heart." In two strides he crossed the space separating them. "Marry me! Please. I love you!" He sank to the brown carpet, clasping her hands and burying his face in her lap. "Just don't leave me. Or—" his voice broke. "Or if you do leave, please don't go back to the drugs. At least I'll have the comfort of knowing you're alive somewhere."

She gaped at him. "You still want me after what I was going to do?"

"I love you." His words were simple, yet the emotion behind them struck me like a blow to the stomach, filling me with longing for Jean-Marc. Suddenly, I was embarrassed to be in the room with them.

Pierre left then, as if knowing he could say nothing more to convince her. He paused at the door. "I'll be at the store, waiting," he said softly.

After his departure, she sobbed in my arms as if her heart would break. "Were you really going to leave?" I asked her.

"I—I don't know. I hadn't decided. I do know that I wasn't going back to the drugs, but I was uncertain about the future and what I would do."

"And now?"

She sniffed. "I love him. It will break his heart if I leave."

"Then don't leave."

She stood quickly. "I've got to go to the store."

I smiled as she ran out the door. I had never doubted she would stay. I suspected she had unconsciously been testing Pierre to see if he really did love her, despite her faults. And both had passed the test. I didn't blame her for wanting to be sure; an eternity was a long time to pledge undying love. Pierre was very special to have seen beyond Paulette's rough exterior to the real woman beneath.

"Ariana!" Pierre said, jolting me back to the present.

I looked up, the memories fading. "Yes?"

"I'd like to stay with her, but where's Marie-Thérèse?"

"At my parents'," I said. "I guess I'd better go and get her. And my own children. They'll be wondering about Paulette."

Pierre stood up. "I appreciate your being here and also taking care of Marie-Thérèse. I'll call you the minute I know anything."

I nodded, remembering that it was my fault Paulette was here in the first place. I wished Jean-Marc was there to hold me, to stave off the chill that cloaked my heart.

"She hasn't had a blessing yet," I said as I left. "But the bishop should be by when he gets my message." I wondered if Pierre would ask where his brother was and what I would say.

"Thanks. I'll take care of it." He sat in my vacated chair and turned his attention back to his wife. I was relieved that in his preoccupation he hadn't asked about Jean-Marc.

I called my parents from the lobby to let them know I was coming, but to my surprise, my mother wasn't there. "She took the children back to your house to get them dressed for that church of yours," my father told me, his voice a bit mocking. "She decided to take them herself when we called and couldn't get hold of Jean-Marc." His words took on a joking tone when he said, "Where is that boy, anyway? I haven't seen him since he left work yesterday afternoon with our newest clients. He was supposed to call me and let me know how it went."

"Well, you know more than I do," I said. "I haven't seen him since Friday night. We had a fight."

There was a pause before my father asked, "What are you saying? You mean he's not at the hospital with you?"

I shook my head, though my father couldn't see. "No," I said in a small voice. "I don't know where he is. He doesn't even know Paulette is sick."

"I'll look for him, Ari. If that's what you want." He was angry, I could tell.

"Would you? I—" I broke off, not knowing how to explain what had happened without sounding like I was whining. Then I began to wonder if my father's involvement would only make things worse between Jean-Marc and me.

"Don't worry. I'll find him." A loud click sounded in my ear.

It was nearly eight o'clock in the morning when I arrived at my apartment building. I pushed my card into the small box that would automatically open the huge metal door of the underground parking garage. It was very dark inside, lit only by overhead lights, which were quite weak compared to the brightness of the morning sun. I came to a quick stop in our numbered spot, sprang from the car, and strode across the rough cement floor, anxious to get home.

Since we lived on the eighth floor, I was glad we had an elevator. Once it had broken and I had lugged André up the steps, listening to the twins complain about how their legs hurt. They would never know what real pain was, at least not for many years. I put my key in the lock and opened the door. The smell of cooking food wafted around me, pulling me into the apartment.

"Mommy!" Josette, named for my mother, Josephine, came running into the small entryway. She was dressed in her church clothes, but her feet were bare. "I missed you!"

"I missed you, too," I said, hugging her.

"Grandma made a cake," Josette informed me with an air of importance. She turned and yelled at the top of her voice, "Marc, come and see! Mommy's here. She's going to eat some cake with us!"

Marc came running from the bedroom, with little André toddling behind. Both smothered me in hugs and kisses. They didn't look any worse for not having had me around for the night.

"There's no cake until after church," my mother said, coming from the kitchen. She was fifty-three but looked younger. Her body was slender, with just a slight thickening at the waist. Only the thin streaks of gray in her dark locks and the deepening wrinkles around her eyes and mouth gave any indication of her true age.

"Oh, Mother, I'm sorry it took so long."

"That's all right, Ari. I'll admit, though, it's been a long night." She let out a weary, lingering breath and walked to the arched opening off the entryway leading to the sitting room. She sank to the sofa while I

opened the blinds to let in the morning sun. Instinctively, I checked my
answering machine. There were no messages from Jean-Marc, only one
from the bishop saying that he and the home teachers were on their way
to the hospital.

"How is Paulette?" my mother asked when I settled on the love seat
across from her.

"Where is Marie-Thérèse?" I asked before replying. As if in answer,
the little girl appeared in the doorway, clutching the doll Paulette had
made. Marie-Thérèse wore one of Josette's dresses, and it was short for
her taller frame. Her face was pinched and red-looking.

"Is my mommy going to die?" she asked, her bottom lip quivering
slightly.

"Goodness, no!" I exclaimed, jumping up to wrap my arms around
her. Until she asked the question, I didn't realize that my faith in the
matter was so strong. "Of course not. Your father's giving her a blessing, you know. She's got pneumonia, but now that she's in the hospital,
everything is going to be all right." I thought I was telling her the truth.

Marie-Thérèse seemed relieved, and I felt bad that I hadn't been
there to comfort her earlier. I hugged her again, more tightly. Marie-
Thérèse was actually lucky; in a few weeks her mother's problems would
most likely be over, but mine with Jean-Marc wouldn't be solved quite
so easily.

"But she will be in the hospital for a few days," I added.

"Then does Marie-Thérèse get to stay with us more days than one?"
Josette asked, her eyes bulging with excitement.

"Yes," I said.

She squealed enthusiastically. "Oh, Marie-Thérèse, can you believe
it? You're going to stay a few nights with us. Finally, I won't be the only
girl here. Mommy doesn't count, 'cause she's a mom."

"Yeah, yeah, we already heard," Marc said. "We're right here. You
don't have to tell us what she said."

Josette ignored him. "Come on, Marie-Thérèse. Let's go play
dress up. I'll be Princess Jasmine, and you be the prince."

"The prince has to be a boy!" Marc protested.

Marie-Thérèse frowned. "I don't want to be a boy."

"You can be a princess, too, and Marc can be the prince."

Her brother hit his forehead in dismay, reminiscent of his father. "Then I'll have to marry both of you!"

"No, André can be the other prince," Josette said.

"He's too little," Marc protested.

"I can tell him what to say."

I watched them with a smile on my lips. My mother stood. "Right now, you'll all go into the kitchen and sit at the table. We're going to eat that breakfast I made. Then we'll go to church. Afterwards, we'll have cake."

My mother was a small woman, as was I, but rarely did her words go unheard by my children, even when she didn't have cake to bribe them. The authority in her voice was unmistakable.

"Thanks, Mother," I murmured as the children raced to the kitchen. We followed at a more sedate pace.

She smiled. "I've enjoyed being with them." Her eyes took on a far-away look.

"Are you thinking of Antoine?" I asked.

She nodded. "Marc is a lot like him."

"I've noticed," I said dryly, pointing at Marc. We had arrived in the kitchen in time to see him teetering on the counter, reaching a hand toward the cake cooling on top of the refrigerator, supposedly out of the sight and minds of certain little four-year-olds. He stepped on the butter on the counter and lost his balance as it squished between his toes. He shrieked as he fell, but I was fast enough to catch him, as I hadn't been during our outing the day before.

"I told him not to." Josette sighed and shook her head, hands on her little hips. I saw my mother swiftly covering her smile. "And I told him not to go up on the wall yesterday. But he did anyway. Boys never listen, do they, Mommy?" Thinking of Jean-Marc, I couldn't have agreed more.

"Marc, how many times have I told you not to climb on the counter?" I asked, setting him down. "You'll cut your chin open again if you're not careful. Didn't you learn your lesson yesterday?" I didn't suppose he had, but I had to say it anyway; as a mother, it was my duty. Just as it was Marc's to ignore me.

"But I was seeing if the cake was cold yet, so we could put on the icing." He grinned at me engagingly, and despite my resolve, I melted. He was so like the brother I had adored.

"Go sit down," I said firmly. He ducked his head and obeyed.

While the children ate, I went into my bedroom for a change of clothes. Mother followed me with André, though she knew I needed to shower. "I already fed him earlier," she explained.

My blinds were pulled shut, and the yellow light coming from the overhead lamp cast strange reflections on my mother's face. Surely these shadows were what made her look so despondent.

"What's wrong, Mother?"

"Nothing." But she sighed.

"Tell me."

Her smile was wistful. "I never could hide anything from you, Ariana." I didn't speak but simply waited for the rest.

She heaved another sigh and sat on my bed, sinking her head onto André's tousled hair. "I want to be baptized."

I nearly slammed my finger in my dresser drawer. "You do? But that's wonderful!" I sat beside her, throwing my arm around her shoulders. "I've waited so long to hear that!" It had been four years since my parents had agreed to listen to the missionary discussions. My mother had attended church with me often, especially in the last year. I hadn't pushed her but had prayed constantly that she would accept the truth. Now it seemed as though she had.

"Why aren't you happy about it?" I asked.

"Oh, Ariana, I'm not like you. From the moment you first knew the Church was true, you forged ahead, not letting anyone persuade you otherwise."

"The Church explained Nette's death," I said softly.

"And Antoine's."

We were silent. Only the cars in the street below broke the quiet.

"When did you first know you wanted to be baptized?" I asked.

"I don't know. It's been a long time now—years. I keep waiting for your father. I thought he would accept the gospel and we'd be baptized together. But Géralde is no closer to accepting it than he ever was."

"Does he know you want to be baptized?"

"No. I haven't had the courage to tell him."

I understood why. My father was a forceful man and assured of his own place in the world. He considered religion a weakness.

"I'm tired of waiting. I want to be baptized, and I want to go to the temple."

"Then you will, Mother. But you'll have to tell him."

She sighed. "Why are men so blind to the truth?"

I snorted. "Tell me about it. Jean-Marc's so busy with work that he doesn't seem to have time for me. Sometimes I feel home is where he goes only to shower and change his clothes."

"It should ease up after the new branch is settled. You'll get used to being married to an important man. I had to."

"He left me," I said abruptly.

"Oh, no! He can't have!"

"That's what I thought."

She set André down and hugged me. "It'll be okay," she murmured.

Would it? I knew if it were up to me, it would be over now. As it was, I couldn't help the gnawing questions. Where was my husband? Could there be someone else? I didn't really believe this last thought. Jean-Marc might be obsessed with success, but he was a good man.

"And we thought marriage ended the struggles." My mother cast me a wry smile.

"The honeymoon is over, huh?" I added. "And the work begins?"

"I guess so."

I glanced at my watch. "I'd better get going, or we'll be late," I said. I couldn't help hoping that Jean-Marc would be at church.

The phone rang, and I flew to the kitchen to answer it.

"Hello, Ariana?"

My hopes plummeted. "Hi, Louise." It was Jean-Marc's mother, not him.

"How are you?"

"Great. And you?"

"Well, I'm worried about Paulette. Pierre called and told me what happened."

"She'll be fine," I said. "She has to be."

"Where's Marie-Thérèse?"

"Here, with us."

"Oh. That's good." She was quiet, but I sensed there was something she wasn't saying.

"So was there another reason you called?" I asked mildly.

She heaved a sigh. "It's Lu-Lu. She's fed up with dating only members. She says there's not enough around. It's gotten worse since she started working as a secretary for that construction company. And now she's going out with this guy she met at a nightclub—Philippe, or something. She brought him home, and I don't like him."

"She's twenty-two now. You can hardly tell her who to date."

Even over the phone, I could hear Louise bristle. "Well, she still lives under my roof!" It was the same argument my parents had used on me all those years ago when I had started drinking after Antoine died. I had simply moved out, thinking to free myself of their constraints. It was the worst thing I could have done, and I didn't want Lu-Lu to rebel as I had. She was old enough to be on her own but not if she parted from her mother in anger.

"She'll get through this. She just needs some time. Don't be too hard on her."

"I thought perhaps you could talk to her. You know, share your experiences with her. She's young for her age, and I'm afraid she'll make a mistake."

I wanted to tell her that mistakes were how we all learned, but I knew only too well how those errors could slice deep into your soul. Look what had happened to me only two days ago—and I was a mature twenty-eight. Still, I wanted to help, if I could, spare my sister-in-law the pain I had endured in my youth. Lu-Lu was immature and had always been shy, and it seemed she was finally breaking out of her shell—but not in the way her mother expected.

"So I thought we'd come down to help Paulette. Or you with the children. If Lu-Lu thought she was needed . . ."

At long last I understood why Louise had called. "You want to get her away from this guy?"

"I guess that's it." Louise's voice was subdued.

"I can always use another hand. Taking care of four children under four is not an easy task. Tell her you're coming to visit for a few weeks and see if she'll come."

"Will you talk with her when we get there?"

"I'll try." But I wouldn't have listened to anyone when I was younger; I hoped Lu-Lu was smarter.

"We'll leave tonight and be there tomorrow," Louise said.

"Why don't you take a plane?"

I could almost hear Louise shudder. She hated airplanes. "No, I like to drive. Besides, it will give Lu-Lu and me a chance to talk."

Or you a chance to preach, I couldn't help thinking.

"We'll see you tomorrow," Louise said. Already, she sounded happier. Strangely, I too felt more content. Maybe things would work out.

I hummed as I drove through the streets, crowded even on Sunday. Ahead of me, I could see my mother's car. Since I planned to stop at the hospital after church, she had driven herself. We were nearly at the chapel when an idea occurred to me. Paulette's mother, Simone, should know about her daughter. I veered to the left, turning away from the church, and drove to a poorer section of Paris where Simone lived. I had once lived there, too.

We stopped outside a run-down apartment building that had to be at least a hundred years old from the appearance of its worn cement exterior. Clothes hung out of windows and on thin lines dangling over the cobblestone road. Some of the windows had small balconies with rusted metal railings that couldn't be trusted to hold anyone's weight. I was glad my children didn't have to live here.

The streets were safe at this hour, but I still searched to be sure there was no apparent danger. "Come on, children." They filed out and gazed around in curiosity. Marc kicked at a pile of loose cobblestones, scattering them. Similar mounds were strewn the length of the street, mixed with refuse.

"Someone needs to fix this road," Marc said.

"Leave the cobblestones alone," I warned, worried more about his church shoes than the rocks.

"It stinks, Mom." Josette pinched her nose.

I hefted André onto my hip. "Follow me, and stay close."

The outside door to the building was ajar, and I could see the lock was broken. The mailboxes just inside the door were rusted and peeling. A foul odor assaulted our senses, and more trash lay strewn about.

"It's dark in here," Marie-Thérèse complained.

"It's not far."

Like the hallway lights, the elevator was broken and had been since I had stayed with Paulette for three months before my first marriage ten years ago. But I hadn't noticed how bad it actually was until I had found a better life. Everything looks pleasant when you are using drugs. I hurried up the stairs, ignoring the way my high heels seemed to stick to the stained marble that had deep grooves worn into its surface.

Simone lived on the second floor, so we hadn't far to climb. As I knocked on the door, the children clung to me in the murky darkness of the hallway. They weren't really scared; they were more thrilled to be in such a curious place. I knew the building, and this adventure would be echoed in their play for many weeks to come.

The door opened, a slice of light cutting through the dark in the hallway, and a woman with greasy dark blonde hair peered out at us. Her colorless eyes seemed unfocused, giving a rather vague feeling. She was taller than I but slightly stooped, so we appeared near the same height. I knew her to be in her mid-forties because she had given birth to Paulette when she was sixteen, yet she looked much older.

"Wha'd ya want?" she asked. The smell of alcohol was on her breath, and in her hand she held a thin homemade cigarette. I wasn't surprised.

"It's Ariana, Simone. I've come to tell you something about Paulette."

"Oh, Ariana," she said, squinting into the dark. "Come in." She backed up and opened the door wide. I took a few steps forward and the children came with me. The hallway inside the apartment was brightly lit but in a terrible chaos. Papers, empty containers, bits of food, and various articles of worn clothing lay haphazardly strewn around, and a thick coat of dust covered everything. "Ya could have called, ya know. I got me a phone now." I couldn't miss the trace of pride in her voice. She picked up a heavy black phone that stood on a tiny table positioned under a mirror in the hall and put it to her ear. She muttered an expletive. "Stupid phone company disconnected me again!"

I shifted André's weight to the other side. "Paulette's in the hospital."

That got her attention. Her face turned to me. "Why?"

"She has a severe case of pneumonia. I'm taking her daughter to see her later, after church. I thought perhaps you'd like to come with us."

Simone stared at the children, her gaze settling on Marie-Thérèse. "Yer Paulette's daughter?" she asked. Marie-Thérèse nodded.

"Why, I ain't seen ya since ya was about two years old, still a baby practically. Not really my fault, ya know. Yer mother don't want to bring ya here. I ain't good enough fer her no more." Her way of speaking clearly showed the accent of the small French village where she had been raised, as well as a lack of formal education, but her speech was mostly an act. She was smart, perhaps one of the most clever people I had ever met.

"That's not really true, Simone. You and I both know she's tried to see you. It's you who has refused."

Simone ignored me. "Come 'ere, child. Let me see ya better." She reached out a bony hand, but Marie-Thérèse took a step back. Simone didn't seem to mind. "Ya look 'xactly like Paulette when she was yer age. A spittin' image." She repeated the last sentence, this time adding a word I would have preferred she not use, especially around the children.

"We really have to be going," I said, retreating into the dark hallway. "Church will begin soon. Would you like us to come back for you?"

The older woman shook her head. "No. She don't want to see me, or she would've called."

"Your phone's disconnected," I reminded her.

Simone glared at me in annoyance. "I ain't up fer preachin' today. That's all she ever does." She reached for the door. "It was good seein' ya, Ariana." I thought she might have added a thank-you, but if she did, it was muffled by the slamming door.

"That was my grandmother?" Marie-Thérèse asked once we were back in the safety of the car.

"Yes."

"Mother told me all about her, but I didn't think she'd look like that."

"How?"

"Sad. I don't know. Like she doesn't have anyone."

I pondered Marie-Thérèse's words on the way to church. Children could be so perceptive. I wanted to explain how Simone's lifestyle had distanced her from her family, but I didn't know how much Paulette wanted Marie-Thérèse to know about the past. And there was also the matter of Simone's refusal to come with us. Paulette would be hurt if she knew.

"I think we'd better not talk about our visit with Simone until your mommy comes home from the hospital," I said to Marie-Thérèse.

"Why?" the older three children chimed.

"Because Simone didn't want to come and see Paulette at the hospital. I think that might hurt her feelings, don't you?"

They thought about it, and then three little faces bobbed up and down. "After Mommy comes home from the hospital, I'll tell her," Marie-Thérèse said.

"We'll both tell her. And perhaps your grandmother will let you visit her again, now that she knows who you are."

"I want to. She smells funny, but I like her."

"She swears, though," Marc said. "We have to tell her not to."

We arrived at the church and piled out of the car. I scanned the parking lot but didn't see my husband or any of the company cars he sometimes used. For the first time, I wondered if our argument would lead to a more permanent separation. Perhaps he had been waiting for an opportunity to leave. The thought sent cold shivers to my heart.

"Where's Daddy?" Josette asked. It was the first time any of them had mentioned their father that day.

"Hurry, kids," I said brightly, trying to distract Josette. "We'll be late." To my relief, she didn't pursue the thought.

My mother's wave attracted my attention. She stood on the cement sidewalk in front of the main entrance to the church. Near her was Marguerite, my longtime friend who had befriended me during the years I had been estranged from my parents. Marguerite and her husband owned several cafés and an apartment building here in Paris.

"Ariana!" my mother cried as they rushed up to me.

I set André down, and he toddled on alone. There were no other members in sight, confirming my idea that we were late. "What is it?" I asked, fearing the worst.

She glanced at the children, who were already scampering to the chapel doors. They were out of hearing range, but even so she lowered her voice. "It's Pierre. He called from the hospital. Paulette's awake, and they want to see you. He says to come immediately—with Jean-Marc. He says not to bring Marie-Thérèse."

"Is Paulette all right?" I asked quickly.

"He wouldn't say."

"Maybe she's having her baby," Marguerite suggested.

"So early?" my mother said. "She's not due yet."

"No. She's got another four months," I said, frowning. "But maybe the pneumonia is causing early labor."

"Pneumonia? Is it bad?" Marguerite asked. I had assumed my mother had already told her about Paulette's condition.

"Bad enough. She's stable but in serious condition. The doctor said the next twenty-four hours will tell."

Marguerite was quiet. "Michelle died of pneumonia." She was talking about her only child, who had died long before I knew the family.

I felt my eyes widen in surprise. "But I thought she died of drugs."

"It was the drugs, but the actual cause was pneumonia. If it hadn't been for the drugs . . ." Her voice faded, and she looked away, concealing her regrets.

"Have you seen Jean-Marc?" I asked. My mother's gaze was sharp, but she said nothing. Both shook their heads.

"You'll have to go without him," my mother said.

I hesitated. "But the children . . . and I'm supposed to teach Paulette's Primary class." I taught Relief Society once a month, but my lesson had been the week before.

"I'll take care of the class," Marguerite said.

"And I'll watch the children." My mother gently pushed me back the way I had come. "They'll be all right. Take as long as you want."

I knew my mother was serious. She always carried one of the twins' old car seats in her car for André, just in case it might be needed. With kisses for the children, I made my way hastily back to my car, casting my eyes about once again for Jean-Marc. My heart called out to him; I missed him more than I had imagined possible.

I drove through the streets of Paris, fearing what I might find awaiting me at the hospital. Still, whatever it was, I felt confident I could handle it alone; after all, I had already faced more tragedy than most people did in a lifetime. It didn't matter that Jean-Marc wasn't with me.

I didn't understand then that refining fires sometimes had to be repeated many times and that we couldn't change the consequences of our earlier choices. I especially didn't fathom that even I could not face this next challenge alone.

CHAPTER FOUR

The hospital halls were oddly quiet, menacingly so, and I seemed to see everything sharply and acutely as if in slow motion. The wheelchairs against a wall were bigger than life, the feather designs on the wallpaper more alive, and the occasional spot on the brown carpet seemed to rivet my attention. The nurses at the desk near Paulette's room looked up as I passed, staring at me with fixed eyes until I glanced in their direction. Immediately their gazes dropped, as if unwilling to meet mine. I walked on and felt eyes on me again, curious and scrutinizing, but when I turned abruptly, they jerked their heads away and focused on their paperwork.

I was sure I imagined their stares and silent refusals to meet my eyes, but nonetheless an overpowering apprehension hung over me. Quickening my pace, I was relieved to see Paulette's room. I rapped on the partially closed door, even as I pushed it open.

The scene made me stop short. Paulette was lying back on the bed. This time she wasn't using the oxygen, but the IV still dripped into her arm. Her eyes were open, and she breathed steadily, if somewhat roughly. In all, she appeared much better than that morning, but there was something disturbing about the way she stared into space, seeming not to see anything.

I coughed, and Pierre, sitting on the edge of the bed with Paulette's hand in his, glanced up. He said something inaudible to Paulette, who started and looked over at me. Her gaunt face crumpled, and she began to cry with heartrending sobs.

I rushed across the room. "What is it, Paulette?"

Her eyes were red-rimmed. "I have AIDS," she said unsteadily.

I felt my eyes grow impossibly wide, and my heart hammered in my ears. Surely this was some kind of hideous joke. AIDS? Acquired

Immune Deficiency Syndrome? "No!" My voice came as a gruesome whisper.

She nodded. "Probably from a dirty needle years ago or . . ."

Or prostitution. My mind completed the sentence she couldn't—or wouldn't—finish. Paulette had done many things in the past to get drugs after Nette's death. But that was over now; she had repented and been forgiven. I couldn't believe the past could come back to haunt her future. It wasn't right.

I glanced at Pierre; his red-streaked, swollen eyes and ghastly pale visage confirmed his wife's words. His overwhelming grief made him appear close to death himself. "Oh, Paulette!" Tears cascaded down my cheeks in silent torrents, and my shoulders convulsed.

She held out her arms, and I went to her. We hugged. It felt strange because she turned her head, as if not wanting me to see her tears.

After a long while, she pulled away. "Marie-Thérèse and Pierre have to be tested. The doctor has agreed to do it today so we'll have the results by morning." The words were matter-of-fact, but I struggled for breath; somehow oxygen seemed to elude me. Marie-Thérèse? Pierre? But of course. AIDS was a highly contagious disease. How could they *not* have it?

"The baby?" I asked carefully.

Pierre sighed. "She has about a 30 percent chance of contracting HIV. If we had known earlier, they could have given Paulette a drug that might prevent the baby from getting the virus. It could be too late, but the specialist has started Paulette on the drug in the hopes that the baby doesn't already have it."

A 30 percent chance of having AIDS! Nearly one in three! The same odds must also apply to Marie-Thérèse. Even now she could have the latent virus in her blood.

"We'll know tomorrow," Pierre said bleakly. "There's a chance that—" He couldn't finish the sentence. The slim possibility that one of them might not have the disease made it too painful for hope.

I wanted to scream out the unfairness of it all. Innocent children! And Pierre, who had never done anything wrong, except perhaps to love a woman back to life. Was that so evil?

The silence in the room was far from tranquil. I could almost feel Paulette's and Pierre's hearts pounding out their hopeless despair. My own feelings threatened to drown me with sorrow. I thought it could get no worse until Paulette spoke again, and it seemed as if my world had been torn from beneath my feet, causing me to fall into an endless void.

"You need to be tested, too. And your family."

"What?" The word felt ripped from my throat.

Paulette closed her eyes and raised a hand to wipe the stream of tears. Pierre reached out to her, but she gently pushed him away.

He faced me. "Dr. Flaubert told us about Paulette's having AIDS this morning. He called in a specialist, and he explained that AIDS is the result of having HIV. AIDS can set in anywhere between six months and eleven years after a person is infected with HIV. They begin to call it AIDS when a patient has signs of two or more sicknesses they call opportunistic diseases. The virus is usually contracted through sexual intercourse, from exposure to contaminated blood or blood products, or from a mother to her child before or during birth. But HIV has also been detected in tears, saliva, urine, and breast milk. It isn't probable, but it's remotely possible that it could be spread through those things as well."

I said nothing, feeling inundated with information that couldn't possibly have anything to do with me. Then I understood why Paulette had turned her face from me during our embrace. It wasn't because she hadn't wanted me to see her tears; it was because she worried she might give me HIV—if I didn't have it already. After all, she had done drugs with my first husband, had perhaps shared needles with him. Who knew when she had become contaminated? Perhaps I too had the virus in my blood, a last bitter present from Jacques. I felt myself backing away from the bed.

HIV in blood? Yesterday, hadn't I taken Paulette to the hospital while she was spitting blood? I had put my arms around her, never thinking I might be exposed to a disease that inevitably kills.

HIV in saliva? Hadn't my children and Marie-Thérèse shared suckers countless times during their young lives?

HIV in urine? Years ago, hadn't I changed Marie-Thérèse's diaper or cleaned up her mistakes when she was potty-training?

The thoughts raced through my mind with a velocity that made me stagger. Had HIV been passed to my own children and Jean-Marc? Were all those I loved destined to die?

It was all I could do not to run from the room.

"I'm sorry," Paulette whispered.

I seemed to remember vividly when she had said those same words the night Nette died.

"I've got to go find Jean-Marc," I managed to say. "He has to know."

Pierre nodded. "The doctor wants to test us all. Could you bring Marie-Thérèse later? We're lucky to be in a hospital that does the tests in its own lab. In some clinics it takes a week for the results. Here they even have a wing for AIDS patients."

I nodded numbly. "I'll bring Marie-Thérèse."

"And don't tell her anything yet," Pierre added. "We want to be the ones."

"Of course."

Once out of their sight, I ran down the hall. Spotting a bathroom, I ducked inside and began washing my hands and arms with the strong-smelling soap, over and over again, as if to wash Paulette's touch from my skin.

AIDS! She had AIDS! Paulette was going to die!

And perhaps take all of us with her.

The hot water seared my skin, but I didn't stop scrubbing, not even when my arms turned red from the heat and tiny beads of blood oozed from the broken flesh. Steam rolled up, covering the mirror and dampening my skin. I sobbed hysterically, and mascara-laden tears blocked my vision and streaked my face. It wasn't fair. It just wasn't fair! How could the Lord let this happen?

I was in the bathroom for a long time, and when I finally emerged, I felt frail and shaky. I passed the nurses' station, once again feeling their eyes on me. Now I understood; they remembered my being with Paulette that morning. They had known about her having AIDS, and they felt pity for us all.

My mind was in too much turmoil to go home. I drove to the Quai of Montebello that ran along the Seine River, opposite Notre Dame. In my growing-up years, this had been one of my favorite places to come with my brother. I walked along the parapets where the booksellers' stalls were located. The stalls were really only large boxes bolted to the stone wall of the quay itself. At night, the boxes would be locked.

My attention drifted from the stalls to the river. I stopped to stare down into the water that lapped softly at the base of the wall below. It held many memories for me, mostly happy ones. Life was good, every minute so precious. Was it now running out?

I wasn't afraid of dying; part of me even longed to be near my brother and Nette. But I was terrified of leaving my children without a mother or of watching them suffer.

Why had this happened?

I watched the boats pass by, staring at the rippling wakes they left in the water. Paulette and I had both come so far. She, especially, had changed her whole life to accept the gospel. She had repented of her sins and been forgiven. What kind of justice was this? I wanted to scream and cry out my pain to my Father, but something inside was also angry. He could have prevented this! Logically, I knew there had to be an explanation, but perhaps I wasn't ready yet to hear it.

Leaving the river, I made my way to my car. I drove slowly, ignoring the impatient honking of the cars behind me. Just as in the hospital, I seemed to see everything under a strange, intense light, as if through a magnifying glass. What was it about death that made life suddenly so precious?

Before I realized where I was going, I found myself near the cemetery where Nette and Antoine were buried. I parked and made my way languidly up the cobblestone path. My foot occasionally hit a loose stone and sent it flying, echoing loudly over the quiet graveyard. I sat on the bench opposite my daughter's grave, my eyes soaking up the quiet green of the grass and trees. Her tombstone was a twin to my brother's; both were made of gray stone with carved scrollwork decorating the top, and they stood nearly as high as my waist. Afternoon sunlight reflected through the leaves and onto the stones and the names carved there, inlaid with gold.

Usually I visited my daughter's grave on the second and fourth Wednesday of every month, right after lunch. I always brought the children—much to the caretaker's dismay—and told them stories of little Antoinette and my life before they were born. I didn't want them ever to forget their older sibling and the pain drugs could cause. Knowing about their sister could only keep them on the right path.

It wasn't the cemetery where Nette had originally been buried. After my marriage to Jean-Marc, my father and I had her moved next to Antoine, for whom she had been named. There I could talk to them both and remember the happy times. Oh, I knew their spirits weren't in the ground beneath the headstones, but coming here gave me a focus, a time out of the real world to concentrate on spiritual things.

Because today was Sunday, there were more visitors than I was accustomed to seeing on my semimonthly trips. Most carried flowers for their loved ones. I paid them no heed but let my head slump into my hands. Tears came again, and I rubbed my eyes to stop the torrent. I had no idea how much time had passed since I left the church, nor did I have the energy to check my wristwatch.

Someone sat down on the bench beside me, and I stiffened. Who would dare to intrude on my sorrow? I darted a glance in the newcomer's direction.

"Hello, Ari." My father slid closer and put his arms around me. "Today's not Wednesday, you know," he murmured against my hair. The cemetery was the one place my father and I met alone. The first time it had happened by accident, but when he discovered four years ago that I visited Nette's and Antoine's graves twice each month, he began to visit on the same days. Sometimes his work wouldn't allow his regular visits, and I would be there alone with only the children and my thoughts for company. Occasionally I was unable to make it at the right time, and he would be alone. It didn't matter; there was always the next time we would visit.

I had never told anyone except Jean-Marc of the time my father and I spent together at the cemetery—not even my mother, though she probably knew, if not from my children, then from my father. It was special, a time for us to be together and talk or just to sit in comfortable silence as the children played nearby.

"Paulette has AIDS," I said, my voice hoarse. I wasn't expecting much sympathy from him. He had warned me all my life about drugs and the consequences of using them. To him, it might even seem a kind of justice.

In thinking this, I misjudged my father. "I'm sorry, Ari," he said. "It doesn't seem fair."

"You already knew?"

He nodded gravely. "Pierre called after you left. He was worried about you. Your mother took Marie-Thérèse to the hospital, and I came to look for you. I hoped to find you here." He held me tightly, smoothing my hair with his strong hands.

"Thanks for coming," I said after a while. "I just couldn't go home. How can I tell my children their favorite aunt is going to die? I haven't even gathered the courage to tell them Jean-Marc has left me."

My father chuckled. "That's not how I heard it."

"What do you mean?" I asked hotly, drawing away from him.

"Jean-Marc told me you threw him out."

"But I didn't—" I stopped. Well, maybe I had. "I was just trying to make a p—" But that didn't matter now. The point was that my father knew where Jean-Marc was. "Where is he?" I demanded.

He shook his head, his voice dripping irony. "For a couple who claim to be married for all eternity, you two aren't communicating very well."

"I never said I was perfect," I retorted. "Just tell me."

"All right, all right." My father raised his hands as if fending me off. "But I'll tell it my way." I sighed and settled back on the bench, knowing I would have to hear the whole story, instead of the part I was most interested in.

"I was very angry after we talked this morning. As I dressed, I planned all the things I would say and do to Jean-Marc once I found him." He paused. The sunlight seemed to reflect off his chiseled features and his graying temples. His trimmed moustache was still a shiny black and seemed to soften his strong face. Not for the first time, I noticed that my father was a handsome man. "Luckily, I calmed down a bit," he continued. "By the time I arrived at the bank, I had begun to think there might be another explanation for his behavior."

"Then he's at the bank?"

He frowned disapprovingly, but I thought I saw a twinkle in his brown eyes. "I remember how before your marriage, Jean-Marc disappeared and didn't call you for two months," he said as if I hadn't spoken. "He ran away then for a reason, and I thought maybe he might have one in this situation. So when I found him asleep on the couch in his office, I didn't kill him at once."

I smiled despite myself. "And?"

"And he told me you two had a fight and that you practically threw his suitcase at him. What else was he supposed to do but leave?"

"That's not the way it was at all," I said. "I felt I had to do something. He's never home. He works more than you do. He neglects the children. And me. It's been going on for years, though I've been so busy with the children, I didn't recognize it until now."

"I'm not the one you should be telling this to."

"But I tried to tell him, and that's why he left."

My father said nothing but gazed out over the tombstones. He put his arm around my shoulders. "You know, your mother and I married very young. She was only nineteen, and I was twenty."

I held my breath in frustration; I had heard this story many times, and I didn't see what it had to do with my situation. However, I had learned that there was no stopping my father once he started. But as he continued, the love in his voice made my resentment fade.

"We were both only children, born late in life to our parents, and they objected to our getting married so early. But Josephine was so beautiful, and I knew that having her as my wife would only give me more purpose, make our lives fulfilled. I was right. I worked hard—and you can see where I am today.

"That's not to say we didn't go through troubles. During those first seven years, we tried to have a baby, but it didn't happen. Your mother grew sad, and I didn't know how to help her. I worked harder to earn money, and it was that money we used to pay for fertility treatments."

"And the treatments got you Antoine and me," I said. My mother had been twenty-seven when she had us, a year younger than I was now.

He smiled. "Yes, but even without the drugs we could have had you both. Your mother's line has a history of fraternal twins—her own mother was one, as you know. We'd wanted a son, but when we got an extra surprise, it was the happiest day of our lives. By that time our parents had died, and I thought that we had already faced the biggest trials we would ever face. Until Antoine was killed."

I saw tears on my father's thick lashes and looked away, embarrassed in spite of our closeness.

"What I'm trying to say, Ari, is that I've learned a lot in my fifty-four years of life. Each day has its hills or mountains, and how each person deals with those problems is different, especially if those people happen to be of the opposite sex."

"What do you mean?"

"Well, for instance, a woman will say, 'André needs a diaper change,' and another woman will understand that the first woman wants her to change the diaper. However, a husband will think, 'Oh,' and go about his business, while the wife becomes angry because he's not doing what she asked. But he thinks that if she had wanted him to change the diaper, she would have said, 'Will you change his diaper?' I see this miscommunication at the bank all the time. In fact, we have a class on it now. Employee relations, you know."

"Jean-Marc has to know how I feel," I said.

My father nodded. "I think he does now. And maybe he did before, but he didn't realize how large the problem has grown."

"Then I did right," I said, "by . . . uh . . . kicking him out." Even as I said the words, I felt ashamed.

"Maybe. But it still doesn't explain why he feels he has to work as hard as he does. There must be some reason. And simply knowing your feelings might not make him change."

I found I didn't really care if the problem between us was solved at all. I only wanted Jean-Marc to come home. Paulette was dying of AIDS, and I felt my reaction to his working late was trivial now. At least he was alive, and I was, too. We could go from there. I refused to consider that one or both of us might have contracted HIV.

"So now what?" I asked.

He sighed. "First, you have to realize that not everyone faces trials the way you do. You tend to go at them head on; Jean-Marc backs away and thinks about it first. One way isn't necessarily better than the other. I've done both in my life, and both have consequences. But one thing I do know is that you can only change yourself, not your spouse. Change has to come from within a person because he wants it. And I learned that the hard way." His voice held memories of the past. A sudden, deep sorrow emanated from him, and I knew it was because Antoine was lost to him forever. While my father had some belief in God, no manner of begging, pleading, or talking on my part could make him realize that he could be sealed to Antoine, that we could be an eternal family.

"What can I change?" I asked, wanting to wipe the sadness from his face. "I haven't been nagging."

He cocked his head back and stared into the blue sky. A white cloud floated across the sun and cast a shadow over us. "That I don't know." He grimaced slightly. "Just when I think I have it figured out, your mother changes the rules."

I bit my lip, knowing that though my mother had not told him of her desire to be baptized, he obviously sensed something in her demeanor.

I kissed his cheek. "Thanks for your advice. When will I ever know as much as you?"

The sadness vanished, and again I caught a gleam in his eyes. "When you're as old as I am, perhaps," he said. "But don't forget that I'll be older then, and I'll still know more than you."

I laughed. One part of me questioned how I could do so in light of Paulette's illness and my own marital problems, but reality seemed far away right then. I stood, crossed the soft grass to Nette's tombstone, and ran my finger over the gold-colored indentations of her name. The edges of the carved stone felt rough against my skin.

I nodded at Antoine's stone and then joined my father. Together we walked back down the path to the black cast-iron gates that separated the graveyard from the world.

"Are the children at your house?" I asked when we reached our cars.

"No. At yours. With Jean-Marc."

My heart seemed to skip a beat. "He's home?"

"I dropped him and the children off before I came here. He wanted to come with me, but," my father's face broke into a wide grin, "I thought he should get a taste of being alone with the children for a while."

I hugged him. "Thanks, Father."

"That's what I'm here for," he said, opening my door.

Smoothing my brown linen skirt around my knees, I slid into the soft bench seat in my car. My father hesitated. "When I talked to Pierre, he said you all needed to be tested tomorrow. And that his and Marie-Thérèse's results will be ready. We'd like to be there, your mother and I."

"I'd like you there," I said softly.

He nodded and closed the door. With a short wave of his hand, he turned and strode to his own car.

On the way home, my mind drifted to Paulette. *Jesus Christ died for our sins,* I thought, *including hers.* I believed that with my whole being; the past was over and gone. Yet why, after Paulette had embraced the gospel and become new, did the past still have the power to destroy her? It simply didn't make sense, and I needed to understand why.

Chapter Five

*I*n my eagerness to see my husband, I fumbled for the keys in my purse. Finally, I opened the door.

"Mommy!" My children ran to me, and I hugged them.

"Why are you crying?" asked Josette, reaching up to wipe away a tear. I caught her hand before it touched me. Until I knew more about HIV, my family would have to take precautions.

"Because I love you so much." They didn't seem to think my answer strange.

"I love you too, Mommy," the twins answered together.

I felt eyes on me and looked up to see Jean-Marc watching us from the kitchen doorway, a wooden stirring spoon in one hand. He wore rumpled suit pants and a white and gray pinstriped shirt. His hair wasn't combed as neatly as usual, and he looked tired, but the green-brown eyes were the same, except today they held no mirth. I stood up and took a few tentative steps toward him. He met me halfway, and we clung together in a tight embrace.

"I missed you," he said, burying his face in my hair.

"I missed you, too." My words sounded like a sob.

He held me back enough to see my face. "After I talked to your dad this morning, I went to church. When I didn't see you there, I got really scared. I couldn't believe it was over between us. Please forgive me!"

I put my finger on his lips, stilling the words, and then kissed him. It was enough just to have him back. He responded fervently, until my head swam from lack of oxygen. For a moment time was suspended, and I was happy and right where I belonged.

"Were you two fighting?" Josette asked.

We broke away to see three curious faces staring up at us. Jean-Marc coughed delicately and moved into the kitchen, drawing me with him.

Dipping the spoon he still held into the enormous pot of soup I had made Friday night, he stirred slowly.

"We're just happy to see each other," he said. His eyes searched my face. "I wish I could have been there for you last night," he said quietly. "How is Paulette?"

"We need to talk."

He looked startled. The spoon dropped from his hand and sank out of sight into the soup.

"Stay here, children." I grabbed Jean-Marc's hand, leaving the spoon submerged in the soup.

"Why?" Marc asked.

"Stay here!" I repeated. They stared with wide eyes as I led Jean-Marc into the hallway and toward our bedroom. The tears were coming, despite my attempt to stop them.

"I know about the AIDS," Jean-Marc said. "I was at your parents' when Pierre called. We went there after church."

"It's not that."

"What's wrong, Ari?" Jean-Marc came close and reached out to touch my face.

"Don't!" I said, remembering the HIV. Then again, we'd been kissing, so a tear hardly seemed important.

"What's wrong? You're scaring me!" He cocked his head back and studied me, his expression unreadable. "I'll be with you through this, Ari. I love you."

I shifted my eyes to the floor. "I hope so," I said softly, "because Paulette's not the only one who may have HIV."

"Pierre!" Jean-Marc looked as if someone had punched him in the stomach and he couldn't find his breath. He slumped to the bed. "Of course! My brother is going to die, isn't he?"

"They don't know, but he probably has it as well. He's probably had it for years."

Jean-Marc put his head in his hand and cried, the tears seeming to dissolve all the problems separating us. My heart went out to him, but I had to tell him the rest. "Marie-Thérèse and Pierre are being tested today, and we need to go in for a test, too."

His eyes grew wide as he reeled from the shock. I tried to comfort him, but he stood up and paced the floor. "No," he said. "It's not possible. We're fine."

"We have to believe that, but we still have to be tested. Tomorrow morning, when the lab opens."

"No." His voice sounded oddly detached. "We don't need to. God wouldn't do this to us."

"Nor to Paulette. Yet she has it."

"We've lost too much already!"

At first I thought he was referring to Antoine and Nette, but from his distant expression, I realized he was thinking of his father. I didn't know much about the man's death, except that it had been from a heart attack. Jean-Marc had never talked about it, saying only that he didn't remember the event very well. I believed he blocked it out; sometimes it was easier to hide pain than to deal with it.

"We need to be tested," I repeated. "And to learn more about AIDS—if only to help Paulette and Pierre."

I thought he might hug me then and reassure me that everything would be all right, but he didn't. He shook his head. "No. I'm not going."

"But we have to know."

"I do know, and I'm not going!" He pushed past me and into the hallway. He didn't stop when he reached the kitchen.

Leaving! Not again. I followed him, stunned. He picked up his briefcase and opened the apartment door.

"Jean-Marc!"

"I've got work to do. I'll be home later."

"On Sunday?" I said. He never went to the office on Sundays. "It can wait. We have to talk about this."

"No, we don't."

"You're running away!" I called after him. "Come back!"

He paused in the hallway, eyes pleading. "Let me go."

I softened, remembering what my father had said about the different ways people handled problems and how I couldn't change him. The only thing I could change about this situation was my attitude. "When will you be home?" With these words he would know that I wanted him back.

"Later."

"Okay." I kissed my hand and then blew on it.

He caught the imaginary kiss with his hand, touched his mouth, and smiled unsteadily. "I love you, Ari." He pushed the elevator button and stared expectantly at the closed double doors.

"Jean-Marc?" An idea had come to me, a flash of memory. One that perhaps could help both of us.

He turned to look at me, eyes guarded. "Yes?"

"Once, you promised me never to try to solve the important things yourself. You said we'd do it together. Do you remember?"

His shoulders slumped. The elevator chimed as it opened, but he made no move toward it. His briefcase slid to the floor as the doors slammed shut again. When he spoke, his voice was teary and full of memories. "Yes. It was when I proposed. I said you were a queen, and I'd do my best to become your king." His eyes met mine, and his voice sounded ragged. "I haven't done too well, have I?"

I gave him a watery smile. "Maybe not tonight or in the past few days, but there's still time."

He walked over to me and hugged me tightly. "What would I ever do without you?"

"Is that why you're afraid of our getting tested? Are you afraid of losing me?"

"Well, it's like this." He held up his hands in a cupping motion, his voicing breaking as he spoke. "Friday morning I felt as if everything was right here in my hands, and now it's suddenly slipping away, and I can't stop it." He opened his fingers and stared down at them.

"What can we do?" I asked him. He probably didn't know, but to ask him might get us both on the right track. He was a priesthood holder, and I had faith that he would rise to the challenge. I wasn't to be disappointed.

"Pray," he said after a long pause. "We need to pray together. And let's start a fast tomorrow."

Jean-Marc retrieved his briefcase and grabbed my hand, holding tightly, as if afraid to let go. We went inside our apartment and turned to face the three pairs of eyes, wide and scared-looking, watching us from the kitchen doorway.

"Come here," Jean-Marc beckoned to them. He led us into the family room where we knelt in a circle, holding hands. The twins were strangely reverent, as if somehow sensing the importance of the moment.

"Dear Heavenly Father," Jean-Marc began. He prayed for Paulette, Pierre, and their children, and then he prayed for us. Instead of imploring the Lord to make us free of HIV, he asked that God's will be done and pleaded for the courage to accept His will.

I was proud of Jean-Marc and the example he set for me and the children. He wasn't perfect, but then, neither was I. We were both merely doing our best.

After the prayer, Josette asked, "What's wrong with Aunt Paulette?"

I looked to Jean-Marc, and he nodded once, sharply.

"She's got a disease called AIDS," I said. "There isn't a cure. And she's going to get very sick."

"You mean die?"

What could I say to my little girl, kneeling on the ground and watching me so intently? She knew little of life and nothing of death— not yet. Eventually she would have to face it—when Paulette died—but surely I could protect her a while longer. I pulled her onto my lap.

"Not right now, honey. Now that the doctors know what she has, they can give her medicine to help her. But like I said, after a few years, she'll be very sick."

Josette's eyes filled with tears. "But does Marie-Thérèse know?"

"Her parents are telling her now."

"I'm going to keep praying for Aunt Paulette," Josette said.

They had more questions, and we answered them to the best of our ability, trying not to scare them but to be truthful. Then Jean-Marc told them about our having to be tested.

"It's just to make sure we don't get sick," he said. He looked at me as he added, "We need to know."

"Could we die?" Marc asked. He didn't seem frightened, only curious, as if dying might be an adventure.

I didn't know what to say. Once I would have reassured him, but now I couldn't. While it was unlikely that Marie-Thérèse or Paulette could have given him HIV, my own life before I was baptized might very well have given him this terrible legacy.

Jean-Marc came to my rescue. "I don't think we should worry too much," he said. "We're all going to be around for a long time. Except, of course, if the tiger gets you. Rrrr!" He flopped onto all fours and pretended to bite Marc's neck.

The twins screamed in delight, their young minds already discounting any danger, but André came to sit in my lap as if sensing I needed something to hold on to. He was a blessing, one I had often taken for granted. I cuddled him, vowing not to make the mistake again. I would cherish each day with all my children. We watched Jean-Marc and the twins playing on the floor until they tired of the game. At last they stretched out on the mauve carpet, panting.

"Now can we get the spoon out of the soup?" Josette asked suddenly, bringing a smile to our faces. "Marc was going to do it, but I wouldn't let him."

"Good for you, Josette. Yes, we can get it out. Does anybody want soup?"

While they were eating, I called the hospital to speak with Pierre.

"Should I come and get Marie-Thérèse?" I asked.

"No. Paulette's asleep, and I'm going to take Marie-Thérèse home tonight. We'll see you tomorrow morning. I'll bring some clothes for Marie-Thérèse, and perhaps you can watch her for a few days."

"Of course. We'd love to have her." My voice wavered. If it turned out Marie-Thérèse had HIV, maybe I wouldn't be so willing.

"Thanks, Ariana."

"Would you like to talk with Jean-Marc?"

"What would I say?" he asked. "It's better to wait until tomorrow. Until I know."

I hung up and went to put the children to bed. The twins went peacefully, but we had waited too long to put André in his crib. The little boy cried irritably as Jean-Marc tried to change his diaper and dress him. Jean-Marc looked upset, but I knew what to do when André acted this way.

I took André from Jean-Marc and whirled him around the room, singing the theme from the latest Disney movie. His tears disappeared, replaced by a smile. I laid him down and tickled his toes softly. In between the tickling, I got him ready for bed. It really wasn't difficult to deal with André; you just had to keep him occupied. The twins had been more exacting.

"I didn't know he ever got like that," Jean-Marc said as I kissed the baby and tucked him under the covers in his crib.

"How many nights have you been here to see how he acted?" I said without thinking. Jean-Marc frowned. "It's because he's tired," I added, relenting. "He doesn't normally do this. There's been too much excitement here tonight."

"Too much for all of us," he said. He peered into the twins' room. Already they were snoring gently.

"Thank you for staying," I said, moving to stand beside him.

"Thank you for reminding me of what I should be doing." He held my hand tightly and glanced back into the darkened room, not looking at me as he spoke the next words. "Ari, are you afraid?"

I nodded. "I am."

His smile flashed so briefly that I wondered if I had imagined it. "Good. Then it's okay for me to be afraid." He laughed but without mirth. "It's funny how it takes a crisis like this before you realize how much you have to lose." He spoke the words in my own heart.

For a long time we said nothing, simply stood in the doorway, watching the sleeping children. Then Jean-Marc reached out to me and drew me close. Our lips met, and for a short time everything was right with the world. We made our way to our bedroom, lit only by the thin moonlight streaming through the blinds. We embraced tightly, neither of us wanting to let go, silently sharing our hopes and fears as only eternal companions could. Whatever the outcome, we were in this together, and nothing—not even death—would defeat us.

I knew my thoughts were brave; in the reality that Paulette and Pierre were living, there would be much more hardship and sorrow. But tonight, I would not borrow others' troubles. Tonight I would be with my husband as if eternity were already ours.

CHAPTER SIX

We awoke early Monday morning to go to the hospital. Jean-Marc made breakfast while I readied the children. The tension in the air was palpable, and André, normally so cheerful, was cranky and crying. Jean-Marc tried to comfort him but was unable to make him feel better. I took the baby from his arms, and after a few minutes he was quiet. Jean-Marc seemed angry, but I didn't understand why. I assumed he was worried about the tests.

We were ready to leave when the doorbell rang. "Who could that be?" I muttered. Jean-Marc opened the door to reveal Louise, a suitcase in either hand.

"I'm here," she announced. She dropped her cases and hugged her son, kissing him several times on each cheek in the French custom. "A young man let me in the door downstairs so I didn't have to buzz you. He was coming out as I arrived."

Jean-Marc darted a questioning glance over his shoulder, and I shrugged apologetically. In the upheaval caused by learning of Paulette's AIDS, I had completely forgotten about Louise's visit.

"Grandma!" shouted the twins, rushing forward with outstretched arms. Jean-Marc stood back to allow them room.

Louise was a plump woman in her late fifties. She had lustrous dark brown hair that showed no signs of graying, though I knew she had help from her hairstylist to make it so. But the youthful hair matched her indomitable spirit. She had been widowed when Jean-Marc was seven and for many years had been the backbone of their family, not only managing their grocery store but supporting both sons on their missions.

"Ariana, as beautiful as ever," she said, coming forward to kiss me.

Jean-Marc and I stood silently, neither of us knowing how to tell her the news about Paulette.

"Where's Lu-Lu?" I asked.

"She went in to work today to finish some things and to tell them she'll be gone for a week. I told her it was a family crisis and that they'd understand if she called from here, but she insisted." Louise sniffed. "She's taking the plane later today. She said for me not to worry about picking her up, either," she added tersely. "Lu-Lu said she knows how to use a taxi."

It seemed that Lu-Lu really was growing up, and her mother wasn't enjoying the process.

Louise heaved a frustrated sigh. "I need to rest. How about showing Grandma to a chair?" she asked the children. Unlike my own mother, she had a few health problems, including an ulcer, varicose veins, and painful arthritis. It had been a relief for her when Pierre had sold their store and she could retire.

"But we're going to the hospital for a test," Josette said.

"Yeah, they take your blood out and everything," Marc added with relish.

Louise glanced up at us, instantly understanding that something terrible had happened. "What's going on?" she demanded.

"It's Paulette," I said.

"The baby?"

I shook my head, glancing at Jean-Marc for help.

"Paulette has AIDS," he explained gently. He repeated everything Pierre had told me at the hospital, leaving nothing out. "Now we all need to be tested."

"Oh, Jean-Marc!" Louise lost her composure and began weeping. He hugged her for long moments as she sobbed.

"I'm going with you," Louise finally said through her tears. She wiped her large hands over her red face, as if to cover the fact that she had been crying.

It was a very subdued group that filed into the hospital. My parents were there waiting, and each picked up one of the twins. With a flash, I remembered how they had picked up Antoine and me at that same age. How young they had been then! And how certain of the future. But Antoine died, and now they were afraid of losing someone they loved again.

The antiseptic smell of the hospital drifted into my nose and seemed to settle in my stomach, making me feel nauseated. I was grateful to feel Jean-Marc's arm around my shoulders; there were no walls between us now.

The nurses at the lab drew blood quickly and efficiently. Little Marc watched in fascination, but Josette squeezed her eyes shut tight. Neither cried, nor did André, but all of the adults had tears in their eyes, stemming from fear of the virus and not from the needle.

"If you call after nine in the morning, we'll give you the results," the nurse said, removing her gloves. Her voice was clipped and remote, making me want to shake her. Our whole lives hung in the balance, but for her it was just another test.

"Thank you," said Jean-Marc.

"Will you stay home to call with me?" I asked quietly as we moved down the hall. He seemed surprised at the question, but I had to know.

"I'll take the whole morning off," he said.

We went to see Paulette. They had moved her to another wing where all the patients were terminally ill, including many with AIDS. To me, even the corridor smelled like death. However, the nurses we saw didn't stare at us with pity, and their smiles were genuine. I guessed Paulette was lucky that this hospital was equipped to deal with her sickness.

"Your mother and I will be in the waiting room," my father said. Once more he held Josette in his arms.

Jean-Marc looked at the twins. "You stay with Grandma and Grandpa."

"But I want to see Marie-Thérèse," Josette protested.

"She's coming home with us," I said. "You and Marc can play with her then."

"And remember, I'll not have any horsing around here," Jean-Marc warned, staring pointedly at Marc.

"Okay," the boy said, the picture of innocence.

"Would you like to leave André with us, too?" my mother asked.

"No, he won't understand anyway." I held my baby tightly.

Jean-Marc's arm went around my shoulders again, and I was comforted.

As we approached the room, our steps slowed in trepidation. Louise knocked and, at a faint sound from inside, pushed open the door.

Paulette lay curled on her side with one arm covering her face. She breathed heavily, and once again we could hear the hiss of the oxygen in the quiet of the room. Pierre, by her side, was strangely calm. His face was still pallid, but the red eyes had disappeared. Marie-Thérèse sat on his lap watching her mother sadly, eyes red and puffy as if she had been crying.

Pierre stood up as we entered, and Marie-Thérèse slipped to the floor. She didn't run to play with André or to greet her grandmother as she normally did but simply regarded us gravely. Jean-Marc stepped forward and silently hugged his brother. No one spoke for a long moment, and the tension in the room built.

"Well?" It was Louise who broke the silence.

Pierre's face was visible over Jean-Marc's shoulder. His lower lip quivered, the only sign of his inner turmoil. He broke away and hugged his mother briefly before speaking. When he did, his voice was low, almost a whisper, and very hoarse. "Marie-Thérèse doesn't have the virus," he said.

"But you do," Louise stated.

He nodded. "I do. Of course, it may be years yet until . . ." His voice dropped away as if he were too tired to finish the explanation or as if to say, "What difference could my words make? It won't change the fact that I'm going to die." The unfinished sentence and the tragic calm on his face revealed more about what he was feeling than any words he could have said.

I didn't know what to do for him. My mind grasped at the only consolation it could find. Marie-Thérèse at least would live! I handed André to Louise and knelt to hug the little girl, unable to stop the tears. "Oh, thank you, Lord," I whispered over and over, hugging her. She clung to me with one arm; in the other she held her rag doll.

"I'm okay, Aunt Ariana," she whispered. "It's Mommy who's sick. But she's going to get better." Her words showed me that like my own children, she had no real understanding of death or the illness that had her mother in its fatal grip.

"Why don't you go out in the waiting room and see your cousins?" Jean-Marc suggested. "They're with Ari's parents," he said in further explanation to Paulette and Pierre.

A smile lit Marie-Thérèse's face. Jean-Marc moved to the door and opened it for her, and then he walked with her down the hall, making sure she was delivered safely into the care of my parents. When he returned, Louise spoke.

"What about the baby?" She had tears on her worn cheeks, but she maintained her composure. She gave André back to me and walked to the head of the bed. One rough hand touched Paulette's hair gingerly.

"They won't know until she's born, unless we want to take a test that may cause her to abort," Paulette said sadly. "We don't want to risk it."

A knock at the door came, and Louise opened it. A nurse entered, carrying a tray of food. She was short, with skin the color of dark chocolate and full lips painted a rich red. "How are you today, Paulette?" she asked kindly.

Paulette groaned, but she let the nurse help her to a sitting position. "I'm not hungry," she said petulantly.

"I know, but you have to eat to keep up your strength. If not for yourself, then for your baby."

It had been the right thing to say. Paulette began to eat, without appetite but steadily.

The nurse chattered happily as she went about her work straightening the pillow, checking the charts, and watching the monitors. "It looks like you're holding steady," she said cheerfully. "That's a good sign."

"This is Giselle," Pierre said to us. "She's been assigned to Paulette."

"Glad to meet you," I said sincerely. She was certainly a lot better than the silent, mean-looking nurse who had taken care of Paulette before.

"And you are?" Giselle's face seemed to shine with a happiness that should be out of place in this room. Instead, I found her manner refreshing.

Pierre made introductions. Giselle looked at each of us intently, as if putting our faces in her memory. "It's nice to meet you all," she said. "It's good to see Paulette has so much support." She turned and faced the bed. "I'll be back in a little while for your tray and to take your temperature and blood pressure before I go off shift. The doctor also wants another blood sample. We need to get you up and home, don't we?"

Paulette nodded, but I could see the fear in her face. Giselle did too. "It's all right," she said. "AIDS is a terrible disease, but you can have a good life for as long as you have left. It's what any of us try to do, really. It's all in the attitude."

I was beginning to like this nurse. She was exactly what we needed.

"We're all here for you," Jean-Marc said after Giselle had left. "Tell us, please, what can we do?"

Pierre looked at him gratefully. "There's nothing now. Just taking care of Marie-Thérèse has been a big help."

"Has she had a blessing?" He motioned to Paulette.

Pierre nodded. "I gave her one yesterday morning."

"Will you watch Marie-Thérèse again, Ariana?" Paulette asked, her spoon pausing in mid-air.

"You know I will."

"Could everybody leave so I can talk with Ariana for a minute?" Paulette asked. The group nodded and filed out the door. Only André stayed with us. He put his hand in my short hair, tugging gently. I pushed his hand away and kissed his forehead.

I waited, but Paulette didn't speak. "So what now?" I asked.

"I'm afraid, Ari," Paulette said. "I mean, I'm going home when I'm over the pneumonia, but I'm afraid of getting Marie-Thérèse sick. For Pierre it's too late, but for her . . ."

"I won't do it," I said, knowing what she was going to ask. "Marie-Thérèse needs you now. She needs to build memories that will last a lifetime, after you're gone. I won't take that away from her."

"Memories of me being sick? Of me wasting away until I die?" Paulette bit her lip to stifle tears. "What good could that possibly do my baby?"

"During the bad days, I'll gladly take her. But don't leave her yet. You have to give her time to adjust. You could have years left. You can't push her aside."

"Not even to protect her?"

"She wouldn't understand. Besides, you've had this for years, and she hasn't gotten it. And now that you know, you can take precautions."

"I'm so afraid," Paulette repeated.

"Just love her like you've been doing. We'll get through somehow."

Tears gathered in the corners of her eyes. A big drop fell and splashed on her white cheek. "Why, Ariana? Why? I can't figure it out.

I thought I was forgiven for my sins, but now I have to pay for them. And so does my family. I don't understand why!"

Those were the same thoughts that had tortured me the day before after I left the cemetery. I still didn't have an answer, so I said nothing. I stared at the floor, unable to help my best friend. Then an idea came. I knew it was the Spirit whispering to me, though I hadn't asked for aid.

"Give it time," I said. "I don't know why, but I have faith. The Lord loves you, Paulette. He does."

"Will you help me?"

I wasn't sure what she was asking. If I would help her understand? Accept? Help her with Marie-Thérèse? Or was she asking if I would help her to die? I thought I might be able to help her with the first three but never the last. I couldn't help her die; surely she wouldn't ask that.

"Whatever you need, Paulette," I heard myself saying. "I love you." I wanted to hug her but didn't dare.

She laid her head back on the pillow. "I love you, too, Ariana."

There was nothing more to say, so I turned and walked to the door. I paused. "Get better, huh? You and I have more memories to make, too."

She gave a short laugh, and to my surprise, it sounded genuine.

When I joined the others, Jean-Marc and my father had already left for work. I felt strangely deserted, though I had known all along that Jean-Marc was planning to leave after our tests. I envied him for being able to bury himself in work and thus not having to think about the possible test results.

"Is there anything we can get for you?" I asked Pierre.

He shook his head. "No. Thank you."

"I'll come back later," Louise said, "to see how she's doing."

"Thanks, Mom." Pierre kissed Marie-Thérèse and then took a few steps backwards. He pointed over his shoulder with his thumb. "I gotta get back to her now. I don't like to leave her alone."

We started slowly down the hall. The twins had overcome their temporary shyness and begun to investigate their surroundings. Accompanied by Marie-Thérèse, they darted in and out of cubbyholes, hallways, and everywhere else they could imagine. I felt like a puppet on a string, with my head jerking from side to side as I tried to keep track of the youngsters. I gave André to my mother and barely managed to stop Marc from going into another patient's room. I grabbed firm hold of my children's hands, and Louise took Marie-Thérèse's. In Louise's other hand she carried a small suitcase for my niece. Linked together, we walked to the elevator.

"Wait!"

I turned to see Nurse Giselle waving at us. We stopped and waited for her to catch up. She was breathless when she arrived, and her wiry black hair puffed about her face. With one hand she patted it down, and with the other she held up a thick booklet.

"It's nearly everything you need to know about AIDS," she said. "I find it helps when everyone in the family knows what to expect. Dispelling any misconceptions can get rid of unnecessary fears, while telling you what to look out for. For example, because HIV has been found in tears and saliva, people suppose they can be infected with the virus by getting a little fluid on them. But the truth is, you'd probably have to drink a quart or more of either liquid before you were at risk of infection. At least that's what they taught me in nursing school." She pushed the booklet into my hands. "This tells it all."

"Thank you." I meant it. Her comments about the tears were especially useful. I felt foolish now, though my fear had been real.

"Have you had many patients die?" Louise asked.

Giselle nodded, her expression sober. "Yes. I have."

"How can you stand it?"

"I make their last moments comfortable," she said. "That's all I can do. The rest is between them and God."

"Do you believe in God?" I asked. The question was instinctive for members like me, who lived in places where there wasn't a large population of Latter-day Saints.

"I do. If anything, working here has helped me to believe that."

"Why?"

"Because I see the peace most of my patients achieve before death. And on their faces after they die. Only God can give them that."

"What religion are you?" asked Louise.

Giselle smiled. Her face was sweet and innocent-looking. "Just of God. That's all."

I wanted to ask her if she had heard of our church, but she glanced at her watch. "I have to go. I need to check on Paulette and give her some medicine." She smiled again and left.

I drove home, feeling lighter than I had expected. Giselle's moving testimony of God's existence had strengthened my own, even if she wasn't a member of the Church.

Thank you, Father, for reminding me, I prayed silently.

The twins argued in the back. André in his car seat and Marie-Thérèse in front both sat silently.

"Mommy," Josette said, "Marie-Thérèse is going to live with us forever now, isn't that right? Marc doesn't believe me."

"Stop arguing now," I said firmly, glaring at them in the rearview mirror. "Marie-Thérèse will live with her parents for a long time to come. Meanwhile, she is always welcome to come to our house to play. She's part of our family."

I stopped the car at a red light as I finished speaking. Louise glanced over, and our eyes met. We both knew Paulette didn't have very long to live compared to a regular life span, even if it might seem a long time to a child. What did the future hold? What of Pierre? And what of the unborn child who might or might not have HIV? I was willing to take care of Marie-Thérèse; I loved her already as my own. But to take the responsibility of a sick infant? To place my own children at risk? I didn't know if I could do it. I couldn't even admit to myself that I didn't want to. It was too much to ask of anyone.

I sighed, pushing the thoughts away. For now, I would take one day at a time. Until the uncertainty of our own tests was over, there would be no point in planning for the future.

CHAPTER SEVEN

I was unable to function normally the rest of the morning. I found myself staring at nothing for long periods of time. When my children spoke to me, I would come out of my trance, only to realize that an hour had passed, and I couldn't remember what had kept me so absorbed.

Finally, I shook myself and concentrated on playing with the children. There were a million things I should be cleaning around the house—a pile of dirty dishes, a tower-high mound of laundry, dust and bits of paper everywhere—but they seemed unimportant now. Instead, I played the brave hero in my children's make-believe game of prince and princess, cutting down pretend foes and protecting them as I might not be able to do in reality.

Josette and Marie-Thérèse draped sheets over their heads and the lower part of their faces; Marc and André wrapped towels around their waists. André tripped repeatedly on his towel during the sword fights, but he didn't cry. He rarely did.

At noon we had a picnic lunch in the bedroom, and afterward, they fell asleep on the blanket as I read them a story. I had a twin on each arm, with André squeezed in next to Josette, his head on my stomach and his short legs thrown casually over his sister. Marie-Thérèse slept next to Josette.

I set the book down and lay back on the pillows. My arms felt stiff, but I didn't move. I wished this moment could last forever, that we would never have to face the reality of tomorrow and the dreaded test results.

I kept telling myself that I didn't feel sick. But then, neither did Pierre.

"Ariana?" Louise called softly from the hall.

"Yes?" I extracted myself carefully from the sleeping children. For all my care, André, who had been the first to sleep, awoke and held out his chubby arms. I picked him up and went into the hall.

"I'm making vegetable soup, if that's okay," Louise said. "Then I'll go back to the hospital. I'd like to take some for Paulette. That hospital food didn't look too appetizing."

"I'll help you," I said. "We'll make extra to serve with the turkey breasts I'm making for the children's dinner." Jean-Marc and I wouldn't be eating because we had begun a fast after lunch.

While we worked, Louise chattered about how Lu-Lu had changed, how she had suddenly become outspoken and had taken to staying out late.

"Maybe she's trying to find herself," I said.

Louise stopped peeling the potatoes. "I think she might be involved in drugs."

My heart must have skipped a beat because I suddenly felt dizzy. I sank abruptly to a chair, staring at André, who sat on the floor playing with a truck and a few miniature people. He wasn't much older than Nette had been when drugs had killed her.

"Will you talk to her?" Louise asked.

"Of course." But I feared it might be too late.

Jean-Marc came home before dinner that evening, carrying a huge bouquet of my favorite white roses. I was content to have him home, whatever the reason. Together we fed the children, and afterwards we washed the dishes, read the Book of Mormon, and had family prayer. Then we set up the cot we kept under Josette's bed for Marie-Thérèse and kissed each child good night. In his room, André curled up in his crib and slept immediately, but the twins seemed to take their father's presence as sign of a holiday, and it was difficult to get them and Marie-Thérèse settled. Because of the test we were more indulgent than usual, and they pushed for full advantage, even without understanding the cause. After a bathroom trip and two drinks of water each, the suddenly dehydrated children finally fell asleep.

The excitement of the evening wasn't over. Louise came home, her face more drawn and weary than I'd ever seen it. "Paulette is dying," she confirmed as we went into the sitting room. "I can see it in her eyes. I'll never forget the look; I remember it so well."

As he hugged his mother, Jean-Marc's eyes were haunted. "We'll get through this together," he murmured. "We're a family."

"Your father was in the hospital for three weeks before he died. He had the same look. Do you remember?"

"No." His whispered voice was slightly self-accusatory.

"How long does she have?" I asked. "Do they know?"

Louise sighed and sank to the couch. "The specialist can only tell me the statistics. That's one of the problems with this disease: it affects everyone differently. He did say that once AIDS sets in, most people die within three years—some a lot sooner. He worries that Paulette has had it for quite some time. Evidently, Dr. Flaubert has been treating Paulette for a variety of what he calls opportunistic infections, without recognizing what was causing the problems in the first place. She's had anemia, bacterial infections, and now pneumonia, which is the leading cause of death among AIDS patients and quite often the first symptom to develop. It wasn't the doctor's fault, really. He didn't have any reason to think she was at risk for AIDS. She never told him about being involved with drugs."

"So what does that mean? Is Paulette coming out of the hospital or not?" I asked. "What does the specialist say?"

"Dr. Medard. His name is Dr. Medard. But he doesn't know. Evidently, people with AIDS get a special kind of pneumonia. At least now that he knows what she has, he can treat it more effectively. But it depends on how far gone her body is. He believes she'll live a couple of months. Longer if she gets over this infection."

"If?" I could hardly believe what I was hearing. I had thought we would have years to come to terms with Paulette's illness.

"What about the girls?"

"Paulette's had HIV for at least six years," Louise said. "Apparently, people can have it up to eleven years before it develops into AIDS. It's transmitted through sexual intercourse, so Pierre," her face seemed to collapse, "had almost no chance to test negative. But according to the doctor, like with Marie-Thérèse, the baby has around a 30 percent chance of having the virus. Had they known sooner, they could have given Paulette a drug that helps prevent it from spreading to the fetus.

They are giving it to Paulette now, but we'll have to wait and see how the tests come out."

I hadn't been asking that question exactly; Pierre had already told me about the drug to help the baby and about it possibly taking HIV eleven years to become AIDS. What I wanted to know was who would take care of the girls when Paulette was gone. I knew Pierre wouldn't be able to do it; he would be fighting for his own life.

"Paulette's being pregnant is another difficulty," Louise continued. "They have to be careful of what they give her because some drugs can hurt the baby."

"Paulette doesn't deserve this," I said.

"No," Jean-Marc agreed. "No one does."

We sat in forlorn silence, broken only by the occasional chiming of the grandfather clock my parents had given us for our wedding.

"I guess it's time for bed," Jean-Marc finally said.

"I made up a bed for you in André's room, Louise," I said. "If Lu-Lu gets here, she can sleep on the couch bed."

"I'm going to wait up for Lu-Lu. She should be here by now. Besides, she'll need to be told." Louise's face showed her worry, one I understood well. It wasn't every day a person learned a brother was going to die. My own world had been shattered when Antoine had been killed.

We started nervously when a loud buzzing broke the silence in the corridor—someone ringing at the outside door downstairs.

"It must be Lu-Lu," Louise said.

Jean-Marc got up from the couch and shuffled to the intercom box in the hallway near the door. Static sounded as he pushed the button. "Who is it?" he asked.

I couldn't make out the answer, but another buzz signaled that Jean-Marc had pushed the button that would open the downstairs door.

"It's Lu-Lu," he confirmed as he came back into the room.

A short time later a quiet knock sounded at the door, and Jean-Marc went to open it. He returned shortly, followed by Lu-Lu. They were not alone.

"Hi, everyone," she said, giving us a wave with her hand as she stood under the arched entryway. She was a feminine version of Jean-Marc, with the same green-brown eyes as her brother. Her short figure was lean and fit, and her dark hair was cut short, similar to my own, but it was newly highlighted with red. She had a thin nose and a wide, laughing mouth. She didn't usually talk much, but I had never seen her without a smile—until tonight.

"This is Philippe Massoni." She motioned to the stranger beside her, a tall youth with shaggy brown hair and a scruffy beard. I could almost have sworn her words were slurred.

Louise stood. "What are you doing here?" She addressed the man directly, her words an accusation.

"When he heard I was flying to Paris, he decided to visit friends himself." Lu-Lu's expression was triumphant.

"We have a family crisis," Jean-Marc said stiffly, standing next to his mother. "No offense meant to you, Philippe, but we need to talk with Lu-Lu."

"But that's what I've come to tell you." Lu-Lu nearly propelled Philippe into the room. The blue eyes that marked his family as likely originating in the northern part of France were dulled, his faded jeans and T-shirt reeked of smoke, and there was a faint aroma of alcohol on his breath. I joined my husband and mother-in-law in opposing this man. I would never forget those smells; they reminded me of Jacques and of Paulette the way she had been before joining the Church. None of us was ready for Lu-Lu's next statement.

"Philippe has asked me to marry him."

We gaped in shocked silence.

"And you said?" Louise finally found her voice.

"I said yes."

"That's great," Jean-Marc said softly. "And what temple will you be getting married in?"

Lu-Lu blinked, and her defiance faded. "Uh, we don't know where or when yet. We've only decided tonight."

I saw the uncertainty in her, even if the others could not. She didn't want to marry outside the temple, but she felt she didn't have a choice. Maybe she thought her love might change Philippe; indeed, love might change him, if anything could. The only obstacle would be if Philippe didn't want to change. My father was right when he said that change had to come from within.

"Well, there's no hurry to decide anything," I said lightly. "We have a problem you need to know about."

"Is it Paulette?" Lu-Lu realized we were serious about the family crisis, that we weren't just trying to get rid of Philippe.

"Yes." I looked at Louise and Jean-Marc, but they said nothing. "She has AIDS," I said gently.

Philippe jerked, and Lu-Lu began to cry. She rushed into her mother's arms.

"Maybe I'd better go," Philippe said after her tears had subsided. He looked uncomfortable. Louise sniffed, and I knew what she thought of Philippe for running out on Lu-Lu at a time like this.

Lu-Lu didn't object. "I'll see you tomorrow." She kissed his cheek.

Philippe nodded toward me and Louise. Jean-Marc held out his hand, but Philippe hesitated.

"It's okay," Jean-Marc said. I could see his eyes glinting in the soft light of the sitting room. He had a half-smile on his face, the one he wore when he teased the twins. "We don't have the virus." He waited until Philippe took his hand. "At least we don't think we have it; we'll find out in the morning."

Philippe pulled his hand away as if he had touched hot coals and then tried to hide it by pulling on his beard.

"Silly," Lu-Lu said, smiling through her tears. "You can't get it from shaking hands."

Philippe didn't seemed convinced. He turned, and Lu-Lu walked with him to the door. "Nice to meet you," he mumbled over his shoulder.

Louise looked about ready to explode, but I cautioned her. "Let it ride for tonight," I said. "We'll decide what to do later." It wasn't really our choice, I knew. But our actions could force Lu-Lu into a quick decision—one she might regret. Lu-Lu was coming back into the room, so there was no time for further discussion. I was glad to see Louise purse her lips and say nothing.

While Jean-Marc explained the details of how we had found out about Paulette, I went to the kitchen to make hot chocolate, forgetting for a moment about our fast. It was really an excuse to escape the tense conversation in the sitting room. As the milk heated, the phone rang.

"Hello?"

"Ariana, it's me," my mother said. Her voice was rough as though from crying.

"Is something wrong?"

"I just wanted to talk with you."

"You told Father, didn't you?" I waited for a response and then prompted, "And?"

Usually my mother was full of words, but tonight I had to drag them from her.

"He got angry. Said he wouldn't allow it."

"And you said?"

"I said I was going to do it anyway, and he said that if I loved the Church more than I loved him, then I should be baptized. Then he went into his study."

I wasn't surprised; Father always retreated to his study when things didn't go as he planned. He liked to control the world around him, and he became upset when someone altered or disagreed with what he believed was right. "Give him time," I said, gently fingering one of the white roses arranged in a large vase in the middle of the table. Their sweet smell contrasted sharply with the horror that had come into our lives, and I was grateful to be reminded of beauty in the midst of our ugly reality.

"I don't have any choice, do I?" my mother said bitterly.

But she did have choices; we all did. Except Paulette.

"The Church is true!" my mother continued. "I can't deny it any longer. But I love him. We've been through everything together, and our love is stronger now than it has ever been. I can't lose him, yet I feel torn. I want to follow the Lord! Doesn't God come first?"

I was unsure what to tell her until I remembered my father's face in the cemetery. "He loves you," I said. "As much as you love him. He has to come around."

"I don't know, Ari. He's so stubborn."

"Well, so was I." We talked more, until the despair faded from her voice.

"Are you still coming over tomorrow?" I asked finally. "To be here when we find out the test results?"

"Of course. Our fighting has nothing to do with you. You're calling the hospital at nine, aren't you?"

"Yes."

"We'll be there for you."

"Thanks."

The milk had long since boiled over onto the stove and had actually put out the fire underneath the gas burner. "I have to go now, Mother. I love you. Will you remind Father about tomorrow?"

"As if he'd forget. But I'll tell him."

I hoped my request would at least force them to talk. Perhaps it might even draw them together and help my father rethink his objection to my mother's baptism. Regrettably, the thought held little hope.

I cleaned up the milk and had started to relight the burner when I remembered the fast. Guiltily, I switched off the gas and went instead to check on the children. The twins' bedroom door was ajar, and I pushed it open wider with my hand. The light from the hallway cut into the room, illuminating it enough to see my children and Marie-Thérèse sleeping peacefully in their beds.

I kissed each soft cheek, marveling at how peaceful they were, how like small angels. *How could Jean-Marc stand to be separated from them so much?* Josette opened her eyes, and her hands went up and around my neck. "I love you, Mommy."

"I love you too, honey." I kissed her again.

Next, I checked on André. He was curled under his blankets, his small head using a stuffed bear for a pillow. The twins would never have fallen asleep alone at that age; I'd had to rock them or pat their backs. But André seemed to prefer to sleep alone.

I went into the sitting room and bade good night to Louise and Lu-Lu. After helping them settle in, Jean-Marc and I retired. A short time later, Jean-Marc's soft snores came quickly and before I knew it, I drifted off to sleep. I had scarcely reached the point of oblivion when a sob reached my subconscious mind and compelled me to wake. It sounded like Josette.

I groaned and rolled from the bed, nearly falling despite the night light in the hall. Jean-Marc's eyes fluttered, but he didn't wake. He never did when the children called, or if he did, he never acknowledged it, as if he felt it was somehow strictly a mother's duty to stay up at night with the children. It hadn't bothered me until André was born, and I had spent most of the nights nursing him and still getting up with the other two. I began to resent his indifference to my dilemma. It seemed one more part of his drawing away from his family.

In the twins' bedroom, I found not Josette but Marie-Thérèse crying and clutching her doll. I sat on her bed and drew her close, rocking her until she slept. She had stayed many times before at our house, but I understood that tonight was different. It wasn't just for fun.

"Life isn't always what we expect," I murmured, stroking her cheek. "Sometimes we need to take one day at a time."

CHAPTER EIGHT

Thin light filtered in through the curtains early Tuesday morning and woke me. I had been dreaming that someone was shining a light into my eyes, but it was only the bright May sun. Birds called loudly to one another in the few trees outside our apartment building. I started and glanced at the clock radio by my bedside. It was only seven—not yet time to call the hospital.

Jean-Marc's soft laugh came from the pillow beside me. He had his elbow bent, propping up his head as he gazed at me with his laughing green-brown eyes. "You are so beautiful," he said. The love in his stare was unmistakable. "I'm so lucky to have you."

I hoped he wasn't feeling emotional because he had some tragic insight about our forthcoming test results. I rolled over next to him. "How long have you been watching me?"

He kissed my nose. "Long enough to know how much I love you."

"I love you, too." I pushed him back on the pillow and laid my head on his chest. I could hear his heart, a calm and steady thumping.

"They're up! They're up!" Marc hurled himself on the bed, yelling with abandon as only small children can do. The others followed Marc, jumping onto the bed and throwing themselves on Jean-Marc excitedly. Even Marie-Thérèse, who didn't appear to remember crying the night before, joined in the wrestling. Someone had helped André out of his crib, and he covered both Jean-Marc and me with slobbery kisses. Far from shattering our peace, the children only added to our special moment.

I loved mornings like this. They were what reminded me of why I had wanted a family in the first place, why Jean-Marc and I had fallen in love.

"I'm going to get you!" Jean-Marc snarled. The twins screamed and jumped to the other side of the bed, but André catapulted himself into his father's arms, growling like a lion cub.

"I know, I'll get Mommy!" Jean-Marc crawled over to me with André still hanging on his neck. He started to bite my arm, working his way up. "Yum, yum." He licked his lips.

"Help!" I squeaked. The twins and Marie-Thérèse were on him in an instant, pulling him off me and laughing almost hysterically when he turned and nibbled on them instead. We played for half an hour before forcing ourselves out of bed. Then I fed the children while Jean-Marc showered and dressed. Louise and Lu-Lu sat in the kitchen with us but declined to eat, and I knew that like Jean-Marc and me, they were fasting.

I was in the bathroom getting ready when the doorbell rang. "It's your parents," Jean-Marc came to tell me. I had him zip up the white dress I had chosen to wear, not only because I could bleach out any stain but because it made me feel pure, not at all like someone who might have a fatal disease.

Together we walked to the sitting room, where Lu-Lu had already made up the sofa bed and now sat silently opposite Louise. My parents still stood, both wearing serious expressions. I smiled and hugged them. There had been a time when they weren't there for me—when Antoine died—but that was all in the past.

"Let's sit and talk," I said.

But it was suddenly hard to find conversation. The minutes ticked slowly by in the oppressive silence. The grandfather clock near the window didn't miss a beat; its pendulum swung back and forth with a steady, unchanging rhythm. I seemed to have to remind myself to breathe. Only the children didn't seem affected. They ran in and out of the room, playing a game that made sense in their minds, if not in ours. Though she played with the others, Marie-Thérèse was not her normal, smiling self but withdrawn and subdued.

"It's nine, Ari. Do you want me to call?" Jean-Marc picked up the phone on the table beside the lamp near the window. It was the phone he had bought last Christmas when I complained about having only one extension in the kitchen.

"Yes," I said in a hollow voice. André toddled to the couch and

climbed into my lap. I wrapped my arms around him, and for once he
didn't struggle at being held too tightly.

My gaze flitted from my parents, to Louise, and to Lu-Lu before
settling on Jean-Marc. In the silence of the room, my breath seemed
loud.

"Yes. I'm calling for the results of my family's blood tests yesterday."
He gave the nurse the information and waited. I closed my eyes and
said a quiet prayer.

I saw the relief on his face before he spoke the words. "Negative. All
negative!" He glanced around the room at the faces of our family before
his eyes came to rest on me. "It's negative, Ari."

I smiled, feeling my lips quiver with emotion. "The phone, Jean-
Marc," I reminded him.

He stared at the receiver in his hand before understanding. He put
it to his ear. "Hello? Are you still there? Thank you. Thank you so
much!" He set the phone in its cradle and came to hug me. I met him
halfway across the room.

Louise was sobbing with relief, as was my own mother. Lu-Lu said
nothing, but tears rolled onto her cheeks.

"What do you say we go and celebrate?" my father asked, putting
his arm around me and squeezing. "An early lunch for all of us. Or a
late breakfast—whatever. I'm starved."

"That's because you've been fasting since yesterday," my mother
said.

"What!" I didn't trust what I was hearing. "I thought you didn't
believe in all that stuff."

My father's face changed color slightly, but I couldn't tell if it was
from embarrassment or anger. "I don't believe in 'all that stuff,'" he said
stiffly. "But I do believe in God. I have since before you were born."

"But he doesn't believe in baptism." My mother's voice was
resentful.

"I don't need a little water to get me to heaven," my father retorted.

"But you do," she replied.

"And I don't need to go to church every week to show I believe in
God," he continued as if she hadn't spoken. She glared at him, and he
glared right back. She opened her mouth to speak.

"Whatever made you do it, thank you," I said quickly. My mother's mouth clamped shut.

"So are we going to eat or not?" Jean-Marc said. "I take it you're treating, eh, Gèralde?"

My father slapped him on the back and chuckled. "I am, my boy, I am."

"Are we going too?" Marc asked me.

"Of course, but not in that." For the first time I noticed his clothes—a green T-shirt, purple shorts, and dark blue socks without shoes. Josette was worse, dressed in a yellow and white striped dress layered over her pink fairy princess costume, with dark blue flowered pants poking out beneath. In her hand she held two pairs of socks, one a deep red and one a light pink, and her white Sunday shoes.

"Which go better?" she asked me. "I think the red is the prettiest."

Brightest was what she should have said.

I glanced at Marie-Thérèse, who wore a pink jumpsuit. It seemed she was the only child in our family with any fashion sense. Either that or Pierre hadn't packed much variety in her little suitcase.

The men were already heading out the door. "Uh, Jean-Marc," I said, "look at *your* children."

He stopped and stared, a smile playing on his lips. "Colorful," he said finally. "But not quite right for a nice restaurant. Back into the bedroom."

It took a short time to get the children presentable. Jean-Marc tried putting on Josette's tights, but she cried because the toes weren't right. I ran from the bedroom where I was gathering diapers for André. "I'll do it," I told Jean-Marc. He seemed relieved.

Minutes later, we were ready to leave. But the joy of our good news was partially diminished as I worried about my parents. Once before, at Antoine's death, our family had been torn apart. Could my mother's love for the Church and my father's rejection of it do the same thing now?

—◦—

Once our early lunch—or breakfast, rather—was over, my father and Jean-Marc went to work. I was amazed at how much better I felt, knowing that my babies and husband were healthy, that I hadn't unknowingly given them HIV.

In the spirit of celebration, I changed from my white dress and packed a snack to take to the playground nearby. The children were exuberant, and I wished I could share their innocence.

"Will you come with us?" I asked Louise as I helped the children into their play clothes. Lu-Lu had already disappeared somewhere with the infamous Philippe.

"No, I want to wait for Lu-Lu," she said wearily.

Once outside, I breathed in the late May air appreciatively. Though the stark heat of summer was not yet upon us, the air was warm with the scent of flowers coming from the landscaped beds in front of the apartment building. I pushed André in his stroller while the twins and Marie-Thérèse skipped on ahead.

The playground wasn't very big. It featured a small sandbox filled with very fine sand surrounded by a cement barrier. To one side of this stood a swing set with two swings and a slide. Below it, the soil was covered with more sand, coarser than what was in the sandbox. That was all. Cement sidewalks with scattered benches made up the rest of the play area. There was no green anywhere. In France, grass was for decoration, not for play.

"I'm going to dig to the bottom this time." Marc's voice was determined as he started for the sandbox. "I have to know what's there."

I smiled. My brother, Antoine, and I had done the same thing at our own playground. The sand had been deep enough to reach our shoulders, the bottom paved with cement. But I wouldn't spoil the surprise. One day my son wouldn't tire of digging, and then he would discover the secret for himself.

My thoughts floated back to Paulette and AIDS. She and Pierre were both going to die! I still couldn't come to terms with it. Hadn't Paulette been forgiven for her terrible past? I had always believed that the Atonement was expansive enough to cover any sin, no matter how grave, aside from murder and denying the Holy Ghost. Any sin. The Savior suffered the pain Paulette bore now and also that which was to come. Then why did she have to go through the agony as well?

For the first time since my marriage, I had a serious question that I was unable to answer with any Church doctrine I was familiar with.

"Mom, it's raining!" Josette tugged on my sleeve.

So it was! I looked up and saw André in the sandbox, sitting contentedly in the large hole Marc had made. With chubby fingers, he patted a large handful of sand into his hair. My oldest son was now building a mountain or a volcano, his goal to reach the bottom of the sandbox discarded for another day. Marie-Thérèse sat on a swing, staring at the sand, her rag doll in her lap.

The rain fell faster, and soon the warm cement was dotted with dark spots where the drops hit and splashed. I breathed in the pungent smell of the wet pavement. I loved the smell now, though once I had despised it for the memories of death it had brought. Those days were over, replaced now by new experiences. A fleeting memory came to mind of a romantic evening when Jean-Marc and I had slept in the rain on a roofless balcony in a hotel near the ocean where we had gone on business several months after our wedding. That was the night I was sure the twins had been conceived. The recollection filled me with tenderness.

Marc began to dance in the rain. Marie-Thérèse left the swing and ran over to him, laughing. André stood up in his hole and fell down again, a smile on his face. Yes, the rain could be a marvelous thing.

I took Josette's hand and whirled her around. She laughed. The others came to join us—even André, who didn't trust his legs on the sand and came crawling.

The smell of wet cement was stronger now as we danced and laughed. The other mothers in the playground were hustling their children away, but we stayed. It was warm, and I saw no danger in letting them play. At least Marie-Thérèse was smiling.

We were soaked by the time we reached the outer door to our building—and covered in wet sand. We stomped off as much as we could outside, but still the children's faces sported adorable splotches of sand, especially André, who wore it in his hair as well.

On the eighth floor, Louise opened the apartment door for us. "Goodness, I didn't realize it was raining! Come on. Let's get you in the bath." She led the children down the hall. I began to follow her, but she stopped me. "Lu-Lu's in the sitting room. Could you talk to her, please?"

"Okay." Something was up. Louise appeared ill, worse than when I had left the apartment. It was as if she had reached the level where she couldn't cope with anything more. I felt sorry for her, and it was an odd sensation. She had always been so strong.

"You're back," Lu-Lu said to me. "That's good. I have something to ask you."

"What is it?" Because I was wet, I didn't sit next to her on the flow-ered sofa. As it was, the sand still clinging to my pant legs tumbled to the carpet. I grimaced.

"I want you to help me plan my wedding."

What! When she had talked about marriage the night before, I had assumed she meant months from now. "When are you planning it for?"

"Next week."

"What's the hurry? Are you pregnant?" I regretted the words imme-diately as I saw her eyes narrow defensively.

"Of course not!" Then more calmly she said, "Paulette's dying," as if that explained everything.

"So you have to get married now?"

She stood up and paced in front of the sofa. "She's going to die. It could be me. It could be Philippe. We have to use what time we have left." She sounded hysterical.

I stepped closer and put my hands on her shoulders, staring into her eyes. "Lu-Lu, you can't live in fear. None of us can. That's not the Lord's way. Fear is of the devil. Now, I'm not saying you shouldn't marry Philippe, but you need to give us all time. Especially your mother."

"She doesn't want me to get married."

"She's just had a severe shock. Her son and daughter-in-law are going to die within years and possibly the baby will, too. Besides us, you're all she has for certain, and by marrying out of the temple, you're going against everything she's ever believed is right. Look at her; she needs time. *You* need time. Don't rush the most important decision you will ever make."

"What if there is no tomorrow for Philippe and me?"

"That's what's so miraculous about marrying in the temple," I said. "Tomorrow will always be there for you, whether in this life or the next."

"So you won't help me?" she asked, her jaw tightening.

"Of course I will. But let's give it more time and do it right. Let your family get through this first crisis. You owe us that at least."

Her face wrinkled in sudden understanding. "Oh, Ari, I'm being selfish, aren't I?"

I smiled. "Yes, but I understand. I remember how I felt when I first thought I was in love."

"With your first husband?"

"Yes. It was a desperate sort of love—quite different from the stronger, more assured love I have for Jean-Marc. It's . . . well, it's eternal. It's hard to explain. Things aren't perfect, but I'll never give up."

Lu-Lu's expression was thoughtful. "I guess we could wait a few months. That would give Mother time to come around."

"And time for us to get to know Philippe. Perhaps we could even get him to listen to the missionary discussions."

"I'd never dare ask!"

That made me laugh. "Silly Lu-Lu! Here you are, all set to marry a man who doesn't even know what you believe in. Never mind—you forget that your family has three returned missionaries. We'll teach him ourselves."

She hugged me. "Thank you, Ari. I'm so glad I can count on you."

"There's just one thing," I said. "I've noticed a change in you. Some of it I think is good, but some of it—" I didn't know how to continue, so I blurted it out. "Lu-Lu, are you taking drugs?"

Her gaze dropped to the floor. "I tried it," she said hesitantly. "But since I found out about Paulette . . . don't worry, I won't do it ever again."

I believed her. Relief hit me, clean and pure in the midst of turmoil. "I hope not," I said, just in case. "That's one thing none of us can tolerate. It's too dangerous."

"I know that now." Her voice was a whisper.

I left her and went to shower and change. In the bathroom, Louise was still washing the children's heads. "Well, did she tell you what she was planning?" she asked.

I nodded. "But she's agreed to wait for a few months."

Louise sighed. "Thank heaven!" Then she shook her head and blinked her eyes as if trying to keep the tears at bay. "I don't know what to do, Ari. It seems as if I'm losing everything. What am I going to do?"

I grabbed her soapy hands. "Believe, for one thing," I said. My own tears began in my sore eyes. "I don't know the answer to everything, like why Paulette and Pierre have HIV, but I do know God lives and that families are eternal. Let's just cling to that for now."

She held my hands tightly. "But what about Lu-Lu?"

I set my jaw as stubbornly as Lu-Lu had set hers. "We have to give Philippe a chance, for Lu-Lu's sake. We'll teach him so much that he'll be baptized or be scared away!"

Louise laughed through her tears. "Of course. Of course," she said.

The children laughed with us, without knowing why. All but Marie-Thérèse, who simply watched us. My heart ached for her, but I didn't know how to soothe her hurt.

After the bath, Louise and Lu-Lu took Marie-Thérèse for a short visit with her parents. I knew I should go, but I was afraid of seeing the death in Paulette's eyes, so I simply made the excuse of having no one to stay with the children. Louise, Lu-Lu, and Marie-Thérèse returned in time for dinner. I served cake for dessert and was rewarded by a smile from my niece.

I had expected Jean-Marc to come home early that night, but he didn't. The children were long in bed, as were Louise and Lu-Lu, before he arrived. The rain had fallen steadily, sounding out a steady and comforting beat on the window. It washed the world clean, as it had me for a brief time that afternoon.

"Hi, Ari." Jean-Marc took me in his arms.

"How did work go?" I decided not to badger him about working late. He was dealing with things in the way that fit him best. I could at least give him that much.

"Good. We settled the Augustin account. And you?"

Unbidden, tears came to my eyes. "We danced in the rain."

His gaze was tender. "You did? I wish I could have been there."

"Me too."

CHAPTER NINE

*T*win shouts filled the silence of the early morning, awakening me from a sound sleep. I yawned and reached out to touch the space beside me. It was empty. The sound of water in the shower, echoing like a torrent of rain, came to my ears so I knew Jean-Marc couldn't hear the twins' complaints. I stretched again and opened my eyes, squinting slightly against the white light streaming in from the curtained window. In the streets below, I could hear the occasional car passing our building.

It seemed too quiet outside, contrasting with the loud children's voices coming from the hall, and a shiver crept up my spine. I snuggled down in my soft blankets, but the warmth didn't take away the sinister chill that seemed to shroud my heart.

The screaming had diminished, but a loud bumping sound forced me out of bed and into the twins' room next door. What had they done now? I sighed when I saw that Marc had pulled the small bookcase down upon himself. Sometimes that child was impossible.

"Marc yelled at us," Josette said, holding tightly to Marie-Thérèse's hand. "And he threw books on the floor again."

I saw that he was unhurt. "Marc Perrault—" I began, but Louise came to his rescue.

"I have breakfast ready," she said, entering the room. "And Pierre's on the phone for you." She looked at the mess of books on the floor. "Don't worry. We'll take care of this right now." She stared at Marc purposefully, and his ever-ready grin vanished.

"But I hurt myself," he protested.

"You're really going to get hurt if you don't pick up those books," Louise threatened mildly. She was used to little boys' excuses and didn't have memories of my brother to cloud her judgment. I tried to hide a smile as Marc quickly grabbed a handful of thin books.

I escaped down the hall and picked up the phone. "Hello?"

"Ariana, can you come to the hospital?" Pierre's voice was calm and oddly detached, yet I could tell he was agitated. There was a quiet desperation inside that rang out as clearly as if he had been screaming.

"What's wrong?" I felt the chill in my heart return.

"It's Paulette; she's taken a turn for the worse. Please, can you come? And bring Marie-Thérèse."

"We'll be right there," I said without hesitation. Paulette was my best friend, and she needed me.

I dressed hurriedly in the white dress of the day before, not stopping to shower or put on makeup. After a quick family prayer, I kissed the twins and André and left them with Louise. Marie-Thérèse held my hand, and with the other she carried the ever-present rag doll. On her face was a wistful smile.

Jean-Marc rode with me in the elevator. "Call if you need me," he said, kissing me good-bye.

"I will." But I completely dismissed the thought. Most likely I wouldn't be able to reach him.

When we entered Paulette's private room, I was sorry I had brought the child. Paulette's condition had noticeably worsened. She lay once more on her side, eyes clenched tight, breath rasping in and out in a grisly pattern, despite the oxygen tube. Marie-Thérèse's smile dimmed, and her large eyes became frightened again.

Pierre stood up and met us halfway across the room, swooping up his little daughter and hugging her. "I missed you," he said, rubbing his unshaven face against her cheek.

She didn't smile. "I missed you, too." She glanced over his shoulder at Paulette. "And Mommy. When is she coming home?"

Pierre sighed. "I don't know yet, honey."

"Is something different today?" I asked, choosing my words carefully so as not to frighten Marie-Thérèse any more than necessary.

Pierre didn't mince his words. "It's the baby. Dr. Medard thinks he could treat her much better if she weren't pregnant. He says her only chance might be to abort the baby. He thinks her life expectancy would be better."

I stared at him. *Abort the baby! How could it come to this?* "And if she doesn't?"

Pierre hugged his daughter close as he replied so softly I scarcely heard the words. "He's afraid she'll never recover from the pneumonia."

Before I could fully digest his words, a feeble voice came from the bed. "Marie-Thérèse?"

"Mommy!" The little girl wriggled from her father's grasp and ran to her mother. Paulette reached out her thin arms and hugged Marie-Thérèse the best she could in her reclining position, struggling to control her grimace of pain.

"How's my baby?" Paulette asked.

"I'm not a baby!"

Paulette smiled. "I can see that. Did you have fun at Aunt Ariana's?"

Marie-Thérèse nodded. "We played tiger with Uncle Jean-Marc yesterday, and last night we had cake and played princess. Do you think I'm pretty as a princess, Mommy?"

"No, you're much prettier than a princess."

Marie-Thérèse smiled, the first real one since we'd danced in the rain the day before. She climbed onto the chair and sat swinging her legs.

"Are you being a good girl?" Pierre asked.

Marie-Thérèse nodded. "I played in the rain, though. I forgot to tell you yesterday."

"If Aunt Ariana let you, then I'm sure it's all right," Paulette said.

Marie-Thérèse beamed. "I love you, Mommy." She leaned forward and touched her mother's lips with a tiny finger and then closed her fist and put it against her little chest.

"I love you, too. So much." Paulette touched Marie-Thérèse's lips and brought the hand to her heart.

Both smiled. I recognized this as a ritual they had done many times before, perhaps at bedtime. The twins had gone through a similar phase the year before, and it had intensified when André was born, as if they needed reassurance of my love. Marie-Thérèse needed such solace now.

"Hey, do you want to go get an ice cream with Daddy?" Pierre asked, patting his rounded belly. "There's a vendor on the corner, and I need to stretch my legs."

Marie-Thérèse nodded. "I'll be right back, Mommy. Don't worry," she said.

Paulette laughed weakly. "Okay, I won't. But don't be gone too long, or I'll miss you."

Marie-Thérèse's face crinkled in a wide smile. She waved and put her hand in her father's.

I walked to the bed and sank to the chair. Paulette looked at me as I took her hand. Thanks to Giselle and the booklet I had devoured over the past few days, I was not so fearful of contracting HIV. Casual touching would not pass the infection. Not even tears or kissing had ever been known to communicate the disease. I had worried for nothing.

"Did Pierre tell you?" she asked.

"About the doctor wanting to abort the baby?"

She nodded. "How can I do something like that? The scriptures say 'Thou shalt not kill.' I feel this baby moving. I know she's alive. And I love her!"

"It sounds like you've made your decision."

Her face seemed more gray than white, as if she had aged in the past week. "I did a lot of things before I joined the Church, Ari. But never murder. I thought I had been forgiven—perhaps not, in light of this disease—but how could I ever be forgiven for killing my baby? I won't do it."

"Not even to save your life?"

She snorted. "I'm dying anyway, Ari. It's only a matter of time." She turned her face into the pillow and hiccupped softly. I smoothed her long hair, wishing I could soothe her pain instead.

"Pierre wants me to do it," she said.

I started. "What?"

"He wants me to abort the baby. He says I need to stay with him and Marie-Thérèse for as long as I can. How can he say that?" Her voice had tears in it, though her eyes were dry. "I don't want to leave them."

"He loves you. He's afraid of living without you."

She nodded slowly. "And perhaps of dying without me. I would be even more afraid if he weren't here." Her face had softened, but now it became resolute. "But he's not thinking about the baby. She deserves a chance to live. How can I take that away? Then they tell me the odds are high that she'll have HIV and that I'll spare her the suffering later. That's what everybody says." She gave a short, bitter laugh. "Kill her now so she won't suffer later. It doesn't make much sense to me—

especially because there is still a chance she won't be infected. I know they're afraid I'm going to die right away if I don't do this, but I can't kill her. I won't." She looked up, eyes pleading. "You'll support me, won't you? You understand."

And I did. "I think I might do the same thing," I said. But how hard it would be! To sacrifice some of my remaining time with my children and husband on the chance of a new life that could be as damaged as my own. "It's the only choice you could make."

"That's what I think," she said. "And I've had a lot of time to consider it." She shifted her position slightly, grimacing, but staying on her side. I knew the doctor was worried about the blood supply to the baby and had ordered Paulette off her back, but the side position was more painful for the pleurisy in her chest.

"You know, the irony of this whole situation would be that the baby will have HIV and I will have killed her anyway, as I have Pierre. In that light, I am already a murderer."

"No, Paulette. No!" I squeezed her hand tightly. "You didn't know you had AIDS; how could you? You wouldn't have infected any of your family if you'd had a choice. It's not the same as murder. Some things we simply can't change, and it's no one's fault. It just is. Like Antoine's death and even Nette's. Nobody wanted them to happen."

"If I hadn't done drugs, none of this would be happening, would it?" Her voice was bitter. "And now it's too late." Tears slid down her cheeks, sluggishly, as if afraid to reach the sharp curve of her jaw. My own face was wet, though I didn't know when the tears had begun. "It's like the scriptures say," she added. "The sins of the parents will be visited upon the heads of the children. My poor baby!"

"I don't know what to tell you, Paulette. I wish I did. But one thing I know is that the Lord loves you. Can you try to hold on to that?"

She nodded. "I'll try. But I'm so afraid. Please," she tightened her grasp on my hand, "don't let me give in and agree to abort the baby! It's not worth it. Please talk to Pierre."

"I will. You just concentrate on making yourself well enough to go home. We're all pulling for you."

As if she hadn't heard me, Paulette lay with her eyes open, staring into space and saying nothing. Then she abruptly focused on my face.

"Your tests. Louise told me they were negative. Were they really, or was she just trying to protect me?" Her voice held dread.

"They were all negative." I was afraid to show my happiness at the fact because it only seemed to emphasize her tragedy.

But Paulette gave a cry of relief, and a fresh batch of tears erupted. "Oh, thank God! Oh, thank you, God!" Her eyes shut tight in prayer, squeezing out more tears. Her reaction proved what kind of a person she was. In her position, I might feel embittered that my friend was free of the disease while I had to suffer. Paulette's honest face showed no such lowly emotion.

"I'm so sorry, Paulette," I said. "I wish more than anything that you didn't have to go through this."

The torrent of tears seemed to abate slightly. "I know, Ari. I know. I'm so grateful I won't have to do this alone. And that my little girl is taken care of and loved."

"She is and always will be," I promised.

"Thank you."

"No, don't thank me. We are friends, sisters. There's nothing more to it."

I stayed with her until she drifted off to sleep and then went to find Pierre. I didn't know what I would say to him, but for Paulette, I had to try.

I found him on the sidewalk in front of the hospital. Both Marie-Thérèse and he were leaning against the rock and cast-iron fence surrounding the perimeter of the hospital grounds, finishing their ice cream. Pierre had only the sugar cone left. Marie-Thérèse had nearly the whole thing but worked at it steadily. She giggled at something her father said, and I smiled wistfully; she was too young to lose her mother and father both.

The afternoon sun was warm against my back, and the cloudless blue sky showed no sign of rain. The sidewalk had few people on it; most would be at their jobs. The traffic seemed heavy as usual, though without the intensity it usually projected. In all, it was a beautiful day in Paris. If only . . .

I shook away the yearning for what couldn't be and walked steadily toward them. "Didn't buy me one, huh?"

They turned. Pierre's smile subsided. "You left her alone?"

"She's asleep. But I made sure the nurse would check in on her. Giselle was coming on shift, and she assured me that Paulette is well monitored."

Pierre's face relaxed, but nevertheless he began walking toward the hospital. I stretched my legs to catch up to him, and Marie-Thérèse skipped on ahead. "She's a good one, Giselle is," he reflected. "We couldn't have asked for a better nurse. She really cares, and she can get Paulette to do things I can't."

"Like have an abortion?"

His face fell, and his lips twisted downward until I wondered if they would fall from his face completely. "She told you I wanted her to abort it, didn't she?"

"*Her,*" I emphasized mildly. "The ultrasound says the baby's a girl. And, yes, Paulette told me you wanted to abort her."

He stopped walking and faced me. Again, I was struck with the similarity between him and Jean-Marc. The eyes were brown, yes, and his voice deeper, but beneath the growing whiskers, he had the same curve of the face and similar expressions. "It's only to save her life. Or to extend it, at least. I don't want to be without her. And it's not fair to deprive the child we do have for one not yet born."

"What about the baby?"

"It's not real to me. Paulette is," he said brusquely.

"But she is real to Paulette. She's been hoping for this child for three years, and she already loves her. She feels her kicking and knows she trusts in her. You're asking Paulette to kill her baby. Don't you see, Pierre? This isn't about me, or you, or even Marie-Thérèse. This is about Paulette and the baby. And if you force her to do what she feels is wrong, then she will have no reason to fight for life, especially when she feels she's already killed you."

His jaw worked convulsively, and his eyes glistened with tears. "She said that?"

I nodded. "Yes. She needs you. And you've got to be there for her."

"How?" he croaked. "I can't let her die."

"It isn't in our hands, is it?"

His gaze was desolate, but I thought I saw a glimmer of acceptance. "And if the baby is born sick, too?"

"Then we'll deal with it when the time comes. We're all here for you—your family, that is. But for now, let's concentrate on getting Paulette home and the baby here safely."

His eyes seemed to lose their wild look. I had done the best I knew how; I could only pray it was the right thing.

We began walking again, catching up to Marie-Thérèse, who waited at the hospital doors, finishing her ice cream. Pierre threw the rest of his cone away and faced me again. "I'd like to keep Marie-Thérèse here with me for a while. Do you think you could come pick her up before dinner?"

"Of course. Either I or your mother will come."

He nodded. "Thank you. The doctor said in the next twenty-four hours we should know what's going to happen, one way or the other. She'll either start getting better or she'll get worse. I—I wanted Marie-Thérèse to spend some time with her in case—" He broke off.

"I understand. And plan on going home to shower or something when we come tonight. We'll sit with Paulette. You need a break."

He rubbed at his face. "I showered last night when Mom came, but I guess I could use a shave."

"Can't have you scaring the nurses now, can we?"

He smiled bleakly. "I guess not. Come on, Marie-Thérèse. Let's go see Mommy." He held out his hand, and she grabbed it trustingly. He took a few steps and then stopped and faced me again.

"Thanks, Ariana." He paused, gathering his thoughts. "You know, I think women must have a special way of seeing things. Giselle believes Paulette should fight for the baby as well, though she didn't say as much aloud. I felt it without her saying anything." He cocked his head back as if pondering something of great importance. When he spoke, his voice was rich and admiring, yet it also held a trace of stark torment. "What is it about women that they can risk their lives to have children? Even in a regular pregnancy, they spend so much time sick and uncomfortable and then have to go through labor. What is it about women that makes them this special? What is it about my Paulette? She's closer to the Savior than I'll ever be. She's willing to die for this baby, as He died for us. I know it's not the same thing, but surely it's as close as a mortal could come." His voice cracked, and the glistening in his eyes became large tears, dropping onto his cheeks. "She is one of the purest people I know, yet she is sure she deserves this disease because of her past. To her, it's the only explanation."

He looked at me, eyes beseeching. "You're good at helping me understand things; perhaps you can help Paulette understand the reason for the AIDS. Please."

I wanted to reassure him, but I couldn't understand it myself. It wasn't as if Paulette was someone who had refused the gospel and who continued joyfully in a contemptible lifestyle. While such people also didn't deserve an agonizing death, it was at least understandable. But she had repented, been married in the temple, and been faithful to all her covenants. Why her? The Lord had the power to save her; why didn't He?

"I'll try," I said woodenly. "I'll think of some way to explain."

Maybe then I would understand it myself.

CHAPTER TEN

I took a detour on the way home, stopping at the café to tell Marguerite and Jules about Paulette. I didn't admit to myself that the reason I was going was to find comfort and perhaps an answer to my question about why Paulette had contracted AIDS.

"I know about the AIDS," Marguerite said. "Your mother called me last Sunday. I haven't told anyone else. I don't really know what to say. It's just like what happened to Michelle."

"Michelle had AIDS?" It seemed that each time we talked about her daughter, I learned something new, something she had held back from me.

Marguerite nodded grimly and leaned over the counter closer to me. "Her body was unable to fight the pneumonia, and she died. It's the most common killer of AIDS patients."

It wasn't what I had come to hear.

Marguerite sighed. "Oh, I'm sorry, Ariana. You didn't want to know that, did you? I'm sorry. It's just such a shock." She came from behind the counter and hugged me. I laid my head on her ample shoulder, fighting tears.

"I want to know why," I murmured. "Why?"

She shook her head, and a few more wisps of gray hair strayed from her bun. "I wonder if we will ever fully understand until we are resurrected."

The bell hanging over the door tinkled, and a group of young people entered. I recognized most of them as youth from our ward. School must have let out, and Marguerite's place was their hangout.

"Hi, Sister Perrault!" they called out as they crowded around the counter, gazing hungrily down at the array of breads and confections. I had been the Young Women's president for more than four years before being released after having André, so I knew most of them by name.

As I greeted them, I couldn't help thinking how different Paulette's life would have been if she had been raised in the Church. They appeared so clean, happy, radiant. They knew why they were on earth and where they were going. Maybe faithful parents could have taught Paulette the dangers of drugs. Maybe she wouldn't have AIDS now. She was every bit as worthy as these young people; why didn't she have a chance?

"I've got to get back to the children," I said abruptly.

Marguerite nodded. "Let me know if I can do anything."

"I will." I turned to go, but her voice stopped me.

"Uh, Ariana?"

"Yes?"

"Do you think she'd like a visit? We didn't know with Michelle until it was too late. I'd like to be there for Paulette."

I smiled. There had been a time, long before either Marguerite or Paulette had been baptized, that Marguerite hadn't approved of Paulette. Yet in the last year or so, they had become good friends. "Of course. She'd love to have you. I think it would mean something to her for you to visit."

There was a flurry of queries from the group surrounding the counter, but I escaped and left Marguerite to deal with it. I had told enough people about Paulette's AIDS already, and each time brought the painful questions.

Next I drove to the cemetery. It was the fourth Wednesday of the month and around my usual time of visiting, but my father was nowhere in sight.

"Paulette's dying," I whispered into the air. The sun shone through the leaves of the large trees lining the cobblestone pathway, leaving a dappled design on the tombstones. The pattern changed as a light wind rippled through the leaves, making it seem to dance across the stones and the short-cropped grass.

Today the cemetery held no answers for me, standing only as a bitter reminder that Paulette's body would soon be resting here. As usual, I knelt down and traced Antoinette's name with a light finger.

"I love you, Nette," I said softly. With a quick wave at my brother's stone, I abandoned the suddenly oppressive silence, leaving the dead to their rest.

Still I didn't go home. The Seine seemed to call to me, and I drove near the Quai de Montebello and the booksellers' stalls. Leaving the car, I crossed the quay and walked through the crowd. I paused, looking over some of the wares: magazines, old prints, engravings, maps, and, of course, books. They sold a variety of other items, some simply junk. The tourists ate it up, but I could also spot a serious collector or two among the crowd, scrutinizing each box for the treasures they might occasionally contain.

Turning my back on the stalls, I stood staring down at the water from the stone wall rising far above the bank. The waves crashed against the sides as a huge boat passed by.

"The water is us," said a voice beside me.

I jerked my head up to see Paulette's mother. On her thin figure she wore a sleeveless summer dress of fluorescent yellow, and her face was painted with more makeup than necessary. Her dark blonde hair wasn't greasy today; in fact, it looked as if it had just been washed. But her eyes still had the unfocused stare I knew to be related to drugs. Anger bubbled inside my heart. This woman should have taught Paulette better. It was her fault Paulette was dying.

"How's that?" My voice was clipped, my face stony.

"The water is us," she repeated. "We're helpless against the trials that come. We can't push them away; we can only go where we're pushed. What good is life when we can't control anythin'?" The desperation in her voice softened my anger, but then she fumbled in a worn brown bag she had slung over her shoulder and grasped a few thin cigarettes. She shoved one into her mouth and drew a great breath, holding it inside for a while before expelling the smoke through her nose. It was an appalling sight, and my heart hardened once again.

"Paulette has AIDS," I said without preamble.

I saw the pain etched on her face and immediately felt sorry, but her response surprised me. "I know." She gazed at the water, and tears trickled down her worn cheeks.

"How?"

"I went to see her. She was sleepin', but a man was there. Her husband, I guess. I didn't go in, but I talked to a nurse—Giselle, I think. Nice girl. When I said who I was, she told me about Paulette."

Now I understood the remark Simone had made about the water.

We were all helpless to change Paulette's condition. My estimation of Simone changed; she did care about Paulette, despite the apathy she had shown when I first went to visit.

"When did you go?"

"Tuesday. Yesterday." She flicked ashes from the cigarette. A few wafted below to the walkway next to the river, and some landed on the stone wall. She brushed them off nervously.

"She's become worse," I said. "They want her to abort the baby."

Simone became more agitated. "Is she goin' to do it?"

"No. But Pierre is afraid she may die sooner because of it."

She closed her eyes. "Some things are worth dyin' fer."

I believed that, but it seemed odd coming from this woman whose lifestyle was so utterly different from mine.

"Are you going to see her again?" I asked to cover my surprise.

"What would I say?"

In her eyes I saw guilt; she knew she was partly at fault. With this insight, my anger dissipated completely. I turned to her. "We can't change this situation, we can only be there for her. For the time she has left."

A flash of gratitude sparked in her eyes. "The nurse said Pierre has it too, but my granddaughter don't. What will happen to her?"

"Pierre may not get sick for a while, but when he does, she'll have a home with me, if that's what Paulette and Pierre want."

"Good. Yer the best one fer the job. You was always good to Paulette, Ariana. Even when ya had a right not to be. I thank ya fer that."

I felt uncomfortable with her thanks. Besides, I wasn't the best one for the job of Marie-Thérèse's mother; Paulette was.

"What about the baby?" Simone said.

"What about her?"

"Will ya take her, too?"

I wanted to say yes, but in reality my decision would depend on if the baby was sick or not. How could I risk an HIV-positive baby constantly around my other children? A simple cut could pass on the virus. It was too much risk. Besides, how could I take care of a sick child without neglecting the others? Jean-Marc certainly was not around to help, and even when he was, I took care of them during the times they were sick or cranky. With four small children to care for, I couldn't do any more. I couldn't.

"It depends on a lot of things," I said ambiguously. "Louise, Pierre's mother, might be able to help take care of her, especially if she has the virus."

"Maybe I can help too, if ya want," Simone said almost eagerly. "I have two days off from waitin' at the bar. Each week, I mean."

Could she be trying to atone for her mistakes? "It's all really up to Paulette," I said. "And she could have years left to decide. We need to pray for her to get well. Regardless, you need to go see her."

"Maybe." Simone turned her face away and leaned over the stone wall. I followed suit. We stood in silence as a fresh breeze drifted up from the water and whispered through our hair. My white dress swirled around my knees.

"How do ya watch yer daughter die?" Simone said, her voice so soft I barely heard the words.

I understood too well what she was saying. Every time I saw Paulette, I wanted to run away and hide. But another experience kept me returning to visit her. I hadn't been there when Nette died, and the guilt I felt at not being with her had been overwhelming. At least I would be there for Paulette, as I hadn't been for Nette.

"Better to be there than not," I replied. "How do you forgive yourself for not holding her during her last moments and saying how much you love her? You have the chance to help your daughter into the next world, as I didn't. Don't miss it, Simone."

Her light eyes met mine, watery but decided. "Yer right, Ariana."

She left me then, and I wandered back to my car. I had already been gone much longer than I had planned, but I didn't hurry. For me everything seemed to slow down, though logically I knew it was probably my own wish to stop Paulette from dying that made each moment stand alone. If only I could stop time!

When I returned to the house, Louise went to visit Paulette and pick up Marie-Thérèse. I began dinner early, with the twins dancing around my feet. Even the normally self-sufficient André played with his toys in front of the stove, wanting to be near me, and I tripped on them each time I passed. Finally, I'd had enough. "Go to your room!" I shouted. "I'm trying to make dinner."

Marc stared at me, and tears welled up in Josette's eyes. André ignored me completely.

"Mommy, are you mad at us? Don't you love us anymore?" my daughter asked.

"Are you going to the hospital again? Can we go next time?" Marc added.

I sighed and sank to the floor to put my arms around them. *How did they always know how to get my attention?*

"The hospital is not really a place for children," I explained.

Josette sniffed. "But Marie-Thérèse goes every day."

"She has to visit her mother."

"What do you do there?" Marc asked.

"Well, what do you think I'm doing?"

"Getting more tests like when the nurse took our blood. Are you sick?" he asked.

I thought I was getting to the bottom of the twins' concern. "Are you afraid Mommy's going into the hospital to stay like Aunt Paulette?" Both nodded, and I hugged them tightly. "Well, I'm not. I promise." I had thought the twins were too young and too removed from the situation to really understand it. I believed their innocence would protect them, but it seemed I was wrong. They could feel pain and worry. It wasn't only Marie-Thérèse we had to safeguard but the twins as well.

I let the dinner sit and went with them to their room, where we played prince and princess. Only occasionally did I find myself losing concentration and wondering how Paulette was doing. I wished Jean-Marc was home to talk things out with me. I almost went to the phone to call, but it wouldn't do any good. They never seemed to know where he was these days.

Louise came home with Marie-Thérèse barely an hour after we had eaten dinner. Her eyes were red and swollen, her face drawn with anxiety. She waited until Marie-Thérèse was playing with the twins before motioning to me. I scooped up André and the pajamas I was putting on him and followed. Louise's steps dragged in the hall, her shoulders hunched as if a massive weight pressed down on her. Paulette's sickness was taking its toll on everyone.

"Paulette's getting worse," she said when we reached the sitting room. "Pierre's beside himself. He doesn't look good."

I paused with André's shirt half over his head. He struggled, and I finished pulling it down quickly. Before I could speak, the apartment door opened.

"Ari?"

"In here, Jean-Marc."

At least he is home in time to kiss the children good night. The cynical thought struck me by surprise. I thought I had begun to accept the situation with his work. *Change yourself,* I thought, remembering my father's words. *You can't change other people.*

Jean-Marc kissed me, taking stock of our glum faces. "What's wrong?"

Louise explained while I pulled on André's pajama bottoms. Jean-Marc slumped to the couch beside me. "Why didn't you call me at work?"

I wrinkled my face at him. "What for? They never know where you are."

A shadow passed over his face, and I could feel his defenses going up. "I was at my desk all day," he said.

Louise coughed. "What are we going to do about Paulette?"

"What can we do?" I asked. "I've been praying, but—"

"Let's begin a family and ward fast," Jean-Marc said. "We can't save Paulette's life in the long run, but she doesn't have to die now. We'll call the bishop and home teachers and give her a blessing. Maybe together we'll have enough faith."

Is that what this was all about? Faith? If so, then my attitude needed changing. I was too busy questioning the Lord for allowing Paulette to have AIDS to have time to pray with faith.

"But she's had a blessing," I said. "Pierre gave her one."

"Then she needs another one," my husband said. "I remember reading that in the early days of the Church, when the elders went to preach the gospel, it was sometimes necessary for them to have blessings each hour to help them through the heavy blizzards. It's no different with Paulette. The first blessing got her through a few days, and now she needs another one for this new ordeal."

Within minutes we were on the phone with the bishop and then with the home teachers and visiting teachers, who would get the message out to the ward. While Jean-Marc finished calling, I read the children a story and put them to bed. Then I called my mother to come and baby-sit while we went to the hospital. Lu-Lu, with her new fiancé tagging along, arrived in the midst of our departure.

Jean-Marc put his arm around the taller Philippe and propelled him back to the door. "So glad you could come, Philippe. And of course we want you to come to the hospital with us. It's about time you met the rest of our family." Philippe started to protest, but Jean-Marc continued, "No, I insist. Don't be shy. If you and Lu-Lu are going to be married, you might as well see how we Mormons operate. We're going to give Paulette a blessing right now."

I had told him my idea of either baptizing Philippe or scaring him away, but I thought he might be overdoing it. Still, Lu-Lu was his sister; he would fight for her as he saw fit.

As Lu-Lu watched Jean-Marc with Philippe, a smile covered her face. "See? I told you my family would try to accept this, Philippe. Let's go with them to the hospital." Under so much pressure, he had no choice but to agree.

I was about to follow them out the door when I remembered Paulette's mother. I went to the phone and called information for her number and then placed the call. I didn't have much hope of reaching her, because her phone had been disconnected, but I prayed silently.

The phone rang, and before it chimed a second time, Simone picked it up. "Hello?" Her voice sounded perplexed.

"It's me, Ariana. Paulette's worsened again, and we're going to the hospital to give her a blessing from the elders in our church. Please, will you meet us there?"

"I don't know."

"It might be the last time you see her," I said bluntly.

"I didn't know my phone was workin' again," she said, as if talking to herself.

"Well?" I waited impatiently. Already the others were in the hall, holding the elevator for me.

"I'll be there." She sounded surprised even as she spoke.

"Good." I hung up the phone and ran out the door. I stepped inside the elevator, waving a farewell to my mother who stood watching. My hand paused at seeing her face, but my momentum forced me into the elevator with the others, and the door closed. What had I seen on her face? She had appeared drawn and tired, but there was something more—a haunting sadness that had nothing to do with Paulette.

We arrived at the hospital at nearly eight-thirty. A nurse with a wide nose and chipmunk cheeks barred the entrance to Paulette's room. "Not so many people tonight. She's in a bad way. Besides, visiting hours are almost over."

"But we have to see her," Jean-Marc said.

"All of you?" The nurse's eyes widened as she saw our bishop and Paulette's home teachers come up behind us. They nodded and smiled their greetings.

"All of us," Jean-Marc said. "These are our ecclesiastical leaders, and we've come to give her a blessing."

"I don't know," the plump nurse said hesitantly. She plucked nervously at the dark hairs escaping from under her nurse's cap. "Does the husband know you're here?"

"No, but—"

"Then I'm afraid you'll have to leave."

"I'm his brother!"

"Well, maybe just you can enter."

"What's the problem?" a familiar voice said behind the big nurse. She turned, revealing Giselle in the quiet light of the hall.

"They all want to see Madame Perrault. I told them it's too risky, that she's weak, but they are insisting." Her nostrils flared at our audacity.

"I'll take care of it," Giselle said to the older woman.

"But—"

"Paulette is my patient. I'll take care of it." Giselle's voice was firm and unyielding, yet somehow sensitive as well. The other nurse nodded and retreated, a relieved expression dominating her stocky features.

"Well?" Giselle asked.

"We've come to give her a blessing," I said before Jean-Marc could respond. His normally cheerful face had darkened, and I worried about what he would say. I wanted the nurse to be on our side. "In our church, some of the men hold the priesthood. Paulette may not live through the night, or the baby either. So we wanted to let the Lord have a chance."

"A blessing," she mused aloud. "Is it done by the laying on of hands?"

I was surprised at the question. "Yes. May we, please?"

Giselle nodded slowly. "But could I . . . Do you mind if I . . ."

"Of course you can stay," I said. "One only needs to have faith in God." I thought perhaps Giselle had more than I did right then.

Jean-Marc knocked softly on the door, and at Pierre's call, he entered. A sad smile creased Pierre's white cheeks as he saw the large group. Silently we filed in, barely fitting in the small room. Philippe stood closest to the door, and beside him Lu-Lu clutched at his hand.

"We've come to give Paulette a blessing," Jean-Marc said softly. "And the bishop has called a ward fast."

Pierre hugged his brother. "I'm so afraid. I can't lose her."

Jean-Marc didn't bother to wipe the tears springing from his eyes. I hadn't seen him cry so earnestly since I was in labor with the twins. "It's going to be all right," he murmured.

The bishop, home teachers, Pierre, and Jean-Marc crowded around the bed. Paulette had been sleeping, but her eyes flew open. Fear glared in her eyes before she recognized the people. Her gaze rested on the bishop. "Am I going to die now?" she asked. Her voice was aloof, her expression detached, as if she didn't really care about the possible response.

He stared a moment before replying. "Are you ready to die?"

"No." But again she spoke with the same lethargy she had shown before. Her despondent manner beckoned to me like a silent appeal. Even her smell reminded me of death.

"Then let's have faith."

She nodded and struggled to sit up. The blips and beeps on the monitors quickened, and Giselle stepped forward. "You need to stay down, Paulette." I watched, feeling helpless, as Giselle pushed her gently back. Once more Paulette's stomach dominated the scene, and for a moment I was angry at the baby who was causing me to lose my friend sooner than was necessary.

Jean-Marc took out the small vial of consecrated oil he always carried with him. "Who will do the anointing?"

Pierre gazed at the bishop. "Will you?"

He nodded. "And you will give her the blessing."

Pierre shook his head almost violently. "I gave her one before. I—I think my faith is lacking in this." I knew he was talking about the baby. He had wanted Paulette to abort her; he didn't feel he could pray to save her now. Pierre turned to Jean-Marc. "Will you do it? You know how much I love her. And you have always had much more faith than I."

"I learned from you," Jean-Marc said, clasping his brother's shoulder. "But I will do it gladly."

The bishop placed a drop of oil on Paulette's scalp. We bowed our heads. Before he could begin, Philippe catapulted forward as the door opened, pushing him further into the room. Simone stood there in the open space, looking awkward in the same bright summer dress I had seen her in that afternoon. Her hair was drawn back into a short ponytail, and her heavy, blood-red lipstick emphasized her thin face.

"Momma!" Paulette gasped.

"I'll leave, if ya want." The vulnerability in Simone was unmistakable.

For the first time, Paulette let her indifferent facade slip, revealing a scared little girl. "I need you to stay," Paulette said succinctly. "Please don't leave."

Simone smiled. "I won't."

The men placed their hands on Paulette's head again, and we bowed our heads. All but Philippe, whose full lips were twisted into an angry frown.

I had never heard such a blessing. The Spirit seemed to pervade the room, filling in the cracks the fear had left in our hearts. "Your sins are forgiven you," Jean-Marc said near the end. "And I command you to become well from the pneumonia in order to deliver your baby in due time." His voice shook as he completed the blessing in the name of Jesus Christ. I heard a strangled cry and opened my eyes. The person making the sound was Philippe, who was standing by the door. He was pale and shaky.

"My sins are forgiven?" Paulette whispered, as if not quite believing. "What does this mean? How can he say that?"

Her question was addressed to no one, but the bishop picked up a set of scriptures from the small bedside table where Pierre had laid them earlier. "Forgiveness with a healing blessing is not new," he said. "In James, chapter five, verses fourteen and fifteen, it says this: 'Is any sick among you? let him call for the elders of the church and let them pray over him, anointing him with oil in the name of the Lord: And the prayer of faith shall save the sick, and the Lord shall raise him up; and if he have committed sins, they shall be forgiven him.'"

Philippe snorted, opened the door, and fled, as if escaping something evil. Lu-Lu ran after him, but the rest of us ignored the interruption.

"It wasn't me, Paulette," Jean-Marc said. "I didn't choose the words."

Paulette looked away. "Thank you, Jean-Marc. Thank you all for coming." She didn't sound convinced. Her eyes closed, and she lay still. Only her rasping breath and the monitor showed she still lived.

"It was beautiful. Thank you for letting me stay," Giselle said. She had tears on her dark face and an unfeigned smile on her red lips. With a final glance at the monitor, she turned to the door. "Five minutes," she said. "Then she really needs to rest."

The bishop and home teachers said their good-byes. Pierre thanked them again, but Paulette didn't open her eyes.

"Can I talk to my daughter?" Simone asked. Pierre nodded, though his expression was doubtful. We turned to leave. "Stay, Ariana," Simone said. "I want ya to hear this."

Paulette opened her eyes as Simone and I approached the bed. Again she had the appearance of a small child. "Am I doing right, Momma?" she asked. "Would you abort your baby to live a little longer?"

"I aborted a baby once," Simone said. "I wasn't married, and my father made me go to the clinic. We was poor, but my father somehow got the money. They said after it was over, I'd forget it and go on. But I never forgot. It ruined my life—and yers."

"How?"

"I felt guilty about killin' that baby. I left home shortly after and got into drugs. It helped me forget. When I got pregnant again, I didn't abort ya, but I was never able to give ya a chance at a good life. Every time I tried to get away from drugs, the guilt wouldn't let me. I'm so sorry."

"It's not your fault, Momma."

"If I hadn't killed that baby, maybe I would have done somethin' with my life, maybe even gotten married to yer father. He wanted to, but I wasn't willin' to give up the drugs, 'cause then I'd have to face my guilt." She paused and reached out a tentative hand to her daughter. "I'm proud of ya, Paulette. Yer brave enough to stand up and do what I never could."

"The situation is different," Paulette said. "You were just a child."

"Maybe. But it don't make what I did right."

A hush fell over the room. "I thought you rejected me," Paulette said with the emotionless voice she had used earlier.

"Never. I just didn't want my life to affect yer bein' happy."

"You won't leave?" The hope was clearly written on my friend's face.

"I'll be here for as long as ya want me." Mother and daughter hugged.

I felt out of place and drifted to the door.

"Ariana, don't leave," Paulette said. "I have to ask you something." I stopped and retraced my steps.

"Will you take care of Marie-Thérèse? Pierre will have to work and won't be able to be with her all the time."

"You're not going to die now!" I said. "Didn't you listen to the blessing?"

She nodded. "I heard, but I know it is based on my faithfulness. And since I was never forgiven for my sins from before, I can't believe it now." She stared into my eyes, entreating me. "Do you believe it? Do you believe God could forgive my sins and still let me get AIDS?"

"Lots of worthy people die."

"That's not an answer. I need to understand." Paulette's face collapsed into pathetic resignation.

I backed away. "I do believe in the blessing," I whispered fiercely. "I do." I practically ran from the room. I didn't know what to tell Paulette. She needed something from me, and I couldn't give it to her.

CHAPTER ELEVEN

*H*e felt something. I know he did," Lu-Lu said jubilantly in the car. Philippe had left the hospital alone, but she had waited to ride home with us.

"He didn't seem impressed," Jean-Marc commented.

"But he felt something." Lu-Lu sounded less sure.

I watched the lights from the oncoming cars and said nothing, playing with the gauzy folds of my white dress, now wrinkled from the long day. Philippe had seemed more scared than anything to me. I dismissed him almost immediately; I was more worried about Paulette. I knew she was supposed to get well, at least temporarily, but somehow I didn't feel she would. I silently berated myself for my lack of faith and for lying to Paulette by telling her I believed in the blessing.

We arrived home well after ten. My mother was up and waiting. Louise told her about the blessing, her face full of hope, but again I said nothing. Leaving the others, I went to check on the children. All were sleeping soundly, even Marie-Thérèse. The rag doll had fallen to the side of the bed, so I picked it up and tucked it next to her small body.

Next, I made my way into the kitchen to clean the dishes I had left after dinner, but my mother must have washed them. I slumped to the table and laid my head on my folded arms. *What's wrong with me, Father?* I prayed silently. *Please help me. Please send an answer so I can help Paulette.* Despite my apparent lack of faith, I did believe my Heavenly Father loved both me and Paulette.

"What's wrong?" my mother asked from the doorway.

I lifted my head. "I could ask you the same thing."

She sighed. "It seems rather petty compared to Paulette's problems." She sank into a chair.

"Well?"

"This evening, right before you called me to baby-sit, I told your father I was going to be baptized no matter what he said. He claimed I loved the Church more than I loved him and that no true God would come between a man and his wife. Then you called, and I left. It's the first time I've ever left without telling him where I was going. He was very angry, so angry he couldn't talk. He just stared at me with his mouth working, up and down. It was awful."

"So what are you going to do?" I asked.

"Can I stay here tonight?"

"It won't help things."

"I know, but I have to think about what I'm going to do. I can't think of living my life without the gospel, and I can't imagine leaving Géralde. I love him. Oh, why does he have to be so stubborn? I'm not asking him to be baptized, just to support my decision." She laid her head down on her arms and sobbed.

It seemed, of late, that people were asking me a lot of questions to which I didn't know the answers. *What should I do?* I asked instinctively of my Heavenly Father, as I had learned to do through the years since I had become a member.

"Would you talk to him?" my mother asked, wiping her face with both hands.

"Now?"

She nodded. "I'll stay here with the children."

"But what will I say?"

Her slender shoulders lifted in a helpless shrug. "I don't know, Ariana. But you always seem to find a way. Please try." I didn't understand what she was talking about, but because of her pleading expression, I had to agree.

In the sitting room, I took Jean-Marc aside. "I'm going to visit my father."

"Now?"

"It's important. My mother wants to be baptized, and they had a fight about it."

"I'll go with you," he said immediately.

"I think I should talk to him alone."

"At least let me drive."

I hugged him, touched that he wanted to be with me. "Thanks. I think I'm tired of being alone."

"Alone?"

My eyes watered. "I've missed you."

"But I'm right here," he said, pulling me close with a smile.

He didn't understand my reference to the many evenings I had already spent alone. I smiled wistfully and turned to grab my white sweater.

We drove the few minutes to my parents' home in comfortable silence. He walked me up the cement steps to the outside door, where I rang the black buzzer. The night was quiet and tranquil, not another person in sight. Stars overhead shone brightly, hovering in their constant vigil.

"Yes?" My father responded quickly, as if he had been waiting.

"It's me, Ariana. May I come up?" The buzzer sounded, and Jean-Marc pulled open the heavy door.

"I'll wait down here," he said, jabbing a finger at the elevator button.

"I won't be long." At least I hoped I wouldn't.

As I rode in the elevator, I wondered what I was doing. It had been a long time since I had been a fearless missionary, accustomed to rejection. "But he's your father," I said aloud. "He can't reject you." But he had once before, when Antoine died.

My father opened the door before I rang the bell. He had his keys in his hand and was pulling on a sweater. For the first time, I noticed the wrinkles around his eyes.

"Going somewhere?"

"To find your mother," he said curtly. "She left. Since you are here, I suppose she's not at your house."

"You suppose wrong."

"Is she okay?" His tone reprimanded my frivolity.

I sighed. "May I come in? She's the reason I'm here."

He stood aside and ushered me into their spacious entryway. I led the way down the short corridor past the kitchen and into their over-sized sitting room. I knew each step well, as I had grown up in this apartment; even the faint smell of spice my mother used to freshen the air was familiar. As always when coming to my parents' house, pleasant memories of Antoine filtered through my mind.

Mother had changed the sitting room since I had been here last, as she occasionally did. A new picture of Christ in Gethsemane had a dominant place over the hearth, and another of the Swiss temple was positioned in the corner by the window where my mother usually sat reading. The couches had been arranged to one side to allow space for a new easy chair, and on the coffee table in front of this chair, a statue of Christ with two children on his lap sat next to a copy of the *Liahona* and my mother's scriptures. I observed all this with some portion of my brain; there had been a time when my mother hadn't dared bring any of her new beliefs into the house.

"She's not okay," I said, settling myself in the easy chair.

My father didn't sit. "What do you mean?"

"She's torn between her love for you and her beliefs. What does it matter if she's baptized? I am, and it has only changed me for the better. Has it ruined our relationship?"

"You are not my wife."

"But I am your daughter. The gospel makes Mother happy; it doesn't take away from your love."

"She'll want me to change—eventually. It'll tear us apart."

I felt my face flush with anger. "Has it torn us apart, Father? No. It was what brought us back together!"

"You're not my wife," he repeated stubbornly.

I stood up. "This is ridiculous. I shouldn't have come. You don't want to listen!" Then I saw it clearly. "You're afraid, aren't you? Afraid that if you let Mother be baptized, you will have to find the truth for yourself. That's it, isn't it? You're afraid!" The idea seemed ludicrous, but there it was. My father was frightened of the truth. For over seven years since I had made up with my parents, I had hoped for their conversion. Now my mother was ready, but fear stood in her way.

I suddenly felt very tired. "I can't do this! You and Mother will just have to work it out. I can't be caught between you. Paulette's dying, and I don't understand why. And all you can think of is your fear of change. You won't even try to learn the truth." I shut my eyes, feeling dizzy. When was the last time I had actually eaten? I had fed the children, but I hadn't been hungry when we began our new fast. "I have to leave."

"Wait!" My father put his hand on my shoulder. "What's wrong, Ari? There's something more, isn't there?"

The anger left me as quickly as it had come, leaving me weak. I sagged, and my father caught me.

"Tell me." He held me close, as he had when I was a child.

"It's Paulette," I said through my tears. "She's looking to me for the answer, but I don't know why this is happening to her, especially after she's worked so hard for forgiveness. I can understand trials, but death? And Pierre too? And possibly the baby? She was forgiven for her sins, but now they've come back to torment her. She feels her sins are being visited upon her innocent family. What kind of forgiveness is that?"

I felt guilty even as I spoke. My father was an unbeliever and certainly not the one I should speak to about my doubts. I should be talking with Jean-Marc. We might have our troubles, but he was a priesthood holder and well versed in the scriptures. Of course, he hadn't been around much lately. When could we have talked? The thought was caustic, but I didn't fight it. It was the truth. Maybe Jean-Marc was trying to escape the situation with Paulette altogether; I certainly wished I could. And now here I was talking with my father, the biggest church critic I had ever known besides my former self. He would surely point out the fruitlessness of my faith.

His next words filled me with astonishment. "It's more complex than that, Ari. I'm surprised you don't know."

I blinked at him. "What?"

"Your church teaches that when a person repents, forgiveness is complete. But repentance doesn't negate the consequences of previous actions. If it did, people could simply repent at the last moment and be cured of anything. For instance, a person who has committed adultery could immediately have the consequences removed. Like a resulting pregnancy could disappear, or the spouse would never leave and sue for divorce. Or perhaps a man caught embezzling would retain his job. Doesn't that sound preposterous? Of course it does. No, the consequences have to be in place; they are unchangeable, and they actually serve as an example to others. Meanwhile, the trial itself refines the person even more. What use is faith if there are no tests? God sent us here to be tested, and what better way for a person to be tested than this? It doesn't mean Paulette was never forgiven or that God is at fault and has abandoned her. There are rules in the universe, and He follows them. Yes, He has the power to change things, but how much more will we learn if we go through it? And those around us?"

My father's speech sounded strangely Mormonized, and I wondered if he had been reading Mother's *Liahona*s. I smiled inwardly at the thought. "But the baby—"

"She is an innocent, to be sure, but any religion in the world will tell you that her innocence makes it a much more potent test. Some of the innocent are sacrificed to stand as witnesses against those who wrong them, but others simply stand as complications to whatever trials are sent to the faithful. It is much easier to suffer yourself than to see someone else suffer for your mistakes—especially in a case like Paulette's, where such a drastic repentance has occurred."

My father's words were difficult to understand. "Are you saying God didn't change the consequences of Paulette's drug use because He wants to test her?"

"Like He tested you." My father's words were gentle. "Your Nette died through no fault of yours, yet had you chosen another path, she wouldn't have died. But does it mean you are to blame? Or that any forgiveness you obtained was tainted? I think not."

I was beginning to understand. "Regardless, Nette still died."

"And Paulette still has AIDS, as she would have had she not repented," my father continued. "We always have a choice in life, but we can't choose the consequences. Those won't change simply because we repent."

I nodded and stepped away from him. "I don't understand it," I said. "You talk like a bishop or something. I never knew you understood the scriptures so well."

He laughed. "It isn't just the members of your church who read scriptures."

"When did you start reading them?"

He appeared startled at my question. "About a year ago."

I smiled. That was about the time my mother had begun attending church regularly. "So Mother's church activity has influenced you." I picked up my mother's scriptures from the table and thumbed through them until I found what I wanted: "And whatsoever thing persuadeth men to do good is of me; for good cometh of none save it be of me."

As I quoted the scripture in Ether, my father's eyebrows drew together tightly.

"That has nothing to do with it." His voice was clipped.

"Yes, it does. Father, I really appreciate what you said to me tonight. It really helped. But I have to point something out. *You* are at a crisis point in your life. *You* have a decision to make, and like Paulette, you can't choose the consequences. Mother loves you more than anything. She also loves the Lord. Please work this out with her." I kissed his cheek and ruffled the top of his hair, as I had as a child when he tucked me into my bed each night. "I love you."

He didn't walk me to the door but stared after me as I left. My own heart was much lighter. I knew my parents still had a long way to go, but whether my father knew it or not, he was on the right path. And, strangely, the Lord had helped *me* by sending me to him. My father had given me at least part of the answer to Paulette's dilemma. Now I would follow up on my earlier feelings and talk to Jean-Marc.

When I stepped off the elevator, Jean-Marc stood up from his seat on the cool marble stair. "How'd it go?"

"All right, I think." I settled on the stair and patted the place beside me. He sat again, looking at me questioningly.

"My father helped me understand something," I said. I noticed my mother's scriptures then. I had forgotten to return them to the table in her sitting room. I let them slide to my lap.

Jean-Marc's face appeared bemused. "And I thought you went to teach him."

I laughed. "Well, we've heard time and time again how the Lord works in mysterious ways. I think my father has been studying religion. Not ours in particular, perhaps, but in general."

He smiled. "So what happened?"

I bit my lower lip. "Well, I couldn't seem to understand why Paulette has AIDS. I mean, I know she did drugs, but she has repented, and it doesn't seem fair for the Lord to let her die like this. She doesn't understand it, either."

He shook his head. "The same question has been plaguing me. Pierre has never done anything wrong in his life, and now he's got it, and eventually he's going to die." His voice was low as he added, "Like my dad."

"My father said these things happen because of consequences, and we can choose our course but not the results." I explained by using the examples my father had given. "But when it comes right down to it, the whole thing is a test, to refine not only Paulette but the rest of us."

Jean-Marc put his arm around me. "I hope we all pass it."

"We won't have to do it alone. We have each other and the Lord." I stared at the swirling patterns in the marble floor. "But I doubted His wisdom," I whispered.

Jean-Marc's hand gently touched my chin and brought my face around to meet his gaze. "We all do it. It's a part of learning. And if we don't keep on learning, we forget."

I knew what he was saying. At the time it had happened, Nette's tragic death had crushed me; but after becoming a member, I had never questioned the Lord about it or anything else He had sent my way. Until now.

"Yet Paulette believes her family is being punished for her sins," I said. "She even quoted scripture to me."

Jean-Marc fingered the scriptures I had taken from my mother's table. "I know where that scripture is—we just had a lesson on it last week in elders quorum. It's in Exodus and again in Numbers. But she has misunderstood it. It is only if a person doesn't repent that the punishments will fall upon their children. Look, here in the Doctrine and Covenants it explains it better."

I read the scripture eagerly. "This is it!"

"What?"

I kissed his lips. "The rest of the answer!" I stuffed the scriptures in my sweater pocket and stood up. Grabbing his hands, I pulled him to his feet. "Come on."

His green-brown eyes sparkled. "You're up to something. Where are we going?"

"To the hospital." My voice was determined.

He grinned. "Right now? What if they don't let us in?"

"They will."

Twenty minutes later, we walked into the hospital and rode up the elevator to the third floor in the wing where the AIDS patients were. Jean-Marc kept trying to duck into deserted corridors when people passed, but I strode ahead without looking around. "You've seen too many American films," I said to him. "The trick is to look like you belong." If my white dress was a bit fuller in the skirt and more gauzy than the nurses' uniforms, such a thing went unnoticed this late at night, especially because of my white nurse-like sweater. For his part, Jean-Marc stood out in his dark suit.

We made it to Paulette's door without being challenged and slipped inside. The room was dark. "You keep watch," I said to Jean-Marc, "and I'll talk with her."

The only light came from blinking machines and through a crack in the heavy curtains. Labored breathing came from the bed. In the dim light I could see the chair next to the bed. It was empty. *Where was Pierre?*

"It's Ariana," I whispered, touching Paulette's shoulder. "Are you awake?"

"Yes." The voice was low and unrecognizable. "I've just been lying here waiting for you."

"How did you know I was coming?"

The thin figure shifted slightly. "If not today, then tomorrow."

I took her hand. It seemed so incredibly fragile, the skin paper-thin and dry like old parchment. "I came to tell you I've found the answer. God *has* forgiven you and loves you! But you see, the consequences can't be changed simply because you repent." Again I explained about the adulterous man and the one who had embezzled, silently thanking my father for his clear examples. "So you see, the Lord didn't let you have AIDS because He didn't forgive you but because He can't go against His own rules and change the outcome. When Nette died, a missionary told me God loves those He tests. He loves you so much!"

"You really think so?" The rasping voice had a touch of wonder.

I nodded, though Paulette could not see me in the dark. "He knew you would stay faithful, no matter what. And when you stand before Him, you can know for a surety the Savior has made your robes white before Him through His sacrifice and through your own faithful endurance. Remember, this life is but a blink in the eternity of things."

I wasn't sure if I was explaining it correctly, but her frail grasp tightened on my hand.

"Thank you! Oh, thank you. And to Him who sent you."

This was my first inkling that I wasn't talking to Paulette. I held the hand for a long time, wondering what to do. Finally, I reached out to the curtain with my free hand and parted it further. Rays from the outside lights surrounding the hospital shone down on the figure in the bed—an old woman, impossibly thin and wrinkled-looking. She was sound asleep, a slight smile on her pale lips.

This wasn't Paulette! I let the curtain drop and crept to the door.

"Finished already?" Jean-Marc asked.

"It's not Paulette!"

"In that case, what took you so long?"

He grabbed me with one hand, the other opening the door. I stared at the number outside the room: 301. Paulette was in 307, three doors down. In my hurry, and with the muted light in the hospital corridor, I had made a mistake.

We glanced up and down the hall. Several nurses passed, but none looked our way. Jean-Marc sprinted down the hall, pulling me with him. He opened Paulette's door.

"Who's there?" Pierre's voice came from the dark.

"It's me, Jean-Marc, and Ariana."

"What are you doing here?" We heard a click, and a soft glow appeared on the headboard of Paulette's bed. Pierre blinked at his watch. "It's nearly midnight."

"I needed to talk to Paulette," I said, feeling suddenly absurd. It could have waited until tomorrow.

"How is she?" Jean-Marc asked.

Pierre frowned. "Not well. I mean, her body is responding to the drugs, but she's not getting better. It's like she's given up." His voice hardened. "Tomorrow, I'm telling the doctor to take the baby, regardless. Either way it will die."

She! my mind shouted.

"But the blessing," Jean-Marc said. "I felt it. I don't understand."

"I do," I said. I crossed to the bed, and despite Pierre's objections, I shook Paulette's shoulder.

"Huh? What?" she said. Her eyes fluttered open and tried to focus on me. "An angel?" she asked. "Oh, it's you, Ariana."

I sat on Pierre's vacated chair. "Having AIDS doesn't mean you aren't forgiven for the past," I began for the third time that evening.

"I've been thinking about it," she said. "My grandfather forced my mother to have an abortion when she was young, and she never recovered. She raised me with drugs, and because of that I am passing this disease to my family. It is the sins of the parents being passed to the third and fourth generations, just as I thought." Her face was glum, her voice hopeless.

I pulled out my mother's scriptures and turned to Doctrine and Covenants 124:52. "'And I will answer judgment, wrath, and indignation, wailing, and anguish, and gnashing of teeth upon their heads, unto the third and fourth generation, so long as they repent not, and hate me, saith the Lord your God.'" I paused to let it sink in. "You see, Paulette, you're not in that category. You love the Lord. You have repented, and He has accepted your repentance. But that doesn't mean He will change the consequences." I launched into my examples and then reminded her of what Elder Tarr had told me so long ago: "The Lord loves those whom He tests. If He didn't, why bother?"

Paulette was crying. "This is too hard!"

"So was losing Nette and Antoine."

She blinked twice, causing large tears to slide down her face in rivulets, and her mouth trembled as she caught her lip in her teeth, biting until the blood came as she had on the night Nette died. "He knew *you* could do it," she said dismally.

"As can you."

"How?" The question came out as a cry.

"One day at a time. And we'll be here for you."

"He loves me," she whispered fiercely. "He loves me."

I nodded. "He does."

"I can do it!" Her voice was stronger, though still filled with an aching sadness.

I glanced over to the door, where our husbands stood watching us. Their faces were full of heartache, yet the pain had been changed by hope.

Paulette sat up alone and hugged me tightly, until my ribs begged for breath. "I love you."

"Then get well. You have a little girl who needs you, and a baby to help grow."

We left Paulette and Pierre, feeling we had done something good. Both Paulette and I had the faith we had lacked earlier, and already she was feeling stronger. The priesthood was healing her body, but my words—no, my father's and Jean-Marc's—had healed her mind and her heart.

The day had been a long one for me, both physically and mentally. I drifted to sleep in the car and almost didn't wake when Jean-Marc parked. He helped me to the apartment, undressed me, and then tucked me into bed tenderly. I felt his love, strong and sure.

"Check the kids?" I asked.

"They're fine," he said, snuggling in beside me.

I knew they were and that my mother was curled up with Josette in her bed as she often was when sleeping over. But knowing and seeing didn't mean the same thing to a mother. I slipped out of the warm bed and went to check on my children and Marie-Thérèse, leaving Jean-Marc to fall asleep.

As he predicted, all the children were covered and slumbering with the peaceful abandon of the innocent. I kissed their rosy cheeks, feeling grateful I would be there tomorrow to see them wake. I considered Paulette one of the most righteous people I knew, but I didn't want her trial, not even to become as close to God as she would be. I remembered all too vividly how savagely the refining fires burned. Even now, as I watched from a distance, my skin felt scorched by the blaze.

CHAPTER TWELVE

Jean-Marc was in the kitchen when I awoke. My mother and Louise were serving a breakfast of juice and hot mush to the twins and Marie-Thérèse, who were seated at the table. The women's eyes were tinged with red and swollen from yesterday's crying, but today both looked happy. Lu-Lu had André on her lap and was spooning in his customary baby cereal.

"Oh, Ariana, the blessing worked!" Louise said.

"What?"

"Pierre called this morning, nearly an hour ago. You got in so late, we didn't want to wake you," she explained. "Now we can finish our fast in thanksgiving, instead of asking for something."

André held out his arms for me, and I leaned down and kissed his cheek. At the table, the twins played a peculiar game with their hot cereal as Marie-Thérèse watched.

"Pierre said Paulette looks much better this morning. They've taken her off the oxygen and everything. He says she got up to use the bathroom and announced she's going home. They're waiting for the doctor to come in this afternoon to see if he'll release her."

Jean-Marc put his arms around me and gave me a kiss. "See what a little faith and fasting can do?"

"Will you take me to the hospital?" Marie-Thérèse asked me.

"Of course I will."

"I want to go!" the twins said in unison.

"But then you won't get to go to the park with me," Lu-Lu said. "I've got suckers," she added enticingly. The twins cheered.

"I wish you could live with us always," Marc said.

"I do, too," Lu-Lu said.

Louise watched her. "I've been thinking of moving here myself. I think Paulette will need us."

Jean-Marc and I glanced at each other. For years we had been trying to get Louise to move to Paris, but she had always refused.

"If you're serious about moving here, Lu-Lu," Louise continued, "Pierre said he could get you a job with his company. He said they could always use a good manager, and you have the training for it, having grown up working in our store."

"What, nepotism?" Lu-Lu said dryly. She sounded far more grown up than I had ever seen her.

"Why not?" Jean-Marc said. "It worked for me." We all laughed. "As for that, I could get you a job at the bank, especially since you've had a few years of college. We have a teller job open."

Lu-Lu appeared thoughtful. "Maybe I'll take you up on that. After all, this is the famous city of love, and I'm certainly ready for some excitement."

Louise frowned, but I was the only one who noticed.

"What about Philippe?" Lu-Lu asked.

Jean-Marc's jaw tightened momentarily. "Him too," he conceded. "I have a job lined up for him, if he wants it. He'll have to cut his hair, shave, and wear a suit, but I'll give him a shot."

Gratitude filled Lu-Lu's face. "Thank you, Jean-Marc. I really think we'll accept. I mean, I'll have to talk with him, but we wanted to move here anyway. This will be the perfect opportunity. I can't wait to tell him!" She stood and handed André to me. "May I use the telephone in the sitting room?"

"Of course," I said.

Jean-Marc smiled, and I knew he was grateful he had supported his sister, despite his disaffection for her fiancé. "Don't worry," he said to Louise. "It's nothing with money, if that's what you're worried about. Philippe will be doing something with the paperwork after the tellers are finished with it."

She sighed. "I just wish I could get her away from him for a few months. That's all it would take, I'm sure."

"How long have you been planning on moving to Paris?" I asked. I knew Louise wouldn't have said anything if the decision hadn't already been made.

"Since I talked to Pierre this morning," she said. "I'm going to give up my apartment in Bordeaux and live with Pierre and Paulette until an apartment in their building opens up. That way I'll be close enough to help when—" she broke off, and I understood why. Now that Paulette was feeling better, it seemed like bad luck to talk about her dying. "I'm going back to Bordeaux today to arrange things, if Lu-Lu will come. I'd better go talk with her."

"But she's taking us to the park," Josette protested as Louise left. The children had been monitoring the conversation without much interest until their outing had been threatened.

"I'll take you," my mother said.

"Do you have suckers?" asked Marc.

My mother smiled. "I can buy some."

"All right then," he agreed.

The buzzer in the hallway rang. "I'll get it," Jean-Marc said.

"Go get dressed," I told the children, seeing they weren't going to eat any more. "Make sure it matches. Marie-Thérèse, you help them decide what to wear, okay?" They scrambled from their chairs and ran down the hall.

I grinned at my mother. "You've been watching my children so much, you might as well move in."

She grimaced and said softly, "I may have to."

"Nonsense. Father may be stubborn, but he's not stupid."

"I hope you're right," she said, heaving a sigh. André held out his arms for her, and she took him from me and held him tightly against her chest. "He certainly is a sensitive child." My mother kissed his soft cheek. I agreed. I didn't know what I had done to deserve such a compassionate little boy, but I was grateful.

"Josephine," my father's voice came from the kitchen doorway. Behind him I saw Jean-Marc's hesitant grin. I knew he had planned this meeting. I only hoped it worked out.

"Géralde." Surprise tinged with hope covered my mother's face. She held André tighter.

My father glanced briefly at me and then back at my mother. "I love you, Josephine. Please come back home." He took the few steps between them and reached for her hands. She shifted André to her hip and let him lift her free hand between his. "I'm sorry for the way I acted," he said. "I had no right to treat you that way."

I started to edge past him to join Jean-Marc in the hallway, but my

father stopped me. "No. Ari, Jean-Marc, I want you both to hear this."
He turned back to my mother. "I had no right to treat you that way,
Josephine," he repeated, "though I do have the right to take steps to
protect my family. I don't want to lose you, and I feel that I will if you
join this church. It will separate us. Please, come home and reconsider.
Attend all you want but don't consent to baptism. Remember, I love
you. Isn't that what's important?"

My mother let André slide to the floor. In her eyes, I thought I saw
all of the things she would like to say, but she knew they were things
my father wasn't ready to hear. "I love you," she whispered, "and yes,
I'll come home."

They held each other in a close embrace, with my father leaning
over to bury his face in her neck. I took André's hand and left the room.

"You planned this," I accused Jean-Marc in the hall.

He shrugged. "It worked, didn't it?"

"For now." I knew that the issue had been shelved, not settled. Just
as Jean-Marc and I had done to our own problems. Perhaps it was good
enough.

Marie-Thérèse and I arrived at the hospital shortly before lunch.
Pierre was in the hall, and he picked up Marie-Thérèse and whirled her
around. "We're taking Mommy home," he said.

She giggled. "I know!"

He set her down, and she ran into her mother's room. Paulette was
standing, pacing the floor. Pierre grinned at me. "I can't get her to rest.
She's like her old self again."

"Then maybe now *you* can get back to your normal self." I patted
his belly, which had shrunk noticeably in the week Paulette had been in
the hospital.

He grinned. "I'm looking forward to it," he said. "Getting back to
normal life, I mean. In fact, I'm going to have to go in to work for a
while this afternoon. I've already taken three full days off as it is. I'm
not worried about vacation time—I still have nearly my whole month's
annual vacation to take—but I left some important things unfinished."

"Why don't you go ahead, and I'll take Paulette home?" I said.
"Then you can take care of whatever and meet us at your house."

"Would you?"

I nodded, and he turned into the room to tell Paulette. I was about to follow when I noticed several nurses and doctors emerging from a room down the hall. Two of the nurses pushed a bed with a still figure on it, a blanket drawn up to obscure the face. I took a few steps down the hall to check the number on the door: room 301. The woman I had talked with last night was dead.

"She died just a few minutes ago," Giselle said, separating herself from the other nurses coming from the room. Her dark cheeks had tears on them, yet her eyes were happy.

"She had AIDS?"

The nurse nodded. "For three years now, she's been fighting for life, though sometimes I wondered why. She was a mean, bitter lady. I often found it hard to take care of her."

"She was your patient then?"

"Yes. But today she was different. This morning when she called for me, I thought she was going to complain about breakfast as she usually did. Instead, she told me she had seen an angel during the night."

I gulped. "An angel?"

Giselle nodded. "At first she thought it was Death come to take her, but then she saw an angel with a flowing white robe who held her hand and told her God had forgiven her and loved her."

"Do you believe her?"

Giselle's even gaze met mine. "Paulette is better today after your husband's blessing, almost miraculously so. It is easier for me to believe in an angel than to see her recover so quickly."

I opened my mouth to confess, but she shook her head. "Angels come in all forms, Ariana, both heavenly and earthly. Sometimes one doesn't know when she will be someone else's angel."

I knew then that she or one of the other nurses had seen me the night before, coming from the dead woman's room. "What was her name?"

"Madeleine. And she died happy, with a smile on her face. I had never seen her smile." Giselle walked away.

When I pushed open the door to Paulette's room, she was waiting for me in the chair beside her bed, an unfinished blessing gown in her hands. It still made me smile in wonder at the idea of Paulette embroidering. It was an art I still had not grasped, though not for lack of diligence on the part of certain sisters from our ward.

Pierre was nowhere in sight, but Marie-Thérèse stared out the window. The thick brown curtains had been drawn back to let in the warm sun. I focused on Paulette. She was still too thin, but her light brown eyes glistened with life.

She nearly bounced from her chair. "Oh, Ariana, thank you so much! Because of you, I'm going home today. At least I will if the doctor ever gets here."

I thought of telling her about the lady in room 301 but decided against it. "It wasn't me, it was the blessing," I said.

"Yes," she agreed, "but you returned my faith to me." She hugged me, and this time I no longer smelled death. She really was going to be okay—for now. I sighed in relief.

"There now, Ari." She patted my back, misconstruing my emotion. "Everything's all right."

"I've missed you. I've been lonely. I don't know what I'd do without you."

"Survive," she said. "You're good at that. We both are."

The door opened, and our conversation died. "Dr. Medard," Paulette said.

This was the AIDS specialist, my first time meeting him. He was a relatively young man of average height, and his face was plain. Nothing to set him apart from a million other faces in the world, except perhaps for his moustache and the compassion in his light brown eyes.

Those eyes now stared at Paulette. "Back in the world of the living, are we?" he asked. He came closer to the bed, and I saw that his moustache hid a cleft lip, repaired in the days before such surgeries had been perfected. Somehow the defect seemed to give him a sense of presence, something that arrested the attention and made me understand he was a man to be admired.

"I feel good," Paulette said. "I'm tired, and my chest still hurts a bit, but I'm well enough to go home."

He frowned. "So it seems. I'm frankly astonished, but from all the tests and from the way you look and feel, I must say there's no reason to keep you here. But I'm a little worried you'll overdo things. Do you have someone to help you?"

She nodded. "My husband's sister and mother are coming to stay with me for a time. And even now, the sisters from my church are lining up at my door to bring meals and do laundry."

The doctor chuckled. "Good, very good. You have to take care of yourself. The next infection you get may be your last. I'll want to see you every few weeks, of course, to make sure you and the baby are progressing well. At any hint of sickness at all, you must come in."

"Okay, okay," Paulette said.

"In that case, you can leave." He smiled again and left the room.

"What happened to your regular doctor?" I asked, remembering the man who resembled a basset hound.

She shook her head. "He's not equipped to deal with AIDS. I'm seeing Dr. Medard permanently now. He's one of the best, and the only doctor around who takes care of pregnant women with AIDS or HIV."

"But he wanted to abort your baby," I protested.

"He wanted to do what was best for me," she said. "Once I explained how important she is to me, he didn't push. It was mostly Pierre."

"Love is an odd thing. Sometimes I don't understand it."

"Me either," she agreed, picking up a sturdy plastic sack packed with her things. She carefully folded the blessing gown and tucked it inside. "Shall we?"

I proffered my arm. "Yes, we shall."

We sauntered out the door and down the hall, with Marie-Thérèse hopping after us. Under her breath, she hummed a melody as she moved from square to square on the linoleum. Unlike the other floors, this one had carpet only in the waiting room.

"Marguerite!" Paulette exclaimed.

I looked to see the robust woman striding down the hall. "But you're all better," she said, staring at Paulette in surprise.

Paulette laughed. "Yes, I am." There was a note of determination in her voice.

Marguerite hugged her. "I'm so glad. Want to celebrate? I'll buy lunch." She glanced at me. "You're still fasting, aren't you? We can break our fast together."

Paulette shook her head. "No offense, Marguerite, but I just want to go home."

The older lady chuckled. "I understand completely."

"But since you're here, there's someone I want you to meet." We were approaching the nurses' station. Giselle stood near it, eyes fastened on a report in her strong hands.

"I'm leaving," Paulette said. "I've come to say good-bye."

"I've never seen anyone recover so quickly," Giselle said to us.

"I'm not surprised," said Marguerite. "Ever since I joined the Church, I've seen many miracles. Why, the fact Paulette is alive today is proof enough."

"You're a member of their church?" the nurse asked. Marguerite nodded. "But I wasn't always."

"Giselle, this is our good friend, Marguerite Geoffrin," I said. "She owns several cafés here in town." As I introduced her, I exchanged knowing glances with Paulette. Marguerite had recently been made a stake missionary, and there was nothing she liked so much as a serious investigator.

"Why don't you two come to the house, and we can talk about it?" Paulette said.

"I wouldn't want to intrude. You need your rest," Giselle said. But the words seemed reluctant.

"Nonsense," Paulette dismissed the thought. "I've done nothing but rest for days. Besides, as my friend, you should come and make sure I'm settled in bed, right?"

"Well, I am getting off now," Giselle said, her black eyes sparkling with amusement. "I'm tired—I've just finished a double shift—but I guess I could come for a while."

"I'll stop off for lunch at the café," Marguerite said. "No sense in going hungry." She turned to Giselle. "Want to come along to help me choose the food?"

"Why not?" Giselle said. "Just let me get my things."

We left the two of them talking like old friends and made our way to the parking lot. I could hear honking in the distance and sounds of traffic. Nearby, a woman getting into a car talked excitedly, and the man with her laughed. They were the usual noises, but each seemed precious. Paulette lived, and I was taking her home!

When we arrived at Paulette's apartment, I called my mother to tell her I wouldn't be home for a while longer. "I don't want to leave

Paulette, at least until Marguerite gets here. She shouldn't be alone at all this first little while."

"We're fine here," my mother said. "We went to the park."

"Did Marc make it to the bottom of the sandbox?"

She chuckled. "No, not yet. In another year or so, perhaps."

I hung up and went to where Paulette was settled on the couch. Marie-Thérèse had covered her mother with a light blanket and now lay cuddled beside her.

"How're you doing?" I asked.

Paulette sighed contently. "Good. Tired but good." The hoarse voice of previous days had all but disappeared. She motioned to her chest. "The pain here is gone, all gone. It's a miracle!"

"I agree."

"Will you hand me the phone? I'd like to call my mother at work." There was a sense of pride as she said the words. "I called her earlier, but she wasn't in. I want her to know that I'm all right."

I did as she asked and then went to the kitchen to make myself scarce. *Paulette has her mother back,* I thought as I took dishes out of the cupboard on which to place the lunch Marguerite would bring. *Something good has come out of this whole mess.*

The buzzer in the hall rang, signaling Marguerite and Giselle's arrival downstairs. I went to let them in. When they stepped out of the elevator, they were smiling—a good sign. "We're eating in the sitting room," I said. I led the way to where Paulette was resting. The apartment had the same basic layout as mine, except the entryway was three times the size and had warm wood strips as flooring instead of cold ceramic tile. Paulette also had two balconies, one off the kitchen and one off the sitting room, whereas I had none.

Marguerite had spared no expense, bringing a variety of food, from soup to pastries, that she or her husband had made themselves.

As we set it out, the phone rang. It was the Relief Society president with a list of sisters who had called to help out by bringing meals or staying with Paulette while Pierre was at work. Paulette hadn't been joking when she told the doctor about the lines of people waiting to help. I hung up and relayed the information.

"The members of your church are doing that?" Giselle asked, her eyebrows rising. "But they just found out about Paulette being released today."

"Oh, we have a sort of network." Marguerite explained about the visiting teachers. "And they probably passed a sheet around on Sunday, asking who would like to help out."

"Can we pray?" Marie-Thérèse now sat on the floor near me, eyeing the meat pastries Marguerite had brought. The others had settled themselves on two comfortable chairs opposite the sofa. "I'm hungry."

"Would you like to offer it?" Paulette asked.

The child shrugged. "Okay." We bowed our heads and folded our arms. Giselle did the same. "Heavenly Father, thank you so much for making Mommy better. I knew You could do it. And thank you for Marguerite bringing the food, especially the pastries. Please bless them and the meat and rice, too. Help us to know if someone needs us so we can help them." She closed in the name of Jesus Christ, and we all said amen.

We began to serve ourselves from the food loaded on the coffee table, but Giselle sat without moving. "How does she know how to pray like that?"

Paulette looked at Giselle in mild surprise. "We taught her, I guess."

"But she talks to God, not at Him. Like she knows Him."

"I do," said Marie-Thérèse. "He's my Father, and Jesus is my Brother. I learned that in Primary."

A sensation of wonder passed over Giselle's face. "I have always believed God was my Father," she said slowly, "and I have always prayed to Him as such. Other people I have met have similar beliefs, yet never have I felt it as now. How can that be?"

I stopped with a piece of bread halfway to my mouth. Paulette lay on the couch in perplexed silence; Marguerite had her mouth full. It was up to me to answer.

"Do you feel warm inside?" I asked.

Giselle nodded. "Tingly. Almost like when your foot goes to sleep, except it feels good."

"That's the Spirit," I said. "Sometimes it comes as a warm feeling or a tingling. Sometimes it's simply a certainty or even like a hug. It's hard to describe, but once you feel it, you can never forget."

Giselle nodded. "I felt it last night when your husband blessed

Paulette," she said. "And that's what interests me. He did it by laying his hands on her head, but where did he get the power? I've never seen anyone recover so quickly. It wasn't possible, and yet," she glanced at Paulette, "there she is. Is your husband a prophet?"

The question startled me until I remembered that she had seen a miracle. "No. But he has received the power of God to heal and to bless. Every worthy male member of our church has this ability."

"Oh." Giselle seemed disappointed. "Then you don't believe in prophets."

"Yes, we do," Marguerite said. "We believe the priesthood was restored to the earth by a latter-day prophet. The living prophet, like those of old, receives the word of God and passes it to the whole Church."

"Marie-Thérèse, go in my bedroom and get the *Liahona* off the table by my Book of Mormon," Paulette said. "It's the conference issue."

"We believe the Lord always reveals things to prophets," Marguerite continued. "Just like in the Bible times. You see, when Jesus was on the earth, He established His Church." She took a blue book from her purse, one with a gold angel on the cover, and grabbed it firmly between the fingers and thumbs of both hands. "Pretend my fingers are Jesus' disciples, and this book is the Church. When Jesus died, the Church remained, guided by apostles and a prophet. But eventually wicked people killed the apostles, one by one." One at a time, Marguerite began lifting her fingers from the book as we watched in fascination. "Until at last, the Church fell." She let the book plummet to her lap. "It broke into many different pieces, as shown by the many different religions of today. Each had a part of the truth, but none held the truth in its entirety. Thus began the dark age of apostasy from the Church of Christ. And so it remained until the Lord decided the time had come to restore His Church." Marguerite stopped like a good missionary did, to give her companions a chance to speak. There was only Paulette or me.

I picked up where Marguerite had left off. "In 1820 a fourteen-year-old boy, Joseph Smith, was searching for the true Church. His family visited various churches, and each chose one to attend, but Joseph couldn't decide which one was true. One day while reading in the Bible, he came across a scripture in James that said, 'If any of you lack wisdom, let him ask of God.' When Joseph read those words, he knew what he had to do." I explained how young Joseph had gone to the woods alone to pray and how he had been answered. Everyone was quiet and intent on my words—even Marie-Thérèse, who had returned with the *Liahona*.

"He saw God the Father and Jesus," I said with quiet conviction. "And through him they restored the true Church to the face of the earth, never to be taken away again. Later Joseph was given the priesthood, and since then it has been passed down through the members of our church."

Marie-Thérèse handed the *Liahona* to Giselle and opened to the page with the general authorities. "See, that's our prophet," she said. "And those are the 'postles."

Giselle took the magazine gingerly in her hands. "A prophet and twelve apostles," she mused. "And who are these?"

Marguerite explained about the Seventies while Paulette's eyes met mine. I saw a contentment there, and instinctively I knew it was because of Giselle's interest in the Church.

"My grandfather always said that Jesus' true Church would have a prophet and twelve apostles," Giselle murmured, as if to herself. "He said they would have the power of God. But he never found a church like that." She touched the picture of our prophet with a brown finger. "A real prophet of God? Could it be true?" I could actually feel the hope and longing in her voice, and for the first time in a week the tears springing to my eyes were from joy, not from sorrow.

"I want to know more," she said. "Please teach me."

"Gladly," Marguerite said. "We'll set up an appointment for you to talk with our missionaries. But for now, take this." She gave the Book of Mormon in her lap to Giselle.

"What is this?" Giselle asked.

"It's a book the Prophet Joseph Smith translated," Paulette answered, her uncertainty about teaching overcome in her eagerness to share the knowledge. "It's a second witness of Jesus Christ. Part of it tells the story of when Jesus visited the people on the American continent. It is the most beautiful book I've ever read. It was what first made me believe in God's love." Her face shone with the strength of her belief.

Giselle stared at the book in awe. "Thank you. I'll be very careful with it."

"Keep it as a gift," Marguerite said. "There are some passages marked and a study guide. Read those first, if you will, and then the missionaries will begin from there."

"May I bring some of my family to listen to the missionaries?" Giselle asked.

Marguerite smiled. "Of course."

Giselle stood abruptly, clutching the book to her chest. "Thank you. I really must be going now."

"But we haven't eaten," Marguerite protested.

"Suddenly, I'm not hungry." In Giselle's eyes I saw a hunger that had nothing to do with food.

"Let her go," I said to Marguerite and then spoke to Giselle. "But leave us your number so we can arrange the discussion with the missionaries."

Giselle pulled a card from her purse and handed it to Marguerite. "Any time in the afternoon is best," she said, "since I normally work the night shift—twelve hours, four days a week. Or I sometimes have the weekend off. Just let me know."

"You can take this, too." Marie-Thérèse picked up the *Liahona* from the table where Giselle had left it. Giselle glanced at Paulette, who nodded.

With her treasures, Giselle went to the door. "Thank you," she said as I walked with her.

When I returned to the others, everyone had begun eating except Paulette. "To think what life would be like without the gospel," she murmured. "I'd quite forgotten. What a wonderful feeling!" She turned to me. "Ariana, will you help me with my mother? I want her to understand how much God loves her."

"Of course," I said automatically. I didn't know how Simone would take to the gospel, but I would do anything to help her.

During the rest of lunch, Paulette and Marie-Thérèse chatted happily about the new baby. Marguerite and I had everything cleared away when Pierre walked in the door. He settled on the floor near his wife, and they exchanged a loving glance.

"I'd better get home," I said, taking the cue.

Marguerite rose. "Me, too."

I kissed Paulette on the cheek and hugged Marie-Thérèse. "Call me if you need anything."

The Lord's love radiated in the room. They looked so happy sitting there as a family, and my heart filled with thanksgiving for this time they had together. The priesthood of God had surely worked a miracle.

CHAPTER THIRTEEN

The summer days slipped away like rats scurrying out of sight behind the garbage bins in the basement parking lot. As Paulette continued to mend, everyone relaxed and began to treat her as they had before we knew she had AIDS. Only I seemed to hold my breath, as if waiting for something dreadful to happen.

Nothing did. My parents had called an unspoken truce and settled again into their lives without discussing the gospel. Neither appeared extremely happy, but at least they were together.

Louise returned from Bordeaux and set about taking care of Paulette while she waited for an apartment to open up in Paulette's building. Lu-Lu stayed with us; I suspected she wanted some time away from her mother.

To our dismay, my sister-in-law persisted with the idea of marrying Philippe, and we had no choice but to go along with it. We tried to fit him into our family, but he mocked our beliefs at every turn. "Crazy. Your family is crazy," I heard him say to her several weeks after Paulette was released from the hospital.

"They are not!" They were out in the hallway near the elevator, but Lu-Lu had left the door ajar as she bade him farewell for the evening.

"If they think a little prayer is going to save your sister-in-law from AIDS, they are crazy. It's incurable, and nearly everyone dies within three years of coming down with the symptoms of AIDS. Three years!" he repeated. "That's not a long time. And your brother has been infected with HIV; it's only a matter of time before he develops AIDS and dies, too. No olive oil and prayer will help him then."

"Philippe!" Lu-Lu chided. "Miracles do happen. I'm not saying Paulette is going to be cured, but I'm telling you she was made well this time by the power of the priesthood."

He snorted derisively. "The doctor's drugs made her well. I tell you, as soon as you are out from under your family's influence, the better I will feel. I love you, Lu-Lu. I'll take care of you." His voice lowered, and I couldn't hear any more from the sitting room where I had been reading before their arrival. I supposed he was kissing her. At first, I hadn't understood her attraction to the man, but once he had cut his shaggy hair and shaved his scruffy beard, he had uncovered a genuinely handsome person. To make things worse, in our view at least, he was succeeding so well in his job at the bank that he was already being considered for a promotion.

"I don't know if I like the way he does things," Jean-Marc said to me late one evening when he had returned home from work. "But it's always done on time and correctly."

"What's wrong with the way he does it?" I asked.

He shook his head. "I don't know exactly. People seem to jump when he calls. He has a sort of magnetism or something. The other workers seem to be in awe, or maybe even afraid, of him."

"That's not good."

"No, it's not. But I don't know what to do about it. I hoped he'd fail and Lu-Lu would see what a loser he is."

"Is he really a loser? Or is it because he's not a member? Lu-Lu loves him so much. Can she be so blind?"

Jean-Marc didn't have an answer, nor did I. Once I had been blinded by the man I thought I loved—my first husband, Jacques. I knew it was all too easy to get caught up in the emotion. Was it true love, or simply the dream of love, that held Lu-Lu in its grip?

"I think she's tired of being alone," Paulette said. It was Sunday and Paulette's first day back at church. In her arms she carried an array of projects and lesson aids for her Primary class.

"Marrying the wrong person is a heavy price to pay for companionship," I countered. "It's worse than being alone."

Paulette sighed. "I know. But we can't expect her to realize that."

"So what do we do?"

"I don't know. Just keep on like we are, I guess."

"Maybe she'll come to her senses in time." My voice didn't hold much hope.

"I'm praying," she said.

Since the onset of her illness, Paulette had changed. She had always been good, but now she seemed more centered, somehow, and more patient. I guess looking at life from her perspective made a difference. It wasn't something I wanted to think about.

We had arrived in Primary opening exercises, and I said good-bye to the twins. They were jumping with excitement at having Paulette back after two weeks of substitutes. "I hope they're not too wild for you," I said.

Paulette smiled. "They won't be." She sat down with the twins near her, but not one of the other class members appeared. I saw several parents peek into the room, but when they saw Paulette they hurried their children away. At first I didn't want to believe it, but when Primary started, only one of the other five children appeared. Children in the other classes stared at Paulette with open curiosity.

Time showed that many of the parents with children in Paulette's class had withdrawn them from Primary when they learned of her illness. They felt it was one thing to let someone with AIDS in the church house but quite another to expose their precious children to the risk at close range. The bishop refused to succumb to pressure to release Paulette, and he worked to educate the ward members and calm their fears. In the end, his effort was in vain, and Paulette decided to resign rather than see the ward divided into two warring factions.

"What hurts most," she said to me, "is that they can think I would actually expose their children to such a grave danger. If there were any risk at all of them getting AIDS—any at all—I wouldn't even *want* to teach."

Part of me carried a heavy guilt because I remembered too well how I had felt upon learning of her AIDS—especially the uncontrollable fear. If I, who loved her so deeply, could feel such a thing, how much more anxiety would accost those who were more distanced?

Marie-Thérèse's Primary teacher was one of the few parents who had backed Paulette, and she treated Marie-Thérèse the same as the other children in her class, never recoiling from her embraces or her outstretched hands. She had calmed the other parents enough so that they hadn't ostracized the little girl because she had infected parents. Her influence had healed my breaking confidence in the members of

our ward in general. She reminded me the Church was still true, even
when sometimes the members didn't act accordingly.

That same first Sunday back also brought another surprise to our
lives—one that gave us unexpected joy.

"I would like you two to stay," Marguerite said to us after church.
"Giselle is coming here after work with a few members of her family for
her first discussion with the missionaries."

I glanced at Jean-Marc. "What do you think?"

"I guess we can stay," he said.

"I meant for you to take the children home," I clarified. "You can
take the car and drop off Pierre and Marie-Thérèse. Paulette and I will
use her car. A missionary discussion is no place for children."

He made a face. "Baby-sitting, huh?"

I laughed. "It's not baby-sitting when they're your own children.
Besides, they need to spend some time with you."

He appeared disconcerted, almost fearful, but he agreed.

The missionaries showed up—two young French elders. We waited
outside in the warmth of the summer sun until Giselle arrived. With
her were four other people, each with skin as dark as hers. One was
older than the rest, and his hair was almost completely white. He had a
benevolence about him that made me want to be his friend.

"My grandfather," Giselle said as she introduced the old man—no,
not old. Though he was aged, he would never seem old.

I held out my hand. "Nice to meet you." But I was more surprised
than anything. From the reverent way Giselle had talked about him, I
had the impression he was already deceased.

"The pleasure is mine." His deep voice was rich and flavorful, his
smile warm and sincere. "Please call me Grandfather," he said when I
asked his name. "I've been called that so long that I don't remember any
other."

"Shall we go in?" the missionaries asked.

"Can we wait a bit?" Giselle scanned the parking lot.

"We have a few more of our family coming," Grandfather
explained.

Another car drove up, and three people emerged. The missionaries
greeted them and started to lead the way up the walk.

Grandfather held up a dark finger. "Just a moment more, if you would," he said politely. He turned to welcome another handful of people, who piled out of a station wagon. The missionaries' jaws dropped.

Our surprise deepened as several more cars drove up to the church to let out people of all ages, dressed in their Sunday best. The skin tones were varied, but all could clearly trace their heritage to Africa.

Next to me Paulette breathed in amazement, and I heard the missionaries make quick arrangements for a larger room. I counted silently; in all, Giselle had brought us twenty-three investigators.

Grandfather noted our astonishment. "I have raised my family to believe in God," he said. "We are searching anxiously for Christ's Church. I have faith that one day my search will come to an end." He held up the Book of Mormon that Marguerite had given to Giselle. "This, I believe, is true. Now I want to hear the rest."

The missionaries appeared dazed for a few moments, and having served a mission myself, I understood their feelings. In France, most missionaries were lucky to have this many investigators during the whole two years they served, never mind in one day.

"Working through the members really works," I heard one elder say quietly, almost under his breath. He was a new missionary, a greenie, and I knew this was a day he would never forget. Nor would I.

We went to the Relief Society room and talked about Heavenly Father and Jesus and the coming forth of the Book of Mormon. Grandfather sat in full patriarchal authority and watched as his family responded to the missionaries, their faces eager. I had a feeling he understood the principles on a level that could only be achieved by one who was already close to the Lord. These people were obviously elect.

Paulette turned to me. "I feel so strange," she whispered. "I love them so much, and I don't even know their names!" She brought her hand to her chest. "I'm so happy." Aside from her own conversion, her experience with Giselle was her first close-up view of missionary work.

"I know," I whispered back. It was the same way I had felt on the day she was baptized. I reached out and held her hand.

At the end of June, a month after Paulette's hospital stay, Louise and Lu-Lu settled into a two-bedroom apartment next to Paulette's. They both seemed content and happy with their move to Paris, and it made me feel easier to know they were near enough to check on Paulette during the day.

Not that she had needed it. She had recuperated quickly, though she didn't gain additional weight as her pregnancy progressed. She faithfully visited Dr. Medard, and aside from a few odd tumor-like growths on her neck, which he was able to remove, and her lack of weight gain, her AIDS seemed to be temporarily arrested. She spent her days with Marie-Thérèse, and in anticipation of the baby, together they busily decorated the third room in their apartment. I often joined them, and we talked for long hours about everything—except her AIDS. By unspoken agreement, it was the one subject we held as taboo.

Mid-July found us in Paulette's sitting room working on new curtains for the baby's room. Paulette fingered the fabric she had purchased six and a half months earlier, when she had found out she was pregnant. It had a charming array of clowns and balloons in pastel colors, with solid stripes setting off the different sections. Because of the design, it had to be arranged just so. It was all too complicated for me, but Paulette had taken to sewing and worked what I considered miracles before my very eyes. I was there more to give support than for anything else, but at least I could cut where she told me, saving her the difficulty of working around her large belly.

As she smoothed the material out over the floor, I videotaped her with the new camera she had made Pierre buy. She wanted to record what moments she could to leave for her children. Her baby might not remember her, but at least she would understand how much Paulette had loved and wanted her.

"There'll be enough for a baby quilt too, I think," Paulette said, smiling up at me.

I was glad the videotape recorder hid my expression. She looked so happy and yet . . . sick. Though Paulette had gained no weight since her hospital stay, the baby had grown. This meant Paulette was thinner than ever, and her bones seemed to stick out awkwardly. The skin on her face stretched tight and was so dry it looked almost brittle. I didn't know what was going on inside her, but obviously her body wasn't taking care of itself as it once had. Each time the thought came, a wave of dread assaulted me until I pushed it somewhere into the back of my mind, firmly out of awareness.

"Mom!" Josette's wail came from Marie-Thérèse's bedroom. "We're trying to dress up, and Marc won't leave!"

"I want to play too," he said.

I walked down the corridor and to the bedroom door. "You all need to play together."

"We are," Josette said. "We just want him to leave until we get our princess dresses on. Boys aren't 'posed to see girls naked!"

I sighed. I appreciated my daughter's modesty, but lately it had been causing problems between the twins.

"She's not naked—she has underwear!" Marc protested, pushing his dark locks out of his eyes. It was long past time for a haircut.

I grabbed him and tossed him into the air, catching him in a tight hug. It took all of my strength, but it got his attention temporarily away from the problem.

He laughed. "Do it again!"

"Me too!" chorused the girls.

I gave them each a turn and then knelt down in front of Marc. "Why don't you come outside the door and knock on it? You can be the visiting prince. Then you get to come in and see the beautiful princesses all ready for the ball."

He thought about this for a moment. "Okay. But why does André get to stay?"

"He's just a baby," Marie-Thérèse said. "He doesn't know any better."

"Oh."

I took Marc's hand and led him out the door. The girls slammed it. "You'd better be ready soon," I yelled through the door, "or the prince won't dance with either of you!"

"I'm going to huff and puff and blow the door down!" Marc howled like a wolf, and behind the door the girls screamed with laughter.

I returned to Paulette. She was scrunched down, trying to cut the fabric. "I'll do it," I said, taking the scissors from her. I sighed. "Sometimes I don't know what to do with those two."

"You're very good with them," she said. "It's a talent I admire."

"What do you mean? You're good with Marie-Thérèse."

"It's not that hard to take care of one."

"What about your Primary class? You handled them pretty well." I knew the minute the words escaped me that it was the wrong thing to say. Paulette's face turned despondent, and a strong feeling of heartache emanated from her.

"I'm sorry," I said quickly, dropping the scissors and crawling across the floor to sit beside her.

"It's not your fault," she said. "You couldn't help their reaction."

I knew that, but I could have kept my tongue from reopening barely closing wounds.

"At least Marie-Thérèse's Primary teacher understands," Paulette said, her pain eased by the memory. She found the good in even this woeful situation.

"Yeah, I guess."

"So what was the problem?" Paulette asked.

"What?"

"In the bedroom with the children."

I snorted. "Josette and her suddenly discovered modesty. Ever since that TV show last month, she won't dress in front of Marc. It's getting so bad I'm thinking about moving her into her own room and letting the boys share. The only problem is that Josette gets scared at night. And besides, André sleeps great by himself."

"Too bad she doesn't have a sister," Paulette said mildly.

"I don't know where I'd fit another child in at this point. Maybe in a few years." I stopped cutting and added, "Maybe when Jean-Marc isn't so busy."

"He's still working late?"

"Every night. He's so good about most things, and I love him more than ever, but . . ." My voice trailed off. I had thought Paulette's illness might make him change his devotion to work, but I guess my father was right when he had said that change had to come from within.

"It's more than work," I said suddenly. "It's like he's afraid of something, but I don't know what. Something that prevents him from opening up completely. I don't know. Maybe I'm making it up."

"Give him time," she said. "Men usually need more of it than we do to get things straight." She lifted her shoulders and let them fall again with an exaggerated sigh. "It's in their nature."

I laughed. That was one thing I could certainly agree with.

The doorbell rang, and Paulette opened it to Louise. She carried a huge box of wedding invitations. "Well, here they are," she said unhappily.

I took one. "They turned out nice."

Louise grimaced. "Unfortunately. And now I have no choice but to address them. Will you help? I wanted to mail them this week. Oh, I can't believe she's going to marry him in less than a month!" She groaned and slumped into a chair opposite the couch. Paulette and I exchanged understanding looks. Lu-Lu was heading straight over a cliff, and there was nothing any of us could do to save her.

As we commiserated together, another visitor came. Simone. Two good things had come out of Paulette's illness: Giselle's introduction to the gospel and then Paulette's reconciliation with her mother. Simone now visited frequently at Paulette's apartment—on the condition that she didn't swear, drink, smoke, or use drugs around Marie-Thérèse. Simone obeyed strictly but had been unable to completely conquer her addictions. Occasionally, she wouldn't appear at Paulette's for a few days. During these times, Paulette had learned to leave her alone. For her part, Marie-Thérèse loved her grandmother and no longer complained about the smell of smoke lingering on her clothing and breath.

After greeting everyone and spending a short time with the children, Simone settled on the sofa to watch Paulette with the curtains. "Them are lookin' real nice," she said. "Ain't no talent ya got from me, that's fer sure."

Paulette looked up. "The women at the church taught me. They could teach you, too, if you wanted."

Simone seemed to bristle without provocation. "Ain't good 'nough fer ya, am I?"

"That's not what I meant." Paulette came to sit with her mother on the sofa. "I just meant that if you wanted to learn, they could teach you. They did me. I've learned so much since I've joined the Church." Louise and I watched, unable to stop what would happen next.

"Well, can they teach ya not to die?" Simone said, lurching to her feet. The careless way she spoke made me wonder if she had been to a bar for a drink before coming here. Or perhaps she had recognized the sickness eating away at her daughter, as I had earlier.

Paulette stared up at her mother calmly. "I'm not afraid to die," she said, lifting her chin slightly. "I'm going to be with Jesus and my Heavenly Father. That's what's so wonderful about the gospel; you don't have to be afraid anymore."

"But what if it ain't true? Did ya ever think of that? What if ya die and that's it? Poof!"

"I know the Church is true, Mother. I know it with my whole being!" Paulette's simple testimony was potent, but it didn't stop the fear in Simone.

"I wish I didn't see ya again. It ain't worth it." Without another word, Simone fled from the room.

"Go after her, Ariana," Paulette pleaded. In her eyes there was no hurt, only compassion for her mother. "She won't listen to me. Please!"

I glanced at Louise, and her face told me she would take care of Paulette, if needed. I hurried to follow Simone, but the elevator had already closed. Throwing open the door to the stairs, I practically plunged down the five flights to the bottom. Simone was just leaving the building, head bowed and shoulders hunched, when I arrived.

What should I say? My thought was a silent prayer.

Down the cement sidewalk she went and then across the street and a half block more until she turned on a side road. I followed from a distance, recognizing the path to the store near Paulette's. To my left there were more apartments, to my right a small forest-like strip of undeveloped land that had a path of logs leading down the gentle slope to the store. It was the only green for miles around, and the children loved to come here, where they were free to romp at will.

Simone stopped halfway down the slope, clutching the remains of a wooden railing that had once run the length of the path. "Go away," she muttered.

"What's really wrong?" I asked. "You picked a fight on purpose."

She stared at her foot as it systematically ground a fallen twig into the dirt. "It ain't true, that bunk about yer church, and I don't like to see my daughter trustin' in stuff that's only goin' to let her down. She's dyin', and that's it." Her despair was easy for me to understand. Not so many years ago, I had been in her position.

I put a gentle hand on her shoulder and said with all the emotion I could muster, "I *know* the gospel's true! Look around you. The very beauty of the world, the exactness of the universe—everything testifies of God, of His love for us! Every blade of grass, every bird that flies, every idea that man has! This is no random accident we see. This is the loving creation of a Supreme Being, a God! It's perfect, and all made for us."

"A perfect world wouldn't have no people dyin' like Paulette," Simone retorted. For the first time, her colorless eyes met mine. "What's perfect about that?"

"That wasn't God's fault, and you know it, Simone! Heavenly Father must let people suffer the consequences of their actions, or no one would learn anything. If He came down and solved all our problems for us, we would never grow. We would never develop faith, because He'd be right there in front of us. Our Father gave us agency because He knew it was best for us. What would life be like if we were forced to do right all the time? Don't you see? Sometimes the innocent have to suffer, but it's not God's fault. It's ours, because of our own choices."

"I wish it was true," Simone said. "I really do. If it is true, I hope ya can make me believe. Or maybe Paulette."

"Wait a minute," I said, pulling back from her. "It's not my responsibility to make you believe. Or Paulette's. It's yours to seek out the truth. Everyone is responsible for their own salvation. You can't put that burden on someone else."

She stared. "Am I doin' that?" Her voice was low, and I knew it wasn't directed at me. "How can I know?"

"You could pray."

"Me?" The word came as a snort. "He won't tell me."

On my mission, I had always been taught to use the Book of Mormon because it would bring the Spirit. I knew it wasn't coincidence that only the day before, my study with the children had led me to 1 Nephi 15.

"There's a story in the scriptures about a man named Nephi," I began. "He was a good man and obeyed the Lord's commandments. But two of his older brothers were wicked, and they complained because they thought the Lord's words, given to them through their prophet father, were difficult to understand. Nephi asked why they hadn't asked the Lord, as he had done, for understanding, and the brothers said they hadn't asked because the Lord wouldn't answer. This makes me assume that perhaps they had tried at some point in their lives and didn't receive an answer." My words seemed to strike a chord in Simone, and she listened intently. "Nephi's response to his brothers was to ask why they did not obey the Lord's commandments. You see, the Lord will not answer those who have hardened their hearts through sin."

"You mean the drugs," Simone said. "He won't answer me while I'm doin' stuff like that."

I nearly smiled. Simone had once again proved how agile her mind was. "Well, you know it's wrong. Your body is a temple, the Lord's temple, His gift to you. He has commanded us to take care of it. I know that if you obey His commandments and ask Him with your whole heart, He will respond."

Her face crumpled. "I can't do it! I can't stop. I've been tryin' real hard, but I can't."

"It's not easy. Drugs are addicting. The Lord knows that. You just need to do your best. It won't happen overnight."

"Paulette quit."

"Not alone."

"No?"

"The ward members helped her."

"But I thought ya couldn't join the Church if you was—I mean, why would they help her?"

"Because she's a child of God, like you are."

"If that's true, I'll go to hell anyway 'cause I can't stop." She gazed into the canopy of green above us. "I want to believe that Paulette will go to heaven and that I'll see her again like she says. But even if it's true, I won't make it there to be with her 'cause of the drugs."

"You're right."

Her eyes flew to mine in surprise. "What?"

"Not without help. But if you want to, you can beat it."

"I do want to! I do!" There was no doubting the fervent emotion in her words.

"There are programs—" I began.

"Too expensive." She dismissed them with a wave of her hand.

"Not for your family and those who love you. We can help, if you'll let us."

"I can't let ya do that."

"Why? Because you don't really want to be free?"

"No, I do! But—"

I took her hands in mine. "I love Paulette. She's my best friend, like the sister I never had. To see you freed of drugs would be the greatest gift ever. Can you deny her that joy? Or me?"

"What if I fail?"

"If you don't try, you have already failed." It was a saying I had heard somewhere, and it seemed to fit.

Calm determination filled Simone. "I want to do it. Please help me."

We walked back to the apartment, and I called a friend from my days working with the Anti-Drug Coalition. The next afternoon Paulette and I checked Simone into a six-month program with constant supervision for the first few weeks and varying stages thereafter. Any setback would return her to constant supervision. If all went well, Simone could gain a work release in two weeks, providing she found a new job; her old one as a barmaid was too tempting. Pierre took care of that, setting her up as a clerk in one of the grocery stores he oversaw.

"You can do it, Mother," Paulette encouraged. Her face shone with happiness.

"I think maybe I can."

Before we turned to leave, Paulette pressed a small package into her mother's hands. I knew it was the Book of Mormon. "Read a chapter a day. It'll help." They hugged as well as they could with Paulette's huge stomach between them, and the glow of their love warmed me.

"Try First Nephi, chapter fifteen," I said. "You might recognize the story."

Chapter Fourteen

The next week, Paulette came down with a severe cold. The doctor, fearing another bout of pneumonia and an early delivery, ordered her to bed, and Louise once again took over running her household. But Paulette seemed to be recovering nicely.

The end of July found me alone in my sitting room, wondering where the days had gone. Lu-Lu's wedding was to be held in a mere two weeks; we had still found no way to stop it. I sighed and gazed out the window into the dark night. My reflection stared back at me, my eyes seeming to fill my whole face, large and pensive. I glanced hurriedly away.

It was Monday, and I had hoped Jean-Marc would come home for family night, which I always held after dinner; but he didn't. I had put the children to bed at their usual time, after reading a Book of Mormon story and singing to them in the dark.

I missed Jean-Marc. A feeling of melancholy settled over me as I thought about our relationship. *How could I reach the part of him that was holding back? And why was he holding back?* I needed to ask him, but I was apprehensive of his reaction. I didn't want him to retreat from me to think things over. *Is this how life is supposed to be?* I wondered. The burdens seemed much heavier than they should have been. I put my head in my hands and sighed.

"Mommy?" Marc and Josette stood in the doorway.

"Is something wrong?" I asked. They nodded and ran to me, burrowing their faces into my body.

"I'm scared," Josette said. "The closet was open, and I could see a man in it."

"Why didn't you shut it?" I asked Marc. He shrugged.

"He was afraid, too."

"Was not!"

"Was too!"

"That's enough!" I hugged them both tightly. "I guess I'll go take care of the man in the closet."

Amidst the giggles, I heard someone at the front door.

"Daddy!" The children ran to the hall and smothered him with chubby arms and wet kisses.

Jean-Marc smiled wearily but returned their embraces. "What? Still awake? I guess the tiger will have to eat you up. Grrr!"

They screamed in delight. Now it would take even longer for them to settle down and sleep. But I forced a smile; at least they were able to spend some time with their father. The wrestling continued until Marc hit his head on the coffee table. He screeched in exaggerated agony.

"Big baby!" Josette taunted.

"It hurts!"

Their argument began in earnest, but it was only a shadow of what I faced daily alone. At least now my husband was here to take care of it. He would sit them down and discuss why they shouldn't argue and how the Lord expected them to act. I turned to face Jean-Marc, but his expression frightened me.

"Go to bed now!" he said. His face wore an ugly frown. "I have enough problems at work; I can't deal with this petty bickering!"

"But I can't go—" Josette began.

"Now!"

"But the closet," Marc wailed.

"One, two, three," Jean-Marc said. Before he had finished counting, the twins were out the door, crying loudly about the monster.

"What was that all about?" I said stiffly. "You didn't even listen to them. They're scared to death because of something they saw in the closet, but you're so busy being sick of their arguing that you don't hear them when they really need you!"

"They were arguing about something stupid," he said. "I just stopped them."

I wondered if he thought I should be grateful. "By yelling at them and not listening? Is that what you want to be to them—someone who comes home at night, just to yell when the mildest of arguments break out?"

"Mildest?"

I nodded, and he gave me a sheepish grin. "I'm sorry. I just got angry. Sometimes I forget they're only four. I'm not with them all day, so I don't have as much patience as you do."

"That's exactly why you should have *more* patience," I retorted. "You haven't had to listen to it all day."

We stared at each other in silence. "Is something else wrong?" he asked. Beneath his calm exterior, I sensed an odd fear.

"It's Monday. Tonight was family night."

He slapped his hand against his forehead. "I forgot."

That's what I thought was so strange. His forgetting didn't go with his character. Something—perhaps fear?—was causing him to act this way.

"They're only four," he said. "It's not like they really need family night."

"Don't they? Wouldn't a lesson on fighting come in handy?" I purposely made my voice light. I turned to leave.

"Where are you going?" he asked.

"To get the man out of the closet."

Jean-Marc followed me to the twins' dark bedroom, where we found them huddled together on Josette's bed. Jean-Marc's face was full of remorse. He strode across the room and swept both children into his arms. "I'm sorry, kids. I didn't know you had a monster in here."

"He's in the closet." Marc wrapped his arms around his father in forgiveness, but Josette pouted a few more seconds before giving in.

I turned on the light and went to open the free-standing closet in the corner. There was nothing in it but clothes. "See? He's gone."

"Your arguing must have scared him away," Jean-Marc said. The twins laughed.

"Maybe he heard you come home, Daddy," Marc said. He scratched his eyebrow. "Why did you miss family night again? We ate cake."

Jean-Marc's eyes met mine. "I don't know." His voice seemed puzzled. "I had to work."

I shrugged and left him with the twins. There was no telling how long he would stay with them now. He was a good man; he just didn't know his children well.

Or know how much I missed him.

André had slept through the entire commotion. As I kissed his little cheek, I marveled again at how good he was. The compelling desire for another child entered my heart, one with Jean-Marc's green-brown eyes, but I pushed it away. I couldn't handle another child, not now.

An hour later, Jean-Marc came to our room. He undressed quickly and climbed into bed, reaching out his arms for me. I moved closer and curled my body into his. I tried to sleep, but Jean-Marc's breathing told me he was wide awake.

"What's wrong?" I asked.

"I was thinking about my father," he said softly. "Why can't I remember him? All I can recall is his voice, not his face."

"What brought this on?"

He sighed. "Something you said earlier. When I was there, with the twins, it came back to me. I began wondering how they would remember me when they got older."

"They'll remember playing tiger," I said, trying to cheer him. Whatever had brought this mood, I welcomed it. If change could only begin within, perhaps it had started tonight.

"I hope so," he said.

So did I.

⁓

The phone rang in the middle of the night, its tone loud and piercing. Thinking it was the smoke alarm, I jerked to a sitting position. "Wake up, Jean-Marc!" I shook him briefly and ran into the hall before realizing it was only the phone. Dread rose within me. A phone ringing in the night only bode ill for those it reached.

"Hello?"

"The baby's coming now!" Pierre blurted out the instant I spoke. I almost cried with relief. At least no one had been killed in a sudden accident. The baby was early, nearly two months, but the doctor had warned us it might happen. In fact, he had even given Paulette drugs to help the baby's lungs develop faster in the event of an early birth.

"Can you come? She wants you here. Louise is staying with Marie-Thérèse."

"I'll be right there!"

Jean-Marc had appeared in the kitchen. "What's up?" He trailed after me as I returned to our room and began dressing.

"The baby's coming. I've got to be there with her."

He sat on the bed, watching me sleepily. "How long will you be?"

"There's no telling. I'll call when she's born."

He nodded. I ran a quick hand through my hair. "You look beautiful," he said.

I could tell he meant it, but I had no time for sentiment. "Now, please," I said, holding his gaze with my own. "If the children cry, get up with them. And don't be upset." Sometimes he could become annoyed if awakened from a sound sleep. I didn't blame him exactly because I got angry too, but as parents we had to contain our irritation at things that in twenty years wouldn't make any difference.

"Of course," he said, sounding offended.

I kissed him and ran out the door.

I was out of breath when I arrived at the hospital. A nurse made me scrub my hands with a sterile brush and special soap, wrapped me in a white gown, and hustled me into the delivery room before I had a chance to think. They were taking every precaution to prevent germs from infecting the premature baby. Paulette lay on the bed heaving, rivulets of perspiration streaming from her forehead. Pierre held her hand, coaching her. Two doctors and three nurses surrounded the bed. One of the doctors was Medard. Each member of the medical staff wore thick rubber gloves, reaching past the elbow, presumably a safeguard against their becoming infected with HIV. I thought I caught a glimpse of plastic lining under their white coats as well.

"I'm here, Paulette," I said.

"Thank you, Ari." She reached out her other hand and grasped mine. Then the contraction began again, and her face contorted in pain.

"Push, Paulette!" the doctor said.

"Oh, it hurts," she moaned. "I can't!"

Seeing her pain, I remembered the experience all too well. "It'll be over soon," I murmured. "And you'll have your little girl."

Paulette glanced at me gratefully. She let go of our hands and grabbed her own legs, bearing down.

"Good! She's coming!"

We watched as the head eased out, and Dr. Medard checked for a cord. "Okay, now push again, Paulette," he said. With a final effort, the baby was born.

"You have a girl," someone said.

"A girl!" Paulette sighed. We had already known from the ultrasound, but ultrasounds had been known to be wrong.

I saw only a glimpse of a tiny baby with dark hair before the second doctor picked her up and carried her to the table and equipment at the side of the room. Only a few inches of scrawny legs hung over his cupped hands. *How can such a tiny thing be alive at all?* I wondered. The doctor set her down, and two of the nurses crowded around him, working quickly. What was wrong? I couldn't see what they were doing, and it scared me that I couldn't hear the baby. I wanted to rush over and see for myself what was happening, but Paulette reached out for my hand, squeezing it tightly. At last we heard a tiny cry.

"Is she all right?" Pierre asked.

"They're stabilizing her," said Dr. Medard. "And cleaning off any blood. Then Dr. Orlan will take her to run more tests since she's so early."

At the words, Dr. Orlan glanced over his shoulder at us. He was part Asian, by the slant of his dark eyes, and it made him seem mysterious in the midst of the more common French features. "She looks good and is breathing well with the oxygen," he said. "I think she'll be fine."

Paulette sobbed her relief, but apparently not all was right. Dr. Medard had continued to work with Paulette and was now asking the nurse for drugs whose names I didn't recognize.

"What's wrong?" Pierre asked with a hint of hysteria in his voice.

"She's hemorrhaging a little, but we'll get it under control," Dr. Medard said. It seemed like long minutes until the man heaved a sigh and stepped back from the bed. He looked up at Paulette and Pierre. "It's stopping now."

"We're taking the baby." Dr. Orlan looked at Pierre. "You can go with the baby, or you can stay with your wife."

Paulette shook her head. "You go with her, Ariana."

I nodded and stood up, but the doctor hesitated. "We usually only let parents come when the babies are so early. It's important for the baby not to be exposed to too many different people at this stage."

Paulette glared at him. "There's nothing usual about my situation."
"I've got AIDS, and my husband is HIV positive. Who do you think is
going to raise this child?"

Pierre nodded. "My sister-in-law is closer than family."

Dr. Orlan appeared to make a quick decision. "Okay, then, come
on."

I followed them as they whisked the baby from the room in a
warmer and down the hall to the other side of the floor, opposite the
delivery rooms. The doctor and nurses paused to open a door with a
sign reading Intensive Care Nursery. The quiet in the room was relieved
by the hum and beeping of the equipment, and occasionally one heard
soft human voices or a weak baby's cry. Incubators were spaced at regular intervals; about ten of the forty box-like chambers were empty. The
rest held tiny babies, some much smaller than Paulette's daughter, all
watched over by attentive nurses or parents. There were no windows as
in the regular nursery, where parents, friends, and family could peer at
the babies. They wanted to keep this nursery as germfree as possible,
and no windows meant fewer people in the area. The array of equipment and the number of personnel, even this early in the morning, were
impressive. I was beginning to appreciate the large and varied nature of
this hospital.

They took the new baby to a corner and continued to work with
her, taking all kinds of tests before bathing her, putting on a miniature
diaper, and taping on numerous thin wires that connected to nearby
monitors. Through it all she whimpered softly, sometimes even crying
loudly. I felt my heart go out to her, as any mother's would at the sound
of a newborn's cry. In between tests, one of the nurses rocked the baby
close to her chest. I was grateful she could do for the child what Paulette
could not.

"How is she?" I asked when they seemed to be finished. Even to me,
my voice sounded distant.

"Thanks to the drugs Dr. Medard gave the mother, the baby's lungs
are pretty well developed," said the doctor. "She seems to be breathing
better now. We only had to give her oxygen for a short time, and that's
pretty unusual this early."

"How much does she weigh?" I asked.

"One point seven kilograms. And she's thirty-six centimeters long."

That was much shorter than André had been and only half of what he'd weighed.

I watched with detached interest, trying to tell myself this tiny, two-hour-old baby with the numerous white wires trailing from her body had nothing to do with me. Yet with her dark hair and enormous brown eyes, she reminded me of my own twins, who had been born three weeks early and had weighed less than two and a half kilograms each. They had been so small and yet so perfect. My earlier desire to have another child returned swiftly and unexpectedly. I stared at my niece, forcing myself to notice how small she really was. If not for the diaper, it would seem she had no bottom at all, just legs that began at the base of a too-slender back.

"Would you like to hold her?" the doctor asked. I didn't—it wouldn't pay to become attached until we knew about the HIV. But he wrapped her body, bare except for the diaper, in a pink blanket that covered all the wires attached to her, and placed her in my arms before I could protest. "It helps to have someone who loves them to cuddle them, if only for a while," he added. "And the blanket will help keep the wires in place."

One of the nurses handed me a bottle of warm milk with a minuscule nipple on the end. It had been a long time since I had used a bottle. André had never taken one, and the twins had only needed one extra a day to supplement my milk until they were old enough for cereal. I was out of practice, and my hand shook. The nurse helped me guide the nipple into the baby's mouth. She sucked, and the whimpering stopped, but almost immediately she choked. I glanced at the nurse anxiously.

"It's all right," she said. "Babies born this early have a problem swallowing and breathing at the same time. She'll receive most of her food for the time being through a tube in her nose. Each day we'll give her the bottle and gradually increase the feedings until we can take the tube off completely."

"When will that be?"

"It depends. But the tube needs to be off before they go home. Try to give her a little more. The faster she learns, the sooner she'll go home."

I did as she asked, but the baby didn't seem happy about it. At last, I handed the bottle back to the nurse and simply rocked her. Soon she closed her eyes, which seemed overly large in her small face, and slept. I gazed at the precious newborn, thinking how cruel life could be, even at the same time a miracle was happening. Had this little baby come from heaven only to go back so soon? We wouldn't know until later in the afternoon if she had HIV.

Despite my determination to the contrary, I felt an immediate and distinct bond with my niece. Was this what Paulette had planned? What did it mean? *Nonsense,* I told myself. *I would feel the same for any new-born who was also a relative. It meant nothing.*

I cuddled her gently for a moment more, until the nurse told me it was time to leave. She placed the infant carefully in an incubator with warm air circulating inside, removing the soft blanket. She checked all the wires while my niece slept peacefully on.

"Don't worry. I'll watch over her," she said kindly. For the first time, I noticed the nurse's features. She was older than I, near fifty by the looks of her. She had a liberal sprinkling of gray in her dark hair and heavy lines around her eyes and mouth, as if she'd done a lot of laughing. "I'm a mother of six and a grandmother too," she added.

"Thank you." I felt comforted to know she would be there, and I knew Paulette would also be grateful.

As I turned to leave, the nurse said, "Only parents and grandparents are allowed to visit here. And you, of course. Are there any siblings?"

"A sister. Four years old."

"She can come in a few days to see the baby."

"How long will the baby be here?"

She smiled. "It really depends. Some are here for a week; others, months. But I would say about a month, give or take a little. Provided, of course, there are no complications."

I retraced my steps to find Paulette, but they had already moved her to a room. When I found her, she glanced up anxiously.

"She's fine," I assured her. "She's breathing on her own, and she looks good."

"Thank heaven!" Paulette said. "They won't let me see her until later. They're worried about how much I bled."

"Why don't you go see her?" I suggested to Pierre.

"Will you stay with Paulette?"

"Of course." I settled in the chair next to her bed.

He left, and Paulette stared after him. "He doesn't look good."

"He's been worried, that's all."

She didn't reply but turned to face me. "How long before we know?" She didn't need to explain further. We all ached to know if this new little baby had HIV.

"This afternoon."

She bit her lip. "I can't nurse her, you know. They won't let me because of the virus—even if she already has it. In many ways, I feel I'm not her mother at all." There was a touching sadness in her voice.

"She's here because of you. And tomorrow, when you hold her in your arms, you'll know you're her mother."

"Thank you, Ari. I'm so glad you're here."

"I'll always be here for you, Paulette. Always."

There were tears on her lashes as her eyes drooped and closed. In a short time, her steady breathing told me she slept.

I let my head drop into my hands, shielding my tired eyes from the bright morning light coming through the blinds. My head ached from lack of sleep, and my heart from something else. There was a hope, an aching, torturous kind of yearning inside me.

I began to pray.

Chapter Fifteen

*A*riana, wake up," a voice said softly. A gentle hand nudged my shoulder.

My eyes flew open. "Oh, Pierre. Did you see her?" I stretched and yawned.

He nodded. "I'd like to give her a blessing. I've called Jean-Marc. He's waiting for you to come home, and then he'll stop by on his way to work. I've gotten it approved with Dr. Orlan."

"She's okay, though, isn't she?" I asked quickly.

"Yes. She's having a little trouble breathing now—they're giving her oxygen again—and her heart rate is slower than it should be. But she's got a strong spirit. I think she'll be all right." I noticed he didn't mention the HIV. The omission was all too obvious.

"What time is it?"

"Seven."

"I'll go home. Jean-Marc will be here soon."

Pierre's nod was absentminded. His gaze was already focused on Paulette, a tender expression filling his face. With a light hand, he touched her cheek as she slept.

I left them and wandered down the hall to the elevator. I didn't notice anyone as I found my way to the car. When I arrived home, the house was bustling. The children were at the table, and Jean-Marc was ready to leave.

"Are you all right?" he asked.

"Yes. I'm just tired."

He kissed me, and we had a family prayer before he hurried out the door. I sank to a kitchen chair and concentrated on answering the children's questions.

Paulette slept the morning and part of the afternoon away. Near three, Louise took Marie-Thérèse to the hospital to see her mother. Afterwards she came to my apartment. I was shocked at how old Louise looked. She walked slowly, hobbling, her face contorting at each step.

"My arthritis is acting up," she said. I helped her sit on the couch.

"I have a baby sister," Marie-Thérèse was saying importantly to the twins. "Only the doctor said I can't see her till tomorrow."

"What's her name?" the twins wanted to know.

"We don't know yet." Marie-Thérèse's voice was matter-of-fact. "We weren't expecting her so soon. But I want to call her Marie."

"That's your name," Marc protested.

She shrugged. "Mommy likes my name."

"Why don't you go to your room to play for a while?" suggested Louise. "I want to talk to your mommy." When the children left, she turned to me, her face grave. "The baby has HIV."

I felt as if someone had kicked me in the stomach. I had been sure she would be healthy, especially since Paulette had been so willing to sacrifice her life to save the baby.

"I have to go to Paulette," I said.

Louise nodded. "I'll stay with the children. I'll walk them over to the park."

"But your arthritis . . ."

She waved it aside. "I'll sit on the bench and watch them. A little walking will do me some good."

When I told the children about going to the park, they nearly broke the door down in their hurry to leave the apartment. "I like it when people have babies," Josette confided to Marie-Thérèse. "We get to play a lot more."

Jean-Marc had taken our car, but Louise gave me the keys to hers. I drove numbly to the hospital, wondering what I would say to my friend.

Paulette wasn't in her room. The doctor had let Pierre wheel her into the ICU to see the new baby. I waited until she came back. Her eyes were wet but strangely elated.

"I held my baby," she said when she saw me.

"How is she?" I glanced at Pierre, but his face was impervious to my scrutiny.

"Better since the blessing," Paulette said. "She doesn't need the oxygen anymore. The doctor seems encouraged—except for the HIV . . ."

I knelt in front of her wheelchair. "I'm sorry," I said. My voice sounded like I might cry at any moment—exactly how I felt.

"She's an angel," Paulette whispered to me, looking more beautiful than I had ever seen her, despite the emaciation of her body. "I'm so grateful to have her any way she is." She held out her arms, and we cried together. Only Pierre's eyes were dry, his dark orbs standing out against the odd pallor of his face.

———

That night Jean-Marc came home early, after I had visited Paulette at the hospital. Carrying a bouquet of white roses and a box of fresh pastries, he announced a second family night. I was baffled and the children were ecstatic, but we all accepted his presence gratefully, without asking why. The lesson he gave was on fighting. I decided my husband still felt guilty for the night before, and I wondered how long it might last. Despite my cynicism, his presence lifted the somber mood that had overcome me since learning the baby was HIV positive.

The next day, when I took Marie-Thérèse to the hospital to see her sister, the feeling of optimism remained. Before taking Marie-Thérèse to the nursery, we stopped to talk with Paulette. She lay listlessly on the bed, staring into space. Her breathing seemed labored, and her eyes had lost a bit of their light.

"Where's Pierre?" I asked. I knew he had taken a week off work to be with her and the new baby.

"He went to see the doctor."

"Are you all right?"

"I've got pneumonia again," she said, frowning. "My body's weak now, I guess. But I'll be okay."

"Does it hurt, Mommy?" Marie-Thérèse asked. She gripped her doll so firmly that her little fingers were turning white.

"Not much, honey. I feel much better seeing my princess."

Marie-Thérèse relaxed and smiled. She climbed onto the bed and lay next to her mother, giving her a full-body hug. Paulette sighed contently, the light coming back to her eyes. I wondered if her arms felt empty without her new baby.

Marie-Thérèse's patience didn't last long. "I'm going to see the baby now," she declared, sliding off the bed. "But what are we going to name her? She has to have a name."

We hadn't told her the baby had HIV and that it might be as little as six months before she developed AIDS. I understood Paulette's dilemma; it was hard to name a child who was almost a part of heaven already.

"You're right," Paulette said. "What should we name her?"

"Marie?"

"That's a wonderful name, but it might get a little confusing, don't you think?"

"Well, Mommy, what do you want to call her?"

Paulette glanced up at me quickly, penetratingly, and then away again. "I once knew a baby named Antoinette. She was very pretty."

"Where is she now?"

"She's in heaven with the angels."

"Is that Josette's sister you're talking about?"

Paulette nodded. I stared at her, but she refused to meet my gaze.

"I like that name," Marie-Thérèse said.

"No," I whispered with an intensity that frightened me. In my experience, people with that name never lived very long. I had named my daughter after my dead brother, Antoine, and after Queen Marie-Antoinette, who had been beheaded during the French Revolution. Naming this new little life Antoinette would be paramount to burying her early.

"Let's think about it some more," Paulette said, meeting my eyes. "We'll talk to Daddy, okay?"

Marie-Thérèse nodded. She turned to me. "Can we go see my sister now?"

As we were leaving the room, we ran into Simone. She was dressed as usual in a summer dress, but today her dark blonde hair was swept up into a bun, and little tendrils of hair fell in wisps against her cheek and neck. It was flattering, and for the first time she almost looked the forty-five she was instead of the sixty most people took her to be. The heavy wrinkles on her face were still there, but her expression was less tense, more content somehow.

"Grandma!" Marie-Thérèse held out her arms and hugged her.

"You look different today," Marie-Thérèse said. For the first time, I noticed Simone wasn't wearing heavy makeup, probably the reason for her more youthful appearance.

"You look great, Simone." I had only seen her twice since her admission to the drug and alcohol program two weeks before, but she had always seemed the same. Not like today.

She smiled. "Thanks. I been experimentin' with my hair and makeup. They teach a lot of stuff at the clinic. Today's my first day out alone. They let me come a day early, seein' as Paulette had her baby and all. I have two hours before I have to go back."

"Did you come to see me?" Paulette called weakly from the bed.

Simone pushed past us. "Of course—and my new granddaughter, if they'll let me."

"Oh, they'll probably let you in, but they may not let you hold her," Paulette said. "Though she is stronger today."

"We're going to the nursery now. Would you like to come?" I asked.

Simone shook her head. "I'll catch up with ya. I want to visit with Paulette fer a while first."

We said good-bye and went toward the nursery. Marie-Thérèse nearly danced with excitement. "My very own sister," she said over and over. "I can't believe it!" Her enthusiasm was catching, and soon I had overcome my dread at seeing the new baby again.

After scrubbing our hands and arms and putting on white robes, we were admitted to the nursery. They almost didn't let Marie-Thérèse bring her doll, but the child insisted. The older nurse who had been there the day before watched over the baby. "You must be the big sister," she said brightly.

The brightness made me wonder if the baby's condition was worsening. "Is she all right?" I asked.

She smiled. "Better than all right. She's doing so wonderfully, you can hold her for a few minutes, if you'd like."

"I . . . uh . . ." I couldn't explain it, but the last thing I wanted was to feel again that strong bond with the baby.

"Oh, goody!" Marie-Thérèse said. "I was hoping I could hold her. I brought my favorite doll to show her." She held her worn rag doll up for the nurse to see. "My mommy made it," she said proudly.

"It's very pretty," the nurse said. "I'm sure your sister will love it.

But let's not get it too close to her yet. Only things that have been sterilized—that means scrubbed clean with special soap—can touch your sister right now because she's so little." She opened the incubator and lifted the baby out. "Have you decided on a name?"

"Probably Antoinette, but we still have to talk with Daddy," Marie-Thérèse said. "Antoinette is Josette's sister who lives in heaven now. Mommy says she was pretty."

The nurse glanced at me questioningly, but I looked away, feeling my face tighten. From the corner of my eye, I saw her wrap the baby in the pink blanket, once again covering the wires.

"Here, honey," the nurse said to Marie-Thérèse. "Sit right here, and I'll help you hold the baby. We have to be very careful because she's so tiny."

"I will." Marie-Thérèse climbed onto the chair. She handed me her doll. "You hold it up so she can see."

So I held the doll up as Marie-Thérèse gazed down into her sister's face for the first time. "You are so beautiful," she cooed. "I just can't believe how perfect you are. See?" She motioned toward the doll with her head. "That's Dolly. When you are older, maybe Mommy will make you one, too." I had never known the doll had a name, but then I had never dreamed Marie-Thérèse would take so quickly to mothering her little sister, either. I hoped it would be a long time before she would have to take on that role.

"Why does she have the little tube in her nose?" Marie-Thérèse asked. The nurse launched into a simple yet thorough explanation, ending with a promise to let Marie-Thérèse help feed the baby a bottle before we left. I wondered if my niece might drop the baby in her excitement, but the nurse didn't take her gentle hands away for an instant.

"What are all these white strings on her?" Marie-Thérèse asked.

"They're wires. They go to these machines right here. They listen to the baby's heartbeat and stuff to make sure she's okay."

"What does that other baby have in its mouth?" Marie-Thérèse tried to point but remembered the baby in her arms.

The nurse motioned to a baby across from us who was being gently cradled by a young mother. "You mean that baby?" Marie-Thérèse nodded and the nurse explained. "She has a mouthpiece to stop her mouth from being deformed because of the respirator. The respirator helps her breathe."

"But my baby's breathing."

"She sure is. She's very lucky. Some babies are born so early they can't even be held. They have to lie under a heat lamp, and the first thing their mothers can do for them is to very gently wet their mouth with a soft sponge."

It seemed Paulette's baby was very lucky indeed. Some of these babies now fighting for their lives in the ICU nursery would never go home with their parents. At least my new niece and her mother would share some time together.

After a while, a second nurse came with a warm bottle for the baby. "Good, the family's here," she said. "It's feeding time." She handed the bottle to our nurse and then went on to the next baby.

Marie-Thérèse grasped the bottle tightly, and the nurse helped her put it into the baby's mouth. "What kind of milk is this?" As with most children, Marie-Thérèse's curiosity knew no bounds.

"Formula," I said.

"Actually," the nurse explained, "it's mother's milk—most of it a donation from the mothers whose babies are here. They usually express much more than their babies can eat, so they give it to the babies whose mothers are unable to nurse for one reason or another. Mother's milk is the best thing we can give them; it will help them grow strong faster. Of course, the milk is gathered under very rigid guidelines, so it's perfectly clean and safe. Because we've had so much success with it, our doctors have fought to keep the program in place."

Like the day before, the baby had problems drinking the milk, but she managed to get some of it down. Marie-Thérèse's face glowed with happiness, and I also felt proud of the effort the baby put out. She seemed strong and willing to try.

"We'd better put her back now," the nurse said when she was asleep. "She hasn't any fat to keep her warm." She laid the baby in the warm incubator.

Marie-Thérèse stood on the chair to better see the baby. "I'll be back, Antoinette," she whispered so softly that I almost didn't understand the words. "As soon as they let me." She helped Dolly wave good-bye to the baby.

We made our way back to Paulette's room, only to find Simone pacing outside.

"Mommy?" Marie-Thérèse walked to the door, but no one was inside.

"What happened?" I asked Simone in a hushed tone.

Her eyes held fear. "Paulette stopped breathin'," she whispered urgently. "I called the nurse, and they worked on her. She's breathin' again, but that's all they'll tell me. They're takin' her to ICU. I waited here to tell you." Tears welled up in her eyes. "Oh, Ariana, I'm afraid."

So was I.

Marie-Thérèse had satisfied herself the room was empty and returned to my side. "They've taken her to another room," I said, "to watch over her better."

"I want to see her." Marie-Thérèse held her doll tightly in her arms. I wondered if she could feel our fear.

"We will, honey."

Her lips trembled. "Is she going to die?"

She had asked me that question once two months before, and I had said no. Then I found out about Paulette's AIDS and understood that she *would* die. I knew Marie-Thérèse's parents had explained about the AIDS then, but two months was a long time in the eyes of a child. To her, everything had been all right again. What should I tell her now?

"No," I found myself saying. "Don't you worry. She's going to be fine."

We made our way to the ICU waiting room, where we talked to several nurses. No one would tell us anything, except that Pierre had been found and was now with Paulette. Simone paced the floor while I called Louise at home. I also called my mother. "I can't leave until I know," I said.

"Everything's fine here. Take as long as you'd like. I'll call Jean-Marc at work and put him on alert."

"Thanks." As I hung up, Giselle, the nurse who had taken care of Paulette before, came into the room. I was relieved to see a familiar face.

"Ariana?" she said.

"What's going on?"

She put her arm around me and drew me away from Simone and Marie-Thérèse. "Paulette's dying. Dr. Medard doesn't think she'll make it through the night. It's not a gradual decline like it was last time but a sudden one. It's time to call your family and say good-bye."

I felt shock on my face, and tears rolled unbidden down my cheeks even as I fought them back. I had known this day would come, but never had I been prepared for it to come so soon. "No! Not yet." I stared at Giselle, begging her to take back her words, but she only nodded gently.

"She died once already, but we brought her back. She seems determined to live, but I don't see how she can hold on. It's a miracle she's alive at all. She's still too weak from having the baby to be able to fight the pneumonia. If it weren't for the AIDS . . ."

"Not now. Oh, please, dear Lord, not now," I murmured.

Giselle squeezed my shoulder. "She keeps asking for you."

"I have to call my mother."

She nodded. "I'll take the others back for a while, and then you can come when I bring them out. We want to keep the excitement down; we never give up hope completely that they'll recover."

Her comment sparked some hope within me. She *had* recovered once. It was still possible for her to do so again—if we could get her another blessing.

I returned to the phone while Giselle led Marie-Thérèse and Simone into the back room. Both looked frightened. I could barely speak as I told my mother what was happening.

"I'll call Louise and Jean-Marc," she said. "We'll all be right there."

Minutes ticked slowly by as I sat alone in the waiting room. The harsh glare of the fluorescent lights made my eyes ache. The now-familiar smell of the hospital—somehow formal and removed from real life—seemed stronger than ever. Yet this was life—and death.

My mother and the children arrived first, followed almost immediately by Louise. Saying nothing, my mother enfolded me in her arms, and I burst into tears. My children crowded around my knees anxiously.

"Is Aunt Paulette going to heaven?" Marc asked.

I nodded. It seemed my mother had prepared them on the drive over.

"Can I say good-bye?" Josette was crying. Large teardrops spilled from her eyes and onto her face.

"Yes. But just for a minute, and then Grandma will stay with you out here." I looked at my mother, who had André in her arms, and she nodded.

A few moments later, Giselle came back with Simone and a tearful Marie-Thérèse. "Who's next?" she asked somberly.

I stood up, taking the twins by the hands. "Can they come? They want to say good-bye."

Giselle hesitated only a moment. "Of course. Come along."

We followed her along the silent corridor. The shiny linoleum squeaked beneath our feet, giving the silence its only relief. The twins clung to my hands tightly. Giselle stopped at a sink, and we had to scrub our hands thoroughly as we had when visiting the baby. Then she brought us to a door, motioned us inside, and continued down the hall alone.

Pierre sat by the bed, holding his wife's limp hand. I was appalled at Paulette's condition. Pain was etched on her face. I could hear her breathing, ragged and harsh, and an oxygen tube dangled from her nose.

"I'm dying," she said when she saw me.

I shook my head. "You can't give up."

"It isn't a question of giving up. It's time."

"Aunt Paulette?" Josette whispered, stepping closer to the bed. "I love you." Tears fell to her cheeks.

"I love you, too."

"I wish you didn't have to go." Marc stood by his sister bravely, but his lower lip quivered, and his eyelashes glinted with moisture. I felt terrible exposing them to death at such a young age, but I knew it would be better for them later on, after Paulette's death. This way there would be closure.

"I'll miss you, too, but I'm going to heaven. I'm not going to be suffering or sick anymore. And we'll see each other soon. You see, Jesus is going to take me in his arms and hug me. Do you know how happy I will be?" Paulette spoke to the children, but her words were for me. I wanted her to cling to life, but at the same time I knew that to waste painfully away, as many AIDS patients did, was not a pleasant way to die. Paulette was trying to tell me that at least she would go quickly and also remind me of the beauty awaiting her in heaven.

"Could you say hi to Antoinette for me?" Josette said. Her words startled me. I knew she was talking about the sister she had never known, but I had already begun to think of Paulette's baby as Antoinette.

Paulette nodded, a faint smile touching her lips. "I will. And I'll tell her all about you and Marc."

"And André," Marc added. "But she probably already knows. She looks down on us, you know."

"Will you look down on Marie-Thérèse?" Josette asked.

"Every day."

Josette nodded in satisfaction. "I'll tell her."

"It's time to go now, children." Taking turns, the children kissed Paulette's cheek. Then they buried their faces in my body. I knew they didn't understand death yet, that over the months to come I would have to help them cope with their aunt's death. I was more grateful than I could express for the wonderful plan of salvation that made eternal families possible. Because of the gospel, I would have answers to their questions.

"Don't go yet, Ariana. I need to talk to you."

"I'll take them back to the waiting room. I'll be right back."

When I arrived in the waiting room, Jean-Marc was with the others. I was surprised; it seemed my mother had been able to reach him. I took his hand gratefully. "How is she?" everyone asked at once. I shook my head and bit my lip to keep it still.

"I have to go back in," I said, trying to keep the dread from my voice. "She wants to talk to me."

"Jean-Marc, go with her," Louise said. "You and Pierre need to give her a blessing. I'll go afterwards."

Yes! A blessing. It had worked the last time. Hope flared in my breast.

"I want to go, too," Marie-Thérèse said. Her face drooped in a frightened frown. I understood her need to be with her mother, and I reached for her hand, feeling her small fingers close around mine. I led them back to the room, stepping more confidently. As we were about to go in, Giselle appeared.

"Going to give her a blessing?" she asked. When we nodded, she said, "Good."

"How is it you're here, instead of in the other wing where you

worked before?" Jean-Marc asked. "Not that we aren't glad to have you."
I had wondered too but hadn't had the presence of mind to ask.

"When an AIDS patient becomes critical and needs the additional
care they can only give here, we like to have someone specifically trained
in AIDS to come over. When I learned it was Paulette, I volunteered.
I'm sort of on loan, you might say. I've worked here enough to know
my way around. Besides," her voice lowered, "even here people are
afraid of getting HIV. It helps to have someone who is used to working
with AIDS patients."

"We're glad you're here," I said.

We turned into the room. Giselle entered and stood near the door.
Marie-Thérèse ran across the room and scrambled up onto the bed as
she had earlier in the day. Paulette's frail arms went around her. The
scene was poignant, tugging at my heart until I thought it would burst.

Jean-Marc greeted his brother with a hug and then pulled out his
oil. "I'll anoint her," he said. "But you need to bless your wife."

"Yes, please," Paulette rasped. "It will make my passing easier."

"You can't die, Paulette," Pierre pleaded. His voice sounded nearly
as bad as hers.

Marie-Thérèse buried her face in her mother's body, and I coughed
gently, reminding them of the child's presence. I moved closer to the
bed to stroke Paulette's leg beneath the blanket. She smiled fleetingly.

The brothers placed their hands on her, and we bowed our heads.
After Jean-Marc finished the anointing, Pierre began the blessing.
Among other things, he blessed Paulette with courage and with a
knowledge of her Father's love. Nowhere did he mention her regaining
her health.

"Thank you," Paulette said when it was over, reaching up to grasp
her husband's hands.

Pierre smiled at her tenderly, but I could see the seething anger in
his eyes. He squeezed her hands and then backed away from the bed.
"I need a breath of air," he said. Without explaining further, he stalked
from the room.

"Go after him," Paulette pleaded.

Jean-Marc and I ran out the door, leaving Giselle and Marie-
Thérèse alone with Paulette.

Pierre was out in the hall with his forehead resting against the wall, and his fists beating uselessly at the stretch of white.

Jean-Marc grabbed his shoulder, bringing him around to face us. "I could have healed her!" Pierre said, gazing at us with fury. "I could have! I felt the power of God within me. It was right there within my grasp." He held out his hand, palm up, and clenched it as he spoke. "I could have made her well, gotten rid of the AIDS completely."

Jean-Marc and I exchanged looks, not knowing what to say. "Then why didn't you?" I asked. More than anything I wanted Paulette to be cured, as impossible as it seemed.

With one hand he wiped tears from his cheeks. "It wasn't right," he whispered hoarsely. "It just wasn't right. I had the power, but I couldn't do it. She isn't going to live. Paulette is supposed to die!"

I shivered at his words, despite the warmth of the corridor. He stared at us defiantly, and then his shoulders crumpled and he began to sob, racked with a torment I remembered so well.

Jean-Marc threw his arms around his brother, but Pierre shrugged him aside. "I should have healed her," he said. "It's my fault she's going to die." He turned on his heel and fled down the hall, leaving us to gaze helplessly after him.

CHAPTER SIXTEEN

*J*ean-Marc stared in the direction his brother had gone. His normally cheerful features were drawn with anxiety, the ever-ready grin replaced by a worried frown. He turned to me without speaking, eyes apologizing for what he wanted to do: leave me and go after his brother.

"Go," I said. "Go after him. He needs you. I'll be fine." He smiled slightly and leaned forward to hug me. "I'll be back as soon as possible." He sprinted down the hail, and I smiled after him wistfully. I felt a great loss at his leaving because I would have to face Paulette alone, but I knew he had to follow his brother. I was losing my best friend; Pierre was losing his wife. There was no comparison.

Reluctantly, I returned to Paulette's room. She looked up as I entered. "Jean-Marc's with him," I said. "He'll be fine."

Paulette appeared relieved. "In some ways this is harder for him," she said.

Giselle nodded. "It really is."

"But there's one thing I have to know." Paulette's gaze met mine and dread washed over me. I had known all along this moment would come.

"Why don't I take Marie-Thérèse back to her grandmothers for a while?" Giselle said.

Marie-Thérèse slid off the bed. "I'll be back, Mommy." She held her finger to her mother's lips and then to her heart.

From somewhere, Paulette found the strength to copy the motion. Her eyes fixed on Marie-Thérèse's as if never wanting to let her go. "I love you more than anything," she said.

"I'll be right back." Giselle led Marie-Thérèse from the room. Paulette and I watched each other, and I wondered what would come next. But my friend lay silently on the bed, saying nothing until Giselle came back into the room and stood on Paulette's other side near the monitors.

"I want to know if you'll take care of my daughters when I'm gone," Paulette said finally.

"You need to fight!" My head spun, and I wondered if I was hyperventilating. Violent sobs racked my body.

She closed her eyes, as if fighting to gather strength. "Don't you think I want to stay? I have just given birth to a beautiful new baby, and I can't even hold her and help her to become strong. Do you know how that feels? I'm going to leave her, and I won't be around to explain why—not to her or to Marie-Thérèse. Who's going to tuck them in each night? Who's going to take care of them? Who will answer their questions in ten years?"

She began to plead in earnest. "And when the time comes, who is going to help my baby understand why she's dying? Who's going to teach her to love God and to find peace in Him, despite the trials? Only *you* can do that."

"But Pierre—"

"Is HIV positive," Giselle said calmly. I turned to her, for the first time feeling resentment against the nurse. This was a private conversation.

My feelings must have shown in my face, because Paulette said, "Giselle is more than a nurse; she's my friend. I asked her to be here when I talked with you." I knew Giselle was taking the missionary discussions and that Paulette had kept in touch with her. I myself had great hopes for the conversion of her family, but that all seemed far removed in this clinical situation.

"Pierre will be around a long time," I said. "A person can be HIV positive for more than ten years without showing any signs of AIDS. It says so in the booklet you gave me."

Paulette looked at Giselle and nodded, as if telling her to go ahead. Giselle's eyes fixed on me. They were a deep brown, filled with love and compassion. "Pierre has cancer, inoperable. It's one of the opportunistic cancers that attack AIDS patients."

I turned my face to Paulette. "When did you find out?" I couldn't believe she hadn't told me.

"Only last week," she said wearily. "We were deciding how to tell everyone, but then the baby came. We didn't have time."

"Well, isn't there something they can do?"

"It's a non-Hodgkin's lymphoma," Giselle said, "called Burkitt's type. These tumors are unusually aggressive, and they don't respond well to chemotherapy."

"So what are you telling me?"

"The doctor thinks he should have a year, maybe more, depending. But he'll become very sick. He won't be capable of taking care of two small children."

"Even if he was and could work," Paulette added, "I want my daughters to have a mother during the day, not a baby-sitter."

"But Pierre's their father! You can't expect Marie-Thérèse to cope with losing both of you at once."

Paulette shook her head. "You're right. We've given this a lot of thought, and we came up with an idea, even before we knew about the cancer. The wall between our apartment and Louise's could be removed, and you could change apartments with her. With the joined apartments you would have five bedrooms—as good as any house in the country."

What she said made sense. As in any big city, houses were a scarce commodity. Most people bought apartments instead, and two linked together was not uncommon, especially for those who were well off.

"You've been saying you wanted to put your boys in a room together," she continued, "but you were afraid Josette would be scared alone. Well, now she can share with Marie-Thérèse. With you and Jean-Marc in one room, and Pierre in ours, you'll still have an extra room for the baby." Her voice dwindled to a whisper. "Or for a nurse, if Pierre needs one. We've got pretty good insurance to pay for a lot of it. Plus our savings."

I shrugged the last bit of information aside. If there was one thing Jean-Marc seemed to be good at, it was making money. My father was also wealthy, and the bank was always giving charitable contributions of some sort. Money was the last thing to worry about. Paulette had obviously been doing a lot of thinking. Belatedly, I wondered if I wouldn't have done the same thing in her situation. Knowing you were dying had certain advantages over the sudden deaths people hoped for.

"I'll understand if you don't want to do it. And I won't hold it against you. It's a risk having an HIV baby around your other children and a lot of extra work." Paulette closed her eyes again. She lay motionless; only her rasping breath told me she still lived. Then her eyes opened. "Louise said she would move in with Pierre and take care of him and the girls until—" She broke off. "I know she means well, but it's not the same thing as having a mom and a dad, and it's not really fair to her. Her health isn't too good."

I knew exactly what she was saying. Louise would do her best, but she couldn't play ball with the children or take them camping or to the beach on vacation. It would be too strenuous for her.

"My mother also volunteered to raise the baby," Paulette continued. "But how, when she works so much? And she can't teach her about the gospel."

Another point well taken. In similar circumstances, I would have chosen Paulette over my parents to raise my children. Being firmly entrenched in the gospel was all-important to me.

"Think about it and tell me later." Paulette seemed to be gasping for breath.

I glanced at Giselle anxiously, but she smiled. "She just needs to rest."

I stared at my friend, lying so helplessly on the bed. I wanted to reassure her, to tell her I would love her babies as my own, but something inside me wouldn't allow me to lie. If I told Paulette I would do it, then I would have no choice but to follow through. I couldn't say the words. Marie-Thérèse I would accept gladly, but the baby? She had HIV and would develop AIDS; with that came all the opportunistic illnesses. I had learned enough to know this was no small favor she asked of me.

"Give me a little time," I said. "I need a little time."

Paulette's eyes drooped. "I'm not going anywhere."

I wasn't too sure she spoke the truth, but I nodded and left the room.

Louise and Simone still sat in the waiting room, but Pierre and Jean-Marc were nowhere to be found. My mother and the children, including Marie-Thérèse, were also gone. "Josephine took them for a snack," Louise said when I asked. "They were getting restless."

"How is she?" Simone motioned to the door with her hand.

I gazed at the ceiling, blinking back the tears. "Not good." I paused and then continued, still not meeting their eyes. "She said she wants me to take care of the girls—to adopt them, so to speak."

"What about Pierre?" asked Louise.

Now I had to look at her, but it made me angry. I shouldn't be the one to tell this woman her son would be dead in a year. "Pierre has cancer," I began tightly, steeling myself against Louise's pain. I repeated what Giselle had told me and then described Paulette's idea for me to move into the apartment. "I can see why she wants this," I said. "But I don't know if I'm able."

"You don't have to do it alone," Simone said. "We'll all take turns. I can take the baby two days a week."

Louise nodded. "And I'll take her two. Lu-Lu can take her part of the time, and that will only leave a day or so for you."

I felt relieved at their words, but inside something asked me what kind of a life the baby would have. Four homes instead of one? And all because she had HIV—something that wasn't her fault to begin with. Didn't the child need a stable home?

"I'm going for a walk." I pushed past them and their plans and ran for the elevator. I thought fleetingly of trying to find my children, but my mother had taken them often enough so I knew they were all right.

I didn't realize where I was going until I ended up at the ICU nursery. Silently, I studied the baby inside the incubator to be sure she was only sleeping and not dead. But her little chest rose and fell at a regular rate—still without the help of an oxygen tube. She seemed so vulnerable, so unprotected with all those wires coming from her, dressed in nothing but a diaper and a small crocheted hat.

Even as I looked at her, I knew I wasn't capable of taking care of her alone. I couldn't even consider having a healthy baby yet, with all the other responsibilities I shouldered alone. I just couldn't.

Maybe it was better for her to die.

I practically fled from the nursery and my macabre thoughts. Before I knew it, I was in my car, driving to the cemetery. Making my way to Nette's grave, I knelt there, crying and wondering how I could tell Paulette I couldn't submit to her dying wish.

I prayed long and earnestly, ignoring the few people in the graveyard who glanced curiously in my direction. Over and over I relived the pain of my daughter's death, remembering how empty my arms had felt then.

I don't know how long I had knelt there when I heard footsteps behind me on the path. *Could it be my father?*

"I thought I might find you here," Jean-Marc said as I looked up at him. He had André in his arms and the twins by his side. André held out his chubby arms for me, and Jean-Marc let him down. All three children greeted me with wet kisses and warm hugs before wandering off to play by the trees. Instinctively I scanned the area for the caretaker, but he was nowhere to be seen.

"They told me what Paulette wanted," he said, sitting beside me.

I said nothing for a moment but gazed at the pattern the sun, filtered by the leaves, displayed on the gravestones. "And?" I finally prompted.

"I think it's a good idea. For the children, I mean. Less of an adjustment in the end. And Pierre will need someone to look out for him when he's no longer able."

Anger flared to life at the comment. "And who will that be?" I said vehemently. "Me? Is that before or after I take care of all the needs of five small children under the age of four? And one with HIV? All by myself? And is that before or after I go crazy?"

"We'll do it together."

I didn't doubt his sincerity, but the idea made me laugh. "You aren't even home for family night! No." I held up my hand to stop him from speaking. "Don't give me that story about how it is all for us. We don't need more money, we need you! By the time you have finished building your empire, the children will be gone and it will be too late. And you and I will be too far apart to do more than say hello."

He stared at me, and I watched anger, fear, and disbelief wrestle for dominance in his face.

"Your priorities are turned around," I continued, standing up and brushing my hands on my pants to clean off the stray pieces of grass clinging to them. "We were supposed to do this together, but who gets up at night when the children need something? Who can calm them when they're upset? Me, that's who. We had the children together, but I'm raising them alone! The fact remains that they are just small children who need to be taught how to act, how to become big people. You have to be patient and enter their world, to try to understand them, even if you think their logic is stupid."

"You always take them from me," he rejoined hotly. "Every time they cry or need something. You won't let me take care of them, even when I *am* home."

His words hit me like a bucket of cold water to my face. Was it possible I was partly responsible for his alienation from the children? I thought back, and yes, I did take them from him when they were upset. But it was only because if I didn't, the crying would go on and Jean-Marc would become impatient. What he needed was to spend more time with them, to understand them, and to grow to love them through service.

My own thoughts condemned me. Perhaps if I had given him more practice during the brief times he was home, he would have learned to be better with them, as I had. Maybe he would have realized how much we all needed him.

"You're a good mother, Ari," Jean-Marc said. "Sometimes I'm jealous because you're so much better with the children than I am." He put his arms around me tentatively. "The point is, I recognize we have a problem, and that I'm a big part of it. Can't we work things out? I want you to be happy, and the children, more than anything else. I want to be a good father."

It seemed we were finished blaming each other; now we could take responsibility for our happiness and not leave it to chance. "I need you to help out more," I said. "That's all." It seemed so simple, yet it wasn't.

He smiled. "That's what Paulette said to me."

"What?"

"Yesterday morning. When I came by to give the baby a blessing. Paulette looked straight into my eyes and asked me what I would be doing if it were you who had AIDS, or me, or one of the children. At first I couldn't believe she'd ask me such a thing, but then I thought about it. And I realized that I certainly wouldn't be working. I'd spend every second with you and the kids, making memories to last long after I was gone. Then it hit me. There are no guarantees in life. We may not have AIDS, but anything could happen to separate us—an accident, another illness, who knows? Life is too short; we never know when it will be taken away. Paulette made me see it's *now* that counts. You're right about my needing to get my priorities straight." He pulled me close and nuzzled my neck with his nose. I hugged him back, wanting to believe.

"Like my father." He spoke softly, but his mouth was so close to my ear that I couldn't mistake the words.

I drew back and stared at him. "Your father?"

He nodded, and when he spoke his voice sounded strangled. "When I went to bless the baby, I had a strange experience—two, really. As Pierre asked me to do the blessing, I suddenly remembered being with my father in the hospital when two missionaries gave him a blessing." Jean-Marc's eyes became unfocused as he remembered. "We were all there: Mom, Pierre, me, and even Lu-Lu. She was almost one—just a baby, really."

"After the blessing, Dad looked solemnly at Pierre and me. I remember what he said, word for word. He said, 'Sons, I'm sorry I haven't been with you more. I've put far too much effort into the store. I thought I was building a secure future for you, but now we'll never have the time to get to know one another. May the Lord forgive my error.' He sighed and shut his eyes, and I remember wanting to run and get the doctor. I was so scared. But then he spoke again. 'At least I have found the true gospel for you. Now use it. Follow the Church programs. Don't neglect your families until it's too late—like I did.' He held out his arms to hug and kiss us. When it was my turn, I ran away. I just ran. I didn't want to kiss him, to feel his tears on my cheeks. I didn't want to smell the death. It was the last time I saw my father alive."

"You remembered all that?"

"It came back in an instant, like I was seeing it in fast motion on a movie screen. Suddenly I could remember the late nights when he would come home and was too tired to do anything with us—play, I mean. Then I realized the real reason I couldn't remember my father was because we had made no memories I wanted to hold on to. I didn't *want* to remember him the way he was." His shoulders shook with emotion. "Isn't that horrible?"

I held his face between my hands. "No. You were only seven. You didn't understand what it was to be a father, to be responsible for supporting a family. That's a heavy burden. Now you know and can forgive him."

"I do understand him," he said. "And I am just like him." His words were desolate.

"Yes," I said. "You love your family as much as he loved you."

"But I ran, Ari. I ran." He gritted his teeth. "Just like I did before our wedding, when I realized how strong and good you were and how weak I was in comparison, and just like I did when you challenged me about my neglecting you and the children. I ran from my father, and I haven't stopped running since. I finally understand that all these months I've been afraid of being close to the children because I'm afraid they'll feel about me the same way I felt about my own father."

"A vicious cycle. The lucky thing is you've realized your error before it's too late."

He hugged me again, squeezing me tightly as if he would never let me go. "I love you so much, Ari. It scares me to think of losing you."

"I love you, too." I hesitated. "So why didn't you tell me this last night?" At least I knew why he had come home early.

"I wanted to surprise you today when I showed you this." He reached into his suit pocket and pulled out an object.

"It's a cellular phone," he said. "I made the company buy it today. In fact, I went straight to the owner—your father." His grin was back. "Now we'll never be more than a phone call apart, wherever I am."

I took the black object and flipped it open. I smiled. "This is exactly what we need."

"It's how the secretary reached me today when your mother called." I pushed the phone in his direction, but he grabbed my hand instead of the phone. "I want you to call me whenever you need me. Whenever you feel I'm neglecting you or the children. Whatever it is, I'll come. I want to make it work between us. I'm through running, forever. You are the most important thing to me, and I want us to be best friends again." His expression was so utterly sincere and full of love that it brought a strange emotion to my breast. I couldn't identify it, except that it was akin to love, only much, much deeper.

"And I promise never to abuse it."

He shrugged and put the phone into his pocket. "Of course you won't." He pulled me close and kissed me, running a gentle hand through my short hair. A little shiver surged down my spine, making me laugh with the exhilaration it brought to my body.

"So this is what the extra family night was about?" I asked gruffly. He could always bring out that special feeling in me.

"It was our first one in a long time," he said. "Oh, I know you always do it with them, but you can't have a real family night without the head of the family." His face was pensive. "The strange thing is that I knew all along what I should be doing, but I figured the children were too young, that it wouldn't make a difference yet. I was wrong."

"There's nothing wrong with making mistakes."

He nodded. "As long as we learn from them."

We stood without speaking for a time, linked together and feeling the strength of our love. Our children had drifted from the trees and were ducking behind some of the tombstones. The caretaker hated it when they played with such abandon; he didn't think they were getting a proper, reserved French upbringing. But the man was nowhere to be seen, and we had more important things to worry about.

"So what are we going to do?" He didn't have to spell it out for me; I knew he was talking about taking care of the baby and Pierre. "He's my brother, and I'm willing to do the work or hire a nurse if it becomes necessary. But regardless, I can't abandon him now."

"Of course we're not going to abandon him. I just don't know if I'm able to do as Paulette asks."

"Don't you think her idea is best for the children?"

I chewed on my lower lip. "I don't know. It would be if I could handle it. I'm not worried about Marie-Thérèse; she's already like one of ours. But the baby—she's going to get AIDS."

"Yes, but maybe not for ten years, and there may be a cure by then. Meanwhile, she needs a real home. I promise I'll be there every night to help; I promise on the strength of my love for you. I will be there. And if I forget, you call me." He touched his breast pocket, where I could see the slight bulge of the phone.

"Aren't you worried our children might get HIV?" I protested. "Certainly our first responsibility is to our own children."

"We can educate ourselves, and we can teach them," Jean-Marc said. "The biggest problem with HIV or AIDS is the fear it brings; that much I'm learning. As long as we are careful, nothing will happen."

"It's not going to be easy."

"But worth it in the end."

His words reminded me of how I had visited my ex-husband in prison after my mission, to forgive him for causing our daughter's death. I had told him something then, when he had wished aloud that he had not hurt me so terribly; and now, nearly six years later, the words echoed in my mind. "But, Jacques," I had said, "the making of a queen or a king is never easy, you know, though terribly worth it in the end."

It had been true then, and nothing had changed since. Still, I fought against the inevitable. "Your mother and Simone said they would take her a few days each week."

"You mean we should shuffle her about? What kind of life is that for a child?" Jean-Marc put his hands on my shoulders and gazed earnestly into my eyes. "I said two things happened when I went to the hospital yesterday. The first was remembering about my father's death; the second was the strange sensation I had when I placed my hands on the baby's head to bless her."

I tore my gaze away from his. Behind him, I saw the oh-so-cold stone marking my daughter's grave. I wanted to cry.

There was a sudden intake of breath. "You felt it too, didn't you, Ari?" Jean-Marc said, moving into my line of sight. His eyes probed my face. "You felt the connection to the baby. Tell me!"

Then I knew the truth. It entered my heart like a sword, stabbing deep and bringing excruciating pain. I was afraid to take care of Paulette's baby not because the other children might contract HIV or because of the additional burden but because I would grow to love her. It would not be just the love of an aunt for a niece but the stronger, more profound love only a mother could feel for her baby. And when the time came, I would have to say good-bye, as I had with Nette. Grief flooded my entire being. How could I watch this new Antoinette die? How could I lose another innocent baby to drugs?

Jean-Marc's face was obscured by my tears. "We can do it," he said softly.

I nodded mutely, and he held me while I cried. I didn't know if he completely understood my fear, but there was time enough to explain later. For now, it was enough to know we loved each other and would face the coming tragedies together.

"Let's go back to the hospital," I said. "We need to talk with Paulette before—" I broke off, unable to complete the sentence.

"Before it's too late," Jean-Marc said.

He rounded up the children while I stepped closer to Nette's grave. As usual, I ran my hand over her name. The sun still played across the gray stone, and I touched the place where the light danced.

I gasped. The stone wasn't cold; it was warm from the sun's light. Or was it from the Son's light? Maybe it was the same thing. The Son of God had given life to the whole world, and all light stemmed from Him—from the Light of Christ.

It was this Light that would sustain me, this Light that would give me the courage to persevere—and to love.

CHAPTER SEVENTEEN

I drove back to the hospital in our car with the twins, while André rode with Jean-Marc in my mother's car. I wondered idly where my mother was and how she would get home. My nose twitched at the smells of the hospital, but the twins skipped to the elevator, unmindful, where Jean-Marc and André waited. I felt a twinge of guilt as I noticed my little boy sleeping in his father's arms. He had obviously missed his nap earlier.

To my surprise, my father was in the ICU waiting room. "I called him to come and get me," my mother said. "I didn't know when you would be back." My father always had use of a company car, and because my mother hated the subway, it was logical for her to call him.

"Has there been any change?" I asked.

She shook her head. "Simone and Louise went to ask the doctor if there's any way Paulette can see the baby. She's very upset."

I knew it was my fault for not being able to give her what she wanted. I sank to the brown floral couch and let my head drop to my hands. "I don't know if I can handle this," I muttered. Jean-Marc passed André to my mother and sat beside me, rubbing my back.

"You can," my mother said. "The Lord will give you the strength."

"We need to fast," I said. I hadn't eaten anything since lunch anyway and didn't feel like I would ever be hungry again.

"We already are," my father replied quietly.

For no reason I could define, his comment made me angry. "You're fasting? Like you did when you thought we might have the virus?" I glared at him. "That's great, Father, but when will you realize that even if Paulette does die right now, she'll be better off than you? When you die, you won't be anywhere near us because you are too proud to accept the truth. You said no one could change another person, and you were right. I'm tired of trying. Only you can change yourself. So do it! I don't want you to fast for Paulette, I want you to fast for yourself. You need to know the truth, or we'll never be an eternal family. You're the only one who is standing in our way!"

Hurt and outrage played on his face, but he kept his temper as I hadn't kept mine. "We'll take the children home," he said. "We'll feed them dinner, and they can have a sleepover."

I dropped my gaze and nodded, once more feeling guilt. I shouldn't have treated my father badly when he was trying so hard to help.

Jean-Marc clapped him on the back. "Thanks, Géralde. We appreciate it."

"You'll let us know?" my mother said.

Jean-Marc kissed her cheek. "Of course."

We kissed the twins and the still-sleeping André good-bye. As they turned to leave, I hugged my father, trying to make amends. "I love you," I whispered past the lump in my throat.

"I know," he said. "I love you, too."

After they left, we tried to see Paulette but weren't allowed. "The doctor's with her. We'll let you know," the nurse on duty told us.

The bishop, our home teachers, and several of the ward members, including Marguerite, stopped by, but we sent them home, promising to call when we had more news. We alternately paced the brown carpet or sat on the ugly couches. It was a relief when the elevator opened to reveal Louise and Simone.

"The baby specialist says she can see the baby," Simone said. "They're arrangin' to roll the incubator into her room."

"Luckily, they have Paulette isolated enough so they feel there's no danger to the baby from the other patients," Louise added.

I knew luck had nothing to do with it, but I didn't feel like speaking.

"How's Pierre?" Jean-Marc asked.

"He seems a little better since you talked with him," Louise said. "But he's still pretty angry. He tries to hide it from Paulette, though."

"This is harder on him than on anyone," Jean-Marc said.

The women nodded at his words. Simone opened her mouth to speak, but the elevator chimed. A second later, Lu-Lu, with Philippe in tow, burst through the double doors.

"I just got your note!" she said, rushing to where we stood. She hugged each of us. "I came home from work and saw the note. I made Philippe bring me immediately."

I glanced at Philippe, whose lank figure leaned nonchalantly against the wall near the elevator. Dressed in a business suit, he stared at his fingernails, as if trying to distance himself from the rest of us.

"Can I see her?" Lu-Lu asked.

"Probably in a while," I said. "The doctor is with her. The nurse won't let anyone in except Pierre and Marie-Thérèse right now."

She nodded. "At least I'm in time to—" She abruptly dropped her head and brought a hand to her face. Her hair tumbled forward and sobs shook her shoulders. Philippe made no move to comfort her.

"There's something else we have to tell you," Louise began. Her voice sounded determined. I turned away as she told Lu-Lu about Pierre's cancer. I couldn't bear to see any more pain. I pretended interest in a painting across the room, but I couldn't shut out the sharp gasp and muffled cries behind me. When Lu-Lu was calmer, I returned to stand beside Jean-Marc.

Louise hugged her daughter. "It's going to be all right."

"But the baby! Pierre can't possibly take care of her alone now. What's going to happen to her?" Lu-Lu hadn't yet been allowed to see the baby—only parents, grandparents, and siblings were allowed in the ICU nursery—but her concern for her niece was touching.

"We can take turns," Simone said. "Together we can do it."

"Yes. It's the only way," Louise agreed.

I watched them talking about the baby, feeling as though things were moving in slow motion, as if in a dream. I knew they meant well, but it *wasn't* the only way.

"I could take her on the weekends," Lu-Lu was saying. Behind her, Philippe straightened, suddenly interested in what his future wife was saying.

"You'll what?" he said, his piercing blue eyes flashing. "Don't you think we'd better talk about this? Do I have to remind you she is HIV positive? I don't think you realize what you're getting into."

"I don't think *you* realize that she's family," Lu-Lu rejoined, accentuating each word. "Family," she repeated. "I'm not going to desert her."

Philippe's face darkened. "And what about us? I thought we were going to be family." They glared at each other, fighting a silent battle with their eyes. The rest of us looked away, waiting for what might come next.

"Maybe it's time to choose," Philippe said through gritted teeth. "Do you want me or them?" He flipped his thumb at us, his voice nearly a sneer. "Make your choice." He shook a finger at her. "I won't come in second to anyone."

Indignant words came boiling to the surface, but I bit them back; this was Lu-Lu's battle, one she had to wage alone. Those of us who loved her could only watch, lest our actions drive her away from us forever. I saw the same emotions on Louise's face and in the way my husband's jaw tightened angrily. I put a restraining hand on his arm.

"It's not a question of coming in second." Lu-Lu's voice pleaded for understanding. "My family needs me."

Philippe's face seemed to be carved from stone. "I'm leaving," he said flatly. "Are you coming?"

Lu-Lu's pleading turned to anger. "My brother's wife, my sister, is dying, and I need to stay here."

"Forget it, then," Philippe growled. "Forget it all." He turned and stomped to the elevator, reminding me of one of the twins in a tantrum. I bit my lip to stop an unbidden smile. Philippe entered the elevator and stared at us defiantly as the door clanged shut.

Lu-Lu's emotions transformed again, this time from anger to hurt, and she exploded. "My whole world is falling apart!" she wailed. "Why does everything bad have to happen at once?"

Louise hugged her daughter. "That's the way life is sometimes," she said soberly. Yet across her lips played the trace of a satisfied smile. I knew exactly how she felt; Lu-Lu may not understand it at the moment, but Philippe's leaving was the one good thing that had happened this night.

Lu-Lu took a shaky breath and stepped back from her mother. Jean-Marc's face caught her attention, and to my surprise she gave a short laugh. "You don't have to fight my battles, brother. I'm not five anymore."

Jean-Marc looked taken aback. He grinned somewhat self-consciously as he let his clenched fists relax. "He shouldn't talk to you like that."

Lu-Lu's smile vanished, but she shook her head as if trying to clear Philippe's actions from it. "So about the baby," she said, turning to her mother. "Together we can do it—take care of her."

Jean-Marc glanced at me. "What do you think, Ari?" His tone told me he would accept any decision I made.

All eyes turned on me, waiting. Once again the world slowed and details stood out: the dark stain on the edge of the brown, low-cut carpet; the blinking lights above the elevator as it changed floors; the strained expression on Louise's face; the wrinkles on Simone's and the additional hair escaping from her bun; and above all, Jean-Marc's intense gaze. I shook my head slowly, wondering on some level why it suddenly felt so heavy.

"Jean-Marc and I will take care of her," I said. "I'm going to tell Paulette that we'll take both the girls as our own." There was a brief silence before the protests began.

"There ain't no need to be a martyr," Simone said.

"We want to help," Louise added. "We're her family, too."

"If I am going to be her mother," I said, "I need to be able to check on her at night, to make sure she's breathing and covered. I need to have time to grow to love her as my own." I paused and then added hurriedly, "That doesn't mean I won't need your help; I will—probably more than I realize. But it will be as we"—I swallowed hard—"her parents, determine."

"We want to offer her a stable life," Jean-Marc added. "Just as any child has the right to live. That's all."

Louise and Simone were nodding. "Of course," Lu-Lu said. "Four homes could never be the same as one."

I was glad the whole thing was settled. Now I just needed to tell Paulette. I went to talk to the nurse at the desk opposite the door leading to the ICU. She called on the telephone. "Are you Ariana?" I nodded. "You can go back now. But just you. Don't forget to scrub."

I glanced over my shoulder and saw Jean-Marc watching me. "I love you," he mouthed. I smiled.

Only Pierre was with Paulette when I entered her room. "Where's Marie-Thérèse?" I asked.

"She went with Giselle," Pierre said. "It was getting a little too much for her in here. Giselle took her on a tour."

Paulette looked wretched and uncomfortable, but her eyes were shining. "They're bringing the baby," she said. "I'll get to hold her." Speaking brought on a bout of coughing, and I cringed inwardly as Pierre tenderly wiped the blood from her mouth. She seemed so weak that I wondered how she would manage holding the baby at all. I opened my mouth to speak but shut it again when the door opened and Dr. Orlan and a nurse entered with the baby.

"Here she is," the doctor said. He rolled the portable incubator close to the bed and opened it, lifting the infant out, once more wrapped in the pink blanket. Her bright eyes were open wide, taking in the new environment. Pierre propped Paulette up in bed, and Dr. Orlan laid the baby in the crook of her arm so that most of the tiny body was resting on the bed. It seemed odd to see her outside the ICU nursery, and I was glad the specialist was there in case something went wrong. The doctor and nurse withdrew and stood near the door, where they talked together in low voices.

"She's so beautiful," Paulette murmured, staring down at her daughter. "She looks a lot like you, don't you think, Pierre?" He nodded but said nothing. I noticed his gaze was fixed on Paulette, not the baby.

All of a sudden the baby started to cry—thin, wailing little sobs that bit into the heart. Paulette tried to rock her but didn't have the strength. In a minute, she lay back on the bed exhausted, rivulets of sweat on her forehead. She began to cry quietly. "I can't help her," she sobbed. I could only imagine how helpless she felt at being unable to comfort her child. "Help her, Pierre," she pleaded.

Pierre reached out for his daughter, moving his hands around awkwardly. After approaching the baby from several directions, he pulled his hands back in frustration. "She's so tiny, I'm afraid I'll hurt her. And I'm afraid I'll pull out her feeding tube. Or the wires."

Paulette's face turned to me. "Ariana?"

I gently picked up the baby, holding her against my body, careful not to pull on the wires. The crying stopped. I felt the bond between us, as I had the first time I held her. Now I understood what it meant.

"You never answered my question." Paulette's voice was strained. "I have to know."

"Of course I'll take care of them," I said. "As if they were my own."

Relief filled their faces. "They will be yours," Pierre said, "after I'm gone." His voice was devoid of feeling.

I gazed at the baby, aware of the powerful emotions of love and fear. She was so utterly precious, and though there was a certain danger in loving this infant, it didn't matter. She was already a part of me.

The doctor and nurse moved restlessly in the background, and I knew they would soon take the baby back to the nursery. I stepped closer to Pierre and placed the infant carefully in his arms. "Jean-Marc and I will fill in for you on earth," I said, "but never forget you will be her parents for all eternity." Pierre's eyes filled with gratitude.

"Thank you," Paulette whispered. "You can't know what this means to me."

"I think maybe I do—a little."

She smiled, and I could sense a peace about her. In her eyes I saw acceptance, and I knew it stemmed from her great faith in her Savior. She coughed again, and this time the surge of blood fell to the blanket. Her body convulsed, and her eyes closed.

Pierre uttered a small cry before handing me the baby and turning to stroke his wife's face. "Paulette, are you okay?" There was no answer.

Dr. Orlan came to the bed, eyes scanning the monitor next to it. His face was grave. "Paulette? Can you hear me?" Her eyes fluttered open briefly, unseeing, and then closed. He punched the emergency button near the bed. In a few moments a second nurse came into the room. "You'd better call Medard," he said. She nodded and left. Dr. Orlan motioned to the baby. "We'd better get her back." The nurse took the baby from me and settled her in the incubator again. I felt a great loss without her. I couldn't help wondering, if I felt that way, how terrible Paulette must feel to be so far away from her baby.

As they took the infant away, Dr. Medard, Giselle, and another nurse crowded into the room, all wearing rubber gloves. They examined Paulette, calling out names and numbers I recognized only from TV shows.

I backed up near the door and out of their way. I was shaking, and my cheeks were wet. Pierre's face was a mask of agony.

"She seems to be stable for now," Dr. Medard said at last, turning a kind face to Pierre. "But she's unconscious. It's only a matter of time." Pierre nodded numbly.

"There's nothing you can do here," the doctor continued. "Why don't you go home and get some sleep?"

Pierre shook his head. "I can't leave her alone. I promised." He sat down and grabbed Paulette's limp hand, ignoring Giselle, who was changing the blood-stained blanket.

"It could be a while."

Pierre didn't appear to hear him. I walked to the bed and stared at Paulette. I expected to see suffering, but her face was calm. Suddenly I could see a glow around her, as if a door to a place filled with light was opening nearby. I glanced around but couldn't find the source. The others didn't seem to notice. Paulette breathed on, but the light disappeared.

I put a hand on Pierre's shoulder, squeezing it reassuringly. "Shall I stay?"

He shook his head. "I'd like to be alone."

"Then would you like me to take Marie-Thérèse home?" I asked. He nodded mutely. I squeezed his shoulder once more and then leaned over to kiss Paulette's white cheek, wishing I could hug her and tell her how much I loved her.

I left the room and walked dejectedly down the hall. I could see Paulette's laughing face in my mind, but the memories held no comfort. As I reached the door to the waiting room, Giselle caught up with me. Her brown face was wet with tears. "Ariana, it's going to be all right," she said. Her fingers on my arm compelled me to stop walking.

"Paulette's dying," I stated, facing her. "She may never wake up."

She nodded. "It was expected. The surprise is that she's holding on so long."

My teeth dug into the soft flesh of my lip. "I never told her good-bye." Could that voice be mine? It sounded like rocks grinding against each other.

"Yes, you did. You told her you would take care of her daughters, didn't you?" I nodded. Her eyes bore into mine. "Then don't you see? You did say good-bye. Until she knew they were safe, she couldn't let go."

I remembered then that when Paulette first discovered she had AIDS, she had asked me to help her. I had feared she meant helping her to die, and I hadn't thought I would be capable of such a thing. But in the end, it seemed I had—twice. By helping her understand and accept the AIDS two months ago and then by agreeing today to take her children, I *had* helped her to die.

"You have been a good friend to her," Giselle said.

"As she has always tried to be for me." I paused and then asked softly, "How much longer do you think Paulette will hang on?"

"I think Paulette is already gone," she said, "or nearly so. Once the light comes—"

"You saw the light?" I asked.

"It's not the first time. Are you surprised?"

"Yes."

"Why? Because I'm not baptized? I may not be a member yet, but I was living the gospel before I ever met Paulette, before Marguerite introduced me to those young missionaries."

I believed her. "Are you saying you are going to be baptized?"

Her smile was serene. "This Sunday. And I'll be forever grateful to Paulette. If she hadn't become sick, I might have never found the true church. Her gift to me is most precious."

"I'd like to come."

"I appreciate your support."

I took her hand. "Thank you for everything you've done for my friend."

"You don't have to thank me. She's my friend, too."

We smiled, and then I went through the double doors to the waiting room. Jean-Marc stood near the door with a sleeping Marie-Thérèse in his arms. His suit was wrinkled, but he didn't seem to mind. He and the others looked up anxiously as I entered. "Well?" Jean-Marc asked. "What's going on? Giselle came and gave me Marie-Thérèse and then disappeared. Did something happen?"

"Paulette has lost consciousness. It's just a matter of time now, the doctor says."

Simone gave a cry and buried her face in her hands. Louise and Lu-Lu tried to comfort her.

"She did get to see the baby," I said. "And I told her what she wanted to know."

Jean-Marc closed his eyes, holding tightly to the little girl in his arms. I saw in his face how he wished he could spare her the pain she would have to face, not once but three times, as those closest to her died from AIDS.

I set my jaw resolutely and wiped away my tears. I couldn't afford to be weak now. I had to take care of Paulette's daughter first. "Come, let's go home. She needs to be in bed."

"I'm stayin' here," Simone said. "I want to see my little girl again."

"We'll stay with you," Louise said. "I don't want to leave Pierre alone, either."

"What about the drug clinic?" Jean-Marc asked Simone. "I thought you had to go back there."

Simone shrugged. "I don't care. It don't matter."

"I called and explained," Louise said. "As long as I am with her, it's okay. I'm sort of a companion. I'll take care of her. You two go on home."

We said good-bye and made our way to the car. As we left the hospital, I felt a ripping sensation in my breast, one that had nothing to do with Paulette. We had left behind the little baby, alone in the hospital, with only the nurses to look after her. Although they were kind, their care could never match that of a mother's. What if she cried? What if she needed me? Now that I knew she was my responsibility, I felt her absence acutely.

I held my head in my hands and let the tears flood my body, purging it. Jean-Marc pulled over, and we held each other until there were no tears left. Then he held my hand as he drove the rest of the way home. When we arrived, he carried Marie-Thérèse to our apartment. I carried Dolly, who had fallen out of the sleeping child's arms.

A short time later, we laid Marie-Thérèse on our bed, removed her shoes, and tucked the covers up around her neck. Normally I insisted on the children wearing pajamas, but there were times when clothes were just as good, and this was one of those times. We slept that night with little Marie-Thérèse between us. During the late hours she awoke, crying for her mother. We soothed her the best we could, but only when Jean-Marc gave her Dolly did she finally return to sleep.

Early Thursday morning, Paulette died. Louise called us from the hospital to tell us she had passed away, never again regaining consciousness. Louise sounded old and tired.

"Pierre doesn't look good," she said. "I'm afraid for him. He loved her so much."

"We'll help him," I said.

By the time Marie-Thérèse awoke, Pierre had arrived at our apartment. She was at the table eating and wondering aloud when her cousins would be home.

Her eyes brightened when she saw her father. "Are we going to go see Mommy?"

Pierre shook his head. He took her in his arms and held her close. "Remember about the sickness Mommy had? Well, in the night Mommy couldn't hold on anymore, and she went to live with Jesus."

Marie-Thérèse cried with heart-wrenching sobs. Pierre cuddled her close for long minutes until they subsided. "Why don't we go somewhere together? For a walk or something."

She nodded, her eyes red and swollen. "Can we take our baby?"

"She's too little to leave the hospital," Pierre said. "But soon."

"Can we go see her? She gets so lonely there."

"No, not now."

I imagined it was difficult for him to go to the hospital. When my baby died, the place had represented a nightmare.

"I can take you to see her later, if you want," I said.

Marie-Thérèse didn't look at me. "Okay," she mumbled. She laid her head against her father's chest.

They left, clinging to each other for support. "He's going to be all right," Jean-Marc said.

"I hope so." But tendrils of worry crept up my spine. Pierre's face was unemotional, as if he had buried any residue of feelings so deep that no one could find them. Paulette had died, and I wondered if part of Pierre, the most vital part, hadn't gone with her. I prayed I was wrong; Marie-Thérèse and that helpless baby in the hospital needed him now.

CHAPTER EIGHTEEN

My mother brought our children home soon after Pierre and Marie-Thérèse left. Her eyes radiated sadness. "I'm so sorry about Paulette," she said. The children were dry-eyed and more curious than sad.

"Do you think she's talking to Nette and Uncle Antoine?" Marc asked brightly.

"No doubt," Jean-Marc said.

"So where's Father?" I asked.

My mother shrugged. "He got up early and left. He didn't say where he was going. I assumed he was at work."

Jean-Marc shook his head. "I called to say I wasn't coming in, but he's not there. It surprises me. We have a big account to settle, and one of us should be there."

"Do you have to go?" I asked. So much for his promises of the day before.

But he smiled. "No. I told the secretary to cancel if your father didn't show up. I'm not leaving you today. We have to make arrangements for Paulette, and I don't think Pierre is the one to do it."

I hugged him. "Thanks for staying."

"He's my brother, and I meant what I said yesterday."

Jean-Marc was on the phone all morning, making arrangements for Paulette's funeral on Saturday. Mother stayed with us, and in the afternoon she watched the children while Jean-Marc and I went to the hospital to see the baby.

"Has my brother been here?" Jean-Marc asked the nurse as he cuddled the infant.

She shook her head. "We have everyone sign in when they come," she said. "He hasn't been here since Tuesday when he brought his wife in the wheelchair." She hesitated before continuing. "I'm really glad she has you two." She motioned to the baby. "She needs someone. I think she'll be ready to go home in a couple of weeks. She's nearly regained her birth weight, and she's having no trouble breathing. God must be looking out for this one."

I ran a hand over her so-soft little cheek. "I think you're right." It was true she would develop AIDS, but her Father in Heaven had not abandoned her. I felt certain she had a mission to accomplish here on earth—an important one that only she could fulfill.

"Do you have a name yet for the baby?" the nurse asked. "We keep calling her Antoinette because of what her sister said."

"We'll talk to her father," Jean-Marc said. "I don't think they had decided yet about a name." I hadn't told him yet about Paulette wanting to call her Antoinette. There hadn't been time.

When we arrived home, the apartment was full of people. Marguerite and several of the other ladies in our ward were there with a huge dinner. Louise and Simone were also seated in the kitchen, looking somber. The twins stood near the counter, staring at a large cake, and André sat in my mother's lap chewing on a roll.

I hugged my old friend. "But how did you know, Marguerite?" Jean-Marc had called the bishop before we left for the hospital, but surely that hadn't been enough time for the women to put together such a feast. Besides the cake, I saw breads, pastries, cheeses, salads, and fruit on the table. On the stove were pans of soup, and through the window in the oven door I could see evidence of a main dish.

"Giselle called us this morning," Marguerite said. "But actually I started cooking last night after visiting the hospital. It makes me feel better to cook. We made two dinners, one for you and one for Pierre and Louise, but we brought them both here when no one answered at Pierre's."

"Where is Pierre?" Jean-Marc asked quickly.

"Don't worry," Louise said. "He's here. He came back a little while ago. He said he couldn't bear to go home. Marie-Thérèse was asleep, and he looked tired so we made him lie down in your room. I peeked in a little while ago, and they were both sleeping."

Jean-Marc appeared relieved. He settled in the only remaining chair at the table, surveying the spread appreciatively. "This all looks good. I don't think we've eaten all day."

Marguerite put her hand on his shoulder. "That's to be expected." She glanced up at me. "We'll be bringing dinner for the next few nights. I'll call to make sure Pierre's still here."

I nodded, touched. When we needed them, the women of the Church were there. It helped to know others were aware of our loss, and, recognizing our pain, were able to jump in and make sure that mundane things like food were taken care of. We hugged and thanked the women as they left.

"Where's Lu-Lu?" I asked.

Louise's expression darkened. "She went to talk to Philippe. I'd hoped she wouldn't, but I guess she loves him."

"Let's wait and see," I said.

"Can we eat now?" Josette whined. "I'm hungry for cake."

"Dinner first, my girl." Jean-Marc stroked her hair.

My mother sighed. "I should go."

"No, stay. There's enough food, if that's what's worrying you," I motioned to the table.

Her eyebrows drew together as she frowned. "No, it's your father. He's not home, and he still hasn't been in to work. I'm worried about him. I should go home in case he calls." There was fear in her voice.

"But he'll call here if you're not home," I said.

"Maybe he can't . . ."

Then I understood; it wasn't his call she feared but the impersonal one, a strange voice like the one who had announced my brother's death that rainy morning so long ago.

"He was agitated after we left the hospital last night," she added. "I think what you said must have bothered him."

I felt my heart sink. All I needed now was to feel guilt for something I had said in my disturbed state. Still, there was one place he might go . . .

"I'm going to look for him," I said. "I think I might know where he is."

Jean-Marc pushed back his chair. "I'm going with you."

"I want to go," Josette wailed.

"Me too," Marc said. "You already went somewhere without us!"

What they were really saying was they needed us with them. Perhaps Paulette's death was real enough to them that they secretly worried about losing us, as well.

"You stay with them," I said to Jean-Marc, putting my hand on his shoulder to prevent him from rising. "They need one of us here, but I have to go find my father. Besides, Pierre may wake up and want to talk." He seemed about to protest, but little Josette climbed on his knee.

"Stay, Daddy."

He nodded. "I will." He reached out to clasp my hand. "But drive carefully." I felt the love in his eyes and bent to kiss his lips.

"I'll be back," I whispered as I drew away, feeling his hot breath mingling with mine. A thankful tenderness welled up inside me. How bittersweet it was to recognize the eternal nature of our relationship— bitter because of Paulette's death but sweet because I could understand how it would continue forever, despite death's toll.

I drove straight to the cemetery and hurried up the cobblestone path. My father sat on the bench opposite Nette's tombstone. He stared into the air, seemingly alone and forlorn, his gray pin-striped suit wrinkled as if he had mistakenly put on a suit meant for the dry cleaner. He wore no tie, and the top buttons on his shirt were open, revealing the dark hairs on his chest. His dark hair and moustache were uncombed. While he didn't look like a vagrant, his appearance wasn't what I was used to from my meticulous father. My foot hit a loose stone, and his head jerked up.

"Ari." His voice was low. He patted the bench and then turned to gaze again over the graveyard.

I settled beside him, and silence fell over us as it had so often over the years. The sun rested low in the sky and no longer sent its rays dancing through the leaves and over the tombstones. The late July air was warm and without the hint of a breeze.

"It's not Wednesday," I said after a time.

His laugh was short. "Or after lunch, either."

At his mention of food, my stomach growled loudly. "Was that my stomach or yours?" I asked.

"Haven't you eaten?"

I shook my head. "Have you?"

"I've been fasting."

"Paulette's dead."

His arm slid around me. "I know. I went to the hospital this morning before coming here."

"Have you been here all day?"

He nodded. "Yes."

"Mother's been worried."

Remorse was etched on his face. "I've been so busy sorting things out, I didn't stop to think that she would worry."

"Well, she has been. She loves you."

His jaw clenched. "I know. I know. And only today did I discover how much."

I turned to stare at him. There was something different about my father, something I hadn't noticed before. "Why are you here?" I asked.

He gazed in the direction of my brother's grave. "I've been fasting—and talking to Antoine."

"Oh?" I hoped my father hadn't taken to seeing ghosts.

"What you said at the hospital touched me. When you stared at me with your righteous indignation, I realized you believed every word you were saying—that even in death Paulette was better off than I am and that I was standing in the way of our becoming an eternal family."

"I was upset." I rotated to face him. His arm dropped from my shoulder.

"But you believed what you were saying and still do. Don't you?"

I thought about it and then slowly nodded, my eyes meeting his. "Yes."

"I realized you meant it, and that decided me. I would fast and ask the Lord if what you said was true." He paused, his stare dropping to his hands, which were now twisting in his lap. "I know you've wanted me to do this for some time, but it seemed so ridiculous to fast about something I already knew was false." He chuckled and looked up. "Imagine my shock when I knelt down this morning in my office, before anyone had arrived, and discovered it was all true." His eyes gleamed with unshed tears.

Abruptly, I knew what was different about my father. He had felt the touch of the Savior's hand. He had a testimony! I smiled, feeling giddy. *My father knows the Church is true!*

"Oh, don't look so pleased," he said testily. "I feel absurd enough as it is. Imagine what I'm going to have to tell your mother. And to think she has put off her baptism because of me!" His head rocked back and forth in amazement. "I don't know if I would have done the same."

"It was you who asked her if she loved the Church more than she loved you," I said dryly.

"That's my point. She picked me."

"The Church doesn't teach women to leave their husbands, no matter how stubborn they are. Maybe she had faith you'd come around."

"Well, I have. I only hope she'll forgive me."

"She will."

He smiled and stood, pulling me to my feet. "Then let's go get something to eat."

"The sisters in the ward brought dinner. There's plenty of food."

"Good. I'm starving."

He waited for me to touch Nette's stone in farewell but paused and turned back to the bench when I began walking. I stopped short, watching him pick up a book which had been on the bench beside him, hidden from my view. The Book of Mormon.

He held it up. "Good reading, this. I'm about finished."

I smiled and leaned against him, breathing in the fragrant air. The evening was perfect. As night approached, the heat that always marked July dissipated, making the evening comfortably warm without being oppressive.

I smoothed the wrinkles in my father's coat. "This needs cleaning."

He stopped and put his hands on my shoulders. Once again I saw the sheen of tears in his eyes. He uttered a sound somewhere between a cry and a laugh. "Oh, Ari! My suit doesn't matter. It doesn't matter at all in the eternal scheme of things!" The laughter dissolved completely into tears, and for the first time in my life I saw my father convulsing with fervent sobs. "Today I learned Antoine is not gone forever and that I will actually be able to hold your little Nette! Oh, Ari. It's all true!"

He dropped his arms from my shoulders and closed his eyes before continuing in a whisper. "How grateful I am to God, and how unworthy I feel of His love! He never gave up on me, not even after all these years I've denied Him. He loves me! He loves my family! I will never look at anything the same way again. Not ever." He opened his eyes and gazed into the western sky. The streaked mixture of oranges, reds, and yellows reflected off the few clouds until the heavens were lit more than they should have been—a bright, natural light, yet strangely poignant.

I reached out and touched his shoulder. I remembered so well my own conversion and how miraculous it had all been. Gratitude once again coursed through me. My father could now take his proper place at the head of our family. We could finally be sealed, and my mother . . . my thoughts stopped there. There wasn't room in my body for the emotions I felt.

"There's not room enough to hold all these feelings," my father said, as if reading my mind. His voice rushed on. "I want to shout, to stop strangers on the street, to sing at the top of my lungs. I want to do radical, outrageous, unheard of things to make people understand the love of God. I feel like Alma in the Book of Mormon, who wanted to shout it with a trumpet to reach the ends of the earth! I understand how he felt!" He whirled around with his hands in the air. Then he stopped, his happy smile subsiding. "It was all because of Paulette and her illness and because of what you said. I went to tell her this morning, to have a nurse deliver the message if they wouldn't let me in, but she was already dead." He hugged me. "I'm so sorry. I know you loved her."

"Love her. I still love her."

"Of course. It's not the end, is it?" Joy covered the pain.

"Pierre's dying, too," I said. "Cancer. We've agreed to take the girls after . . ."

"We'll help you, Ari. I wasn't there for you when Antoine died, but I will be now."

"Jean-Marc won't be working so much." I resumed my steps on the path.

My father nodded. "He works too much, anyway."

"Not anymore. I don't care if it means less money."

"Once I would have been appalled, but you're right. Money means nothing. Absolutely nothing."

A faraway look shadowed his face. "Paulette," he said softly. "Can you picture her now, Ari? Wrapped in the arms of her Savior? I envy her that. Can you imagine the sheer bliss of that hug?"

I could, though perhaps faintly. When I had first learned that families could be eternally together, my jubilation had far exceeded anything I had ever felt.

We walked back to the parking lot in silence. My father turned to me before I opened the door of my car. "What is my new little grand-daughter's name?" he asked.

"I don't know yet." I still didn't want to name her Antoinette.

I drove through Paris, thinking about the baby. I wanted to stop at the hospital and be with her, but I knew my other children needed me as well. I prayed she would be watched over. I felt that she would; she had a special connection with heaven. Surely Paulette, now released from her frail, earthly body, was at her side, loving her and comforting her. The warmth of the Spirit flooded through me, testifying of the truthfulness of my thought. At that moment, I knew without a doubt that Paulette was happier than she had ever been on earth.

When my father and I arrived home, Pierre and Marie-Thérèse were sitting at the table with everyone else, finishing their meal. My father took my mother's hand and drew her close, kissing her tenderly.

"I'm sorry I worried you," he said. "But I have something impor-tant to tell you." My mother's face grew worried, but my father laughed joyfully. He knelt down on the hard, tiled floor and took her hands in his. "My dear, dear, Josephine. How much I love you! Thank you for not giving up on me!" The room had gone silent as we watched them, captivated by the strong love emanating from my father. Even the chil-dren were enthralled and for once didn't interrupt.

"Will you do me the honor of being sealed to me for all eternity in the temple of the Lord?" he asked humbly. There was a stunned shock—everyone knew my father's views on how religion was simply a crutch for weak people.

My mother's eyes opened wide. "You mean—?"

He nodded. "Oh, yes. I do. It's true—all of it!"

Mother pulled him up and embraced him. This time her tears were from happiness.

"Why is Grandma crying?" asked Josette.

"Grandpa's getting baptized," I said, translating the adult conversation.

Cheers and clapping exploded into the room. Questions and com-ments shot out from all directions.

"It's about time."

"I can't believe it!"

"But he said he'd never be baptized!" little Marc said, not wanting to be outdone.

"Sometimes never is just around the corner," Jean-Marc fluffed our son's hair. "You never know when you'll stumble over it." Marc scampered out of the kitchen to look around the corner, and we all laughed.

My father gently wiped my mother's tears and then released her and walked over to Pierre. "I have your wife to thank for my conversion. It took this to make me find the answers. She was—is—a wonderful person. I'm sorry for her death, but I'm glad she is with the Savior." The laughter died, and once again the stark realization of Paulette's death hit us.

"Thank you." For a moment, peace seemed to light Pierre's face.

I grabbed a roll from the table and bit through the flaky crust to the soft inner white, but my appetite had left me.

"Can we go see the baby?" Marie-Thérèse asked. "I really want to see her."

Pierre was quiet. His expression was so agonized that I imagined we could actually hear his pain.

"I'll take you tomorrow," I said.

Her lips drew into a pout. "I don't want you. I want Daddy to go."

"Well, what ya goin' to name her?" Simone said, cutting into the silence left by Marie-Thérèse's remark. Her voice was rough with unspoken emotion.

"Did Paulette have a preference?" Louise asked.

"We didn't talk about it," Pierre said. "We didn't pick a name."

"Yes," Marie-Thérèse corrected. "Antoinette. Mommy wanted to name her after Josette's sister in heaven. She said she was really pretty."

"Are you sure?" Louise asked, glancing at me. I could feel my lips clamp tightly together, and I wondered if my expression showed my apprehension.

"Yes, it was Antoinette, wasn't it, Aunt Ariana?" Marie-Thérèse's eyes turned on me, challenging and angry. I couldn't understand her attitude toward me when we had always been such good friends, and this made me willing to back her up, despite my reluctance to name the baby Antoinette.

"Paulette did mention it yesterday before she went into the ICU," I said. "Maybe we could name her Antoinette Pauline," I added, voicing a thought that had been in the back of my mind. "Then we could call her Pauline after her mother."

"It's perfect fer her," Simone said. "The name means 'small in stature but big in love.' That's why I named her Paulette in the first place. She was so tiny, but I felt so much love. It seemed to fit somehow."

We all waited for Pierre's response. "Fine," he said without feeling. "Whatever you think Paulette would like."

So Paulette's daughter became Antoinette Pauline Perrault instead of "the baby." Marie-Thérèse seemed content with the name, though she still kept her distance from me. I didn't know what to make of her new rejection, but I would give her all the time she needed.

It was Pierre who concerned us now.

CHAPTER NINETEEN

*B*y Pierre's request there was a short viewing, attended only by members of the family and held Saturday morning just before the funeral. The funeral director opened the top part of the casket and left the room. I hadn't seen Paulette since I had told her I would take care of her babies. As then, she looked peaceful, though they had not gotten her makeup quite right. It didn't matter; she was no longer in the body.

For the first time, I saw Pierre cry. His body convulsed almost violently, and somehow I knew he stopped short of throwing himself over Paulette only because of Marie-Thérèse. Louise held him against her ample bosom until the wild shaking had relented. Then Pierre took Marie-Thérèse's hand and walked up to the casket. He kissed his wife's pale cheek, and silent tears splashed onto her face, smearing the makeup. Marie-Thérèse was crying, but she held out a trembling hand to touch her mother's red lips and then held it to her heart.

"I love you, Mommy," she whispered.

Pierre picked her up and stepped back into the semicircle we had made around the casket. Not a face was dry except for André's, and he didn't understand what was happening. *Or perhaps he understands better than any of us,* I thought.

"Shall we pray?" my father asked. It was strange to see him standing up as the patriarch of the joined families. Louise and Simone looked at him gratefully.

"May I offer it?" Jean-Marc said to his brother.

"Please." Pierre's voice was hardly more than a whisper. He clutched Marie-Thérèse as though he were drowning.

After the prayer, we each filed past the casket, bidding Paulette a private farewell. When all had said their good-byes, Pierre tenderly covered Paulette's face with her temple veil and stepped back from the casket. The funeral director must have been watching from the door, because when we finished, he was quick to come in and close the lid. He reached under the curtain to unlock the brakes on the metal frame holding the casket and rolled it into the main room where friends were gathering.

Marie-Thérèse was still crying. I longed to reach out for her, but when I tried, she shook my hand away. How was I to take care of her if she didn't let me? *I'll find a way,* I promised silently as they rolled Paulette from the room.

People gathered in the large room where the funeral would be held. Elisabeth and René, old friends of Paulette and the Perrault family, had come from Bordeaux with their two little boys. Monique, the nurse who had first introduced me to the gospel, also attended with her husband and three children. Many of the ward members were there as well, including the parents of the students in Paulette's former Primary class, the same ones who had shut her out from teaching. Their faces showed their regret, and this somehow comforted me. The mood was somber as people shared their memories of Paulette. Pierre took no part in the service but had asked me to speak.

"Paulette has been my friend for many years," I began. "I know of no one who has so turned their life around, no one who is more pure. She gave up the time she had left on this earth to save her baby's life." My words stopped, and sobs shook me. *My baby,* I thought. *She died early to save the baby she would give me to raise, as she hadn't been able to save Nette.* Pauline's sweet little face danced before my eyes, and the growing love I felt for her swelled even more in my heart because of Paulette's sacrifice. *What a precious gift!*

I don't know how long I stood there crying before Jean-Marc rose and gently led me from the pulpit. I clung to him. He settled me beside my parents and then took the stand himself.

"I know we all loved Paulette," he began. "But I can't help thinking that she might be a little upset at us today. We have remembered her but not once mentioned the thing most dear to her heart besides her family. I feel I should do so now." He paused and stared out over the audience. An air of expectancy filled the room.

He continued, "If Paulette were here, I think she might say it like this: Once there was a child born who came to save the world, not in but from their sins. He loved us so much that He willingly gave up His life so that we can live again. So that Paulette can live again! Think of it! Think of families being forever. I know as surely as I'm standing here that Paulette is alive, that we will all see her again. I'm sure she would ask us to remember our Savior today, to lift up our hearts and sing with joy for His everlasting love!"

Of course! Jean-Marc was right. Paulette would have us remember the Savior. And who knew how many countless lives Jean-Marc's testimony would touch that day? Nonmember neighbors and friends in the room couldn't help but feel the Spirit bear strong witness of the truth. My husband had taken this somber occasion and turned it into a giant missionary discussion.

"Paulette has made her transition from mortal life to the eternities triumphantly," Jean-Marc declared. "Let us all redouble our efforts to obey the commandments and turn to our Savior." He concluded with his testimony. The mood in the room had changed from sadness to one of hope and love.

After the service, I gathered my children about me and headed for the car, steeling myself for the burial. At the cemetery, birds sang overhead, flying carelessly across the clear blue sky as the casket was lowered into the warm, protecting earth. This time I didn't feel the devastation I felt when Antoine and Nette died. I knew where Paulette was and that I would see her again. It made things much easier.

Nearby, I could see Louise holding Marie-Thérèse and whispering in her ear. I hoped she was telling her the things I would like to say, given the chance. My arms ached to hold her, to start fulfilling Paulette's last wish, but I would have to be patient.

The next day we attended church as a family, including both my parents. Only Pierre declined to attend. Marie-Thérèse took her cue from him, and reluctantly, we left them both home. Later we went to the baptisms.

We had settled in our seats in the chapel when Giselle and her grandfather entered. Giselle was beautiful and radiant, dressed in white, but it was Grandfather who held our attention. The white clothing across his barrel chest contrasted sharply with his ebony skin and yet matched the hair on his head. His countenance was regal, and a sense of unmistakable greatness hung about him. A row of dark faces, also dressed in white, trailed after him—his posterity. I found myself smiling.

"Pierre should be here," Jean-Marc whispered, a grin covering his face. "He'd like this."

"But who's baptizing them?" I asked. Neither of the missionaries who had taught the discussions was dressed in white.

The mystery was solved when we went into the room with the font, and Grandfather took his place in the water to baptize Giselle.

"He was baptized earlier this week so he could receive the Aaronic Priesthood," Marguerite explained from the seat behind us. "He said that to make sure none of his children doubted the truthfulness of the gospel, he would baptize them all himself!"

And so he did. His deep voice seemed never to tire as he said the words that would set his family on the path to salvation. After the baptisms, both Giselle and her grandfather came up to us.

"Congratulations," I said, hugging them.

"How are you doing?" Giselle asked.

"Pretty good, actually."

"Paulette told me to check up on you."

I felt a rush of emotion. It was as if Paulette were there in the room, telling me how much she loved me.

Grandfather bent down to talk to my children on their level. He and Giselle were the only members of their family to live within our ward boundaries, so the children knew him fairly well. He rose and addressed us. "Time with them now will save a hundred sleepless nights later."

"I'm beginning to understand that," Jean-Marc said.

"You know," Grandfather continued, "I have accomplished many things in my long life, but none equals the pleasure of having a righteous child."

"Well, I think you must be feeling pretty good then." Jean-Marc motioned to his descendants.

Grandfather's eyes twinkled, and a warm smile stretched his lips. "Yes," he said, nodding. "This is a pretty good day."

Pierre and Marie-Thérèse stayed with us while the workmen took down the wall in their kitchen that separated their apartment from Louise's. Louise hadn't wanted to move into our apartment because of its larger size, and she and Lu-Lu were staying with my parents until they found a smaller one. We put our apartment up for sale and began to pack. I was grateful for the activity, as it kept my mind from my troubles with Marie-Thérèse.

Lu-Lu had tried to make up with Philippe, but he refused to forgive her for her choice at the hospital. Unhappily, she called off the wedding and notified the guests.

"I'm so sorry," she said to me a week after Paulette's death. She had asked me to call the caterer and florist to cancel and get back what money I could.

"Why?" I asked. "It's not your fault."

"But it is. I shouldn't have upset him so. Then maybe he would still love me and we would be getting married. Then you wouldn't have to call." Her voice sounded despondent.

"Don't be ridiculous!" I said. "Your only mistake was to become engaged to him in the first place."

"What?" Her eyes flashed angrily.

"At last, a spark of life," I teased. "Don't you see how much pain you've been spared? The many times you would drag your kids to church alone because he refuses to go? You are so lucky."

"But I love him!"

"You can't go through life not being yourself around someone. With him you're afraid to speak your mind. You can't even be with us without endangering his self-confidence." I grabbed her hand. "Lu-Lu, that's not love. Believe me, I know. Please listen."

"I didn't know you didn't like Philippe. You never said anything before."

"Only because you wouldn't listen. But we've been praying so hard that what was best for you would happen."

She sniffed. "So have I."

"And our prayers have been answered," I said. She frowned abjectly. I shook my head. "Oh, Lu-Lu, there's so much more out there—so much that doesn't involve Philippe! Love will happen when you least expect it. Until then, look outside yourself and see who you can help. It will get your mind off Philippe."

"But it hurts!"

I hugged her. "I know. But it will go away, and you'll be able to look back on it with a different view. Just as someday we'll remember Paulette without the pain. You need to be happy within yourself," I added. "You can't rely on a man to make you happy, just on yourself and on the Lord. Only then can you be confident and whole enough to enter an eternal relationship. Until then, just take it one day at a time."

Her arms tightened around me. "Thanks, Ariana. It doesn't seem so now, but if you say so, I believe you."

"Good," I whispered. I only hoped Philippe wouldn't realize what he had lost before she was over him completely.

Pierre came into the kitchen for a drink of water. We said hello, but he appeared not to hear.

"Is he always like that?" Lu-Lu asked, coming out of her self-absorption.

I nodded. The whole time Pierre had stayed with us he had said little, walking around as if in a trance. We had given him André's room for privacy, moving the little boy's crib to ours. Now Pierre spent most of his time in the room, sleeping or simply staring at the teddy bear wallpaper. He didn't visit little Pauline in the hospital or leave the apartment at all, except for doctor's appointments and his radiation and chemotherapy treatments. I didn't know what to do for him.

Daily, I visited Pauline, who was growing stronger and gaining weight steadily. She took more milk at each visit and used the feeding tube less. The doctor was sure she would be able to go home soon. Marie-Thérèse accompanied me on my increasingly longer visits but only to see her sister. She refused to speak to me during our outings or at home, and even with her father she had become reserved and cautious. Only with Jean-Marc was she her old self. She talked incessantly to him and insisted on sitting next to him at the table. Josette began to feel displaced in her father's affection, and it showed in her treatment of her cousin.

"I want her to go home," she said on Monday during family night, almost two weeks after Paulette's death. She glared at Marie-Thérèse, who sat on Jean-Marc's lap, clutching Dolly in her arms. We were in the front room playing a board game—always a difficult challenge with the twins. As usual, Pierre had retired to his room early, claiming exhaustion.

"Josette!" I reproved her sharply. My daughter had made no attempt to lower her voice, and Marie-Thérèse glared at her.

"But she gets all the attention. She still has a dad, but she only wants mine."

Marie-Thérèse was crying now, and Jean-Marc comforted her. He looked sternly at Josette. "That's enough. You and I will discuss this later."

Josette's tears began at her father's tone, and in frustration I started to cry—but in loud, fake sobs. The girls looked up immediately to see if my tears were real. Grinning, little Marc did his best pretend wailing, and then Jean-Marc joined us. Soon only André was quiet, staring at us curiously. Despite herself Josette laughed, accompanied by Marie-Thérèse, though she resisted looking at me.

When all the tears were giggles, Jean-Marc fixed his eyes on the children, moving slowly from face to face. "We're a family now," he said. "We're all staying together. We'll be moving next week to Marie-Thérèse's house, only it's bigger now because they've finished taking out the wall to Grandma Louise's old apartment. You four children will live like brothers and sisters. That's the way it is."

"And my baby?" Marie-Thérèse asked.

"She'll be coming, too," I said.

Marie-Thérèse, staring at her hands, appeared relieved. "Good. I really want her."

What she wanted was to not lose any more loved ones from her life. My feelings echoed hers.

"But before we get the baby, we'll need a bigger car." Marc's tone was matter-of-fact. "We don't have enough seat belts."

Jean-Marc smiled. "How about us men going to look for one tomorrow?"

"Yeah!"

"I want to go!" Josette said.

"Me too!" Marie-Thérèse added.

Jean-Marc looked at me, but I shook my head. "You got yourself into it, and now you're stuck. I've done it before with all of them." I smiled and added helpfully, "I'll keep André."

He grimaced, but I could tell he was enjoying the idea. "Okay, I'll take you all." The children cheered.

"I get the front!" Marc shouted.

"No, you had it last time!"

"It's my turn!"

My husband's eyes met mine, and we both sighed. But inside I felt happy.

———

Moving day, the Tuesday three weeks after baby Pauline's birth, came sooner than expected. Pierre had returned to work the day before, but Jean-Marc and my father took the day off to supervise the movers. Louise, Simone, and Marguerite were in our new apartment, cleaning and putting things away as they arrived. Josette and Marie-Thérèse squealed excitedly at having their own room away from the boys, and Marc stoically accepted sharing with little André. Both rooms were in the part of the apartment that had been Louise's.

I went into the nursery Paulette had so painstakingly arranged for her darling baby. We had taken Marie-Thérèse's old room next to where the baby would sleep. On the other side of the nursery was Pierre's room—the one he had shared with Paulette. I had removed all of her things, either giving them away or keeping them for the girls when they were older. Pierre hadn't wanted to return to the room, but I insisted he be where he could hear his baby cry and go to her, should she need him.

When I had made the suggestion, he stared at me, looking strange without the thick head of hair he had sported before starting the chemotherapy. "She won't need me," he said. "She'll have you and Jean-Marc."

I wondered if perhaps we had been wrong in stepping in to help Pierre so much, in spite of Paulette's wish. But then I thought of Pauline's precious little face, and I knew I had to do it for her. I couldn't let her feel abandoned. Still, I hadn't expected that Pierre would try to completely abdicate his responsibilities.

At one o'clock, Jean-Marc, Simone, and I took the children to the hospital in our new van, leaving my father and Louise to finish things at the house. Pierre was notably absent, as he had insisted he couldn't take any more days off work.

In the nursery, I dressed Pauline in a warm but frilly outfit Marie-Thérèse and I had bought the day before. She was still tiny, just under two-and-a-half kilograms, and the clothes were big. We laughed as I wrapped her in the baby quilt Paulette had made from material left over from the new curtains. I fingered the pattern, remembering how many times I had seen the fabric in Paulette's loving hands as she worked on it.

I carried Pauline to the van, wrapped snugly in her mother's love. It felt wonderful, and not just a little strange, to be holding my new baby without all the wires and the feeding tube. I buckled her into the new car seat next to André's and then sat on her other side to make sure she didn't cry. The children bounced on their seats with excitement, and I felt like joining them.

"Now remember what we've taught you," Jean-Marc said as he started the engine. "What do you do if the baby spits up?"

"Tell Mom or you so you can watch while we put gloves on and clean it with a cloth," Marc said.

"Then we put it in the special basket," Josette added. "And throw the gloves away."

"Or if it's a lot, we let you clean it," Marie-Thérèse said.

"Then what do you do?"

"Wash our hands with soap," said the chorus.

"And what if you see blood? Do you touch it? Or try to clean it up?"

"No!" all three children said emphatically.

"What about dirty or wet diapers?"

"Only with gloves," they said.

Jean-Marc continued to drill them on everything that might happen with the baby. They knew all the answers; it seemed we had them prepared well. We had tried to instill not fear but caution. We wanted them to love Pauline and to be prepared to help her for however long she would be with us, not to turn away from her because of the infection.

Despite all my worrying about the virus passing to the healthy children, the doctor had been much more worried about our caring for the baby. "Since her immune system is damaged, keeping her free from sickness will be your chief concern," he said. "You need to watch for signs such as cough, diarrhea, or any odd behavior that might signal an infection. Anything at all needs to be reported immediately."

We had been told to keep Pauline inside and away from people outside the family until she was stronger, at about six or seven months, and then she could go out only if it was good weather. It wasn't only because of her HIV; most premature babies were too fragile to fight off even the normal germs coming from outsiders. As with any premature baby, anyone who did stay with Pauline was required to take a CPR class, and all the adults in our family took it, including Pierre. I hopeed we would never have to use it.

As we gathered for dinner, Pierre came home from work. He glanced around at the changes in the apartment, and I thought his face showed relief; I had altered things enough so the memories of Paulette wouldn't assault him at every turn. Then his eyes rested on the baby in her carrier sitting on the large kitchen table. He studied her, and for a moment I thought he might go to her, but he didn't. He slumped into a chair and stared at his food listlessly.

"Daddy," Marie-Thérèse said, "I missed you." She climbed onto his lap. As usual, she carried Dolly in her arms.

Pierre managed a smile. "Missed me? But I was only gone to work."

"Do you have to go again?"

"Yes, tomorrow."

"We brought Pauline home. Isn't she beautiful? I've never seen a baby so beautiful."

Pierre grunted. Marie-Thérèse tried to turn in his lap. Clutching the doll made her clumsy, and she knocked Pierre's fork to the floor.

"Marie-Thérèse!" he said sharply.

Her face fell. "But I love you, Daddy," she wailed.

"Pick up the fork," he said. She slid off his lap and retrieved the fork, her face puckered in a fearsome scowl. Pierre took it but made no move to comfort her. I longed to go to her, but I knew she wouldn't accept me. I met Jean-Marc's eyes over the table, begging him to do something. He shook his head at me.

"I love you, Daddy," Marie-Thérèse said again.

"I love you, too," Pierre said.

"I want to hug you." Marie-Thérèse held out her arms. Pierre sighed wearily but did as she requested. Then he pushed his chair back from the table and lurched to his feet.

"I'm not hungry," he said. "I'm really tired." He left the kitchen, and I stood staring after his ever-thinning frame. The doctor had warned us he would change as the effects of the cancer progressed, not only in body but in spirit, but surely not this soon. And why his utter rejection of Pauline?

"I just love him," Marie-Thérèse said softly. It was a phrase that had become common on her lips since her mother's death. If her father showed even the slightest irritation, she would say the words over and over, whining, until he gazed directly in her eyes and responded with his own feelings of love. It was irritating at best and grated on us all, even though I knew it was only because she was not getting what she desperately needed. But Paulette wasn't coming back, and Marie-Thérèse wouldn't let me fill her place. There was only Pierre, who seemed too wrapped up in his own private misery to notice his daughter's cry for help.

Jean-Marc picked up Marie-Thérèse and danced her around the kitchen. "I bet I can eat dinner faster than you," he taunted, coaxing a reluctant smile. The tension dissolved, and we passed the rest of the evening in peace. At bedtime we gathered the children around us, as we had begun doing since Paulette's death, and read the scriptures. We sat on the floor in the girls' room and Jean-Marc read aloud, acting out some of the parts to keep the children's attention. This was how I had always imagined life with my family. Jean-Marc had so far kept his promise to me and tried to place us first, though some nights he still had to work late.

Pauline wriggled faintly in my arms. She opened her eyes and stared at me with eyes seeming far too wise for someone only three weeks old. She was still so tiny, yet I sensed a strong spirit there. Pauline—little but big in love. The name fit her well.

I cuddled her close, loving her. I felt a soft touch on my shoulder and looked up to see André watching me. He reached out and stroked the baby with surprisingly gentle fingers, his face bursting into a grin. "Baby," he said. I helped him sit in my lap and placed the baby on top of his short legs. His smile grew wider. "Baby," he said again.

That night, we put Pauline in her crib and turned on the small machine we had purchased to monitor her breathing. Because of her size and the HIV infection, we had felt it best to keep it on her, just in case. We bought another device that allowed us to hear any sound in the room. It comforted me to know that though she was so far away from me, I could hear even her tiniest cry at night. My other children had always been in the same room with us for at least the first few months, but with Pauline we had to consider Pierre. "He has to have a chance to know her," Jean-Marc said when I had reconsidered putting her in the room alone. "And he won't if we keep her in our room." Reluctantly, I agreed.

The days went by quickly with my new responsibilities, and some-times I wondered if I would make it through. I had forgotten what work a new baby was and how much time was necessary for her care. Though she had completely captured my heart, Pauline quickly turned into a demanding, fussy baby, with a surprisingly loud voice for one so small. The burden grew heavier as Pierre became more sickly and could work only part time. He spent more time in bed than out of it, staring at the wall and only grunting in response to my questions. He never thanked me for the care I gave him, and each day he withdrew more from Marie-Thérèse.

Louise and my mother came over often to help, as did Simone on her days off. Still, it was all I could do sometimes to keep my sanity. Even with the relatives helping, Pauline's care fell mostly to me and Jean-Marc. When he walked in the door at night, I usually plopped the baby in his arms, crying or not.

"And to think I once complained because you wouldn't let me take care of the children when they cried," he said one day when Pauline was six and a half weeks old. The baby was crying, and nothing I did would stop her.

I glared at him. "I've had it! Do you know what your sweet little children did today? They colored all over the kitchen walls with crayons while I was rocking Pauline!" The baby had stopped crying as I said the last words, and my voice seemed conspicuous in the abrupt silence.

Jean-Marc's eyebrows drew together, and he made a sympathetic noise.

"And we've no food," I added. "We're eating leftovers again."

He shifted Pauline to one arm and put the other around me. For once, the baby didn't cry. "I love you," he said. "And we'll get by some-how."

"'This, too, shall pass,' eh?" I quoted.

He smiled. "Something like that. Why don't I watch the children while you go out for a while?"

"I could go to the grocery store."

A key turned in the lock, and Pierre entered. He hadn't gone into work until after lunch, but already he appeared exhausted. "What's wrong?" he said, immediately noticing my flushed face. I saw him glance at the baby and away again quickly.

"The children wrote on the walls in the kitchen," Jean-Marc said.

Pierre's mouth twisted in his gaunt face, and he stomped down the hall, making more noise than I had believed possible for a man who had grown so thin. I followed him, with Jean-Marc close behind.

Marie-Thérèse looked up from the wall she was cleaning with a rag. She saw her father's grim face and dropped the wet cloth onto the white linoleum floor. "But I love you, Daddy," she said before he could speak.

"You know better than this," he said. "After you clean up, you'll go to your room."

She began to cry. "I don't love you, Daddy. Never, never!" Tears streamed down her cheeks as she faced him defiantly. "And I don't like you, either!"

Pierre gave a strangled gasp and then whirled and made his way down the hall. Marie-Thérèse stared forlornly after him.

I ran after Pierre. I reached his room before he had completely shut the door and elbowed my way in. "She didn't mean it, Pierre!" I said. "She just needs you. You haven't been here for her, and she's afraid of losing you like she did Paulette."

"She *is* going to lose me," Pierre grated sarcastically. His face seemed heavily marked by black despair. "I'm dying. I can barely work any-more. The doctor says I probably have only a few months left. Before long, I won't be able to get out of bed!"

"You're not so sick that you can't love your daughter," I retorted. "She won't let me do it; you're the only one."

He pulled up the leg of his trousers. Covering his calf were strange growths, standing out dark and ugly against his thin, white leg. I gasped and recoiled.

He laughed mirthlessly. "Another opportunistic cancer," he rasped. "It's eating away at the outside while the other cancer eats at the inside."

"How long have you had it?"

He shrugged. "A month now."

"Does it hurt?"

His smile was bitter. "Oh, yes." His eyes narrowed as he added, glancing toward a large picture of Paulette and Marie-Thérèse hanging on the wall above his dresser, "But it's nothing compared to the feeling in my heart."

I felt his hopelessness, but I was also fighting for my best friend's child, my child. "And you're a grown man," I said acidly. "How do you think Marie-Thérèse feels? She's hurting just as badly as you are, maybe worse, because she feels she's lost you as well." He glared at me, but I wasn't through. "And Pauline needs you, too. Don't for a minute think that she's too young to feel your rejection. You and Paulette wanted a baby, and it was Paulette who made the decision to save her life when no one else wanted to." I shook my finger at him. "You have to come to grips with that. *Your* wife chose to give *your* baby a chance at life. It's not Pauline's fault. Stop blaming her for her mother's death."

"She's going to die." Pierre's face was stricken.

"We're all going to die someday. Our job is to survive until then and try to be happy." I purposely made my voice hard. "And don't tell me you're enduring to the end. Enduring isn't standing idly by and letting life sweep you away. It's making the best of what you've been given. If you ever want to see Paulette again, maybe you should think of that. Eternal families take work." I turned from him and strode from the room.

Outside in the hall, Jean-Marc waited with the baby. "Did you hear what I said?" I asked.

"He had to be told," Jean-Marc said. "It should have been me."

"You love him too much. He's your brother. But I love the girls more than I love him."

"Where are you going?" he asked as I passed him.

"To see Marie-Thérèse. We've something to settle between us."

He nodded, and I felt perhaps he stopped himself from saying it was long past due. I felt a stab of guilt; he was right. She was just a child, and whatever it was that stopped her from letting me love her, it couldn't continue—especially if Pierre wouldn't come to his senses.

I found Marie-Thérèse alone in her room. The door was slightly ajar, and I pushed it open far enough to squeeze in. She sat on the floor, facing the window, holding her doll to her chest and rocking it as she sang. Her voice was thin and high and shook with feeling.

"Heavenly Father, are you really there? And do you hear and answer ev'ry child's prayer?" I realized that Marie-Thérèse's prayer was actually a song she had learned in Primary.

"Please, send my mommy back," she whispered when she couldn't remember any more words to the song.

I must have moved, because she turned. Her lips drew together as she saw who I was, and she turned back to face the window.

"We need to talk," I said, sitting on the floor beside her. She said nothing, so I plunged ahead. "I know I can never take the place of your mommy, but we've always been such good friends. Can't you tell me what's wrong? Why are you angry with me?"

Marie-Thérèse's face darkened, and she clamped her lips together tightly.

"I love you," I said.

"No, you don't."

"Yes, I do. And before your mom died, I promised her I would take care of you. That's why we all live together now. I'll always love you, no matter what."

Her face turned in my direction, eyes challenging. "You said my mommy wasn't going to die, but she did."

Of course! I had told her that, and I had believed at the time she wouldn't die—at least not right then. How was I to know Paulette would die so abruptly? But at least I now understood the problem. In Marie-Thérèse's eyes, I had lied. How could she believe me when I said I would always love her?

I sensed a waiting about the child, as if she wanted to give me a chance. "I thought I was telling you the truth," I said. There was passion and conviction in my voice, but I wondered if she would understand it. "I didn't think she would die, not for a long time. I just kept telling myself she wouldn't. I guess I thought if I said it enough, it wouldn't happen."

Marie-Thérèse watched me for a moment before saying softly, "She could come back. Heavenly Father could make her come. He can do anything. Can't He?" The last two words were spoken tremulously, as if she was afraid this too was a lie.

"He can, but He won't," I said. "There are certain laws He also lives by. Because your Mommy got AIDS, she had to die, no matter how much we hurt or how much Heavenly Father hurts with us. Now we have to show how we can grow strong and learn how to get along without her. And you needn't worry about your mommy. She's with Jesus now, with no more pain or hospital beds, and she's looking down on all of us, waiting for us to be together again."

Her eyes dropped, and I thought I had lost. "Oh, please, Marie-Thérèse! Please, let me love you. I miss your mommy so much. Can't we help each other? I don't know if I can do this without you!"

I saw the tears on her lashes and reached out to draw her close. To my extreme relief, she didn't pull away. "I love you so much," I said, to make sure she understood. "And I'll always love you. Always."

She still didn't meet my gaze, but now she clung to me, letting her rag doll slip to the floor. As at Giselle's baptism, I felt Paulette's presence warming me, and I knew she was with us.

"We're fine," I whispered. "Just fine."

CHAPTER TWENTY

Sunday, several days after my confrontation with Pierre, dawned bright and tense. He hadn't emerged from his room all the day before, though I thought I had heard someone in the kitchen during the night. An air of expectancy had seemed to settle over the house. The children were abnormally quiet—except Pauline, who cried a great deal, as usual, squeezing her tiny fists together and howling with all her might until I gave her whatever she desired. Lately, she wanted only to be held in the rocking chair in her room. The automatic swing we bought wouldn't do; she wanted human contact. She demanded almost constant attention, as if she had too much energy for her little body. Tomorrow she would be seven weeks old, though she was still smaller than most newborns.

I hummed to myself that morning as I rocked Pauline in her room. André sat on the floor in front of me, dressed in his Sunday clothes and playing with some toys. Jean-Marc was in the bedroom dressing the children. As usual, Josette was whining because her tights weren't quite right, and Jean-Marc sounded exasperated. I knew he was tired from lack of sleep—we had both paced the floor with Pauline last night—yet I stilled the urge to rush to Josette and take over. My husband had been right about my never letting him solve the problems with the children, and I had been practicing sitting back and watching. It seemed to be working. More and more often the children turned to him when he was home, leaving me more time for the household—or, more accurately, for Pauline.

I stared at her face. She wasn't sleeping, just watching me. I knew if I stopped rocking she would cry. She favored Pierre rather than Paulette, with abundant dark hair and intense brown eyes. There was no hint of illness yet about her, only the urgency to experience life.

André lurched to his feet and held onto my knee, swaying as I rocked. A grin nearly split his face. "Such a big boy," I cooed. As usual when looking at him, I marveled at how good he was. Then it hit me; my Father had known all along I would be raising Pauline and had given me the steady and serene André because He had known I would be overwhelmed. I reached out and patted his tousled brown locks. "I love you, André." He giggled and reached for my hand. In my arms, Pauline gave a small cry, as if suspecting my attention had shifted.

"Well, we're ready," Jean-Marc said, coming into the baby's room. It was his turn to go to church with the children. Since the baby could not leave the house except for doctor's visits, we took turns staying at home with her. Pierre was usually in the house, too, as he hadn't returned to church since Paulette's death, but we were afraid to leave her with him because he had never looked twice at her in the same day.

"Remember to come home right after, just in case Simone is late," I said. "She's working and was worried about getting here on time. I may not have time to get there on the subway." Today at the baptisms after church, my parents would become members. Since the day of Paulette's death, my father had been taking the missionary discussions and searching out every minute aspect of the Church, as was his thorough nature. Finally, he and my mother were being baptized. Simone had agreed to watch Pauline while Jean-Marc and I attended together. I felt comfortable leaving the baby with Simone as I had never imagined I might. The subtle changes that had begun in her since entering the clinic had continued, though she still refused to accept the missionaries.

"I'll be here," Jean-Marc assured me. "And if Simone's not here, you'll go on ahead and I'll meet you at the church."

"And probably miss the baptisms," I said.

He kissed me. "Don't worry about it. Since I'm baptizing them, they won't start without me."

"Don't be too sure," I said lightly. "My father's pretty determined now that he's learned everything he can. If Simone is late, maybe I should stay." I grimaced even as I said the words.

"It'll work out," Jean-Marc said confidently. His grin was infectious. "Now kiss Mom, kids, and let's be on our way." The twins came exuberantly, Marie-Thérèse shyly, and André sedately, as usual. I felt especially grateful for Marie-Thérèse's acceptance of me. Her little face seemed less tragic now. If only Pierre could be there for her.

Pauline had fallen asleep, but I didn't move from the rocker. I was content to hold her and enjoy these moments of peace. Later, I warmed a bottle. As I fed her, I held her close and studied the tiny, perfect features so superbly masking the time bomb ticking away inside her.

The minutes turned into hours, and when my family arrived home from church, I jerked awake in the chair. My body felt stiff and sore, and I tried to stretch my back. Pauline awoke with the movement and smiled as she always did after a good sleep. I grinned back, helplessly drawn to her charm.

The phone rang, and I stumbled to my feet to answer it, but Pierre had come out of his room and beat me to the kitchen. "Okay, I'll tell her," he said into the phone.

"What?" I asked.

He didn't meet my gaze, and I sensed an embarrassment about him. "Simone can't come. She says she has to stay at work."

I groaned. Jean-Marc came into the kitchen with André in his arms and the others scattering around his feet like little yellow chicks. Except for Marie-Thérèse's slightly lighter hair on a head poking an inch above the others, the three could pass as triplets. "Then Pierre will have to watch his daughter," Jean-Marc said firmly.

Pierre's eyes widened, and he shook his head, backing away. "I can't."

"Yes, you can." Jean-Marc let André slide to the floor and took Pauline from my arms. "You know how to rock her and feed her. If you don't remember from when Marie-Thérèse was little, you have seen us doing it enough." He tried to give the baby to his brother, but Pierre retreated down the hall. He went into his room and slammed the door. I heard the lock click firmly into place.

"She's your daughter," my husband yelled through the door, "and it's about time you took your responsibility. You've had time to adjust. Now stop feeling sorry for yourself and do something with the time you have left. Is this how you want your daughters to remember you—a man whose spirit has been broken? What kind of example is that?"

There was no answer. "Well, we're leaving," Jean-Marc said through the door. "Ari's parents need our support today, and we haven't left this apartment together since we brought your baby home. *Your* baby, Pierre! We're going to leave her in her crib, and you're taking care of her!" He stomped away from the door and into Pauline's room. Gently, he laid the baby in her crib, stroking her cheek for a moment so the sudden change wouldn't make her cry.

"No!" I whispered. "What if he doesn't take care of her?"

"Ari, I know what I'm doing. Please take the children and wait in the hall."

I wanted to rebel, but his eyes pleaded. "Come on, children." I ushered them out, stopping only to collect my purse on the small table beneath the mirror in the entryway.

As I opened the door, Jean-Marc ducked into our room for an instant and then out again. He glanced over his shoulder. "We're leaving, Pierre," he declared.

I heard Pauline start wailing in her room, realizing she was alone. My heart constricted, and I tried to go back into the apartment.

"No," Jean-Marc said, stopping me. The children watched us with anxious faces.

"I'm her mother. I won't leave her without knowing."

Jean-Marc shut the door and put his arm around me. "Of course we won't leave her." Out of his pocket he drew the baby monitor and held it out to me.

I grabbed it and switched it on. Now we could hear Pauline's shrill cry even more loudly. Marie-Thérèse's eyes held tears; I too wanted to cry. We huddled together in the hall around the monitor in Jean-Marc's hand.

"Let's go get her," little Marc said, voicing my feelings.

"Wait a minute more," Jean-Marc said. His tearful gaze met mine. "It's the only way, Ari. They need each other, and this is the only way I know. It's like me with our children. I need to be with them and take care of them, even when they are being difficult—no, *especially* when they are being difficult."

The resentment building in my heart dissolved. Leaving Pauline alone, so little and helpless, was hard, but we had to balance her needs now against a possible relationship with her father for however long they had left.

The crying went on and on, seemingly forever, though it could only have been a few minutes. Then a new sound: stiff steps, a low mumbling. "They left," came Pierre's puzzled voice. "They really left!" Pauline screamed even louder.

"Shhh, baby. Be quiet. Just be quiet." His voice was rough, and I wondered if he might hurt her.

Jean-Marc saw my thought. "It's Pierre," he reminded me. "He loves her. He's her father."

"Pauline!" Pierre's voice came through the monitor, sounding frustrated. "Please stop crying!" Then, "Okay, come here." The cries changed slightly but didn't stop. "There, there," Pierre mumbled.

"I've got you. Don't cry." The cries lessened to a whimper and then ceased completely.

"See? It's okay. I've got you. You're not alone." Pierre's voice sounded odd now. "Don't worry. I'm not going to leave you alone." Again we heard crying, soft sobs, but they came from Pierre, not Pauline. "Hi, little one," he murmured. "I guess it's time we met. I'm your daddy. Yes, I am." He paused before adding hoarsely, "And I love you. I'm so sorry, Pauline. I love you so much!"

I looked up to see Jean-Marc watching me. His hand was gentle as he touched my cheek, wiping a stray tear. "It's going to be all right, Ari. He just needs time alone with her." I nodded.

"So are we going?" Marc asked. Now that Pauline was no longer crying, his child's brain had moved on. "I don't want to miss Grandpa getting baptized."

"Me either," Josette said.

Jean-Marc glanced at me questioningly, and I gave a sharp nod. "Okay," he said. "Go push the button on the elevator."

"It's my turn!"

"No, mine!"

I left Jean-Marc to sort it out and focused on Marie-Thérèse. She still stared at the white monitor in my hands. Pierre was singing a song so softly I couldn't make out the words or recognize the tune.

"He's singing 'Tell Me Why,'" Marie-Thérèse said, a smile playing on her lips. As she said it, I recognized a few lines from the song I had known as a child:

> Tell me why life is so beautiful.
> Tell me why life is so happy.

Tell me why, dear Mademoiselle.

Is it because you love me?

"He used to sing that to me before Mom—" She broke off and transferred her gaze to me. "Is he back?" she asked. Her expression was hopeful but tinged with caution. "Do you think he'll love me now?"

I hugged her. "He has always loved you. He just misses your mom, and he's a little scared, like you are. But I think he's back. I think everything's going to be okay now."

She seemed relieved. "I'm glad. I missed him."

"Me too," I said. "Me too."

The elevator chimed, and I picked her up and carried her inside where the others waited. There would be time later for her to be with Pierre. Right now, he and Pauline needed to get to know each other without interruptions.

I didn't know if I was right about leaving Pauline with Pierre; it didn't matter. I was only doing the best I knew how; it was all any of us could do.

———

At the church, my father was pacing in the hall, already dressed in white. "Oh, you're here," he said. Jean-Marc went to change while my father led us to where my mother was seated. Louise and Lu-Lu were with her.

"They look so happy," Lu-Lu whispered to me.

I smiled. My parents were holding hands, and occasionally their eyes met and held as if exchanging deepest thoughts. "They know they'll be together forever," I said.

"Do you really believe that?" Lu-Lu asked.

The question startled me. "Don't you?"

"I—I guess so. I just didn't realize how important it was. When Philippe and I were planning to get married, I just thought about now and about how much I loved him. But take your parents. They've been together so long, and yet they nearly broke up because of their different beliefs. I wonder if that's what would have happened to Philippe and me."

"You never know. But it seems likely, given his attitude toward the Church."

"I could never imagine choosing the Church over a man I loved," Lu-Lu said. "But maybe I was wrong. I mean, like with Paulette and Pierre, their love will go on forever. Had Philippe and I been in their position, our love would have been over, with no hope."

"Do you have a testimony of the Church?" I asked.

Lu-Lu paused in thought. "I don't think I did, or I would never have settled for marriage outside the temple," she said. "But I believe now."

"That's a beginning," I said. "Now what are you going to do about it?"

"What do you mean?"

I laughed. "Don't look so startled. All I mean is that a secure knowledge of the gospel always leads people to want to help others. Do you remember when my father decided to be baptized? Well, when I found him in the cemetery that day, I thought I might have to stop him from jumping up on a park bench somewhere and proclaiming the gospel with one of those loudspeakers."

"Really?" Lu-Lu giggled at the idea.

I nodded. "It wasn't a bit like him. Do you know he passed out a Book of Mormon to everyone at the bank?"

"He didn't!"

"He did. The board members weren't too happy when they heard."

Her eyes grew wide. "What did he do?"

"He gave them each a long overdue raise—and a Book of Mormon!" The idea of him doing so made us both laugh.

"Shhh, you two," my father whispered. "It's beginning."

I turned to say just one more thing. "Family is one of the most important things we preach in the gospel," I said. "I never realized how important family was until I went on a mission. It was then I knew that the best work I could ever do was at home, with those I love. Don't settle for what won't make you happy in the long run. It's not worth it!"

She nodded. "I think I've been luckier than I deserve," she said. "My family has always been strong. I wonder if I . . ." Her voice drained away. "Thanks, Ari. I've got some thinking to do." She turned to listen to the speaker.

A short time later, when my father emerged from the water, I knew I had never been happier in my entire life. *We did it, Antoine,* I said silently. *Our family is whole!*

Jean-Marc met my gaze from where he stood in the font, waiting for my mother. *I love you,* he mouthed.

Life was sometimes hard but so worth it.

—————

When we arrived home, Pierre met us at the door with tiny Pauline asleep in his arms. His face was worried.

"What's wrong?" I asked anxiously, checking Pauline for any visual signs of sickness.

"It's Simone," Pierre said.

"What?"

"The clinic called. She's supposed to be here or at work, but when they were doing random checking, they found out she's not at either place."

I frowned. "Oh, no! For over two months she's been without drugs. Two months! What if . . ." My voice trailed off.

"I don't believe it," Jean-Marc said. "She was doing so well."

"Was she?" I asked. She had been upset at Paulette's death but less than I expected. Perhaps stark realization had finally struck. "I have to find her," I said.

Jean-Marc nodded. "Pierre and I will stay with the children."

"No, I want to go with Ariana," Pierre said.

"Are you sure you're up to it?" I didn't try to keep the surprise from my voice.

He nodded once, decisively. "Yes. She's Paulette's mother. It's time I took responsibility for my family and their happiness." He handed Pauline to Jean-Marc and knelt near Marie-Thérèse. "I'm going to find Grandma Simone, and when I come back, you and I are going to have a talk."

Marie-Thérèse beamed. "What if I'm asleep?" she asked, her smile fading.

Pierre kissed her nose. "Then I'll wake you right up."

"Thank you, Daddy. And I love you." Her arms went up around his neck.

"I love you, too."

I bade farewell to the twins, and Jean-Marc blew me a kiss. I grabbed it in mid-air and slapped it on my cheek. Pierre pulled on a cap over his bald head and opened the door.

We started by searching the bars and cafés near Simone's house and then near ours and the clinic. We found nothing. It was embarrassing entering the places reeking of alcohol and smoke, but we plunged doggedly on. We began checking the small stores lining the streets, though many were closed for the Sabbath. The afternoon sun began to fade.

"Where could she be?" Pierre said.

I shook my head. In his eyes I saw the same guilt I was feeling. If only we had been more supportive, if only we had paid her more heed. "It's not our fault," I said. "It's her choice to change or not."

"Like it was mine to reject my daughter."

I said nothing, just watched him.

"You were right all along," he continued. "You and Paulette. That baby is a gift from God."

"Shall we pray?" I asked.

He grinned, and I could see the old Pierre shining through. "I'll offer it." We stood together and prayed in a little alleyway off the main street. Afterwards we walked on.

"Now, where might she go?" I mumbled. I couldn't help feeling that the answer was within my grasp.

"She wouldn't try to hurt herself, would she?" Pierre asked. "Like throw herself in the Seine or anything."

I grabbed his arms. "The Seine, yes!"

Without explaining, I propelled him back to the car. I drove straight to the Quai de Montebello and the booksellers' stalls. We left the car and hurried to the stone wall overlooking the Seine, eyes searching through the thin crowd of tourists.

"There!" Pierre pointed, and I saw her, looking out over the water.

"Simone!" I cried. She turned her head and watched our approach.

"Where have you been?" Pierre asked. "We've been searching everywhere."

She turned her gaze back to the gentle waves below. "I've been watchin' the water. And wonderin' how God made it."

"What?" Pierre said, but I smiled.

Simone focused on Pierre. "Ya thought I went to a bar, didn't ya? Or back to drugs?" Pierre nodded, shamefaced. There was no trace of substance abuse in Simone's manner. She laughed. "Don't feel bad. I almost did." There were tears in her voice. "I was missin' Paulette and thinkin' about yer little baby. I got depressed and planned to go to a bar and order a vodka and a couple joints to begin with, but then I stopped here first. A man came up to me, and we got to talkin' about how water is made—you know, them molecules and stuff. He told me how the world always has the same amount of water in it, and how it recycles. It evaporates, goes up and comes back as rain, or people use it. It was so fascinatin', such a perfect system. I knew God made it." She glanced my way briefly. "So I prayed." She stopped.

"And?" Pierre asked anxiously.

"He answered, of course," Simone said. "I guess I'll be seein' them missionaries of yers after all. And don't be shocked, but I ain't too sure if I won't go back to school, study science or somethin'."

Pierre hugged her. "Paulette would be proud."

"Proud?" Simone asked doubtfully. She thumbed heavenward. "More than likely, she's up there askin' what the h—, uh, beans took me so long."

We took Simone back to the clinic. She had to undergo a drug test, but given the circumstances of her daughter's recent death, the personnel were understanding—especially when the tests came out negative. Pierre and I went home, exhausted but happy.

"We have been blessed," Pierre said to me. "Don't let me ever forget it."

CHAPTER TWENTY-ONE

*A*fter his baptism that Sunday, my father threw himself into church work like a man starved for any touch of the Spirit. Through his efforts, the genealogical line I had been sporadically working on doubled in size the first week. My mother blossomed with her newfound happiness. "I'll never ask for another thing," she vowed. "The Lord has been so very good to me."

My parents were the only ones newly baptized, but they were not the only ones who began a new life. That day it seemed we all started anew—learning from the past, throwing out everything that held us back, and holding on to only that which made us strong and sealed us as survivors.

Pierre's budding relationship with Pauline healed something inside him, something none of us had been able to reach. It made him stronger physically, as though the love inside helped fight the cancers that ate at his body. Even with his growing strength, he didn't return to work full time. He wanted to spend whatever moments he had left with his little girls, building memories to last them the rest of their lives. He unearthed the videotape recorder Paulette had made him buy, and we spent outrageous sums on videotape in order to record every moment we wanted to hold dear.

In November, when Marie-Thérèse turned five, we celebrated at the house. At nearly four months, Pauline was still too small to go out in the cold weather, so we contented ourselves in having a family party with more presents than any little girl had a right to. Josette couldn't hide her envy, but Marie-Thérèse was more than willing to share her bounty.

One of Simone's presents turned out to be the best. She had carefully wrapped a certificate the bishop had filled out for her baptism that coming Sunday. She had originally planned to wait until her drug program was complete, but she decided that having the Holy Ghost with her would make the last six weeks in the clinic easier to bear. She had been clean for four and a half months.

Marie-Thérèse handed Simone a money bank I had given her. "Then you'll need this," she said. "To save money for a trip to the temple."

Simone hugged it to her body. "Oh, thank you!"

"Well, that's all the presents," I said, stooping down to gather wrapping paper from the floor in the sitting room.

"I have an announcement," Lu-Lu said suddenly. She had been bursting with a secret since she arrived, and I felt dread at hearing it, fearing that Philippe had come to his senses and wanted to marry her after all.

"I'm going on a mission," she said brightly. "I'm tired of waiting for something good to happen. I'm going to be like Ari and go out and try to make a difference." She turned to Jean-Marc. "And who knows? Maybe I'll meet my future spouse on my mission, like you did." We hugged her, offering congratulations. I saw sharp relief on Louise's face. She, too, had been worried by the impending announcement.

My father stared at Lu-Lu enviously. "I wish I could go." Abruptly his eyes glazed over, and he seemed far away. "Why, I *can* go! Not yet, perhaps, but retirement is not too far off." He faced my mother. "What do you think?"

She laughed. "You? Retire? I'll believe it when I see it."

"You've got another ten years before you can even think about retiring," Jean-Marc said.

My father's eyes glistened with a fervor which before I had only seen him demonstrate toward his work. "It's not too soon to begin planning," he said. We laughed. To think that less than four months ago, my father had never even read the Book of Mormon! A miracle had happened before our eyes.

"Enough of this," I said. "Who wants cake?" A chorus of voices shouting "I do!" followed me into the kitchen.

Lu-Lu helped me serve. "So what made you decide to go on a mission?" I asked.

"I want to help people understand how much God loves them," she replied. "It's like you said. Once I began to understand how important and true the gospel is, I wanted to share it."

"Kind of like a virus, ain't it?" Simone said inelegantly. "Ya know, catchin'." I wasn't sure I liked the analogy, but she had a point.

The phone rang. "It's for you, Lu-Lu," Jean-Marc said.

"I'll get it in the sitting room," she said. "There's too much noise here."

When she had left, Jean-Marc came up to me. "It's Philippe," he said quietly. "On the telephone."

I groaned and closed my eyes. "Not now." I went into the large entryway where I could see Lu-Lu talking in the sitting room. When she put the phone in its cradle, she was crying.

"Are you all right?" I asked.

"He wanted me back," she said. "And I wanted to say yes. I still love him. But I know the Church is true. If he wants me, he'll have to come on my terms. I'm not trading eternity for what I can see right now. Like you tried to tell me when your parents were baptized, it's not worth settling. There's too much at stake."

"I'm proud of you," I said.

She came to me and buried her face in my shoulder. "I'm all right. I really am. It just hurts because I know Philippe won't be changing any time soon."

"I guess it's good you're going on a mission then, isn't it?"

She smiled. "Yeah, I guess so."

A feeling of love pervaded the room, drying Lu-Lu's tears. I knew there would be hard times yet ahead of her, but more than half the battle was already won. We joined the others for a beautiful evening of family togetherness. Love and laughter filled the apartment as never before.

"Happy?" Jean-Marc asked, pulling me close in a tight embrace.

"Oh, yes," I said. I knew that our happiness was ever so much more precious because it hadn't come easily.

The evening had gone well, but later, long after the children were in bed, I started from a sudden sleep, my heart pounding frantically. I hurried out of bed and into Pauline's room. Had she become sick? She had seemed so well earlier. *Not my baby!* I cried silently. *Not yet—it's too soon!*

Jean-Marc was already in the room, staring down at a sleeping Pauline. "She's all right," he whispered. "The crying isn't coming from here."

Now that I knew Pauline was safe, I smiled in wonder that Jean-Marc, who had once slept so soundly, had awakened before me. Pauline certainly had us all trained. "Let's check the others," I said.

We met Pierre coming from the girls' room. "It's Marie-Thérèse," he said, wringing his hands. "She's crying. I can't get her to stop." He looked up at the ceiling, blinking rapidly, and in the dim light I could see the tears. "She's calling for her mommy."

I pushed past him and into the room. Marie-Thérèse was sitting up in bed, clutching her rag doll and rocking back and forth, whimpering.

"Mommy! Oh, Mommy, where are you?"

I sat on the bed and drew her unresisting body onto my lap. "I'm here, Marie-Thérèse. I'm here for you. It's going to be all right." She clung to me and the whimpering stopped, but her little chest still shook with silent sobs. I held her, not knowing what to do. I had thought she had accepted her mother's death, but it seemed that acceptance was not a complete healing.

After a long time the shaking subsided, and Marie-Thérèse spoke. "I can't see her anymore."

"What do you mean?"

"In my mind, when I close my eyes. She's not there. Her face isn't there. I don't remember what she looks like."

I had experienced the same thing myself. At times I could see Paulette so clearly, but at others I could only remember the way she had made me feel.

"Are you afraid you're going to forget her?" I asked. Marie-Thérèse gave a large sniff and nodded. I hugged her. "You know, sometimes when we're not with a person, we can't remember too well what they look like. But that doesn't stop us from loving them. Not ever. We can hold them in our hearts, even if we can't hold them in our minds. Our hearts will never forget."

Then I had an idea. I picked up Marie-Thérèse and carried her into the hall. "We need a picture of Paulette," I said to the brothers who hovered anxiously near the door. "And a flashlight."

"I'll get the flashlight," Jean-Marc said.

I glanced at Pierre. "I want a good picture," I said. "A large one we can hang near Marie-Thérèse's bed."

He disappeared, and I carried the little girl back to her bed. Soon the others were back. We hung the picture and gave Marie-Thérèse the flashlight. She turned it on, shining it onto her mother's face. It was the large picture from Pierre's own room, taken at the time of Marie-Thérèse's birth. Paulette was staring down at the new baby with love etched unmistakably on her face.

Marie-Thérèse nodded, her expression solemn. "Now I won't forget."

I pointed to her chest. "Remember what I said. You won't ever forget her in your heart, even if you can't remember her face."

She nodded and then reached out a finger and touched my lips, closing her hand tightly and lifing it to her heart. "Thank you."

Her special link with her mother, and she had used it with me! For a moment I could only stare, marveling at the miracle. Then I brought my own finger to her lips and held it to my heart. "I love you, Marie-Thérèse," I whispered.

She smiled, and for a moment I saw Paulette in her face. "I know," she said simply.

I kissed her and stood up to leave. Jean-Marc did the same, but Pierre settled on the floor beside the bed. "I'll stay here for a while, until she falls asleep."

The rest of the night passed quickly, with only Pauline's feedings to break it up. When it was my time for one of the three nightly feedings, I checked in on Marie-Thérèse, but she slept soundly. Pierre was asleep on her floor, and I covered him with an extra quilt.

Early in the morning, I heard someone enter Pauline's room. I listened to the monitor but heard nothing more, so I arose and went in. Marie-Thérèse stood on the bathroom stool near the crib. The bright morning light streaming in through the windows made an aura of light around her body, bringing out the highlights in her hair like a halo. In her hands, she held the cloth doll Paulette had made.

She glanced up as I entered. "She's awake," she said.

"Did you sleep okay?"

She nodded. "Do you know why I'm here?"

"You wanted to say good morning to Pauline?"

The little head shook. "No, I came to give her a present."

"What is it?" I asked, wondering which of her new birthday gifts would go to the baby.

"You'll see." Marie-Thérèse stared at her sister. "I have something for you," she said softly. She lifted the rag doll over the side of the crib and settled it next to the baby. "Mommy made it. She would have made one for you, too, but since she can't, I want you to have this one."

Her face was somber, and I wondered why she would give away something that meant so much to her. She felt my gaze and looked up at me.

"Pauline won't remember Mommy at all," she explained. "She won't even remember when she sees a picture. I want her to have a part of Mommy."

I put my arm around her. "You're a wonderful sister," I said. "And I'm sure if you ever want to borrow Dolly for a while, Pauline won't mind."

The baby had discovered the doll, and her tiny hands reached out for it clumsily, pulling it closer. Because she had been born prematurely, her development was behind that of a normal baby her age, so the motion was unexpected. Marie-Thérèse gave a cry of delight. "See? She likes it! She's trying to get it! She never did that! Do you think she knows Mommy made it?"

"Who knows?" I said. The diffused light in the room seemed to grow stronger, though I knew it was only my imagination. This, I decided, was a little piece of heaven on earth. This quiet moment alone with my new daughters.

—⁓—

February came with its endless wetness and melancholy grays. The twins turned five, and Lu-Lu left on a mission to the south of France. Pierre's condition had worsened, yet he clung to life, despite the pain, if only for his daughters. By May he was completely bedridden, and Louise moved into our house to help me care for him. "There's no sense in getting a nurse," she said as she settled her belongings into Pauline's room. "I'm his mother, and I want to do it."

Jean-Marc moved Pauline's crib into our room, and the baby monitor became Louise's way of knowing if Pierre needed her. I worried that despair would fall over our household, and some days it did, but it never stayed for long.

"It seems as though I can see right through him to heaven," Jean-Marc said to me one day. The children were in bed, and we sat cuddled together on the sofa. I could feel his breath on my neck.

"I know what you mean," I said. "It's as if heaven is closer than we ordinarily know. It's a comfort, and yet—"

"He doesn't even look like himself."

I knew what he meant. Pierre was so thin now that he seemed hardly bigger than a child under the blanket. His gaunt face resembled a skeleton more than a living human, with dry skin stretched taut over his face.

A sob shook Jean-Marc. "I don't want to let him go."

"I know." There was nothing I could do but hold him.

"Have I kept my promise to you?" he asked abruptly. "To be the husband you wanted?"

I faced him. "You're not perfect," I said. "But neither am I. And you have come home on time at least half the time." I kissed his lips. "I am happy, if that's what you're asking."

"It is. I want you and the children to be happy for as long as we have left."

"We have eternity."

"I know. But sometimes it's hard to remember."

"We have to remember. We *have* to."

The children enjoyed having Pierre at home all the time. He often read them stories of Jesus, filling our house with enough hope to get us through the hard days.

"It's all in the attitude," he said to me at the end of June. The children were sitting around him on the double bed he used, holding handfuls of books for Pierre to read. "We can choose to be happy in any circumstance. We can choose to have faith. It's our choice! I feel so grateful to the Lord for everything."

He appeared tired, so I motioned the children off the bed. "Let's go make Pierre some lunch," I said. The twins and André jumped off the bed and raced each other from the room. I picked up Pauline, who was nearly eleven months old.

"Can I carry the food, Mom—I mean, Aunt Ariana?" Consternation filled Marie-Thérèse's face at the slip. Pierre and I glanced at each other with concern. Though I had longed for this day, I feared anything I might say would make the situation worse.

"Come here." Pierre motioned to his daughter. She climbed onto the bed next to him, her face downcast. "Are you worried because you called Ariana Mom?" he asked. She nodded. "I know what you mean. It's hard not to call her that when she does all the stuff mothers do."

Her light brown eyes lifted to meet his. "Do you think Mommy would be mad?"

He shook his head. "No. It's kind of like how you call Simone, Louise, and Josephine Grandma. They don't mind that you call the others that, too; it doesn't take away from them."

"But they *are* all my grandmas, except Grandma Josephine. She's not my real grandma. She's Josette's and Marc's."

Pierre's eyebrows drew together slightly. "Well, I've got a better example, then. You know how Heavenly Father and Heavenly Mother are your parents in heaven?"

She nodded. "Yeah."

"You see, they lent you to your mom and me to raise here on earth. Do you think they mind if you call me Father or Daddy? Of course they don't. And with Mommy, it's just like that. She's lending you to Aunt Ariana to raise. I'm sure she wouldn't mind if you called her Mom." Marie-Thérèse didn't seem convinced, and Pierre continued quickly, "If you're still worried, maybe you could always refer to your mommy as Mommy, and you could always call Ariana just plain Mom. That way they would each have their own special name, like your grandmas. Does that sound good?"

A slow smile spread over her face. She slid off the bed, glancing up at me shyly, waiting.

"I would love that," I said. She ducked her head and ran out of the room, giggling self-consciously.

"Thank you, Pierre." I wondered if he realized what he had imparted to both his daughter and to me. By giving Marie-Thérèse permission to call me Mom, he had paved the way for many future transitions.

"Paulette knew this day would come," he said softly. "And she was right; a child needs a mother."

Pierre died two weeks later, passing away in his sleep, his pain at last ended and the torment on his face forever stilled. After a brief time of grieving, the children rebounded, but Jean-Marc seemed to go into a depression. Once again he began to spend long hours at work. I knew he was only trying to forget his loss, but after waiting three weeks for him to return to normal, I called him on his cellular phone.

"It's time to come home," I said. "You're taking a vacation."

"I am?"

"Yes. I've cleared it with the boss."

His chuckle was low. "I'm doing it again, aren't I?"

"Yes."

"Why didn't you tell me?"

"I *am* telling you. Now come home."

His step was a little lighter as we carried our suitcases to the van and set off for a long-overdue vacation, just us and our five children.

We made the long drive to Deauville, on the western coast of France—a crowded, internationally famous seaside resort where the children could play in the ocean. There were also horse racing and boat sailing to keep people occupied, but my interest was simply to spend time with my family. It didn't matter what we chose to do.

"Hmm," Jean-Marc said when we arrived in Deauville the next morning. "Isn't that the place with the balcony?"

"The very one," I said with a smile. I had in fact reserved the same suite we had stayed in the night the twins were conceived.

We settled in the rooms and headed for the beach.

"Thank you," Jean-Marc said. "This is exactly what I needed."

"It's what we all needed."

"I love you so much, Ari." His voice was gruff. He reached out and cradled my face with one hand, his thumb moving under my eye and wiping off the sand clinging to my cheek.

A loud crying spoiled the moment, and I jerked away to focus on Pauline, who was trying to spit out a mouthful of sand.

"I told her not to eat it," said Josette.

André grabbed a cloth from the picnic basket and with clumsy fingers tried to sweep the sand out of the one-year-old's mouth. I noticed he was careful not to get the saliva on himself, though such an amount would never pass the HIV virus; we had taught him well. At his ministrations, Pauline cried harder.

"She needs a drink," little Marc said helpfully.

I sighed and pulled Pauline onto my lap. "Spit it out."

"Hold it there! What a great picture!" Jean-Marc pulled out both the camera and the videotape recorder.

"Me too! Get me too!" chorused the other children.

"Can I be by you, Mom?" Marie-Thérèse asked.

"Sure."

I posed for the camera, for some reason remembering the day I had filmed Paulette making the baby curtains. As always, I felt a stab of heartache when I remembered my friend. It wasn't the aching grief I had felt when she died but more the longing for what could have been, for what would be one day. Until then, I would do my best to satisfy the role that had been thrust upon me.

"Smile!" Jean-Marc said, poking the camera in my face.

Upon us, I amended silently. Paulette had given us a gift most precious: this little toddler in my arms. I lowered my face to her soft halo of brown hair and breathed deeply the baby scent of her. She was so precious to me. In dying, Paulette had given me more than what had been taken away—just as the eternal gift of her testimony had forever changed the lives of so many others who had been important to her.

Jean-Marc put down the camera and came to my side. We held hands as we watched our children playing in the sand, dancing barely out of the waves' reach, as if taunting the ocean. Their cherished faces crinkled in wide smiles, and laughter sounded over the crowded beach.

I felt alive as I never had before; every moment seemed priceless. How incredibly beautiful the world was! How unique! I would live each moment to its fullest.

Pauline's tears had ended, along with her patience, and she wriggled, trying to leave my lap and crawl to the gritty sand. For a moment I resisted, thinking of the future. As yet she had shown no signs of the illnesses that marked AIDS, and though it might seem like holding water in my cupped hands, I would try to hold on to her forever. Hold on to her as I hadn't been able to do with my beloved little Nette. At least until the time came to say good-bye.

In the meantime, the future always held the chance of a cure. I never let go of the hope—or the faith that the Lord knew what He was doing, what He was building in us. And who knew but that the time would shortly come when the Savior Himself would put His hands on her head and make her whole?

I let Pauline go, and she giggled softly as she reached the end of the towel. Promptly, she picked up a handful of sand and tried to bring it to her mouth. "Oh, no, you don't," Jean-Marc chided, reaching for her.

I laughed softly and gazed out over the ocean. The waves lapped lazily onto the shore in steady repetition, reminding me of the gentle waves in the River Seine. I watched, recalling vividly what Simone had said the first day we had met at the stone wall above the riverbank near the booksellers' stalls.

"The water is us," she had said. "We're helpless against the trials that come. We can't push them away; we can only go where we're pushed. What good is life when we can't control anythin'?"

I smiled at the memory, understanding much more than I had that day. We *were* like the river water, as she had suggested, being tossed to and fro by the wind and the wakes of the boats. But when the boats were gone and the wind ceased, the water remained in its place. Like the water, we too remained when the problems and trials were over, falling back into our lives as before until the next waves came to test our endurance. And always, we were cradled in the banks of our Father's firm hands.

"Do you think it might rain tonight?" Jean-Marc asked, scanning the sky hopefully. "I thought we might sleep out on the balcony," he added, his voice teasing.

"You want to get wet?" I asked, jumping to my feet. Laughing, I pulled him to the frothy waves. In his arms, Pauline giggled.

Yes, water was mighty and resilient, as we were. We, the children of God!

ARIANA

A New
Beginning

Ten Years Later

CHAPTER ONE

*T*he late November sunlight peeked faintly through the heavy layering of clouds in the sky. The dark billows threatened rain, but I didn't care. Anything was better than what I had faced at home scarcely half an hour earlier. I pulled my long coat tightly about my body and sat down on the stone bench opposite my daughter's grave.

I always go to the graveyard when I am troubled. Somehow it seems to make everything clearer. But today things were about to get worse. A lot worse.

My bare hands slid into my pockets, and one hand touched paper. *What's this?* A smile played on my lips as I brought it out and recognized Jean-Marc's bold script. My husband had occasionally written to me during our nearly seventeen years of marriage, but it was uncommon enough to be unexpected. There was nothing to tell me this note was different. I felt only as if he were at the cemetery with me, warming my chilled hands in his.

"This is just what I need," I whispered softly. Jean-Marc was a good man who had a tendency toward tender, emotion-filled displays of love. He had mellowed over the years, and now his temper rarely surfaced; it was a pity his manner hadn't spilled over to all of our five children. I could still see fifteen-year-old Josette's face, her pretty features contorted with anger. It was she who had driven me here this afternoon.

Marie-Thérèse and I had just returned from the shopping spree I had promised for her sixteenth birthday. She had wanted to find something special for her first date the next week, and I had wanted to give it to her. Though my adopted daughter had grown into a beautiful, self-assured young woman, she was considerably reserved around people outside the family, and I was surprised she had accepted the date at all. Of course he was a member of our church, and of course he would be well-behaved. My Marie-Thérèse would choose no other. I had hoped to help make the experience a positive one.

Twelve-year-old André had met us at the door to our apartment. "Going somewhere?" I asked.

"To Grandma Simone's," he answered.

I nodded. Simone was the grandmother of my two adopted daughters on their mother's side. She had only recently settled into an apartment within walking distance.

"Where are the others?"

"Josette's in her room. Dad and Marc went to fix Grandma Simone's sink. Pauline went with them." That last sentence surprised me. André was rarely without Pauline; though Marc and Josette were the twins, André and Pauline were just as close.

"I was sleeping when they left," André added sheepishly, answering my unspoken question.

"I wonder why he didn't call a plumber like we usually do," I said.

At that point, Josette swept into the large entryway, slipping slightly on the polished wood floor. "You took long enough!" she exclaimed. Her dark brown eyes flashed as she surveyed her sister's purchases. "You got one of those jackets?" She turned to me quickly, her long dark hair fanning out around her. "But you wouldn't buy me one!"

"I said you'd have to wait until your birthday for a second jacket, that's all," I explained calmly. "It was your choice to pick out the clothes you did when school started. *You* picked the nylon coat, not me."

Josette's lips drew together in a pout, marring her perfect face. She fingered the rich brown leather her sister had chosen. "You'll let me borrow it, won't you?"

Marie-Thérèse hesitated, and I understood all too well her dilemma. Once Josette was given permission to borrow something, it was almost like giving it away; she wouldn't ask a second time. Besides, she didn't care well for her things. Stains and rips were common in her clothing.

Marie-Thérèse brushed back her light brown locks with a lean hand. Her freckled nose curved slightly upward, giving her a delicate, pixie appearance. "We'll see," she said.

Her tone didn't fool Josette. "You think you're so great just because you get to go out alone with a boy. I'm the popular one; *I'm* the one who should be going!" She turned to me. "Mom, please let me go! Practically everyone's asking me!"

"Not until you're sixteen."

She fumed with exasperation as her anger grew. Though I knew it stemmed from frustration, it bothered me that she had to react so violently. Couldn't she take lessons from her sister?

"A few months," she said, nearly bursting. "It's just a few months' difference! I'll bet if Marie-Thérèse had wanted to go a little early, you would have let her, wouldn't you?"

I didn't answer. The truth was, I probably would have. Marie-Thérèse was a good judge of character, and she always behaved appropriately. Josette was too volatile, and I feared her immature nature and extraordinary beauty would get her into trouble.

"You just love her better than me, don't you, Mom?" Josette cried. "All my life, you've put her above me, just 'cause she's a little older. It's not fair!" She glared at both of us.

Marie-Thérèse turned pale. She darted a nervous glance at me before making her way around Josette, running through the kitchen and down the hall to the room they had shared since childhood.

"You're such an idiot." The slow drawl came from André, who up until then had watched the display in silence.

Josette whirled to face him, her dark hair once again flying, giving me the impression of a cat arching angrily to face a dog. "What!"

"Mom doesn't love her better than you. She's just trying to make up for Marie-Thérèse not having her real mother!"

Am I doing that? I thought. Aloud I said, "Don't call your sister names, André. And I'm not trying to make up for anything. I love all of you."

"Sorry, Mom." He was instantly contrite. André had always been the child most attuned to my feelings. Ever since he was a baby, he had given me practically no trouble.

Josette stomped into the kitchen, muttering something under her breath about nosy little brothers. André laughed. "Don't worry. She'll get over it." He kissed my cheek. "I'm leaving now." Coat in hand, he disappeared through the door.

I followed Josette into the kitchen. The dishes from lunch were still sitting on the table. I knew it was her turn to clean up.

"Please change your mind," she pleaded. "I'm old enough. Why can't you see that?" A flash of memory came to mind—a memory of me at the same age. There was no doubt who Josette got her nature from. Had I ever been so young and innocent? So passionate?

"Whose turn is it to clean up?" I asked lightly.

Her face darkened a shade. "Mine," she muttered. "That's all you care about. Dishes and your precious Marie-Thérèse!"

I faced her, my patience fading. "Enough! That's enough!"

Her mouth was open, but it clamped shut as she recognized the seriousness in my voice.

I stalked to the door. "When I get back, I'd better find a lot of things changed around here," I declared. "Especially your attitude!" I grabbed my coat from its hanger in the closet near the door and left the apartment.

Now at the graveyard on the outskirts of Paris, I pondered my life since Jean-Marc and I had adopted our young nieces after losing their parents to AIDS. We'd had our problems, but life had been very good. It was hard to believe that ten more years had passed and I would soon be forty. Forty! *Where did the years go?*

There was only one thing I really regretted. I had wanted to have a child with Jean-Marc's green-brown eyes. I had thought it might happen in the years after we had adopted the girls, but I had been disappointed. Perhaps that was one more reason why I had been given Paulette's children to raise. The Lord knew that I would never have any more of my own.

Our three biological children all resembled me. Oh, André had his father's firm jaw, but each had my oval face and dark brown eyes, as well as my thick, unruly brown tresses instead of Jean-Marc's more manageable hair. Marie-Thérèse, of course, looked like her mother. Little Pauline, with her round face, resembled my husband more than anyone; she took after her father, Pierre, Jean-Marc's brother. But none of the children had those extraordinary green-brown eyes.

Feeling a bit foolish, I smiled and laughed aloud, purposely steering my mind back to the letter in my hand. Becoming sentimental seemed to go with turning forty. Something to do with holding on to youth, I supposed.

Jean-Marc had used a simple sheet of lined paper with holes that told me he had taken it from the six-ring binder he always carried in his briefcase. Not very romantic, but at least he had thought to write to me.

It was the four-day-old date that first gave me an inkling that something wasn't right; it was odd for my husband to have kept silent about it for so long. His usual way would be to contrive something to force me to look in my pocket. He would have taken me out for dinner and asked me to hold the car keys, or some such thing. *Why was this different?*

These thoughts raced through my mind as I focused on the words and their meaning:

My Dearest Ari,

Have I told you recently how much I love you? Every day you grow more beautiful to me. I don't know how to tell you that I've failed you. I guess by writing this letter, I'm running from having to face you, but I have learned over the years that I can't solve the big things alone. This is one of those things, Ari.

My pulse quickened fearfully, and my hand went to my heart. I didn't want to read the rest. Regardless, my eyes moved relentlessly down the page.

The bank is failing. I've done everything I know to do and have employed the best people to try to stop it, but I can't. It's my fault because I approve all the decisions, but I daresay that several of my employees will be investigated. I suspect they have been embezzling since before your father turned the bank over to me last year—perhaps for many years before that.

Everything we have is tied up in the bank. Everything. I don't know what we're going to do. Our insurance will end next month, and there are Pauline's treatments and special drugs. The children's college and mission funds are gone, too, though we might recover a portion later on. The funds were not insured as they should have been, as the company promised they were—one more thing to be investigated. I just don't know where to go from here. I guess I need to find the heart to start over.

I'm sorry, so very sorry I have failed you. Please forgive me.

Jean-Marc

I blinked twice and shook my head, but the words on the page before me did not change. My heart thudded dully in my chest, and a queasy feeling gripped my stomach. *Everything gone? But how? Why?* I reread the letter slowly, letting realization penetrate my soggy brain.

Fear was my first emotion—What would we do? How would we pay the bills?—but anger came close on its heels as I instinctively tried to protect myself. We were too old to have to start over! It wasn't fair— we had worked so hard to save and be frugal. Now that the children were older, our life together, Jean-Marc's and mine, was supposed to allow us more time to explore our relationship. We shouldn't have to worry about eking out a living!

The more I thought along these lines, the angrier I grew. I imagined confronting those who had wronged us, seeing them locked away forever behind thick prison bars. They could never replace the comfortable security they had stolen from my life. What about my children? What about little Pauline, who needed a daily dose of expensive drugs for her HIV treatments? All our careful plans for the future now lay in ruins. Could this really be happening?

The anger intensified. Minutes ticked away into an hour as I became absorbed by my fury. Intertwined so intimately with the fear, I felt it eating away at my soul. I knew I should make it stop; yet, in some indescribable way, I wanted to feel the sharp pain because it seemed to further justify my wrath.

Jumping to my feet, I began to pace back and forth before the headstones of my brother, Antoine, and my daughter Nette. The normally brilliant green grass of the graveyard was faded with the cold, and the trees had lost many of their leaves; yet there was a strange, austere beauty here, even during this time of year. The frail light reflected off the scrollwork on top of the gray stone on Antoine's grave and seemed to send a brief, piercing flash that stopped me abruptly.

The panic I had yielded myself to was suddenly overcome by another emotion, a stronger one of compassion. Poor Jean-Marc! How long had he known? How many months had he tortured himself with these same visions as he tried to shield his family? If I felt the devastation this clearly, how deeply his must run! He had always been confident of his ability to support us—what must he be feeling now?

This new emotion was welcome; it coated my anger, sweet over sour. I had to get to Jean-Marc.

My feet nearly ran down the cobblestone path, boots crunching on loose pebbles, but I hesitated before reaching the black cast-iron gate. I stared at the menacing, pointed tips that topped the fence surrounding the graveyard. Even in the diluted light, they gleamed like inky arrows.

What would I say to my husband? What had I to offer him, except perhaps my own anger at the situation? No; before I faced him, I needed to have something to offer, something to start us in a positive direction. I knew he must be deeply wounded at what he saw as his failure, and my reaction would be a defining moment.

I sighed aloud. "Thank you, Father," I prayed. I didn't want to think about what I might have said had I discovered this note in Jean-Marc's presence. Whatever it was that made him write instead of telling me himself had worked to our advantage.

I methodically retraced my steps and sat again on the stone bench, drawing from my pocket the now-crumpled letter. My coat had opened, and I smoothed the paper out over the thick black leggings I wore underneath a semi-dressy gray sweater. The fear in my husband's simple words was obvious, and it renewed the trepidation in my own heart. I wondered if our lives had changed forever in this short moment of time.

I stopped myself. It was only money. What did it matter as long as we still had each other? Our love had already suffered through much more than this. "You'll get work," I practiced saying aloud. "I can, too, now that the children are older. It's not that big a deal. We'll get through this."

That was when I heard steps to my left, on the path that led to the gate and my car parked beyond. I wiped the tears off my cheeks with hands stiff from the cold. I glanced up, thinking to nod and smile at the stranger as he passed. Our eyes met and held. For a moment I didn't recognize the man with the longish dark blond hair who stared at me. His head cocked slightly backward and to the side in an oddly familiar way, and in his gloved hands he held a bouquet of white roses.

White roses!

At once the flowers bridged the seventeen years between us, and his features became even more familiar: the lean face, the dark brown eyes, the slight cleft in his chin—all spelling out a certain rugged handsomeness. The compelling smile on his full lips made his expression almost boyishly eager, and I sensed the magnetism that had always hung about him. I stood, trying to gain the advantage height might give me. It made no difference; he was taller still. *Why was it that just when you thought things couldn't get any worse, they did?*

Lifting my chin slightly, I gazed into the face of the man I had once loved so desperately—the dashing playboy who had nearly destroyed my life, the man who had killed my daughter, my precious Nette. I had hoped never to see him again.

My heart hammered in my ears as I spoke. "Hello, Jacques."

CHAPTER TWO

My voice was remarkably calm, given the circumstance. Jacques shifted nervously, moving the bouquet of flowers from one hand to the other.

"It's you who's been bringing the roses," I said. I had found them several times next to Nette's grave in the past month and believed they had been put there by my father, recently returned from a mission to Canada with my mother.

He glanced over at the stone. "It seemed the thing to do." His breath made a hint of a white cloud as it reached the cold air. I tried to stifle the indignation that threatened to bubble to the surface. After all, he had every right to be here; Nette was his daughter, too.

We stood in awkward silence for a long minute.

"Now that we've met, do you mind talking for a while?" Jacques' voice was hesitant, with a touch of pleading.

I had closed that chapter in my life; the nightmare of Nette's death had nothing to do with my present. Not once had I imagined this moment would come; not once had I wished for it. Yet here it was, and I couldn't deny my sudden curiosity. "All right." I inclined my head toward the bench. My backside was already cold from my long vigil, but my head whirled. I would rather sit than faint from the shock of seeing him.

"I've dreamed of us meeting like this," he began. I chewed the inside of my cheek and said nothing. He gave me a tentative grin. "I wanted to tell you that I beat the drugs. I was paroled a year and two months after you came to see me at the prison." He paused before adding quietly, "I don't think you'll ever know how much it meant to me to know you forgave me for what happened. It was the only thing that got me through my time at the prison. That and this picture." He slid a hand inside his long coat and drew out a photograph of our daughter, taken when she was seven months old, a month before her death. It was worn and dog-eared. "I've had copies made, of course, but I keep this always close to me so that I can remember her. Whenever I have a tough decision, she helps me."

I too felt she helped me. That was why I came so often to the grave-yard. "You've changed, Jacques."

He relaxed. "I hoped you'd see that."

"So what have you been doing all these years?"

"I've been in Nice with my father."

I couldn't conceal my surprise. "I thought he would have nothing to do with you." The man had, in fact, kicked Jacques out of his home long before we had met.

"He wouldn't, at first. But when he realized I was serious about changing my life, he gave me a position in his company."

"What company is that?" I knew enough of Jacques to be leery of anything he said, changed or not.

He smiled. "Carpet." He replaced the photograph in his pocket and took out a card with his name embossed in gold letters.

For the first time, I noticed that his coat was a rich wool, and his shoes looked as expensive as those my husband wore. I stared at the card. "Carpet? You sell carpet?"

His laugh came easily. "Not really. I mean, I make the decisions, but I'm not actually in the showrooms. Believe it or not, I'm the president and chairman of the board now, though it wasn't easy. My father started me at the bottom. I had to actually lay the stuff for my first two years before he'd trust me to do anything else."

Once again our gazes locked. "Wise man, your father."

He nodded. "At some things. I only wish he could have helped before . . ."

I turned away. We shared a past, that was true, but I didn't want to have a connection with him now. Whatever he wished about the past was not my concern.

"What about you, Ariana?" His voice caressed my name.

"What about me?"

"Did that guy Jean-Marc ever come back?"

I nodded. "We got married. In April, it'll be seventeen years. We have five children."

His eyebrows lifted. I noticed they were a darker color than his hair. "So many?"

"Three are ours. The other two are Paulette's. She died, you know. Of AIDS."

His expression dimmed. "I knew she had it; the hospital called to inform me. I guess she had me on the list of people who might have been at risk. I didn't know she died."

"She did. Two months later—right after she gave birth to her baby, Pauline. She's buried over there." My hand waved in the direction beyond Nette's grave. Then I reached for my wallet inside the breast pocket of my fur-lined leather coat. The family picture I showed him was fairly recent. "That's Pauline," I said. "She's eleven."

"She looks a lot like your husband."

"She takes after her father, Jean-Marc's brother. He also died from AIDS, a year after Paulette."

"I'm sorry."

"Don't be. We're doing well, and I know where they are."

His eyes bored into mine, slightly challenging, but something in my face must have convinced him. "Yeah, I guess you probably do." He studied the picture. "And who is this?"

"Josette. She and Marc are twins. They're fifteen, but Josette thinks she's going on twenty."

As he studied my daughter's picture, the lean edges of his face softened. "She looks just like you did when your hair was longer." He glanced up. "You haven't changed all that much. You're a beautiful woman, Ariana."

I knew my cheeks must be streaked from crying, and my short hair had not seen a comb since early that morning, but Jacques had always known just the thing to say. I had always felt beautiful around him. Tears pricked behind my eyes, and a tenderness grew inside me. For the first time since my remarriage, I wondered what my life would have been like had circumstances been different . . . had Jacques and I been able to hold on to our love.

I bit my lip and forced my voice to be even. "Thank you." I pointed again to the picture. "This is my son André."

He nodded. "And this must be Paulette's other daughter."

"Marie-Thérèse," I acknowledged. "She looks a lot like her mother, except that her hair is a little lighter and her nose kind of turns up a bit at the end."

"The resemblance to Paulette is striking, like with you and—what was her name? Josette?"

"Yes, Josette."

We sat silently for a few minutes, staring at the picture. "Marie-Thérèse is the oldest," I added to fill the silence. "She turned sixteen yesterday."

"You love her very much, don't you?"

I nodded. "And Pauline."

"They're lucky to have you. But how is it they didn't contract the virus?"

Tears spilled over before I could stop them, and his face showed concern. He scooted closer and put a tentative hand on my shoulder.

"They have it, don't they?"

"Just Pauline. It's been eleven years now. She's had some pretty serious illnesses lately, but she's still okay. She has to take medication every day." I looked up at him. "They named Pauline after Nette, you know. Her full name is Antoinette Pauline."

He pulled me closer into a loose embrace. I resisted, but the shocks of the day had sapped my energy. Jean-Marc and I were penniless, Josette's temper was out of control, and telling Jacques about Pauline only made things worse. It was too much for me to bear, and for a moment I let my head rest on his shoulder as we sat on the bench.

He patted my back. "I'm sorry, Ariana. I had always imagined you were happy."

That gave me strength to extract myself from his arms. "Oh, but I have been! Jean-Marc is so good to me. I love him, and I love my life with him and the children."

His eyebrows drew together, and I sensed disbelief. "Then why are you so sad? It's not just Pauline, is it?"

I felt the paper in my pocket. "Just some things that happened today, that's all. Tomorrow will be better."

He grinned. "That's my Ariana. You were always so positive."

I wasn't his Ariana any longer and hadn't been for many years. It bothered me to hear him say it. "Why have you come to Paris?" I asked.

"We've moved the company headquarters here."

"That's nice." Glancing at my watch, I saw that I'd been at the cemetery for more than two hours. "I'd better get home." I stood to leave, and the wallet on my lap plummeted to the cobblestones in front of the bench. Jacques bent swiftly to scoop it up. When he straightened beside me he was staring at a picture that had fallen out of the wallet. It was the twins at less than a year old.

"They look like Nette."

"They are her brother and sister," I said, more sharply than I'd intended. His face looked pained.

I softened. "Didn't you ever marry again? Don't you have children?"

He shook his head. "No." He seemed about to say more but stopped himself. Handing back the picture, he said, "You'd better get going. Your family needs you."

I nodded. And though I felt a little strange doing it in front of him, I crossed to Nette's headstone and bent to touch the letters in her name. When I rose, Jacques was there beside me. He stooped and arranged the white flowers in the vase cemented at the base of the waist-high structure. He was close enough for me to smell the tantalizing aroma of his aftershave. For no reason I could define, my heart began to beat erratically.

"Good-bye," I said hastily.

"Wait!"

I paused. His brown eyes studied me, as if taking in every bit of my face, memorizing it. He held out a single white rose in his hand, which was shaking slightly despite his warm glove. "Here."

I took the flower in my bare hands. The white rose had always been my favorite.

"You have my card," he said. "If you ever need me for anything—money, to talk, anything at all—please, please call."

"I'm fine, really," I lied. I knew he must still be trying to atone for the accident that had taken our daughter's life.

I backed away. "Didn't you listen to the missionaries?"

"The what? Oh, you mean those young foreign men. I did hear them, but then they made some rule about them not coming to the prison. I meant to look them up after I got out, but we lost touch. Once I was back with my father, it hardly seemed important. I had already stopped the drugs."

I wanted to tell him that there was so much more to it, but I felt too uneasy in his presence. Besides, now that I had his card, I could always send in the referral. "Good-bye," I said.

"Good-bye."

This time he let me go, but I could sense his eyes, searing and intense, following me on the pathway. I felt strange leaving him alone with Nette, but there was nothing he could do to her now. Cold had seeped into every part of my body, yet somehow I felt hot inside. Alive.

"Mom!" Josette was waiting by the cemetery gate. She was dressed warmly, yet her nose was red with cold. Instinctively, I cast a backwards glance at where Jacques still stood by Nette's grave, though the distance made him quite unrecognizable. *How long had Josette been watching us?* I clutched the rose stem even more tightly in my hand, feeling the thorns bite into my skin.

"What are you doing here?"

Her expression was guarded. "I knew you would probably come here. I wanted to say I was sorry about how I acted."

I put an arm around her shoulder and pulled her close. "I'm glad you came." This was the part of Josette that I admired. She was always repentant and worried constantly that something might happen to us. As a child, she had mothered her siblings so much they rebelled. Now her concern for me was shining through, and it made me want to hug and kiss her as I had done when she was young.

"I cleaned the kitchen."

I smiled. "Good." She must have done it quickly and then caught the subway to the cemetery.

As we walked in the direction of my car, Josette looked over her shoulder. "Who is that man?"

"Just someone I used to know." I couldn't keep the nostalgia from my voice.

"Someone special?" she asked curiously.

"No, not anymore."

Suspicion clouded her face. "Then why did he give you the rose?"

Without thinking, I brought it to my face and breathed in the sweet fragrance. I said nothing to Josette but opened the door to our van. She slid in next to me as I fumbled for the keys with frozen hands.

"Tell me, Mother—who was it? I saw you hug him while you were sitting on that bench. Tell me, who is he and why did he give you that rose?" Her voice bordered on hysteria.

I turned to face her. "It's not what you think." I looked down at my left hand, which still held the flower. When I opened it, I saw the drying bits of blood where the thorns had pierced my soft skin. It was what Jacques had always done to me, coming with a beautiful cover and ending up wounding me—and much more deeply than this.

"Here." I handed her the rose. "Keep it."

"Who is he?" she pressed.

"He brought the roses for his daughter and gave me one, that's all." She waited for more.

"It was Jacques," I said finally. "Your older sister's father."

"Nette's father?" she gasped. "What does he want?"

She had pinpointed it exactly. "I don't know."

But I wondered if I did. The way he had stared at me wasn't the way one looks at a friend or even an ex-wife. Then I felt absurd. It had been twenty years since our marriage ended and seventeen since I had last seen him. Jacques could have no hidden motives.

Why did he have to come back now? I thought. Yet even as I thought it, an unquenchable curiosity rose to the surface. Jacques was no longer the dashing, impetuous boy I had loved but a successful businessman. I couldn't help thinking that he knew exactly how to get what he wanted.

CHAPTER THREE

*I*n the parking garage under our building, I heard my older son before I saw him. The clank and rolling of wheels on the rough cement echoed in the nearly empty expanse before Marc burst from behind one of the thick supporting pillars.

"Marc, you scared me!" Josette said, looking up at him. A sudden growth spurt had left him taller than Jean-Marc—not that my husband had ever been very tall.

Marc laughed, grinning as he hugged me and kissed my cheeks. "Mom, you gotta see this." In an instant, he whirled from me and zoomed away at top speed on his roller blades, swerving occasionally to avoid parked cars, his dark, short-cropped hair ruffling from the velocity. He came back even faster, this time steering toward a ramp he had set up in the middle of the garage.

"Marc, no!" I heard Josette scream. But he was far from hearing her. He leaped at the end of the ramp, spinning in a circle before hitting the cement. He nearly toppled and smashed into a car but recovered at the last minute.

He came up to us grinning. "See, I can do it!"

I closed my eyes for a second. There were some things I would prefer never to see my children do, but I had to allow them a measure of agency. "I see," I said. "I'm impressed. But where's your helmet?" My judgment with Marc was often clouded by the fact that he so closely resembled my impetuous brother, Antoine, but not so completely that I couldn't reprove him when necessary.

Josette frowned. "And your knee pads? What would you have done if you had fallen? Marc, you have to think. I don't want to be the one to pick your guts up off the floor." There was nothing ladylike about her words or her grimace.

Marc's grin widened. "Oh, don't worry, Jose. Nothing's going to happen." He skated in a circle near her, his expression taunting.

"Promise me you'll never do it again without your helmet!" she pleaded.

His smile dimmed. "You're really frightened, aren't you?" She looked away and didn't answer. Marc skated into her line of sight. "I'm sorry, Jose. If it means that much to you, I'll promise."

Josette's smile was genuine. "Thanks."

He held up his finger. "On one condition." He paused dramatically. "You have to go blading with me." He skated to the row of small storage units that flanked the garage, stopping short before the one marked 5-B. Pulling a set of keys from his pocket, he opened the door to grab Josette's roller blades and two helmets.

Josette opened her mouth. "But—"

"No buts," he said.

She threw back her head and laughed. "Okay, you win. But you're buying the hot chocolate at the café."

"Deal."

"Here, Mom." Josette pushed the white rose into my hand and ran to her brother. I watched them, remembering my own childhood. I hoped they would always be so close.

"Be home before dinner," I shouted after them.

Marc flashed me his teasing grin. "Maybe." I knew he would do his best.

As the elevator climbed the five flights, my mind returned to the problem of what I would say when I faced Jean-Marc. The bank's failing was a problem, to be sure; but together we could overcome this. Jean-Marc would get another job, and maybe I could, too, for a time. We would simply limit ourselves to only the necessary spending, and somehow we'd get through.

I tried not to dwell on the problem of Pauline's costly treatments. We had made sure that she had the best doctors and the most expensive drugs, which alone consumed more than two-thirds the salary of the average person. Our insurance had paid a great deal, but now that would end. And our savings . . .

The anger I had first felt when learning about the bank came back, but this time I channeled it into plans for the future. I rapidly calculated what I would need to support my family. It had been a long time since I'd had to worry about such things, but I had always been good with numbers.

I walked into the apartment and was greeted in the entryway by André and Pauline.

"We fixed the sink," André said. "And it was mostly me. Dad couldn't figure out how to get the pipe off, but I found out how." He was nearly bursting with pride.

I hugged him. "Good." But my stomach twisted; now I knew why Jean-Marc hadn't called a professional as he usually did when either of the two single grandmothers needed something fixed. There were a lot of things we would have to do ourselves for a while. And a lot of things the grandmothers would have to pay for themselves.

Pauline lifted her face for a kiss. "I missed you. Where have you been?"

I glanced at the rose. "The cemetery. Would you put this in water for me?"

She accept the flower, her sweet round face eager. "I love roses."

I removed my coat as André watched me. "What's wrong, Mom?" Sometimes he was too sensitive.

"There is something, André, but I need to talk to your father. Where is he?"

"In your room, I think."

"Thanks." I gave him an encouraging smile before making my way down the hall, but André's face was pensive. For the second time that day, I felt eyes following me.

Jean-Marc stood by the window, his shoulder leaning into the wall as he fingered the lace curtains. His boyishly handsome face was bleak, his eyes far away. He started slightly when he heard me enter, and his ever-ready grin came to the surface, though it didn't reach his eyes. How could I have missed these signs?

"Ari! Where have you been?" He held out his arms.

I didn't reply but drew out the letter. His face fell, and tears came to his eyes. It had been a long time since I had seen him cry—ten years to be exact—since his brother's death. I went to him, and for a long, silent moment we held each other.

"I'm sorry," he murmured finally.

"It's not your fault."

He released me and paced the room. "It's my responsibility to support our family, and I've failed. Oh, I know it's not my fault, but I can't help thinking that somehow I could have stopped it." He came to an abrupt standstill. "And what am I going to tell your father? He's worked hard all his life, and now that he's retired, I've ruined everything he worked for. I've no idea how much he's lost."

"He'll get by, and so will we," I said. "Jean-Marc, we still have each other, and our family. No matter what, I love you!"

A relieved smile touched his lips. He crossed the room and buried his face in my neck. "That's just what I needed to hear."

His lips found mine, and we kissed fervently. Against my will, a picture of Jacques came to my mind. I pushed it away. My love for Jean-Marc was eternal and filled my whole soul; there was no room for Jacques, past or present.

"So where do we go from here?" I asked when we finally drew apart.

Fear and determination mingled on his face. "I'll look for a job beginning next week. I'll have some things to finish up at the bank, but basically government investigators are taking over. I have to answer any questions they may have."

"You'll easily get a job with your qualifications."

He grimaced. "I'm not too sure. The unemployment rate is very high right now, and being the president of a failed bank won't exactly look good on my resume."

"But it's not your fault! What about the employees who've been embezzling?"

He shook his head. "It's going to take a long time for the dust to clear on this one. I think we're going to have to face a lot of accusations ourselves."

"What do you mean?"

"The press has to point the finger at someone, and unfortunately, I'm that someone."

"Preposterous!"

Despite the seriousness of the situation, Jean-Marc broke into a grin. "You sound like your father."

I smiled back. "Speaking of which, shouldn't you call him?"

The grin vanished. "Yes, I'll have them come over tonight."

"Afterwards we'll talk to the children."

His nod seemed painful, and I reached out to stroke his cheek. "It's hard," I said softly, "but not nearly so hard as the last trial. I've been thinking; I could get work, too. You know, temporarily—until we get things settled."

I was unprepared for the intensity of his reaction. "No! Ari, no! It hasn't come to that, not yet. The children need you at home."

"The children are in school all day."

"Please don't do this—not yet," he implored. "Just give me a chance. I can support you; I can. I don't want you to have to work like my mother did. You see how her health has suffered from working and raising a family alone. You won't have to do that—not while I'm alive." His determination to care for me moved me like I hadn't imagined it might. I knew his reaction was old-fashioned and perhaps even a bit chauvinistic, but I loved him for it.

"You're a queen, my Ari," he whispered, his voice low. "Please let me treat you like one."

I kissed him again, passionately, and this time there was nothing of Jacques to destroy the moment. "I love you so much," I said through my tears.

"Not nearly as much as I love you."

———

Pauline and I were in the kitchen cleaning up after dinner when my parents arrived. Jean-Marc had already explained the situation over the phone, but he and my father immediately shut themselves in the sitting room to talk business while my mother came into the kitchen. Pauline sang happily as she worked, bringing a smile to our faces. André still sat at the kitchen table reading a book, but the twins and Marie-Thérèse had gone into the TV room.

Our apartment was actually two joined together, so our kitchen was double the normal size. The extra sitting room had first served as a play-room and now was used as the TV room. We also had five bedrooms. Marc and André shared one, as did Josette and Marie-Thérèse. Pauline had her own room, and Jean-Marc and I had the fourth. The remaining room was used for projects and for guests. With three grandmothers, one grandfather, and a single aunt in Paris, all of whom loved to spend time with our children, it was used frequently.

"So how are you adjusting to being back in normal life?" I asked my mother. Her hair was a silvery white, and she held her head with an undeniable grace. Her figure, though not as trim as in her youth, was still slender and firm. She was a striking woman, even at sixty-four.

She laughed. "Serving a mission was fun, but I rather prefer France," she said. "In Quebec the people are great, but I missed you and the kids."

"How's Father taking being home from the mission?"

To my surprise, she frowned. "He wants to go again. There or somewhere else. He's already got the papers."

"But you just got back!" In fact, only a month had gone by since their first year of missionary service had ended.

My mother sighed. "If it weren't for this new calling, he would have put in the papers already."

Father had been called as a counselor in the stake presidency upon his return from Canada. I had seen him only four times in that month. One of those times had been when I went for a temple recommend. "He's been busy, I take it."

"I hardly see him," she grumbled. "It's much worse than when he worked at the bank. At least then he came home. Now he visits members every day and night. Him at sixty-five! It's like he is going to single-handedly counsel every member in Paris, as well as convert all the rest of the population!"

I laughed, remembering the zeal my father had shown upon his baptism eleven years earlier. "It'll calm down, Mother. Don't worry. It's the missionary spirit."

The phone rang, and I went to answer it. "Hello?"

"Is this Madame Perrault?"

"It is."

The caller identified himself as working for Paris's largest newspaper and launched into his attack. "What do you have to say to the allegations that your husband stole millions of francs from the bank of which he was president, causing it to fail and costing thousands of people their life savings?"

I gasped. "You don't know what you're talking about!"

"Don't I? Well, according to my sources, I do know what I'm talking about. Where is the money, Madame Perrault?"

I hung up immediately.

"What's wrong, Mom?" André was at my side in an instant.

"You're completely white," my mother said.

"Was it a crank call?" André asked.

Pauline wiggled past her brother and put her arms around me. "I love you, Mom." She was young enough to have faith that her love could cure anything. There was a lot of love in our house, and while it could ease this situation, it couldn't fix it completely—or shield us from every bit of cruelty people might throw our way. I had just seen the first inkling of what the next few months might hold.

I sent the children to the TV room before explaining to my mother what had happened. "I'm sorry," she said. "Unfortunately, things are bound to get worse before they get better."

"It'll be hard, I'm sure," I replied. "But nothing compared to what we've already faced."

"Oh, but it will be." Her face was earnest. "Work is a man's life. I mean, it's tied up with who he is—the way a woman's life is tied up with her children." She shook her head. "I can't explain it exactly, but such a crushing failure is like a kind of death to Jean-Marc. He is much like your own father in that way."

"I don't know," I said. She couldn't know what she was talking about. This was my husband. He loved me, and come what may, we would get through this problem.

I excused myself and went to the sitting room. Through the thin wood partition that separated it from the entryway, I could hear my father's voice. "How many times did I teach you to diversify your assets?" he was saying.

"I know," Jean-Marc agonized. "But I thought that having all my funds controlled by our bank would make them safer somehow."

"Well, you're welcome to any savings I have from my accounts at other banks," my father said. "Though that's precious little when you see how many we are."

"I don't want your money, Géralde. I'm just relieved you'll still have enough to support yourself and Josephine."

"We'll have enough to scrape by, but we won't be going on another mission soon."

"I'm sorry."

"Enough. It happened; it's over. Now you have to go on from here." My father's voice was gruff, and I winced inwardly. He, of all people, should be sympathetic to Jean-Marc's position.

I pushed back the folding room divider. Jean-Marc glanced up at me from the long blue couch, my father from the chair by the corner table lamp. They waited expectantly in silence, and I could hear the pendulum of our grandfather clock ticking softly as it swung back and forth.

"Someone from one of the newspapers called," I announced. "They know the bank has failed and are trying to place the blame on you." Jean-Marc's face paled, and I almost kicked myself. My father wasn't the only one who could be insensitive.

My father nodded his white head, trimmed by gray traces of once-black hair. His upper lip still looked odd without the moustache he had worn for forty years. That distinguishing feature had been the first thing to go after receiving his mission call. "That is to be expected," he said. "A lot of people will be angry." He glanced at Jean-Marc. "You had better call and give them a statement. At least they'll have some of the truth."

"And we have to tell the children tonight," I added. "We can't have them hearing about it somewhere else."

Jean-Marc nodded slowly. "Yes. Gather them together, if you will, while I make the call." There was a deep sadness in his eyes, one I wished I could wipe away. He turned abruptly and picked up the phone on the table near the window.

"We'll be waiting in the TV room," I said.

Jean-Marc nodded again. As I retreated from the room, the grandfather clock in the corner chimed nine times. The sound followed in my wake, echoing hollowly, almost menacingly, off the walls in the room.

We were waiting when Jean-Marc and my father came into the TV room. I had turned the television off, and silence reigned. Marc was sprawled on his stomach on the light blue carpet. Josette lay next to him, using his back as a prop for her elbow. They talked in playful undertones about their adventure in roller blading that afternoon. I sat on the worn sofa that I'd had since before my marriage to Jean-Marc, with Pauline snuggled close by. On her other side sat my mother, with André resting on the floor near her feet, his arms circling his knees, his dark eyes filled with worry. Marie-Thérèse sat in an armchair across from us, her light brown eyes calm.

We began our family council with a prayer, and then the children listened intently as their father explained the circumstances. I watched their expressions anxiously. Shock, disbelief, and anger were their first emotions, but these were quickly replaced by courage and determination.

"So you'll get a new job," Marc said, a bright smile returning to his face. "We're behind you, Dad."

"We could all do something," Josette suggested.

Jean-Marc sighed. "Perhaps. But for now, let's see how it goes."

I knew he was determined to support his family as he had always done. No matter that he had worked in his own family grocery store from a very young age; he wanted his family to have all the advantages he'd never had.

"Your father's a smart man," my mother told the kids. "He'll figure it out."

"Until then, we'll need to tighten our belts, so to speak," Jean-Marc said. "No more movies or eating out for a while. Or buying clothes. We're lucky we've followed the prophet's counsel to stay out of debt. We worked very hard to pay off the apartment early, but we still have food and utilities." He paused before adding, "And medical expenses."

"Will we change schools?" Pauline asked. All the children attended a private school, as I had as a child. It had become even more important to us since Pauline joined our family; she had special needs that might be overlooked in a public environment. She loved both her school and her teachers. We were rather overprotective of our youngest family member, and though it was for good cause, she sometimes longed for freedom—which, to some extent, school allowed her.

Jean-Marc shook his head. "No. We're paid up through the year." I knew that was only a month away, but I refused to worry about it now.

Marie-Thérèse came to her feet. "I have some money I'd like to contribute. It's in my room."

"Me too!" the other children were quick to join in. We had been generous to them for many years, and it seemed they were now willing to give back what they could. I was touched, and the heavy burden seemed lighter.

We pooled the money, including some I had stashed away as part of the emergency money the Church had counseled us to keep in our seventy-two-hour kits. For a few weeks life would go on as normal, maybe more if I stretched the meals. Surely by then Jean-Marc would have found a new job.

We said family prayer and read from the scriptures before saying good night. When I visited the children's rooms as I always did at bedtime, Josette patted her bed for me to sit. Marie-Thérèse was still in the bathroom, and we were alone.

"Mom, how do you know when you're in love?" Josette asked.

An indulgent smile came to my lips. "Well, it feels right," I said. "And of course you have to pray about it."

"Does your heart pound and your head feel light?"

"At first maybe. It also makes you want to sing with joy and laugh out loud. But you need to be careful that it's not just infatuation."

"Does it matter how old he is?"

I gazed at her suspiciously. "Just how old?"

She shrugged. "Oh, I don't know. Twenty or so, I guess."

"Did you meet someone you like?" I had always known that if one of my children were to give me trouble in this respect, it would be Josette—but surely not this soon!

Her face broke into a radiant smile. "Don't look so worried, Mom. I talked to a man a few times. He was nice, that's all."

"Good," I said. "Just remember—"

"Who you are," she finished.

"Not just who you are," I clarified, "but who you are destined to become. A queen in heaven. Don't ever forget that."

"I know, I know." Her voice was slightly subdued. "But what if I never find a man in the Church to marry?"

What was it about girls and their desire to marry so young? Didn't they realize that there was an eternity to be married, that their youth was to prepare and to have fun? They would be washing dishes, changing diapers, and making meals for many years to come. After the first week or so it lost its appeal, only then it was too late. Better to experience life and then settle down with a worthy man who would share the burdens. As often as I said this, my daughter still didn't understand—and probably wouldn't until she married.

"I mean, I don't want to end up like Aunt Lu-Lu," Josette added. Lu-Lu was Jean-Marc's younger sister, who was thirty-three and still single. She lived a short distance away with her mother, Louise, and worked as a manager at Jean-Marc's bank—or had until this disaster. She and her mother were currently visiting relatives in Bordeaux and were due to return home next week.

"Lu-Lu nearly got married once," I told her. "But she decided she wasn't going to settle for someone outside the Church. She wanted a temple marriage, and so she changed her mind and served a mission instead. She helped baptize a few remarkable people. And she'll get married yet, you'll see. It isn't for lack of offers, either. She wants to find the right one—the one who will help make her a queen. The best is always worth waiting for."

"I get it," Josette said in exasperation. But I noticed she was smiling. Her face grew somber in a rare moment of reflection. "I know the Church is true, Mom. I won't let you down."

I kissed her cheek. "I know, honey."

How grateful I was for the gospel and for her budding testimony! That, above all, would keep her out of trouble.

It was long after I had retired to my own bed that I remembered Jacques and our meeting at the cemetery. It seemed trivial now, but I had wanted to mention it to Jean-Marc. Somehow not doing so seemed dishonest.

I stroked my husband's shoulder in the dark. He was curled away from me, toward the wall, and light snores filled the otherwise complete silence in the room. My confession—for so it suddenly seemed—could wait for another day.

Later, I would wish that I had awakened him.

CHAPTER FOUR

The headlines in the papers for the next few days heralded the whole crisis at the bank, and Jean-Marc's name was always mentioned, usually unfavorably. Only a few of the papers wrote the truth as we knew it, and even they partially blamed him. We quickly learned not to answer the telephone until the answering machine picked up to tell us who was on the other end. Each day, the machine filled with hateful messages.

Lu-Lu and Louise cut short their visit to Bordeaux when they read the papers. Their dismay was evident, but so was their determination to give us all the support they could.

"I have a bit to spare." Louise pressed a few small bills into my hand. She was a short, stout woman in her late sixties. With her strong spirit and her hair dyed a rich brown, she appeared younger. "My money wasn't in that bank." But I knew her retirement check was meager, and much of it went to the doctor for her health problems. She suffered from an ulcer, varicose veins, and painful arthritis, all of which had grown worse with age. Recently, she had developed diabetes. Though the apartment she shared with Lu-Lu was paid for, she couldn't have much left over, especially now that Lu-Lu was also out of a job.

"I'll find something soon," Lu-Lu said brightly. "I'm not picky." She was a female version of her brother, even to the green-brown eyes, except that she wore her short brown hair with a flourish of dyed red highlights.

"I can't settle for anything that won't support my family." Jean-Marc's voice was tight and angry.

"I didn't mean . . ." Lu-Lu began, but he waved her aside wearily.

"I know. I'm sorry I'm so touchy." The truth was that his tension was mounting daily, and I had to be careful of each word I said to him.

Our ward rallied around us, even those who had temporarily lost investments, and their faith sustained ours. In the beginning we refused monetary help, though I didn't know how much longer we would be able to do so. Our health insurance would soon run out, and to keep it we would have to pay an exorbitant rate—that or pay for Pauline's treatments ourselves. I was sick with constant worry, though I tried not to let it show. The twins and Pauline went about life as usual, but André grew pensive.

Marie-Thérèse spoke little, but her thoughts must have been working overtime. "Here," she said to me on Friday, the evening of her first date. Her hand held a small roll of bills.

"What's this?" I asked.

She didn't meet my gaze. "Just some money I had. I'm sorry I didn't give it to you on Saturday when Dad told us."

I could certainly use it, but it wasn't like her to hold back. Before I could question her, Josette flounced into the room. She was still jealous about Marie-Thérèse's date but loved her sister enough to be excited as well. "Where's your jacket?" she demanded. "It goes perfectly with what you're wearing. Alain won't be able to take his eyes off you."

"We're just friends," Marie-Thérèse said automatically. She nervously adjusted her silk blouse so that it fell attractively over the matching jade skirt. Her feet shuffled nervously in high heels.

"So where's the jacket?" Josette probed.

"I'm not going to wear it."

Glancing down at the money in my hand, I knew exactly what my adopted daughter had done. Part of me wanted to make her take back the money, but I didn't want to reject her sacrifice. I put my arms around her. "Thank you," I whispered. "I'll make it up to you, I promise."

There were tears in her eyes. "You already have, Mom. Many times."

A vision of her as a child, set adrift in a sea of pain, came to my mind. There was a bond between us that was in some ways stronger than the one I shared with my birth children, and even with Pauline, who was everyone's favorite.

"You'll wear mine," I said, going to the closet and pulling out the full-length leather coat with the fur lining.

"You never let me wear it!" Josette protested.

"Your sister has made a sacrifice for us, and I will make this one for her."

"What?" Josette hadn't understood any of the exchange between us.

The buzzer rang, telling us that Alain was at the outside door. I punched the button to let him in. Jean-Marc came into the entryway, and the rest of the family followed. Even Grandma Simone, Grandma Louise, and Lu-Lu were on hand for a picture.

Alain was an average-looking boy with black hair and gray eyes. He was the same height as Marie-Thérèse, who had always been tall, like her natural mother. Though Alain was a member of our stake and we knew his family, he appeared as nervous as Marie-Thérèse.

"I understand how he feels," Jean-Marc whispered to me. He cast me a boyish grin, and for a moment I could see no trace of his constant worry. "I was so nervous when we went out on our first date."

"That was hardly the same thing," I whispered back. "We were already engaged when we had our first date." We had fallen in love through letters exchanged during my mission.

"I was still worried you'd find out who I really was and get rid of me then and there." We both giggled and tried to hide it. Everyone gazed at us, but we didn't offer to explain.

"Well, the rest of the gang's waiting downstairs," Alain said. "We're going to catch a movie."

I was glad to hear they were going out in a group like most of the young people usually did. "Have fun!" we called after them.

It was a strange moment for me, seeing my little girl leave. This was the beginning of a new phase in our lives, one that would end when our children left home. The many years in its making now seemed few.

———

As the first weeks of December dragged by with no sign of a job for Jean-Marc, his wavering confidence dwindled. Every day he met with the heads of different companies, but always he was refused. He grew depressed, as I should have expected, and nothing I said made a difference.

"Just pretend you're a missionary," I said lightly one day after the children had left for school.

He didn't appreciate my humor. "It's as if I've been blackballed." He set his cup of hot milk untouched on the table. "Like someone has warned people not to hire me. I explain and explain that what happened could not be avoided, but they don't hear what I'm saying."

"After the investigation is over, then they'll know." I had faith the truth would come out and also that people would forget. Already the angry phone calls had decreased to almost nothing.

His face darkened. "But it might be too late. We need money *now.*" We both knew that our cash was gone, and only our credit card stood between us and hunger. Soon we would have to rely on relatives and charity to get by. "I'm thinking I'll have to find something out of Paris."

The suggestion shook me. "But our life is here! Our apartment, the school, the ward, our family."

"I know, but what else can I do?"

Approaching the table where he sat, I laid a hand on his shoulder. "I could work for a while."

He pulled away from my touch, as he had been doing of late. "I can do it, Ari. Don't lose faith in me!" He stood, his face sorrowful.

"It's not a question of losing faith in you! I know you, I know your intentions, but why can't I help out?"

"Just a bit longer," he pleaded.

"All right," I said, watching his face relax. But I didn't mean it. There was an empty ache growing inside me, and it wasn't because of the lack of food—at least not yet. This crisis had hit Jean-Marc in his weakest spot, and it was fast becoming a wedge between us. He was unable to help his family, and his pride wouldn't allow me to do so. I could only hold onto hope and pray that things would soon change.

Jean-Marc left the house, and I felt utterly alone. Shaking myself, I cleaned the kitchen vigorously, until the heat of action released some of my tension. Afterward, I went to the cemetery for my regular semi-monthly visit: the second and fourth Wednesday of each month. I wondered if my father would be there as he had been so often in the past; I thought I could use some of his sage advice.

I used the subway; it would take longer but was decidedly cheaper than spending the gas for the trip. Gasoline prices, like unemployment, had risen drastically. It was cold in the train and even colder in the streets. I couldn't remember it ever being so wintry in Paris. Of course that meant higher bills; we had central heating, a must with little

Pauline being so susceptible to illness. Many in Paris and the surrounding cities were not so lucky, especially in the older areas. I knew there would be deaths because of the cold. If it became worse, I wouldn't let Pauline out, even to go to school.

I blew on my cold hands and then fished my gloves out of my coat pocket. Signs of Christmas were everywhere: nativities and decorations in store windows and in the streets, even strings of lights announcing the Lord's birth. Usually the season brought a rush of joy to my heart but not now. Though Christmas no longer brought the unspeakable delight to my children that it had when they were small, I knew they would be disappointed this year. Why did I always wait until the last minute to buy their few gifts? Why couldn't I be like many of the sisters in my ward who were finished with their Christmas purchases before October? Perhaps because money had never before been a problem.

After leaving the underground train, I had a healthy walk to the graveyard. I drew my coat tightly about my body and wrapped a wool scarf around my head and neck, but the freezing air crept in despite my efforts. Staring at the cement sidewalk, I tucked my chin inside the scarf, warming myself with my breath. At long last I saw the cast-iron gates and the cobblestone path leading inside.

There were actually three paths winding through the cemetery, dotted every so often by stone benches. Upon entering, I took the middle one which ran through the center of the graveyard and joined again with the others on the far side. Paulette and Pierre's graves were off this path, allowing me to stop a while before walking to the end and curving onto the path leading back to where Nette and Antoine were buried. I didn't mind the extra steps this cost me, because I enjoyed the peaceful atmosphere in the cemetery. The headstones were varied, from small plaques to statues and the occasional small building erected by rich families long ago. These had vaults plunging into the earth where the dead slept, with small chapels overhead where relatives had once prayed.

Some might think graveyards eerie, macabre, or even evil, associating them with strange or supernatural occurrences. I knew better. I saw them not only as the serene resting places they were but as the glorious sites of happy family reunions they would become. It wasn't difficult to imagine these people's joyful faces at the Resurrection, when at last loved ones would be forever joined. Mental images of the hugs and expressions of affection that would be exchanged—all in the light of our Savior's great love—brought tears to my eyes. Not the searing, painful kind but the ones that came when joy knew no bounds. I had earned this view from my past trials, and now this place was my refuge, my place of security.

But when I reached Nette's grave, I was not alone. A man sat on the stone bench opposite her grave, staring into space. From a distance I thought it was my father, and my step quickened, but I slowed when I recognized Jacques. I knew I should leave and return after he had gone, but I pushed aside the thought. I had come a long way to visit my daughter; his presence should make no difference.

At the base of Nette's grave stood a huge bouquet of white roses. I was grateful, as I had no money to take flowers myself. Heat seeped into my blood—heat that came from within. I welcomed its warmth, while not looking too closely at its source.

"Hello." I had to remove my chin from my scarf to speak, and the skin, damp from my breath, seemed to freeze instantly. Gasping slightly as the air pierced my lungs with its sharp fingers, I quickly shoved my chin and mouth back into the folds of my scarf.

Jacques looked up, feigning surprise. But I knew he had been expecting me. Perhaps he had seen me through the trees or when I had entered the gates. "Hello, Ariana. What brings you here today?" A cloud of warm breath filled the space between us, hovering slightly before mixing with the colder air.

I very nearly told him that my visits were regular but bit my tongue instead. He was a stranger to me now, not a friend. "What a coincidence that we should visit again on the same day," I said instead. This time the cold on my uncovered face wasn't such a shock.

"Isn't it?" he agreed, shifting to one side of the bench to allow me to sit.

I settled as far away from him as possible. He looked much as he had two and a half weeks earlier at our first meeting, yet there was a melancholy about his eyes and his full lips that I hadn't noticed before. And today his face, tinged red by the cold, was unshaven; I could see the hairs, a darker blond than those on his head, giving him an even more rugged appearance. During our brief marriage, I had always loved it when he left it like that. After three days it would be soft, and I would rub my cheek against his repeatedly. Then it would grow too long and he would shave it; but always after a few weeks he would let it grow again, just for me. The long-forgotten memory provoked a tenderness I didn't know I could feel toward him.

"As to what brings me here, nothing really, just a little peace and quiet," I said quickly to rid myself of the unwanted emotion.

"My father died." Jacques' voice held regret.

My eyes met his. "I'm sorry. When?"

"Last week. He'd been sick, but I wasn't expecting it this soon. He was all the family I had left."

We sat in silence for long minutes. Jacques was obviously grieving, but I didn't know how to comfort him. I couldn't even reassure my own husband.

"You're sad, Ariana," Jacques said. "I didn't mean to make you so."

"It's not you." I blinked back a stray tear. "I've just had a few problems of my own these past few weeks."

He sat up straighter. "Is there anything I can do?" he asked almost eagerly.

"No."

His eyes probed my face, what little of it was open to the frosty air. "You can't hide it from me. Your eyes are so large and sad, I could fall into them and never find my way out. What is wrong, Ariana? Tell me."

While often wanting in originality, Jacques had never lacked passion. I wasn't fooled, of course, but something in me longed to tell him my troubles—whether because of his own confession of his father's death or the way he complimented me, I couldn't say. But there it was. He was warm, friendly, romantic, and his emotions did not cut into me the way Jean-Marc's were doing. If only my husband could find a job and redeem his broken self-esteem!

"I'm fine," I said. "And you're still the charmer, aren't you? Though your grammar is better now."

"I went to school. There was nothing else to do in prison, and then my father insisted I finish. He was right; you were both right. But I am serious about helping you."

"What makes you think I need help?"

He cocked his head and smiled at me, a lazy sort of grin I once loved. "Instinct." The word was loaded with animal magnetism and innuendos I didn't want to understand.

"Come on," he continued. "I read the papers. I know what's going on. Besides, I owe you. I'll always owe you . . . for Nette."

"Talk about something else." I turned away stiffly. His words made me angry.

He stood. "I really must be going. I have a company to run." He rotated on his heel, pulling gloved hands from his pockets. "Good-bye."

Something had fallen out of his coat, and I bent to retrieve a small roll of large bills. Enough to pay the insurance for another month. Enough to pay the bills and buy groceries. And maybe enough to buy a present for each child. Never had I been so tempted to take what wasn't mine. Jacques did owe me in some way, my mind rationalized, and he had as much as told me to take it.

"Wait!" I called before the temptation could sink deeper. "You dropped this." I held out the bills on my open palm.

He stared at me for a full minute before crossing to where I still sat on the bench. "I don't think it's mine," he said, fingering the cash. His touch seemed to go right through my glove to my flesh. "Why don't you keep it?"

"I saw it fall out of your pocket," I said. "Please take it." I didn't need or want help from him. Besides, how would I explain such a thing to my husband?

He took the cash with one hand, the other coming up to stroke my cheek. I pulled away as if touched by fire. Was that longing in his eyes or simply my imagination? His smile faltered. "You're a strong woman, Ariana. You never cease to amaze me. I think I still love you." Without another word, he turned and sauntered down the pathway, leaving me staring after his lean frame.

I cried. I didn't really know why. Perhaps because I didn't want to feel anything for Jacques, and I couldn't deny there was something in my heart. He was the picture of understanding, of confidence, while Jean-Marc seemed only to push me away.

"Nonsense," I said aloud. "It's this crisis, that's all." Logically, I knew I loved Jean-Marc more than I had ever imagined I could love anyone, including Jacques. It was the timing of the situation that confused the issue.

Before leaving the cemetery, I bent at Nette's stone and withdrew a rose, sniffing its sweet fragrance. Its whiteness seemed to stand as a symbol of purity, of young love untroubled by adult miseries.

"I'll just take one," I told Nette, "to remember you by." But in that I deceived only myself.

Upon leaving the graveyard, I went to visit Marguerite Geoffrin, my longtime friend and fellow member of the Church. She and her husband, Jules, owned two cafés and an apartment building in Paris. In my youth, I had worked for them. The café they still worked in was located on the main floor of their apartment building, sharing the space with their living quarters. It was a small café but warm and cheery, despite the large windows facing the cold street. Their well-kept building was situated in a run-down area of town, and at night the streets were unsafe. The threat, however, had diminished over the years because of the large numbers of Church youth who had adopted the café as their hangout.

Marguerite was at the counter, and she looked up as I entered. She was helping a customer, but it was obvious the lunch rush was over. For the first time, I noticed that the indomitable Marguerite was growing older. Her once gray-speckled hair was white, and her skin decidedly wrinkled. Her thick arms and strong fingers had seen much work, and a weariness seemed to exude from her.

"You work too much, Marguerite," I said.

She smiled, the fatigue vanishing almost instantly. "How good to see you. How are you holding up?"

I grimaced. "Not too well, to tell the truth. Jean-Marc still hasn't found work, and he stubbornly refuses to let me try."

"You could work here. Not at the counter but at the books. Jules isn't as sharp as he used to be."

"Could I? I mean if . . ." I trailed off, not wanting to think the worst. "What is it about Jean-Marc? I don't understand him."

"He wants to take care of you. That's not so bad."

"But I feel so helpless. I want to do something to help him, to help our family. Sometimes I think he's more old-fashioned than my father!" As I spoke, I eyed one of the meat pastries inside the glass counter. My stomach rumbled, reminding me that it needed more than the hot chocolate and toast I'd eaten for breakfast.

Marguerite pulled out a pastry and set it before me on a small plate. "On the house." She watched me for a moment before adding, "What else is wrong?" She had been my friend for too many years for me to hide anything from her.

I laid the white rose on the counter; it was now turning brown from the cold it had endured outside, or perhaps from the abrupt change of temperature inside the warm café. "I saw Jacques at the cemetery."

She took in a sharp breath. "Him!" Marguerite sounded angry and offended all at once.

The pastry made my mouth water, and I bit into the flaky crust before replying. "He's changed some. Do you believe he's the president of the most successful carpet company in France? Hard to accept, I know."

"Could it really be true?" Marguerite's doubts brought my own to the surface.

I shrugged, popping the rest of the pastry in my mouth. "It doesn't really matter. He has nothing to do with us."

"Good. My, but you're hungry! Haven't you been eating? You've lost weight, haven't you?" The hefty Marguerite thought nearly everyone was underweight, but this time she was right. I didn't know if not eating as much as usual came from stress or from instinctively wanting to save food for my children.

Marguerite began pulling out a variety of meat pastries and cakes from the counter and packing them into a carry-out sack. When I opened my mouth to protest, she cut me off with a wave of her hand. "I know you say you don't need help yet, but that's nonsense. With no income for three weeks and nothing in the bank—"

"But—"

"No buts." She grabbed my hands where they rested on the counter and stared into my eyes. "Ariana, it's time to let your friends and family help. You don't have to face this alone. We want to do something. Please let us."

"Thank you."

She smiled and handed me the bag. "There will be more. Count on it."

I kissed her cheeks gratefully and walked out into the streets. A thick blanket of swirling fog had risen while I was in the café; now it grew heavier by the minute, giving me the odd feeling of walking in a dream world. People on the streets appeared as if out of nowhere and then disappeared behind me just as quickly, fading from both sight and memory. For long moments I was alone in the white expanse as I tried to find the opening to the subway. At these times, an ominous feeling overtook me. I could walk forever and never find my way back into the real world. The thought was unsettling, but real fear came when I felt unseen eyes on me, just out of sight. I could almost feel someone's breath on the back of my neck, but when I turned, no one was there.

I gave a sigh of relief when the dark opening of the subway beckoned. Taking the steps in twos, I ran down the stairs, leaving much of the fog behind. As I waited for the train, I noticed the rose in my hand was very dark now and held none of its former beauty. The fragrance was gone as well, or my nose was too cold to do its job. Either way, the rose was of no use to me. Spying a large square garbage can, I threw it in.

Lights from the darkened tunnel signaled the train's approach. It came to a stop, and the doors slid open. Before entering, I scanned the strangers next to me on the long cement platform, but none of the faces were familiar.

Even so, I couldn't help the feeling that the unseen eyes continued to watch me. Shivering, I took my seat and pulled my coat and scarf more tightly about my cold body, hugging the warm pastries to my chest for what little heat they had to offer.

CHAPTER FIVE

*T*hat evening as Jean-Marc arrived home, the bishop stopped by. He was carrying a ten-kilo sack of rice and a check for a substantial amount of money. "I know you say you don't want help," he said. "But people in the ward have anonymously donated funds."

"Thank you." I took the money before Jean-Marc could refuse. As the mother of five growing children, I couldn't be overly concerned with pride. I turned to my husband. "All these years we've paid our fast offerings and helped others. Did we regret donating that money? Of course not. And neither do they."

"Exactly," the bishop said. "This is the way the Lord has of taking care of His children." He turned to go. "You'll let me know how things go?"

Jean-Marc inclined his head. "Thank you."

When the bishop had gone, Jean-Marc turned to me with a defeated air. "No luck again. I guess it's just as well he came by." He stopped and then added quickly, "I did get a lead from one of the men I talked to today. He's got a company in Bordeaux. I think I should go there and see. I can stay with some old friends."

I didn't want him to go, but the despair in his eyes begged for my support. "All right," I said calmly. "If that's what you need to do. We'll be here waiting for you when you come back."

"I'm not running, Ari."

"I know." But I wondered if he was trying to escape from our troubles. Then I decided that even if he was, maybe it wasn't so bad. He had been under extreme pressure. "Everything's going to be okay," I told him.

His green-brown eyes met mine. "I know it will. I just don't know how long it will take."

The next day Jean-Marc left Paris, heading for his home city of Bordeaux in our family van. Before leaving, he kissed each of us. "You obey your mother," he said to the children. "And help out all you can."

I hugged him tightly. "I'll miss you."

"I'll miss you, too." He kissed me, but it was quick and unsatisfying, as all our kisses had been in the last weeks.

"Check in every now and then," I called after him. "I have to know you're all right, money or no." He had a cell phone, but I didn't know how much longer we could afford that luxury.

"I'll be fine." The elevators clanged shut behind him, and the hallway seemed empty and forbidding. I sighed and shut the apartment door.

"It's raining, Mom," André said. "Maybe Pauline should stay home from school."

I glanced out the window and frowned. "I think you're right."

"Oh, please let me go, Mom. I'll promise not to play in the puddles."

"No, I'm sorry. I don't want you to get sick." There was silence; we all knew what that meant.

André put his arm around Pauline. "Don't worry, Dolly," he said, using her childhood nickname. Marie-Thérèse had given Pauline the rag doll her mother had made before her death, and Pauline had carried Dolly with her constantly. When the doll had become too old to repair further, it had at last been retired to the chest in Pauline's room, but the name had somehow transferred itself to the child, though only André used it now. "I'll bring your homework and play a game with you when I get home," he added.

Pauline's sunny smile blossomed. "Thank you, André. You're the best brother."

"What about me?" Marc teased.

Pauline laughed. "Will you play a game, too?"

"We'll all play," Josette said. None of the other children could resist Pauline.

"And I'll bring you a chocolate," said Marie-Thérèse.

Pauline giggled. "I think I'll stay home every day."

"We'd better get going or our train will leave without us." Marie-Thérèse's upturned nose twitched as if she were fighting a cold.

"You stay out of the rain, too," I said to her.

The children were scarcely out the door when my mother appeared, her arms full of groceries. "You can't be doing this," I said as she settled herself at the large table. It wasn't the first time she had brought food.

"Of course we can. We're not as well off as we were before the bank failed, but we're getting by. Your father seems to think we'll recover some of the loss when the investigators finish up at the bank."

"I hope so. Where is Father?"

She sighed. "Counseling some members. You know, he works much more than he ever did now that he's retired."

"But that's Church work. It's not the same thing."

"Isn't it?" She gazed at the floor. "You know, when he was baptized I said I'd never ask the Lord for another thing. But I always thought that when we got old, we'd spend time together, just the two of us. Sometimes I don't want to share him with the Church." Her voice sounded resentful.

"Tell him how you feel," I said.

"Maybe."

The next few days were dreary and colder than ever. I missed Jean-Marc, and though I loved my children, they were poor company. With the money the bishop had given us, I paid the insurance and numerous other bills that had piled up. There was little left for food, but Marguerite and other members were generous with their gifts. I often found bags of food anonymously left outside the door to our apartment.

Jean-Marc called on his cell phone each night he was away, the frustration evident in his voice. "It was a bad lead," he said. "The company doesn't even want to hire; in fact, they're cutting back. I don't understand. If I didn't know better, I'd say someone was trying to sabotage me."

I laughed, grasping at the trace of mirth in his voice. "It's because something better is out there waiting. You'll see."

"Are you keeping warm?" he asked. "It's been colder here than I've ever seen it. Some of the people who don't have central heating have been moved to shelters." The gentle flow of his voice faltered. "An old woman died last night. It was in all the papers here. She refused to go to the shelter, and she died of exposure."

"We're fine. I've been keeping Pauline home from school, though."

"That's good."

"When are you coming home?"

"In a few days. I wanted to try to get something before Christmas." His voice grew husky. "I love you, Ari."

"And I love you. No matter what." But I hung up the phone feeling utterly alone.

That night I woke up because of the cold. Stumbling down the hall and through the kitchen, I opened the small closet that housed our furnace. The pilot light was out, and I had no idea how to relight it. The apartment I had grown up in hadn't had central heating, and since marrying Jean-Marc, I had left those things to him.

"It can't be too hard," I said to myself.

"What is it, Mom?" Marc appeared in the hallway, rubbing the sleep from his eyes as he had done as a child.

"Do you know how to light this?"

He shrugged. "No."

"Oh, here are the instructions. 'For relighting, shut off gas and wait for it to clear. Then turn on and light with match.' Doesn't sound too hard, except which knob is the pilot? The printing is too faded."

"What's going on?" André asked, appearing behind us. "Why is it so cold?"

"The pilot's gone out. We're trying to figure out how to light it."

"I can do it," he said. "I've watched Dad before." This didn't surprise me, as he always seemed to see everything. He squatted down and took the matches from my hand. "Let's see," he murmured, striking one. "I just turn this knob and put this here." There was a sudden flare, and a small explosion knocked us backward onto the carpet in the hall.

"Are you all right?" I asked my sons. The loud noise had left a ringing in my ears.

André jumped to his feet to help me up. "It looked so easy when Dad did it."

"At least there's no fire," I said. The gust of air caused by the small explosion had put out the flame.

"What happened?" Marie-Thérèse and Josette came running down the hall.

As the boys explained, I worked on the furnace. Try as I might, I couldn't get it to light, and I worried that the explosion had caused irreparable damage. "I guess we'll have to get out the electric heaters," I said at last. That meant I would have to stay awake all night because of the fire hazard, but it was better than having my children freeze. I wondered when this strange cold spell would end.

"Everyone to my bedroom." I handed each son a portable heater. We tramped through the kitchen, where there had once been a wall separating the conjoined apartments, and down the other hallway to my room.

"Mom, Pauline's window is open!" André had gone into her room to wake her.

I followed him quickly and found him shutting the window. "Pauline," I said, "wake up!" It was hard to believe she had slept through so much noise.

Her eyes fluttered open. "What's wrong?" she asked sleepily.

"Why did you open the window?"

"I was hot."

I put a quick hand to her forehead; she didn't feel hot. "Come on. We're going to have a sleepover in my room."

"Why?"

I left the older girls to explain and walked into my room. Marc and André were busily setting up the electric heaters. "Girls in the bed, boys on the floor," I said. They went about happily arranging the blankets.

Josette insisted on sleeping on the floor with the boys. "It's too crowded in the bed," she said.

I tucked Pauline under the covers and plugged in the heaters. Soon the room was warm. "I wish we could sleep like this every night," Pauline said. "But I miss Daddy."

"So do I."

I tried to stay awake, but my eyes shut against my will. The next thing I knew, André was shaking my shoulder. "Wake up, Mom! There's a fire!"

Any hint of sleep fled from my mind. I jumped from the bed to help Josette and Marc, who were using their pillows to pound out a fire by the door where one of the heaters had been. "Go get the fire extinguisher!" I yelled to André. He nodded and slipped past the fire and ran in the direction of the kitchen.

It wasn't a big fire, but it blackened a large portion of the wall by the door before we managed to extinguish it. The carpet had big holes with melted strands surrounding them. Marc's blanket was a total loss. The elaborate cedar chest my parents had given me when I married was singed on one end, but the precious contents, memories of my own and my children's earlier years, were untouched. I fingered the marred wood, feeling a brief anger at the damage.

"I'm sorry, Mom," Marc said, noting my frown. "I scooted closer to the heater, and before I knew it, my blanket went poof!"

The realization that it could have been so much worse washed over me like a wave. I hugged him. "It's all right."

A cough from the bed brought my attention to Pauline. "It's smoky in here," she said.

I opened the window to clear the air and wrapped her in my quilt to keep her warm. Her face glistened, and I didn't like the sluggish way she turned to look at me. When I touched her forehead, it burned like fire.

"Go call Grandma Josephine," I said. "Tell her to come quick! We need her to take Pauline to the doctor!" A stunned silence filled the room, as André gave a strangled cry and ran out the door.

After André finished talking with my mother, I called Jean-Marc's cell.

"Hello?"

"It's me," I said. "Pauline's sick. She's got a fever. I don't know if it's serious or not."

"What did the doctor say?"

"We haven't gone yet. Mother's going to take us. We're waiting for her."

"I'm coming right home."

"What about the job?"

"My family is more important."

"Thank you," I said. "I'm scared." Even though he was hundreds of kilometers away and wouldn't be able to arrive before evening, the idea of his coming made me feel better.

"It's going to be okay. I love you. I'll be there soon."

I hung up and dressed myself with trembling fingers. My parents arrived shortly, and my father wrapped Pauline in a blanket and carried her to the car. Then we all squeezed into their car and drove to the AIDS clinic near the hospital where our doctor worked. The children were grave, and tears streaked André's face as my father carried Pauline inside.

Dr. Medard was at the clinic. He was in his mid-forties, a man of average height whose plain face was enhanced by compassionate light brown eyes and a thick moustache that hid a cleft lip. A strong presence surrounded him. "How's my favorite patient?" he asked. He had tended Pauline since the day he had guided her head from her mother's womb, and I knew his words were sincere.

Pauline giggled weakly, and a concerned frown came to his face. After a few minutes of examination, he decided to admit her to the hospital. "Don't worry," he said, touching my arm lightly. "I'll take care of her."

It was hours before the blood tests came in so we knew exactly what was wrong. I waited at the hospital, battling my fears and praying, while my parents took the other children home. Everything had the surreal appearance of a bad dream. Finally the doctor came with the news.

Because of her HIV, Pauline's T-cell count had dropped dangerously low from the previous month; this, combined with the cold weather, had led to pneumonia. The drop in T-cells showed that the virus had mutated and become immune to the old drugs. We had known this would happen eventually and that we'd been lucky it had taken so long. For the past year she had been showing signs of AIDS, meaning that the HIV was widely spread in her system, leaving her open to many opportunistic diseases.

"I recommend giving her a protease inhibitor," Dr. Medard said.

I knew what that meant. It was part of a relatively new mixture called a "cocktail" treatment. It consisted of two of the old drugs and a new one called a protease inhibitor. Most patients rebounded for months after receiving the medicine, and it was being hailed as a possible lead to a cure. But there was a downside as well; 10 percent of the patients began to fail again after nine months or so on the drugs. For them, there would be no second chance.

"Do I have your permission?" Dr. Medard asked.

I nodded. He had already tried the other drugs, and this was all that was left. Both of us feared that she would develop an immunity to the protease inhibitors, leaving her nothing else to take. Still, I agreed to the treatment. While this drug was a last chance for Pauline, it would give her precious time until a cure could be found.

The cocktail mixture was very expensive, more so than the other drugs, and it worried me that we didn't have any money coming in. I made a hasty decision: when Jean-Marc arrived home tonight, he would have to agree to my going to work.

"Mom, don't cry. I'm okay," Pauline said after they had begun the medication. Her eyes were beginning to droop with the sedative they had given her.

I wiped the tears away. "I know. I just worry."

A smile spread across her lips. "I love you."

"I love you, too."

Her eyes closed, and I watched her sleep. If a bit thinner than some girls her age, she seemed so healthy and so full of life. She had always seemed so, even as an infant.

A cough from the doorway distracted me from my reverie. I glanced up and smiled at Simone, my adopted daughters' grandmother and my good friend. She wore a flowered dress as usual but had thick tights underneath to ward off the cold.

"How ya doin'?" Her nearly colorless eyes had a green tint today, a reflection from the green flowers on her dress.

"All right. She's asleep now. I think she'll be home in a few days."

Simone approached the bed and settled in a chair near mine. "Your mother called me, and I went to your apartment to help the kids dress for school. Man, that place is cold. I'm glad my whole apartment buildin' only has one heatin' system in the basement. When it goes out, I just call the manager."

I sighed. "It's never been a problem before."

We sat in silence for a moment. "Oh, here. I got your mail. It came just as I was leavin'." She fumbled in her purse and handed me the letters.

"Don't you have to be at the university?" I asked. Simone had been taking courses since her baptism ten years before. She was close to completing a degree in physical science and now taught part time. It had been rewarding to see the changes in her life, from her new job to mastering correct verb conjugation. Also, to my regret, she had all but

lost the colorful accent of the small French village where she had
grown up.

"Naw, I took the day off when I heard about Pauline," she said.
"I've an in with the boss." Actually, Simone was dating the head of her
department, who happened to be an older widower she had met at a
stake function. They had been dating for nearly two years, and he
wanted to marry her, but at age fifty-six, she feared making a big mistake. Poor Frédéric held on, completely under her spell.

"When are you going to finally marry him?" I asked. The question
was more habit than anything else; we always teased her.

"Maybe someday."

We fell into silence as I thumbed through the mail. A letter from
our health insurance company caught my eye. I opened it quickly. The
check I had sent them slid out of the envelope and to the floor. I felt
the blood drain from my face. "They've cancelled our insurance!"

"What!" Simone's eyes narrowed, and she grabbed the letter from
my hands. "'In accordance with articles thirty-seven point two and
sixty-five point one, we hereby terminate health insurance coverage
for . . . '" Simone read on, but I didn't hear the rest.

What am I going to do? The heater broken, my room burned, and
Christmas less than two weeks away. I had to find some relief. I needed
money, a lot of it. Today.

The answer came, and before I knew it, I spoke aloud. "I'll ask
Jacques."

"What?" Simone said. "Where'd that come from?"

"I met him in the cemetery visiting Nette. He's read the papers, and
he's offered me help. I know it may be difficult to believe, but he's a real
businessman now. President of a carpet compay, he said."

"Impossible to believe is more like it," she said. "That boy was never
anythin' but trouble. You'll stay away from him, if you know what's
good for ya." She waved the insurance company's letter under my nose.
"We can fight this. I'm sure there's been a mistake. You don't have to go
to him."

"Don't worry. I'm not a child anymore. I've been through with
Jacques for a long time now. But I won't see Pauline's treatments held
up for anything, especially not my pride. You know as well as I do that

the public system won't allow the care she's been getting. If Jacques can help and wants to, why shouldn't I let him?"

Simone didn't seem convinced. "I wouldn't be surprised if he wasn't lyin' to you even now." She snorted. "President of a carpet company. Of a drug ring, I'll bet."

"But his father really did work in carpet," I told her. "And here's the card he gave me." Why I came to his defense, I didn't know. Perhaps because of the roses he placed at our daughter's grave; perhaps because I needed it to be true. "I never met Jacques' father, though, because he'd already kicked Jacques out before we met."

Simone rolled her eyes expressively. "That, I believe."

"Will you stay with Pauline?"

"What about Jean-Marc?"

I shrugged. "He won't be here until later. When the hospital finishes the paperwork, they'll call the insurance, and then they'll know we've been cancelled. I don't know what else to do." I gazed at her, pleading for understanding.

Her wrinkled face softened. "Go, then."

I kissed Pauline's cheek and nearly flew from the room, bumping into someone outside the door. "Josette!" I exclaimed. "What are you doing here? You're supposed to be in school!"

"I did go, but I just couldn't stay there. I had to see if Pauline's okay." She glanced toward the door, which was closing behind me.

"She's fine. We're not going to let anything happen to her."

Josette sniffed. "It's my fault she's here. She asked me if she could open her window a little last night. Her room was so hot, I didn't see any harm in it. I meant to go back and shut it, but I forgot."

I hugged her. "You couldn't have known the heater would go out, and you couldn't have known her T-cell count was low. It's not your fault." I helped her dry her tears as we walked down the hall.

"Where are we going?"

"You're going back to school."

"But Pauline—"

"Grandma Simone's with her." I stopped walking. "Pauline's going to be fine. They have some new drugs. Don't worry. All we need now is money." I felt in my pocket for Jacques' card. "And I know just where to get it."

Josette's sharp eyes spied the name on the card. "Who?"

"Nette's father."

"You're going to ask him!" she said, aghast. When I nodded, she quickly added, "Can I come?"

The building where Jacques worked was located between the hospital and the school. It wouldn't take long for the detour, and I had to admit I would enjoy the company. "All right," I said. She smiled. Linking arms, we left the hospital.

In the subway, I began to have second thoughts. Simone was probably right; Jacques had always lied to me. What if I arrived and found nothing at the address? Or what if it was an illegal business? That had happened before. But the desperate part of me held on to a slim thread of hope.

CHAPTER SIX

The cold bit into me as we left the underground station and traced our way through the streets of the busy commercial area. People filled the sidewalks, jostling each other as they passed. Small mom-and-pop businesses flanked the narrow road, and cafés beckoned with their fragrant wares. There was a hum of expectancy in the icy, late-morning air. Despite the cold, it seemed, life continued on at its breakneck speed.

It seemed to take forever to find the address, but when we did, we hesitated outside. "Wow! Look at that place!" Josette said. The tall building was impressive, and the huge sign in front even more so. In bold, gilded lettering it read: *Preference Carpets.* I took a deep breath and opened the glass door. Inside, a new smell permeated the air. The walls were papered with gray designs etched with gold, giving it a prosperous appearance. The rich carpet was a shade of darker gray with elaborate patterns in the weave. A blonde receptionist smiled up at us as we entered, but her smile was tight and somehow false.

"May I help you?"

My confidence had returned. There was no way Jacques would go to all this trouble to fool me. "I'd like to see Jacques de Cotte," I said.

Her hazel eyes narrowed, and she clicked her long nails on the polished surface of the desk. "Do you have an appointment?"

I bit my lip. "No, but I think he'll want to see me. Tell him it's Ariana. He'll know."

Reluctantly she spoke into a phone, a look of surprise coming over her pretty face. "He'll see you now," she said. "Go down the hall, and it's the last door on the left."

"Stay here, Josette." I didn't know what might be said between us, and I didn't want her to be affected. "I won't be long."

I left her and practically sprinted down the soft carpet before she could voice the protest on her lips. As I raised my hand to knock, Jacques opened the door.

"Ariana! I'm so glad you came." The warmth in his voice reminded me of a time we had been in love. He reached for my hand and started to bring it to his lips. I pulled gently away.

I followed him into the large office. It boasted the same carpet as in the lobby but of a darker shade. A huge mahogany desk stood opposite the doors, dominating the room. Behind this was a large, gilt-framed painting of Queen Marie-Antoinette. To the left side sprawled an expensive-looking leather couch in chestnut; bookcases and filing cabinets lined the right wall. There were other pictures of places I didn't recognize, also in gilt frames, and a small old-fashioned world globe decorated the desk.

"I came to ask you for help," I said bluntly when he had shut the door behind us. "For Pauline." I showed him the insurance letter and explained what had happened the night before. "I can't risk a delay in the drugs. I don't like to do this, but I need help. I swear I'll pay back every franc."

"Of course I'll help. I'm glad you felt you could come to me." He skirted his desk and pulled open a drawer, taking out an oversized check ledger. He laid it down on top of the papers covering his desk and began to write.

"I didn't know what else to do," I confessed.

He glanced up, a wry smile twisting his lips. "Sometimes I wish you weren't quite so honest."

"I'm sorry. I just—"

He waved, dismissing the words. "It's okay. What about your husband? How does he feel about this?"

"About what?"

"About you coming here."

I shook my head. "I haven't told him—yet. There hasn't been time. It happened so fast. He's out of town right now; he'll be back soon." Now that he had brought it up, I began to worry about what Jean-Marc might say. I shoved the thoughts away; it was too late now.

"I hope it won't cause problems between you." He said the words, but they lacked the ring of truth.

"Why should it? It's for Pauline, and we'll pay you back."

"Hmm."

I didn't know what that meant, so I said nothing.

"Here you go." As I took the check, his hand grabbed mine. "Would you like to talk about it?"

I nearly wanted to cry at the sincere sympathy I heard in his voice. "No," I managed. "I—I should get back to the hospital."

He released my hand slowly, letting it slide over his long fingers. "I'll walk you to the door."

In awkward silence, we returned to where Josette waited. She sat in a chair near the reception desk, her face buried in a magazine, but looked up when she felt us coming. Her eyes widened. "You!" she said accusingly.

I was about to protest when I realized she was staring at Jacques. He gazed back at her, his expression inscrutable. I glanced back and forth between them, feeling the air sizzling with tension. "Do you two know each other?"

Jacques swallowed hard and then smiled. "Yes, Josette and I have met. It's nice to see you again." He inclined his head toward her. "But I need to get back to work. Please feel free to come back, Ariana. I enjoyed seeing you." He made a hasty retreat down the hall.

Josette's glare followed him. "That's your—your, uh, ex-husband?" she asked when she finally found her voice. There was unmistakable pain in her words.

"How do you know him?" Suspicion had always come to my mind where Jacques was concerned.

"He came to the school. He was giving a grant or something. I was one of the students who accepted it. Remember that thank-you speech I had to write?"

"But that was more than three months ago!"

"Afterward, he took us across the street for a pastry," she continued as if I hadn't spoken, "and then the others left, and we kept talking. I could tell he liked being with me." She lowered her head, and I saw a tear splash to the gray carpet.

"Didn't he tell you his name?"

"Yes, but I didn't connect it. There are a thousand Jacques around.

I didn't know his last name. I thought he liked me!" Hurt and anger played across her face.

Terror struck in my heart. "Did you see him again?" I asked sharply.

"Just a couple of times. And only at that café. Sometimes he'd be there after I got out of school."

"What did you talk about?"

Her face darkened. "You, mostly. I thought he liked me. *Me.* But all the time he was asking me about *you.*"

"What did you tell him?"

Her face crumpled. "I don't know. Everything, I guess."

"Did you tell him about me going to the cemetery?"

She nodded, and a tear slid down her cheek. "I'm sorry, Mom. He was so nice and good-looking." She didn't have to apologize; I knew too well how charming Jacques could be.

"It's not your fault. It's his."

"I haven't seen him for at least a week," Josette said. "I wondered why he'd stayed away so long."

"Excuse me?" The receptionist had come up behind us, a malicious glint in her eyes. "I couldn't help but hear what you were saying." She tossed her head in the direction of Jacques' office. "He's like that," she said softly. "He leads people on. But it's all a game with him." The bitterness in her voice was raw, but it calmed Josette's tears.

"He cares about few things other than money," she continued spitefully. "He is, however, hung up on some woman. Problem is, she's married. I don't blame her for not looking twice at him. He's not a nice person. A few weeks ago, he was on the phone, calling practically every businessman in town, offering bribes and services if they'd do something to some poor guy. I don't know what. Not kill him or anything like that, but something about business, probably a competitor. I only know about it because he made me keep calling a few of the company presidents he didn't get hold of the first time."

A door slammed somewhere, and the receptionist jumped guiltily, giving me the impression she had been caught gossiping before. "I'd better get back to my desk," she said nervously, bringing a long red nail to her teeth. She didn't bite it, only nibbled briefly, and then hurried away.

"You go on to school," I said to Josette.

"What are you going to do?"

"I've got a few more words to say to Monsieur de Cotte."

"I want to see!" Revenge flared in her eyes.

"This is not your battle. I'll let you know how it goes."

Reluctantly, she turned and left the building, shivering at the penetrating cold. I waited until she was out of sight before going back to Jacques' office.

"Wait!" the receptionist called after me. I ignored her.

I opened Jacques' door without knocking, pushing it with more force than necessary. He was setting down the phone as I entered, surprise written on his face. "Ariana!"

"You used my daughter!" I accused.

He stood and came around the desk. "It wasn't like that."

"No? But it wasn't a coincidence we met at the graveyard, was it?"

"The first time it was."

"Maybe. That was a Saturday. But you knew I would be there last week. You planned our meeting!"

The calm, businesslike exterior vanished. "Is that so bad? I read the papers, and I wanted to see if you were okay. I swear that's the only reason I let you see me."

"Let me see you? What do you mean? Have you been spying on me?" Indignation colored all of my other emotions. I remembered all too vividly how I had felt someone following me in the fog after we had met at the cemetery last week. Now I thought I knew who it might have been.

His face darkened, but in an instant it was gone. "I wanted to see you, and when Josette told me how you always visited the cemetery, I went there. I didn't ever approach you. For nearly three months I watched from a distance."

For three months he had invaded my privacy! "Why?"

He stepped away from me and began pacing the room, running a hand through his dark blond locks. "You can't imagine what it's been like for me these past years since I got out of prison. I tried to make a life! I tried to forget you! But my life is so empty. Oh, I've been out with women, but every time I get close, I realize it's you I'm trying to replace. It's you I see when I close my eyes." He stopped pacing and faced me earnestly. "You are the most beautiful, caring woman I've ever known,

Ariana. It was my worst mistake to let you go. I finally decided to do something about it."

I felt stunned, but at least now I knew why Jacques suddenly seemed so sensitive to my needs.

"What life we had together is over, Jacques," I said. "There can be nothing else."

"Why?"

The question seemed so simple to him, but to me the complications were obvious. My love for Jean-Marc and my family was the main thing; my deep belief in God another. I was building for eternity, while Jacques understood nothing of such things but lived only for the gratification he could get in this life.

"I don't love you." Surely this was a reason he could understand.

He closed his eyes tightly, emphasizing the slight wrinkles around them. "I can take care of you," he whispered. "I love you enough for both of us. You loved me once; I can make you love me again—just give me a chance!"

I shook my head slowly. "You had all your chances, Jacques. I'm sorry, but I love my husband and will stay with him. I would never leave him." Then I added softly, "Nor would he ever abandon me."

"Like I did?"

I said nothing, allowing his words to stand as testimony.

"I thought you forgave me." His voice was anguished.

"I did. For everything."

"Then why can't you love me?" The words seemed to hang in the air between us, heavy with yearning. Then he drew a shuddering breath, blinking rapidly. A strong hand lifted to halt my answer, and his head shook back and forth as if moved by hidden strings. "No, don't answer that." The calm demeanor was once again masking his face. "I can wait."

You'll be waiting forever, I vowed.

I searched in my coat pocket and drew out the check he had given me. "I can't accept this. I was wrong to come here."

"Keep it," he said tersely, pushing back my hand.

"I shouldn't have come. I need to talk with my husband, and together we'll decide what to do." Now that I was removed from the hospital and all the tragic memories, I saw that my flight to Jacques had been premature, if not completely unnecessary. Somehow Jean-Marc and I would come through, as we always had.

"Him?" Jacques' expression was one of disdain, and I felt myself bristle. "Your husband can't even get a job. Not in Paris and not even in Bordeaux! He can't care for you the way I can."

"How do you know about Bordeaux?" I asked, suddenly suspicious. It was reasonable that Josette had told him of Jean-Marc's failure to obtain work, but she had not seen Jacques since Jean-Marc decided to go to Bordeaux. The story the receptionist had told us came back to me. What if Jean-Marc was the man Jacques had been sabotaging? It was apparent I was the married woman he claimed to love.

Jacques didn't respond to my question. "Tell me!" I demanded. "I have a right to know!"

"I heard it in business circles," he said lamely. Though his expression was unchanged, I could tell he was lying.

"You set it up, didn't you?" Anger swept through me like a cleansing fire, freeing me from the pity I felt for him. "You're the reason Jean-Marc can't find a job! Tell me!" I was yelling, moving closer to him. "Did you think his not having a job would make me leave him? How little you know about real love!"

"You're here, aren't you?" His voice was hard.

"For Pauline! I'm here for Pauline."

He gave me a sardonic grin. "Are you?"

"How dare you manipulate me!" I held his check up and ripped it repeatedly before throwing it in his face. The little pieces fluttered slowly to the carpet like dainty snowflakes on a sea of cold gray. Several landed on his broad shoulders, and one caught in a fold of his jacket sleeve. "I can't be bought," I said, gritting my teeth.

He reached out his hand and touched my jaw, gently and caressingly. "I wasn't trying to buy you, Ariana." His voice had softened again, taking me by surprise. "We were marrried once. Why won't you believe that I still care about you?"

It was at that moment the door burst open. My heart skipped a beat when I saw Jean-Marc standing there, his face livid. I was all too aware of Jacques' hand still reaching out for me, and his declaration of love freshly fading into ominous silence.

Jean-Marc nearly leaped into the office, filling it to capacity with his presence, though there was still ample physical space in the room. Simultaneously, I stepped back, and Jacques' arm fell to his side.

"I'm sorry. He just got by me." The receptionist, partially blocked from view by my husband, stood in the hall, twisting her hands nervously. But I thought her eyes quickly squelched a hint of amusement.

"That's all right, Charlotte. You may leave," Jacques said. A relieved expression passed over her face, and she vanished.

Jean-Marc's fists clenched, and the furrow in his brow deepened. He didn't look at me, but kept his eyes fastened on Jacques, as if sizing him up. Jacques met his angry glare with a haughty stare of his own. Jean-Marc was shorter than Jacques, almost as short as I was, but his build was slightly heavier than Jacques' panther-like leanness. They seemed to be an even match, but I was afraid for my husband. Jacques, once a practiced bar fighter, would have no mercy, whereas my husband was basically gentle and compassionate. I hurried to him and grabbed his arm, tugging him in the direction of the door.

But when Jean-Marc spoke, his voice was steady and showed no sign of the wrath his face couldn't hide. "My wife and I will be going now."

"What, no introductions?" There was no mistaking the irony in Jacques' voice or in his half-smile. It was as if he meant to make a mockery of the situation.

Jean-Marc's eyes narrowed. "I know you," he grated. "I've seen your works." I knew he referred to Jacques' past mistakes, and it made me wonder that he could still be so angry at Jacques when I, who had been wronged, had forgiven him.

"Come on. Let's go," I said.

Jacques' smile faded. "This isn't over yet, Ariana!"

I turned a stony face in his direction. "Yes, it is, Jacques. I never want to see you again!"

He took two strides and reached out to place a hand on my arm, but Jean-Marc stopped him. "Leave my wife alone," he warned. "*My wife.*"

Jacques snorted. "What if she doesn't want me to?"

"I do," I said.

"I can take care of her!" Jacques growled, ignoring me.

"Like you did the last time?" Jean-Marc challenged.

I gasped and ran from the room. Men were impossible! Let them beat each other senseless, if that was what they were determined to do!

Yet I was overcome with relief when Jean-Marc followed me down the hall. The receptionist gazed at us with open curiosity, mouth opened to voice a question, but I stormed past her. She would have to find another victim.

Jean-Marc caught up to me outside the building as I paused to wrap my scarf around my head. "Why did you come here?" he asked, turning me around to face him. "Why did you go to *him?*" The cold in the streets seeped into my soul, and I couldn't speak.

"Tell me, Ari! What's going on?" His pain added to my guilt.

"Pauline," I said. "I wanted to protect her. I just didn't know what else to do!"

"Why didn't you tell me about meeting him before? I saw Josette coming from the building, and she told me everything. About how you met him at the cemetery." His voice emphasized his feelings of hurt, as did the torment in his eyes.

I took his hands in mine and felt sad when he recoiled from my touch. "It wasn't important! I never planned on seeing him at all, but then the problems with our private insurance, and Pauline getting sick and all—" I broke off, tears coming despite my attempt to stop them. People in the streets were beginning to stare. "I was desperate," I cried. "I know now that I was wrong, but you were gone, and I felt so helpless! I knew this cold would bring death, but I never imagined it could be in my own family!"

A familiar tenderness came into those splendid green-brown eyes. He pulled me close, and for a moment I let myself go weak in the circle of his arms. His cheek touched mine, and I could feel his face grow slippery with the salt water coursing from my eyes.

He pulled back enough to wipe the tears from my cheeks with his bare fingers. "Come," he said, glancing at the many passersby. "Let's go somewhere a bit more quiet."

Hands linked, we searched the frigid streets for a café that was uncrowded and reasonably priced. We found one in a quiet side street, though we knew that soon the lunch rush would begin and our peace would end. The restaurant was Chinese, and the decor transported me away, if temporarily, from my problems. We were led to a corner table for two, where the low lights and unobtrusive waitress added to the romantic atmosphere. Relaxing slightly, I ordered sweet and sour chicken with rice; Jean-Marc ordered egg rolls.

"How did you get here so quickly?" I asked.

"I took a plane right after you called. One of my cousins will be bringing the van back for us in a few days. He had to come to Paris anyway and jumped at the chance." He grimaced. "Unfortunately, the plane fare is one more bill on our credit card."

"Did you see Pauline?"

A grin stole over his face. "Yes, but she was sleeping. Simone was with her and told me where you'd gone. She remembered the address, and I came after you. That woman's got a sharp mind."

"She's going to be all right," I said, not wanting to talk about Jacques. "Pauline, I mean."

"I know. I gave her a blessing. Some of the brethren from our ward were there, and they assisted."

His words were like a balm to my soul, flooding me with sweet comfort. I gazed into his handsome face. "Thank you for telling me."

We sat in easy silence until the food came. I ate hungrily, having eaten nothing that morning.

"Did you mean what you said to Jacques?" Jean-Marc asked abruptly.

My eyes snapped from my plate to his face. I sensed a vulnerability about him that I had never seen before. "What did I say?"

"That you never wanted to see him again."

"I did mean it," I said fervently.

"Good."

"He's one of the reasons you haven't been able to find work," I added, explaining in detail what I'd learned from both the receptionist and Jacques. "It seems he's promised favors to those who don't help you." I shook my head sadly. "Jacques always wanted power, but look how he uses it."

Instead of my words setting him at rest by making him understand that his failure to obtain work was not completely his fault, Jean-Marc became more agitated. He tapped his forefinger steadily against the edge of the plate in front of him, and the muscles in his jaw worked. "At least now I know what I'm up against." Then his voice grew soft. "But I still wish you hadn't gone to him."

"So do I. It doesn't matter, though. He's out of our lives forever."

I hoped I was right. Once again I had been fooled into thinking Jacques had changed, but though he had left the drugs behind, he hadn't really changed at all.

Neither had our situation.

"Marguerite's offered me work," I told Jean-Marc, "doing the books for her café. I want to do it." His face seemed pained, but I rushed on. "I *have* to help. You have to let me feel that I'm contributing to my family in this crisis. If I'm busy, I won't get so desperate. It's what I feel I have to do. When things get back to normal, I'll gladly step down because I'd rather be at home with our children, but you know as well as I do that we have to have some income. With the apartment and van paid for, we have too many assets to depend on public welfare or the Church for any extended period of time."

He nodded slowly. "I've been an idiot. I know I should have let you help, like how you let Marie-Thérèse return her jacket."

"Exactly. We all need to pull together. We're a family; that's what we're supposed to do."

He let out a long sigh. "I never imagined it would come to this. I'm supposed to take care of you."

"We're supposed to take care of each other," I corrected, "and that's exactly what we're going to do."

His grin was back, a ghost of its usual brilliance, but at least it was there. "Maybe Marguerite has a job for me, too, even if it's waiting tables. A job is a job, and until I find something better, I also need to do something."

I nodded, a smile coming to my face at the idea of him working in a café instead of being president of a bank. "Who knows?" I said. "We might have fun."

"As long as we're together." The grin vanished, and his voice seemed almost questioning. I smiled and put my hand in his.

We finished our meal and left for the hospital. Jean-Marc's step seemed lighter, but there was a lingering doubt in my own heart. Why had I really gone to see Jacques? Had I a second motive, hidden even from myself? I had to admit that some small part of me had enjoyed the way he had stared at me with such yearning. But wasn't that because of the tension my husband and I had been going through—the neglect I felt and my own helplessness? Yes, that had to be why. But now we were a house united, and together we couldn't fall. I wouldn't let Jacques' overt determination interfere with my happiness.

Something told me that convincing Jacques might not be so easy.

CHAPTER SEVEN

When we returned to the hospital, Pauline's room was alive with visitors: Aimee, Pauline's Primary teacher; Grandfather, the stake patriarch; and Jules and Marguerite Geoffrin. Pauline was very popular with the ward members, and because she wasn't in critical condition, visitors could come and go as they pleased. The little girl sat up in bed, her eyes bright as she opened a present.

She gasped as she saw the doll with a fine porcelain face. "Oh, but, Grandfather, you shouldn't have!" She ran a finger over the dark colored hair and cheeks. "Why, she looks just like Giselle!"

Grandfather, as everybody in our ward had called him since his baptism eleven years ago, chuckled, his dark eyes beaming almost as excitedly as my daughter's. He had white hair and ebony skin and seemed somehow ageless, though I knew he had great-grandchildren. "I thought so too. And when you see her, tell her I said so." Giselle was his granddaughter who used to work in the AIDS wing at the hospital until she married our bishop's son and gave birth to the first of her five beautiful children, all different interracial shades of brown. She still lived in the ward and was expecting her sixth little boy. Her oldest was nine.

Grandfather straightened. "I'd better be getting along. But you get well, hear?"

Pauline nodded. "I will. I'm probably going home tomorrow. At least, that's what the doctor said a while ago when my daddy gave me a blessing." She sighed and held up her small hands. "I'm good 'nough to go right now, but no one believes me!"

Grandfather's deep chuckle filled the room. He glanced up and saw us by the door. "Ah, the parents," he said. He neared us and, taking my hands in his, said, "That child is special. You can feel the love radiating from her. The life! It makes me feel young just to be around her." The deep wrinkles around his brown eyes seemed only to give him more character instead of age.

"I never realized you were old," I said.

He squeezed my hands and looked heavenward. "I'm not going anywhere yet, but when I do, I'm going to talk to someone up there about Pauline. And about you." His smile filled his whole face. "Everything is going to be all right."

"Thank you." I believed it would be when he said it like that, as if he were a wise man who could see beyond the veil.

He left, followed by Aimee. "Call me if you need anything," she said. I knew her own three children kept her busy, but her offer was sincere.

"How are you doing?" Marguerite kissed my cheeks and then put a motherly arm around Jean-Marc.

"We've been worried," Jules added a bit gruffly, as if embarrassed to admit such a thing. He too kissed my cheeks. "Is there anything we can do?"

Before I could answer, Pauline called out from the bed. "Mom, come and look at it!" She held up the doll, her face like a ray of sunshine. Pauline was used to receiving presents, as she had been sick so often in her young life, especially of late. But always the marvel of each gift stayed with her, making the giver feel as if he were the one who had received something special.

I went to the bed and hugged her. Doing so seemed to drain the tension out of my body as well as the worry. "It's beautiful," I said, sitting on the edge of her bed.

"I guess we'd better get back to the café." Marguerite moved slowly toward the door.

I stood up. "There is one thing you could do." I glanced at Jean-Marc, and he nodded encouragingly. "If the job is still open, I'd like to do the books for the café."

"And I'd like to know if there's something I might be able to do," Jean-Marc put in quickly, "either in your apartment building or in the café. Something temporary, until I find a permanent job. I'll do good work for you."

Jules and Marguerite exchanged a long look, seeming to communicate silently or to agree on something they had previously discussed.

Then Jules brought a strong-looking hand to his face, rubbing his grizzly chin. His gray hair seemed more sparse than I remembered. "What we had in mind was a little different, but let me put it to you and see if you're interested."

A puzzled expression came over Jean-Marc's face. "What do you have in mind?"

"Retiring," Jules said. "I've worked forty-five years, and I'm tired. My old bones don't move the way they used to, and Marguerite and I have decided to go somewhere warm. Our niece, Colette, and her husband have agreed to buy out our half share in our other café, but we were feeling reluctant to give up interest completely in our original one. It holds a lot of memories for us. So we'd about decided to find someone to manage the café and apartment building, at least for a year, until we decided for sure what we wanted to do. But neither of us was looking forward to trying to find someone to run it. There are so many stories of old people being robbed blind. But we'd feel safe with you two."

"We'd planned to include our apartment in the package," Marguerite said, "but it wouldn't be big enough for your family. Still, it has another entrance from the regular apartment building, so we could just wall in the opening to the café and rent it out like any other."

"It'd be up to you how you did it," Jules said. "It's not easy, but it's a decent living. We'd be fair with the wage for taking care of the building, and we'd give you a percentage of the café profits. You'd pay the bills and wages, hire employees to replace us, everything. Fact is, it'd be a relief if you'd do it."

"A year, you say?" asked Jean-Marc. I could see a spark of real interest in his eyes. Managing a small café and four-story building was not the same as managing a successful bank, but it would have its challenges—and a paycheck. The twelve—thirteen with the Geoffrins' flat—low-priced, well-kept units were in high demand, and Jean-Marc would have time to keep them rented and still be free to search for another job.

"We'd want a year's agreement," Jules said. "But if you got something else, you could hire someone to do the maintenance, just as long as you still made sure everything ran smoothly."

Jean-Marc's gaze turned to me. "Well?"

"We could do it," I said. "We could actually work at the café as well, at least the children and I could. I've done it before, and it can be very rewarding. The children will love it."

"Can I help too?" Pauline asked.

I smiled. "See? She wants to work already."

Jean-Marc began to discuss the minute details with the Geoffrins, while I turned to my daughter and began to brush her long, dark hair. "I'm good at wiping tables, aren't I, Mom?" she asked.

"I'm sure we'll find something you can do." We had to take precautions because of the HIV. Fear overshadowed compassion in many people.

"I could even be a greeter. I'm good at talking to people, and I could show them to their tables."

"It isn't exactly that kind of restaurant."

"Still, it's going to be fun."

Engrossed as I was in our conversation, I didn't notice when Simone pushed open the half-closed door. "So you're back," she said, capturing my attention. "I've got a surprise for you." She motioned to someone in the hall. A tall man with red hair and clear blue eyes came into view. He was huskier than I remembered, and it was strange seeing him in casual clothing instead of a suit, but recognition didn't fail me.

"You!" I gasped.

He grinned. "Didn't they tell you?" He waved vaguely in the direction of the Geoffrins and Jean-Marc. Pauline grinned, enjoying her part in the little secret.

In three steps I crossed the room and threw myself into the arms of the faithful returned missionary who had helped bring the gospel to me so many years before. "Elder Kenneth Tarr! I can't believe it."

He stepped back far enough to study me. "Why, Ariana, you're a remarkable woman! The years have been kind to you."

"You old flatterer," I said. "What brings you to Paris, Elder?"

He shook his head. "Not Elder anymore, though you could call me Dr. Tarr if that makes you feel better. I earned a doctorate in French," he explained. "I teach at Brigham Young University. Can you believe it? Me with that horrible accent I had on my mission." He shivered in exaggeration. "Anyway, I finally decided it was time to bring my wife and children to see France, so I took a sabbatical from the university and arranged to teach at a school here for a semester. We'll be here about five months."

His French hadn't been faultless during his mission but never that bad. Regardless, now his mastery of the language had improved to such a point that I might believe he was a French immigrant and not an American.

"This is my wife, Kathy," he said, bringing a slender woman forward. I realized she had been at his side all along, but in my excitement at seeing the elder who had baptized me, I had overlooked her. She was pretty, with honey blonde hair, green eyes, and a ready smile. She seemed very young, though I knew from Kenneth's occasional letters that she was only a few years my junior.

"Hi, nice to meet you," she spoke in halting French.

"Kathy doesn't speak much French," Kenneth said, "but she's picking it up quickly."

"It's very nice to meet you," I replied slowly. "Your husband is very special to me." I was happy when she seemed to understand. I glanced back at Kenneth. "Why didn't you tell us you were coming?"

He threw back his head and laughed. "When I arranged to stay in Marguerite's building, I asked her to keep it a secret, and she did. We've been communicating by letter and phone for months now. My family and I arrived yesterday. We heard about your daughter through Marguerite and Jules, and we came to the hospital an hour ago. We met Jean-Marc and Pauline, but you weren't here."

"It's really great to see you," I said. "I can't think of a better Christmas present." Jean-Marc came over to stand at my side. He put an arm around my shoulders. "I owe you so much for your persistence," I continued. "I don't know where I would be without the gospel."

"Teaching you was one of the greatest moments of my mission. You had been prepared to receive the gospel. Tough testing but worth it." Kenneth looked around the hospital room. "It seems you're being tested again."

It was my turn to laugh. "Yes, but we'll come through. I can see the light at the end already, thanks to Marguerite and Jules." I leaned against my husband, feeling contentment. Things were better, if not completely perfect, and we would work at it.

"Let's go out and celebrate tonight," Kenneth said enthusiastically.

"My treat. And just us adults. We can get our kids together later. I want to see Paris! It's been so long since I've been here!"

"I'll drive," Jules offered.

Kenneth smiled. "That's good. My wife and I aren't much use at that. You Parisians drive way too fast." He pretended to wipe his brow. "Whew! And I thought Provo traffic was getting bad."

We made arrangements for Jules to pick us up later that evening at the apartment. The Tarrs and Geoffrins left together, planning where we would go. When their voices had faded down the hall, Jean-Marc and I sat together by Pauline's bedside.

"What do you think?" he asked softly.

I knew he was talking about running the café. "I heard a saying once on my mission that wherever a door is shut, God opens a window."

He grinned. "And this is our window?"

"Well, there are several in the café," Pauline put in.

"Ha-ha."

"Uh," Simone interrupted, popping her head in the door. "I've been talkin' with your insurance company, and I think I'll get things ironed out, but I'll need your records. It seems someone has done something with the computer at the company. They're firin' one of their employees because of it." She shook her head. "It's too bad. They don't understand why he did it. And he just got new carpet in his apartment, or so the other employees say. I wonder how he'll pay for it without a job."

Her words made me start, and Jean-Marc's teeth ground together. Simone, unaware of our reactions, continued blithely, "I'll be goin' now. But I'll check in later in case you need me. Frédéric will want to know what's happenin'." Her lips curved in a girlish smile. She blew us a kiss and whisked out the door.

"It's probably a coincidence," I said.

"Nothing can be considered a coincidence where Jacques is concerned." A dark shadow passed over his face. "I just had an awful thought." Standing, he pulled his cell phone from his suit pocket. "I'll be right back."

"Is Dad okay?" Pauline asked, staring after him.

I followed her gaze. "I think so. He's just had a few shocks today."

"Good. When he comes back, I'm going to have to talk with him."

I hid a smile behind my hand. If anyone could lighten Jean-Marc's mood, it would be Pauline. She perfectly embodied the meaning of her name: small in stature, big in love.

When Jean-Marc returned a short time later, he didn't explain his odd behavior, and I didn't question him about it. When he was ready, he would tell me, as he always did. Pauline made him sit with her and describe his airplane trip, and then she fell asleep contentedly in his arms.

After school let out that afternoon, the other children met us at the hospital. Pauline was awake and in high spirits. Her siblings seemed relieved when they learned she would most likely be coming home the next day.

"We'd better make sure the heat's on first," André said. His eyes hadn't moved from Pauline since he arrived, and his expression was unusually sullen.

"What?" Jean-Marc asked. In all the excitement, I hadn't yet explained about the heater or the fire.

"It's a long story," I said.

"Oh, yeah, guess what? We completely forgot to tell you. We're going to own a café!" Pauline chose that moment to make the announcement to the others.

"We're thinking about managing one," Jean-Marc corrected. "Perhaps now is as good a time as any to have a family council about it." He explained Jules' idea, and the children immediately became excited.

"We could actually work there after school," Josette said, her face blushing. "Think of all the people we'd meet!"

"Boys, you mean," Marc said. Josette punched him.

"What about me?" asked Pauline. "Can I work, too?"

"I'm sure there'll be something you can do," Marie-Thérèse said, echoing my earlier words.

The vote was cast and the decision unanimous: we would try our luck at the café. That didn't mean Jean-Marc would stop looking for a job; it just meant he could take his time and pick what he wanted. We would run the café ourselves, with only the help from three longtime employees, all of whom were also members of our ward.

Next, we discussed the private school and decided to try public education for a time, except for Pauline. Jean-Marc was reluctant to have any of them change schools, but together the children and I convinced him.

"You never went to a private school," I pointed out, "and you turned out fine." Sending the children to a private school was what people in our former position normally did, and it was difficult for Jean-Marc to let go completely; it seemed tantamount to admitting that he would never recover his position.

"Besides, it's only until you're rich again, Dad." This show of Marc's utter faith in his father won Jean-Marc over. There would be a few things we had to change but never our faith in his abilities.

Louise, Jean-Marc's mother, came to sit with Pauline, and with the exception of André, who insisted on staying, we went home. The children wandered into the kitchen for a snack and to do their homework, while Jean-Marc and I went to the bedroom to change for our night out. The closet where the heater had blown was scorched and ugly, but the bedroom wall was worse. One-fourth of the wall was completely blackened; the wallpaper along the dark stain was curled, the edges brown. The holes in the carpet seemed larger and blacker than I remembered.

"Tough night, huh?" Jean-Marc's grin was sympathetic.

I nodded. "You could say that." I began to recount the night's events, this time leaving nothing out.

He came over and circled his arms lightly around me. "Are you okay?"

"I am now. Are you?"

"Yeah." But his voice was worried. I wondered if it had something to do with the phone call he had made at the hospital earlier.

The doorbell rang, and we heard the children run to answer it. Excited cries filled the air. Casting puzzled glances at each other, Jean-Marc and I hurried down the hall to the entryway. Our three teenagers were bent over a large cloth sack of the brightest red, pulling out new articles of clothing, toys, and even food.

"It's Father Christmas's bag," Marc exclaimed.

"Merry Christmas to Josette." Marie-Thérèse read the card on a leather coat almost identical to the one she had returned to the store. Josette squealed and grabbed for it.

"Here's another just like it for you, Marie-Thérèse," Marc said, rummaging farther into the sack. "And look—a new pair of roller blades for me. Wow! These are the best!"

There were more items in the bag, each addressed to one of the children, and each horribly expensive. "Did you catch any sign of who delivered it?" I asked. The children shook their heads.

"One of the neighbors must have let them in the downstairs," Jean-Marc mused. "We could ask them if they recognized who it was."

"It must be from the ward," I said. "Or from a group of the members together."

"This is the best Christmas ever!" Josette cried. She shoved her arms into the jacket and danced around us, eyes flashing. "It's like they knew exactly what we all wanted."

Jean-Marc smiled. "They sure know how to cheer you guys up. I wonder why it wasn't wrapped, though. What do you say we wrap them all up to put under the Christmas tree? You three have seen them, but that doesn't mean André and Pauline shouldn't have a surprise."

"Let's do it!" Marie-Thérèse said.

"Even the jacket?" Josette said reluctantly.

"Don't be so selfish," Marie-Thérèse said. Josette threw daggers with her eyes but finally agreed.

A tiny beeping sound came from Jean-Marc's pocket. He quickly retrieved his cell phone from deep inside his suit coat. "Go ahead," he said to us, retreating into the kitchen. "I'll be right back."

"Mom, here's one at the bottom addressed to you," Marc said. He had taken the presents one at a time from the red bag and now held a sturdy oblong box tied with a thick red ribbon. I knelt on the floor next to the children and studied it.

"Open it, Mom," they urged.

"Maybe I should save it for Christmas."

Marie-Thérèse wrinkled her freckled nose. "I don't know. The rest of this stuff wasn't wrapped. What if it's something that should be opened now? It looks like flowers."

"You *have* to open it," Josette pleaded. "I'll die if I have to wait to see what it is!"

"Go on," Jean-Marc encouraged, coming from behind. "We can't have Josette dying now."

With so much urging, I grew excited to see what the white box held inside. My hand reached for the ribbon and untied the bow. Carefully, I lifted the lid. As I saw the contents, a sinking feeling pierced my stomach, and I had to fight the urge to run to the bathroom and lose what little food remained from my lunch.

"How beautiful!" the girls chimed together.

Marc shrugged. "It's okay."

"Exquisite," Jean-Marc said. "Just like you, Ari."

Nestled in the folds of the softest tissue paper was a delicate flower made from the finest crystal—if the store name on the tag could be believed. A flawless, dainty white rose.

"What's wrong, Ari?" Jean-Marc asked. "You've suddenly turned white. Marie-Thérèse, go get your mother a drink."

"No, I'm fine," I said. "I'll go myself. Kids, you clean up these things." I arose, leaving the white box with its rose behind on the polished wooden floor.

Jean-Marc followed me to the kitchen, carrying the glass rose. "Better put this up. They might break it." I took it from him and placed it in the garbage can. "What! But it's your favorite!" he exclaimed.

"It's from Jacques."

His eyes widened. "How do you know?"

"I just do." I motioned over my shoulder through the door where we could see the children in the entryway. "Every single thing in there is exactly what the children wanted. Jacques pumped Josette for this information, and at the cemetery he gave me a white rose. This glass rose is his way of telling me these presents are from him. Why can't he leave us alone?"

Jean-Marc's face darkened. "I should have hit him," he muttered.

"No, we did the right thing."

"You don't understand. That call I got a few minutes ago—I asked them earlier this afternoon to check the possibility of bribery as a motive for the employees at the bank who were caught stealing. One of them admits to having been bribed, and he's agreed to testify, but he doesn't know the person who paid him. The authorities think they will never know. I think it's been a setup, systematically put in place over a very long time."

"You think Jacques is involved?" The idea seemed ludicrous.

He sighed. "We'll never know, I think. But we have to tread carefully where Jacques is concerned."

"Shall we return the presents?" I asked reluctantly. The children were so happy with the unexpected windfall, and the objects were exactly what I might have bought them. They would never understand the reasons for sending them back, and trying to explain it would make things worse for me.

Jean-Marc considered, and I sensed he was also loath to steal their joy. "Let them have their innocence," he said finally. His lips curved into a smile. "And I will write Jacques a thank-you note and send him a check to cover the items. We'll get an advance on the credit card."

"I don't want the rose."

Jean-Marc retrieved it from the garbage. "This I will send back with the check. If anyone is going to buy you something as elegant as this, it's going to be me."

I could only hope that would be the end of it.

That evening, Jules came by early to help Jean-Marc fix the furnace. He brought some supplies from his own stock, and they managed to get it working in a little over an hour. Jules also brought some painting supplies so that on another day we could fix the wall in our room. The insurance would most likely pay for the carpet. After they cleaned up, we went to pick up Kenneth and his wife for dinner.

"I get the feeling people aren't used to big families," Kathy said in her awkward French. "We've been here two days, and whenever we take the children with us, we turn around to find people counting us. Then they ask Ken if all eight are ours!"

"They did that to me when mine were little," I said, laughing. "And I only had five. It *is* unusual to have so many."

"Oh, look, Kathy! There's the Eiffel Tower!" Kenneth's red head bobbed enthusiastically. "We tried to find it yesterday. I was driving, and Kathy was guiding us with the map. We never found it."

Kathy sat with Marguerite and me in the backseat of Jules' car. "It's my fault," she confessed, leaning over conspiratorially. "There are so many naked statues! I get too distracted by the scenery to pay attention to the map!" We giggled almost uncontrollably. It was true; there seemed to be statues on almost every corner, many of them wearing nothing but fig leaves or even less. I could imagine such a thing would be distracting for someone not accustomed to the sight.

For the first time that day my body relaxed, and I silently thanked my Father for sending Kathy to put things into perspective. It wasn't until we left the restaurant that my worries came flooding back. Jacques sat at a table near the entrance, watching me. Both he and the important-looking man with him seemed to exude power. Dishes clanked, people talked, but for me the world stopped. Our eyes met for a brief instant, his questioning, mine angry. Before the others could notice, I turned away. I told myself it was a coincidence, just one more in a long line. But for some inexplicable reason, I felt his fate was tied up with mine.

The thought made me furious.

I clung to Jean-Marc's hand as we stopped in at the hospital to say good night to our daughter. Nothing would come between us, I promised silently. Nothing.

CHAPTER EIGHT

*T*he next day Pauline came home to continue her recovery, and life returned to normal. There were only a few days of school left before Christmas, but even when she was better, she wouldn't be leaving home as long as the cold lingered. Jean-Marc and I used the extra time at home to fix the wall in our room and to supervise the carpet layers. We sanded and revarnished the burned parts of my cedar chest. It didn't look like new, but I was satisfied.

After finishing at the apartment, we asked Louise to sit with Pauline while we went over things at the café with Marguerite and Jules. Christmas fever was in the air, and the feeling buoyed up our hearts, giving us hope. Celebrating the Savior's birth would mark our own new start in life.

"So have you settled on a destination yet?" I asked Marguerite. She and Jules were debating where to buy their retirement home. He wanted to find a place in the Algarve on the southern coast of Portugal, where it was warm almost all year round, but she was worried about the language barrier.

"I'm not leaving France," she said. "No matter what Jules says. But I wouldn't mind visiting Portugal. I think we'll go there after Christmas."

Sunday came, two days before Christmas, and I was thankful for the day of rest. We dressed Pauline warmly, and for the first time since leaving the hospital ten days earlier, she left the house. At the church, everyone eagerly waited to see Elder Tarr and his family. He had visited another ward the previous Sunday, but the news had spread about his being back in France. Today there were many visitors from other wards and branches who had come to see one of their favorite former missionaries.

"Who's that?" Josette whispered as they came up the walk.

That turned out to be the Tarrs' eldest son, seventeen-year-old Kenny. He was tall and rather gangly, with his mother's honey blond hair and his father's blue eyes. He didn't seem any different from a hundred other young people I had met over the years, but my daughters jostled each other as they vied for position at the glass door.

"He's cute!" Josette exclaimed. Yet when the family came in the foyer, she suddenly pretended not to care; she preferred to be chased than to give chase. "Oh, yeah, nice to meet you," she said with easy nonchalance. But her gaze darkened when Kenny sat by Marie-Thérèse in the chapel, talking animatedly in English. Marie-Thérèse's hard studying in her second language was paying off.

I sighed, wondering how long the jealousy would last between the two girls.

"Where's André?" Pauline asked, drawing my attention.

"What?" I scanned the crowd, but André was nowhere to be found.

"He's been acting strange," Pauline said. "I'm worried."

I stood and walked to the front of the chapel where Jean-Marc, as second counselor in the bishopric, was sitting with the bishop and the first counselor. "Have you seen André?" I asked.

"No. He was with us in the van. I'm sure he'll show up."

An uneasy feeling gripped my heart. "I'm going to look for him."

I met my mother in the hall. She wore an angry frown, and her face was flushed. "Have you seen André?" I asked, thinking he was possibly the reason for her distress.

She stopped short. "Is he missing?"

"It's probably nothing. You know how boys are."

"Do I!" she said emphatically. Behind me in the chapel, the inspiring strains of the opening hymn filled the air. They didn't seem to soothe my mother's soul. "Your father left me to go on the subway. Can you believe counseling someone this early on a Sunday morning? I've had it! He's available for everyone except me! I don't even know why I'm here. I hate sitting through sacrament meeting alone."

"Aren't you exaggerating?" I asked. The financial ruin had been hard on everyone, but my mother's chief pastime of decorating and buying things for everyone had been abruptly curtailed. Now, with my father's busy calling as first counselor in the stake presidency, she had been left too much alone with nothing to do.

She sighed. "Probably. Here, I'll help you look for André."

We walked down the hall, eyes searching. "Have you noticed anything odd about André?" I asked.

"Well, now that you mention it, he has seemed sort of withdrawn. I thought he was worried about beginning a new school or something."

"Ariana!" Giselle, the hugely pregnant granddaughter of Grandfather, the stake patriarch, motioned to me from a closet near the kitchen. As the Primary president, she had her own closet to store projects.

"What is it?"

"It's André," she said quietly. "I saw him through the kitchen door. I prayed about what to do, and then you showed up. You'd better go see for yourself. I'm so sorry."

Dread made my steps slow, but soon my mother and I were peering out the kitchen door into the cold winter outside. Seated next to the garbage can were André and another boy, huddled together in their coats for warmth. Gray smoke curled its way lazily to join with the white billows covering the sky above. The puffs of smoke weren't stemming from hot breath meeting the cold air but from little sticks of poison held in young fingers.

"André!" I could hardly believe my perfect little boy sat there smoking. He started at my words. The other boy jumped to his feet and thrust his hands behind his back. André coughed and dropped his cigarette to the cement. "Come on," I said. "You have some explaining to do."

A short time later, Jean-Marc and I were in the bishop's office alone with our son. He sat on a padded chair, bottom lip thrust out, eyelids half shut as he glared at us.

"Why?" Jean-Marc demanded. "We want to know why."

He shrugged. "I wanted to try it. So I did."

"But you know that smoking is wrong," I said. "It's bad for your body and will lead to other things. Why would you break the Lord's commandments?"

"It ain't true. None of it!" The words seemed to burst from him.

"What isn't true?" Jean-Marc asked.

"All that junk about the Church. Pauline's still going to die!"

"What!" I exclaimed. "No, she's not going to die. We are going to fight every minute to keep her with us."

"But it won't do any good, in the end." He looked up at me, and I could see the pain in his eyes. "Can you tell me that she'll be okay forever? Of course you can't. All my life I've watched out for her, but I can't help her in the end. No one can. I used to pray that God would take me instead of her, but you know, I don't think there is a God at all."

"But there is!" I said.

"Then He doesn't care about us. Pauline shouldn't have to suffer."

Jean-Marc and I bore our testimonies to him, but André kept his gaze glued to the carpet, showing no emotion. I put my arms around him and cried. For the first time, he showed signs of remorse. He hugged me back. "Please don't do it again," I whispered.

"Okay." But his voice sounded hollow, and I wondered if I had lost my innocent little boy forever. Growing up wasn't easy.

Christmas Eve fell on Monday night, and we celebrated with our whole family at the apartment. At midnight we opened our few presents and sang Christmas carols. Then we sat down at the long table, loaded with Christmas goodies brought by our relatives. As we ate dinner, joyful conversation filled the air. Only André was silent, though Pauline's healthy exuberance made up for his lack of sociability.

"I'm excited to start my new job," Lu-Lu said to me. Only a week earlier, she had finally found a position. "I'm not making as much as before, but at least it's at a bank."

"You'll work your way up quickly," said my father.

"I am a little worried about it being so close to that bomb site," Lu-Lu said with a shiver. Earlier in the year, there had been a bombing at a government building near the bank where she would be working. The authorities were investigating Islamic extremists who claimed responsibility for the explosion that had killed eight and injured many others. The attacks had continued randomly the year before, but for months everything had been quiet.

"That's the safest place to be," Jean-Marc said. "Near where they've already bombed."

"I wouldn't worry about it, Aunt Lu-Lu," Marc said. "They arrested about a hundred guys. I'm sure they've found the ones who've been doing it."

The phone interrupted the conversation. "It's for you, Géralde," Jean-Marc said.

My father stood and reached for the phone. "Hello! Yes. Merry Christmas to you! Really? All right. Why don't you meet me down at the church, and I'll help you figure it out." He replaced the receiver.

My mother's happy expression faded, but she said nothing as my father kissed her and made his way to the door. "I have to help Brother Lucien with a problem," he explained.

"Can't it wait?" I asked.

My father's face went blank. "But I'm happy to help. I'm glad to be able to give him the benefit of my experience."

"Sometimes it's good to learn from making mistakes." I didn't know what Brother Lucien's problem was, but it didn't seem important enough to break my mother's heart. Especially on Christmas.

"I'll be back soon," my father said.

But when we had cleaned up the dinner and the children had fallen to sleep on the floor in the TV room, he still had not returned. My mother ended up sleeping alone in the guest room. I tried not to notice how old she appeared.

When we arrived in the solitude of our bedroom, Jean-Marc held out a small gift, wrapped in gold paper. Earlier, I had given him a belt to hold the tools he would need as a building manager, and he had given me an apron to use in the café. We had agreed to keep the gifts simple this year. Due to the lack of money, it hadn't been difficult.

"You already gave me a present," I murmured.

"But this is special." He pushed it into my hands.

I opened it slowly, relishing the moment. Jean-Marc had occasionally surprised me over the years, but we had grown to know each other so well that surprise gifts challenged our creativity. With all the other problems in our lives, I didn't know where he'd found the time.

A small box covered in black velour nestled inside the gold paper. I knew instantly that the contents must be jewelry. I had never appreciated precious metals and stones the way my mother did, though Jean-Marc had bought me a beautiful collection of them over the years, and now I tried not to show my disappointment. How silly to be disappointed with a gift you hadn't planned on receiving at all! The human mind was sometimes so unpredictable.

Then I gasped. The box held an intricately designed yellow gold pin, featuring a rose cast in white gold. "I've never seen anything so beautiful!" I breathed. "Where did you find it?"

Jean-Marc smiled. "I returned that glass rose Jacques sent. But I wanted to know when he bought it, so I went to the store to check it out. They couldn't tell me, but I found this staring up at me. I knew it had to be yours. I bought it on our credit card."

"I do love it," I said. "But the cost! We don't have the—"

He put gentle fingers on my lips to stop the flow of words. "Sometimes a person has to do what he feels is best. I know how much you enjoy white roses, and now you'll always have one with you and be able to remember how much I love you when we're apart."

I met his gaze with my own, trying to convince him with my sincerity. "But I know you love me. I don't need anything to prove that." Truth was, I worried more about our next meal than anything else.

My thoughts must have been plain on my face. "I know we haven't been in debt since we paid off the apartment," he said, "but I *need* you to have this."

The phrasing of his words sparked my curiosity. "Does this have something to do with Jacques?"

He glanced away for a second as if collecting his thoughts. "Maybe. I guess it threw me when he gave you the glass rose. It had always been something between us. I never thought about your life before, with him. I never imagined he knew you so intimately." He stared at the ground. "I guess that's stupid of me. After all, you were his wife, and you had a child together."

His voice was tortured, and I silently berated myself for letting Jacques back into my life, however temporarily. Jean-Marc's feelings of inadequacy had only increased because of my actions. "I love you," I said, hugging him. "And I love this pin. I'll wear it always."

He sighed, trying to hide his relief. I wondered if he thought it would keep me safe from Jacques.

The next day we immersed ourselves completely in the café and the building above it. The café had two full-time employees, Dauphine and Hélène, and Dauphine's daughter, Annette, worked part-time. Since they were members of our church, we knew them well—especially Dauphine, who had been at the café since I had worked there before my mission. All three were excited to have us as the new managers.

"We'll be working too," Marie-Thérèse said. "We have to fill the places left by Jules and Marguerite."

"I can work extra," Annette said. "I only have my college classes in the morning now."

"Thank you," I said. "That might be best. The café seems to be busier than when I worked here, and we'll probably need three people in the day and more at night."

So it was decided. Dauphine and Hélène would come early in the morning to start the baking and work until four. After helping the children off to their new public school, I would keep busy with the books and the ordering. If needed for the breakfast rush, I would help the women. Jean-Marc would be on hand to pick up the food or handle work in the building. At noon, Annette would come in and work until closing. Again I would be around to work an hour or so during the lunch rush, if needed. At four Dauphine and Hélène would go home, but Marc, Marie-Thérèse, Josette, and André would help Annette, taking time out to do their homework when business was slow.

"I'll write," Marguerite said as she kissed me the morning she left for the Algarve in Portugal. "Let us know what's happening."

I smiled widely. "I will. And thanks so much. I don't know what we'd do without this opportunity."

I thought it would be awkward slipping into my new role, but instead I found it challenging and fun. I especially loved balancing the books. The children also learned quickly. Marie-Thérèse proved to be the most faithful and efficient, and even Pauline did well washing the dishes in the back. Josette was popular with the younger crowd and could work fast, but she often went out and sat with the customers, forgetting that she was supposed to be working. Marc stayed in the back, learning how to cook with Annette, though sometimes he spent more time watching the pretty girl than learning from her. At first it was André who saved the food from burning—until he began showing up less and less, using schoolwork and other excuses to separate himself further from us. Several times he appeared at the café with boys I would just as soon forbid him to see.

Sometimes I felt as if my little boy were floundering in the middle of a raging ocean and I was helpless to prevent him from drowning. I knew that if I could just put his feet on solid ground, he would find his way, but he seemed out of my reach. Only when he was with Pauline did I see the twelve-year-old boy he had once been instead of the stranger he had become. My heart ached, but neither Jean-Marc nor I knew how to save him.

Jean-Marc was another problem. He learned his job thoroughly and worked hard, but the light faded from his eyes. Each afternoon that he could get away, he diligently searched for a new job and each time found nothing. He hurt in a way I couldn't heal.

"How are you doing?" I asked him once.

"A job is a job," he replied. "At least we are supporting our family." But I knew that managing the building and café no longer appealed to him and that each day he spent there, another little piece of him died.

I prayed for my family fervently at night. Desperately hoping for a change, I forgot that sometimes the Lord's answers are different from our own.

CHAPTER NINE

*O*ur phone rang early one morning in January, jolting both Jean-Marc and me from the bed. Yawning, I went to the kitchen to answer it. "Ariana?" It was Dauphine. "I'm sick. I can't come in today."

My heart dropped. Today was Monday, Hélène's day off. I normally took her place because Mondays were slow, but I couldn't do it alone. "That's all right," I said. "Take care of yourself." I hung up and called Hélène, but there was no answer. I vaguely remembered her saying something about visiting her daughter.

"What's wrong?" Jean-Marc noticed my expression.

"Dauphine's sick, and I can't reach Hélène. What should I do? Maybe the girls will have to stay home from school."

"I'll help you. We can do it alone. It's only for breakfast."

I smiled. "At least we can give in a try."

A few hours later found us at the café, juggling the jobs the women handled easily with long practice. A long line formed at the counter. "Here, take these," I said to Jean-Marc, pulling out a batch of fresh-baked meat pastries. They were ones Annette had made a few days earlier and put in the freezer. Most of the pastries we bought daily from a bakery, but the meat pies and the bread we made ourselves.

There were more people than I had ever seen on a Monday, probably because the dreadful cold spell had passed, and our confusion grew. Jean-Marc and I rushed around, feeling a bit lost and bumping into each other constantly. When the bread ran low, I mixed up a new batch, rushed out to the front to help Jean-Marc, and then back to get the bread. To my surprise, it turned out edible, if not perfect.

"You have flour on your nose," Jean-Marc said, laughing. I glanced up and found him watching me from the doorway. I laughed. Behind him I could see the counter where, at last, no one waited for help. "We make a good team," he added.

I grimaced. "I'm just glad Annette will be in this afternoon. I don't think I can handle lunch and dinner." Pastries and bread for breakfast were one thing; real food was something else entirely.

He grinned and hugged me. "Me either." I kissed his nose and ran my hand through his hair, leaving streaks of flour.

"Whoops," I said.

But he laughed. "Flour and all, this has been a fun morning."

I agreed. I hadn't felt so close to him since before he lost his job.

The bells on the door jingled, signalling more customers. At the same time the phone rang. "You answer that," I said. "I'll go up front."

I wished I hadn't. Jacques stared at me, dark eyes narrowing. "Why are you here?" he asked bluntly.

"I'm working." Pride stopped me from explaining further. Frankly, it was none of his business.

"It didn't need come to this. I have plenty to take care of you."

"I can take care of myself," I said. "If you hadn't interfered in the first place, I wouldn't be here."

"Don't blame me. You had a choice."

I could see the fire in his eyes. "And I chose this."

He frowned, and I noticed his eyes taking in the gold pin on my blouse. "You sent back what I gave you," he said, his voice deceptively light, hiding an anger I recognized only because I knew him so well. "Why?"

"Because—" I broke off, not knowing how to explain.

"Did *he* make you?"

I shook my head slowly. "Jean-Marc doesn't *make* me do anything. We are partners." I touched the pin lightly, without thinking.

"He gave you that." It wasn't a question.

"Are you eating anything?" I countered.

He shook his head. "Suddenly, I'm not hungry." His eyes fastened on my face. "You know where to find me." Before I could respond he strode from the café, his lean figure reminding me of a caged tiger. I sighed.

"What's wrong?" Jean-Marc asked, coming from the back. "You're white as a ghost."

"Jacques was here."

As anger filled Jean-Marc's face, I knew Jacques' visit had been planned. He knew I was working at the café and that Jean-Marc was with me. Why wouldn't he leave us alone?

——————

After that day, Jean-Marc helped out more at the café. We worked side by side, and those were moments I knew I would remember forever. I learned things about him I had only guessed at before, and my love for him grew. The sadness he felt at his business failure was partially swallowed up in our love, but it hurt me to know that though he also enjoyed the time we spent together, he longed to feel as strong as he once had, to find a new identity. His inability to find a job and take care of his family ate constantly at his soul.

Good news came at the end of January. Some of the missing bank funds had been found, and the government had agreed to cover others. Jean-Marc called my parents over to the café to hear the news.

"Maybe we could go on another mission," my father said excitedly. We lounged at a table in the nearly deserted café, shortly after the lunch rush had ended.

"How wonderful." The irony in my mother's response fell heavily on my ears, but my father seemed not to notice.

"What about your calling?" I asked.

"Hmm. I do have a few people I'm working with. I guess I can't let them down."

My mother stood and without saying a word turned and walked out the door. "Where are you going?" my father called after her retreating figure. If she heard, she didn't let on. We watched in silence as she disappeared from sight.

"What's that all about?" My father shook his head. "I don't understand what's getting into her. Well, at least she left the car." The midsized vehicle sat in the weak sun in front of the café, its white paint shining.

"Do you have a minute to talk?" I asked. Perhaps I could help him understand as he had helped me so many times in the past.

He glanced at his watch. "Well, I have a meeting in about twenty minutes, and I'm visiting inactives tonight." He stood and kissed my cheek. "We'll talk later."

"When?"

"Well, it can't be tomorrow. I'm helping at a service project, painting someone's apartment. And the next day I have to help some members go over their finances. I don't know how long it will take; they've got themselves into a fairly serious situation. What about after church on Sunday? I should have more time. Oh, wait, I have to—"

Jean-Marc stood and pushed him gently back into his seat. "Give her a minute, Géralde. Or does she need to make an appointment through the stake executive secretary?"

His face darkened at Jean-Marc's audacity, but my husband met his gaze without flinching. My father dropped his eyes and sighed. "All right. Talk."

"The sink is leaking, and I'm getting pretty good at fixing things like that." Jean-Marc winked at me and left us alone. He passed Dauphine and Annette, who were busy restocking the open space under the glass counter with delicious pastries and sandwiches. In the kitchen, Hélène prepared soups for dinner.

"I haven't seen you since Christmas," I began.

"That's true. The holidays are a busy time. People get depressed, and they call me. Take Brother Lucien, for instance. His testimony's been wavering, and I've set up a complete schedule of reading and study for him. I check in with him each day." He smiled in satisfaction. "And then there are the Gilberts, who simply can't deal with their teenagers. I have to see them each day, too." My father's voice droned on, detailing how he went about helping the families with whom he worked. As he talked, I realized that he wasn't helping them so much as he was controlling their lives.

"Don't you think that every day is a little too often for counseling?"

My father's eyebrows rose. "But they need me. They'll fail if I don't keep on them. And I'm good at it, too. I'm so grateful to be a part of the true Church! I feel alive each day, knowing I can actually do the members some good."

"By *making* them behave?" It sounded a little too pat to me.

His lips pursed in obvious annoyance. "They come to me, Ariana. They want help."

"What about Mother?"

"What about her?"

"How does she feel about this?"

He stared at me blankly. "She's happy I can help so many people."

"She *wishes* you were around more."

"But we have eternity to be together. I'm fighting to help others have that same blessing."

"At her expense?"

His head shook back and forth vigorously. "I love your mother. She is the most important thing in the world to me."

"Then maybe you ought to worry about *her* testimony."

My father glanced at his watch and stood, pulling his black coat around him. "I have to be going. We'll talk about this later."

"When, in another month?" I muttered.

"What?"

I sighed. "Nothing."

He bent down and kissed me on both cheeks. "Your mother's all right. She just needs something to do."

That was the first thing he had said that made sense. Maybe I could help my mother by asking her to fill in at the café occasionally. She had never worked outside the home before, but she was an excellent cook. She made a special cake with egg yolk frosting that had always been a family favorite. Adding it to the menu could only make business better. We would call it "The Josephine."

"Ariana!" I looked up to see Lu-Lu coming toward me. Her face was flushed, and a nervous energy radiated from her.

"What's wrong?" I started to rise, but Lu-Lu launched herself into a chair and flopped her head and arms onto the table, nearly upsetting it.

"I can't believe it. Him after all these years!" Her voice was a mixture of pain and disbelief.

I smoothed her short locks. "Who? Tell me!" If Jacques had been bothering my sister-in-law, so help me I wouldn't be responsible for what I would do. "Did Jacques—"

She lifted her head from her arms. "Jacques? What does he have to do with this? No, I mean Philippe!" Now her stress made more sense. It wasn't every day a woman came face to face with a man she had almost married. In my own situation with Jacques, I could appreciate her reaction. Lu-Lu had once loved Philippe enough to defy her family's wishes, despite the fact that he was arrogant, controlling, and completely against the Church. He had dumped her during the crisis of

Paulette's death and then came crawling back, but she had recognized the greater importance of gospel truths. Still, even after serving a mission, she had never found anyone to replace him.

"How did it happen?"

She sniffed. "I'm being considered for a promotion at work, and I'm waiting to be interviewed by this bigwig from the main branch. When he comes in, I'm staring at some papers I've brought to show him, and, lo and behold, I look up and there he is staring at me, just staring. He was as surprised as I was." She moaned and buried her face once more in her arms. "Eleven years," she muttered. "Eleven years! And I felt like it was just yesterday. I almost threw myself into his arms!"

"Then what?"

"Nothing," she wailed. "He kept staring, and I felt my face go red. Then he coughed a couple of times, like he was trying to clear his throat, and he walked out and left me there. I was so mortified that I left my papers on the desk and fled. Oh! How will I ever dare to show my face there again?"

"You'd better do it quickly if you want to keep your job."

"Who cares about the job?" she retorted. "I can't work with Philippe as my boss!"

"Maybe you won't have to work directly with him," I pointed out.

"He's been married," she said as if I hadn't spoken. "Twice, I think. He has two children by the second wife, a girl and a boy." Her breath came rapidly, and I worried she might hyperventilate. I stroked her head again, wishing I could soothe her pain. Her head lifted again, and her striking eyes met mine. "They could have been my children, Ariana. All these years, I've known I chose the right thing, but seeing him . . . I . . . ." Tears coursed down her red cheeks. "I think I still love him!"

It wasn't exactly what I had expected, but I should have known. Lu-Lu had grown into a beautiful, poised woman of thirty-three; it wasn't easy to reduce her to a sniveling idiot. "What are you going to do?" I asked.

Her shoulders slumped. "There's nothing I can do."

"He obviously feels something for you, too—if his reaction is any indication."

"It doesn't matter." Her words were desolate. "I'm not going after what isn't mine. I won't come between a husband and wife. No matter how I feel."

I was happy to hear it. Philippe had been a cruel, selfish man, and unless he'd changed a great deal, Lu-Lu would only end up hurt again.

Jean-Marc came out of the kitchen whistling. He held a wrench in his hand, and his smile told me the sink was fixed. I shook my head when he started toward us, and he nodded. I felt a rush of love for him flow through me. We knew each other so well that communication didn't always have to be verbal.

"I think I'll walk to the subway station and meet the children," he called. I waved and blew him a kiss, but Lu-Lu kept her tear-streaked face averted from her brother.

She wiped her face with her hands and smiled weakly. "I guess I'd better get back to the bank. Thanks for helping me out."

I hadn't done anything except listen. If only my parents' problem could be solved so easily. "Any time, Lu-Lu."

As she was leaving, Ken and Kathy came into the café with their eight children, and Lu-Lu paused to talk with them. Their oldest son looked eagerly around for Josette and Marie-Thérèse, and the others pushed two tables together so the whole family could fit. Their presence filled the café. One of the customers, an older man, was finishing up his meal and made no secret about counting their cherubic faces in unconcealed amazement. The two-year-old smiled at him and crawled under his table near the door. Kathy dived after her.

"She threw the ladder to the bunk beds out the window in the back," Kathy said in English, pulling the kicking little girl into her arms. Ken had gotten into the habit of translating for her when she wanted to explain something more detailed. "The older children were throwing a ball up through the window and back down again. They wouldn't let her do it, so she decided to get into the act herself. She threw the first thing she could find that wasn't too heavy. Then she cried because when she tried to throw it toward the window, it hit her in the head!"

I laughed and Ken shook his head. "Children never cease to amaze me," he said.

"I guess I should be grateful it wasn't my new clock," Kathy continued. Again Ken translated. "It's a beautiful piece I found at a flea market last week. I had stored it in their room on the dresser near the window. It's pretty heavy, and I didn't think they could hurt it. But when I went into her room, she was on a chair trying to push it out the window. I just saved it from smashing into a million pieces."

"Or smashing any heads," Ken added.

To my surprise, I found I envied them. Yes, having small children was a constant challenge, but the life and new perceptions each one brought into the family made it worth every tear shed. Most women my age were thankful their childbearing years were behind them, but I didn't feel that way. My babies had been born so close together that many days I had been under too much stress to enjoy them. Now I looked forward to having grandbabies to love.

Next, things happened so quickly that I couldn't remember afterward in what order they came. Out of the corner of my eye, I saw a group of young teenagers from our ward open the door to the café. Then the earth rocked and a series of loud booming noises filled the air. Someone bumped into me, and I lost my balance. I felt Lu-Lu catching me as an abrupt sucking sound came, like a swift intake of air, and then utter silence.

Ken helped Kathy to her feet. The toddler in her arms broke the silence with loud screams, and everyone else stared at each other with horrified expressions.

Before the shock had diminished, a man burst through the door to the café. "There's been a bomb let off in the subway station down the street!" he shouted. "There's got to be a hundred people trapped in there! Call the police! The ambulance! Hurry!"

His urgency spurred Annette to action, but I felt my life draining as if from an open wound. My children were due on the train. Jean-Marc had gone to meet them.

Lu-Lu's face held the same terror as mine. "Oh, dear Lord," she prayed. "Please, not the children!"

Ken understood our fear. Having lived in the apartment building for five weeks, he knew our family's schedule. "Go," he said. "We'll help out here if they need us." Already the café was filling with people talking excitedly about the explosion.

I ran quickly over the cobblestone sidewalk, pushing past the crowds of people that had appeared to sate their curiosity. Muffled curses and exclamations followed in my wake, but I didn't stop. "My children," I said once when a wiry man in a police uniform blocked my path. His stern face softened, and he let me by. Lu-Lu followed me closely.

All around me was confusion and noise. Cries, shouts, and wailing echoed through the streets. My heart pounded as if it would break through the fragile confines of my chest.

I was near the opening now, but only rubble marked where stairs had once led down into the underground station. A good portion of the street had erupted into a gaping cavity. People leaned curiously around the edges of the hole, and even as I watched, the ground under a man's feet crumbled. He fell, vanishing from my sight.

"Get away! Get away!" cried a group of men in uniform who emerged from one of the first emergency vehicles to arrive on the scene. They quickly strung a bright yellow ribbon around the area and began herding people away. I ducked under the ribbon and pushed forward through the crowd, my eyes scanning the people moving slowly away from the explosion site, some holding broken arms, others with faces and bodies covered with soot and bloody scrapes. Bedlam reigned, and the terror in my heart reached a feverish peak. My lips moved in silent, desperate prayer.

Then Jean-Marc lurched into view, with an arm around Pauline. André and Marie-Thérèse flanked him. Josette's head bobbed behind them, and I saw that Jean-Marc had hold of her arm and was pulling her along. All seemed healthy and whole. Relief flooded me—until I realized that Marc was missing.

CHAPTER TEN

I ran to Jean-Marc and the children. Pauline launched herself into my arms. She was dressed warmly, as usual, but even through the thick layers I could feel her thin body shaking. Her eyes were wide and fearful, more so than I had seen them during any of her illnesses.

André was silent and brooding, and Marie-Thérèse's face tragic, but it was Josette who captured my attention. Muddy tears streaked her cheeks as she pulled violently on her father's hand. "Marc," she moaned helplessly, "I have to get Marc! Oh, please let me go. It's all my fault! I told him not to go."

I gave Jean-Marc a questioning look. He shook his head. "I can't find him." His voice broke on the last word, and tears flooded his eyes.

"What happened? Where is he?"

"André and Pauline went ahead when they saw Dad," Josette said through her tears. "But Marc had his roller blades and wanted to put them on to see if he could jump the gate. I went a little ways, and that was when the explosions came. I fell down, but I was okay. Marc was coming toward me and we started to leave, but then we heard a woman crying. She was somewhere down under all that dirt. Marc stopped and went back." Josette hiccupped loudly. "He climbed up on top of the train. I told him not to go, but he just laughed and skated over to the edge. The next thing I know, the whole train shifts and he disappears! I tried to find him, but a man grabbed me and brought me up to the top. We need to find him! I can't bear for him to be dead! I can't live without him!" Her eyes begged me to make everything all right, and with my whole heart I wanted to. Little Marc, so much like my brother, Antoine—fearless, brave, and more than a little foolish. I had always hoped Josette would be able to keep Marc out of serious peril, as I hadn't my own twin brother.

Josette sobbed uncontrollably, and there were tears on my other children's faces—all except André, whose emotion manifested itself only in his tightly clenched jaw.

"Take them," Jean-Marc said, thrusting Josette's hand into mine. "I have to find him." His voice grated, and I recognized his terror, for it was my own. I nodded and held tightly to Josette, who tried to pull away and follow her father. Pauline wept against my side, arms clinging to my waist, while Marie-Thérèse gently stroked her hair. Lu-Lu reached out to comfort André, but he dodged her hand and plunged into the crowd after Jean-Marc.

Instinctively I followed, drawing my daughters along. Josette, understanding where we were going, weaved through the thinning crowd. I could see Jean-Marc ahead, with André close behind, but an official stepped in front of them.

"You have to leave the area," he said.

Jean-Marc shook his head. "My son's in there. I have to find him!"

The policeman frowned, pity showing clearly on his face. "Just stay here. We'll have trained men here in a few minutes to rescue the survivors."

Jean-Marc grabbed the taller man by the shoulders. "It's my son!" he repeated. "And I will look for him!" He pushed the man backward and ran to the edge of the hole, dropping out of sight. André ducked under the policeman's arm and also disappeared.

Josette tried to follow, but I pulled her back. "No!" I screamed in her face. "It's too dangerous!"

Some of the policemen emerged from the hole carrying injured and sobbing survivors. A flurry of ambulances arrived, but there weren't enough trained personnel to help the wounded. "Run back to the café and bring supplies," I yelled to Lu-Lu. She nodded and motioned for Marie-Thérèse to help.

Josette pulled on me, trying to break my hold. I drew her close. "You stay near me," I said firmly. "If you don't, I'll take you back to the café. There are a lot of people who need help, and we are the only ones here to do it. Now, leave Marc to your father, and show me that you are grown up by taking care of Pauline."

"Okay, Mom," she said, subdued.

Assured that she wouldn't run for the subway, I pushed Pauline toward her and ran to help several victims whom the rescue workers had found in the rubble. A man bled profusely from an arm, and a woman suffered from a head wound. It took me three tries to tear a strip of cloth from my apron—the one Jean-Marc had given me for Christmas—and my hands shook as I tied the knot.

"Let me help." Josette was standing over me. With a deft twist, she tore a piece of cloth from the bottom of her skirt and wrapped it around the woman's head. I smiled grimly and moved to the next victim, glancing often toward the ugly hole that had swallowed my husband and son.

Finally, I saw Jean-Marc and André emerging, carrying in their arms a limp figure with long blonde hair. They carried her to us and then disappeared once more. Tears slid down my cheeks as I turned to help the woman.

Lu-Lu and Marie-Thérèse returned shortly after the camera crews and more ambulance workers arrived. Police pushed the crowd back further, but working among the victims, we were left alone. One woman I saw was completely burned. A man in his mid-twenties sobbed heartbrokenly at her side. I didn't know how he could even recognize the body.

"They're newlyweds from Tours," I heard a very young nurse say of the unfortunate couple. "They came to spend their honeymoon in Paris." She hiccupped loudly, her voice bordering on hysteria. "He identified her solely by her new wedding ring. I've never seen anything so horrible! There's nothing I can do for her. Or for him."

I wanted to spare my little Pauline the ghastly horror, but in her young life she had already seen much. Many of her friends at the clinic had died of AIDS—long, painful deaths caused by cancer, pneumonia, and even parasites with unpronounceable names. After ambulance workers had covered the woman's body, Pauline left my side. Without saying a word, she flung her arms around the weeping bridegroom and cried with him. He held onto her like a drowning man, his face contorting with anguish, but less than before, now that it was shared.

My husband came up from the cavity, covered with sweat-streaked dust, and again deposited someone who was not Marc. Lu-Lu rushed to help the man, but I saw by her face that it was too late. The ambulances filled up, but more arrived to cart away both the dead and the living. The panic of the moment subsided, but still there was no Marc.

Jean-Marc carried out another woman, barely conscious and bleeding profusely from multiple wounds on her extremities and her left side. Again Lu-Lu raced to the victim. I tore another strip off my apron, as I had no more bandages, and went to help Lu-Lu. The shapely woman appeared to be in her late twenties. She had auburn hair, high cheekbones, and perfectly groomed eyebrows—a beauty by any standard.

"Oh, dear Father," prayed Lu-Lu, parting the woman's hair to uncover a large, bloody lump on the left side of her head. Slippery red fluid mixed with the long auburn strands. Her lids fluttered open, revealing a striking gray on the right side. The left eye was completely dilated. I wasn't sure what that meant, but I thought it might be due to the shock of her head wound. "Thank the Lord for that young man," she mumbled. "If it wasn't for him, I would have died!"

Josette stiffened at my side. "That's her, Mom. That's her! I recognize her voice!"

"What young man?" I cried. "Where is he?"

She rolled her head back and forth slowly. "I don't know," she said through heavy gasps. "He pulled me out, and then the ceiling caved in. If he hadn't been wearing those skates, maybe he would have—"

Josette wailed and ran to the edge of the crater. The woman stopped talking, and her eyes closed. Lu-Lu bent to lift her up, struggling under the weight. "I'm taking her to an ambulance," she said. "I'm afraid she's dying."

I wanted to help but felt torn. Pauline appeared at our side with the new bridegroom. "Let me help," he rasped with a voice hoarse from his tears.

When I reached Josette, a dozen or so men were climbing wearily out of the hole. "I think that's all there are," a short, swarthy-looking man said.

"No! My brother! He's down there, too!" Josette's lips quivered as her eyes begged for help.

He gazed at her kindly. "There ain't no one else there, girl. And if there was, he's dead by now."

"No!" Josette screamed, echoing my own emotions.

"He's down there," I said firmly, hoping to convince them. I put a detaining hand on his arm. "Please. A lady just told us how he pulled her out. He was wearing roller blades."

The man shook his head, and the others did the same. "I'm sorry."

A dirty child ran up from the rubble behind them, and it was only by his voice that I recognized André. "My father needs help!" he yelled. "He's found another."

Josette cried out. "Is it Marc?"

André's face crumpled, though it was hard to tell beneath the dirt. "He's wearing roller blades."

"Don't worry, Madame. We'll get him out," the swarthy man said.

The group headed back into the deep recesses of the subway. I scrambled down the rubble and followed. A layer of broken cement and glass covered the area, dotted by unrecognizable pieces of metal. I could see the train ahead, most of which was blackened by fire. It was through this and to the other side that André led the men. I held Josette back and clasped André to me before he could protest, not wanting him to risk his life further. His face was a mask of devastation, as if he had seen too much. I ached to comfort him. This was an experience that would mark him for life, and I knew that Marc's survival was important not only for himself but for my sensitive André. I didn't want him to become an angry adolescent, bent on punishing the world and himself for the horrors he had seen.

Now that they knew where to look, it took only minutes for the men to lift the rubble covering our son. Jean-Marc appeared from the wreck of the train, cradling a deathly still Marc to his chest. He was unconscious, but when we removed his helmet, we could see no signs of head injury.

"He's still breathing," Jean-Marc said.

"If he lives, it'll be because of that helmet," the swarthy man said. He and the others headed back to the rim of the hole, and we followed more slowly.

"Josette, run ahead and get a doctor or an ambulance worker," I said. "And a stretcher." She obeyed quickly.

Marc moaned and coughed, but he didn't open his eyes. He looked worse with each passing minute. "A blessing," I whispered urgently. "Give him a blessing! André, help me clear a place."

Jean-Marc laid our son on the ground, with his head cradled in my lap. No one paid attention to us as Jean-Marc reverently said the words of the prayer. No great claim of healing came, just the understanding that circumstances would depend on our faith.

As we finished, Josette returned with two ambulance workers and a stretcher. They worked over Marc, taking his vital signs and inserting an IV. Before taking him to the ambulance, they removed the roller blades and left them on the ground. Josette swooped them up and held them tightly to her chest, her face pale and strained. I noticed they were the new ones Jacques had sent at Christmas.

"Go with him," Jean-Marc said to me. "I'll bring the children along in the van." I cast him a grateful smile. Holding onto Marc's limp hands, I watched my family fade from sight through the small window in the back of the ambulance.

Upon arriving at the hospital, Marc's vital signs deteriorated rapidly, and the emergency room doctor rushed him into surgery. Despite my badgering, the nurses could tell me nothing of his condition. Details of the bombing filtered to me as I paced in the waiting room along with families of the other victims. Eight people were dead and thirty-three hospitalized, four of whom were in critical condition, including the beautiful woman Marc had risked his life to save. Nearly a hundred others had been treated for minor wounds and released.

Jean-Marc, Lu-Lu, and the children arrived. I felt some comfort in my husband's embrace, but without Marc's laughing face, the room felt empty. Josette still clutched the roller blades, and André's sullenness surfaced once again. Of the whole family, Pauline was the most calm. "Heavenly Father will take care of Marc," she said confidently.

"You don't *know* that," sneered André. It was the first time I had ever heard him talk that way to Pauline.

But she smiled, half mysteriously. "But I do. He always takes care of us."

"Like He did your parents!" André didn't wait for her reply but whirled and ran from us.

"He doesn't understand," Pauline said softly, staring after him.

"I'll try to find him," Jean-Marc said. "I'll be right back."

I nodded. "And I'll call my parents." But after waiting my turn at the pay phone, there was no answer in their apartment. I left a message on the machine and hung up.

The doctor came out from where he had been for over two hours with Marc. "We've stopped the internal bleeding," he told me. "Only there are some other complications." He paused and glanced briefly at the television in the room.

The camera crews showed some of the nearly two thousand policemen and soldiers with machine guns patrolling the streets from Paris to the western sea coast. Policemen stopped cars for random searches, and others erected large barricades around schools throughout all of France, fearing an attack similar to the one on a school in Lyon several years before. People avoided the subway stations, especially school children, causing the roads to be packed with both cars and pedestrians. Taxis were in constant use. The news reporter interviewed people on the streets near the bombing; excitement and fear vied for dominance in their faces.

"Marc's kidneys are severely damaged," the doctor continued, dragging his eyes away from the surrealistic report. "He's stable, and for now we can use dialysis, but we'll need to find a kidney for him."

"What!" My initial relief had turned to dismay. I couldn't believe I was hearing his words correctly. Marc had to be all right!

"When the cement from the bombing fell on him, it damaged his kidneys to such an extent that they cannot function. It also caused a great deal of internal bleeding, and frankly, I've seen less severe cases die on the operating table. But he's a strong boy, and I think he'll pull through."

"If we find him a kidney," Jean-Marc said, almost bitterly.

"Even without," the doctor clarified. "People can use the dialysis machine for months, but they are not the ideal. All his blood will have to be purified at least three times a week, and it's taxing for the body. He probably won't have the same energy as before, and the treatments will leave scars on his arms."

Lu-Lu nodded. "I knew a man who was on dialysis for a year and was scarred from his wrists clear up his arms, and even on his legs. It was horrible. They are deep and ugly scars, and to this day he won't wear a short-sleeved shirt because people stare and ask questions."

"She's right," the doctor said. "Dialysis has saved many lives, but it's not easy or pretty."

Josette let out a small cry, voicing my own turbulent emotions, and the doctor looked at her kindly. "I only tell you these things to prepare you. You'll learn a lot more along the way."

"What exactly does a kidney do?" Pauline asked.

"The kidney cleans and filters the blood, helps red blood cell production, regulates blood pressure, and several other things. It is vital to your body, but we can now use a machine to do some of the work the kidney usually does."

"Isn't there any other way to clean the blood?" I asked.

"There are portable machines, which are less expensive, but they are all just a temporary fix. Nothing is as good as a kidney."

"So how do we get a kidney?" I asked. Fear strengthened my resolve. Now that I knew my son was going to survive, I would somehow find the best for him. The faintness that had overcome me with the doctor's announcement was already vanishing.

"There are two ways you can go about this," the doctor said. "And, of course, you'll have to discuss the options with your own doctor as soon as you can. You can either find an organ donor from an accident victim or use a family donor. In the case of an outside donor, we put Marc on a waiting list and start praying. When a kidney becomes available, it is given to the patient whose tissues are the best match, meaning there is less chance for rejection. Of course, in any case immunosuppressive medications have to be taken for the rest of the patient's life. Rejection can occur suddenly, even after many years. The good news is that kidneys are the most common of transplants and are often the easiest to maintain."

I couldn't see anything easy or common in the situation. No one I ever knew had needed such a treatment. Despite my determination to be strong, I longed to cry until there were no more tears left.

"What about the people who died in the bombing?" Marie-Thérèse asked softly. "Could any of them be a match?"

The doctor lowered his voice. "I looked into that before coming to talk with you. Of the eight people who died in the accident, all but two are beyond transplant hope. Of those remaining two, one of the families refuses to let any organs be used, and the other has both kidneys already on the way to other hospitals for people who need them. But it's unlikely they would have been a decent match anyway, and they won't throw away a perfectly good kidney on someone who is likely to reject it. Marc's blood type is fairly rare, which complicates things. Are any of you the same blood type?"

"I am," Jean-Marc spoke up quickly, his face alight with hope. "I'll give him a kidney."

"Is there anyone else?" the doctor asked. "Though parents often give kidneys to their children, sibling donors are usually better matches."

"No." I shook my head. The girls, André, and I had a more common blood type.

"And they have to be at least eighteen," the doctor added. That would exempt all of the children, anyway.

"My mother has the same blood type," Jean-Marc said.

"How old is she?"

"Nearly seventy. But she's not in very good health. She has diabetes, among other things."

"Then she wouldn't be a likely candidate." The doctor smiled. "But *you* seem healthy enough."

"Can we see him?" Josette interrupted. It was what I wanted more than anything right then.

The doctor regarded her for a minute. "You must be his twin sister."

"Yes," she answered softly. "And it's my fault. I didn't stop him."

"You can't blame yourself," the doctor said. "He was awake before the operation and mentioned you. He said to tell you that he was wearing his helmet like he promised. Personally, I think that's what saved his life."

Tears dimmed my vision. Josette *had* taken care of Marc!

"You can see him for a few minutes," the doctor said, "but he won't really wake up for a couple of hours. Keep it quiet."

We waited until nearly midnight for Marc to awaken. Though he acted groggy and said little that made sense, at least he recognized us. We were all so grateful for his life that we knelt down right then and there, thanking our Father in Heaven. When Marc fell back to sleep, we left the hospital. Lu-Lu had gone on ahead with Pauline, but Marie-Thérèse and Josette had stayed with Jean-Marc and me. We had no idea where André was but hoped he had gone home.

"Ariana!" It was my father, coming toward us, seemingly out of nowhere. It surprised me that he hadn't come earlier.

"When did you hear?" Tears sprang to my eyes, and I wanted him to hold and comfort me as he had when I was a young child.

He came toward me, his unsmiling face gray under the stark white of his hair. Wrinkles stood out clearly on his brow and around his eyes. He looked older than I had ever seen him. "I'm sorry about Marc," he said. "I didn't know, or I would have come sooner. But that's not why I'm here." He paused before rushing on. "Your mother's missing. I've been searching for her for hours."

"But where could she be?" Now at least I understood why they had not been in contact.

"There was a message on the machine." His expression was pained. "She said that I loved the Church more than I loved her." Those were the same words my father had said to my mother when she had wanted to join the Church eleven years earlier. Now they had come back to haunt him.

"She's not here," I protested.

He frowned. "Not listed. But two of the bombing victims have not yet been identified."

My heart nearly stopped beating, and I felt the blood drain from my face. The all-too-vivid picture of the weeping bridegroom identifying his wife by her wedding ring came to my mind. My mother had left the café on foot shortly before the explosion. Depending on what she had done before heading to the subway, she might have been caught in the worst of the blast. Perhaps she had even paused that fateful few minutes to leave a message on the answering machine. No wonder my father appeared so ill!

No! I thought. *No!*

The possibility was too much for me to take. The room wavered and spun, and for the first time since I was eighteen and pregnant with my first child, I fainted.

CHAPTER ELEVEN

J ean-Marc must have caught me as I fell, for he was holding me as I awoke. A nurse waved a foul-smelling mixture under my nose. I opened my eyes and gasped, pushing her hand away. The girls and my father stared at me anxiously. Jean-Marc stroked my cheek. "I'm taking you home," he murmured in my ear.

"When was the last time you ate?" the nurse asked. "You've been here all evening with your son."

"I'm fine. But my mother . . ."

My father's jaw tightened. "I'll take care of that. I should have been more careful in telling you, what with Marc's accident and all. Don't worry, everything will be all right." He kissed my cheeks. "You go on home now, and let me worry about your mother."

Marie-Thérèse had found an apple somewhere and gave it to me. Jean-Marc and Josette helped me out to the van, though I felt all right now that the original shock was fading. At home, Pauline and André—who had gone home after all—slept peacefully in their beds, and Lu-Lu was in the guest room. We woke her up, but she had heard nothing from my mother. Jean-Marc offered a prayer, and we snuggled together in bed. To my surprise, I slept soundly and without bad dreams. When I awoke, Jean-Marc was in the kitchen, and my father was on the phone.

"They're not your mother," Jean-Marc said. "The burned bodies at the hospital. One turned out to be a man, and the other is wearing jewelry that isn't your mother's."

I sagged against him wearily. "Thank heaven!" Of course my mother was still missing, but she was a grown woman and could take care of herself. Most likely her anger toward my father had prompted her to stay at a hotel that night.

Later that morning, Jean-Marc and I met with a transplant specialist our regular doctor had recommended. Dr. Albert Juppe was about the same height as Jean-Marc but stocky, with plump fingers and black hair. As we entered his office, he sat back in his chair, seemingly relaxed; yet his intense black eyes showed concern for our son and love of his work, inspiring confidence. In a concise manner, he explained the specific details of kidney transplants. Because of his age and good health, Marc was an excellent candidate for a transplant, though he might have to wait for more than three years because of his rare blood type.

"You see," Dr. Juppe said, "there are several types of matching and tissue typing we must do to match a kidney with a recipient. One is blood type, and the rarer yours is, the longer you usually have to wait to find a match. Other typing can help determine which of the people on the list within the same blood type will be a better match for the donor kidney. One of these tests, called human leukocyte antigen typing, or HLA typing, is a blood test that determines if the two people involved have similar antigens."

"Antigens?" I asked.

"Yes. Each person has six different antigens, and we try to find as close a match as possible. Having all six match would be like having your identical twin give you one of his kidneys, and it doesn't happen often. A family member, especially a sibling, is generally a closer match than a total stranger. Though we can transplant when there are zero matches, the better the match, the less immunosuppression medication you have to take. In the case of the list, there are a number of factors involved, but Marc will most likely be waiting a long time.

"Your best bet would be a family donor," Dr. Juppe continued. "Though I have to tell you at this point that one of the patients at the hospital, who is in critical condition, seems to be a good match for Marc." He glanced at the papers in front of him. "A Madame Danielle Massoni, whose husband gave permission for me to talk with you about the case."

Massoni. The name was familiar to me, but I couldn't place why.

Dr. Juppe cleared his throat. "Danielle is listed as a future donor, though like Marc, one of her kidneys was irreparably damaged when the debris from the bombing fell on her. But because Marc is at this hospital, it is very possible he could receive her remaining kidney, especially if you talked to the family. Knowing you, they could request that the kidney be given to Marc."

"But she's not even dead!" I exclaimed. "How could we ask something like that?" I remembered how the doctor in the emergency room had told us we should pray once Marc was on the waiting list, but how could we pray for a kidney? How could we pray that someone else would die so that our son could live?

Jean-Marc shook his head. "It is something we could pursue," he said. "But we can't just wait for someone to die. I'll give Marc one of my kidneys. Surely I would be a better match for my son."

"Presumably. But we'll have to do a workup to make sure you're healthy, etc. That way if we need it, we'll be ready."

"Let's do it then," Jean-Marc said. "I want Marc well as soon as possible."

"The test results usually take about a week," the doctor cautioned. "But that'll be better for Marc, anyway, as he is too weak right now for a transplant." He paused, picking up a schedule on the desk with his thick fingers. "I have some time today for some of the tests if you're able."

"What is the success rate for the transplants?" I asked. The doctor had explained that while donating a kidney was generally safe, it still involved major surgery. We needed to be prepared in case Marc rejected my husband's loving gift.

"With living donors we have about 90 to 95 percent success in the first year as opposed to 85 percent with cadaveric donations," Dr. Juppe said. "Don't worry. We'll do everything we can to ensure that the transplant runs smoothly."

Before the tests, we drove to the hospital to visit Marc. It took longer than usual to make our way through the streets. Once, we were pulled over and our van searched by police. I didn't mind; I hoped they would find whoever was responsible for the bombing. Like many others, I had kept my children home from school for fear of more attacks. Josette and Marie-Thérèse were helping out at the café, more to keep themselves busy than anything else, and I had left André and Pauline at home with Grandma Louise.

At the hospital, Marc was more lucid than the previous night but still very weak. "I'm sorry," he said, as we entered the room.

I smiled, kissing his cheek. "Next time there's a bomb, run!"

"I'll keep that in mind," he said. Then a wide grin covered his bruised and scraped face. "But I saved that lady, you know. The nurses say she told them all about the boy with roller blades." The grin faded, and he strained slightly, as if trying to sit up, grimacing with the pain. "Only she's not doing so well now, and they're worried she's going to die. They say her husband's about crazy because of it and that her children can't do anything but cry. I'm not supposed to know, but I hear them talking. One nurse said she had a subdural hematoma, and they had to drill a burr-hole to fix it. Later, I asked the doctor what that meant, and he said it happens when someone gets a bad blow to the head. The hematoma grows and squishes the brain, and they have to put in a needle and let out the blood and stuff." He stared at us anxiously. "I don't want her to die! Will you help me pray for her?"

"Of course we will," Jean-Marc said. I nodded in agreement. I was proud of my son and his faith.

Marc sighed and relaxed. "Her name is Danielle Massoni."

I bit my lip and glanced over at Jean-Marc, but I saw he didn't recognize the name of the woman Dr. Juppe had told us could be a possible kidney donor. Was that why the name had seemed familiar? But I didn't remember Marc mentioning it before.

"We'll pray for her." I was happy I could say it and mean it. Because of Jean-Marc, we didn't need her kidney.

"I'm going to give you one of my kidneys," Jean-Marc said, punching Marc lightly on the arm. "Imagine that. You're going to have a piece of me inside of you!"

Marc chuckled. "I've been thinking about that since you mentioned it last night. That'll be twice you helped give me life."

Jean-Marc grinned. "I'm glad to do it." The love in his voice brought happy tears to my eyes. Even in the midst of this hardship, we were blessed.

I went back to the café to get some work done while Jean-Marc went for his tests. Upon arriving at the café, I sent the girls to the hospital to see Marc. Both went eagerly. Louise brought Pauline to the café shortly before dinner, but André had refused to come. Worry grew in my mind, but I had to push it aside. First I had to get through Marc's problems.

Many of the ward members came by the café to ask how Marc was doing. Not one had heard from my mother. Some of the women began planning fund-raisers to pay for the transplant. Thanks to Simone's hard work, our insurance had been reinstated; but there would be much it wouldn't cover. I was glad the Church members were there to offer support, because I couldn't deal with the problems alone. Each time I thought too deeply, a desperate fear—like the one I had felt on the day I had asked Jacques for help—came over me. But I had learned that fear wasn't constructive. I needed to focus on one thing at a time and go from there. Living in fear came from the devil, but trust in the Lord conquered those feelings.

Simone also stopped by the café to see how I was doing. "I'm beginnin' a fund for Marc's transplant at the college," she said.

I hugged her. "Thanks."

"Well, I'd best be gettin' along."

"Wait! Have you seen my mother?" Was it my imagination, or did she shift her weight nervously at the question?

"I've been at the hospital. She wasn't there." Glancing at her watch, she added, "I've got to go."

I watched her leave. *Why is she in such a hurry?* Probably she had a class to teach or, more likely, she wanted to see her boyfriend, Frédéric. She wasn't a blushing schoolgirl, but I knew she loved him.

Lu-Lu came in shortly after the girls returned from the hospital. "I wasn't fired," she announced. "It's strange, but no one really noticed I was gone. Philippe came back, but he didn't say anything about my not being there. Everyone thought we were together talking, so they never missed me."

"Did you get the promotion?" I asked.

She grimaced. "I doubt it. But the curious thing is that no one did, at least not yet. Philippe was supposed to call today with his recommendation, but he never did. I heard he was having family problems. One of the girls told me he and his wife were separating."

It seemed suspicious that Philippe's marriage was in trouble the day after Lu-Lu appeared on the scene. I couldn't help but think the two might be connected.

"Shall we go visit Marc?" Lu-Lu asked.

"Sure. Let's go."

Pauline went with us to the hospital but stayed only a short time in the room. Marc was sleeping, so there wasn't much to do but watch him breathe, as I had so done often when he was a child.

When we were ready to go, I kissed his forehead and went to find Pauline. She was reading a book in the waiting room.

"Let's go home," I said.

"I wish you had come sooner," she said. "There was a man here asking me questions."

I stiffened. "What about?"

She gazed at me innocently. "He was so sad, Mom. I asked him why, and he said his wife was dying and he felt bad. I told him he would see her again, and he asked me all sorts of questions about that. I told him the thirteen Articles of Faith." Her face beamed. "I remembered all of them, but I think I got the last one a little messed up. He didn't seem to care. He shook my hand and said thank you."

"That was all?" I asked suspiciously. Was this real or just another part of Jacques' plan?

Pauline nodded. "Except he showed me a picture of a little girl. She's only five." The corners of her mouth turned downward into a frown. "She's going to be so sad if her mother dies. I wanted to help her."

"Maybe you have," I said, hugging her. "Maybe you have."

We went by the café and picked up the girls and then drove home. All the lights in the apartment were on, and my father was pacing in the kitchen. Jean-Marc sat with André at the table.

"We've called everyone we know," my father said. "I just don't know where your mother is." He ran a hand through his short hair. "How can she do this to me?"

"Maybe she thought you wouldn't notice," I said softly.

He whirled on me, his dark eyes flashing. "How could she think that? I love her!"

"I'm not the one you should be telling." I glared back at him.

"Stop it, you two," Jean-Marc said. "Wait a minute." He slapped his forehead with his open palm, as if remembering something important. "There is one place I didn't think to look."

Hope blossomed on my father's gray face. "Where?" he demanded.

"Simone's."

I stared at him doubtfully. "I saw her today, and she didn't mention anything."

"Did you ask her directly?" Jean-Marc asked.

"Yes, but she said she'd been at the hospital and hadn't seen her." I hesitated. "Come to think of it, she did seem like she was avoiding answering me."

"Ah-ha." My father left the kitchen, stopping at the apartment door only to throw his long coat carelessly over his shoulders. But his steps faltered in the outside hall, and before the door closed, it was pushed open again as he backed into the entryway.

"What if she won't see me?" he asked, not turning to face us. "Why is she doing this?" Once it had been I who had gone to him for help; I wished I could help him now.

"I think you know," I said.

He shut his eyes, letting his head droop. "Maybe I do. But how do I fix it?" He didn't wait for an answer but slowly retraced his steps to the outer hall, shutting the door softly behind him.

"Look at that," André said mockingly. His sharp eyes had taken it all in. "This is what the Church does to people." Then he disappeared into the glaringly empty room he had once shared with his brother.

Jean-Marc followed him. I never knew what passed between them, but it made no apparent difference in André's attitude. Marc was still in serious condition, but I greatly feared it was André who needed the real help—a spiritual surgery we didn't know how to perform.

CHAPTER TWELVE

*T*he next day we went earlier than normal to the café to finish our work in time to be at the hospital for Marc when they hooked him up for a dialysis treatment. Slowly, the blood flowed into the machine to be purified and then back into Marc's body. He took it stoically, as he always had the unpleasant things in life, staring in fascination at the catheter entering the cut in the flesh of his arm, making a scar he would carry for life.

Jean-Marc paced. Seeing this process made him even more eager to give one of his kidneys to Marc. The doctor had promised to notify us as soon as the test results were ready, but I was in no hurry. According to the doctor, Marc wouldn't be strong enough for the operation for at least a week, perhaps a day earlier if his steady progress continued.

During the long process, I left and telephoned Simone. "Where is she?" I asked bluntly.

Simone sighed. "Okay, she's here. Your father already called, but she wouldn't talk to him."

"She'll talk to me. Put her on."

There was a brief pause as Simone obeyed. "Hi, Ari." My mother's voice sounded apologetic.

"You worried me," I said.

"I'm sorry. I just needed to get away. I feel bad that I haven't been there for you. I didn't hear about Marc until yesterday. Please forgive me?"

"Sure. But are you coming to see Marc?"

"Yes, this afternoon. We'll talk then, okay?"

I smiled, though she couldn't see me. "All right."

"I love you."

"I love you, too." I hung up, feeling happier now that I knew for sure where my mother was staying.

"Mother's at Simone's," I said to Jean-Marc as I reentered Marc's room.

"That figures. Simone always was kind of sneaky."

I laughed and settled on a chair next to Marc's bed. "At least Mother is safe. She's coming to see Marc later in the afternoon."

"Good," Marc said. "I miss her."

My husband gave Marc's leg a squeeze. "I've got a few things to fix at the apartments. And I'm going to talk with another bank today." He bent and kissed me on the cheek. "Take care of yourself. I'll be back later."

I wanted to question him about the bank where he was going, but each time I probed, he became distressed and slightly hostile—reactions stemming, I believed, from his insecurity. It was best to leave him be, to play a supportive role without asking for anything in return. Standing, I threw my arms around him. "I love you! Good luck."

A flash of gratitude touched his face. He kissed me. "Thanks, Ari." I watched him leave, my heart full of tender emotions toward him.

In the late afternoon, after the lengthy dialysis treatment was finished, I went to stretch my legs and get a drink of water in the waiting room. There, I overheard a couple of nurses talking about Danielle Massoni, the woman Marc had pulled from the rubble. Their news worried me. As I turned to go back to my son, a voice called to me.

"Mom!" Pauline skipped out of the elevator, followed by André and Lu-Lu. "Did you find Grandma?" Pauline asked.

I nodded. "She's at Grandma Simone's. She said she'd come by."

"How's Marc?" Lu-Lu asked. Pauline was already wandering down the hall to his room, but André stayed nearby. He stared dismally at an impressionist painting above the green couch, his eyes dark and intense.

"Doing really well," I said.

"Then why do you look so worried?"

I sighed. "It's that lady he saved. You know, the really beautiful one you carried to the ambulance?"

"Danielle. She said her name was Danielle."

"Well, she's not improving at all. She's slipped into a coma. I heard two nurses talking about it just now. I don't dare tell Marc."

"Have you met the family?" Lu-Lu asked.

I shook my head. "No. I haven't been here all that much, and when

I am, I'm in Marc's room. Pauline met the husband, I think yesterday evening. Remember that man she talked to? That must be him."

"So much devastation because of that bomb," Lu-Lu said. "It just isn't right. Pauline said he has a five-year-old daughter."

"Marc heard they have two children, a boy and a girl," I added.

We both sighed and turned to go down the hall when the elevator opened. "Dad," André said. "And Grandpa."

Jean-Marc and my father caught up with us, both wearing business suits. It had been so long since I had seen my husband dressed that way, except for church, that I looked at him twice. But it was my father's presence that occupied my thoughts. "Jean-Marc Perrault," I muttered under my breath. "You're setting up my parents. You know Mother is coming this afternoon."

A boyish grin filled his face, and his green-brown eyes twinkled. "The safest place for a meeting," he returned in a whisper. "After all, if a fight breaks out, we have doctors at hand."

I almost laughed aloud at the suggestion of my parents fighting physically. Their fights may have involved yelling or running away but never hitting or other physical abuse. "You're the one who'll probably get in trouble," I said. The words bounced off the white walls in the corridor and seemed to come back to me like a promise. I shrugged the odd feeling aside.

"They have to talk," Jean-Marc insisted. "Running away does no good. I know." He was right to some extent, but I knew that if my father hadn't been so stubborn, he would have listened before it reached this point. I pursed my lips and followed him into Marc's room.

"Wow, I'm getting popular," Marc said.

We laughed, all but André. "Where'd Dolly go?" His use of his pet name for Pauline didn't escape me.

Marc shrugged. "She said she wanted to visit a friend down the hall. Don't worry. She can take care of herself."

The room was comfortably crowded, but it became overwhelmingly so when the door swung open and my mother walked in. She wore her nearly white hair swept elegantly on top of her head to reveal the graceful curve of her neck. Beneath her open coat she wore a gray skirt and white blouse.

"Josephine!" My father took a step toward her.

She gripped her purse tightly. "Géralde."

"Where have you been?" Relief and anger played over his face before he squelched the emotions with a stern frown.

"Ari," my mother chided.

I raised my hands. "Don't look at me. Blame him." I pointed an accusing finger at Jean-Marc, whose grin matched Marc's.

"This is better than TV," Marc said from the bed.

The door opened again, and the room became even smaller when Dr. Juppe entered. "Uh, I'm glad to catch you here," he said. "I came to check on Marc, but I have news about your tests." His last words hung ominously in the air.

"What is it?" Jean-Marc said quickly.

Dr. Juppe glanced at my parents, but they made no move to give us privacy. "My parents," I explained.

He nodded and turned to Jean-Marc. "I'm afraid you can't give your kidney to Marc. All the results aren't in yet, but one thing is sure: one of your kidneys isn't working as well as it should. I can't fix it."

Jean-Marc's jaw clenched. "So, give the other to Marc. I'll live with the defective one."

The doctor shook his head. "It wouldn't be enough to keep you alive. I'm afraid we'll just have to wait for a donor, unless you have other friends and family to be tested." He continued, explaining the reason for the kidney's impaired function with medical names I didn't recognize. "The good news is that medication will prevent the same thing from happening to your other kidney," he finished.

The color had fled from Jean-Marc's face, leaving it as gray as my father's had been when he thought my mother was dead.

"I've put Marc on the list, but your quickest bet would be the patient I mentioned before. They don't think she'll last the night."

"You mean the lady Marc saved!" Lu-Lu said. "Danielle."

Marc's smile vanished. "She can't die! She can't! I don't want her kidney. I'll wait for another!"

Jean-Marc sighed heavily and slumped to a chair. "I'm sorry, Marc."

Marc turned his face away and squeezed his eyes shut. A single tear appeared in the corner of one eye.

The doctor left, and we sat there in gloomy silence. Jean-Marc looked up at me in utter defeat. "I've failed again, Ari."

I grabbed his hands. "It's not your fault! Don't worry. We'll find a kidney for Marc. Everything's going to be all right." I didn't know that for sure, but I had to be strong. This news had been a sharp blow to Jean-Marc's already damaged confidence.

"You couldn't have known," Lu-Lu added. "None of us could have." My parents moved forward, united in an instinctive desire to comfort us. An awkward silence fell as we struggled to accept this new information.

The door opened again, and this time Pauline appeared. But she was not alone; a tall, brown-haired man and two subdued young children stood with her. The youngest, a girl, had one hand in Pauline's; the other clutched his father's leg. Even after more than a decade, I still recognized the man's bleak face.

"Philippe!" Lu-Lu exclaimed.

"It *is* you," he breathed, his blue eyes boring into hers. "I wasn't sure, but I hoped when I found out Pauline's last name today."

"What are you doing here?" Jean-Marc asked, his voice hard.

Philippe nodded, as if he hadn't expected to be well received. He put a gentle hand on Pauline's shoulder. "I've been talking with Pauline here." He addressed us all, but he had eyes only for Lu-Lu. "She's an incredible little girl. I wish I could have understood that when I walked out all those years ago."

His words brought the memories back vividly. Lu-Lu had wanted to support her family during Paulette's AIDS crisis, had even wanted to help raise the premature Pauline. But Philippe had wanted nothing to do with a baby who had HIV.

"I was wrong," Philippe continued, "about a lot of things." His voice broke. His moist eyes rose to include the rest of us. "But I came to ask your help. My wife's dying. She was in the bombing. She's in a coma now, and they say she's not going to make it. But Pauline here," he cast a grateful look at my daughter, "reminded me of how her mother was healed long enough to give birth to her. Please," he begged in a wavering voice, "I don't want my children to lose their mother. God knows I haven't been good to her, but I know I was wrong. I knew the minute I saw you at the bank. You brought it all back." He made a tentative step toward Lu-Lu. Once again he spoke only to her. "I lost you eleven years ago, just as I'm losing her now, and it was my fault. *I'm* the one who needs to change. And now it's too late—unless your family will give her a blessing. Even after all these years, I've never forgotten the feeling I had when your brother gave his sister-in-law that blessing, though heaven knows I've tried. But that blessing saved Paulette, and she was able to give birth to Pauline. I want that blessing for my wife. Please, can you forgive me enough for that? If not for me or for her, then for our children?"

Once Philippe had denied the miracle of the priesthood, and now he asked for its blessing.

The little girl and boy stared up at us with their sad gray eyes. Both had auburn hair and high cheekbones, probably inherited from their mother, though I could see Philippe's handsome features in their faces as well. I wanted to help them and save their mother, even if it meant Lu-Lu would never have another chance with Philippe. But there was something else complicating the matter. Danielle Massoni, the woman whose death would save my son months of torment and even his life, the same woman my son and later Lu-Lu had tried to save, was none other than Philippe Massoni's wife. Now I knew why her last name had seemed so familiar to me.

"Your wife is Danielle," I said. Lu-Lu gasped and held her hand to her heart.

Philippe nodded. "Please, will you help?"

Marc's tears ceased, and he responded eagerly. "Oh, Dad, please. I don't want her to die. I can stand the dialysis for a while longer. I'm not a girl; I don't care about the scars. I don't want her kidney! Please give her the blessing!"

"*He's* the boy who needs the kidney?" Philippe said, the color draining from his face. "I didn't know."

"He's our oldest son," I said.

Philippe nodded. "Marc, isn't it? I remembered he was named after his father." His eyes flicked to Jean-Marc and then away quickly. He didn't say another word but simply waited.

"Well?" Marc demanded, staring at his father.

Jean-Marc lumbered to his feet, sighing wearily. "Of course we'll give Danielle a blessing." He glanced at my father, who nodded sharply, his face drawn and tense.

Pauline smiled in her innocence. "See, I told you they would bless her. Grandpa 'specially likes to bless people. He almost never comes over to see me, because he's always doing it."

My father's mouth opened slightly in protest, but he didn't speak. Surprise, with a touch of sadness, lingered in his expression.

"I'll pay you anything you ask," Philippe said, dormant hope springing to life in his face. "Anything at all. I know that won't make up for the kidney, but it should help find a new one." It seemed as if he was almost begging. I wondered if he was trying to ensure that they would give him a real blessing and not just lip service. How little he knew about the gospel—or my husband!

Jean-Marc's eyes met his. "No," he said firmly. "The priesthood is not for sale. Not now or ever." He glanced back at Marc before continuing. "It's not even ours but was given to us by God to bless those in need. If I refused to bless your wife, I would be refusing my God." His voice sounded rough against my ears. "And I cannot do that."

"Not even to save your own son?" Philippe asked. Curiosity had dampened some of the obvious fear he felt for his wife.

Jean-Marc's face saddened, and he glanced in my direction. "Marc will be fine," I said. "We have our faith."

Philippe nodded. "Then you have more than I."

"That's not true." I took a step in his direction. "You came to us and asked for a blessing. That's a beginning of faith."

Uncertainty crossed his features, softening the bleakness. "Perhaps you're right."

"She is," Jean-Marc said.

Philippe had always excelled in convincing others to his way of thinking, but even so it took some long, hard talking to get us all, Marc included, into his wife's room for the blessing. Marc's eyes danced with enjoyment as he watched Philippe negotiate with the nurses. Finally, they moved Marc to a portable bed, and we rolled him into the room.

Danielle lay deathly still, her striking face marred by the many bruises and the heavy bandaging on her head, but for the first time I noticed her resemblance to Lu-Lu. Her hair was long, but the auburn color was nearly that of my sister-in-law's. That Lu-Lu used hair dye to achieve the effect on her normally dark brown hair made no difference in the end. Danielle's build and rounded face also mirrored Lu-Lu's, and I remembered that she too had striking eyes, though of a different color.

The two women might be taken as sisters. Could that be why Philippe had chosen Danielle? Did he still love Lu-Lu?

I glanced at Philippe. He watched his wife with obvious concern, but his gaze occasionally rested on my sister-in-law, soft and regretful. She eyed him in the same manner and appeared close to tears. I wished I could take her away from there, but I knew by the stubborn set of her jaw that she was determined to see this experience through.

"I'll anoint," said Jean-Marc.

My father regarded him silently for a long moment. "I think you should give the blessing. It was you Philippe asked. I wasn't even a member when Paulette died." They both glanced at Philippe, who nodded anxiously.

"All right," Jean-Marc agreed. I saw that he was reluctant, but I knew he wouldn't let his personal feelings for Philippe color the words—at least he would try not to let that happen.

After the anointing, he began slowly and hesitatingly. He told Danielle that the Lord was aware of her trials and had heard her many tearful pleadings. He promised her that she would be made well. It was a simple blessing, shorter than Jean-Marc's usual, but powerful all the same.

"That's it?" Philippe asked.

"Now it's up to our faith." Jean-Marc bent down until he was at eye level with Danielle's children. "Do you believe in Jesus?" Both children darted a frightened glance in their father's direction, disclosing that this had been a point of contention in their parents' relationship.

When Philippe said nothing, the little girl meekly replied, "Yes."

"That's good," said Jean-Marc, "because He does exist, and He loves you! Do you believe that?" This time both children nodded. "Then I promise you He will make your mommy well." Without another word, he stood and left the room. André followed him, a dark expression on his face. Lu-Lu and my mother were in tears, and even Marc, flat on his bed, looked misty-eyed. In another situation, I might have teased him.

"Oh, you big baby," Pauline said, laying her cheek against her brother's. "I told you she wasn't going to die, but you just didn't listen." Marc nearly choked with laughter.

"Thank you, Pauline," Philippe said. His voice was steady, and his face showed no sign of tears, yet I sensed he had been touched. "Thank you all." We left the family alone, Lu-Lu staring over her shoulder long after the door had closed behind them.

Both Jean-Marc and André had vanished, and I hoped they were together. The revelations of the day had not been easy on any of us but even less so on them. Jean-Marc blamed himself for his inability to help Marc, and I knew this was one more thing André would blame on the Church. And I could understand his response. A blessing to save Danielle's life would necessarily deprive his brother of the organ he needed. The paradox didn't seem fair. Even within myself I sensed a struggle, but I felt content that we had done everything we could do. Now Danielle's life was in the hands of the Lord.

We settled Marc in his room. He looked tired and satisfied. "I want to sleep now," he said with a grin. "So go home!"

"You don't have to kick us out," Pauline protested. I laughed, but my parents and Lu-Lu were silent, each intent on their inner thoughts.

"Are you coming home, Josephine?" My father waited until we stood in front of the elevator doors in the deserted waiting room before asking the question.

"I don't know," she said, not meeting his gaze. "I think that depends on you."

My father paced, flexing his hands. "I'm trying to do my best. You know how much I've longed to retire so that I could dedicate myself to the Lord. It's just that there's so little time left for me to help people recognize the truth!"

"But you work too hard! And don't give me that line about it being only this last year. You've been this way ever since you were baptized. How many times did you spend your evenings tracting with the missionaries? Supervising them? How many times have you stayed out all night counseling people who are perfectly capable of handling their own problems? You don't have time to eat—you've lost weight."

"Me? Who cares about me?"

"I do! You'll work yourself into the grave."

"But I'm already baptized. I know the truth. It doesn't matter if I die."

My mother sniffed. "It matters to me—or doesn't that mean anything?"

"That does mean something, but I am not as important as they are."

"Yes, you are, Grandpa!" Pauline had been listening to their argument with increasing dismay. "You told me when I was baptized that I was special to Jesus because I accepted Him. So that means you're special, too! Jesus loves you. He doesn't want you to die from so much work!"

"She's right, Father," I said. "We have accepted the covenant, and the Lord loves us even more for doing so. But I think He would want you to take time to smell the roses. After all, He made them for us, didn't He?"

My father scanned the circle of faces. "Maybe you're right."

"I always thought," my mother said, "that the Church is supposed to be important in your life but never above your own family. Above me. Dedication to the Lord is one thing, but Church work comes after your family. I just want to spend more time with you, that's all."

"I'm supposed to treat my wife as the Lord did His Church," my father mused. A sigh escaped him. "Oh, what have I done?"

My mother hugged him, and Pauline, Lu-Lu, and I joined in. "This is nice," he murmured. We embraced for a moment more and then separated, staring at each other in the awkwardness that always seems to follow an emotional display.

"Why hasn't this blasted elevator come?" Father asked.

I hid a smile. "It helps if you push the button."

"Yeah, but we didn't want to disturb you," Lu-Lu added.

Pauline giggled. "I'll do it!"

We rode down the two floors in comfortable silence. When the doors banged open, we found Jean-Marc and André waiting in the lobby.

Jean-Marc jumped toward us. "Is Marc okay?"

"Yes," I returned. "In fact, better than okay. He said to thank you."

A touch of irony marked his next words. "Thank me?" he mumbled. "When I took his two best chances away?"

I grabbed onto his hands. "You did what you had to do."

"I know. But that doesn't make it any easier."

My father coughed. "What do you say we go and buy some roses?"

"What?" Jean-Marc asked.

Father put his arm around my husband's drooping shoulders. "I've got a mind to smell them, Jean-Marc. Didn't you know the Lord made them for us to smell?"

"Of course," Jean-Marc replied, recapturing some of his former cheerfulness. "Did you think that He said, 'Hmm, I think I'll make a few people to take care of those roses'?"

This evoked a smile, even from André.

"Come on," I said. "Let's go home."

CHAPTER THIRTEEN

In the morning Danielle Massoni regained consciousness, and during the next week she slowly recuperated. As the swelling and bleeding in her brain diminished, the doctors declared a miracle. By contrast, Marc's health deteriorated. Except for the kidneys, his internal wounds healed, but he lacked the energy that had characterized him. The marks on his arms from the dialysis were deep and ugly. He said he didn't mind, but at times I caught him staring at them with a wistful expression. Despite his weakness, the doctor allowed him to go home after seven days, as long as he promised to take things slowly.

We went back to work or to school, except for Marc, who needed to recover further before he would be allowed to return to his normal schedule. While on dialysis, he had to adhere to a strict diet, and this depressed him further. Louise stayed with him during the time we spent at work. Jean-Marc and I talked about getting him a portable dialysis machine which could cleanse his blood as he slept and which the doctor claimed was less taxing on his system. The expense was exorbitant. Money was an increasing problem, though the fund-raisers were well underway. Each day I prayed for Marc, but even as I did, I pictured the devastation another family would feel if my prayer were answered.

On Monday, a week and a half after the bombing, my father came into the café alone. He walked with an air of confidence and vitality, and his face appeared rested.

"Where's Mother?" I asked, looking up from the small desk in the office where I worked on the café finances.

A smile stretched his lips. "Getting her hair done," he said. "I think she's had enough of togetherness for a while."

I laughed. My father had a tendency to overdo things, and it would take time for my parents to come to a happy medium. "How are the members you've been working with?"

"Fine," he said. "I still call them every day, but I only see them once a week. The odd thing to me is that they actually seem to be doing better without so much . . ."

"Interference?" I supplied.

He smiled wryly. "I guess so. I think I'm realizing that even after everything I do for them, they will have to make the choice to follow the Savior. I can't force them to be good the rest of their lives."

"Like with our children." The burdens of the past few months weighed heavily upon me, and I sometimes wished I could curl up in bed and stay there without moving for a week.

His gaze became sympathetic. "André will find his way. He's very young yet."

I blinked back the tears. "Will he? Somehow I keep wondering what I could have done to prevent this. He was always such a good, undemanding child. Did I neglect him? Pauline was so demanding as a young child; in caring for her, did I overlook his needs? I always tried to be fair. What could I have done differently?"

"Don't, Ari." He leaned over and covered my hand with his. "I tortured myself with those same questions when you were a teenager. The fact is, it doesn't matter what we could have done; it's what we do now that we need to worry about."

He was right. Worrying about the past wouldn't change the present, and doing so would only waste precious energy. I needed to concentrate on loving my little boy and bringing him back to himself.

My father glanced at his watch. "I'd better get back to your mother. I just wanted to see how you were doing."

I smiled. "Thanks, Father." It meant more than I could say to have him back in my life once more—with his heart and not merely the occasional physical display he had offered in recent years.

Laying my head down on the desk, I prayed long and hard. The next thing I knew, Lu-Lu was shaking me. "Wake up, Ariana! Wake up! Are you okay?"

I tried to push her hand away. "I'm fine. I must have fallen asleep. Would you please quit shaking me?" The violent motion threatened to topple me over. The room whirled.

"Sorry." Her hand dropped. "I only have a few minutes on my lunch break, and I had to talk with you."

"So talk," I said, yawning into my hand. The nap had made me feel considerably better; I hoped the Lord would excuse my interrupted prayers.

"I got the promotion," Lu-Lu announced.

"Well, that's great, isn't it?"

"I started yesterday. I'm head of business accounts. I'll be working with Philippe each day." Her voice had taken on an indeterminate note, as if she couldn't make up her mind whether working with Philippe was a blessing or a curse.

"Is that a problem?" I asked gently.

She began to pace in front of the desk, occasionally bumping into the other chair, though she appeared oblivious to it. "His wife is coming home from the hospital," she said, pretending indifference. "At first I thought he gave me the job because he was grateful for the blessing, but sometimes when he looks at me, I get all shaky inside and I want to . . . to . . ." She sat abruptly in the chair, and all signs of pretense fled from her demeanor. "Oh, Ari! Can I still love him after all these years? And he me? What about his wife and those two adorable children? So help me, I think sometimes it would have been better if—" She broke off, staring at me aghast.

"If she had died?"

"Oh, what have I become, Ari?" Her head flopped onto the desk, cradled in her hands. "Dear Lord," she muttered, "forgive me!"

I grabbed her hands from beneath her face, forcing her to look at me. "I'm sorry, Lu-Lu. I really am."

"I wished I'd never met Danielle. Or seen Philippe again. It only reminds me of what I can never have!" She pulled away from my grasp, sprang to her feet, and ran from the office.

"Wait!" I called. But she was already gone.

Lu-Lu's overt loneliness and longing had called up a melancholy I couldn't explain, and I felt like crying. "The beginnings of a midlife crisis," I said aloud. In about a month and a half, I would be forty. I sighed.

"Would you like some lunch?" Dauphine asked, holding out a platter with a bowl of soup and a large roll.

Suddenly I felt ravenous. "Yes," I said eagerly, "but you needn't serve me."

She smiled. "I wanted to. You've been under a lot of stress lately, and you're looking peaked." She set the platter on my desk. "You have to keep up your strength for the family."

I heard the genuine concern in her voice. "Thanks, Dauphine. You're a good friend."

"I know." She turned on her heel and went back to work. I heard many customers coming in, but Annette had already arrived, and with Hélène, they could easily handle the lunch crowd. If not, they would call me.

I bit into the fresh-baked roll, which tasted like a slice of heaven. Since working in the café, I hadn't had to worry about feeding my family; there wasn't a shortage of food anymore. With all the delicious array, both Jean-Marc and I had gained a few kilos, even with all the tension of his not finding a job. The stout Marguerite would be happy.

"At least we'll die fat," Jean-Marc had joked. Being a woman, I hadn't found the comment particularly humorous.

"Hello," said a cheery voice. I looked up to see Ken standing in the open door, his red hair seeming even brighter in the stark light of my office. "Got room for one more?" He carried a plate of food in his hand.

"Sure. Come on in." I motioned for him to set his food on the desk.

He took a bite and swallowed before speaking. "How are you holding up?"

"Good. How is your family?"

"Fine."

We sat in silence for a long time, both concentrating on our meal, and then Ken dropped his fork onto his fast-emptying plate with a clatter. "I don't know why I'm here, actually. I just felt I should come." Through the door, I saw Hélène bringing a new pot of soup to the front counter.

"I'm glad to have you." It wasn't unusual for him to come to the café; he often ate here. Of late, he and many others in the ward had taken to coming to the café to see how we were faring, and I appreciated their support.

The vegetable soup was perfect, not too spicy, not too bland. I enjoyed it immensely. The peace echoed silently in the room, and I nearly jumped when the heavy black phone on the desk rang shrilly.

"Hello?" I hoped it was my mother. I wanted to talk with her about adding her special birthday cake to my menu.

"Hi, Ari." It was Jean-Marc.

"How'd it go?" I asked. He had been to an interview that morning and then taken Marc for his dialysis treatment.

"Not well," he said. His voice sounded strained.

I sighed. Jacques and the shortage of high-paying jobs had really worked against Jean-Marc. "Maybe next time." I made my voice purposely light.

"It's not that, Ari. It's Marc."

My heart beat faster. "What happened?"

"He collapsed before they could do the treatment. They don't seem to know why. They got him on the bed and conscious again, but they've had to admit him. They think it might be the injuries from the bombing. He seems a little better now, but . . ." What he left unspoken was his fear, but I knew him well.

"I'll be right there," I said. "Wait for me."

"I've got so much to do at the apartments. There are two showers that need fixing, and . . ."

"It doesn't matter. I'll find help." I hung up the phone and sprang to my feet.

"It's Marc," I said in answer to Ken's silent question. "He's had a setback. They don't know why."

"I'll come with you."

"Do you know how to fix showers?"

He smiled a bit crookedly. "Of course. I'm a teacher with eight children; I've had to learn to be self-sufficient. Tell me about these showers while I drive you to the hospital. Come on. My car's outside." Since Jean-Marc had our van, I didn't protest. I was grateful for Ken's company.

We reached the hospital and found Marc sleeping in his room, with Jean-Marc pacing outside. His face was tortured. "Why did this have to happen?" he asked. I knew he really didn't need an answer, so I hugged him. Ken did the same.

"Would you give him a blessing?" Jean-Marc asked Ken. That he didn't want to do it himself showed the great stress he was under. His self-doubt was showing clearly.

"I would be honored." Ken's clear blue eyes were full of compassion.

The two men gave Marc a blessing, and Ken left, saying he would take care of our showers as soon as he taught his last class that afternoon. The blessing comforted me somewhat, but the doctor's words weren't encouraging.

"I wish we could get him a kidney," he said. "He simply isn't doing well on dialysis. As good as dialysis has become, a working kidney is about ten times more effective, and a lot less time-consuming. And with his recent injuries, I'm particularly worried about his getting an infection that would make it so he couldn't use the dialysis at all." I knew that would result in death, and I scarcely heard the doctor's next words. "And since there is a history of diabetes on your husband's side of the family, that could also cause complications if it were to manifest in Marc. Besides, he's young. He shouldn't have to live off a machine. I absolutely feel he would be better off with a kidney. Do you have any friends who might be willing to donate? Maybe members of your church group?"

"I don't know," I said. "Is it that serious?" I had thought a patient could go twenty years or more on dialysis, or at least until the technicians couldn't get access into the body because of collapsing veins or excessive scar tissue. This new information was startling and unwelcome, and I was afraid to learn the ugly details. Before, I had simply focused on the twenty years as a cat grabs at a frail piece of yarn, but that was no longer possible.

The doctor nodded. "I feel it would be best. Like I said before, I'm worried about potential infection."

Marc looked so helpless in the bed, made even more so because of his relaxed state. I could almost see in his stead the little boy he had been. I loved him more than I could express, and my heart ached at seeing him so ill.

"I wish it could have been me in that explosion instead of him," Jean-Marc said, voicing my own thoughts. "I keep wishing I could turn back the clock and change things." But we couldn't. Marc would have to suffer for his brave impulsiveness, regardless of our futile desire to protect him.

Before going home, we stopped at the café to pick up the children. Annette was busily cleaning the last dishes in the kitchen prior to locking up. Pauline and André sat at one of the tables staring at some schoolbooks, and Josette and Marie-Thérèse were arguing near the counter.

"He asked *me* out," Marie-Thérèse said in her reserved way. "Not you."

"That's because Mom won't let me go," Josette taunted. "But just wait until next week—that's ten more days, not counting today. Then I'll be sixteen, and he'll have nothing more to do with you!"

"He wouldn't want you with the games you play!" Marie-Thérèse shouted, finally losing her temper. Though she was attractive, she had none of the radiant passion that was Josette's, and today she was obviously feeling the lack. From my point of view, Marie-Thérèse was much better off; she would be loved for who she was, not for her appearance. Yet I figured it would be many years before either girl would learn this lesson.

"You big—"

"Girls," Jean-Marc interrupted. They both started. We had come in through the front door, but their discussion was so heated they hadn't noticed us.

"You have a date?" I asked Marie-Thérèse.

She nodded. "With Kenny."

I pictured Ken's oldest child. At least he wouldn't be a lasting problem between the two girls, because the family would be returning to America at the end of the college semester.

"It's just because I can't go!" Josette asserted, turning to me. "And it's your fault. If you didn't love her more than you love your own flesh and—"

"That's enough!" I declared. "Marie-Thérèse is every bit as much my daughter as you are. And love has nothing to do with why you won't be allowed on dates until you're sixteen. I don't want to hear this argument again. Ever. Or you will wait until you're eighteen for your first date!"

Josette looked abashed, if not completely repentant, and I knew she would comply with my order. She talked big but ultimately wanted our approval. As yet I didn't worry overly about her going behind my back. As vocal and headstrong as she could be, she was rarely secretly rebellious. I suspected she worried privately about hurting me. She had always been protective in her passionate way.

"We need to talk with you," Jean-Marc said. "It's about your brother."

More tension entered the room. Pauline slammed her book shut and jumped up from the table. "Is he all right? I dreamed last night that he was gone and I couldn't find him. But there he was when I woke up."

I crossed to where she stood and placed a comforting arm around her. "He got sick again. He has to stay in the hospital a few days. He needs a kidney."

"I wish I could give him mine," she said sadly. Of course there was no chance of that, even had she been the same blood type and the required eighteen years old. Exchanging kidney failure for HIV infection wasn't an option.

"We should have let that lady die," André muttered.

"What!" Jean-Marc and I exchanged shocked glances.

"Then Marc would be home and everything would be fine," he insisted. "It's all your fault, Dad. You shouldn't have blessed her."

"Then those two little children wouldn't have a mother!" I said. "What about them?"

"I don't care." But his eyes showed his pain.

Jean-Marc looked at his son for a long time. "I know this is a difficult situation. And I understand how you feel. Don't you think I feel the same way?"

André stared at the ground, but he appeared to be listening.

"What happened was the Lord's will," Jean-Marc continued. "I couldn't change it. At least you understand that without the blessing, the woman would have died. Doesn't that show you God lives and loves His children?"

"What about Marc?" André didn't raise his head.

"Can you trust in the Lord a little longer?" asked Jean-Marc.

"I don't know." This time there were tears in my son's voice.

"Then just trust in me. And in your mother."

"Okay," came the mumbled response.

The crisis of the moment ended, we piled in the van and drove home.

CHAPTER FOURTEEN

*T*he next few days we spent hours on the phone, calling every-one we knew about finding a kidney. We called old friends like René and Elisabeth in Bordeaux; Monique, the nurse who had intro-duced me to the gospel; and Colette, Marguerite's niece. None of them had the same blood type. "I'm so sorry," each said. "If I could give my kidney, I would do so gladly."

Each time I hung up the phone I grew more depressed, but I con-soled myself with the knowledge that these old friends and their grow-ing families had remained strong in the gospel and in their commitment to the Lord. In the days that followed, donations toward Marc's future transplant flooded in from them, tangible symbols of their love and support.

In our desperation, we turned to newspaper ads. A few people came forward, but the only tissue matches were a man who had high blood pressure and a woman who had diabetes, both of whom were dis-qualified. In our ward were several children who had the same blood type, as well as two pregnant women, leaving us exactly where we had started. Outside our circle of family and friends, we found little sup-port. Finding a kidney simply didn't have the importance of finding a liver or other organ that was immediately needed to sustain life.

Marc was released from the hospital after only two days and seemed to be growing stronger. He was depressed, however, and dreaded the dialysis treatments. The loss of his smiles and good-natured quips was the most difficult for me to take. I threw myself into finding him a kid-ney, but discouragement slowly ate at my determination.

"Is there anyone you've forgotten?" asked Ken. He and Kathy were at our house visiting on Wednesday evening. They had come with Kenny, who had taken Marie-Thérèse to see a movie, leaving behind a glowering Josette. "I've written home to Provo but haven't had any luck. Marc's blood type doesn't match those who are willing. People are very concerned about losing a part of themselves. What if they should come to need it later in life?"

"I can't fault them," I said. "Before this happened, I wouldn't have wanted to do it for someone I didn't know."

Jean-Marc shook his head. "Me either. I guess we just have to wait for one from the waiting list."

"I can't bear to think that he'll have to endure this for perhaps years," I said. "Having to depend on a machine for the rest of his life. What a waste of precious time. He's only fifteen!"

"If only—" Jean-Marc broke off. I knew he felt guilty for being unable to help Marc himself.

"It's not your fault," I said for the millionth time. "It's just chance. I mean, I could have been born with the same blood type. It would have simplified matters." Thinking about this brought another paradox to light. My first daughter, Nette, had been the same blood type as Marc. If she had lived, perhaps she would have been able to donate, and we wouldn't be in this bind. Then again, if she hadn't died, I would not have joined the Church when I did or met and married Jean-Marc, meaning Marc would never have been born. So the point was moot.

Or was it?

At that moment, an intense revelation shot through me—a burst of pure understanding I had overlooked. Nette had been the same blood type as Marc—and she hadn't gotten it through me! I gasped, standing abruptly. Without excusing myself from our guests, I ran from the sitting room and down the hall to my bedroom. I threw open the fire-damaged cedar chest where I kept Nette's memories. Hands shaking, I fumbled for medical papers two decades old.

I began to cry with relief.

"What is it?" Jean-Marc had followed me, concern written on his face.

"Nette had the same blood type as Marc," I said bluntly. "She got it from Jacques."

"Him!" Jean-Marc's exclamation held disbelief and anger.

I looked up into his eyes, pleading. "He told me he would do anything for me. *Anything*. Why not this?"

"Not Jacques. Anyone but him."

Now it was my turn to become angry. "Marc's our son! I'm as reluctant to ask Jacques for anything as you are. But we can't let this chance for Marc slip by, can we?"

"Can you imagine how Marc would feel, knowing he had a piece of your first husband inside him?" Revulsion filled his voice.

"We might have to wait for more than three years to find a match. Three years! Can you watch Marc hooked up to a machine for that long when there's another alternative? How will *that* affect him? And what about the infection the doctor mentioned? I think if we handle it openly, Marc won't care about Jacques being the donor. At least he'll know another person didn't have to *die* to give him a chance at a better quality of life."

My husband sat wearily on the bed, the fight dying in his eyes. "Do you miss him, Ari?" he asked me softly. "Do you miss the life he could give you?"

I stared at him aghast. "How could you ever think such a thing?"

His face was a mask of sorrow. "I never did before. He wasn't important in our lives. But now it comes to me that you were married to this man, slept with him, had his child, and even loved him."

I took his words literally. "I didn't suspect that you were holding my past against me like this." A bitter taste invaded my mouth.

He jumped up and grabbed my hands. "No. Never that, Ari! You were more beautiful and pure on the day we married than any other bride on earth or in heaven." He paused, sucking in a deep breath. "It's me. I can't help but wonder if he wouldn't have made you a better husband in the long run. If maybe you wouldn't rather have him as the father of your children, have him holding you at night. You did love him once. And before me." His voice broke on the last word, as if he couldn't bear to think of it.

"The love I had for Jacques was simply the need of a love-starved child," I said, feeling the passion with which I meant the words. "I was a *child*. That was all. I chose you, and you are my life now. You can't denounce our love or yourself because of what happened so long ago. I love *you*."

"Then don't go to him, Ari." There was pain in the words.

I had never expected to have to choose between my husband and my child. The two should always be on the same side. Then a thought occurred to me. With the dialysis, Marc was not in immediate danger of dying; there was still time for Jean-Marc to change his mind—at least as long as the infection the doctor worried about never appeared.

I touched his face, running my fingers over the six o'clock shadow on his chin. "All right." But inside, I was still upset that he could put his feelings before our child.

He seemed relieved, and yet at the same time I sensed his guilt increase. I could not change that; Jean-Marc would have to deal with his own demons.

The next few days did not alter Jean-Marc's attitude. Each time Marc went for his lengthy dialysis treatments, his father was at his side. I knew it relieved some of his imagined culpability. I didn't go with them because each time the sight would make my stomach churn, and I would become lightheaded. In some odd way, Marc's discomfort became my own.

At the café on Friday, five days before the twins' birthday, my head and heart felt heavy. I had finished the accounts for the week, but I had no desire to go home to an empty house. Jean-Marc was at the dialysis center with Marc, and the children were in school. I shut the door to my office and sobbed as quietly as possible to prevent Dauphine and Hélène from hearing.

I didn't understand my feelings. There was a great deal wrong with my life, but even more had gone right. Pauline hadn't had any more tumors or odd illnesses since beginning the protease inhibitors, the ward had raised a great deal of money for Marc's transplant, and we were paying the bills with our part of the profits from the café and apartment building. It wasn't the living to which we were accustomed, but our family was together, and we always had the hope of eternity.

A brisk knock at the door jolted me from my self-pity. I wiped the tears quickly with my fingers and the backs of my hands and made my way to the door. My mother, dressed in a loose smock, more casual than her normal attire, stood in the kitchen. Hélène, at the stove, cast a brief eye in our direction but, seeing my face, glanced hurriedly away.

"Come in, Mother," I said.

"You've been crying." Crossing to my desk, she pulled a couple of tissues out of the box on the desk and began to wipe under my eyes. Black mascara stained the soft white. "What's wrong?"

"The same. I think I'm mostly just tired or maybe getting a cold. I don't seem able to cope as well as I should."

"You're doing fine, given the circumstances. You can't be strong every minute." She dabbed a bit more at my face and then surveyed me. "There, now you look better." She paused before asking, "Has Jean-Marc changed his mind about approaching Jacques?" My mother was the only person I had told about the discovery and the ensuing confrontation with Jean-Marc.

"No," I said sadly. "I haven't asked him. But maybe he's right."

"I don't agree. Marc has to be put first."

I said nothing, not knowing what she expected of me.

"Why don't you go home and take a nap?"

"I like to be here for the lunch rush, in case they can't handle it. Annette sometimes gets out of class late."

"She's already arrived. And I can be here, just in case."

"You?" I asked incredulously.

"Don't look surprised. I've come to make a few cakes, as you suggested." Pulling her purse from her shoulder, she fished out a large apron. She shook it out and tied it over her dress. Now I understood why she was outfitted so casually. Mother was going to bake.

"But where's Father?"

"Out visiting."

I raised my eyebrows. "Back to his old ways?"

"No," she said, seeming embarrassed. "He's doing everything I could ask of him, but—" she bit her lip—"I realized that it wasn't just his fault, our problems. I need to have something to interest me besides him. Just because we're old doesn't mean we have to sit around in our rocking chairs and stare at each other."

I grinned despite my dark mood. "Good for you."

"Now go home and rest," she countered, kissing my cheeks. "Things will be all right here."

I did as she asked, but on the way home I stopped briefly at the cemetery to place a rose at Nette's grave. Not wanting to risk meeting Jacques again, my visits had been irregular and never on my accustomed

Wednesday. A bouquet of white roses already graced the base of the tombstone, revealing that Jacques had come within the past few days. *If only Jean-Marc would agree to let me ask Jacques!* Of course, I could go without his approval; but I felt that to do so would risk our marriage, and I couldn't bear to do that.

Why did everything have to be so complicated?

Pondering the problem only added to my frustration, and I gave it up willingly. Instead, I drove home, kicked off my shoes, and curled up in bed, not bothering to remove my white blouse or brown linen jumper. I had been home for less than two hours when a sound woke me from a restless sleep. I yawned and walked down the hall, my stockinged feet making no noise on the soft carpet. Immediately the voices of my husband and oldest son came to me.

"I'm a little tired," Marc was saying. "I think I'll go to my room and read. I have a lot of homework to catch up on."

"Sounds like a good idea," Jean-Marc said with forced cheerfulness. "But are you hungry? I could bring you a snack."

Marc made a disgusted sound. "Snacking isn't fun for me anymore with this diet." He sighed. "I'm not hungry, anyway. But thanks, Dad."

I paused outside the kitchen, pasting a smile on my face before entering. But a new voice stopped me.

"Are you okay?" It was Ken.

"Yeah, but . . ." There was a long pause from Jean-Marc. "I hate seeing him like that. He used to be so full of life and laughter. You know, always teasing everyone."

"And you feel it's your fault."

My smile died. A scraping noise echoed in the silence, a chair being pulled back from the table. Jean-Marc sighed. "Logically, I know I couldn't have stopped it. But I can't help thinking that if I hadn't blown it at the bank, then—"

"Then you wouldn't have been working at the café, and the children wouldn't have been in the station when it was bombed. But that's crazy. You can't change the past."

"I know. I know. But now there's good old Jacques, with his money *and* an extra kidney. He can give my son what I can't. How do you think that makes me feel?"

"Rotten," sympathized Ken.

"One part of me wants nothing to do with him, but the other wants to help my son. I keep rationalizing that Marc will get another kidney from somewhere else, but how much time will he lose? And how much more will he suffer because I don't want to accept anything from my wife's ex-husband? I don't want to be indebted to him. In fact, I'd like to shoot him and get it over with."

Ken chuckled dryly. "Not an easy situation."

"Easy?" Jean-Marc snorted. "He's caused nothing but trouble in Ari's life and now in mine. The agents investigating the bank failure are sure that at least one of the employees who mishandled funds was accepting bribes to do so."

"And you think Jacques had something to do with it?"

"No. Yes . . . I don't know. But with him going to most of the major banking corporations and promising them favors to not hire me, I can't help but be suspicious. And then that mess with the insurance. What am I supposed to think? I've tried to ignore the man and go about my life, but in the business world, I'm effectively shut out. Those who don't believe the rumors that I stole money still want to stay away from any connection to me."

"You'll have to go outside your profession."

Jean-Marc didn't reply, and I thought of the café. My husband had gone outside his profession, way out, and all in the name of supporting his family.

"There is something you may be overlooking," Ken said. "I mean, why did Jacques show up now, after all these years? What circumstances brought him to this point? Could all of this be that he was supposed to be here when Marc needed him?"

I had thought of that myself, though had never dared to voice the words to Jean-Marc.

"Marc doesn't need him; he needs a kidney."

"Which Jacques may have to give," countered Ken. "And maybe he needs to do it."

"What do you mean?" A touch of anger colored Jean-Marc's voice.

Another scraping noise sounded as Ken settled at the table. "When I first met Ariana," he began, "it was the day of her brother's funeral. I stopped her during a street meeting. You should have seen her. She looked remarkably like Josette—young, slender, passionate, and just dawning on great beauty. She turned on me, eyes blazing, and told me to get lost, but I sensed the need in her. For nearly two years I prayed to find her again and that she would let me help her. Now, this wasn't just for her, as I would like you to believe, but I needed to find her for *me*. I needed to gain a testimony that the Lord could save a life so destroyed. I hadn't had much proof of that during my missionary service, and I began to doubt. My faith wore thin—until I met Ariana again and saw how much the Lord loved her and how my prayers had been answered. Watching her become converted to the gospel planted in my heart the seed of the strong testimony I have today. In fact, she was the only person I baptized during my whole mission."

"Really? The way she talks about you, it's like you were the most spiritual person she had ever met."

Ken laughed. "Maybe right then I was, because that was what she needed. The Lord can work miracles, even with such poor material as me."

"So, are you saying that Jacques needs something from us?" Jean-Marc asked.

"I really don't know. But I don't believe in coincidence. He's here for a reason."

"Yeah, to convince Ari what a lousy provider I am," Jean-Marc said in a harsh voice. "He wants her back, you know."

"Can you blame him?"

Jean-Marc gave a short laugh. "You sure know how to put things in perspective."

"Like I said, I don't believe in coincidence without reason. Perhaps that's why I'm here in France this year instead of next. To put things in perspective. Who can say? But what I do know is that Jacques seems willing to do most anything to win Ariana back. What are you willing to do for her?"

"It all comes down to the kidney, doesn't it?" Jean-Marc said sadly. "Ari wants it, I want it, and Marc needs it. I just wish it wasn't Jacques."

"Maybe it won't be. We don't know the medical particulars. For all we know, Jacques is on dialysis himself. The drugs he used years ago could have ruined his kidneys."

"One can only hope." From his voice, I knew Jean-Marc was smiling.

I changed my mind about going into the kitchen, afraid to spoil the moment, and instead retraced my steps to my room. The blankets no longer held the warmth from my nap, but I curled under them anyway, wondering what Jean-Marc would do. Silently, I prayed.

It wasn't long before Jean-Marc came into the room, humming under his breath. "Ari! What are you doing here?"

I felt my face flush, but I didn't confess that I had been eavesdropping. "I didn't feel well. I haven't been able to sleep much this week."

He crossed the room and sat on the bed, one hand reaching out to check my forehead. "No fever," he said, but his face showed worry.

"I'm fine. I slept a little. I'm about to get up and go to the café. Are you going there now?"

He stood and crossed to the dresser. "Yes. I have appointments to interview some couples for the upcoming vacancy at the apartments. I wanted to change first." The clothes he wore were casual and rumpled from his stint at the dialysis center. He reached for a suit. "I actually enjoy this part of the job," he said, grinning slightly.

"How did it go at the center?"

His grin vanished. "The same." He let the suit fall back onto its hanger and turned to face me. "Ari, I've been thinking."

"Yes?"

He glanced over to where the February sun shone through the window, sending fingers of warm light into the room. "I think maybe I've been wrong about not asking Jacques to help with the kidney. We can ask him, if you want."

I knew how much the words cost him, and the turmoil raging in his heart. Slipping from the bed, I walked over to him, placing my arms around his waist. "Are you sure?"

He shook his head. "Not really. But I don't see any other way right now."

I nodded. "That's how I feel."

"Then we'll ask him. It can't hurt."

"*I'll* ask him," I said, remembering the last time they had faced each other.

His face was troubled. "I don't want you to go alone."

"You have to trust me."

"It's Jacques I don't trust." He sighed. "When will you go?"

I glanced at my watch. "Right now, I guess. I'll meet you at the café afterward. The children will be there shortly, anyway."

"Okay, then." His arms wrapped around me tightly, and I could feel his breath, hot on my cheek. "Remember how much I love you."

I pulled away and fingered the white gold rose pinned near my heart. "I never forget. But if I did, I have this to remind me." I kissed him. "I love you."

Pulling apart, we both went about changing our clothing. My linen jumper was wrinkled, and I couldn't face Jacques that way. Doubt and apprehension assailed me. What if Jacques wouldn't help? What if going to him caused even more problems?

I wished I didn't have to go.

CHAPTER FIFTEEN

*J*ean-Marc and I left the apartment at the same time, and he insisted on driving me to Jacques' office. I kissed him once on the lips before exiting the van. He touched my cheek and his sad green-brown eyes watched me leave. I smiled. *It's all right,* I mouthed. He nodded and drove off. I shivered in my leather coat with the warm lining. Not from the cold but from dread. Setting my jaw, I tossed my head and pulled open the door.

As before, the opulent aspect of the company caught my attention. The lush carpet seemed to drag at my feet, and the inlaid gold on the wall mocked my purpose. The same blonde receptionist sat at the desk, a phone to her ear and her hands on a computer keyboard.

I approached the desk, and Charlotte—if I recalled her name correctly—glanced up from the screen. She paused in mid-speech, staring. I knew she remembered the scenes with my daughter and husband. She quickly finished her conversation and hung up the phone. "May I help you?" she asked. Blatant curiosity filled her face.

"I'm here to see Jacques de Cotte. I don't have an appointment, but he'll see me, if he's in."

"And you are?"

"Ariana."

"If you'll tell me your last name and what it's about, I'll ring him," she said in a brittle voice.

I didn't want to satisfy her curiosity, especially with the way she adored to gossip. "Just tell him I'm here."

She hesitated but evidently remembering the way I had been received before, she picked up the phone. "A woman named Ariana is here to see you. She refused to tell me the nature of her business." Jacques' answer was not to her liking. Her eyes widened, and her lips drew together tightly, as if tasting something bitter. "You can go on down," she said irritably, not bothering to tell me where. But I remembered all too well.

"Thank you," I said politely. She smiled, but I could feel a hostile glare boring into my back as I marched to Jacques' office. If I had ever held any regard in her eyes, I had lost it by refusing to answer her questions.

Jacques opened the door before I arrived, eyes alight with pleasure. "Ariana. How wonderful to see you. I'm glad you came." He had his hand outstretched, and I felt compelled to offer mine. Jacques held it for longer than necessary, but in the light of what I had come seeking, I decided not to mention it.

His gaze fell to the pin Jean-Marc had given me, and his jubilance faded. "What brings you here?" he asked, leading me to the couch on the left side of his desk. A painting in a beveled frame above the couch stopped me cold; it hadn't been there before. The picture was of me, taken by one of my friends on the day Jacques and I were married, more than twenty-one years earlier. Jacques had obviously paid someone a great deal of money to copy the cheap photograph, and the painted copy was far better than the original. The younger me smiled out at the world with the intense, innocent expression of the very young, passion flaming in my deep brown eyes. That day, I thought I knew what love was. How was I to know that my feelings were only a hint of what was to come later with Jean-Marc?

"Do you like it?" Jacques asked.

"I do, but—"

"But you object to my having it."

"Yes."

He sighed. "Why are you here?"

I sat abruptly on the couch, the picture forgotten. How could I say it? I had never been one for coating the truth or making allusions, but then I had never before asked someone for a body part.

"I need your help," I said finally.

"Is it Pauline?"

I shook my head and felt a slight smile tug at my lips. "No. In fact, now that she's on her new drug mix, she hasn't had any problems at all. It's like a miracle. I think they're nearing a cure."

He smiled. "I'm glad, Ariana. I know if anyone deserves for that to happen, it's you. It's good to see you smile."

"But my son isn't doing so well."

"I saw the newspapers. I'm sorry to hear about his problems. But I thought they had released him."

"They have. Only he went back in and then out again." I sighed. "It's just not a life for a young boy. No camping trips or vacations, just every other day hooked up to that impersonal dialysis machine. I sometimes imagine it sucking the life right out of him." I didn't look at Jacques as I spoke but kept my eyes on the gray carpet, not wanting him to see my tears.

Jacques waited, but when I didn't explain further, he stood and crossed to the desk. He pulled out a drawer. "How much do you need?" It was a simple question, and his voice held only kindness, but for some undefined reason it rankled me.

"I don't want money. I want you."

A glint of something flared in his eyes before I could correct my mistake. "Or part of you," I added hastily. "Your kidney."

He gaped at me. "You've got to be kidding!"

"I'm not."

He searched my face. "You're serious." The pen dropped from his hand and clattered to the desk. "You're actually asking me for my kidney."

Feeling the height disadvantage, I stood. "You're the same blood type as my son, and you said if I ever needed help I should—"

"I meant money, of course," he said, beginning to pace. One hand ran through his hair, pushing it back from his eyes. "Or comfort, or someone to talk to, or—" He stopped talking and faced me. "Do you know what giving a kidney is like? The risk of major surgery, six weeks of recovery, not to mention a lot of pain. What makes you think I would be willing to do that? What makes you think I could take six weeks away from my company, even if I wanted to?"

His reaction surprised me. "And I thought I'd have to explain the risks to you," I said dryly. "Where did you learn all that?"

"I read," he said defensively. Now *that* I knew was a lie. The Jacques of old would have done anything to avoid a book, and I had ample proof that he hadn't really changed. No, more than likely he had gained this information while spying on me and my family, planning his next move. The thought made me uncomfortable.

"Does your husband know you're here?" he asked.

"Yes," I said, glad that it was true. "He didn't want to ask. Neither did I, but Marc . . . he's . . . well, he's just not the same. He might have to wait years because of his blood type; there are others on the list with the same type, and they've been waiting for years already. And now the doctor is worried Marc'll get an infection—because of complications with the injuries caused in the bombing—that will make it so he can't use dialysis. If that happens, he'll have to get a new kidney or . . . or die. Then I remembered you, and how you were the same blood type. I thought you might help." A tear fell from my eyes onto my cheek, sliding downward.

Jacques watched my face for a brief second, following the progress of the tear. When he spoke, his voice was soft, almost aching. "I should have known when I told you I would help that it wouldn't be something easy. I'd planned to fight to win you back—but a kidney?" His grin held no mirth. "I'm rather attached to it. To both of them."

"You don't need both." But I knew my request was excessive. "Oh, I shouldn't have come." As I started for the door, his hand closed around my upper arm, a hard, tight grasp.

"I didn't exactly say no," he said with a touch of arrogance.

"You didn't exactly jump up and say yes, either."

"Give me some time to think about it."

I stared pointedly at my arm, and he released it.

"You can think about it and call me. I'll send you a packet of information." I turned to leave.

"Wait!"

"Yes?"

He appeared to make a rapid decision. "How badly do you want this kidney?"

"What do you mean?" I asked slowly.

"What are you willing to do for it?"

His implication was insulting, and my eyes narrowed. "I'm willing to come here to ask my ex-husband to help me. I'm willing to risk upsetting my family by having you be the donor. I'm willing to humble myself and beg, if necessary. Isn't that enough? What can you be thinking?"

His lean features weren't hard but needy, imploring. "I'll give you my kidney, but I want you to give us another shot. I'll take care of you, your children, whatever. Only come back. I'll be the man you can love."

The idea was ludicrous, and I wondered that he didn't see it. Though Jacques' declaration would make a good fantasy or dream for a young girl, and even perhaps for me on a day I was feeling neglected by my husband, that's all it could ever amount to—a dream, an ethereal vision brought by the wings of foolish imagination. It wasn't even something I wanted to consider. It was absurd in the extreme. Trade a kidney for eternity? For my family? For the passion and love that Jean-Marc and I shared, however currently strained by circumstances of the past few months? There was no contest. Once, I had doubted my own motives in coming to see Jacques. But no longer.

My swift anger dimmed in the light of knowing my family was eternal, and nothing Jacques could do would change that. By contrast, he was an unhappy man, alone with his blind desires. A great sadness overwhelmed me. "Oh, Jacques," I said. "You don't understand."

"I can't live my life without you!" he returned almost angrily. "Life has no meaning. Without you, there's simply . . . nothing."

"No meaning?" I nearly laughed. "Life has *every* meaning. We are children of God; doesn't that mean anything to you? Children of a God who loves us! We have so much potential, so much inside. This life is but a blink in the eternity of time. If only you could see the world as I see it, Jacques!"

"I want to," he said, coming closer and reaching for my hands. "That's why I want you with me."

"The gospel teaches us truths you've never even imagined," I continued, stepping away from him. "You can be happy! Service, prayer, faith, knowledge—these are what bring it about, all based on the love of our Savior."

A feral sound came from the back of his throat. "What I need is *you.*"

I edged toward the door, seeing the futility of trying to answer him. Anything I could tell Jacques about the Savior and the gospel would be swallowed up in his obsession with the past. Why couldn't he let go?

"Well?" he asked.

"No. Not even if I weren't married. The past is over."

"It's not!" He grabbed my shoulder, his look wild and ruthless. "Isn't that why you're here? You think I *owe* you because of what I did to Nette, don't you? That's why you think you can come and ask me for such a thing. But I tell you, I didn't mean to hurt Nette! There's not a day that goes by that I don't think about her and cry."

My shoulder ached under his rough grasp, but his sincerity touched my soul. "I know, I know." I met his stare, and he must have found what he needed in my eyes, because his grip slowly lessened. So did my fear.

"I'm sorry, Ariana." The muscles in his jaw worked convulsively. "I hope I didn't hurt you."

"You didn't," I lied, rubbing my shoulder. I started toward the door again. "I didn't come because of Nette," I added. "I came because you told me to and because Marc needs you. There's nothing more to it."

A sardonic mask covered his face. "You have my answer."

Having reached the safety of the door, I paused, glancing one last time at the lifelike painting of my youthful self. "Yes, I guess I do."

With effort, I refrained from slamming the door, shutting it carefully and quietly as if a baby slept inside. I half expected Jacques to follow me, but he didn't. A great relief washed through my trembling body. *Whatever possessed me to come here?* It seemed a mother's love knew few bounds.

I wandered back down the long hallway. Charlotte wasn't working. She sat back in her chair while the screen saver on her computer sent a flurry of fish swimming lazily across the screen. She glared at me. "I can't believe you came to ask him to risk surgery like that," she said, her voice sharper than the long, clear nails drumming relentlessly on top of the papers near the keyboard.

Her vehemence struck me as comical, since the last time I visited she was the one who had gossiped behind Jacques' back. "How did you know?"

Her face reddened, and I knew that somehow she had listened on their intercom system. Perhaps Jacques had accidentally left his end open. It didn't really matter.

"Good-bye," I said.

She practically vaulted from her seat. "He'll win in the end," she insisted, and this time her voice was bitter. "He always gets what he wants."

"Not with me." Some nuance in her expression begged me to continue, and despite my former resolve to give this woman nothing to gossip about, I obliged. "I'm happy with my life and my future. Jacques lives only in the past. I don't want him."

"Do you really mean it?"

Those five words held hope, and in a shower of inspiration, I realized this woman's frustration came not because of spite or boredom but because she actually *loved* Jacques. And more, she didn't realize it yet.

"I mean it." I tried to keep the pity from my voice.

She sniffed and sat again in her chair. "Not that I care, of course."

"Of course. And I'm sorry."

I turned and left before she asked me to explain. What was I sorry for? Sorry for her and her impossible love? Sorry that I had misjudged her? Sorry that Jacques was so awful? Yes, all of it. But most of all because he wouldn't give Marc his kidney.

I thought about what Charlotte had said about Jacques always getting what he wanted. Ridiculous. No one ever got that. Take my own life, for example. I was happy more times than not, sometimes deliriously so, and still life denied me some things.

Like a kidney.

I shoved the thought aside. "It must be for the best," I said aloud. The dark clouds overhead threatened rain, and I hurried to the subway. They still hadn't completely repaired the station by the café, but at least the trains were going through. Jean-Marc would be waiting and wondering.

Chapter Sixteen

*T*he café was alive with business. The older ladies had already gone home, but my oldest daughters and Annette handled the rush with the exuberance of youth. I passed them with a smile and a wave. I noticed that young Kenny was in the line, and both Marie-Thérèse and Josette were working feverishly to be the one to help him.

The kitchen was loaded with cakes my mother had baked earlier, frosted with the yellow-orange mixture. "They're a hit," Annette said. "We've used up several already." It seems my mother had found an interest and an outlet at last—one that didn't involve my father.

Through the open office door, I could see Jean-Marc and Pauline. My daughter flung herself at me for a hug, as if it had been a week since we had last spoken instead of only that morning. "Oh, Mom, I missed you!"

Joy cut through the sadness of the day. "I love you too, Pauline." Sometimes it seemed that she had been born simply to love us. Behind her, Jean-Marc smiled.

"Come and eat with Dad," she said. "I want to go out and wait for André."

"He's not here?"

"Josette said he stayed after school to hang out." He had been doing that a lot lately since the children changed schools, though it wasn't something we allowed without reason. We would have to talk with him again.

Pauline chattered on. "I have a talk in Primary on Sunday, and he said he'd help me write it." André was a year and a half her senior, and she was in the habit of having him help with schoolwork, but she had usually asked me to help with Church talks.

"Do you want me to find a story for you?" I volunteered. "I'm not too busy."

"No," she said, picking up a stack of Church magazines from the desk. "I think it's something André needs to do."

How keen her insight! André did need this link to the Lord. Anything we tried seemed to fail or bounce off the invisible wall he had built around himself. On our order, he went to church each Sunday, though reluctantly and with a bad attitude. In class, he either disrupted or stared sullenly out the window. Twice we'd found him in the halls. I consoled myself by thinking that at least he hadn't been smoking, but I knew he could hide that fact if he wanted.

"Good idea," I said. Pauline flashed me her merry grin and danced away.

I sank onto a chair, feeling Jean-Marc's eyes on me. "How'd it go?"

Frowning and shaking my head, I reached for one of the meat cakes on a plate sitting on the desk. "He won't do it."

Jean-Marc nodded. "Well, we tried." I could tell he was relieved.

Frustration made me angry. "You're glad," I accused.

"I guess I am, in some way. I don't want Jacques in our lives."

I nearly shouted, "And you think *I* do?" An inner part of me felt surprised at the intense, almost irrational emotion I displayed. "You just can't get it through your head—can you?—that I only want what's best for Marc. I don't care about Jacques—not as a man, anyway." I stood, accidentally knocking over the chair. "I wish you'd get over your inferiority complex, or your middle-age crisis, or whatever it is that's bothering you, and just love me." *And I want a part of each and every aspect of your life,* I almost added. *Even part of the rejection you face each day as you search for work.* I could help him deal with that, couldn't I? But he wouldn't talk about his failures, not to me.

"Ari, calm down. Let's talk about this." His expression was baffled, but there was irritation, even outrage, there as well.

"I just can't talk to you anymore."

"Fine."

We glared at each other, both hurt but not wanting to be the one to back down. I knew I was wrong. We were both wrong. But I didn't really care whose fault it was; I just wanted things back to normal. Fighting the tears, I stalked out of the office, leaving Jean-Marc alone.

I held in my emotions until later that night after the children went to bed. Then I sobbed quietly in the bathroom, feeling a terrible loneliness surge through my aching heart. *Should I say I'm sorry to Jean-Marc?* I thought. *Sorry for what?* a caustic voice inside me replied. *Sorry for wanting to improve your son's life? Maybe even save it? Or sorry for wanting to be a full part of Jean-Marc's life?*

I went to bed, tears dried, but the heartache still all-encompassing. There, I clutched my knees to my chest in the fetal position. Jean-Marc lay on his side of the bed, silent and unmoving. Minutes ticked slowly by. Then he reached out a hand and touched my shoulder. I didn't respond, and after a long moment he pulled away. I could hear him awake beside me, just out of my reach, hugging his misery to his chest as did I. It was a long time before I finally slept.

The next morning found me cleaning between the cracks on my tiled kitchen floor, a task I had long neglected because of my work at the café. The cleaning fluid seemed unusually pungent, but the scrubbing action gave vent to the remaining frustrations eating at my soul. After we awakened, Jean-Marc and I had talked as if nothing had happened last night, neither caring to bring up the pain again. As a result, the words and feelings we had exchanged still sat like a heavy lump of iron in my stomach, making me feel out of sorts with everyone and everything. I wanted to make up with my husband so that my world could be at peace once more, but I had missed my opportunity.

Jean-Marc had already left, taking André with him to fix the blinds in one of the apartments. The girls had gone to the café, though not to work. We had hired three other people from our ward to take their places on Saturday. We felt the children needed a free day as much as we did, and Saturday usually ended up as such. They found plenty of time during the weekday lulls at the café to finish their homework, leaving Saturday for play. But play to them meant other teenagers, especially boys—but at least they were Mormon ones. So they went to the café, where the youth in our ward hung out. I stayed home, nursing my grief. Marc was in the apartment, too, but had already returned to his room for a nap. Once, he would have been zooming in the basement garage on his roller blades. Perhaps, in time, he would do so again.

The buzzer below rang. *Who could it be?* I picked myself up off the floor and let my brush drop. I punched the intercom. "Who is it?"

"It's me, Lu-Lu."

I buzzed her in, left the apartment door ajar, and went back to my scrubbing. The elevator bell dinged, and Lu-Lu swept in. I stood up to greet her. Her dress was immaculate and set off her slender figure. Glancing down at my own body, I made a commitment to stay away from the pastries at the café. I was still trim, but it seemed middle age was coming to my waist.

"He's going to leave her," she announced, tossing her short hair. Its red highlights glinted more overtly than I remembered.

"What!"

"Philippe loves me. He said so. As soon as his wife's stronger and can take care of herself, he's going to tell her, and we're going to get married as we should have eleven years ago."

My cleaning brush clattered to the ground. "Lu-Lu, think what you're saying! You know you weren't supposed to marry Philippe; you've said so a million times. And what do you mean, breaking up his marriage? What about Danielle, his wife? What about his children? And he may have changed enough to ask for a blessing when there was nothing else left to do, but that doesn't mean he'll marry you in the temple. Lu-Lu, *think!*"

She had bent to pick up the brush as I spoke, and now she fiddled with it in her hand. "I *am* thinking. And I love Philippe! I want to be with him. I do believe that we weren't supposed to marry back then, but who knows why? Maybe I can't have children, and that's the only way those little spirits could come to earth." Her look pleaded for understanding. "Oh, Ariana, I'm so tired of being alone. I know Philippe won't be able to take me to the temple, but I can't wait my whole life, can I? I've been given this chance with Philippe again, a second chance at love. Can you blame me if I take it?"

Her words screamed out her sincerity, but they also reeked of poor judgment and immaturity. "Coming between a man and wife isn't right," I said. "Don't you see that?"

"They were separating anyway!" she said with more than a little despair. She bent down and began to scrub furiously at the tile where I had left off. "They were. She was going to leave him. Then the accident happened."

"And Philippe underwent a change. He recognized his errors, or some of them. I understood that he was going to try again with his wife, if given the chance."

"What are you saying?" Lu-Lu scrubbed harder. That she would risk soiling her dress in this mundane task showed her troubled frame of mind. A detached part of me wondered how I could get her to finish the rest of the floor. I sat on a chair to watch.

"I'm saying you haven't given them a chance. How do you know Danielle still wants to get rid of him?" With every fiber of my being, I felt my sister-in-law was making a mistake. She had kept herself pure too many years to settle for anything less than an eternal relationship.

Her hands worked violently with the brush on the tile but always in the same spot.

I sighed and knelt down on the tile, placing my hands over hers. "Stop. It's clean there."

She glanced down and heaved a shuddering breath. "Ari, what am I going to do?"

"I don't know. Only you can decide. But if there is something left in their marriage, you have no right to come between them. They are *married*. That's sacred, even out of the temple."

"I need to talk to Danielle," she said abruptly.

I didn't know if that was a good idea.

"Then I'll know how she feels. If she's just waiting to leave him again, then—"

"And if she's not?"

"She is! I know it!" She stared at the white tile a full minute before saying in a soft voice, "Will you go with me, Ari?"

"What, me? Right now? Is she even home from the hospital?"

Lu-Lu nodded. "She went home three days ago. She has a temporary nanny to take care of the children and a nurse who comes in daily. But Philippe has a meeting. He won't be there. It'll be the perfect opportunity. We'll say we wanted to see how she was doing."

"I would like to know," I said. "Marc keeps asking about her." I brightened. "Hey, we could take Marc. He's feeling stronger now, I think. Getting him out of the house might be just what he needs to cheer him up. The doctor won't let him go to school yet, but this ought to be all right."

"That would be perfect," Lu-Lu agreed.

Leaning over, I mopped up some of the dirty residue on the floor.

"Ar-r-i-i-i," agonized Lu-Lu.

"Well, I can't just leave it to dry, can I?"

"I'll clean the whole floor for you later, if we can go now."

"It's a deal. And I'll hold you to it, too. I'll go change and get Marc. Don't worry—I'll be quick."

I knocked at Marc's room. "Come in," he said. He lay on his bed, stomach down, staring at a pair of roller blades on the floor.

"How are you feeling?" I asked. I wondered that the position didn't hurt his surgery scars.

"Better," he said. He paused before adding, "How long do you think it'll be before the doctor says I can go blading?"

"I'm not sure. We'll have to wait and see."

He sighed. "I guess it doesn't really matter. I don't feel much like going, anyway." His eyes rose to meet mine. "Will I ever want to go again, do you think? Will I ever be like I was before?"

I bit my lip, wondering what to say. Sitting on his bed, I curled over his body, cradling him and stroking his back as I hadn't done since he was a child. He was bigger than I was now. He rolled slightly and brought an arm up to circle my neck. "I think you will," I said, "if you want to. Until then, let's take it one day at a time."

He nodded. "Thanks, Mom."

I straightened. "Aunt Lu-Lu and I thought we'd go see Danielle Massoni. She's out of the hospital now. How 'bout it? Want to go?"

He sat up, a smile coming back to his face. "Oh, sure. I'd like to go. She's really pretty, isn't she?"

I laughed and punched his shoulder. "Typical male."

A few minutes later, we were ready to leave. But the buzzer at the outside door rang again, and this time Simone was on the other side. "We'll be right down," Lu-Lu said. "We're leaving."

"No, I've got something in my hands. I have to come up," Simone replied.

We waited, Marc sitting in a chair, Lu-Lu pacing, and me watching the two of them. "Here I am," Simone called as she entered the apartment carrying a pastry box in her hand.

"What's this for?" I questioned. "The twins' birthday isn't until Wednesday."

Simone's thin lips curled in a smile. "It's not for them. It's for me."

"It's not your birthday."

"No, but I am celebratin'. Where are the others? I want to tell everybody together."

"Sorry. They're at the café."

Simone's face drooped. "Oh." But whatever her secret, it wouldn't let her stay depressed. "I guess you'll have to do," she said. With a flourish and a fairly good imitation of a bugle trumpeting, she threw off the top of the cake box. In bold letters, it read: *Congratulations on your wedding!*

Lu-Lu's eyes darted to mine in consternation. In them I read the same question I was asking myself: *How did Simone know about Lu-Lu wanting to marry Philippe?*

"Frédéric and I are finally gettin' married," Simone announced. "So don't I get some congratulations or somethin'? What is with you two? I thought ya'd be happy. You've been tellin' me for the past year that I ought to marry him."

"That's great, Grandma!" Marc said. Lu-Lu and I joined in, perhaps a little too heartily. Simone didn't seem to notice.

"We're goin' to wait until spring, of course, but Frédéric was determined to celebrate my answer now. He bought me this cake. We thought we could have a little party."

Marc's eye's danced almost like before the accident. "We could do it tonight."

"Sure, we need a party," I said.

"But right now we're going to see Danielle Massoni," Lu-Lu said pointedly.

"That lady Marc saved?" Simone said. "I think I'll go with you, if ya don't mind."

"Sure. Why not?" Lu-Lu said. But she didn't seem very happy at the added company. "Come on. Let's go." She led the way to the elevator and from there to her car, parked out front. Soon we were hurtling through the streets of Paris with a velocity to make the strongest stomach ill. In the backseat Marc and I stared at each other, with me feeling as green as he looked. Simone threw back her head and laughed with glee. Lu-Lu only glared ahead in determination.

Like us, the Massonis lived in a wealthy area of town. The February air was filled with the tantalizing smells coming from a corner bakery. Lu-Lu stopped and bought an assortment of pastries for the Massoni children. We rang the gold buzzer at the outside door, and when we announced ourselves, the door clicked open.

"That was quick," Marc commented.

"She must want to see us," Simone said. "Probably to thank you for savin' her life."

Marc beamed. "You think?"

It wasn't Danielle but a teenaged girl with short brown hair who let us in. Behind her in the wide, circular entryway peered the two children we had seen at the hospital, both excited but reserved. "Mommy's in there," the little girl said, pointing across the rich rugs scattered across the wooden floor to a door that was half ajar.

We looked at the nanny, and she nodded. "She said for you to go right in. She's in her bedroom. I'm fixing lunch—will you be staying?"

"I don't think so." Lu-Lu spoke at the same time Simone said, "Sure." The girl frowned in confusion.

"We'll just stay a while," I said. "We have other plans for lunch."

She smiled at me gratefully. "Go on in, then."

We followed the children into the room. Danielle Massoni sat up in bed, a mound of matching pillows supporting her back. The bed was large, and the pictures and other decorations made it obvious that this was a room shared by a married couple. Lu-Lu's face tensed with added pain. "I brought the children some pastries," she said in a wavering voice.

Danielle smiled up at us, her lips full and inviting. Her high cheekbones made her seem young and fragile. Yellowish bruises ran along one cheek and on her forehead, and her left arm sported an ugly scar. "Oh, thank you! Look, children, this can be your dessert. What do you say?"

"Thank you," the children chimed in sweet, high voices.

"I'm so glad you came!" Danielle said, her voice like soft velvet. "I've been telling Philippe that I have to go see you and thank you for what you did for me. I'm so grateful! But he refuses to let me until I'm up and about." Her beautiful gray eyes rested on Marc. "You're the boy who saved me in the bombing, aren't you? How brave you were! I couldn't believe it when I saw you skating over that train. Until I saw you, I was sure I was going to die! How can I ever thank you?"

"Aw, it was nothin'." Marc hung his head and looked pleased.

"Not to me, it wasn't. Nor to my family. If it weren't for you, my children wouldn't have a mother!" Danielle wiped away a tear and focused on Lu-Lu. "And don't I remember you? Yes, you took me to the ambulance. They say if you hadn't gotten me there so quickly, I would have died before I reached the hospital. What a family you are! I can't believe that you could help me, not knowing where your own nephew was." She grabbed Lu-Lu's hand. "Thank you so much!"

"Uh . . . you're . . . welcome," Lu-Lu managed. "It wasn't just me, though. A man helped me carry you."

"I didn't know that," Danielle said. "I wonder who he was."

"A man in the bombing," Lu-Lu murmured. "He lost his wife."

Danielle's lovely face fell. "Oh, that's sad. I hope he's all right."

"We never saw him again," Lu-Lu said. "So we don't know."

"We'll have to pray for him," Danielle said softly. We stood in silence for a long minute.

"So how are things with you now?" I asked before we could dwell on the sadness any longer.

She smiled at me. "Are you Marc's mother?"

I nodded. "And Pauline's. I understand she came to visit you a few times in the hospital after you woke up. I worried that she would be intruding."

"Oh, never." Danielle's sincerity couldn't be questioned. She was honest and warm, completely unlike the austere woman I had envisioned. "Pauline is like a ray of sunshine. She's told me all about your family. And about the blessing your husband gave me. It was beautiful."

"You heard it?" Marc asked in surprise.

Danielle grinned as if a giggle were about to burst from her lips. "No, not really. But Philippe and the children told me." Her smile dimmed. "You know, that was the first time my husband turned to God for help. I've been trying all these years to get him to go to church or something, but he was dead set against it. He wouldn't even let us talk about such things." The children had climbed up on the bed on either side of her, both snuggling against her body. She put an arm around each of them. "But I taught them about Jesus," Danielle continued. "I know He exists and loves us. I used to go to church when I was small, and they told me stories. I still have a Bible, and I read it to the children when Philippe isn't home."

"So you and Philippe aren't getting along?" Lu-Lu asked. Only I seemed to hear the desperation in her voice.

"We weren't before the accident," Danielle replied innocently. "We were even separating. But he's changed now, and I'm so hopeful." Her eyes seemed luminous in the quiet light of the room. "He doesn't mind when I talk about Jesus now, and he spends more time with us. And he's nice. Sometimes he could be so—" She broke off, as if afraid of saying too much.

"You can tell us," I said, "if you want. We knew Philippe a long time ago. We care about him." At least Lu-Lu did.

Her smile was back, childlike and engaging. "That's right. I remember him saying that your husband gave him his first banking job. You must know, then, that his mother died when he was a baby." I hadn't known that, but Lu-Lu was nodding. "His father raised him," Danielle continued. "He was a stern man and very hard on Philippe, not very loving. He never gave him a kind look or a hug. As a result, my husband became angry at everything. He didn't believe in God, yet at the same time he wanted to somehow punish whoever had taken his mother away." She sighed. "I've never seen anyone so lost. I guess that was what attracted me to him in the first place." She scanned our faces. "I thought I could fix that. Underneath, he's really a good person. He'd been married before for about a year, but it didn't work out. He was pretty bitter about it, but I thought I could fix that, too.

"After we married, Philippe insisted I stay home with the children. He said he didn't want them growing up without a mother like he did. I've loved being home with them, but Philippe and I kept having problems. I didn't know what to do. He's a good father, and he loves his children, but the anger wouldn't leave. So I finally decided I would have to leave to save them."

There was no doubting that whatever decision Danielle had made before the bombing, she still loved her husband.

"You said things had changed," Simone prompted.

"Yes. He's better now." Her smile lit up her face with unveiled hope. "I think my miraculous recovery is making him understand that there is a God who loves him. And that makes all the difference."

"I've got something to ask you," Lu-Lu said. There were tears in her eyes and a fatal expression on her pale face. I feared that she might say something to hurt this innocent woman in the bed; but before I could interfere, Lu-Lu rushed on. "I'd like you to come to our church." Her mouth was open to say more, but no words came out.

"Why, I'd love to!" Danielle said enthusiastically. "Wouldn't we, children?" They nodded, and the little boy whispered something in her ear. "Yes, I'm sure they'll have stories about Jesus," Danielle said. Then she gazed up at Lu-Lu. "Thank you for asking. I was hoping you would. I think we could be friends, if you like." She shrugged her shoulders in embarrassment. "I mean, with staying at home and all, I don't get out much. You know, to meet people."

"I'd like to be your friend," Lu-Lu said steadily. I was proud of her reaction, though I suspected that inside her dreams were shattered. I felt like crying at her nobility.

"Are you all members of the same church?" Danielle asked.

"Yes, but I wasn't for a long time," Simone said. "I had some drug problems to work out, but my family stood by me."

"I've always been curious about religion," Danielle said. "Sometimes I see those foreign missionaries in the streets with suits and short hair. I almost stopped them once, but I knew Philippe would be angry."

Marc grinned. "Those are probably our missionaries. We have a lot from America, but a lot from here, too. When I get older, I'm going to go on a mission." His face darkened, and his voice became very soft. "At least I was. I don't know if I can, being on dialysis and all."

It was something I hadn't thought of. How would his future missionary service be affected if he was tied to a machine every other day for hours on end? Marc's goal to serve a two-year mission had been an unwavering part of his plans since his childhood; could saving another's life ruin that hope forever? I wasn't familiar enough with Church policy to know where they stood on situations like Marc's.

Danielle frowned, and the room seemed darker because of it. "Oh, I am sorry. If I hadn't damaged one of my kidneys, I would gladly give it to you!" How cruel fate had been to Marc, letting two chances slide away!

"What's done is done," Simone said kindly, though her voice was gruff.

"We have faith that something will come up," Lu-Lu said. I thought she might be talking about herself as well. She was keeping her emotions under control, but her eyes begged me to help her escape.

Somehow Lu-Lu made it through the rest of the visit, and we returned to my apartment. Simone left, and Marc retired to his room for a rest. Lu-Lu and I sat on the sofa in the living room, and only then did she vent her feelings.

"Why couldn't she be cold and uncaring?" Lu-Lu sobbed. "Why does she have to be so . . . so innocent and loving? You can see how much she adores Philippe, and he loves her, too. I think I knew it all along."

"I thought you said he loved you."

"He did, and I think he does. But he loves her too; I can tell by the way he talks about her. Plus she's the mother of his children. They can make it together if I let them."

She buried her head in my shoulder as the children had done when they were small, crying in earnest now. I looked up to see Marc's worried face in the doorway. I shook my head at him and raised a warning finger for him to keep silent. He nodded and crept away. Lu-Lu cried harder and clung tighter to me. I put my arms around her and simply rocked back and forth with her on the couch, letting her sob out her grief. I didn't know what else to do for her. As with Marc's problem, only time could ease this wound.

CHAPTER SEVENTEEN

That night, we had Simone's party. Frédéric beamed as I had never seen him do since his first wife's death. He was fifty-nine, older than Simone by three years, and his hair was nearly white, contrasting with his darker eyebrows. His dark, expressive eyes were intelligent.

"This is one of the happiest days of my life." Frédéric stood in front of the group, raising his crystal goblet full of purple grape juice. "For years, with your help, I've been trying to convince this beautiful woman to marry me, and at last she has agreed. It is times like these when we are truly thankful . . ." Frédéric continued. He was as verbose as Simone was direct.

"Oh, drink your juice and sit down," Simone said, her gruff manner masking her embarrassment.

"Not until I tell you how much I love you."

Simone flushed. "You just did. Now, do you want to get married or not?"

Frédéric smiled, not in the least daunted. "A toast to my beautiful bride to be." We drank deeply. "This wine is not as sweet as your lips."

"Wine?" Simone said.

"Juice just didn't sound right," he supplied. "It doesn't make me feel in the least as I do when I kiss you."

"Will you sit down?" Simone's face turned an even darker shade of red. I laughed aloud. Never had I seen her so flustered.

From across the table, I felt Jean-Marc's eyes on me. He smiled when I looked his way, though his expression was unreadable. His hand reached out tentatively, and I placed mine in his. Our argument might still be unresolved, but I knew he loved me.

Late Wednesday afternoon came and with it signs of a family birth-day party. We invited Ken and his family as well, so there was quite a crowd to wish the twins well on their sixteenth birthday. Mother made one of her special cakes, and Dauphine worked an extra shift at the café so we wouldn't have to worry about work.

In the midst of furious present-opening in the TV room, the phone rang. I kept my eyes on the twins sitting near me on the couch as I answered. "Hello?"

"Hello. Am I speaking with Madame Perrault?"

"Yes, this is she."

"This is Dr. Juppe. I'm calling about a kidney for Marc."

I stood in my excitement. "A kidney!" I nearly screamed the words, and abruptly everyone in the room fell silent, except for Kathy's youngest child, who played loudly with a toy airplane. Marie-Thérèse grabbed her, and the noise stopped.

"A kidney!" Pauline shouted. "Marc, I bet they found you a kidney!"

"Do we have to come right now?" I said into the phone. We had been told that when a kidney became available, we would have only a short time to get to the transplant unit. "We're right in the middle of a birthday party, but that's all right." In my nervousness, I was babbling.

"A birthday? Oh, that's right, Marc is turning sixteen this week. Tell him happy birthday."

"With that kidney, I think you already have."

"No, no. I thought you understood," Dr. Juppe said. "This is none of my doing. The man said he had talked with you. This will be a live-donor transplant. Marc needs to come in tomorrow and be admitted for the last few tests, and if everything matches, we'll do the transplant early Friday morning."

My mouth refused to work, and it was three tries before I managed the words: "A live donor? Who?"

"Jacques de Cotte."

I sat down in shock.

"Are you still there?" Dr. Juppe asked.

"Yes, yes. Go on."

He gave me the details and hung up. Immediately, family and friends bombarded me with questions about when and where. I answered, and they all showed the same shock I felt when learning the kidney would come from a live donor.

"But who would be so kind?" Louise asked. Jean-Marc's mother had been upset when the doctor refused to let her donate because of her ill health.

Jean-Marc's eyes bore into mine. "It's Jacques, isn't it?"

I nodded, and this brought another flurry of questions from my children, but none seemed overly concerned about Jacques being my ex-husband.

"He must be a pretty nice guy, after all," Marc said.

"He's cute, too." Josette seemed to have forgotten the way Jacques had pumped her for information.

Before the party wound to an end, we knelt and my father offered a prayer of thanks for Jacques' decision. I wondered why he had changed his mind, and part of me felt uneasy.

"See, the Lord has His own way of doing things," Ken said, slapping Jean-Marc on the back as he left.

The children retired to their rooms, leaving only Jean-Marc and me. He sat in the easy chair, his hand plucking at the armrest, staring into space.

"Let's go to bed," I said.

He didn't reply but sat quietly, his eyes fixed on something I couldn't see. I wondered if he was upset at the turn of events. We had never resolved our feelings stemming from the fight the Friday before. With each passing day, it had become easier to forget that the discussion had ever taken place.

"What is it?" I asked.

"I went to see Jacques after you did," he said, not meeting my gaze. "Saturday morning. I felt bad about our fight and knew how disappointed you were. I wanted to do anything to make you happy again. I told Jacques he was a coward, that he talked a lot but never came through. He asked me what I would do if the situation were reversed, and I told him that as much as I hated him, I wouldn't hold it against his son. And, funny thing is, I meant it. He said he didn't hate me, that he didn't care about me one way or the other or about my son. He only wanted what was originally his. You. I told him you were free to make your own choices. He said that was good because he knew you still had feelings for him and that he would win you in the end. He was so darned confident. Sitting there, smiling."

Jean-Marc's eyes finally met mine. "And, Ari, I have to say that I went there wanting to beat some sense into him, but when he sat there smiling, it was as if I could suddenly see through him. He was so sad and so utterly alone." Jean-Marc pulled me onto his lap, kissing my cheek and nuzzling my neck with his nose. "No matter how rich and successful he becomes, he would never have you. While I, on the other hand, have you and the children. That's all that's important."

I hugged his head to my chest. "But you've known that all along."

"It's a lesson I keep having to learn. I've been so down on myself for what I haven't been able to do that I forget what I have done. Being a good husband and successful father is more important than my failing at work." He pulled back and gazed at me. "I haven't been fair to you, Ari. I haven't shared my trials with you. I wanted to protect you, but it's just driven you away. That was why you felt you had to run to Jacques when Pauline got sick. You couldn't trust me."

I tried to speak, but he wouldn't let me. "Oh, I know it's not as simple as that, but what it boils down to is that because I was so miserable, I wasn't there for you. You know, Jacques may be a slimy, lowlife creep, but he cares about you and about how you feel. That's why he wants to help Marc. He's being more of a man than I was."

"I don't think he could ever be the man you are," I said, meaning it. "But I don't want to force him to give up part of his body. This has to be a willing gift."

Jean-Marc nodded. "I told Jacques that on Saturday, when I suddenly felt so sorry for him. I said that neither of us wanted to force him and that the decision would have to be his. Forcing someone to do something wasn't right, I said, and unless the decision was made freely, it wouldn't be any decision at all. He said he'd think about it, and I left."

I wondered if Jean-Marc's comment had reminded Jacques of how he had tried to coerce me to going back to him. But that problem was in the past, and Marc would still receive his kidney—if they were a good match. I snuggled closer to Jean-Marc, pushing all thoughts of Jacques to the back of my mind.

"I got two job offers yesterday," Jean-Marc said.

Warmth spread through me, not at the information but at the voluntary sharing of it. "And?"

He snorted. "They both offered less than we make managing the apartment and café. I think it's best I stay there until I can find something better. At least this way, I get to be with you."

I smiled at his sentimentality. He was right; it was good being together. "Listen, the rain," I said. His arms tightened, and for a long time we listened, just the two of us.

———

The next day went quickly. There were many tests, and Jean-Marc and I spent much of the day shuttling back and forth between the café and Marc's room at the hospital. When we couldn't be with our son, Grandma Louise stayed in our place. We were to get the final test results by late afternoon and learn whether or not the transplant would take place the next day.

At the appointed time, Dr. Juppe came to Marc's room, smiling. "It's a go," he said. "Everything is matching up better than I expected. At least as good as some kidneys I transplanted twenty years ago that are still working. I'm very hopeful."

"Yes!" Marc said from the bed. Jean-Marc, Louise, and I smiled.

"We should go see Jacques," I said. Jean-Marc nodded.

"Tell him thanks for me," Marc said.

"Take your time," Louise said. "I'll stay with Marc."

The room was dark, and Jacques was watching TV. He grinned up at us when we came in. "I passed the test, huh?" he said. "The doctor just left. I guess I have no excuse now."

"You don't have to do this," I reminded him.

He met my eyes, and for the first time I could see him instead of his desire to relive the past. "Yes. I do need to."

I nodded. "Well, we came to say thank you and to see how you're doing."

"Is there anything we can do for you?" Jean-Marc asked.

Jacques' smile faded. "Could you come and see me tomorrow before the surgery? I'd appreciate it."

I smiled. "Of course. We'll be here."

We turned to leave. "Would you like to see a little TV?" Jacques asked. There was an odd, lonely touch to his voice. When we hesitated, he added hastily, "You probably have to get back to your son."

"Actually, my mother-in-law is with him," I said. "But I have to go to the café to see how the girls are doing. I'm bringing them back to see Marc."

"I'll stay." Jean-Marc looked at the TV, pretending interest in the show.

"I'll check in later with the girls," I said. "But first I'll have to take André and Pauline to my mother's." They didn't allow children younger than fourteen to visit at the transplant unit.

"Take your time." Jean-Marc settled in a chair beside the bed, while Jacques watched him with cautious eyes. I left, swallowing the growing lump in my throat.

Later, I took the girls to see Jacques before going to spend time with their brother. Both Josette and Marie-Thérèse had wanted to thank Jacques for his sacrifice. We found him and Jean-Marc still watching the TV. They looked up and smiled.

"Hi." Josette practically bounced near the bed.

"How are you?" Jacques asked tentatively.

"Good. I wanted to thank you for helping my brother."

"I'm glad to do it. And maybe you can like me a little again. I'm sorry if I hurt you."

She shrugged, shifting her weight from one foot to the other. "It's okay."

Jacques smiled and turned to Marie-Thérèse. "You must be Paulette's daughter. You look like her. We were friends in the old days. I cared about Paulette; I was sorry to hear about her death."

"Thank you." She held out her hand. "It's nice to meet you."

Jacques shook it warmly. "No, the pleasure is all mine."

We stayed for another twenty minutes, talking or simply looking at the television. The girls pestered Jacques with questions about his life, but there was little to tell.

"How did you meet Mom?" Josette asked. I glanced warily at Jean-Marc, and he sat up in his chair, ready to interfere should Jacques say anything to embarrass me or our daughters.

"We met at a nightclub," Jacques said. "It was her birthday, and we danced practically all night. I couldn't take my eyes off her. She was very beautiful." He paused. "You remind me very much of her at that age, Josette." She flushed prettily and didn't think to ask more questions. I admired Jacques for changing the subject so skillfully.

"We should be getting to Marc," I suggested.

Jacques hid a yawn. "Believe it or not, I'm tired." I thought he said it only to be polite; it was a side of him I hadn't often seen.

"We'll see you tomorrow," Jean-Marc said. "We'd like to give you a priesthood blessing, if you don't mind."

Jacques shook his head. "I don't think so. I won't need it."

"But it can help." Josette appeared surprised at his refusal.

"Thanks, but no." Jacques' voice was final.

"Whatever you want," I said. "Regardless, thank you."

He smiled. "You're welcome." We left together, not looking back.

—⁓—

At seven the next morning, Jean-Marc and I visited Jacques before they took him into surgery. "How are the girls?" he asked.

"A little worried," I said. "They're out in the waiting room now."

Jacques himself acted nervous. "Do you mind saying a prayer for me, Ariana?" he asked. "I mean while I'm in there." He had refused the offer of a blessing, but as the time for surgery neared, he was apparently growing anxious.

"Sure," I said.

The nurses came in and made the bed ready to wheel from the room. "See you later," Jacques said a little breathlessly. We watched him until he reached the end of the hallway, where the nurses entered the double doors.

We went back to Marc's room where Ken, Father, and Jean-Marc gathered around the bed for yet another blessing. I was fasting and feeling very sick, but the blessing calmed my spirit.

Marc must have read something in my face. "Oh, Mom, don't worry," he said with a grin. "I'm going to be fine. I think in a couple of months, I'll be able to go roller blading."

"Well, maybe in three." I searched his eyes. "You're not afraid?"

"I was, but I'm feeling fine now. Don't worry."

I wondered if Marc had inherited his father's way of trying to protect me. I wanted to shelter and comfort my little boy, but instead, he took upon himself that role. For a moment, I felt as if my deceased brother was there, helping him know what to say. Antoine had always taken care of me, in life or death.

"Mom," Marc said, "once, when I was little, you told me that all knowledge comes from the light of Christ. That means the knowledge of this transplant also came from Him, and I sort of feel He's going to be there, helping the doctor."

"I think you're right," I agreed, hugging him.

They took Marc away, leaving us to wait in his room, praying and talking softly. Occasionally, we checked in with the rest of our family and a group of friends in the waiting room. The two operations were timed so that as the kidney was taken from Jacques, Marc was already being opened to receive it. Minutes ticked slowly but steadily toward the nearly three hours it took for the surgery. At last Dr. Juppe entered the room, smiling.

"Everything seems to be going well," he announced. "The minute I hooked the new kidney up, it started working. Sometimes they don't start right away, and that always makes me nervous, but with Marc, it went very smoothly. Only time will tell for sure, but I am very hopeful for a long twenty or thirty years with this kidney."

"Thank you," Jean-Marc said.

"Yes, thank you," I repeated. "We appreciate everything you've done."

Dr. Juppe's chubby face crinkled in a smile. "It's what you pay me for." But we knew that his compassion went far beyond the payment we would give him.

"When can we see him?" I asked.

"He'll be in recovery for about an hour, and then we'll bring him back here. He'll still be pretty groggy, though."

We went to the waiting room to share the news. Family, friends, and ward leaders stood as we walked into the room. "Well?" Pauline nearly danced with excitement. Even André had lost his sullen look, if temporarily.

"He's fine," Marc said. "The kidney's already working."

"How's Jacques?" Josette asked.

I started guiltily. Since learning about Marc, I hadn't thought even once about Jacques, who had given him this chance. "I haven't heard," I said, "but I'm sure he's fine."

With the good news, the crowd began to disperse. They all wanted to see Marc, but for a few days only two visitors at a time would be allowed in. My parents took our children back to their schools, while Louise and Lu-Lu stayed to wait for a turn to see Marc.

When they wheeled Marc back into his room, he was tired but ecstatic. "I had a dream," he said. His face glowed. "I'm going on a mission, Mom! I may not go very far away, and I'll have to take my pills, but I am going!"

We talked for a while longer, but it was obvious he still needed to sleep off the effects of the anesthetic. Finally, we decided to let Louise and Lu-Lu in to visit while we grabbed a late lunch. To our surprise, Ken was in the waiting room with Louise and Lu-Lu. The bright color of his flaming hair brought warmth to the bleak environment. "I thought I'd see how Marc is doing," he said. "I couldn't come by earlier because of work. Louise and Lu-Lu tell me everything is going well."

"It's looking good," I said. With the crowd of supporters, I hadn't noticed his earlier absence.

"We're just about to eat lunch. Want to come?" Jean-Marc asked.

"If I'm buying," Ken said. "After what you guys have been through, you deserve a good meal."

Jean-Marc paused, his face suddenly thoughtful. "Maybe we should check on Jacques first." Ever since Josette had asked about him, I'd wondered how he was doing, but the nurse we had seen didn't have any information.

"He doesn't have anyone," I said. "We really should go see him." I glanced at Ken. "But they probably won't let more than two in."

He shrugged. "I'll wait out here. I have plenty of time."

We tried to go to Jacques' room, but he wasn't there. A strange fear gripped my heart and was reflected by the expression in my husband's eyes. "He should be here already," he muttered.

We asked the head nurse and finally received some news. "He's still in recovery," she said. "He had some complications with bleeding. You won't be able to see him for a while. I'll tell the doctor you were asking."

Jean-Marc and I stared at each other. What exactly was going on?

We weren't allowed to see Jacques until the next day. Dr. Juppe came into Marc's room, where we had smuggled Pauline in to see him, but the doctor didn't seem to notice. "Monsieur de Cotte is asking to see you."

"Is he all right?" The words burst from my mouth.

The doctor shook his head, and his voice was grave. "He has developed blood clots in his lungs and an infection as well. It's pretty serious. There is always a risk of blood clots after surgery, but coupled with the great deal of blood he lost . . . well, would you like to see him? He doesn't seem to have any family."

"He doesn't," I said.

We went to Jacques' room. Thin wires connected him to a monitor, and oxygen went in through a tube to his nose. Pain was etched across his lean face, and at the sight, guilt assailed me. It was my fault he was there.

"Ariana," Jacques said softly. "Thanks for coming."

"After what you did for my son? I will always be grateful."

"How is Marc?" he asked with effort.

"Doing fine. The kidney seems to be working well. I'm sorry about your complications."

He tried to shrug but gave it up. "I'm glad to help him."

"You need a blessing," Jean-Marc said. "Will you please let us give you one?"

Jacques studied us without speaking. "Does it mean that much?" he asked finally.

"You've done everything you can for Marc; now let us do what we can for you," I said. "Please."

"Okay."

Jean-Marc glanced at me. "I'll call someone." To Jacques he said, "I'll be right back."

"Don't worry. Your wife is safe with me," Jacques said, a flicker of humor passing over his face. "Besides, she chose you every time, even when I bribed her with my kidney."

"What?" Jean-Marc said, uncomprehending.

"Never mind." Jacques closed his eyes and seemed near death, though surely the doctor would have told us if he was so critical, wouldn't he? Silence settled over the room, cold and unforgiving.

Casting a sorrowful look at Jacques, Jean-Marc hurried from the room.

"I'm dying," Jacques said into the quiet. The stark words held no regret.

"No."

"Look at us," Jacques continued as if I hadn't spoken. "We've come full circle, you and I."

"Full circle?" I couldn't tear my eyes away from his stare.

"I took Nette away from you, but I gave you everything I could for your Marc. Does that make it okay? Can I finally rest?"

"What do you mean? Nette's death was an accident."

"But it came from an earlier choice I made to use drugs," he countered. "A terrible choice. But this, what I did yesterday, was good." His laugh was low. "I don't mean this in a bad way, Ariana, but if I weren't going to die, I think I could live without you now. I think I've given you enough. Perhaps not as much as I took, but enough."

A sudden understanding filled my mind. Jacques had never really wanted me but had yearned to compensate me for my great loss. In some way, his gift to my son had erased that debt, and now Jacques planned to let himself die. *Why?* My mind searched for the answer, but I found none. A conscience can be a terrible thing.

"You must fight, Jacques! You can't give up."

His grin was sardonic. "I don't want to fight anymore. I'm tired. You have what you need. Jean-Marc is a good man."

"This isn't about me. It's about you and your life."

He frowned. "My life ended when our daughter died."

"No, it didn't. If it had, you wouldn't be here to help Marc. Look at me—my life went on. I know you didn't want Nette's death to happen. I forgave you. Why can't you put it behind you?"

"I thought I could," he said dully. "But something inside me won't let me ever forget."

"You don't need to forget completely. Just get beyond it."

"Get beyond the fact that I killed my daughter?" Irony tainted his words, and a single tear trickled down his cheek. "How? I tried. Please, don't talk about it anymore. I'm so tired." His pallor convinced me he told the truth, and for fear of upsetting him and further depleting his strength, I said nothing.

It seemed like a long time before Jean-Marc returned with Ken in tow. Jean-Marc did the anointing, and then Ken gave the blessing. Near the end, the words seemed to strike a chord within me: "Your past can be forgiven and forgotten," Ken said, "but only in and through the Lord Jesus Christ."

The blessing held the answer! I had survived my terrible trials and lived a happy, fulfilling life because I had accepted my Savior. He had made me strong and had taken upon Himself the pain I could not bear. But Jacques had trusted in the arm of flesh. Because he could never make complete restitution, he could not heal himself, and he didn't know how to let the Savior fill the void. He had simply gone through the motions of living, while all the time, guilt and sorrow had become twin aches inside his tortured heart. No wonder he could not go on. No wonder he wanted to die!

A silence filled the room when the blessing had been concluded. "Do you understand what I've said?" Ken asked. "Or what the Lord has said through me?"

Jacques nodded, wheezing slightly. "I think so." Then he added, as if musing aloud to himself, "Could it be so easy?"

"The strait and narrow way is never easy," Jean-Marc said. "In fact, it can be a pretty tight squeeze. But belief in Jesus is the easy part. The beginning."

Like when the Israelites had only to gaze upon the staff of Moses and be saved, I thought. *We must look to our Savior to find our salvation.*

Jacques' eyes met mine. "And the rest. Is it hard?"

I nodded. "But terribly worth it in the end."

"You said that once, long ago. But only now did I hear."

A commotion in the hall made us turn. The door burst open to reveal Charlotte, Jacques' receptionist, fighting off two nurses. "I will see him!" she shouted.

"It's all right," I said. "Let her in."

"I'm sorry," the nurse said apologetically. "She said she was his sister, and when I told her he already had too many visitors, she went"—the nurse glanced warily at the wild-eyed Charlotte—"crazy."

"Sister?" Jacques said in puzzlement.

Charlotte rushed to his side. "I told them that so they'd let me in. I can't believe you're here and that you gave away your kidney! I've been searching all over for you!"

Jacques' eyes showed his surprise. "I told you I was taking a vacation and that I'd check in."

"But you always leave a number. I was . . ." Her voice drained away, and she looked around the room, as if realizing for the first time that they weren't alone. "I was worried," she finished lamely.

Knowing the woman's feelings for Jacques, I wasn't surprised to see her here or at the intensity of her emotions, but Jacques continued to stare at her in confusion. "Why are you here?" he asked weakly.

"To see you," she said, lowering her voice. "I'll take care of you."

Some inkling of the situation found its way to Jacques' brain. I thought I saw a glimpse of life come to his eyes. He glanced at me and then back again at Charlotte, as if wondering when this thing had come about. I nearly laughed aloud.

"Please," the nurse said. "You can't all stay. He's in very serious condition."

"We're just leaving," I said. "Good-bye, Jacques."

He hardly took his eyes off Charlotte. "Good-bye, Ariana."

CHAPTER EIGHTEEN

*J*acques didn't die. He had to stay in the hospital three weeks, a week longer than Marc, but he left without a trace of the complications that had beset him. The doctor felt confident he could return to his normal schedule a month or so after his release. As for us, our lives were changed dramatically by Jacques' gift. Marc gained strength daily, and though he had a strict follow-up regimen, it was nowhere the time-consuming monster dialysis had been. His cheerful nature returned, and so did his impetuousness and teasing. We didn't mind.

The many fund-raisers paid for most of the transplant costs not already covered by insurance, and once more we had something to be grateful for. We felt fortunate that because of others' generosity, we would not be in financial ruin the rest of our lives.

The Sunday after Marc's release, Danielle and her children attended church. Jean-Marc was at home with Marc, but the rest of our family met them in the foyer. To our surprise, Philippe accompanied his family. The bruises on Danielle's face had disappeared, leaving only her vitality and innocence. She walked over to us, an unmistakable bounce in her steps, clinging to her husband's arm.

"How wonderful to see you again!" She hugged each of us, and we hugged her back. "I heard about your son's transplant. Philippe told me. I knew the Lord wouldn't let him down. He's such a good boy."

"I'm so glad you came," I said.

"I am, too," Lu-Lu agreed. I watched her carefully. She tried to avoid Philippe's steady gaze, but it seemed like a magnet, ever pulling on her.

"Why don't you come meet the missionaries, Danielle?" Simone said. "And my fiancé. I'm gettin' married, you know." Danielle cast a smile in our direction and let Simone lead her and the two children to where the missionaries stood near the chapel door. My children followed, Pauline already deep in conversation with Danielle's daughter.

Philippe glanced at my face, as if asking for privacy, but Lu-Lu stayed me with a shaky hand. Philippe shrugged. "Why have you been avoiding me?" he asked.

"I haven't."

"Yes, you have. What about our plans? I thought you cared for me."

Lu-Lu stared across the room at Danielle. Feeling her gaze, Danielle glanced up and waved. The happiness in her face was all too obvious. "Danielle loves you," Lu-Lu said. "Don't you see it?"

Philippe blinked twice, making me feel he had not expected this vein of thought. He stared at his wife. She winked and blew him a kiss.

"And you love her too," Lu-Lu added. "Knowing that, there can never be anything between us. You need to make the best of what you have."

Philippe seemed about to protest, but his eyes again went to his family. His eyebrows drew together in deep thought while we waited silently. At last, his mouth closed, and he turned to Lu-Lu. "I'm sorry, Lu-Lu, if I hurt you. I didn't mean to. I never wanted to. You are very special to me."

He took a step away, but Lu-Lu's hand stopped him. She gazed earnestly into his face. "Make Danielle happy. Promise?"

Philippe nodded. "I promise."

He walked across the room and took his wife by the arm. "Shouldn't you sit down?" I heard him say. "You don't want to overdo it." Simone led them into the chapel.

"He wasn't hard to convince," Lu-Lu said forlornly.

I put an arm around her. "He already knew he loved her."

"Did he love me at all?" Lu-Lu blinked back the tears.

"I think so. And I think he was afraid of hurting you again. He really must have changed, if he could risk his feelings. But it's obvious that he loves his family, too."

"Then it's all for the best. But why do I feel so empty? Why am I alone?"

"There will be someone. There will. Someone as special as you are."

"Only if a miracle happens," Lu-Lu said.

"A miracle? Well, why not? Look at the way Marc got his kidney.

Look at the way I found the gospel. This is the church of miracles! Miracles follow faith."

"Thanks, Ariana," Lu-Lu managed. "I do believe the Lord loves me. And maybe I was an instrument to save Danielle's marriage. But that doesn't stop it from hurting. Maybe it will one day." She turned on her heel, heading blindly to the rest room.

The service was beginning, and my family had already taken their accustomed seats. Philippe and Danielle sat next to them. Frédéric, Simone's fiancé, nearly beamed with his new happiness. Josette and Marie-Thérèse were making eyes at Kenny two rows behind, and Pauline drew a picture for Danielle's children. Where was my youngest son?

"Poor Aunt Lu-Lu," said a voice beside me. It was André. I knew his sensitive nature was once again wounded by the seeming injustice of the situation. Leave it to him to have noticed his aunt's dilemma.

"Oh, I don't know. Let's wait and see. Come on, it's about to start." I reached for his arm.

"I need to use the bathroom," he said, escaping me. His brooding expression returned. He left and didn't reappear until time to go home. I prayed silently for a change of heart, that something could reach him before it was too late.

~

"Danielle was at church," Josette said to Jean-Marc when we arrived home. "And her husband, too. She is such a nice lady, and beautiful, too."

"Not as pretty as Aunt Lu-Lu," André said.

Josette stared at him. "What does she have to do with Danielle?" Before André could reply, she rushed on. "Mom, Kenny asked me to go to a movie on Friday. Can I go?"

Marie-Thérèse's face turned a bright red. "He asked you! You asked him, was more like it. I'm the one he likes. He asked me to go on Saturday."

"Did not!"

"Did too! I don't know why you just can't find your own boyfriend, instead of trying to steal mine!"

"He likes me!" Josette shrieked.

"Does not!"

"He's using both of you!" André inserted.

"No, he really likes *me*," Josette protested. "He just feels sorry for Marie-Thérèse."

"It's you he feels sorry for!" Marie-Thérèse retorted.

"That's enough!" Jean-Marc and I said together.

Pauline stamped her little foot on the white tile of the kitchen floor. "I'm so sick of hearing about Kenny or some other boy. Who cares about them? Our family is what matters. Sisters are more important than any *boy!*"

Jean-Marc smiled. "'Out of the mouths of babes,'" he quoted.

"Pauline's right," I said. "Boyfriends will come and go, but sisters never change. I think you two have lost sight of what's really important. In a few months Kenny will go back to America, and most likely you will never see him again, either of you. Is he worth breaking up the best sister friendship you've ever known?"

The girls were silent, both pouting and glaring at each other for long minutes. Finally, Marie-Thérèse relented. "I do miss doing stuff with you," she said hesitantly.

Josette's face softened. "I can't believe he asked both of us. I think Kenny needs a lesson."

A smile transformed Marie-Thérèse's face. "Yes . . . and we're just the ones who can do it!"

"Let's work it out together," Josette said, a wicked glint in her eyes. "Deal."

The older girls hugged Pauline. "Thanks," they said together.

"Finally, some sense around here," Pauline said with a grin. Jean-Marc and I laughed, but André didn't crack a smile.

I sighed, remembering the other problem tugging at my heart. "Where were you at church today?"

Jean-Marc looked disapprovingly at his son. "I thought we talked about this."

"You talked. I listened," André said belligerently.

"We only want what's best for you," I said.

"Then just leave me alone." He stalked from the kitchen, heading out the apartment door before we could protest.

Jean-Marc sighed. "We have to do something about him."

I nodded. "But what?" Now that our crisis with Marc was over, perhaps we could help André.

"We'll think of something," he said. "We can't let things go on this way." Pauline stared at us with brown eyes huge in her small face. But she remained silent.

Girlish laughter reached our ears. "That'll teach him," Josette said, coming into the kitchen. "We called all the girls from church, every one of them."

Marie-Thérèse giggled. "Now Kenny'll have *no* dates!"

"Hey! What's going on here?" Josette asked, noting our somber faces. "Did something happen?"

"It's André," I said.

She frowned. "What happened?"

I sighed. "Oh, nothing. Your father and I will deal with it. Can you girls get lunch? I'm feeling tired." What I really wanted was some time alone with Jean-Marc to plan what we should do.

"Sure, Mom." Marie-Thérèse was already moving to the refrigerator.

I ended up taking a nap, while Jean-Marc searched the scriptures for an answer. I hadn't meant to sleep, but the constant worry of the last few months had taken its toll. When I awoke, the sun was already far in the west, and I was alone in the room. My stomach growled; I had missed lunch, and it was already near dinnertime. Stretching, I pulled my weary body from the bed.

Jean-Marc met me coming down the hall, his face grim. "I've just had a call from the police," he said. "They've picked up André and some other boys. We have to go get him at the police station."

"What!" I caught my breath. *My little boy in a police station!* "What did he do?"

"I'll explain on the way. My mother is already here to keep an eye on Marc." He led me down the hall to the entryway and helped me put on my coat.

"Can't I go with you?" Pauline asked tearfully.

I shook my head. "You can see him when we get back." The girls watched us with frightened eyes as we left the apartment. Louise's face was sad.

"Tell me what happened," I said in the van.

"Apparently, André and some other boys were on the Champs-Elysées when a group of tourists nearby came up missing some money. The boys were seen taking it. The police caught up to them shortly after someone in the group tried to buy drugs from a police plant."

"André couldn't be involved in that!"

"I didn't think so, either. The policemen have determined that André had nothing to do with the buying part at least, so they aren't holding him. The boys also had a hefty amount of alcohol and cigarettes on them, presumably purchased with the stolen money."

"André stealing?" I felt like crying.

"Let's wait and see what he says."

We drove the rest of the way in dark silence. I tapped my foot restlessly, wishing I had driven so that I had something to occupy my mind. When we arrived, Jean-Marc made no move to get out of the van. I shut my door again and faced him. "What?"

"I'm not too sure what to say to him. I think we should pray."

"Good idea." For myself, I was torn between beating André to a mushy pulp and hugging him in relief that he was all right. As the shock lessened, I began to lean more and more toward the beating idea.

We prayed good and long. I felt my anger and fear lessen. "Okay," Jean-Marc said. "I think I can go in now." His face was more relaxed.

Inside the police station, a tired-looking man in his fifties was at the front desk. A few long-haired youths stood talking with uniformed officers. An elderly couple sat near the door, waiting. Jean-Marc went up to the desk. "Someone called about my son." I could hear the embarrassment in his voice. "I'm here to pick him up."

The man's eyes were kind. "His name?"

"André Perrault."

"But of course. I was the one who called you." A hint of a smile flickered on his lips. "I did what you asked on the phone. We just happened to have one of our undercover cops here, and we put him in your son's cell for awhile. That helped, I think."

"What's this?" I asked, indignant.

"I asked them to give him a good scare," Jean-Marc explained. "If he has to have this experience, I want it to be his last."

"But he's only twelve, not a hardened criminal!"

The man at the desk held up a hand. "Oh, we didn't hurt him,

Madame. We only showed him the truth of what being in jail is like. A little bit, anyway. I've talked with him. Your son is a good boy. He's not like the others. Now, if one of you will sign here, we'll turn him over to you."

"Thank you. We appreciate your help." Jean-Marc pulled the paper closer and signed it with a flourish.

While we waited for André, a policeman came out of a side door with an older boy. He had a handsome grin and a hardened expression that reminded me of Jacques when he was younger. The old couple by the door stood to greet him, their shoulders drooping in resignation. I assumed they were his grandparents.

"Mom! Dad!"

I turned to see our son emerging from the same door the other boy had come from. His face showed stark relief at seeing us. I held out my arms and hugged him. When we separated, Jean-Marc put his arm around André's shoulders and gently propelled him to the door.

Once in the van, Jean-Marc didn't start the engine. He turned in his seat to face André. "I want an explanation."

André frowned, and tears welled up in his eyes. "I'm sorry. I really am. I didn't know they stole the money. I didn't! I promise!"

"You also promised me you wouldn't smoke," I said.

"I didn't. Honest. I just held it in my hand so they wouldn't think I was a sissy or something."

"And how do you feel now?" Jean-Marc asked.

André stared at the ground and said nothing.

"Being with those boys is not a good thing," I said. "They were buying drugs. And you know where that can lead. Remember your sister?"

"I didn't know," he protested.

"Don't you see how wrong they are?" Jean-Marc said. "You can't be with people like that."

"But I can help them," André said. "I can. I could even introduce them to the Church or something."

"By pretending to smoke yourself?" I asked. "If you don't live your religion by obeying God's commandments, you can't possibly share it with others."

He was silent for a long moment. "I won't do it anymore. I don't want to go back to jail. It was horrible!" He shuddered.

Jean-Marc turned back to the front. With a deft twist, he brought the engine to life. "This isn't over yet. We'll have to think of a punishment. This is very serious, and it may take us a while to decide. Until then, you will stay with one of us unless you are at school."

André bent forward and stared at the floor resentfully. I saw a tear drop to the ground. Whatever treatment he had experienced in the jail had made an impression on him, but it hadn't changed everything. I reached over the seat and touched his head. "I love you," I murmured. "We both do. It won't be easy, but you can earn our trust again."

He didn't reply.

When we got home, the older girls were full of questions. André answered them tersely. Pauline didn't look at her brother or speak to him but whirled and stomped into the kitchen. After seeing Louise to the door, Jean-Marc and I checked on Marc, who was sleeping in his room. Then we went to the kitchen to start dinner. Serious voices stopped us in the hall. "What's wrong, Dolly?" André was saying.

"You think you're so smart!" Pauline taunted.

"What did I do? What's wrong with you?"

"I'm sad, that's what. And it's your fault."

"Why?"

"Because you don't want to be with me."

"Of course I want to be with you! I'm here, aren't I? Didn't I just ask you to play a game with me?"

"Why should I?"

André's voice showed his confusion. "Well, you don't have to, if you don't want."

"How come you don't stay with me all the time like you used to?" Pauline challenged. "You don't care about me anymore, is that it? You used to do everything with me, but now you stay at school or hang out with bad boys. And now you've been in jail. What are you doing? Why aren't we friends anymore?"

Along with Pauline, I waited for an answer. Our lives had been so hectic lately that I hadn't been able to pay attention to how André's change was affecting our youngest daughter. Jean-Marc and I stared worriedly at each other when André's voice came, rough and full of tears.

"I just don't want you to die," he said.

"But I'm not going to," Pauline replied. "I'm better than ever. I haven't been sick since we had that fire." That was true. The new protease inhibitors had done better than I had dared hope.

"It's only a matter of time," André said sullenly.

"No, it's not. Danielle got better, and Marc got a new kidney."

"No one ever gets better from HIV."

There was silence, and Jean-Marc motioned me into the kitchen. We arrived in time to see little Pauline shrug. "You just never understand," she said. "Even if I go early to live with my parents and Jesus, I'll be happy." She frowned suddenly, and tears gathered in her eyes. "But you will make me sad, because I'll wait for you there, and you'll never come because you don't believe." Pauline started to cry, and André looked stricken.

"But I—I—"

"Do you believe?" Jean-Marc asked gently, grasping his shoulder as I took Pauline into my arms.

André fought his emotions bravely, but there was no denying his strong feelings for his sister. "I do believe, Pauline! I do. I just get so scared." He came closer, and Pauline turned from me to face him.

"You don't have to be afraid. Jesus will take care of us."

"That's right," Jean-Marc said. "We can't live in fear. That's too big a burden for anyone. Let the Lord have it."

Tears glistened on André's eyelashes. "I don't know how."

"But we can show you." I hadn't realized until then that André's rebellion stemmed from fear. It seemed he wanted to distance himself from his sister and all those he cared about so as not to feel any more pain. Pauline and I pulled André into our circle, hugging him tightly.

"I'll always love you," Pauline whispered. "Just please be my brother again."

"I will, Dolly," André said, remorse evident in his eyes. "I'll never leave you again."

"Well, you'll have to go to school," I said lightly. So much emotion threatened to overcome us all.

A smile flickered on André's lips. "You know what I mean."

"Yeah," I said.

He hugged me again. "I'm sorry."

I squeezed his shoulder. "I love you."

Jean-Marc grabbed André in a bear hug. André pretended nonchalance, but I saw the gladness in his eyes and the way his arms tightened about his father. Gratitude to the Lord filled my heart until I almost felt dizzy. *The Lord loves us,* I thought.

"What's going on?" Josette asked. She and Marie-Thérèse came into the kitchen. "Did we miss something again?"

The rest of us laughed. Yes, something had happened, but it wasn't anything I could explain. Once I had scoffed at the idea of Pauline believing love could solve the world's problems, but now I knew better. Pauline's love *could* cure anything. And maybe other love could, too. Lu-Lu loved Philippe and Danielle enough to give up Philippe a second time; and Charlotte's love—and the Lord's—might just cure Jacques. We had come full circle, all of us, to a new beginning. Or almost, anyway. Oh, I knew the change of heart I had prayed for wouldn't come to André in one conversation, but he had taken the first step. More often than not, that was the hardest step to take.

Jean-Marc and the children retired to the TV room, where Marc rested on the couch. Jean-Marc sat in the armchair with Pauline on his lap and the others at his feet, their scriptures open. Since the twins were four, Jean-Marc had read scriptures each night to the children near dinnertime. He had always made it fun, and now I hoped this relationship would pay off with André.

I made dinner, enjoying the precious silence, my thoughts turning to Lu-Lu. She had been at Danielle's side during Relief Society but disappeared before Philippe returned from priesthood with the missionaries. I wondered what she would do next. Seeing Philippe every day wouldn't be easy for her, for either of them. Before long, something would have to change.

I didn't have long to wait. On Monday morning, Philippe visited the café. Jean-Marc was in the apartments, but I called and asked him to come down.

"Thanks for seeing me," Philippe said. "I'm here because Lu-Lu resigned this morning. I know she's quitting because of me, to protect Danielle. But that isn't right. I should be the one to go. It's my family."

"So what are you going to do?" Jean-Marc asked.

"I'm changing jobs," Philippe said. "I've been offered a position by another banking firm, and I'm going to take it."

"What does this have to do with us?" I asked.

Philippe smiled ruefully. "Well, I feel some obligation to the company I'm working for. As the manager of several of the Paris branches, I'm leaving them in something of a bind, unless I can find a replacement. I thought of Jean-Marc." He paused before adding hastily, "You gave me my first job at your bank. I'll be forever grateful."

"I did it because of my sister," Jean-Marc said.

"I know. But it gave me the chance I needed. Who knows where I would have ended up if not for you?"

"How does your company feel about this?" Jean-Marc asked. We both knew the firm was larger than ours had been and that Philippe's job entailed as much responsibility as Jean-Marc had shouldered as the president of our bank. "I'm not exactly on the banking profession's good list right now," he added.

Philippe snorted. "The failure wasn't your fault, and anybody worth anything knows that. I talked to the board of directors this morning, and they are willing to give you a chance. I won't lie to you and say there was no opposition. A couple of old men said they had inside information that you were no good, but I stood up for you. The job is yours, if you want it."

"I'll take it. And thank you."

Philippe shook his head. "Don't thank me. I'm doing it for the same reason you gave me a chance. For Lu-Lu. And for what you and your son did for my wife."

They shook hands, and Philippe walked out the front door of the café, looking for all the world like a man who'd had a great burden lifted from his shoulders.

Jean-Marc grinned at me, his green-brown eyes twinkling with a trace of their former light. "What do you think of that?"

"I would never have believed it. It's a miracle."

"They won't regret it. I'll show them how good I am."

I smiled. Already his confidence was returning.

"What about Lu-Lu?" he asked. "Do you think she'll be okay?"

"I don't know. I just don't know."

CHAPTER NINETEEN

*O*n a Saturday in mid-March, two weeks after Marc came home
from the hospital, I celebrated my fortieth birthday. Jean-Marc
planned to take me out to dinner, but as I readied myself in the bathroom, I felt a wave of queasiness and wondered if I hadn't picked up a
bug from the extra hours I was putting in at the café. Jean-Marc had
started work at the bank two weeks earlier, and we had both put in extra
hours to take care of the apartments. Only yesterday we had found
someone to take over maintenance, though I still hadn't decided what to
do about the café. Now that Jean-Marc was working again, my small
income wasn't necessary. The novelty of being in the café had faded, and
I found myself longing to be home with my family.

"Forty years old," I murmured to the bathroom mirror. On my face
was a myriad of small wrinkles I had never noticed before, but inside I
felt the same.

"Hello, beautiful!" Jean-Marc appeared behind me, wrapping an
arm around my waist and kissing my neck. "Surprise!" He brought his
other hand around to present me with a large bouquet of the purest
white roses. "Happy birthday!"

I turned, kissing him. "Thank you!" Burying my nose in the
flowers, I breathed in their sweet fragrance.

"Mom, you look beautiful," Pauline said from the door. André was
at her side.

"Doesn't she though?" Jean-Marc whistled appreciatively.

"Not yet," I said. "I have to finish my hair and makeup."

"No, you don't," my husband insisted. "You're always beautiful."

I snorted. "Right." I turned to André. "Learn well from your father.
When your wife looks lousy, you tell her how wonderful she looks.
Flattery goes a long way."

Jean-Marc shook his head. "No, André. It's not like that at all. When you look at the woman you love, she will always be beautiful to you."

I opened my mouth and then closed it again without saying anything. Jean-Marc smiled, and our eyes met in the mirror above the white roses. *Oh, how I love that man!*

"Aunt Lu-Lu's here," Marc said, calling from the hall. "Come on, André. Let's play a game of chess."

"Why's Lu-Lu here?" I asked.

"Don't know," Marc said. The children scattered.

I laid the flowers on the edge of the sink and added a touch of blush to my cheeks. The skirt part of my dress was tighter than I remembered, but Jean-Marc's loving gaze didn't seem to notice the middle-age spread I was so conscious of. I felt beautiful.

"Tell Lu-Lu I'll be right there," I told Jean-Marc.

In the kitchen I found Lu-Lu on her knees, scrubbing the white tiles on the floor with gloved hands. "I told you I'd do it for you, and I never did. If you went with me to Danielle's. Remember?"

"Yes. But I wasn't going to hold you to it, not really."

"I have nothing else to do."

"I'm sorry." I tried unsuccessfully to hide my pity, but she waved it aside.

"Consider it part of your birthday present." She pointed to a package on the table. "I did bring you one. It's a book. I didn't know what else to get you, and I figured you'd be having a lot of time on your hands once you quit managing the café."

I smiled. Lu-Lu obviously had no idea how much work a family with five children took or how far behind I was in my housework—or maybe she did, since she had dressed in her old sweatsuit and even now scrubbed diligently at the stains on my floor.

"Thanks," I said. "But we were planning on having a family party tomorrow after church. You're invited."

"I must have forgotten." Lu-Lu's eyes seemed far away.

"How are you holding up?"

She sniffed. "Well. It's easier not seeing Philippe every day, and I'm glad I kept my job. I enjoy it, and working with Jean-Marc is like old times." She paused in her work, her eyes glued to the ground. "Danielle and I are becoming good friends. She comes to see me sometimes at work, and we have lunch together. She's been seeing the missionaries, and she told me yesterday that she wants to be baptized—and the children, too, when they're older."

"But that's wonderful!" I exclaimed.

Lu-Lu's smile finally reached her eyes. "It is, isn't it? You know, I love Danielle like a sister, and that somehow makes up for losing Philippe. I lost him, but I gained her." She shook her head. "I don't know. It sounds silly when I say it that way. But I'm glad I didn't hurt Danielle."

My sister-in-law, the martyr, I thought with a trace of pride. Then aloud, "Will Philippe let her be baptized?" I knew he hadn't come to church again since that day Lu-Lu had rejected him.

Lu-Lu nodded. "Danielle says so. I guess we'll wait and see."

The buzzer in the hallway rang. Pauline ran to answer it, pushing the button without asking who was there. Jean-Marc frowned. "You really should ask, Pauline," he said. "You never know who might be there."

She grinned innocently. "It's just another person come to wish Mom a happy birthday. Or Grandma Simone. Or maybe Grandma Louise is feeling better." Since the older girls had gone out with their friends, Simone had volunteered to stay with the children while we had our date. We normally asked Louise, because Simone's fiancé didn't like to be without her on a Saturday night; but Louise's diabetes was acting up, so Simone was filling in. Though the children were old enough to stay by themselves, I worried about Marc having a relapse and wouldn't leave him without an adult until he was fully recovered.

"We'll see." Jean-Marc turned to me. "Shall we go?"

I nodded. "Give me a kiss, Pauline. Where are André and Marc?"

"They're playing chess in the living room," she answered.

The doorbell rang, and I went to kiss my sons while Jean-Marc answered the door. It wasn't Simone or even Louise. A strange man followed Jean-Marc into the spacious living room, shifting his weight awkwardly as we stared. He had medium brown hair and eyes, with a slightly prominent nose and sharp chin. His strong-looking features seemed vaguely familiar, yet I couldn't remember ever having seen him. The boys glanced up from their game.

"This is Jourdain Debre," Jean-Marc said. "He's looking for Pauline."

"For me?" Pauline asked, bouncing up from the couch. "Why? I don't know you."

"No, but we have a mutual acquaintance," the man said.

I motioned to the couch. "Please, have a seat, Monsieur Debre."

The man obliged. "Please, call me Jourdain."

"Don't I know you from somewhere?" Lu-Lu asked from the doorway. Evidently, it didn't take much for her to lose interest in cleaning.

Jourdain smiled, and his average-looking face became quite handsome. "It's not me. It's my younger brother you met, though we look quite a bit alike." His dark eyes didn't leave Lu-Lu's face, and now it was her turn to shift nervously. She put her hands, still clad in the cleaning gloves, behind her back.

"Your brother?" she prompted.

Jourdain's face clouded, and his smile dimmed. "Guillaume and his wife, Nicole, were in the bombing of the subway. She died. Burned to death."

"The newlyweds!" I said, remembering the man Pauline had hugged and who had helped carry Danielle to the ambulance.

Jourdain nodded.

"I remember him," Pauline said. "He was so sad."

"Guillaume remembers you too," Jourdain said, turning his attention to Pauline. "He wanted to thank you for your kindness. But he couldn't bear to come himself. He took Nicole's death very hard." He slipped a hand inside his overcoat to an inner pocket, withdrawing a small ring. "Nicole used to wear this on her little finger," he continued. "My brother wanted you to have it." He held out the ring with a steady hand. Across the front the gold twisted to form the word LOVE. Pauline hesitated.

"Guillaume gave this ring to Nicole when they were children, about your age. Please take it. He says it will make him feel better knowing it's with a little girl who has as much love inside her as Nicole did."

Pauline glanced at me, and I nodded. She took the ring in her small fingers. "Thank you," she said. "I guess I can keep it for her until I see her in heaven."

Jourdain looked at Pauline in surprise but said nothing.

"How's he doing, your brother?" asked Lu-Lu.

Jourdain shook his head. "Not well. They were childhood sweethearts, though when they went away to different colleges, things cooled off considerably. But after college, when their jobs brought them together again, they rediscovered their love. I've never seen anyone so happy as they were on the day they married. Two days later, she was dead." He frowned worriedly. "I try to tell him that he'll see her again, but he just laughs, sort of bitter like, you know, and says that I have no proof of it. And he's right, I don't." He gazed at Pauline again, as if remembering what she had said.

She felt his stare and looked up. "I tried to tell him that too. I told him my parents were there in heaven, that they'd look after her, but he didn't believe. I think he has to learn to trust Jesus. Lots of people have trouble doing that." Pauline squeezed André's arm as she said this. Grinning, he shrugged her off.

"Your parents?" Jourdain asked.

"Pauline is our adopted daughter," I explained. "My husband's brother and sister-in-law died shortly after Pauline's birth, and we adopted her and her sister."

"But we're sealed to our parents," Pauline said.

"Sealed?" Jourdain's question held an unmistakable intensity.

Jean-Marc sat down opposite Jourdain. "Yes. We believe that God has restored the sealing power through modern-day prophets—the power that transcends death and binds loved ones together forever."

"What is this church?"

"The Church of Jesus Christ of Latter-day Saints," Lu-Lu replied.

"I think I saw a news clip about that a few weeks ago. Do you have missionaries with short hair and white shirts and dark suits?"

"That's us," Marc said. "I'm going to be one soon. Well, when I'm older."

"Me, too." André's words were the best birthday present he could have given me.

"Tell me more," Jourdain said. "I like hearing about various churches. I've studied more than thirty different religions so far. I almost became a preacher in one, but I couldn't reconcile myself with some of the doctrine."

"We'd be glad to talk with you," Jean-Marc said. "But today is my wife's birthday, and we have plans this evening."

Jourdain stood up hastily. "Oh, I'm sorry. I didn't mean to intrude."

"It's no intrusion at all," Jean-Marc said. "We're very happy you came by and even happier to have the chance to share our beliefs with you. They bring us a lot of peace."

"It's strange, but I can feel that here," Jourdain said. "There's a peace in this house. Like it's a haven from the world."

I smiled. "We try to make it so."

"That's the Spirit and the priesthood," Marc said. "It makes the apartment feel like that."

"The priesthood!" Jourdain's exclamation wasn't a question but more a recognition of something he already knew or had studied.

"The power to act in the name of God," recited the boys together. "It has to be given by the laying on of hands."

A curious light came into Jourdain's face. "I read about that once."

"You can come to church with us tomorrow," Pauline invited. Not for the first time, I thought what a wonderful missionary she would make.

"Yes, we'd be glad to have you." Jean-Marc took a piece of paper and jotted down the church's address and our phone number. "Please feel free to call anytime," he said, handing Jourdain the paper.

"Thank you. I'd love to learn more." Jourdain smiled. "I can't believe it was my brother who brought me here. He doesn't put much stock in religion."

"Maybe it will make him feel better to know that he helped save a woman's life," Lu-Lu said. "He helped me take my friend Danielle to the ambulance. If we hadn't gotten her there so quickly, or had waited until they got around to her, she would have died."

"I pulled her from the wreckage," Marc put in. "Only I got caught myself."

"But of course. I remember reading about that in the papers," Jourdain said. "You are quite the hero, that's for sure. But I didn't know Guillaume had helped anyone. It might give him some comfort to know." He edged to the door. "I guess I'd better leave you to your evening." Still the man paused, seeming reluctant to leave.

"I'm not doing anything tonight," Lu-Lu offered abruptly. "I could talk to you about the Church. I was a missionary once."

"Could you, really?" Jourdain said. "I mean, I'm not doing much, either. I'm a bachelor, you know, and I work a lot. Religion is sort of a hobby with me, though. I keep thinking I'll find something important." His gaze deepened, and Lu-Lu flushed becomingly. She looked positively radiant.

"You might at that," she said.

"Could we go somewhere?" Jourdain asked. "I mean, I know this good couple"—he motioned to Jean-Marc and me—"wouldn't feel comfortable with a stranger in their house while they're gone, and I don't want to ruin their plans."

"Sure." Lu-Lu looked down at her outfit and then to Jourdain's nice dress slacks and button-down shirt. "I'm not dressed to go out, but I live nearby. Maybe we could stop, and I could change."

"Sounds great."

We watched them leave together, hiding our smiles. "Well, it looks like Lu-Lu forgot about the floor again," I said.

Jean-Marc grinned. "It hasn't hurt it to wait this long."

I punched him. "Is that a negative reference to my housework? Be careful, Monsieur Perrault, or it'll be *your* assignment!"

He caught me in his arms and kissed my cheek. "Whatever you want, I'll do."

"Yeah, right," I said dryly. "Trying to sweet-talk me again." I never could think clearly when he held me that way.

The doorbell rang a second time, but the children were too engrossed in their game to notice. "It must be Simone," I said. "I bet Lu-Lu let her in downstairs."

We were surprised again. Jacques and Charlotte stood in the hallway, the elevator clanging shut behind them. "Come in," I said hesitantly.

"We'll only stay a minute," Jacques said. He walked deliberately, as we would expect from a man who'd been released from the hospital only a week earlier. Charlotte supported his arm, though more for closeness, I thought, than for any help her thin frame might offer.

Under his arm Jacques carried a large, rectangular object wrapped in white tissue paper. "I knew it was your birthday, Ariana, and I brought you this." He hesitated. "Only it's not really for you but for Jean-Marc."

"Thank you," Jean-Marc said. "But we are already indebted to you for helping our son."

Jacques stared at me. "I was only doing what I should have done in the first place, and it has brought me so much more." He put his arm around Charlotte. "We got married, you know. Yesterday. We're leaving on our honeymoon as soon as I'm up to it."

Married! I thought.

"Congratulations!" Jean-Marc and I said together.

"Thank you. Well, we must be going." Jacques turned and opened the door. "Good-bye, Ariana, Jean-Marc. Thanks for everything."

As they left, I noticed that Jacques' lean, hungry look had disappeared and in its stead resided an unusual contentment. I felt happy Charlotte could give him that.

Jean-Marc opened Jacques' package. Inside was the painting of me that had hung over the couch in Jacques' office. "Wow!" Jean-Marc exclaimed.

"Look, there's a note."

Jean-Marc opened the folded paper and read aloud. "To Jean-Marc. Here is Ariana, almost as beautiful as she is today. She was always meant for you. Take care of her. Jacques." My eyes misted over at the magnitude of Jacques' gift, both the physical one and the far more important acknowledgment of my eternal relationship with Jean-Marc.

"One thing he got right for sure," Jean-Marc said. "You are more beautiful now than ever." I thought I might always be so to him. For eternity. He hugged me, and I hugged him back, enjoying the feel of his arms.

Then without warning, bile rose in my throat. Uttering a muffled cry, I ran for the bathroom. Jean-Marc followed anxiously. By the time I reached the bathroom, the urge was gone and I sat wearily on the side of the tub, face in my hands.

What is wrong with me? Am I sick?

The answer came, so simply that I wondered why I hadn't recognized it before. The past few months of extreme fatigue, the occasional dizziness, the constant tears, the emotional displays, and the extra pounds. No, I wasn't just suffering from the trials or giving way to the middle-age spread. I was pregnant!

"What's wrong, Ari? You're as white as the tub. Are you sick?" He knelt beside me and took my hands from my face.

I shook my head and then nodded and started to cry.

"What is it, Ari? Is it Jacques? Did his visit upset you?"

How dumb can I be? I thought. I had attributed the few months of a lighter menstrual flow and then finally a complete lack to stress, undernourishment, or possibly an early change of life. It had happened to my mother about this age, and the symptoms I'd been having were easy to shrug off. The fact that my last two pregnancies had followed the same unusual pattern had never entered my head.

"Ari! What is it?" The torment in Jean-Marc's voice spurred me to action.

"I'm pregnant!"

He blinked twice, a slow grin spreading over his face. "Pregnant? Really?"

"Well, I think so, but . . ."

He slapped his open palm against his forehead. "Why, of course you're pregnant! I should have known. I've seen the signs." He hugged me. "How wonderful!"

"But we're too old to be parents!" I protested. *How could this happen?* After so many years of wanting another child and finally accepting that it was not going to happen—then bang!

He pulled back to see my face. "What do you mean, too old? I hate to be the one to break it to you, but whether you're pregnant or not, we're still parents."

"But to a baby?"

He laughed. "We can do it. And you'll have a lot of help this time, with the children being older." His arms tightened around me again.

Now that the initial shock was fading, the joy came through. I could almost feel the tiny miracle in my arms, hear the satisfied sighs as it slept. "A baby!" I murmured into my husband's shoulder. "Well, it had better have your eyes."

CHAPTER TWENTY

A month later, Jean-Marc and the boys went on an all-day fathers and sons outing with the youth of the ward. The girls and I sat in the living room, planning to spend the day together reading, talking, and making things for the baby. The room shone brightly, lit by the warm April sun that sparkled into the room through the open sliding glass door that led to the wide balcony. The grandfather clock chimed its deep, resounding bongs, marking two o'clock. Lu-Lu had just arrived.

"Jourdain said yes!" she cried triumphantly as she burst into the living room. "He's going to be baptized next week!" A mere month had passed since we had met the man, but we shared Lu-Lu's excitement.

"That's wonderful," I said, looking up from the pregnancy book I was reading. Lu-Lu's face glowed with the radiance of a woman newly in love. It was good to see her so happy.

"Now maybe you can get a baby, too," Pauline said. In her hands was a small needlepoint square she was working for a baby quilt she and the other girls were making together for the new baby. Grandma Louise had shown them how to make the tiny stitches two weeks ago, and Pauline certainly had her mother's talent for it—a talent she shared with Marie-Thérèse. Pauline was already on her tenth and last square. Marie-Thérèse had finished her ten and seven of Josette's as well.

Lu-Lu's face darkened. "I don't know about that."

"But why not?" asked Josette. She too had needlepoint in her hands, her first square, but the uneven stitches looked more like vague flowers than plump teddy bears.

Pauline looked up from the cloth. "But I thought you said the other day that you thought he loved—"

"Girls, that's enough." I propped the open book on my stomach.

586

At five months along, my belly had grown but was not yet to the point of being uncomfortable.

Lu-Lu heaved a sigh and flopped to the couch. "I don't know," she wailed.

"At least he said yes to baptism," I said. Jourdain had turned out to be one of those special people who recognize the truth instantly when they hear it. I wasn't surprised today by Lu-Lu's news.

"He asked me to marry him," Lu-Lu blurted out.

"What!" I said.

"How romantic!" Josette clapped her hands.

"I'm so happy for you," Marie-Thérèse said.

"I knew it! I knew it!" Pauline dropped her needlework and hugged Lu-Lu.

Lu-Lu frowned. "I said no."

We all stared at her aghast. "But you love him!" Josette said.

"But how do I know whether he's getting baptized because he believes in the Church or because he loves me?"

"Lu-Lu, that's ridiculous—" I began. But it wasn't ridiculous. It was possible, and in Lu-Lu's eyes, too scary for chance. She had been waiting for an eternal love for a long time.

The phone rang into the silence, and we all jumped. Pauline picked up the receiver. "Daddy?" she asked. Jean-Marc had promised to call if he and the boys were going to be late. Pauline held the phone away from her mouth. "It's not Daddy," she said. "It's for Aunt Lu-Lu."

Lu-Lu took the phone. "Hello? This is Lu-Lu. Who's this? . . . You want me to what?" She hung up the phone.

"Who was it?" I asked.

"Some crazy person saying something about looking out the window. Like I'm going to do something so idiotic just because someone pretending to know me calls and tells me to."

"Right. Like we even care what they are doing," Josette added.

We waited for a full second before rushing out onto the balcony. Lu-Lu's jaw dropped. "Well, tie a bib around my neck and call me baby!" she exclaimed.

"Let me see!" The girls jostled for position against the railing.

Five flights below on the cobblestone stood Jourdain, the missionaries, and several of his friends, who worked in building construction with him. Jourdain and his friends had guitars, and the American elder had a violin. Portable microphones and speakers carried the sound up to our disbelieving ears. Almost all the windows in the nearby apartments showed the curious faces of our neighbors.

Not one of the musicians below knew how to play, or so it seemed. They strummed in uneven chords while Jourdain sang: "Oh, Lu-Lu, I'm so blue. My life means nothing without you. Oh, please, oh, please, *mon petite choux*—my little cabbage—marry me for eternity. I need you. Oh, oh, oh, oh, oh—you have to be mine, or I'll stay here all day, until the police haul me away. Let me know before these fantastic missionaries get sent home for shirking their duties. You wouldn't want to do that to them. So marry me! Jourdain and Lu-Lu were meant to be. . . ." More nonsense followed, throwing us into fits of laughter.

"They're really bad," Marie-Thérèse said.

Josette sighed. "He looks so cute. Oh, say yes, Aunt Lu-Lu."

Jourdain stopped singing and put his mouth closer to the microphone. "This is how the American missionary told me they do it in America. Frankly, I feel stupid, but I won't take no for an answer. I understand why you're worried but give me a year to prove myself. Will that be enough? I'll wait until we can go through the temple. I love you!"

Lu-Lu was crying. "Come up, you fool," she shouted. "And stop that racket!"

The American missionary grabbed at one of the microphones. "Only if you'll marry him."

Lu-Lu glanced around at the crowd growing on the sidewalk. "Okay, okay. Just get up here!"

But the motley band didn't want to give it up so easily. They insisted on doing one more crazy, spur-of-the-moment song before Lu-Lu and the girls went down and dragged them inside to a heathy round of applause from the gawking neighbors.

So it was that Lu-Lu became engaged.

Caught up in so much romance, Simone and her Frédéric finally set their wedding date for early May. "But what temple should we do it in?" Simone asked.

"In Germany," Frédéric said.

"The one is Switzerland is closer," I said.

"Switzerland, then," Frédéric said, while at the same time Simone muttered, "Germany."

I shook my head. "One would think you're not ready for marriage."

To prove me wrong, they were married and sealed in the Swiss temple two weeks later. Both beamed with contentment.

We returned from the temple in time to attend Danielle's baptism. Philippe still didn't show interest in attending church, but he supported his wife and children. "I think he'll come around one day," Danielle said. "I just have to keep loving him." If there was anyone to do that, it would be Danielle.

In mid-August, I gave birth to a healthy baby boy with a round face and chubby little hands. We named him Louis-Géralde after Jean-Marc's mother and my father. He filled a place in our family that had been glaringly vacant, although it wasn't until he was born that I even realized the void.

When he was three weeks old, we took friends and family to my parents' mountain cabin for a few days of celebration. The air was fresh and clean, and various shades of green dominated the tree-filled slopes. My children roamed in the woods with their grandparents, while the rest of the adults relaxed near the cabin. I stood backwards against the porch railing, gazing at my husband and Jules, who sat on the wooden bench near the cabin door, and at Marguerite, who rocked my baby in the crickety old chair my grandmother had used with my father. The Geoffrins had come from the Algarve in Portugal to settle the sale of their property and had joined my parents and my family at the cabin.

A fresh breeze rustled through the leaves and stirred a few locks that had escaped from the hair I had swept up onto my head. Knowing that I was to be the mother of a young baby, I had let it grow long enough to pull back out of the reach of chubby hands. Though the breeze was cool, I didn't feel cold in the off-white sweater Marguerite had brought me from Portugal.

"He's a fine young man," Jules said, watching Louis-Géralde.

"He'll be the next kidney donor for Marc," Jean-Marc said. I didn't find the comment funny, but the twinkle in his eyes told me he was teasing. I had to admit to myself, though, that it might one day become necessary for Louis-Géralde to make such a sacrifice.

"How is Marc?" Marguerite asked.

"He's doing great," I said. "He had a brief bout of rejection a few months ago, but they controlled it with medication. We have every reason to hope Jacques' kidney will last twenty or thirty years." I smiled. "It's so good to see Marc back to his normal self. He's even roller blading again, though he seems to be a trifle more cautious." For this I could only be thankful.

"What about you?" Jean-Marc asked the older couple. "Are you coming back to Paris?"

Marguerite laughed. "Believe it or not, Jules and I love Portugal. The coast is so warm and pretty. We've had an offer for the café, and we're going to accept it. The new owner has agreed to give Dauphine a lifetime contract to run the café."

"Now you two are off the hook for making sure things are running smoothly," Jules added.

"I'm going to miss you both," I said.

Marguerite kissed Louis-Géralde's tiny cheek. "We'll be back to visit. You and the children are like family."

André came in from the forest, letting a huge bundle of sticks he had gathered fall to the ground in front of the cabin. He vaulted up the stairs to Marguerite's side. "Can I hold him?" he asked, brushing himself clean. Marguerite passed him the baby, and he kissed his brother tenderly, tucking the soft quilt the girls had made around his body.

I gazed happily upon the scene. André was doing better, for now anyway, and I was overjoyed to have my caring child back again. He had developed a unique relationship with little Louis-Géralde, which I knew was a great blessing. If Pauline was called back to her Heavenly Father early, he would have this new brother to cling to, as would we all.

However, Pauline showed no signs of illness. She thrived under the new medications, and I prayed that in these drugs the cure had at last been found or soon would be. We had come so far on hope and faith; it wouldn't do to turn back now. Grandfather, the stake patriarch, had passed away peacefully at ninety-five years of age shortly after Louis-Géralde's birth, and I wondered if he wasn't keeping his promise to "talk to somebody up there about Pauline." That night at the cabin, a vision of her wedding came to me: a beautiful bride with a sunny smile, dressed in white and kneeling before an altar across from a light-haired man who loved her very much. I didn't know if it was in this life or the next; but then, did it really matter? Eternity was closer than we knew.

The next year, Jourdain and Lu-Lu went to the Swiss temple. As they were sealed for time and all eternity, I realized how each had made choices in their lives that had kept them worthy to be in the temple of the Lord that day. Lu-Lu had found her soulmate, and he was as pure and clean as she had striven to keep herself all those long, lonely years. He had been prepared for her, despite his lack of the gospel, and their love was stronger for the waiting.

"I'm so glad we have an eternity," Jourdain said to her as they knelt across the altar. "I'll need at least that long to show you how much I love you." Lu-Lu, radiant with her love, smiled and stroked his hand.

Jean-Marc pulled me close and whispered, "I wish *I* had said that. That's exactly how I feel."

I smiled. How could I not be happy? "I love you, too," I said.

When we returned to France and our waiting children, I found a thick letter on the kitchen table from my parents, who were serving another mission, this time in Belgium. Behind it was another letter, thin but even more interesting. I ripped it open.

"Who's it from?" Jean-Marc asked.

"Charlotte," I said. "Look." We read the words together.

Dear Ari and Jean-Marc,

I wanted to tell you that the missionaries you sent have taught me a lot, and I'm planning to join the Church. I had hoped to be baptized with Jacques, but he has some Word of Wisdom problems to work out and some other concerns, so I'll go ahead alone.

"She must mean his business dealings and his involvement with the employees who caused the bank failure," Jean-Marc interrupted. I agreed.

Jacques is cooperating with the authorities and trying to do everything in his power to make amends. We both hope your life is going well. Thank you for everything.

"She's sent a picture," I said.

Jean-Marc whistled. "She's expecting," he said, stating the obvious.

Their coming baby was not the only marked difference. The maliciousness in Charlotte's eyes had faded, and the pursed lips had softened to a relaxed smile. Jacques appeared younger and more carefree than I remembered him. Both looked happy.

"Why is it that women are more susceptible to the promptings of the Spirit?" Jean-Marc asked. "Danielle has been baptized for almost a year now, and Philippe still won't listen to the missionaries."

I laughed. "Because men are stubborn," I explained. "But we women are more persistent. Both Danielle and Charlotte will win their men over in the end." I wasn't worried about Jacques or Philippe; they both knew now that Jesus lived and loved them. The rest would come in time.

"Mom, can I go out on a date tonight?" Josette asked. She had just finished a lengthy conversation on the phone.

"That depends where you are going and who you are going with."

"You'll like him," Marie-Thérèse interjected. "He's a new boy in Aunt Lu-Lu's apartment building. We met him when we went to water her plants while you were gone."

I stared at her suspiciously. "You don't like him too, do you?"

"Are you kidding?" Josette said. "If Marie-Thérèse liked him, she could have him."

Marie-Thérèse smiled. "No man will ever come between us again," she declared.

"Yeah, yeah," I said. They had proclaimed the same words to anyone who would listen ever since Kenny had returned to America. I knew one day that a man *would* come between them, but hopefully that would be far in the future. And when it did happen, they would be exchanging their sister relationship for the stronger one of husband and wife.

"Besides, I'm doing an extra shift at the café tonight," Marie-Thérèse said.

A cry came from the baby's room. "You go get him," Jean-Marc said. "I'll check out this boy. Unless you'd rather."

"No, you're much better at it than I am," I said. Josette groaned. The baby wailed louder.

⁓

Louis-Géralde, my surprise gift from heaven, keeps me busy. Yet I can't imagine not having him here. The powerful love that swells in my heart each time I look at him whispers of eternity and tells me he was meant to be mine. His laughter fills the house, and his eyes—yes, those eyes, the same wonderful green-brown color of his father's—sparkle with mischief and expectation of things to come.

Each day is a new beginning, and my life has just begun.

ABOUT THE AUTHOR

Rachel Ann Nunes (pronounced noon-esh) learned to read when she was four, beginning a lifetime fascination with the written word. She began writing in the seventh grade and is now the author of more than two dozen published books, including *Fields of Home* and the award-winning picture book *Daughter of a King.* Her most recent picture book, *The Secret of the King,* was chosen by the Governor's Commission on Literacy to be awarded to all Utah grade schools as part of the "Read with a Child for 20 Minutes per Day" program.

Rachel and her husband, TJ, have six children. She loves camping with her family, traveling, meeting new people, and, of course, writing. She writes Monday through Friday in her home office, often with a child on her lap, taking frequent breaks to build Lego towers, practice phonics, or jump on the trampoline with the kids.

She loves hearing from her readers. You can write to her at Rachel@RachelAnnNunes.com. To enjoy her monthly newsletter or to sign up to hear about new releases, visit her Web site, www.RachelAnn Nunes.com.